AGE OF STEEL

- RISE OF MANKIND 4 -

JEZ CAJIAO

Copyright © 2023 by R J Cajiao
Published through MAH Publishings Ltd

Audio production was handled by Neil Hellegars in collaboration with Tantor Media
Editing by Michelle Dunbar
Editing by Faith Williams
Cover by Marko Drazic
Typography by May Dawney Designs
Formatting and additional editing by Emily Godhand

This is a work of fiction, all characters, places, spells, realities and secrets of the Upper and Lower Realms are entirely my own work, and if they offend you, it's not intentional. Probably.

TABLE OF CONTENTS

THANKS, AND AN EXPLANATION...

Hey everybody! Okay, First of all, I need to thank my team, producing a book isn't a one man job, not at all, and over the last few months we've had some internal changes. Some of the team have retired to follow their own dreams, others have moved on, and new members have joined us, through it all, all the stress and constant changes five people have made it possible to continue and to get everything out on time.

Chrissy, first and foremost. You took on extra jobs for me, you kept the kids distracted and you put up with my grumbling and rants at all hours, making sure that when the kids did realize they'd not seen me for days (and most of Christmas) it was smoothed over.

Thank you my love, always.

Geneva and Kristen. You kept picking up the slack, and making time in the schedule for little things like meetings and chasing people, miniatures and printing, adverts, edits, shipping and even getting presents sorted for me for Xmas. Thank you both so much.

Emily. The last few months were hard, and you did, and redid your work over and over thanks to issues on our side and confusion. You handled it all with good grace, and always lied when I apologized, saying it was fine. I know you were swearing at me from your side of the keyboard. Thank you.

May. When cover art turnaround was tight, and we had literally hours to do typography, when sizing issues threw everything off and when I damn well needed help, you fit me in and sorted it with a laugh and a smile. Thank you, it means a lot.

There are hundreds of others I could spend this time thanking, but I'm going to focus on those five this time around, so again thank you all!

Now: An explanation!

Rise of Mankind was always intended to be a six book series, and I stuck with that for as long as I could, but unfortunately I need to change that now. As these things do, the story has grown, and part of that growth, was the potential for a lot more of the base building and research, growth and development to be included.

I'd not intended originally to include so much, being more of a war and battles kind of a guy, but this feels right for the story, and frankly, a lot of people mentioned that they felt the levels were being breezed past.

The levels of growth were coming later and later in the books, because there was so much of each to cover, and rather than force the story to fit the constraints of the book? I decided to adjust my plan.

As such book 4 remains Age of Steel, but book 5 is now Age of Forged Steel, named for the additional time spent refining and developing the potential of the Steel dungeon.

Book 6 will now be Age of Glass, with Age of Neutronium as book 7, and probably book 8, the final in the series, as Age of War, or possibly Conquest.

Anyway, I hope that the three people who read this section, or those that don't skip ahead if Neil narrates it, are glad I've explained that!

Thanks everyone, and I hope you enjoy the book!

-Jez, 27th January, 2023

PROLOGUE

Robin clambered up the hill; the pressed tarmac that formed the narrow path was buckled and broken by roots. The trees on either side leaned inward, creating a shadowed and private path that made it nearly impossible to see the creatures lying in wait.

"Come on, everyone," Robin called over her shoulder, in a hoarse whisper. Looking back at the bedraggled and tired refugees, she cursed. There was just no way they could keep this up.

The group had been together for about four days now: running, hiding, fighting, and raiding abandoned buildings in equal measure. Four days…it felt like a lifetime. Hell, for some it *had* been a lifetime—certainly the end of one, anyway.

The fire that had driven them all from their homes had started small. Nobody knew how, either. Or, if they did, they weren't saying. Once it had taken hold, though, without the fire department's machines, without access to pressurized water, and without the heroes that the fire department had provided, the blaze quickly grew out of control.

It raced through the terraced houses in almost no time at all, and as the blaze grew stronger, the flames leaping and spinning, they spread.

It had only been one house at the end of a residential street at first, and then a single street. For almost a full day, they'd hoped it would stay that way. They'd battled the flames as they spread to the next house, and then the next. Communities banded together, trying to fight the blaze. Everybody understood that although it might not be their property now, soon it would be if they didn't stop it.

They formed human chains, dredging up old buckets from garden sheds, half full of plaster from renovations, most cracked or filled with random detritus. Duct tape had been found, and cracks sealed…enough to make it work for now, anyway.

They'd turned out in their hundreds—men, women, and children—standing in the streets to form a great chain as the fires spread. People ran from the beach all the way up to the main road—across what had, until the fall, been one of the busiest roads in the area—and past the sunken gas storage containers.

Once, they'd been full practically year-round, swollen and proud, filled with the gas stores that would see the commercial city of Sunderland through the winter months, just in case.

Certainly, Robin had never known a time—beyond when those selfish arseholes in the companies had sold all their gas in the summer, rather than planning for the winter—when they'd not been at least half filled.

Fortunately, by the time the fires came, they'd been low, almost empty.

The human chains fought on, but the fires were relentless. They tried to save their neighbors' homes, then their own, and then finally, desperately, just trying to save what was left of their damn city.

The shipbuilding, coal, and salt industries that Sunderland was built upon meant that most of the older districts were terraced: row upon row of old houses pressed up against each other, cheek by jowl.

Once the first house fire had taken hold, it couldn't be stopped. People had moved to the ends of the rows, frantically felling trees, dousing the surrounding area, and concentrating on limiting the spread.

People fighting a blaze on one street celebrated, coughing and exhausted but believing they'd won, only to stare in horror as the blazes others had lost control of rolled in behind them, unheeded and unseen, closing off all avenues of retreat.

It'd all been in vain. Dozens had died of smoke inhalation in the first few hours, as the still air seemed to join the fight against the locals. Then came the secondary fires, spreading out and around the areas people frantically fought in, and the dozens became hundreds.

The heat grew and grew, streets becoming estates, becoming entire towns as the flames climbed higher, until the people fled, grim-faced and terrified, headed inland.

The hundreds of dispossessed became thousands, became tens of thousands. They died in droves—burned, asphyxiated, trapped under collapsed buildings— and with them died the only ones who could have helped them.

The fire brigade was overwhelmed by the speed of the blaze. Their long-term allies in service, the police, ran to help, and the hospitals became burdened in short order, filled with the survivors of that heroism.

Passing people, desperate to save their homes, were pressed into service, dragging bodies out and wounded people in. Seeing no hope, many gave up there and then, at the sight of the piled bodies in the hallways.

The medical staff fought on past the point of exhaustion. Nurses, dull-eyed and broken, carried bodies from the beds, making room for the next one, desperately searching for those they could save.

People on long-term ventilation had died already. Anything that required electricity to maintain it had long since failed in the single night of the fall. That had created a small amount of physical space, but the massive influx of burn victims quickly exhausted the limited supplies the hospital carried.

Teams were broken into triage, treatment, and disposal. People whose entire lives had been spent saving others were forced to condemn those they could have saved under normal circumstances to die, alone and in pain, in droves. Only those they knew beyond doubt could be saved were given the chance.

The next morning saw more than a few of those doctors, nurses, and medical staff stepping off roofs, overdosing, or finding other ways to escape the terror the new world inflicted. Unable to deal with the things they'd seen, and the things they'd been forced to do, the despair grew; the flames ringed the hospital, before finally rolling in to consume it and all within as well.

Among the terror and the horror, there were heroes still.

Those rare few, who went house to house, rescuing people, racing into the flames again and again, struggling up the stairs of houses to carry unconscious kids and more down the same stairs, hissing as their skin burned and their clothes caught fire, then moving to the next house, and the next.

Robin hadn't been one of those rescued, having finished a night shift. She hated her job; she'd had three days off and had decided to spend as much of it online as possible. She'd spent time before work the night before buying enough food, drinks, and general crap to ensure she didn't need to leave the house for several days. When she got home, she'd settled in for a marathon gaming session, only to find the power out.

Furious, she'd gone to bed, resolving to deal with the day when she needed to. Waking mid-afternoon to the sounds of kids playing football against the wall of her house, she'd gritted her teeth, and gone to put her music on, thinking to drown them out, but the power still wasn't on.

Whereas the majority in the deprived area she lived in were furious over whatever paranoia and drugs-induced "plan" they believed the government was enacting, she was secretly fine with it, gathering up several books that had been recently delivered and cooking—on her gas cooker—a massive breakfast. She'd then crawled into her comfiest chair and started to read.

Hours passed, and then days. As the world around her grew stranger and more frantic, she buried herself in the worlds she'd fled to as a child, realizing that if the power wasn't on, nobody was going to be hounding her to show up for her shift.

She'd never been popular as a child, not like the sunny, smiling girls around her, the ones who'd loved the pretty cartoons and everything that was pink, giggling, and cute.

Instead, she'd been the quiet child, the one who read and watched, the one who didn't shine like the stars at school but struggled to get good grades and to get through.

Her father had been abusive, and her mother uncaring, resentful that they'd "ruined their lives" by getting pregnant with her so young. Their own parents had viewed their "disgrace"—a child born out of wedlock—as all the reason they'd needed to turn their back on them.

Robin had grown up unwanted—by her parents and by her peers—and she rebelled, wearing black and spikes. Deliberately turning her face from the one that society said she should show, she spiraled down into herself.

When she'd moved out, getting a job in a shitty factory by the river and earning her first paycheck that her parents hadn't been able to take from her, she'd bought a basic gaming PC, having never been able to afford one before.

The world she found inside—filled with dragons, with heroes and heroines who threw magic and kicked ass, where the worlds her beloved books shared with her were suddenly accessible…to her avatar, at least—was literally life changing.

A child with few friends, she suddenly had hundreds, others like her. Loners who'd believed they were forever to be on the outside were suddenly a keystroke away.

Weeks became months, and she changed, dressing differently, not changing to pinks and happy makeup, but changing inside. She felt worthy, and rather than feeling that the world hated her, she began to open up.

Her friends in the games taught her that she was indeed worthy, and she spent her time desperately waiting to return to them. Work was always a pain, but as time passed and she began to speak to others, she found it more bearable.

Men in the factory tried to flirt with her, and she compared them to the characters she loved, the heroes and the knights, the kings and the mages, and she found them wanting. She ignored them, and the women who came on to her as well, eventually deciding that until "the one" came, there was little for her outside of the games and books.

Years passed, and Robin grew to manage her cell in the factory, running the small team of "loners," as the factory called them. The weirdos nobody wanted to work with, often pushed into manual jobs like this, became some of her first real friends.

They made the hours between the shift change whistles more bearable. Even so, she kept her distance.

Then, as the world ended, as electricity vanished and the games were taken from her, she retreated to her books again.

Days passed, and she eventually left the house, gathering up the little food she could find, paying in paper and hard coins, finding the few places that had anything were only accepting that, and she went on, hiding away, and waited for things to get better.

Then came the days of the fire.

She'd seen what was coming through the small windows of her flat, seen the way the smoke had built, and the glow on the horizon, and she took the bags she'd packed.

One was her battered old work backpack, and the other a hiking one, left by the tenant before her. She'd filled them both with a mixture of her most precious books, her dwindling food, and the basic amenities, including a toilet roll. That wasn't a luxury; it was a damn necessity.

She'd also taken the sword that she'd bought by mail order seemingly forever ago, a decoration that was now worth its weight in gold. She'd rigged a sheathe for it over her shoulder, and just because she needed a slightly less lethal option…she pocketed the telescopic baton she'd bought as well.

Then she'd dressed in her work overalls, smiling as she unfolded the freshly treated full-body covering. They were awkward to get into, and hot as all hell, but they were also insanely sturdy, built to give you a little protection in a heavy steelworks.

The material was fire-retardant, thick and strong, and that was what she needed right now. Dressed in that, she'd locked the door to her little flat and had set off marching, resolving to head farther inland, to the next city over. If any of the local councils had their act together, it was more likely to be Newcastle, rather than Sunderland. She'd spent her life here, after all; she knew how useless and corrupt her local councilor was.

Barely ten minutes passed before someone had seen her, stomping along in her work boots and overalls, hiking backpack on her back, normal backpack on her chest, and her prized samurai sword sticking out over a shoulder.

There'd been two of them. They'd seen her hair bound up in a ponytail, the "goodies" that she must have had in her bags, and the sword, and had decided that, as a woman, she was an easy target.

She'd tried to talk her way past them. Then, seeing the pair of them working their way up to it, and having experienced violence from her father, she did as she had the last time he'd tried to beat her, and she did it before they could.

The telescopic baton she pulled out of her pocket was illegal in the UK, but that just meant that it was marketed as an "extendable pole" from the mail order sites.

The pair of assholes, who'd been threatening her with a stiletto knife, looked at it in confusion, not understanding…until she'd flicked it, and the baton extended to its full, and lethal, length.

She'd not hesitated, swinging hard and sending the blade skittering across the pavement. The asshole's wrist snapped with an audible crack.

Then, the dam burst. She'd struck again and again, whipping it across and smashing the lead ball at the tip into their arms, legs, sides, and back. They frantically fled, screaming for help.

She'd stood there, stunned.

It'd been so…*easy*.

Instead of running, or being the victim, instead of being beaten, she'd attacked, and *they'd* broken. She'd picked the stiletto up, closed the blade away, and set off, a little worried that someone would send the police after her. Realistically, she knew the police were far too busy to care.

She joined others, smoke stained and weary, heading inland. Long lines of staggering people turned their back on their homes and fled.

Hours passed, and the flames grew higher behind her. She stopped to help a young family, the father struggling to carry two crying kids, while the mother pushed a stroller full of the million things kids needed, and had a third strapped to her chest in a sling. She'd not wanted to be involved, believing she was better off being alone, but the stumbling man ahead of her, and the twin girls who clung to him, wailing, tugged at her heart.

She assisted him, catching him as he stumbled, wordlessly, and then taking up station by his elbow, helping as they struggled up a muddy hill.

"Thank you…" he gasped, sitting on a rock and cradling both kids to him. Sweat ran in rivulets down his face, lines in the soot making him look even worse. "You managed to grab a few things then?" He nodded to her bags.

"I was…I was ready to go." She glanced at the mother as she stopped as well, putting the parking brake on and rubbing her back with a groan. "Are you both…I don't know. Are you headed anywhere particular?" she asked awkwardly, looking away, wanting to hear whether there was news, but being uncomfortable with the closeness.

"My father lives in Washington. It's a few miles ahead, that's all." The woman smiled tiredly. "He wanted us to stay with him the other day when we visited. Now I guess he gets what he wanted…"

"Yeah, not like we can go home, is it," the husband muttered, looking back behind them.

Robin turned, following his gaze, and gasped, having been watching him all the way up the hill, and having been down too low prior to that to see.

Now, looking back at the city, the residential estates still surrounding them, even here, all that could be seen was a firestorm.

The flames of a few dozen houses had become hundreds, all ablaze, and as she stared, something caught her eye. At first, she'd thought it was something picked up by the winds and flames and carried aloft.

Then she saw it twist around, and dive into the flames, before lifting and dancing again, cavorting through the rising inferno. Even at this distance, its joy clear.

"Is that…is that a…?" she whispered, staring in shock.

"There's more," the man said woodenly. "Haven't you seen them?" He pointed to the right, in the distance, where a line of houses was being steadily consumed until—

One of the creatures appeared from the flames, flipping over and diving into the houses, vanishing into the roof, as if insubstantial, only to explode into the sky seconds later as the flames roared into frantic life.

"What is it?" Robin asked, fascinated and horrified in equal measure.

"Nobody knows, but they love the fire. We thought it was just a normal fire, until the first one appeared," he whispered. "Did you feel the explosion?"

"The ground shaking?"

"It was the old gas storage…something must have been left in it, and when the pipes went up…that was it. It exploded and the flames just rolled out, unstoppable," his wife or partner whispered, shaking her head.

"Hopefully the creatures will stay here," he said, muttering it again, before kissing the heads of his children held tight in his arms.

"Look, do you…do you need help?" Robin asked softly, not wanting to, not really, but unable to turn away.

"Please." He nodded slowly. "Please, yes."

"I'll carry one of them?" Robin offered, nodding to the children, and he indicated one with his chin.

"You can put your bags on here, if you want." The mother nodded to the stroller, and Robin did, but only the front backpack, the lighter one, that freed up some space for her to carry the child.

Other parents soon gravitated to one another automatically as they set off. People going in the same direction moved in and offered a hand. Some children ran back and forth, others clung to their parents, sobbing, and here and there…

Robin turned from the dull-eyed stare of a man cradling his child as he stumbled past. The trail of blood behind him and the stillness, the horrified thousand-yard stare made it clear that his child would never run and shout again.

It didn't take long for the first of the predators to arrive, drawn by the helpless mass of people. Young men and women moved in, picking those they liked the look of, and carved them out of the crowd.

When it happened nearby, Robin watched the thug who stepped up to another young woman ahead, reaching out and grabbing the necklace she wore and pulling it loose with a grin, uncaring of those around him. It crystallized the new world for her.

"Here," Robin said softly to the father, Jakob, who took his daughter back with a forced smile, before seeing what she'd seen.

"Don't. It's not worth it."

"It is to me," Robin replied. "Mind if I leave this with you?" She didn't wait for a response from Emma, the mother, as she dumped her hiking backpack on the stroller, and pulled the baton free.

"Robin…" Emma shook her head in a wide-eyed warning, getting only a hesitant smile in return.

There were three groups between the thug and Robin. He was busy, having moved to staring down an older man, knife held threateningly as he waited for the man to back down, sure of his superiority and the right to take what he wanted. That meant that by the time he saw Robin, it was too late.

The first blow was hard and fast, from the side, an overhead blow that sent the knife flying. The second and third blows landed, hitting the collarbone, and then the chin, each breaking bones. The last sent him crashing to the ground, unconscious, the tip of his tongue severed by his own teeth.

"Move," she ordered the older man, unthinkingly.

He nodded frantically, babbling his thanks and rushing around the unconscious figure.

Robin paused, looking down at him, and around at the others. So many were slowing, and yet none of them went to help him, or to help his victim.

She shook her head, picking up the knife and moving back to the others, slipping it into the band of her belt. But it wouldn't be long before she'd draw the baton again.

Each time, the group around her coalesced, moving in tighter and banding together, and ten minutes after the next one, the first of them asked for a knife, or the cricket bat.

The predators who moved alone saw them and attempted to loop around, to avoid the slowly growing group…only to be hunted down instead.

Her group grew faster and faster as more joined them, bringing their own weapons. And the march went on, even as the creatures circled, the predators in the dark places feeding on the human assholes as often as the "cattle" they attacked.

CHAPTER ONE

The sun rose slowly in the distance. The reds and golds that filled the sky far to the east fought with the blues and blacks that continued overhead and vanished into the west.

I stood there, leaning on the Lightning converter, enjoying the reassuring feeling of Lightning mana as it slid into, and from, me. The multitude of converters all around me picked up and disseminated the beginnings of a fresh storm, making the air feel heavy with the promise of it.

I pulled up the first of my notifications. My good mood shriveled as the names of the dead accumulated again. I swallowed hard, forcing myself to read them all, before banishing it finally, again seeing the smiles and hearing the laughter of missing friends.

"You know, not all of us need to be fucking soaked all the time, you bastard," Chris muttered from behind me.

I looked over, smiling despite myself, and spoke quietly as he wove around the various nodes to reach me.

"You're up early," I pointed out.

"Yeah, well, I might have had a bit too much to drink. I was awake throwing up, checked and saw that Jo was moving around and got her to heal my hangover. After that? Coffee."

"Surprised you didn't go back to bed."

"I tried. Becky is sprawled across the entire thing. Believe me, you'd think she was a dragon when she first wakes up, breathes fire and all that…"

"Enjoys a good 'lancing'?"

"You know it."

I grinned. "Shame she's stuck with you then, really."

"You dick."

"Love you too, mate."

"You know, I checked, saw you were up here, and thought I'd come and see my old mate, maybe check on you and make sure you were all right. Instead, I get abuse." Chris sighed, sitting on the ground and staring up at the sky sullenly as the first raindrops fell.

"You mean you thought about something you wanted and saw I was up here, and you'd chance it?"

"Never!" he replied, pretending to be shocked. "You wound me, sir."

"So, you don't want anything?"

"Well…" He drew the word out and winked at me, before blowing out a long breath and shrugging. "I suppose I might as well just say it. I'm leaving."

I looked at him, stunned, and he grinned.

"Got you, ya fucker. Seriously though, I need to get away for a few days. Maybe a week." He bit his lip and looked out across the roof. "I need an excuse, but I also need to go. So, you know, don't expect me to stick to whatever excuse we come up with."

"Is this the bond?" I sat down.

He nodded. "It's a weird thing, mate. It's not like when you have a pet, all right? You know when you have a dog, say, and the dog dies, and you don't want another for years? Then you get over things and maybe get another?"

"Yeah?"

"It's not like that."

"Fuck's sake, then why mention it?"

"Because it's relevant, I guess. Well, sort of." Chris scratched the back of his head, then stretched as he clearly thought about how to describe what he was feeling. "Right, okay, so think about the dog. They die and you feel terrible. You miss them like crazy, and you don't want another. This is like that, but it's not as well."

"I feel like I'm betraying Simo's memory by wanting to 'replace' him like this, but also? I feel like I'm missing half of my fucking soul. All my senses are dulled, like to below Becky's. Before I bonded Simo, I had better hearing than her, you know that? It was just something I accepted. I could hear things a little before she did. It helped in the forest."

"Right?"

"Now?" He growled, clearly frustrated. "Now I keep asking her to repeat herself! I can't sleep, everything tastes like shit…But worst of all? It's like an itch I can't scratch. I guess this is what cold turkey feels like, from coke or something."

"Is it not better to do that?" I asked carefully. "I mean, if it's like an addiction, you've already started, so why not continue? I mean, I know it's not going to be easy, but…"

"No," Chris said gloomily. "Look, maybe drugs was the wrong comparison, but I need it."

"Sure sounds like an addiction to me," I said softly, watching him.

"Yeah, I suppose it does." He shrugged. "The thing is, you know how you explained your class? How you grow stronger and become, I don't know, more lightning-y?"

"Really, 'lightning-y' is the best you can do?"

"Look, you know what I mean." He picked up a small shard of bone and frowned at it, then shook his head and tossed it over the side of the wall. "I'm like that. I'm a druid, and I form a soul bond as part of it. I don't need it, not to level, but to grow in *power*? Half of the druid abilities come from the bonded familiar. With Simo, I got faster reactions, better smell, taste, and hearing, and I…I don't know. I was starting to sense things, like the locations of people and more around me without realizing it. My abilities were growing stronger, but now…?" He shrugged, staring out through the slowly falling rain and across the slick rooftops.

"It's going backward?" I asked, and he nodded.

"Yeah, it's like going blind, deaf, and…fuck knows what smell is, but losing that as well," he whispered, still staring.

"Okay," I agreed, getting a fast flick of the eyes from him before he looked back out across the rooftops.

"What?"

"Okay," I repeated. "I'll cover for you. Fuck it. Look, we need the area scouted, right?"

"Yeah?"

"Do you need to be alone?"

"Yeah. No animal worth the effort is going to come close to a bunch of us all marching around and farting."

"Not sure how you'll find anything that wants to bond with you, to be fair, but I'd make sure you're downwind, rather than the other way around," I suggested, smiling. "But seriously, how about this? We get you set up, whatever gear you need, and you go out on patrol with Mike and a small team. We talk to him, quiet-like so he knows, and then you leave them once you find something that seems interesting. If you don't find anything? You come back, and you keep going each day?"

"I can't be back in and out. And Becky will want to come with me."

"Then you find something Becky wants more, and you set her up to do that, then volunteer to go scouting, and you take off. Look, mate, I don't like it, I'll be honest, but you're your own man. You don't need my fucking permission to leave, or Becky's."

"I know that, you arse," he snapped. "But I need to be able to come back! I don't want to go, man. I feel like I'm dropping you in the shit by going, but..."

"But you need to go," I finished for him, getting a nod. "Look, Chris, we've got some time...or I think so, anyway. The Unlife Pantheon?"

"You said they'd declared war?"

"They have, some dick called Balthazar, but..." I paused, wondering how to explain what I now "knew." "I can feel him—shut it!" I snapped, seeing the way Chris opened his mouth to speak.

"Spoilsport," he replied with a grin.

"Right, well, I can feel them, their presence, okay? It's weird as well, because there's three pantheons, not five as the prompt said. Yeah, Dickless is dead, but that still leaves four, or it should, and they're coming."

"You can sense them?" He sat up and looked from me back out at the surrounding buildings. "Where?"

"Far out. I can't see a map or anything, but the sense I get? It's *far* out, like I don't think they're in this *country*. The east coast is what, ten, twelve miles? Then it's all sea till you hit Europe."

"Right? Wait, you think they're all the way over there?" He grinned. "That's great!"

"Why?"

"Look, man—no planes, no real ships, all the machines are dead, right?" He shrugged. "No stress. They're not coming this way till they discover proper old-school sailing! And how many people can do that? A decent storm, like the ones you're learning to control, and boom! All lost at sea—nice easy win."

"Yeah, man, this is why I'm glad you're not in charge," I said flatly, getting a pretend "hurt" face from him. "First of all, there's the Channel Tunnel. If they're coming all this way, they can march to the south and go through that..."

"We blow it up then."

"It's four hundred miles to the south, you idiot. You know what we've faced here—you think this is only local? Imagine the shit we'd need to wade through to get to the south!"

"They'll face the same."

"Yeah, they will, except they're the dead. All they have to do is overwhelm anything they come across and resummon the dead as they fall. Then they raise whatever beast they killed, and they're growing stronger by the day, instead of being weakened as we would be."

"Crap. But okay, we'd get stronger as well. And we could recruit as we go, raise an army, hit the army depots, resupply with ammo and…"

"And they might just march off the beach, and across the seabed," I finished for him. "It's not like they need air, right?"

"Shit."

"Exactly," I agreed. "I can feel a stronger pull to the southeast, which I think is Balthazar. Then there's one due east, fainter and farther away, I think. Then weakest of all, far, far to the west…probably somewhere in America…there's the third."

"Think that the stronger, closer one might be two of them?"

"I…shit, yeah, that makes sense, I suppose." I sighed. "I should have thought about that."

"So, what are you two plotting?" a new voice asked and we both shifted, looking back toward the door as Markus walked toward us. "Do you want some company?"

I nodded, gesturing to the ground nearby.

"Here." Chris frowned, then grinned as a bench appeared, making me smile as he did a "jazz hands" wave, before standing up and moving to sit on the other end, as Markus sank onto it with a sigh.

"You know, getting old is a pain, boys. I admit, it's better than the alternative, but I ache." Markus stretched his legs out and rubbed his knees. "So, again I ask, what are you reprobates plotting?"

"Just talking about the future," I said. "Basically, the undead? I don't think they're nearby; I think they're in Europe and America."

"Both a bad and a good thing then." Markus grunted. "Good, because we have time to prepare; bad, because should nobody oppose them, then the continents may become playgrounds of the undead."

"Exactly."

"So, I expect you have a plan?" He quirked one eyebrow in question.

"Not a plan," I admitted. "More of an outline…"

"Which is?"

"We grow and we level," I said firmly. "The undead were a massive problem, but should we move on and upward in technology? Let's face it—they're bags of bones. A rail gun should be able to kill them in their thousands. A God-rod? We just need to aim it, boom. Job's done."

"God-rod?" Markus frowned at the unfamiliar term.

"It's a theoretical orbital weapon. Think of a spear, make it of some daft metal and take it up, fire it down, boom. It's non-nuclear, so no fallout, and cheap to produce, but massively indiscriminate. And a damn long way off, technologically, from where we are now."

"So what's the point in mentioning it?" Chris asked.

"It's an example," I said. "Like fighter jets and so on—fly over the undead armies and fucking bomb them into the ground. Look, we've begun the upgrade to Iron. It's another full two days before it's finished, which gives us a good idea of how big of an upgrade it is. But for whatever reason, we still have access to the systems, so we've got that going for us. I think we need to make the most of this time."

"Training and looting?" Markus guessed, and I nodded.

"Basically, yes. We lost a shitload of our people in the fight with the undead, and most of our experienced dungeon creatures as well. We need to rebuild and solidify our hold on the area, then we start looting as fast as we can."

"Same as before?" Chris asked. "Tech as the priority?"

"Yeah, and people," I said after a few seconds, noticing the smile I got from Markus.

"Anything else can be replaced, but the people," he said simply, and I grunted.

"True, but there's a few people we don't want near us as well." I glanced at Chris meaningfully.

"Those two." Chris spat on the ground. "They're like fucking cockroaches. Nothing can kill them."

"What's this?" Markus asked, confused, and I smiled grimly.

"My old neighbors," I said. "They lived below me. You remember I was in a three-story house with a flat on each level? Well, they moved in a few months back, and basically ruined the place, they're that unpleasant."

He smiled and leaned forward. "Come now, lad, some people can be a little…"

"They called the police on Matt the first time they met him, said there was a 'criminal type skulking around,'" Chris pointed out.

"Well, you do look—" Markus said, only to be cut off by me.

"I'd just finished work and they were moving in; I offered to help them carry the boxes up to their flat."

"And?"

"And they accused me of trying to rob them. So I left them to it, only to find they'd called the police and said they'd found me rifling through their boxes and had stolen things from them," I finished sourly. "They found the missing stuff in another box, or the police did anyway, but I still spent two hours in a cell. Never got so much as an apology. And considering I worked in IT, with high-level security clearance for some of our clients *required* as part of the job? Had they managed to make it stick, I'd have lost my job, and probably my career."

"They're basically the stupidest kind of racists, and like all cockroaches, they're survivors. They came in with the last load of survivors, and they're already trying to claim they need better apartments and so on," Chris said. "I say we should just shoot them. Make it look like an accident."

"Nah, I'm not wasting a bullet," I muttered, before grinning. "I'd love to send them into the training dungeon, though."

"Oh, gods yes!" Chris agreed, nodding. "Please. Look, I'll stay. We just need a few things, like a wraith, a few corpse lords, maybe a behemoth…"

"Now, now boys." Markus shook his head and smiled at us. "It seems they're indeed unpleasant, and yet I'd imagine that given the situation, they'll soon adjust to the realities of life. You watch—they'll be useful members of society yet…"

"Well, they could feed the pigs?" Chris suggested.

"We don't have any pigs," I pointed out. "And what would we feed them if we did?"

"Those two, clearly." He smiled. "We just chop them up and feed them to—"

"Now Chris," Markus said firmly. "I know you don't mean that, but considering the number of new refugees? Many will have no clue you're joking, so let's pretend that anything you say can be heard, hmmm?"

"I wasn't joking," Chris muttered, before sighing and nodding at Markus. "All right. *But* you go spend some time with them, all right? You and Clarissa, see how long you last."

"I will," Markus said with a gentle smile. "Now, moving on. I believe Barry wants to join us, and is planning on bringing the entirety of his settlement under your banner?"

I nodded, sighing. "Yeah, looks like it."

"So, if that's the case, what's the plan?" he asked.

I hesitated then stood, cracking my back and laying one hand on the converter again, shivering slightly at the boost in regeneration I received, as I drained the mana it'd gathered.

"Okay, I think if we're going to talk about this, we need to really talk. We need to get the others and sit down," I said. "The entire leadership group needs in on this, including Clarissa, because we're going to have a busy few days."

"Well, lad, it's still early yet. Older folk like myself might be up and about, but there was a lot of celebrating done last night," he warned, and I nodded.

"I know, but we need to get the ball rolling." I looked out. The buildings we'd destroyed recently surrounding the dungeon had made the area feel larger, but I knew it was an illusion. We had nowhere near enough space, especially not for the soon-to-arrive influx, should Barry still want to bring his people to join us.

I sighed, and reached out, checking on Jack, my cybernetic panthera. Basically a hitherto unknown variant on a giant cat base, entirely constructed of wood, glass, plastic, and metal, Jack had been rebuilt from a basic dog shape into something like a much stockier and vicious-looking panther.

Overall, he was fucking terrifying to be on the wrong side of, and after returning from the battle yesterday, I'd ordered him out to scout the area continually, judging that nobody else was in any fit state to do it.

I felt him roaming the area still, a fast blur of a connection letting me know that he was intact—had a few more scuffs and bits of damage, but that was it, basically. I nodded at that reassurance and dismissed him from my mind.

We moved back inside, heading down a few floors to the canteen level, determined that although we didn't want to wake people after the last few days we'd all had, simply grabbing people as they arrived would work well enough. Chris diverted, dumping a few bits of cutlery and condiments he grabbed from a stand, then snagged a table off to one side. Then he was back and examining the food on offer, as I smiled greetings at the volunteers who manned the counter.

Whereas some of us had been fighting for our lives yesterday, many of the dungeon's population simply weren't suited to that life. Some were exempt due to age, others due to personal beliefs or preferences.

That made them sound less valued than the fighters, but in truth they certainly weren't. Any group, be that a city, a village, or whatever, required gatherers and supporters as much as they did soldiers and hunters.

For an army to run, fight, and defend, the warriors and soldiers and so on needed to not be making their uniforms, their weapons, and everything else.

Essentially, cleaning the toilets was a shitty job—literally—but if it wasn't done, it became a breeding ground for viruses and more. Then people got sick, couldn't fight, and the entire force ended up dizzy and shitting themselves when enemies came.

It was ridiculous, but it was true, and that was just one example of one of the least glamorous jobs. When it came to actual weapons research, armor crafting, and all that? It just grew more and more complicated and important.

There was a damn good reason back in medieval times the local lord was the only one fully armored for a long time. Making that shit and maintaining it required a massive base of dedicated and skilled people. Expanding that into an entire army?

For every soldier, we needed at least two "regular" people, and we didn't even have most of the shitty infrastructure costs they all had back in those days to contend with. I shook my head and moved up as Chris collected his food.

I moved along the line, picking a few bits of food out, not overly interested, but I needed to eat. Then, moving to our table, I noticed the subdued atmosphere around the room.

"We lost a lot of people," I said softly to Chris as I sat next to him, and he nodded, looking around.

"It's true." Markus smiled, sadly. "But you know that's not why they're being quiet, don't you?"

"No?"

"They don't want to interrupt you or any of the fighters. They know what we all went through yesterday, some of it at least. They saw the state of us when we came back. They saw the bodies, and they saw the look in our eyes. I saw it too."

"You were there with us…"

"I was, lad, but I'm considerably older. I see things a little differently, and war, well, it's a young man's game. As you get older, you learn to see the world through new eyes. Don't get me wrong—the fight was necessary, and there was no way to avoid it, but when you're young, your blood runs a lot hotter."

"You're just speaking in meaningless platitudes now." Chris frowned at him, then summoned a can of Red Bull to the table in front of himself.

"Thanks." I grabbed it and winked as I cracked it, taking a swig. He glared at me, then summoned a second, as Markus went on.

"You remember how dead everyone was? Then the sudden desperation when they realized we won? The desperate drinking, the overly loud laughter, the way everyone was chasing each other around the bedrooms?"

"Well…" I paused, remembering the arguments I heard: people close to blows one minute, then, well, enjoying blows the next, really. The way that people had acted, and how everyone from Dante to the soldiers had been necking booze and eyeing each other. The desperate desire to prove they were alive, to themselves as much as anyone else.

"Yeah, yeah, I saw that, and yeah, I can guess what you mean," I said.

"That can be boiled down to 'I'm alive, and so are you,'" Markus said. "This morning, though, people are waking up early. Some of them will start drinking again to dull the memories of yesterday; others are looking to dull their memories with work, or their partners. Some will go back to sleep, some will, well…There will be many nightmares, and people needing to talk, even if they don't know it."

"I get that, although I'd not thought about it like that," I admitted, smiling and kissing Kelly's cheek as she slid into the chair next to me. "But what's that got to do with people being quiet?"

"They feel it." He shrugged. "They don't know what you, we, or all of us are experiencing and feeling, but they know we're on edge. They know we're a little broken, and as such, they're trying to be a little extra considerate."

"It seems weird…" I started, only to have Markus shake his head.

"No, it's not, lad. What's happening here is a community growing. As we all lived before, side by side but never interacting, it would have been strange. Now, however? We're like a village in the wilds, surrounded by enemies. We're only as strong as each other, so we all have to care about the person next to us."

We sat there for a few minutes, eating and enjoying a drink. The table gradually grew cluttered with drink cans, teapots, coffee cups and more as others wandered in, grabbing food and pulling up a chair.

Soon the entire group was there, with Markus shifting around so that Clarissa could sit with us. Chris and I had been joined by our partners, Kelly and Becky; Ashley and Sarah with Dante, Griffiths, Barry, Rhodes and Ramnik, Jeffrey, Patrick, Finn and John. Others milled around, but most left us to it. Tulio stood against the wall nearby, watching us and Anna, his wife, with their kids, at the same time.

Last to arrive were Aly and Amy, the little girl who had started the ball rolling to all of this shamelessly clambering through the mass of people to sit on Kelly's knee as if that were just her rightful place.

She then whispered her breakfast order to her aunt, who promptly summoned a veritable mountain of pancakes, complete with melted chocolate, strawberries, and honey.

I saw the look Mike gave Kelly, and I clapped my hands together, drawing everyone's attention before he could say anything.

"Okay, people, time to get this shitshow started," I declared.

CHAPTER TWO

"There's no easy way to say this, so I'll just say it, and fuck convention," I said simply. "The last few days have been horrendous. We've lost friends and family, we've lost a shitload of mana, and we've lost a horrific number of summoned creatures that were created to protect the dungeon and all of us.

"The simple truth is, winning was better than losing—yeah, obviously, but we were nearly broken by it. Now's the time to rebuild, to rearm and to sort this place out. As usual, though, we'll never have as much time as we need. So, Barry, you said yesterday you don't want to be allies anymore?"

I paused, quirking a slight smile as he straightened up, glancing around at the sudden frowns he was getting from the others, and nearly choked on his coffee as he tried to respond.

"Instead, you want to join us, is that right?" I finished, grinning at him as he glared at me. "Considering everything you now know, are you sure about that? You'd be stepping down as leader of your community. Yeah, you'll have a place on my council—which a majority of are here now—but you'll be *one* of the council, that's all. Not its leader."

"I'd have done it ages ago for that alone," he replied sadly, shaking his head.

I winced, remembering him telling me about his wife, and the decision she'd made when, once again, he hadn't come home as promised.

"I'm sorry…"

He cleared his throat and forced his tears back as he spoke. "No, it's okay. And yeah, I want to join, and to bring my people."

"How many are there?" I shifted in my seat to face him more squarely down the table.

"Just under five thousand, last I heard anyway. Probably more now. A few join every day."

"Well, fuck," I muttered as others whistled and cursed.

"We were in the middle of a housing estate. There were literally a hundred thousand and more in the area. We managed to save five thousand, and hundreds of those are the people you brought to us," he said, and I nodded, blowing out a long breath.

"Yeah, I remember." I chewed on my lip as I thought, then shook my head. "We can't take that many…" I said slowly, then waved at Barry as his frown deepened. "Not *yet*."

"It's room inside the walls that's the first issue." Kelly gestured to the outside with one hand. "To fit that many people inside, we need to build facilities, and we need to push the walls out, possibly claiming another entire section of the city and then begin the conversion of that into accommodation and food production."

"That'll take time, though. Days at least, probably weeks. Add to that, the second issue, and please don't take this the wrong way, Barry, but it's security. I trust *you*, and you'll have, what? A few dozen to a hundred or so you actually trust?"

Barry sat up from where he'd started to slouch. "I trust—"

"You trust your people—yes, I get that in a general way. But seriously, mate? You sent an order to them to send their 'best' to us, and they sent the people they most wanted rid of. That's the exact opposite. Now, I don't deny it was understandable. After all, why would they make their lives harder? They probably thought that the others were sending their 'good' people and they could sneak a few of the troublemakers in, get rid of them."

I paused, struggling with my words. "They didn't try to fuck us, Barry, and they didn't try to fuck you. Honestly, I believe that. *But*...they disobeyed you, and they put us at even more risk, all while we were working our asses off to help you. You then brought a load of people to help us, people you made damn sure of, and you saw how many of the fighters quit as soon as they had the chance." I shook my head, holding a hand up and gesturing for him to wait as he tried to speak.

"This is the exact problem, Barry. You had to physically lead your people here to fight. We'd already been defending you, and your people had seen us, yet they still took the opportunity to back out. Some of them at least," I corrected, flicking a finger in Dante's direction.

"Dante here has been insanely useful and has more than earned his place with us. SO!" I sat forward, tapping one hand on the table, as my mind raced. "This is how we're going to do this. As always, I'll listen to your input, people, if you think I'm wrong, but for now? We start small."

Silence greeted my proclamation, and I nodded, looking around at them all.

"We'll make a plan for a massive expansion—housing, food production, all of it—enough for more than double the people you have there. That should give us a breather, and let us plan for the future, *but*..." I held up one hand. "We'll be limiting the influx for right now, to a hundred people.

"That's for two reasons. First and foremost, space. We literally don't have the quarters or the space right now. We need to level a good-size area, enclose it with walls, and then begin construction, create living areas, quarters, food production, all of it.

"Secondly, security and..." I paused, frowning. "Fuck, I don't know the word for it, means something like the personality of the group?"

"Ethos?" Griffiths asked.

I snapped my fingers, pointing at him. "That'll do, thank you." I smiled. "Okay, the current dungeon 'ethos' is clear: we all work, we're all family, and although there's been a few dicks, beyond that, we've been good. We bring in five thousand people, most of whom are used to sitting on their asses and refusing to work? Nope. The whole outlook will change.

"Add to that, we basically have a luxury settlement going on here, which is insane because all we have is food, hot water, and a degree of safety, but..."

"That's luxury, believe me," Barry insisted. "I get it, though. You want to assimilate people in groups, make sure they fit, and you can cull the assholes—"

"Remove, yes; cull, no," I said. "Well, if they're criminal fuckheads, rapists, murderers, etc., then yeah, a sharp knife and a few feet of soil. But that's not what I meant." I rubbed at my jaw and looked around, making eye contact with as many as I could, as I thought.

"I want to bring people in, give them a safe home, but we need to trust them, and they need to want to be one of us, not to just sit and take. Don't get me wrong. I understand there are people, among our number as well, who literally just sit and stare at the wall; they lost everything and they're just waiting to die. I get that, genuinely I do. But it's a tiny portion of us, and—"

"And it's a majority of my people," Barry admitted. "Yeah, all right, look. We've got about five thousand people. Of that? Maybe five hundred work. They clear houses, they cook, they look after each other. Then there's the fighters, mainly ex-military, and there's a good three hundred of them. They're mostly back there still."

He broke off at the glare I gave him and snorted. "What? You thought I'd leave the entire settlement unprotected? Fuck, no. I brought the ones I knew had the best chance, and they left their gear behind, which is why they were the worst equipped. If I'd brought their gear, the settlement would have been stripped and burned when I returned."

"We kitted you out…"

"I know, and we lost more than half of those I brought with us. We were fighting with gear we were unfamiliar with, and we damn well knew we'd lose people, yet we still came to help," he growled, before Kelly interrupted him.

"Barry, it's okay. We're not having a go at you. It's obvious you'd do that, when we stop and think. It just wasn't something we'd considered before, that's all. You were there with us, risking your life by our side, after all."

"Point," I muttered, before nodding firmly. "Sorry, Barry, just…you know," I finished lamely.

"Yeah, I do," he agreed, understanding that I was referencing the way they'd dropped us in the shit each time so far.

"So, we'll take a hundred, and believe me, Barry, these better be people who contribute, all right?" I said, getting a grunt and a nod. "Okay, they'll start integrating, and we'll find them room and jobs. While they're getting settled, we'll expand…But which section?" I muttered, rubbing my chin as I thought.

"How about the south, toward the river?" Ashley suggested diffidently. "You said before you pushed out down that way to put the converters in the river, right?"

"Yeah…" I gestured for her to go on.

"Well, there's a load of hotels along the river. That's ready-made accommodation, right?" she suggested, and I glanced over at Clarissa and Aly, seeing the considering looks on their faces.

"It *could* work," Aly said after sitting back and clearly pulling the map up in her vision. "The issue would be security, and how far we go."

"Explain," I ordered, having a good idea of what she was thinking. I was thinking the same, but wanted to hear it, and have the others hear it too.

"The bigger hotels are to the right, if we're facing south. We have no walls there, so we'd need to absorb the quayside for a good half mile to take them into the dungeon, as the line of claimed territory is nowhere near them. Then once we've claimed the outer ring, it'd need a hell of a lot of walls raising…in fact—" She broke off, and I shook my head, seeing the same issue.

"Our territory would have to be massively increased to take that much land under our control, like four or five times what we hold now. Add to that, the cost of the walls alone would be insane, never mind things like closing off the sewage pipes and more so that nothing can come up inside the territory."

"What about claiming another section?" Chris suggested. "You said before you could set up a node of sorts, and grow a new area from that. What about doing that?"

"Again, the cost would be insane." I shook my head. "Also, when we come to expand to that area eventually, it'd have been massively inefficient as we absorb that back into the dungeon."

"I'm sorry." Ashley settled back and looked embarrassed.

"No, no…don't be," I said. "That's the point of us all sitting here, to consider the options."

"North?" Clarissa suggested, frowning as she clearly tried to be half in and half out of the dungeon sense to evaluate the area on a map. "Northeast, I mean? That block there, the Bigg Market and the buildings behind it."

"We've claimed this side of the market," I agreed. "It'd be a lot less effort to claim that section. But that's mainly shops and offices, so we'd spend a fortune building living quarters."

"What about mana storage?" Aly suggested, staring fixedly into the distance as she worked in the dungeon sense. "What if we went all out? Build a shitload more storage—we already made some, after all. We claim the area, then flatten it, like really go all out, have everyone stripping and absorbing the buildings. We flatten and clear the whole section, build the wall so we know we're all safe, then we start building and we go upward."

"Like build our own hotel, you mean?" Mike frowned.

"No, you mean our own *skyscraper*," I guessed, nodding along.

"Exactly." She banished the screens from her vision and sat forward, looking around. "Whatever we do, this problem will raise its head again, so what if we plan for it now? It makes sense. Matt, you wanted a beacon, right? Something that says to anyone who sees it that here we are, and to come to us for safety and security?"

"Yeah, except we can't deliver that yet."

"No, but it's not going to be built in the next few days. I'm saying we claim the area, strip the buildings and start demolishing them, build more storage nodes and get ready. Then build up and up, with the intention that it becomes the new official 'heart' of the dungeon. Nobody who comes needs to know where the real heart is. We prepare, then build upward, going level by level, and accept more people as each section is complete."

"How big an area?" I asked, considering it.

"Two minutes…" We waited as Aly worked through a few different systems, before coming back to us all. "Okay, best guess, that section to the northeast covers roughly about forty thousand square meters."

"Fuck," I muttered, eyes wide. "That's huge!"

"That's what she said," Chris muttered, before being elbowed by Becky.

"She did, yeah," I agreed, winking at Kelly. "It just wasn't about you, mate! Okay, seriously though, my flat in Jesmond was big. It was seventy square meters, and I had a spare bedroom. If the average house is what, a hundred square meters? That gives us two decent large bedrooms, bathrooms, and so on…"

"We wouldn't need kitchens," Aly said. "They're nice to have, but we plain don't need them. People can convert a bedroom into a kitchen, or have it in their living space if they really want one."

"Okay, so if we're aiming for the long-term here, we need, what? Two bedrooms? A bathroom and a living area?" I suggested, looking around.

"A mixture," Barry said. "We've got a lot of families with three and four kids…have some apartments with extra rooms, others with just one."

"Could you make it by level?" Dante asked, and I frowned, thinking we'd covered that. "I mean have like, a single bedroom apartment floor, then a bunch of two-beds, then a floor that's all three- and four-beds, with maybe a floor that's a general area for people to gather inside that's safe?"

"Yeah." I nodded. "That'd probably be a good idea to be fair. Lot of couples and singles out there, after all…"

"You could build those four floors, and then repeat?" he suggested, getting excited. "That way, everyone gets a chance at a nice apartment, somewhere to live that's safe and—"

"Maybe make two floors of single apartments?" Griffiths suggested. "I know a lot of soldiers would kill for a little section to call their own."

"We can do that." I ran it through my head. "So let's say a single apartment is fifty meters square: a bedroom, bathroom, and a living area. A two-bed is seventy-five and a three is a hundred. We limit it to that for now. Some families are massive, I know, but if need be, we can make an adjustment on the fly and knock a wall down between two three-bedroom apartments maybe."

"Okay, so if we work on a twenty-thousand-square meter floorplan, to start with…" Aly created a bundle of blank pages on the table before her, and a pen, then started to sketch and make notes.

"That means…" she said after a few minutes of calculations, a rough drawing of a square building on the paper before her. "If we change it and make it twenty-*three* thousand meters, because we need things like stairs, and corridors—we plan for twenty thousand as 'usable space' being four hundred single apartments on the singleton floor. So eight hundred for each pair of floors, with two hundred and sixty on the two-bed floor, and two hundred on the three-bed. That gets us an average of…"

Again, she sat for a minute, doing calculations.

"Okay, based on half the singleton apartments being actual singles, and half couples, and the two-beds being three people on average, with the three-beds being for four people…we could accommodate two thousand, seven hundred, and eighty people over four floors."

"Holy shit," I muttered, stunned by the numbers in a single block.

"This is just rough calculations, so I might be wrong, but this is going to cost…a fuckload." Aly winced, shaking her head. "Honestly, I don't even know how to work this out, but it's going to be a *lot* of mana, like more than we've generated since the beginning to now, I think."

"Simple question," Barry said flatly. "How secure will this be?"

"Pretty goddamn secure." I shrugged. "The walls will be reinforced by the dungeon core, the windows essentially transparent crystal. Plus, it'll be inside the dungeon radius, so we can drop summoned creatures anywhere we need to, make the entire roof into a trap if we start getting enemy fliers, set up corpse lords on the roof with ballistae, have roaming wraiths and impai…"

"So you'll have a totally secure place?" he asked.

I shook my head slowly. "Nowhere is totally secure."

"But compared to Saltwell Park?"

"Fuck, yeah, it'll be massively more secure," I said.

"Much more secure, more comfortable, and most likely better in every way when it comes to things like food and so on? So you could take everyone, or even just half to start with?"

"Yeah," I admitted, before leaning on the table and drawing a deep breath. "But like I said, I'm not taking a massive amount of people."

"Dammit, Matt, these are goddamn families we're talking about!" he snapped. "You could take the families. I'll keep the assholes and the normal folk. Take the families and kids and—"

"We're not doing it, Barry," I said. "No, wait." I held up one hand and looked around at the table around me, before going on. "You sent a hundred people to us a few days back, supposedly your best, people who were looking to better themselves and work in exchange for a fair wage."

"Shit," Barry growled, shaking his head and knowing what I was about to say, as we'd covered it once already.

"Exactly. We asked for your best, and only *seven* stayed. The rest ran. This brings us to the next point, though: one was recognized by Kelly…You knew she worked in the local court, yeah?"

"Yeah, she said," he admitted, deflating.

"Exactly. So she'd recognized him as being a known pervert, and probably a rapist." I sat back and spread my hands in a "what now" gesture. "What happens when we accept them into the dungeon? What happens if they try that shit here? Because I'll be very clear—I don't want perverts and rapists inside my walls under any circumstances. Make no mistake here, Barry, I rule here with my council's advice…but I *do* rule here. This isn't a democracy. As much as I don't want to be a king or whatever? I will make the final decision. And again, if someone thinks to kill me and try to claim the dungeon? It'll die. Everyone ends up on the streets as the dungeon dies and everything built by it fails…"

I was fairly sure that wasn't true. Kelly, Aly, and most of my inner circle knew that, but they stayed quiet, understanding the reasons for my words.

"I'll take families, and I'll take hard workers. I'll even take criminals…" I saw how John and Kelly jerked at that, but I went on. "On the understanding that their crime has been paid for, and genuinely. No violent asshole who got away with it because they intimidated the witnesses."

"They could serve in the army?" Griffiths suggested, clearly not liking the idea, but open to it as well.

"Perhaps there could be a tier system," I said after a few seconds of thought. "People who you can vouch for, and I mean *you,* Barry," I said, "they'll be accepted on a provisional basis straightaway. Not the ones your people suggest, not the people you once bumped into in the pub and seemed all right, but the ones you *know* are good. And believe me, if they fuck us over? There will be consequences."

I looked around slowly; everyone was watching me and waiting. "That goes for all of you. You know someone in there, someone you personally vouch for? Yeah, you've earned my trust...provisional room at the inn." I smiled at how Dante straightened, and I nodded to him. He'd mentioned his mother being back there still.

"And the rest? I mean, there's always some assholes, but their families?" Barry asked in a flat tone. "What am I supposed to do? Just tell them it's tough and they can die?"

"No. The assholes, the real ones, will be given a space as well...well, not the rapists and so on. I'm sorry, but fuck that shit. They'll get some supplies and be told to head south or north or wherever. But they go, or they die. The ones who are dicks, but not to that level? They'll be given a chance. The vast majority will be given quarters...but in Saltwell Park."

CHAPTER THREE

"What?" Barry asked, confused.

"The idea of setting up a dungeon node was a good one—we just make it in Saltwell Park instead," I said. "Clarissa, how long would it take to expand to the park? A straight line, as much as possible?"

"It's about two, maybe three miles..." she replied, stunned. "It'd take weeks?"

"No, I don't think so," Aly disagreed. "Working in shifts, two people constantly on just that, no stopping for anything else—yeah, it'd be boring as all hell, literally take a step, pause, expand, take another step..." Aly zoned out as she ran the numbers, before sitting back up and wincing as she looked at me.

"Roughly six days. It's just under three miles, as the crow flies. With two shifts working back-to-back, it shouldn't be an issue, and that covers us for brain-dead exhaustion as well."

"Brain-dead?" Clarissa looked annoyed.

"She means whoever's doing it is going to be bored to all hell, that's all." I glared at Aly, who had the good grace to wince, before apologizing.

"Sorry, Clarissa. I didn't mean that. I've done it, remember? I know how dull it can be," she said, getting a glare and crossed arms from the older lady as her only response.

"Okay, moving on!" I said hastily. "I agree with the plan to the northeast section. Clarissa, if you and your people can concentrate on that, please? I'd like you to expand along from the northeastern corner of the training dungeon on Dean Street, all the way up Grey Street, and turning west on Market Street, down Grainger Street, and returning to our current walls along Westgate Road. Does that make sense?"

"It does. It's also a fair bit larger than we discussed."

I nodded. "It is. And as you'll also have the team working to expand to Saltwell Park, I think it's best to do the outer loop first. Then we can raise the walls, seal the underground, and move into the buildings and 'fill in' the area afterward, basically."

"It's a hell of a space to claim, boy. You know it'll take awhile, right? You don't expect it all done in a few days?"

"No, I expect a week at the earliest, just to claim the outer ring," I assured her, and she relaxed. We both knew it could be done in less time, and we both knew the other knew that. But the simple truth was, there were a million jobs to do, and although her team had worked their asses off already, expanding the border of the dungeon as fast as they could, it took mana to do it, and mental effort.

There was no point in breaking people now that we'd gotten the local area more or less pacified.

"So, as we were saying, Barry." I turned back to him. "What we'll do is take your people on, yes, but we won't be opening the dungeon to everyone. We'll open the current area to a select few, namely the people we know we can trust. That's including any who have bled and fought for us, and their immediate families— wives, husbands, and kids, etc. No third cousins twice removed. I'll go that far. The rest can stay where they are. And in a week or so, we'll start raising the new walls and building the city block we were talking about, in the center of the park."

I smiled ruefully. "I know it sounds like I'm giving with one hand and taking away with the other, but a lot of those people? They're not helping. They wouldn't help you when you asked for them to do anything. They sit and they eat, drink, and wait for something to change. My people here? *Our* people, if you still want to join?"

I gestured to where people were coming in to breakfast, seeing the smiles and the jokes. Some people looked terrible, clearly grieving, having lost people in the fight yesterday, and yet, still they were there, putting a brave face on and asking what they could do to help.

"They're working, mate. They understand that if they don't help, we're all fucked. The people at the park will have to learn this. They don't have to go fighting if they're unsuited to it. They don't have to crawl through sewers or stand on the front line, *but they have to work*. They can strip the surrounding buildings, they can help to teach the kids, they can feed those who can't feed themselves."

"They can craft, they can clean, they can fucking well tell jokes and help people. I don't care—they just have to contribute," I finished.

"And if they won't?" Barry asked quietly but firmly. "Matt, I agree, you know that, but some of these people are in shock. They're broken. They won't interact beyond feeding and shitting." He shook his head. "Honestly, it pisses me off, but I can't just ignore them and leave them to starve…"

"And neither will we. If they're not criminal, if they're not assholes, but they just refuse? If they can work, but they won't?" I asked, making sure he understood I meant by choice, not medical or mental capability. "Then they'll have a space in a barracks or rooms inside the walls at Saltwell. They'll have the most basic food prepared as it is now. They'll be offered a safe place to exist, until they're ready to earn more."

"Earn?"

"Everyone will be paid," I said. "I'll not let people starve, again. Everyone will be given a wage, even if it's just a handful of copper a day, and that will cover the basic meals. But if they want to better themselves? Then they work and help. Medically, they'll all be healed, so that's no excuse not to help. And if they're in shock, etc.? They'll be helped. It's the terminally fucking lazy and unhelpful this is aimed toward, not those who are broken."

"If they want more than the basic subsistence life, then they'll help. It makes sense," Griffiths said, before breathing out slowly and shaking his head. "I need to add, Matt, that we stayed because it was the right thing to do. We can't stay forever, though. I'm sorry."

"You had lives down south," I agreed, nodding. "I know, and I figured this might happen, so how about a compromise?"

"I'm listening."

"When we talked and I said a year, before we could provide transport and so on, it was on the grounds that we thought it would take months to reach Iron as the core. Now?" I shrugged, gesturing around us. "The upgrade is in progress already, and should be done in the next few days. As much as I hate that undead asshole? He brought an insane amount of mana to the door, and we found ways to make more. Give me three months." I paused, seeing the way he opened his mouth to refuse, and I went on.

"Give me three months, run our forces with Sarah as your second, and Mike as the overall military leader of the dungeon. Markus and Jeffrey and the others will help as trainers as well. Build us an army, I'll get you transport to return south, and when the time comes? I'll provide you with reinforcements to make sure you get there."

"Dungeon creatures?" he asked, and I shook my head.

"No. Although, if I thought it'd work, I'd say yes. I think that if they go too far from the dungeon, they'd fail and die, but that's just a guess. No, I mean we'll develop transport systems. Iron as a core is a massive upgrade from Bronze, but the next in line? Steel? That has to come with more options. Give me three months—rest, recover, and help me. We'll consolidate the local area, make sure it's safe, and then push out, try to link up with the other bases in the area."

"And Otterburn?" Rhodes asked, interjecting.

"What about it?" I asked, confused, as it was in the wrong fucking direction. "I know Catterick is on the way south. Yeah, it's a bit farther away than Otterburn but—"

"It's a fully functioning training facility, as well as a main secure base for the North of England. If you want ammunition, equipment, and, more importantly, soldiers? That's the place we need to go."

"You said it was overrun by possessed people with black veins. I don't see them joining us…"

"You've got healers," Griffiths said slowly. "Look, Rhodes is right. That base is heavily equipped. We're talking the kind of equipment that can't fall into the hands of people who don't know what they're doing. And anyone in the area who knows about it? They'll head straight for it and be taken down by whatever has taken the base over. You've got a shitfull of magic. Surely we could do something once we got there…"

"Wait, you want *me* to go there?" I blinked, stunned.

"Why not?" Griffiths asked.

"Because the dungeon—"

"You said before you were leaving Aly and the others in charge. Either they weren't really or you're lying about the dungeon dying," he said flatly, getting a glare from me. "Yeah, that's what I thought. Look, Matt, you want our help? Fine, here's the deal. Two months. Two months, we'll stay and help you, provided I can talk my people into this. Because if they say no? I'm not shooting them for leaving me and heading back home."

"Of course not…"

"Exactly." He nodded. "So, two months and we'll clear the area, train your people, play nice and all of it. In that time, you get us transport, and you help us check the Otterburn camp out. If there's nothing we can do to save those people, then we evaluate the defenses, and we either raid it and escape with the gear, or we pull back. The one thing I won't accept, though, is abandoning soldiers in need without at least trying." He sat back, folding his arms, and I glared at him.

"*If* we can get transport up and running," Aly said softly, and I looked to her in question. "If…and that's a big if, okay? But *if* it's possible, it might be worth it? But…transport won't be ready in two months. Maybe, and I mean *maybe*, I could do it in three. But two?"

"Mike?" I asked, and he glanced at me, confused.

"What?"

"Get me an ice cream, will you?" I said sarcastically, then snorted. "What the hell do you think, you idiot? What do you think of this!"

"If we can check it out from a vehicle? Fuck, yes," he said. "That camp is loaded for bear. There's enough ammo that we could be set for years. But more than that? If we can save the soldiers? We have to try."

"I'll agree to trying, *if* we can get transport, and on the condition that if we work toward hitting that base, you give me three months," I hedged.

"Matt…" Griffiths said slowly, starting to shake his head, and I went on quickly.

"Just hear me out." I held up a hand, waiting until he nodded. "I'm saying three months, because preparing a raid, from some kind of transport in two months, hitting the base, and, yeah, doing our best to save everyone, is one thing. Planning enough transports and outfitting an entire team to get to London? That's like five or six times as far. Whatever transport we figure out will need to be adjusted, issues we find fixed…all that crap."

"You seemed to think it was a done deal before."

"I hoped it was, and I still do, but we need to wait and see," I said. "If we can, then we will. But the dungeon? We genuinely don't know if it will survive without me. Aly doesn't have the class to take it over. So, most likely? It *would* die. The walls and all should stay, but the rest? Probably lost."

"About what we thought," Rhodes said with a grin.

"So, anything else?" I looked around.

"Yeah, next steps," Mike said firmly. "We've got the overall plan, and it sounds good, but where do we start?"

"Shit. Okay, Barry? Take your people home, spread the word, and tell them what the situation is, and that in the coming weeks, we'll be taking over the camp and building a more secure one. Make it clear that they help, or they get the most basic of everything only. If they're known criminals? They can join the army and work off their time, provided they're not capital crimes. Capital crimes are murder, rape, terrorism, espionage, and attacking a member of my people. Make that last one very fucking clear. They join and hurt someone in here? They'll regret it for the last seconds of their life."

"They're not criminals, Matt!" he snapped. "Most of them are good people. Yeah, there's some assholes, but I bet you've got plenty of them here as well."

"We probably do, but we're starting a new day here, mate, and absorbing thousands into the group uncontrolled would be madness, you know that," I said firmly, before looking around. "Okay, while Barry's sorting that out, we're going all out. We need to strip the local area like never before. We've already hit the areas we knew would have easy and high profit targets—the pear shop, the IT hubs, all that shit. Now it's time to clear the rest. We'll be splitting our focus. Those who don't want to be a fighter or a mage, that's for you. Aly and Finn, find any prospective crafters and gather them up, see what we can get started with, and get them leveling."

She nodded, and I turned to Ramnik.

"Ramnik, gather the mages, and we'll start planning for the future. Magic changed the course of the battle yesterday, and we need more of it."

"I've got some ideas," Ramnik said, and I nodded.

"Glad to hear it. Okay, after this? Meditation on the roof, and we can talk about it. Patrick?"

"Yeah?" Patrick glanced from Ramnik to me.

"I know…Monk class. Well, you use mana, just channeling it through your body instead of using it externally, right?"

"Yes?"

"So, join us for meditation, and we'll see what we can do. Might be that your methods and mine are totally different, but fuck it, we can discuss the various options, see if anything helps—" I broke off as Griffiths lifted a hand for attention. "Really, dude?"

"Well, you were concentrating," he said with a wry smile. "So, I'm down to seven soldiers. Any chance of us joining in with the magic lessons?"

"Makes sense…" I muttered, before looking over at Aly. "I was just going to have us sit on the roof with the converters and meditate, but I suppose it doesn't really matter where…"

"It makes sense to do it where the converters are," Aly disagreed. "Maybe do it in relays? Have say, ten at a time come and join you?"

"If it's an issue…" Griffiths offered, and I shook my head.

"No, no, it makes sense. Leave me with it, and we'll come up with a plan today, okay?"

"Griffiths?" Mike said, and he glanced over, curious. "You weren't about for the conversation before, but there's another army base in the area, the Fifth Fusiliers, about two, two and a half miles from here, with a few smaller bases dotted around, like the REME and artillery centers."

"Right?"

"So, we were talking before about heading out and examining the bases, see if they're secure. If so, trying to recruit them and fold them into the dungeon's forces and—" I broke off as Mike dropped his head into his hands and groaned, and Griffiths shook his head firmly. "What?"

"They're the army, Matt," Mike said, before banging his forehead on the table. "They won't just fold into your forces, for fuck's sake!"

"I know it won't be easy but—"

"Matt, I think what Mike means to say is that the army won't obey you. We have specific orders when the shit hits the fan. We secure our bases, and we protect civilians," Griffiths clarified.

"Yeah, okay. You're all heading back to the south, I know…"

"We are, or we plan to, but those who have a base in the area will be looking to take the area over and secure it themselves. They'll be searching for *elected* civilian command, such as the local members of Parliament and, failing that, council leaders. That's what they should be doing. Then they'll secure the area as best they can. With the creatures coming and going, the general shit that's happening? If you stroll up and say 'Hey, I'm a Dungeon Lord; you serve me now,' they'll shoot you."

"I wasn't going to fucking say that," I growled. "I'm not an idiot."

"You sure?" Mike asked, and I glared at him.

"Seriously, though, if you want the local forces to fold in with you as the best option?" Griffiths asked, and I nodded. "They'll need to understand that you're *not* a threat, but that you're powerful enough to *be* a threat and a potential home for them. You need to show you're securing the area, protecting people, and you're offering a real alternative. As things are?" He gestured around vaguely. "They'll probably refuse, or try to fold you under *their* command."

"That's not happening," I said firmly.

"And that's another point, Matt. You're a nice guy, really you are, but you're not a democratically elected leader. As you said before, you're the boss. Great, fine, totally understand that. But I've spent the last few days seeing everything that's going on. Had you said that when we first met? I'd be thinking 'warlord,' not ally. I'd have been considering removing you from power for the good of the area."

"It'd end badly," I warned him.

"I know, and I'm not looking at that, as I said. But you need to understand that first impressions count massively. I'd seriously recommend we don't reach out to that base until the local area is pacified and secure. Get the walls up, get the base in Saltwell Park underway, get a command center that looks the part—rather than us discussing the future of the country, and probably the world, over breakfast and beers in a public dining room."

He gestured around the room, and I winced, seeing how many people were sitting quietly, eating their breakfast on nearby tables and listening to the plans. I trusted them, and I had nothing to hide, but still…

"I agree," Mike said, and others around the table nodded. "To be clear, I wasn't about to suggest we reach out to that base, but I needed to make sure you were aware of their existence. I think a few days of preparation, and then we should make overtures to them, scout it at least, and have Ashley use her class to make the introductions."

I paused, glancing at Ashley, then nodded. The Courtesan class wasn't as she'd originally feared, a glorified hooker. Instead, it was a spymaster, diplomat, assassin, and alchemist rolled into one.

She was perfect for it, having spent her life as the "beautiful one" of her groups, and being hounded by people who wanted to own her, rather than love her for herself.

She and her younger sister had won the genetic lottery, both around five and a half foot, stunningly beautiful and naturally athletic, as well as intelligent, considerably beyond the average. Ashley had seen the way people had reacted to her from a young age, and had resolved to make the most of it, on her terms.

She wore makeup and had cosmetic surgery, but she used it and viewed it much in the way that Mike viewed wearing his body armor and servicing his rifle.

It was her armor, taking what she'd been given naturally, and instead of slipping into the role of an influencer, or kept woman, as most people thought she should, hanging off the arm of a footballer or being a model, she'd hidden behind a perfect smile, gliding through life and working her ass off.

She'd seen the threats all around her, and she'd promised and flirted, danced and dined, and played the game, but never allowed anyone too close.

When the world had ended, and the animals had come knocking, expecting to make her "theirs," they'd found a woman smarter than all of them put together, and hard as diamond. She'd played one off against another until she'd come to the dungeon and been given the opportunity to get her hands on real weapons.

When she'd leveled, the system had recognized her talents, and had rewarded her accordingly, augmenting her already amazing natural charisma—and expensively "enhanced" physique—with bonuses that helped her to reach new heights.

Amusingly for the rest of us, that was when she'd met Dante.

Dante was a pyromancer, a boy fascinated by fire to such a degree that he'd developed a Fire mage's ability *naturally*, and with the sheer balls and brains to make the most of it. He was an innocent in many ways—gangly, awkward, and regularly picked on growing up, and certainly after the fall.

He'd even had his club, literally a glorified stick, stolen from him by another volunteer. Yet still, when the majority had fled, he'd stood tall and had come with Kelly and the others, to help save the dungeon.

He'd met Ashley and had fallen head over heels in love with her, attracted by the obvious looks, but spending more and more time in awe of her mind.

His bravery and innocence made an impression on her, where shining gold and abs you could bounce a quarter off of, publicly worshipped footballers, and the gleaming smiles of male models had all failed.

After the battle yesterday, when we'd almost all damn well died, and he'd channeled literal hellfires onto our enemies, she'd fought with spear and sword, rallying troops and leading them in pitched battle, defending him and the other mages. After the fight, finding that they were both alive?

She'd made damn sure he was no longer "innocent." And by the stunned grin on his face as he sat with her, hands held under the table, they were both feeling as if they'd gotten the better end of the deal.

I paused then, and actually looked at the pair of them, realizing that Dante was a hell of a lot more than I'd given him credit for when we'd first met, and more than society had conditioned me to expect. He *was* brave, honorable, and intelligent, after all. Sure, he was a normal guy, a few years younger mentally than his physical age, not out of his teens yet, with a scraggly beard that he clearly thought a "wizard" should have, skinny and with a face pock-marked with acne, but he was a good guy.

"I'll go," Ashley said, before shrugging. "It is my job, after all." She smiled.

Dante nodded and opened his mouth to volunteer as well, when I cut him off, speaking firmly.

"Thank you, Ashley. We'll see what we decide, but it makes sense to send you, and to make sure you have an escort. For now, though, I agree. Let's get the dungeon sorted out, *then* we can look farther afield." I paused, reordering my thoughts before moving on.

"Okay..." I frowned and looked around. "We've covered the immediate plans for expansion, bringing the park in and dealing with issues there, the local army bases and your people, Griffiths, the mages...what's next?"

"Research and development, crafting, and security," Aly said.

CHAPTER FOUR

"Okay, well, research wise, the dungeon is upgrading, so the normal systems like automated research and so on are off-line, meaning it's all down to you and your people, right?" I asked Aly, getting a nod.

"It is, and for now, with most of the deeper systems off-line with the upgrade, I'm focusing on equipment, as that's something we can improve very easily. There's no point in wasting my time on armor or weapons, frankly. Once the upgrade is complete, we'll have access to more materials and higher technology, so whatever I do now, it may well unlock anyway. Instead, I'm working on tools and crafting gear, creating 'blanks' for things like leather, ingots, hammers, and chisels, all that kind of thing. Basically, everything the crafters will need."

"Okay, so you're doing that, and...?"

"I'm waiting to hear what the mighty Dungeon Lord of Newcastle wants me to do," Aly prompted, and I nodded, finally getting what she'd been hinting at.

"Right! Okay, what we do is focus on the advanced kobold design and—"

"It's done."

"What?"

"It's done," Aly repeated, before taking a deep breath and settling back more comfortably. "Okay, look, you know when you and a few other idiots went all batshit and leapt off the walls? When you spent literally a full day fighting with the corpse lords and basically showing off? Well, *some* of us were working."

"I did tell you the next morning, Matt, but you were still a bit out of it," Kelly apologized. "I talked to Aly, when we realized how much mana was coming in, and I pushed the advanced kobold research forward, completing that. Then we researched the common variant of the corpse lords, and because the bar was filling faster than we could spend it, we had the system run up armor for them. Then we started spending on summons instead."

"I remember...vaguely," I muttered, frowning.

"We made more control capacity generators, upping the limit to two hundred and forty, then spent most of the windfall on summoning common corpse lords, replacement kobolds, and equipping everyone."

"Then the core upgrade kicked in..." I remembered, nodding. "It's still in progress, but yeah, okay, that makes more sense. I saw something about the kobolds when I woke up that day and dismissed it, I think..."

"You'd fought on the front lines against the undead for most of a day with your team. Hell, you had people chanting your name while they watched. Do you remember how many you killed?" Griffiths asked, smiling and shaking his head as I frowned, trying to remember. "Over two *thousand*. Just lifting a single small weight two thousand times in a day would have broken most men. Even enhanced as we all are now, fighting like that? It was impressive."

"It wasn't just me," I corrected, shrugging uncomfortably.

"Yeah, but most of us took goddamn breaks," Chris said. "But noooo, Mr. Godling here has to try to show us all up…"

I glared at him and got a wink.

"Well, just you wait, mate. One day you'll grow up and get to play with the big boys," I shot back, getting the finger.

"Moving on before you children start another argument…" Aly sighed. "We need a plan for the dungeon, Matt. *Yes*, we've got one for the accommodations, and we need to discuss the farms we finished as well, but for now? The dungeon needs an overarching plan, as well as a new layout."

"She's right." Markus shifted forward and gestured at the rough drawing Aly had done. "I don't know about the rest of the plans, like the research and so on—no clue what that's about, and frankly I'd rather not worry about it—but we need to plan for it for the military, and we need a dedicated space to work…"

"And the research section needs to be increased in size, and capacity," Aly said. "As things stand, it's all working, just, but when we do bring more people in? It's going to be a mess unless we plan this out now."

"Okay…" I muttered, agreeing wholeheartedly. "Let's stop, roll it back a step." I picked out a section of paper, then snorted and tossed it aside, starting to absorb everything but the drawings on the table instead.

In less than a minute, it was clear, the few drinks people weren't finished with having been swept up protectively, or replaced if they weren't fast enough.

I spread the paper back out and drew the outline of the land we had so far, starting on the left and angling up to the right, down to the farthest right-hand section, and then back up to the left, making a rough triangle.

"Okay, so this is the area we have, or will soon be claiming," I said, then started to sketch in the current buildings.

"This is the dungeon building…" I went from slightly in on the left-most or west side, and along a little in a straight line. "This is the training dungeon…" A second block was created down and to the east. "And this is the living quarters." I filled in the section to the south of the dungeon building and due west of the training dungeon.

"You know, you're a shit artist, mate," Chris said after a few seconds of silence.

"I hate you," I muttered, getting a laugh from several of the others. "Right. Before you all give me more grief about this shit, let's try to plan this out."

I paused, thinking, then added the castle in at the bottom right. But rather than the broken and crumbling ruin, I drew it out with the original, as far as I could tell, walls.

"Uh-oh…he's got a plan," Chris muttered.

"Fuck, I'm out," Aly said, quickly trying to get up and pretending to panic. "Mike, move—run, man, run!"

"Okay, you lot!" I said loudly, ignoring the byplay. "This is what I'm thinking. We demolish the rest of the buildings on the promontory around the castle—what's there again?"

"The Moot Hall." Kelly sighed. "It's a nice old building, made in the nineteen hundreds, I think…"

"Is it any use?"

"Well…it could be…"

"Would it be better used by us as it is, or flattened and rebuilt?" I asked more firmly.

"Flattened," she admitted after a few seconds of struggling with herself. "The rooms are all shapes and sizes, the plumbing is—"

"Flattened then." I shrugged, not getting emotional about it. "Everything here…" I marked the area that was currently full of the remaining buildings around the castle. "Can go. We repair the castle, make walls that are actually appropriate to a fucking castle, and use that as a holding zone. That's going to be the official entrance to the dungeon. People want to come in? They enter there. We'll make some normal accommodation for visitors and various storage areas, medical and so on, and we make a central building that looks like it can hold against a fucking army—"

"You said that the accommodations would be secure," Barry interrupted.

"And it will," I assured him. "This isn't a fallback position." I grinned evilly.

"It's a trap." Griffiths hunched forward and frowned. "It'd be an expensive one, though."

"Exactly. If we're going to make this into a real home? Sooner or later, people will come, looking to take it from us. What we do is make this the research and leadership *public* building. People will want to point to something and say, 'That's it.'"

"You want to put my wife in there as bait?" Mike asked slowly, glaring at me.

"Yeah, and the rest of the government types, you know, the head of the forces, etc., we'll all have our official space here." I tapped the drawing, then looked around and made sure that nobody outside our little group could hear me as I went on.

"Yes and no. First of all, we need a public place that people can point to as the heart of the dungeon. We need it to be impressive and visible. We'll make it secure as fuck as well, though—solid stone, glass that can shrug off a howitzer shell…that kinda shit.

"It'll be the public building, but it'll have an escape tunnel, one that we can seal shut with meters of solid stone behind our people if they have to retreat.

"There's a cavern underneath us, and it's a big one. What we'll actually be doing is setting up, when we can, a secondary fallback point there. We'll also have tunnels we design so that they can be collapsed leading out to the other sections. Then we build high, lethally defended walls around the rest of the compound. If anyone wants to attack us like the undead did? They come in, and we close the gates behind them, turn this area…"

I gestured to the open area around my new "castle" and grinned. "We turn this into a killing ground."

"Evil…I like it. What else?" Rhodes asked.

I nodded to the accommodation block we'd already made to the south of the dungeon. "That," I said simply. "We build a new accommodation for everyone— better, safer and stronger, with more room…the works. Then we convert this and the buildings next to it into the barracks and a training zone.

"The south becomes the defense and training areas. The middle is the training dungeon, nice and close to the barracks. And as far as the new people care? *That's* the dungeon. This building here remains the true heart of the dungeon, but we'll also be beefing up the walls and roof, etc. This will stay as *our* accommodation for now, although eventually we'll sort out nice apartments, I imagine, and the canteen and so on will stay here as well.

"Eventually it'll be used for other things, no doubt, but for now? Best people just think of it as I'm weird and live in the basement, and you all put up with that. You're welcome to claim better rooms, though. We'll convert as much space as you need."

"What about the rest?" Aly asked, and I nodded.

"The old printing press and the triangle tip due north of here, we'll convert into the crafting hall, slowly, because we've not got that many crafters. That's a lot of space, but still…"

"That's only half the space we'll be holding."

"And that's because the northeast quarter will be accommodations and construction. We flatten this section…" I drew a circle around the buildings immediately to the east of the dungeon and north of the training section, including the building I dropped on the undead dickhead.

"Then we begin construction. We'll build the accommodation block as a skyscraper, heavily reinforced underneath, then make each floor from there upward, aim for the first four floors as we discussed, two with single apartments, one with twos and one with threes. Then, I don't know, a canteen floor? With loads of seating and an area for the kids to chill, away from their families? Something like that? Maybe somewhere for people to hang out."

"I can do that," Aly agreed, nodding. "It makes sense to give them somewhere that's theirs and that's safe."

"Okay, any other changes?" I asked, getting a handful of additional recommendations as we went.

"What about the rest of that block to the north?" Mike frowned. "It's a big space…"

"We clear it," I said. "We clear it all and make it additional farmland for now. Should we need to, we can make another tower. But honestly, I think this will do for now. And we're better off making somewhere people can just walk around and work in safety out there."

"Question. Maybe you've covered this, but…" Griffiths asked slowly. "Why grow food at all? You can magic it up, can't you?"

"It's a fair point," I admitted. "The growing plants will help us generate nature mana, and life, which the converters can harness for us. The food itself will be cheap to produce, hopefully, and…"

"And it gives people something to do to keep them busy?" Rhodes guessed shrewdly.

"Well, yes and no. Yes, it's good for that, but more, with the nature magic we have access to, we should be able to strengthen the crops, make them the best versions of themselves we can grow. Then harvesting them for the table or for potions, we'll just keep improving the 'standard,' basically. Also, it'll provide resources that anyone from outside can identify, and it'll play down the 'dungeon' side of things. We don't want to be too tasty a target."

"I'd say growing food will make you that regardless," Griffiths said.

"It's a game of minimizing the risks, but there's no way to be without them and still recruit. We give people what they expect to see, and then we deal with the consequences." I shrugged, sitting back and noting Aly making a quick few notes, then wiping the table clear in the dungeon sense, making sure nobody could study the details later.

I grimaced at the thought of not being able to fully trust "my people," but I understood it, and approved. "So, what else was on the list?" I asked, aware of the insane flashing of the notifications I had waiting.

"Finn, can you give us a crafting update, please?" Aly said distractedly, as she made a few more notes.

"It's happening?" he replied. "There's not much more to say at this point. I have a dozen others with me, and we're all working on the same few stations, taking turns and basically getting in each other's way. Ideally, we need a crafting hall, with a station each, like a tailor's area, a blacksmith's, and so on, but honestly? As much as we need it, it'd also be overkill right now. I need to make things clear so you're not getting too excited here, but for things like the potion bag I made yesterday?"

"Yeah?"

"That took me two days." He shrugged. "To make it, I had to plan it all out, cut it to shape, stitch it, make things like pockets, belt loops, a drawstring…I know it sounds like there's not that much to it, and yes, it's massively easier than it was at first, thanks to things like the leather being provided, ready tanned and treated…but it takes damn time! If I had a sewing machine? It'd be a case of one an hour, probably, but by hand, it takes time.

"I can make more of them, making them better each time, or you can copy the first one. I know we have the potions, and we can replicate them, but as we covered the other day, each and every one is the same. To improve them? We need time and practice."

"And the other crafters?"

"Much the same. Basically, I've got a guy working on a spear at the minute. It should be done in the next day or so, and it's frankly shit compared to the ones we have right now, but he's learning. In a few days, he'll be able to make a better one than he can today, and then as time goes on? More and more."

"It seems mad," I admitted, toying with my can. "That we can summon things like this, I mean, and hopefully soon we'll be able to make weapons that there's no way we should be able to make by hand, rail guns and shit, and we're wasting people's time learning to make spears—"

"But that's just it!" Finn interrupted, sitting forward excitedly. "It's not a waste! Look, yeah, a spear he makes, it's not a lethal weapon—it really isn't, and yeah, Aly can take it, blow it up in the research system and replace the parts with new ones. It's made of bronze and iron as that's the very best we can do now. But the guy who's making it right now? Once he understands his craft a bit more, he'll be able to help in the research node to make a better spear. He'll understand the spear in ways that Aly never can."

"It's true," Aly agreed. "I'm working on everything and nothing. I get a general understanding of things, but having a blacksmith, or a leatherworker working with their hands and then working with the research details? They can make things much better than I can. They can make the parts of, say…a rifle. They could make them out of bronze or iron or whatever as we level the core and get the systems we need, but as they learn? As they study the research systems? They'll be able to make improvements that I just can't."

"That's the next step for the crafters and research teams," Finn said, getting a nod of agreement from Aly. "We need to start working on a research and development block, like the housing area. Scientists and crafters working together to create wonders. You want rail guns? That's how we get them. Engineers and armorers working on guns, taking system information and learning!"

"We need that," Griffiths said. "Look, Matt, as much as we need to move on, and yes, we do, we also need to look at the bigger picture. You say you'll get us transport and more? Great. Being realistic, though? We go south, find our families and our friends, and then what? You think we're going to just forget about you?"

"No. You want to work on the rail guns and spaceships, fighter jets and I don't know, lasers or whatever? Well, give us a few days with our people to get things sorted, then I'm betting we'll be heading straight back up here."

"Really?" I had it in my head that they'd be gone, and that was it, but…it made sense. After all, why would they stay in the South, not even considering the fact that the North was *obviously* God's country—literally now—but realistically, rebuilding civilization around the dungeon was just logical.

"It's something that's yet to be decided, and it may be that I'm overruled," Griffiths said. "Add to that, I'm a captain, and although I believe that it's logical to ally with you, and be part of the dungeon—and yes…I'll take orders from you, provided they're not bloody stupid—my superiors may think differently."

"And they might decide to make a play for the dungeon," Mike pointed out, getting a glare from Griffiths. "Hey, you know them. The upper officers? Most aren't too bad, but yeah, some, though? If they see a chance to seize power? They'll try to take it."

"Are civilian politicians any better?" Rhodes argued, and I held up my hands, moving to head off an argument before it could get worse.

"Whoa!" I snapped, patting the air. "Yeah, there'll be some assholes at the top, I've no doubt…turds always float. And as to politicians? Fuck yeah, they'd be worse…" It was a long-held belief of mine that anyone who wanted to be a politician was proved to be unsuitable by that desire alone.

"Matt, the army won't just salute and fall in, obeying you—" Griffiths started, and I nodded, holding a hand up again.

"I know, okay? I know. You've got a point, though, and that's why we have these discussions, so we get everything out and come up with plans. Yes, no doubt some fuck nugget will try to take command based on the fact they lied successfully enough that people thought they gave a shit…"

"Had one of those already," Barry muttered. He paused as people looked over at him and he shrugged. "He kept issuing orders, and confusing things. People died, so I shot him."

"And there's a permanent solution to politicians!" Patrick interjected happily, only to receive a glare from John.

"I was a copper because I believed in the rule of law, and keeping people safe," he interjected. "So we need to address *that* as well…"

"Fuck's sake, Barry," I muttered, rubbing the bridge of my nose with a finger and thumb. "Okay, OKAY!" I raised my voice. "This is what we're doing. Griffiths, you and your people work with the fighters we have. You'll be kitted out with the same gear we had for the fight, and you'll have your guns for backup—"

"We're almost all out of ammo," Mike said, then winced and held a hand up in apology.

"You'll have your guns for backup, and we'll work on the ammo situation," I repeated grimly. "You work with Mike and make goddamn sure the buildings around us are empty. Send out a squad to the nearest smaller bases, the artillery sites and so on—not the big one. Ashley, you go with them. See if you can recruit any soldiers in there, and if so? Great. If the site looks abandoned, hit it, recover any weapons and ammo you can. The next few days is that, on fucking steroids. We know there are others in the area. Get out there, find me ammo and allies, and see if you can find where the hell those assholes got the military gear from in the first place." I paused, making sure they understood, before I went on.

"While you're doing that, we'll build up the dungeon, make more and better dungeon creatures, and lay the groundwork for the dungeon's place in the world. We'll get ourselves laid out and straightened up. As we agreed, appearances matter, and I get that."

I looked around, seeing how damn scruffy we were, and sighed. "We'll also need a tailor to work on a uniform or something, I guess…"

"I don't think we need to worry quite that far," Kelly whispered, taking my hand and holding it, gently supporting me, as I let out a relieved breath.

"I hope not," I said. "Okay, so while you're doing that, and we're sorting the dungeon out, we'll also be sorting out our *people*. A lot of them are working their arses off stripping the local buildings, and although we desperately needed that, and still do, a lot of them want something different. It's time we addressed that, too."

"Like what?" Chris asked, surprised.

"Like recruiting more crafters, more researchers, people to work in the fields that we make," I said. "Finn's point about the equipment is a damn good one. We need to practice and learn."

"I need more volunteers as well," Jo interjected. "I have a few medical trained staff, and they've worked wonders, all having gotten the healer basic class, but I don't see any way we could have too many healers, not the way the world is going. Now's the time to train them."

"Good point," I agreed. "So, Clarissa, you're in charge of people, you and your council. I need, and I hate saying this, considering how many have just died for us, but I need more volunteers to fight. I need volunteers for healers, for the fields and researchers. Find me any you can from the teams that are stripping the buildings."

"I'll ask," she said, and I nodded, appreciating the fact she wasn't saying anything else about our losses from the fighters.

"Okay, people, that's plenty to be getting on with. I'm going to summon some more kobolds for Beta to break in, after meditating on the roof. Mages, with me." I climbed to my feet, feeling as if we'd done nothing but chase our own goddamn tails in the entire meeting.

CHAPTER FIVE

Half an hour later, I sat on the rooftop. The gentle rain of early this morning had passed, and a steady breeze had sprung up, making the rooftop almost uncomfortably cool. I sat, trying to find that special meditative trance, as the others sat around me, finally learning that a little space was my goddamn right as the Dungeon Lord. It was also helped by the fact I sat in the middle of a Storm, Lightning, and Thunder converter.

Where before I'd found the meditation easily, this morning I couldn't focus. Every time I managed it, sinking into myself and following the fast-flowing mana as it raced along my channels, a noise, a sudden fly buzzing around my ear, or a badly timed fart by one of the others jerked me out of it.

There were so many details that were new. The Arcanist class I'd taken…it changed everything! I'd been used to my place in things, magically, anyway; now I started to see that I was more like a goldfish in a bowl, sitting on the shelf of a cruise ship, having no goddamn clue about the rest of the world around me.

In taking the Arcanist class, a thousand tiny and overt details became obvious as the minutes passed. I concentrated and the world seemed to blur, rolling away as I fell inward, sinking ever downward into my mana channels.

The first seconds were strange, as a thousand details tried to distract me— everything from the tingle of unfamiliar mana rolling across my skin, to the cells and their interactions as mana seemed to reinforce them.

I ignored it all, picking out the channels of power, and imagining myself as a boat on a river. I dipped into, and began to flow along, the racing river inside me, the lightning leaping joyously to carry me along.

Seconds passed, changing to minutes, as I reveled in the power. My mana channels were growing, and my body, once seemingly a receptacle for lightning only, was starting to accept more and more again, and I could feel it.

Where the mana had once spread out, now it coalesced, becoming tighter and tighter. The power grew more intense as it flowed through those hoops and loops that Thor had once shown me.

I raced round the outer edge of my body, feeling the speed building as I raced along the channels. I allowed myself to circle twice, just relaxing and sinking deeper, burying myself away from all the concerns of the world and my dungeon, even as a slight tickle at the edge of my consciousness informed me that the fucking cat was somewhere nearby, and watching.

Eventually though, rather than racing past, I flowed inward, finding myself at the core. It towered over me, a giant multifaceted star surrounded by whips of nuclear fire. As before, the closer I came to the core, the clearer the star became.

It grew in my vision, shifting as the world around me reoriented. The mana that raced past on all sides became a mélange of thousands of different aspects.

The star shifted as I drew close. The fire that it seemed to be made of changed to glowing arcs, then paths, before finally into the massive pillars that swept out in interlocking arcs, dipping into the mana and drawing more and more of their aspect free.

I "landed" on the central pillar, a single massive strand, seemingly a mile or more across. I "stood" there, staring up, feeling the purity of the mana beneath and all around me.

Pure mana could be and do *anything*: it could be absorbed by any creature, and it worked to be whatever we needed. If we were injured, it healed us; it protected us, smote our enemies and more, provided we could interact with it, reaching out and forcing it to bend to our will.

Pure mana, though, wasn't natural.

As mana interacted with everything around us, it changed. It passed through a blazing house? It became "fire" aspected. Or through a dead body? Death.

The worst part was that, as near as we could tell, life generated mana, so it seemed "life" was pretty much the default; then it got mixed with other things.

It meant that everything was always changing, and as I looked up at the massive spire of pure mana, the sea of mana around it seemed to want to *be* it, and also to *absorb* it.

There was a lot I was missing, I knew. So many minor details stood out, like the way that if life created mana, but then was easily taken over by other kinds, how did any of it still exist outside of the bodies of the living? After all, Air mana was a thing...

Why didn't the mana that floated past at all times become air? Why did everything seem to change into pure mana to cast, and to create individual things, and yet cost so much less to create certain things out of mana?

Why was it cheaper to create an undead from Unlife mana, when pure was distilled from the Unlife? Surely it should be the other way around?

I didn't know, and instead of wasting my time worrying about it, I banished it from my mind, focusing on the pillars as they flew past, moving, unhappily, to the Water pillar.

I was at forty-nine percent affinity, and although it meant the damn thing no longer made me want to vomit, damn, I still didn't like it much.

I "knelt" on it, seeming to become solid and human in shape as I laid a hand to the mass below my hand, feeling the ridged lines, the solidity...and wondering what the hell it meant that it was solid here.

I could feel the flow beneath my hand, as the Water mana was drawn slowly upward, siphoned from the corrupted mass all around me and slid into the Water pillar, being slowly purified and stored, as more and more was pulled free.

Taking a deep breath, I reached down and pulled, feeling the draw increase. It wasn't much, but the longer I pulled at it, the more I felt the change, until finally...I was shaken from my meditation by the new prompt.

Congratulations!

Through careful study and manipulation, both of internal structures
and through the alignment of your soul, you have increased your
[Water Affinity] from [49%] to [50%].

Continue to study to raise this affinity further!

Your current evolutionary position is: Thunderstorm: 7%

Increase your capacity to reach the next level of Evolution.

7...7...7...7...7...

I stared at it, frowning, then looked all around, seeing the way the others sat silent…apart from one dickhead who kept chanting to himself.

"Ramnik," I whispered, before coughing and trying again. "Ramnik!"

She flinched, blinking and looking around, seemingly having been expecting something weird.

"Yes, Matt?" she asked carefully as I clearly fucked everyone's meditation up.

"Have you managed to land on your core yet?"

"Land…?"

"Fuck," I muttered, rubbing at my face and thinking how best to describe this. "Okay, we talked about your core, yeah?" I asked, both to her and the others around me I could sense listening. "Once you have that, draw in as close as you can. The world seems to change. The tiny stream of corrupted mana that the core is busy purifying becomes a sea all around you. You understand?"

"I…you land on it?" she asked again. "It's your core…you should observe it, and—"

"Yeah, you fucking land on it. Visualize yourself as a person, as *you*, landing on it. I just pressed my hands to a spire I've been having issues with, and *pulled*. I increased my affinity by a single point, and yeah, I'm knackered now…" I paused as I realized it was true: my heart hammered as if I'd been for a run, pounding the pavement for a good while. "It's not easy," I finished lamely.

"But you can increase your affinity?" she asked. "And it didn't damage its opposite?"

"What, and reduce it?" My eyes grew wide as I frantically pulled the notes up and scanned through them, before sagging in relief. "No," I said. "My Fire is still at seventy-six, thank fuck."

"So you can increase your affinity through effort…can you also increase it—"

"You can get rewards from the system. Like when I took Arcanist, I got a sixty percent increase I could assign," I interrupted her.

"Yes, I did as well. I was unsure if that was something you could only do once, however…"

"I got it once before as well, can't remember why," I muttered, and she nodded, smiling faintly before speaking in a louder voice to make sure everyone could hear.

"Okay then, those of you who are happy working on a single aspect, please continue to do so. Those who wish a more specific future? Consider the various affinities you have, and work toward that."

"What?" I asked, confused.

"Most people have a single affinity that is markedly higher than the others," Dante pointed out. "I'm Fire, pretty obviously, but there are other aspects of Fire that I could focus on, like the spell Inferno? The one that's in the focal orb?"

"Yeah?"

"There's an actual affinity for Inferno, which is a second-tier form of mana, Fire and Air combined. So if I wanted to focus on that specifically, I could raise my Air to be close to my Fire, and we think that the next time I get the chance to specialize, I'd get that as an option."

"Fuck, man, why didn't you tell me!" I growled, pulling my affinities up and searching quickly through them. I found what I was looking for a few seconds later, and cursed, before shaking myself as I clambered to my feet. I sighed, forcing a reassuring smile as I told him *It was okay, not your fault, mate*, and I set off in search of the crafters, having a sudden suspicion.

I paused in the doorway, turning back and calling out to them. "Nobody's seen that fucking cat around, have they?" I asked, getting stammered apologies that made me curse even more as I set off again. "Goddamn fluffy shitbag…I'll get him yet," I growled, half-formed plots involving catnip, kitty litter, and fucking popping candy roaming around my mind.

I could feel the little bastard nearby, and yet like all his furry-arsed kind, he was hiding when he was needed.

I forced myself to stop at the bottom of the first flight of the stairs, twisting aside and entering into one of the nearby rooms, moving away from the door and sitting in the far corner. I needed to act on the thought I'd had before but…

But I was always fucking running. My entire life felt like I was racing from decision to decision, and I hated that. I was used to working in IT, after all. If you ran around like a headless chicken in that field, absolutely *nothing* would get done. A friend of mine, Daniel, had been a sort of IT troubleshooter as well as a planner.

The bosses would have him in their meetings, and would tell him "this is what we'll do." Then they'd all fuck off for lunch and to schmooze another client, practically dislocating their own shoulders as they patted themselves on their backs that hard, while he worked literal IT sorcery and actually made it all work.

I couldn't do it, not at his level, but he was always calm, always collected and methodical and logical. He was like the fucking Spock of the IT world.

I needed some of that, some calm and collected planning. The first step, though, before I could do any of that, was to sort out my goddamn notifications, basically so they'd piss off and stop bothering me.

Congratulations, First Lord of the Storm!

As the first leader of a Local Pantheon to kill an opposing God, you have been granted the following Boons!

- +10 to a single Stat
- +2 Spells
- +2 Class Skill points

That was a simple one, and I'd seen it before, but hey, I'd not done anything with it yet, and the spells and class ability points would be massively important. The plus ten to a single attribute? Hell yes.

I put it aside, determined to be logical, and read through all the prompts before assigning the points, just in case.

Congratulations!

You have killed the following:
- 1x Enemy God, Lord of the Dead Daedalus, Level 28, 8,470 XP
- 2087x Mindless Undead Shamblers, Level 1-19, 18,554 XP

Total XP earned: 27,024 XP

A party under your command killed the following:
- 1107x Undead Legionnaires, Level 2-13, 34,495 XP
- 6016x Mindless Undead Shamblers, Level 1-16, 36,221 XP
- 1x Guardian Abomination, Level 11, 285 XP
- Wayne Kerr, Level 17, 2,145 XP

Total Party XP earned: 73,146 XP

As party leader, you receive 25% of all XP earned.
Total XP awarded 27,024+(73,146x0.25=18,286.5)=45,310
Partial XP is lost to the ether.

Current XP to next level stands at 53,986/25,000

You have 18 unspent Stat Points, and 10 unspent Skill Points.

*

Congratulations, First Lord of the Storm!

As you have entered a formal war with another local pantheon, the Pantheon of Unlife.

You have received a 10% boost for the duration of said conflict.

Please select this now:
Ambient Mana Generation: Yes/No
Mana Regeneration: Yes/No
Health Regeneration: Yes/No
Melee Damage: Yes/No
Ranged Damage: Yes/No

The boosts that have been selected by both sides will be awarded to the winner of the conflict as permanent boons!

Good luck!

I paused with this one, as it was a seriously important decision to make. I considered reaching out to the others, to ask for opinions, but I knew, in my heart, that this was one of those decisions I needed to make alone.

The Ambient Mana Generation was clearly for an area, when I looked at it, rather than a person, the feeling of a space clear in my mind. It'd cover roughly a square mile, presumably intended to help act as a training ground by spawning more powerful monsters inside it. Or...it could help a dungeon, which made me smile straightaway.

Mana regeneration? That'd be nice as well. After all, it'd literally boost me by a little. And I got a feeling this one was for people, a group specifically, so there had to be a way to designate my people as "dungeon followers" or some shit to make sure they all got it. I thought about it for a few seconds, then sighed.

It'd do me fuck all real help personally, as my mana was something like eighteen points an hour regenerating, so a ten percent boost for that, considering "partial points are lost to the ether" as the system gloried in reminding us, I'd basically get a single point extra an hour. It might help my people, though, so I'd consider it for that.

Next was Health Regeneration. That was a different level. Mana would be a nice thing, sure, yeah, but as long as my people could get out of combat? An extra ten percent on the speed they regenerated their Health, though? That could be literally life-saving.

That was a serious possibility.

The last two options were an extra ten percent damage to either melee or ranged damage.

Now, that made no real sense to me, how the hell they could make that work. After all, it wasn't as if the creators of the system were standing around, adding an extra stab or punch or whatever to the outcome…

I paused, listening to the tickle of intuition and following where it led, focusing on the damage that we did to each other, regardless of the kind.

It came down to the actual muscles we used and our Perception usually, I knew, like how Mike did more damage than I did, even if we used the same bullets and rifle, simply because he got a bonus to the damage he dealt through his increased Perception.

Again, the recognition of "Perception" tickled at me, and I followed that.

Perception…did the damage we received have something to do with if we believed it, then? No…that made no sense; if that was the case, a headshot from behind or when you were asleep wouldn't have any effect until you knew about it.

No, it had to be a function of the Perception itself, perhaps…perhaps the way you looked at a target? The extra ten percent was simply their way to "qualify" the damage to us, and the description, but that actual effect was that it came about because it was a solid increase to our Perception ability?

So we targeted someone, through the scope of the rifle for example, and because of our increased Perception, we simply aimed better? We were more likely to hit a target, and to do damage, because we saw it a little clearer?

Thinking back to the time I'd dumped a load of points into my Rifles skill, and I'd shot the shit out of the wraiths, that made a lot more sense: the bullets hadn't hit harder; they'd just been more likely to hit. I'd been better at tracking and hitting the fuckers!

That was it, I felt. It was a solid Perception increase, not a numbered one, which would have made more sense to me, but a subtle one, where it adjusted the things you saw…

That freaked me out a little, as I started to wonder about the aliens twisting our vision, making us see what they wanted…but ultimately I shook it off. Paranoia was a dangerous thing, especially after the fall of mankind.

I hesitated for a few seconds, then I chose the Health Regeneration.

I did it for two solid reasons. First and foremost, I wanted my people to live. This might be the difference between that for some of them, and as their leader, I had to think about them first.

Secondly…I had a feeling that if I picked something, and the undead dick picked it as well, I'd end up with two of the same bonuses when I killed them all.

The Life Regeneration was the least fucking likely for them to choose, and I wanted them all! I was guessing he'd pick Melee, which was a sensible option, but I was planning on stopping them getting close enough to land any blows anyway, thanks to the fact that the fucker was highly unlikely to have any clue that in addition to being the First Lord of the Storm…I was also a fucking Dungeon Lord.

I was betting he wouldn't expect me to have a fucking dungeon, especially not one that I could research heavy weapons in, and use against him!

I grinned at the surprise that fucker was in for, and I read on.

You have completed a Quest!

Quest!
Defend the Dungeon! (3)

The Lich Lord you slew spoke of its master, the Lord of the Dead. You have found the enemy God, and have defeated him in combat, protecting your dungeon against his invasive influence and earning the following bonuses:

- +6 to top three Attributes
- +1 Spell
- +2 Class Skill Points
- 20,000 XP

Bonus: *Additional Citizens of dubious morality*

I nodded at that. I'd damn well earned those rewards, but the goddamn "citizens of dubious morality" was all I fucking needed. Adding the twenty thousand from the Defend the Dungeon quest took me up to seventy-three thousand, nine hundred, and eighty-six, shooting me all the way from level 21 to 23, and gained me another eighteen points to spend.

You have gained additional Stat Points in the following areas through constant effort.

- +2 Agility
- +3 Constitution
- +4 Dexterity
- +3 Endurance
- +1 Intelligence
- +3 Luck
- +2 Perception
- +2 Strength
- +1 Wisdom

Continue to work hard to increase these or other stats…

I pulled up my stat sheet, comparing it and my new gains, and let out a low whistle at the difference. Between the optional "plus ten" that I could sink anywhere I wanted, that brought me up to twenty-eight new points to allocate, and the "plus six to top three attributes" dropped neatly into Dexterity, Endurance, and Luck.

Clearly even the system thought I was a lucky fuck who slid through shit by the skin of his teeth.

Name: Matt, First Lord of the Storm	
Modifiers: None	
Species: Thunderstorm	**Bonus:** None
Level: 23	**Progress to next level:** 18,986/35,000
Control: 34	**Dungeon Capacity**: 628 points (34x2=68+560=628)
Host Powers: 1 (Enhanced Regeneration)	**Class Spells:** 8 **Class Abilities**: 15

Stat	Current Points	Description	Effect	Progress to Next Level
Agility	33	Governs dodge and movement	Heightened chance to dodge attacks 66%+20%= 86%	77/100
Charisma	20	Governs likely success to charm, seduce, or threaten	30% more likely to succeed in events that require seduction, persuasion, or threats (10%+ (10x2) = 30)	58/100
Constitution	28	Governs Health and Health Regeneration	HP: 28x30 = 840	27/100
Dexterity	37	Governs ability with weapons and crafting	+37% Increased chance of improved result +13 to melee damage.	48/100
Endurance	35	Governs Stamina and Stamina Regeneration	Stamina: 35x40 = 1,400	56/100
Intelligence	38	Governs base manapool, standard intellectual capacity, plus Control when combined with Wisdom and divided by 2	Mana: 38x40=1520 Control: 38+30/2=34	37/100
Luck	35	Governs overall chance of bonuses and critical hits	+50% increased chance of positive outcome	17/100
Perception	26	Governs ranged damage and chance to spot hidden items/traps	+16 to all ranged attacks	88/100
Strength	32	Governs damage with melee weapons and carrying capacity	+44 to all damage with Melee weapons	54/100
Wisdom	30	Governs mana regeneration and Control, when combined with Intelligence and divided by two	19 mana regenerated per hour Control: 38+30/2 = 34 (30x10/8=37.5x2/2=37)	55/100

I looked the full screen over, frowning in thought. I needed to make the most of this, and not just because I had class skill points to allocate, but because this was the long game I needed to play.

I was gaining power steadily, but mainly? It was my magic that was the game changer. Sometimes it was the ability to go all "Lord of the Storm" and smash the shit outta things. Other times it was the versatility of my spells and summoned creatures.

Less and less, as part of the team, though, was it my sheer physical capabilities. That seemed insane, when I looked at the fact that the most-used stats for the fights recently were Dexterity, from wielding my weapons, and Endurance, from the goddamn stamina to go toe-to-toe with the undead for literally hours.

The decider was Luck. If I'd not been bloody stupid and distracted, determined to imbue that damn spear with the excessive mana I'd had after the storm, we'd have all died.

The mana I'd needed to imbue the weapons hadn't been excessive, but the fact I was always scrabbling for it? That had led me to panic in my use. I needed to be more stable, more reasoned, and fucking smarter.

Yeah, maybe in the future physical strength would be a bigger thing, and no doubt it'd be important regardless—there'd always be a need to kick someone's ass, after all—but...

I needed to grow up. If I'd had the Wrath of the Heavens spell? With a kick-ass manapool? I could have wiped the floor with so many of the undead we'd faced, it wasn't even funny.

The thought of facing the wraiths and the abomination and so on when the dungeon had first been surrounded?

I could have stood on the walls and fucking *nuked* them.

I needed to accept that I was a ranged fighter, unless everything was going to shit. I had magic, and hopefully we'd have rail guns and shit soon. Getting up close and dirty with my enemies just gave them a chance they didn't deserve.

I paused, thinking about the asshole Amadeus, and that the shield he'd been using was linked to his undead. If we'd had a rail gun and decent walls? I could have sniped that fucker and called it a day.

No—although I needed to even things out, so I didn't end up fucked up again—I was reassessing my build.

I had twenty-eight points, and Charisma was my lowest, at only twenty. I dropped another six points into it, bringing it up to twenty-six, so at least I wasn't ashamed of it. Two points into Constitution, bringing that to thirty, and boosting my Health to twelve hundred points.

Four points into Perception, because I had to find the fuckers to kill them, and that left me with sixteen points.

Sixteen points...I needed to improve my Wisdom and my Intelligence scores. That was basically where I was aiming now, as clearly magic was the way to go.

I did a little math, trying to figure out the most bang for my buck, as my cousins would have said, I think.

I could add all of it into one area, but that would risk unbalancing me massively, and I'd learned my lesson there. I could drop twelve points into my Intelligence, going from thirty-eight to fifty, and fifteen hundred and twenty mana to three fuckin' thousand...

That was tempting. Shit, that was *insanely* tempting!

That would leave me six points to put into my Wisdom, taking it from thirty, and eighteen mana an hour regenerated, to…*Wait, what the hell?*

My mana regeneration had taken a serious jump at some point. I pulled back the stats screen, then stared, confused as all fuck. It took a few minutes of searching, but I found the damn notification, eventually, and I even vaguely remembered it, more or less. It'd tried to open when I woke up after the full day of fighting, when Aly had been at the door to get us to go and assault the brewery. I vaguely remembered pushing it aside…meaning to come back to it, and then finding out that I'd literally just flashed Aly. Again.

It'd kinda distracted me. I pulled the details up again, seeing at that point it'd been regarding just Earth, and that just now I'd hit Water as well?

I'd been at forty-nine out of fifty, but had literally just reached fifty in it now. I'd gained Earth and Water to my Air and Fire. That, in turn, meant that as I no longer had access to only the most basic building blocks of the storm, Fire and Air, the regeneration speed had massively improved.

Congratulations, Dungeon Lord and First Lord of the Storm!

Due to raising your Earth and Water Affinities both past fifty points [52 and 50] and your Air and Fire past seventy [72 and 76], you have reached the minimum threshold of [50] across all four elements, and can now draw from each in regaining your own mana.

Remember, you are limited only by your perceptions…

I grunted, then dismissed it, far more interested in the fact I'd doubled my mana regeneration. And I finally knew how the hell I could improve it further!

Yeah, the better I did with Lightning and Storm overall, in the right situations—like a fucking *storm*—I'd be able to refill my mana much faster. But…*if* I could get all the basic elements past fifty percent? It'd mean I would be back in the game for mana regeneration!

I bet if I got them higher, I'd be able to improve them as well!

I grinned, a new plan there at last. I was irritated that I'd not seen the difference before now, but…basically, looking at the numbers, it was easy to see why I'd not noticed before.

I had over fifteen hundred mana, and even with the new boost, it'd take…I ran the numbers in my head, grunting as I did so, annoyed that I'd been so excited there.

Forty hours.

Forty fucking hours to recover my mana fully.

"Well, that makes it kinda easy to pick then," I muttered. I had eighteen points to spend. Two points into Intelligence, although not nearly as impressive, still moved me from thirty-eight to forty, and my mana from fifteen hundred and twenty to two thousand mana.

Then the remaining sixteen points into Wisdom…thirty points to forty-six, and my mana regen from thirty-seven an hour to fifty-seven.

Admittedly, with my mana getting higher, it was going to take almost as long to refill as before, but at least I'd get a few more shots off now.

Also, my control point score had been increased, making life slightly easier as I'd gained another twenty points.

I reached out, planning to bring up the details for the advanced kobolds next, before cursing and clambering back to my feet.

I needed to deal with too many goddamn things, and right now, the kobolds were farther down that list. I'd had a serious realization on the roof, and now that the notifications were out of the way? It was time to make the most of that.

I'd assign the spells and class abilities once I'd gotten this done, and I'd had some time to think. It wasn't like I needed them immediately.

CHAPTER SIX

I jogged down the stairs, hurrying past the few people inside as they stepped aside, questions rising as the Dungeon Lord raced past.

It didn't take me long. The next building over to the north had been the old printers', where once thousands upon thousands of copies of the local newspaper had been printed daily.

Now, as I physically entered it for the first time, instead of selecting it in the dungeon sense and making vague changes, I was stunned by the difference from the building I remembered seeing in the system.

The interior was high ceilinged and split into two, with a subtle reek of chicken shit, literally, still hanging in the air from my ill-advised order that the harvesters collect chickens awhile back.

Now there were people working with the harvesters, sorting their finds in one side, including what looked like a handful of bullets, thank the gods, while the other had been changed into a crafting station…of sorts.

As Finn and the others had said that morning, they desperately needed more space, but in reality, space wasn't the problem. They had an absolute *shitload* of space; what they didn't have much of was workbenches or equipment.

Most of the room was empty, with piled parts here and there, such as the stack of fifty ingots, and the small stack of leather and pelts.

The issue was that most of the crafters sat around on shitty plastic chairs, leaning on and working around small folding tables, or blatantly looted office desks, while a handful of them worked in a specialist crafting station, and others kept themselves busy or stood talking, clearly awaiting their turn.

"Finn," I greeted, moving over, and nodding to him where he sat, feet up on a desk. He had a bundle of leather rolled on his stomach as he worked a needle through the edges, clearly following a pattern he could see.

"Two minutes," he mumbled around a mouthful of needles and general crap. Actually, that was what I assumed he said, as the actual words were more like "Moo mimutsh."

I didn't have to wait long though, as he finished the section he was working on. He tied a tiny knot and then snapped the strip free, laying the leather pile aside and taking the mess from his mouth, and smiled at me.

"Hey, Matt, so…to what do we owe the pleasure of your company in 'craft-town'?" He climbed to his feet.

"I've got a few questions, and frankly, I needed to see this," I admitted. "In the dungeon sense, I can see there's desks, and that you're all working here, but…"

"But it's basically a wire drawing," he agreed, nodding. "I was planning on bringing you down here, to be honest, to show you what we're doing and why it's not the easiest working environment."

"Yeah, that's clear," I muttered. "Okay, so first of all, you said you had a blacksmith down here, right?"

"Tim." He pointed to a man who'd been clearly bored when I'd arrived, and who now looked scared, having been caught sitting around, clearly *not* busy when the "boss" arrived.

He'd grabbed a file and was working on a section of bronze, trying to look busy, and as we headed in his direction, he grew visibly worried.

"Matt, this is Tim the blacksmith; Tim, Matt, the Dungeon Lord." Finn introduced us, and I winced, seeing the worry on the man's face.

"Dungeon Lord...sir." Tim bowed his head, and then jerked a quick bow before I could stop him.

"Tim, it's fine. Please don't do that," I said. "Look, you're the blacksmith, right?"

"Yessir."

"What's your affinity to metal?"

He frowned.

"Your affinity," I repeated, seeing the confusion and cursing myself. "Okay, you've got your systems access, right? The screens you can see, and the information?"

"Uh...yes, Dungeon Lord?"

"Pull them up and slide all the way to the right, then concentrate on 'pulling' the screen upward and seeing what's below." I guided him through the next few screens until he had his affinities front and center. "Okay, you've got that...now, look for metal. Let me know what it is, please." I crossed my fingers.

"Ummm, fifty-seven?"

"What's your highest?" I asked, waiting.

"That's it. The next is nature, at thirty-eight."

"Fuck, yes!" I crowed, grinning widely. "Okay, now why did you want to be a blacksmith? And this is important, so please, for fuck's sake, be honest with me, all right?"

"I..." He paused then sighed, scratching the back of his neck as if embarrassed as he looked at the floor. "I'm clumsy," he admitted after a few seconds. "Always was, always will be, I guess. Metalworking just seems to work a bit more than anything else, and when I make mistakes, it's not as bad. I tried pottery once. Ex-wife made me try..."

"And?" I asked.

"Broke the pottery wheel," he said, shame clear on his face. "I'm sorry, Dungeon Lord. I don't know why I thought I could do this. I'll go back to clearing the buildings..." He turned, clearly desperate to leave, when I grabbed his arm and turned him back to face me.

"Tim, how would you like to get better at being a blacksmith, and at all metalworking?" I smiled. "I think I've found a way to 'fix' our affinities a little, and I'm betting that we can improve your skills as they're linked to it."

"Really?" He seemed confused and nervous. "I don't know, Dungeon Lord. Maybe its best if I just—"

"How about this?" I purred. "You spend the next forty-eight hours doing as I ask, trying, and I mean *really* trying, and I'll power-level you myself to get your first class?"

"Power lev—" He froze, eyes going wide, before nodding frantically. "Yes, yes, please, Dungeon—"

"That's fine." I cut him off, grinning and looking around, trying to figure somewhere a bit more comfortable to sit, and not wanting to have others try this until I knew it worked and it wasn't a massive waste of their time. "Okay, let's go over there…" I pointed to the far wall. "Finn, you can come if you want, but until we know this works? Don't share it around, okay?"

He nodded, and the pair followed me, moving over to the twin sofas I summoned and dropped into place, before sitting down on one end, grinning at the stunned look on Tim's face.

"It's good to be the boss," I admitted, winking at him. "Plus, you're going to need somewhere to sit." I checked the mana that was available, and designated the expenditure, selecting the spot next to Tim, and ordering it there for now, glad that we'd found we could move things around later when we needed to.

"Okay, so…ever tried meditation?" I summoned the new device and grinned as the Metal mana converter started to grow and glow. The motes of light were dragged inward and spiraled around as the dungeon got to work.

An hour and a half later, I was much less hopeful about the whole Metal and blacksmith situation. I left the crafting hall, climbing up the stairs onto the roof, and looked around, seeing the surrounding area with my own eyes again.

If it worked? It'd be fantastic, truly it would. But the chances? Tim took to meditation with the natural skill and grace of a one-legged duckling in an arse-kicking competition.

I moved over to the right-hand side of the roof, looking down at the shattered tarmac and filth-covered pavements, seeing them as they'd been a few weeks ago, soaking wet as I'd staggered along them, drunk, in the early hours after meeting Kelly.

Then I saw the streets as they'd been only a matter of hours ago, massively overrun by howling undead, destroyed creatures in their hundreds littering the ground.

I remembered dropping down into the middle of it, fighting my way to the front next to a pair of corpse lords and fighting the undead between them, mechanically.

I remembered the burn of muscles pushed past mortal limits, and the steady, steely determination that not one inch would they take from me.

Looking around at the other buildings around me, standing mostly silent, grey and abandoned, I wondered at the changes in my life.

A sudden movement caught my eyes in the building opposite, as one of my people walked past an open window, deeper inside what had once been the local cloth market.

They worked like ants, constantly and steadily, stripping the buildings room by room, level by level, and I sighed. There was so much to do, every day, and I frantically tried to do it all. My friends helped—they did so massively, to be fair to them—as did everyone else. But still, I felt the harder we worked, the more there was to do.

Even now, seeing the way my people worked their asses off, I couldn't help but think that it was a shitty and ineffective way to do it.

I had more than six hundred control points now. A skeletal laborer cost a mere two points—as well as a hundred mana, admittedly—but still.

The building I was atop was the farthest north we had. I jogged across the rope bridge we'd made between the old printers' and the last of the buildings that formed the triangle tip of this section of the dungeon.

The buildings to the west, or my left from here, had included the old Idol's bar, and had been destroyed in the battle with the Coronaught Queen, and the subsequent annihilation of her brood and corpse. The building at the south of that block, the old student accommodation building, had been wiped out by the laborers. The one between was still in progress, getting smashed down as I watched.

That, when finished, would provide a good-sized clear area around the dungeon. But there was still a section of the block on that side that would be left standing, including an old church.

That building had literally become the haunt of unholy creatures like the Jiangshi and randomly spawning undead. I wasn't that bothered about demolishing it, but I winced at the thought of Clarissa's words, should I do it without discussion with the local priest at least.

I left it for now, and faced due north instead, across the remaining section of the Bigg Market.

The buildings there were mainly shops, some smaller hotels, and a lot of bars, and I nodded to myself. It was time to make this a little more efficient.

I checked the mana reserves, finding that between the people who were working on absorbing and the various collectors' production, I had a grand total of three hundred and seventy mana now, a number that rose and fell constantly, indicating that Aly was hard at work somewhere.

"Well, time to get to work, I guess," I muttered, sitting on the edge of the roof and dangling my legs over the side. I summoned three of the larger skeletal creations on the road below me, then a pair of bright-red baseball caps that had been absorbed at some point, and settled them on their heads to make them look both a little less scary, and a bit more ridiculous, should people see them unexpectedly.

I sent them to the edge of the block opposite, it having already been picked as our next acquisition, and ordered them to strip anything metal out of the building.

I figured that was the best way to get them to bring the tech, as trying to explain "bring me computers" was going to result in a random load of shit being dumped.

The third one, though, I ordered to stay where it was, eyeing the construct with a critical eye. I'd not done this for a few days—I'd been busy, after all—but activated Forced Evolution and Imbue at once, working as I had before to slide twenty-five percent Earth mana into the solid creation.

It started to shake, the bones clattering, as the light in its eyes grew, and I frantically shoved more and more pure mana at it, in the hope that it would stabilize the creation.

Cracks grew along the bones, splintering and sending flakes of bone tumbling free, fading from sight as they fell toward the ground.

I winced, and I expected to lose it.

As the seconds passed, though, I frowned. The damn thing was still there. The glow in its eyes grew, fresh growths seeming to inch from the cracks in the bones, like mold growing, but instead it was…stone!

I watched, open-mouthed, as I guessed that the dungeon was creating an *elemental*. I'd poured Earth into the creation, up to what I thought was the maximum, to create this form. Then, once it'd settled and stabilized, I'd done it again, exceeding the original maximum that the system wanted to allow.

The changes rolled on. The stone grew outward, looking like some kind of weird, stop-motion accumulation of stone—like a stalactite that was steadily flowing outward, consuming the bone, then spreading further.

The seconds turned to minutes. The creature seemed in pain. Its head rolled around, the light in the eyes flared wildly, then died away, then flared again, until a new message popped up.

Congratulations!

You have created your first Golem: Bone Golem.
Dungeon Golems are creations of the dungeon, imbued with limited intelligence, and are expensive to maintain, but over time, the various forms can prove to be highly prized creations.

Each Dungeon can maintain a limited number of true Golems. At your current evolutionary epoch and capacity, you may support 0 Golems…

The golem shuddered. Then a cry filled the air, one clearly filled with pain, and I collapsed, rolling back onto the rooftop—fortunately—and clutching at my chest.

The pain that ripped through me was horrific. More notifications flared to life, and I realized that the voice that had cried out in pain was my own.

Beware, Dungeon Lord!

In creating a creature that your Dungeon was unable to support, you have tied it to your own health pool, donating the requisite mana and HP to keep it active.

Bone Golem: 1000 Mana & 1000 HP per day.

I stared at it, my heart stuttering and stopping as my Health dropped, literally streaming from me in a red mist of blood and floating to my creation, ready to grant it life…by damn well nearly killing me!

I forced myself upright, staring at the golem as it continued to grow. The stone flooded across the bones, and I reached out with my abilities and the dungeon sense at the same time, selecting it with everything I had, and cutting the link, before collapsing, facedown, on the roof.

Blood ran from my nose and mouth, rolling down my arm and dripping from senseless fingers. The steady *drip-drip-drip* drew the attention of one of a trio of people who'd come running, drawn by the shouts and the appearance of the golem, as well as its sudden collapse.

"Hey!" someone shouted, and I forced myself to move, dragging myself to the edge and peering blearily over the edge, trying to focus on the faces below.

"Wha?" I mumbled.

"Shit!" someone cried. "It's the boss!"

I flinched, half rolling backward, and stared around, trying to spot whoever the boss was, and get my brain to reboot, when a handful of extremely dangerous words floated up.

"Kelly! Just get her. She'll know what to do…"

"No!" I panicked, lunging forward and almost falling over the side of the building. "Don't…do that!"

"But—"

"Magic went wrong…that's all. She doesn't need to know," I got out, before shaking my head and wiping at the blood, smearing it across my face accidentally. "Just…leave it, okay?" I ordered.

"Are you sure…"

"Yes!" I called, finally able to focus, and groaning in pain as I did so. "Thank you!"

I slid down the low wall that ran all around the edge, dropping my head into my hands as the trio departed. I blew out a long breath, sliding down the retaining wall to sit with my back against it, staring out across the pigeon shit-covered roof.

"Fuck, that was close…" I closed my eyes. The last damn thing any man needed, especially when he'd just fucked up, was his partner hearing all about it.

I sat there for a few minutes, until I judged my brain wasn't actually going to seep out of my ears and float away, before finally reaching out to the dungeon again, and looking for the golem.

It was dead, well and truly, a collection of parts that were laid haphazardly in the road, looking much like any number of random bones and trash lying around.

"Holy crap, that hurt." I forced myself to turn and sit on the wall again, legs dangling and looking over the side, shaking my head in disbelief at the mess below.

Well, I'd found that I could create a golem, and those fuckers were dangerous! That was weird, though, as one of my damn spells could create a "normal" Earth golem, and that thing was a meter high. The bone golem hadn't been that much bigger, and the way things had been phrased…I was fairly sure there was a research option somewhere to get damn elementals, so what the hell had happened?

I started digging, trying to figure it out, but got nowhere, resolving after half an hour that I'd leave it to Aly, once I'd figured out how the hell I was going to ask without letting on that I'd nearly damn well killed myself. Instead, trying to distract myself, I reached out and pulled up the notification I'd dismissed a few days ago when I'd been too damn busy.

Congratulations!

Uncommon Kobold has been upgraded to Advanced Kobold!

Advanced Kobolds are an almost entirely different species from the base creature, significantly closer to their draconic ancestry. They develop intrinsically magical characteristics and a wide variation of form, from the Heavy Kobold warrior to the highly agile Scout.

Note: Advanced Kobolds have a significantly higher level of intelligence than the baseline version, resulting in a much higher chance of rebellion, should the creature be mistreated…be warned!

Optional Research Project Unlocked!

Draconic Bloodline

Where kobolds in general are accepted to be descended from the greater dragons, through a series of extremely poor personal—and sexual—choices by their ancestors, occasionally a latent Draconic Bloodline will become evident, rising in an otherwise lower life form, and granting them a significant gift from their ancestor.

Note: Draconic Bloodlines, once activated, cannot be reversed. A formerly loyal minion may decide to leave, to follow a biological imperative, or to destroy their former master to punish them for their treatment. Beware.

Do you wish to add Draconic Bloodline to your research list?

0/500,000 mana charge invested.

Yes/No

I read it and reread it, first of all because the new version of kobolds sounded awesome, and basically? I was looking at getting a version of a fucking dragon here. I liked that a *lot*.

Secondly, there was an option to "awaken latent draconic bloodlines," which was sodding amazing. Yes, it was a risk—fuck, it was a risk—but…Beta was awesome. She was around here somewhere, causing trouble, no doubt, but she was still a baseline unevolved, uncommon kobold.

As time went on, she'd grow less and less relevant to the kobolds I summoned. Regardless of how powerful and experienced she might grow, she was always going to be limited by her original variant and species.

If these kobolds were bigger and stronger, as well as fucking smarter, putting her in charge of them might be a serious mistake.

Some creatures, the goblins primarily, fought among themselves for rank. Should some freshly spawned dickbag decide it wanted to lead and gut Beta?

I didn't know what I'd do.

I reminded myself that, yeah, they were my minions, and I occasionally burned or exploded one. I also sent them into fights, knowing they'd die, determined to save a "real" person's life by their sacrifice, and yeah…I was going to have to create some more goddamn researchers, which meant Aly being pissed at me again.

I had no emotional attachment to the normal kobolds, although Beta had been with me for a while now. I grumbled a bit under my breath, then pulled up the details for the advanced kobolds, swearing at the cost difference.

Where the uncommon baseline had been twenty-five mana each, and three control points, the advanced…well.

A skeletal laborer was a hundred mana to summon; corpse lords, with their abilities and all, were two thousand mana, and ten control points. But these fuckers? Two thousand, five hundred points to summon, and they were summoned individually! It wasn't even that I got three of the fuckers for that!

They were twenty-five goddamn control points each! This was insane. There was no way these fuckers could be worth that. Realistically, there was just…just…

"Ah, fuck it. Who am I kidding?" I muttered, glaring at the details. I knew I was going to summon one of them, and soon.

CHAPTER SEVEN

I took a long breath, frowning over the details as I assessed the current incomings and outgoings of the dungeon, before nodding in satisfaction.

I had three spells, which could be sorted now or later really, but I also had four class skill points to spend. And if I was going to start messing about with the kobolds, or any of the various creatures, really, it was time to get these spent.

First and foremost, I had the three spells to choose, and looking over the options, well…

<u>**Spells:**</u>

Class selection: Arcane Dungeon Lord

<u>Summon Demon:</u> Summon a Demon. Formed entirely of your power and imbued with terrible purpose, the Demon exists to see your will achieved, and will allow nothing to stand between it and its goal.

<u>Incinerate:</u> Cast a blast of terrible heat at a target, achieving up to 1000 degrees of heat in a single location. Note: This spell has lessening effects, depending on the area covered, and ranks from 0 (10cm) to 5 (1000cm). (1)

Evolution: Atomic Furnace: Select a location and summon the power of the sun to turn all inside that area to glass! Note: This spell has lessening effects, depending on the area covered, and ranks from 0 (1m) to 5 (1000m).

<u>Eternal Winter:</u> The depths of space are places of terrible cold; why not share that knowledge with your enemies? It's likely to leave a lasting impression on anything that's caught inside the AOE. Note: This spell has lessening effects, depending on the area covered, and ranks from 0 (1m) to 5 (1000m).

<u>Tame:</u> Tame a creature, adding it to your Dungeon lists. (Selected) (1)

Evolution: Affinity Boost! As you Tame a creature, you can now choose to imbue it with an elemental affinity. The higher your own affinity, the higher the chance the gift will result in a successful union.

<u>Conversion:</u> Creatures you encounter out in the wild, be they sentient or not, should all be part of your domain. Convert the heretic to your side! This spell ranks in levels from 0 (Unfriendly) to 5 (Sworn Nemesis).

<u>Examine:</u> This spell allows the nascent Dungeon Lord to divine details about a target that are hidden from the eyes of most mortals. This skill ranks in levels from 0 (Curious) to 5 (All-Knowing). (1)

Evolution: Secret Knowledge! Those you encounter frequently have their own agendas; why not make them share that information?

This skill ranks in levels from 0 (Fears) to 5 (Darkest Secret).

Summon Elemental*:* Summon an Elemental to do your bidding. Note: This spell will summon a creature of the Elemental Planes, depending on your ability, to serve you for a short period of time, and ranks from 0 (Lesser) to 5 (Elemental Lord).

Lightning Bolt: Cast a blast of Lightning at your target, stunning and possibly frying them with the power of electricity. Note: This spell has lessening effects, depending on the area traveled, and ranks from 0 (50,000V) to 5 (150,000mV). (1)

Evolution: Lightning Storm! Select a location and unleash the true power of the Storm! Note: This spell has lessening effects, depending on the area covered, and ranks from 0 (10m) to 5 (10km). (1)

Of the spells I had access to…well, Incinerate had served me damn well so far, and to move that up a rank to Atomic Furnace? Well, it was an easy call there, especially because I was going from up to ten centimeters to up to a meter that I could "turn to glass."

I still had access to both Lightning Bolt and Lightning Storm I saw, so clearly I kept the original version *as well* as receiving the augmented one, which was frankly awesome.

I was torn for the other two spells, though, first and foremost because Summon Demon sounded fucking awesome. The description sounded like it'd be seriously kick-ass as well, notably because the fucker didn't have ranks, it was a "fire and forget" as far as I was concerned: summon the fucker, turn it loose, and let it do its job.

Hell, I could, in theory, summon the fucker and send it off to kill the other Unlife gods, if it was powerful enough. Awesome. If not? Well, shit happened. It wasn't as though they'd be any *less* pissed at me.

The issue was that I wanted the evolution to Tame as well, gifting the creatures we'd tamed an elemental boost. It was literally how we ended up with lightning horses or some shit.

But…

Conversion allowed me to convert enemy creatures to my side, and the potential of that? This wasn't like Tame, as near as I could tell, where essentially I could "tame" a dumb creature. Like the way I'd beaten the crap out of the dogs the goblins had been riding, and then I'd tamed them.

The levels on this specifically said "unfriendly" to "sworn nemesis," so…I could apparently convert creatures that were actively my enemies to my side?

Admittedly that was close to Tame as well; they both had similar focuses, but, as with so much of the crap I dealt with, I wished I had access to a wiki at the minute! The system didn't care about our views, we knew that, so there's no way it'd use two different skills unless there was a damn reason.

I gritted my teeth…and went for it. I selected Atomic Furnace, affinity boost, and…Summon Demon. It was a last-second choice, going more on instinct than anything else, but the more I thought about it? The more I wanted a secret trump card, just in case.

I moved on, pulling up the class skills, and grinned at the four points I had to spend.

Class Skills:

Class selection: Arcane Dungeon Lord

Imbue*:* You may choose to give freely of your own manapool to imbue an item or creature of the Dungeon with magic. This ability can fail, and spectacularly so; however, creations of wondrous might can also be brought into being. Be wary. (Selected)

Evolution*: Foresight:* No longer are your creations the chance things they were…now see the true potential of a creature!

Monster Master*:* No longer do the creatures of the Dungeon view you with apathy or irritation when you pass by. Now they are devoted to you! This skill ranks in levels from 0 (Interested) to 5 (Worshipful). (Current level: 0, Interested)

Evolution: Lord of All! The creatures of your Dungeon know their true master, and those who follow willingly can now receive arcane gifts that match their level of devotion!

Arcane Breeder*:* Some Dungeon Lords wish for only the purest strains to survive, while others enjoy the randomness of evolution…select the genes you wish to see and promote them!

Artificer: You may gift magical artifacts to your creations, and when combined with Foresight, these creatures will gain significant bonuses to magical item creation and replication. This skill ranks in levels from 0 (Curiosity) to 5 (Legendary). (Current level: 0, Curiosity)

Arcane Pets*:* Your sentient Dungeon inhabitants can gather and breed pets, but where before there was an element of random chance, now you may lure those you wish into the range of your tamers. This skill ranks in levels from 0 (Magical) to 5 (Legendary Creatures).

Insatiable Curiosity*:* Random Sentient Dungeon Creatures will now have the chance to be spawned with an Insatiable Curiosity. These creatures can be put to work in your Research Nodes to increase Research by a staggering degree. This skill ranks in levels from 0 (Incompetent) to 5 (Genius). (Current level: 2, Interested)

Evolution: Magical Researcher! Before, your researchers were generalists, plodding along at their task, be that a better toilet seat or a converter; now they stand a chance at developing true magical gifts, and at learning the secrets of creation! This skill ranks in levels from 0 (Novice) to 5 (Master). (Current level: 0, Novice)

Manafield: Your Dungeon's Manafield will now passively expand at 10% more than the previous rate, enabling greater growth in a shorter period of time. This skill ranks in levels from 0 (Restricted) to 5 (Expansive). (Current Level: 1, Limited)

Evolution: Tides of Mana! All life creates mana, as do elemental interactions. Now, through the wonders of gravitational magic, you can start to draw more mana into the area of your Dungeon. This skill ranks in levels from 0 (Gentle) to 5 (Vortex). (Current Level: 0, Gentle)

Reach Out and Touch Me: Your Dungeon is no longer only controllable when you are within its own environs. Now you can interact with it at increasing distances. This skill ranks in levels from 0 (Local) to 5 (Interstellar). (Current level: 0, Local)

Evolution: Gates! No longer is the Dungeon a distant creation; this skill unlocks the creation of the Gates, transportals that can be built inside the Dungeon and activated at a remote location to provide a stable link between the two points.

This skill ranks in levels from 0 (Single Gate) to 5 (Unlimited).

I took Foresight straightaway. As much as I knew it wasn't going to be that simple—I fucking *knew* it—I still had to hope. That left me with three more class skills, one of which was just a blatantly obvious choice.

I took the Gates option, selecting a single transportal and hissing in pain as the knowledge "downloaded" into me, and the dungeon.

Where Foresight had been a tingle at the back of the mind, transportals were insane levels of math. The equations that governed intergalactic fucking warp tech was in this research path, I suddenly knew, as were…

I focused on the portal, finding that once the billions of lines of "code" were parsed through? The reality was simple; even if I could barely grasp the *how*, I understood the *why*.

Transportals were points of fixed space-time where two points were made one. That was an insanely simplistic description, but it was accurate as well.

The ether was different everywhere you went, even if only slightly. What the portals did was make two points exactly the same. Gravity, mana, sub-atomic particles—all of it: literally, they made a line of space inside the portal frame exactly duplicate another.

As two *exact* instances cannot coexist, the intervening space simply ceased to exist, as they became one. Stepping through this portal, you stepped out of the other.

I could feel the mass of data hovering, ready to render me insensate, and I shuddered, turning aside mentally. I didn't need to know the exact *how*, just that it fucking *did* work.

The data was downloaded into the dungeon instead and I sighed in relief. The central portal was unlocked, although it'd need to be built yet, and the "tether" for the other end as well.

The central portal could make dozens easily, but the tethers were individuals, and were linked directly only. I could go through one here to, say, Saltwell Park, but I couldn't go from that one to another I got somewhere else.

For now at least, I'd have to return to the center, then go out again. That was fine, though; it was still a hell of an improvement! I pulled the details up and looked over the last two choices. I was tempted, seriously so, to drop them both into one area, like Insatiable Curiosity, and take it from level two all the way to four.

I'd only need one more to max it out, and that would make a hell of a difference. Although…*Arcane Pets*…

The description was that they could be "lured in range of your tamers." That was me. I could lure them in range, and then I could tame them, creating an awesome cavalry or…

Cavalry.

My mind fixated on that word, as it went wild with possibilities from the recent fight. Despite myself, I grinned widely.

"Oh, fuck yes…" I muttered, nodding. "That's a plan right there…but not for right now."

I forced myself to go back to it, rereading the options from start to finish. I had Imbue, and now Foresight, so they were out. Monster Master was more or less tempting, mainly because I was thinking if I dropped two points into that, or one and one into Lord of All, then maybe the orcs would be usable.

Then I thought of the limited interactions with the fuckers, and my desire to fireball them all on general principles rose. Nope, fuck that shit.

Arcane Breeder was tempting. After all, so far I'd been summoning the creatures as I needed them. But really, if I were to create a breeding den, they could start breeding themselves, and I could encourage certain traits, it said? It'd theoretically let me develop more and more dungeon creatures.

I regarded it for a minute, then shook my head. Nope, not for now at least.

Artificer was tempting. I'd already taken one level of it, after all, and it literally was a case of "gifting" magical artifacts to the researchers, as near as I could tell. With Foresight that I'd now taken? They should be able to start breaking down things like the focal orbs and reproducing them. Dumping two points into there would get it to halfway and give them a far better chance of success.

That was a serious contender, and I put it aside to look at again.

Pets and Curiosity I'd already considered, and was tempted by, as I was by Magical Researcher. I had a single point in there as well, and it seemed like that would be synergistic with the Artificer option. So, one or the other—or hell, both points—into one would work well.

Lastly, though…there was the long game to consider. Manafield and Tides of Mana were both seriously tempting. I had two points in the first and one in the second, gaining me an increase of twenty percent to the expansion of the dungeon's influence, and a "gentle" pull on the mana in the atmosphere around us.

Rather than risking draining the area of mana, it would instead pull more and more mana inward.

It was perhaps the least "fun" option of them all. It'd gain me nothing personally, and it'd have no real effect as anyone could see it, but…it'd keep the mana coming. It'd give us some stability in the future.

I didn't want to take it—really, I didn't. I wanted so many of the others, but I couldn't risk it. I had no right to risk it for everyone else, so I selected the second option for Tides of Mana, moving from Gentle to Steady, then putting the final point into Magical Researcher, moving that from Novice to Apprentice, and blew out a long breath.

I loved doing this, and I damn well hated it as well. Genuinely I did, because there was always the knowledge that I might have just fucked up massively.

I could have dropped all four points into any of the damn sections and improved it, rather than basically going for the Jack-of-all-Trades approach.

It was who I was, though. I knew that specialists were far more valuable, and more powerful, as the Undead assholes I'd faced so far had been. They'd been able to raise tens of thousands of undead slaves and throw them at us. In comparison, I felt weak as shit at times.

But…I was still here. They weren't, and damn if that didn't prove my theory against "glass cannons."

That was because I'd spread myself out, learning a bit of everything, and being able to address any situation, or so I hoped, rather than being awesome in a single one.

I already regretted taking the Tides of Mana rather than dropping both points into the researchers. It certainly wasn't a case of the research option being the best one—not by any stretch of the imagination, either—but fuck it. If we were going to change this building into a research outpost, or the "castle" into one, or the government building or whatever, either way, I damn well needed researchers.

I also needed Beta and her kobolds.

Standing, I turned slowly, staring outward as much as inward, meshing the sense of the dungeon with my own instincts and eyes. In only a few minutes, I had her.

She had been sitting in the churchyard of the old cathedral, the remains of her team with her. Frank the rottweiler had died, facing the well-dwelling abomination; Foxtrot and Zucc, the hunter and rogue respectively, had been killed by Dickless, and Mirr the assassin was crushed and ripped apart by Wayne Kerr.

Her little team of elites had gone from seven, counting Frank, to three, and they were mourning. She'd sensed me looking for her, I assumed, as almost the same time I "found" her, she had poked her head around the corner and looked up at me in question.

I headed to her, and she did the same, jogging along with the other two, Starr the shaman and Stumpy the hunter. I had to smile at them, as they clambered up a ladder, pausing as they reached the top and spread out, helping each other, before running toward me.

They moved like humanoid raptors, all bobbing and weaving, fast movements, then pausing and looking around, and yet…they were clearly insanely intelligent, as well as operating as a team at an almost instinctive level.

Beta came to a stop before me, straightening up and letting loose a questioning "chirp," blinking as the other two drew to a halt on either side.

The three were the same baseline "level," in the they were uncommon kobolds. But Beta was the first warrior variant, and one of the original trio I first summoned. Stumpy, as a "hunter" variant, and one who'd lost a significant section of his tail in the fight for the dungeon, was slightly bigger than her, with a metal blade attached to the remains of his tail.

He had a collection of blades now, two crossbows, and a few random traps hanging from his belts; pouches and bags hung here and there. He'd apparently decided to paint himself, or had been painted, considering his left arm and a line down his face had a red line down them, then poorly scrawled "tattoos" that looked as if he'd let some kids at him with a packet of crayons.

He also had several small trophies: fangs, varying in length from a standard human canine to something that I hoped had come from a carnifex. *If it hadn't...*

I shrugged and glanced at Starr. The colorful and badass shaman watched me patiently, his multicolored plumage and weighing eyes making me nod to him in automatic respect.

He'd gathered a few potions from somewhere, and had them tied to his belt, along with a pair of daggers and several random bangles, as if he'd raided a young girls' accessory shop. He looked badass with it, though, despite the several Hello Kitty charms woven into his necklace.

Beta stood proudly between them, heavily muscled and scarred, sporting dozens of throwing daggers, a pair of crossbows, a compound bow with a quiver of arrows on her back, bolts on her right hip, and...

And she had a tiny, filthy, white fluffy kitten in a pouch on her left hip. Its squashed face peered up and out at me, bright-blue eyes gleaming as it watched me silently.

"Hello," I whispered.

Beta, seeing the direction of my gaze, reached down and flipped the cover of the pouch back, stroking the kitten with one taloned finger, before closing it again and glaring at me, as if daring me to do something to her pet.

Instantly, the many, *many* kobolds I'd accidentally fried and blown up in experiments reared their heads in my mind. I coughed, wincing before offering a smile, even as I tried not to wonder at the best mixture of eleven herbs and spices to add to the krispy kobold platters...

"Looks like you've made a friend!" I said, getting a nod from Beta and then the others of her team. As the silence stretched out, I thought about what I wanted to say, and then just went for it.

"Beta, Starr, Stumpy. You've all earned my respect, and anything you want to ask for, if you can show me what you want, it's yours," I said. "I know you have quarters set up above the training dungeon. Do you need anything for them?"

Silence.

After a couple of seconds, Beta shook her head slowly, making me wonder whether she really understood or not. Fuck it. I shrugged, moving on.

"Well, if you do need anything, tell me and..."

Starr surprised us all by stepping forward. He waited, making sure I was paying attention, then he tapped his potions, one at a time, showing them to me.

Two were clearly attempts at healing potions, a dull red glimmer filling them, but cloudy as all hell. The third…it looked like it was a bottle full of mud, basically.

"You want more potions?" I asked, getting a sharp nod, before he offered the muddy one to me. I took it and used my Examine spell.

Potion of Darkness	Potion
This is a weak potion of Darkness. Upon the breaking of the potion container, a small cloud of smoke and dirt will be released, confusing any who hunt using sight or smell. Depending on the environment, this cloud will last up to a minute.	
Durability 4/10	Potion Strength: Weak

I read the details, grunting as I realized that not only was this his own creation, but it was a potion we didn't, to the best of my knowledge, have access to.

"You made this?" I asked.

Another sharp nod.

"Can you make more?"

Again, a nod.

"Okay, we need you to work with Ashley…" I muttered to myself, before sighing as I finally realized his damn point.

"I'm sorry," I said to the three of them. "It never occurred to me that you'd want to do crafting like this, which is clearly fucking stupid. Okay, I took the Artificer class skill for the dungeon. That replaced the standard Crafter one with a focus on magical artifacts, so I guess that's a good first step. Hmmm." I rubbed my chin, thinking quickly before nodding to myself.

"Okay, I'll sort out some crafting spaces for you. Although, you know you're allowed to use the crafting spaces the humans use, don't you?" I got three sets of unblinking stares, and I sighed.

"Okay, I'll sort it," I promised, straightening up and nodding to them. I could understand it, really. I hadn't told them they could use the crafters' stations, and to be fair, even if they'd thought to go and use it? The few crafters we had were all queuing for the spaces, so I guess they'd have walked away as soon as they saw it.

Add to that, I didn't even know whether Ashley had a bedroom beyond the alchemy workshop, and considering she and Dante were both basically hormonal late teens and early twenties in the first days of their relationship? The sights the kobolds might end up seeing…

I shook my head.

They needed access to a real crafting station, and somewhere that they could use in peace.

"I actually wanted to see you all for a different reason." I looked from one to another. "Beta, you know that I have access to…fuck, this is going to be complicated to explain," I muttered, rubbing my face with one hand.

"I can summon more evolved versions of your species, do you understand?" I asked, getting a strange look from her.

She cocked her head to one side, her reptilian lineage clear as she examined me with first one eye, then the other, before slowly nodding.

"Okay…the new ones I can summon to help you, I'm going to summon a few of them directly for *you*. They're to be part of your team, and then over the next few days, I'll be summoning others. They'll be formed into a new security force, to defend the dungeon, and to fight where I need them. But you and your team? You'll be my elites. I want you to train, and to make the most of these new additions. Do you understand?"

I stood for a couple of seconds, wondering whether I'd just babbled a load of shit to a half-sapient lizard, when she finally nodded, then pointed to the ground, and hissed something to the other two, having them back up, before looking at me expectantly, as if to say, *Well? Get a move on, bitch.*

CHAPTER EIGHT

"Okay," I muttered, having not really planned to do it right now, but not really having any reason, beyond the mana cost, to put it off. "These will be the first of their kind, Beta, so we'll need to arrange armor and so on for them as well."

I sat down, getting comfortable, and looked up at the way they still stood, waiting. "You might as well settle down, guys. It'll be a few minutes at least," I assured them, checking the details.

Two thousand five hundred mana each for these fuckers, and twenty-five control points. I couldn't help but shake my head in amazement at the increase in the cost.

They better be a literal step away from goddamn dragons for that price, I decided, before dipping into the dungeon sense and reaching out to Aly.

I shared my plan with her, getting a request to wait, as she wanted to see the new members of the dungeon as they arrived, as well as the obvious impression of how much easier it'd be for her to adjust their gear, once she'd seen them in the flesh.

I agreed, sharing my location, and then slid "sideways" through the dungeon sense, finding myself at the pile of steadily building equipment ready for assimilation.

I glanced it over, disappointed by just how little good shit there was. It was mainly crap: some monitors and TVs, several dozen telephones, the high-tech office kind, as well as a load of older models. Piles of wiring and occasional junction boxes, office lighting, plug sockets that had been physically ripped out of the walls—I'd have to have a word about that; if it was our people and not the undead doing that, it was a massive effort for little payoff…no need to waste their time—and a collection of things like coffee machines, PayPoints, and more.

I started at the top, permeating anything that looked vaguely like it could possibly be useful later, but absorbing anything and everything I could as I went.

Only a few minutes passed before I sensed Aly joining me and heard her question about timescales.

I shared the information on the cost with her, and grinned to myself at her muttered swearing, before she settled in and got to work with me.

I sensed the others, Tulio especially, as his mind brushed up against my own. Seeing we were working steadily, he joined us, switching from a more general absorption of everything, into focusing on higher tech and helping.

It still took a buttload longer than I wanted, before most of the pile was gone, and I finally had enough to summon three new kobolds.

I blinked out of the dungeon sense, finding Aly stretching her back and Beta and her team playing a game with a painted set of knuckle bones. The kitten sat in her lap, happy as I'd ever seen an animal, getting stroked and cooed to.

"If you'd told me you weren't ready, I'd have kept on with my own work," Aly grumbled, and I snorted.

"Yeah, and you'd have been using the mana as fast as I could get it!" I pointed out, getting a shrug and a "get on with it" wave from her.

I took a deep breath, selected the "kobold" option, and designated the spot I wanted them to appear. I chose to make one at a time and deal with them individually, just in case they were dicks, like the orcs had been.

The bright lights of the dungeon flared, gathering like a thousand fireflies to "print" the new creature. It was a weird process, considering it was literally "printed" from light before me, and yet...

I watched the sections that were completed gradually dull from the bright-white light to the correct hue, meaning that the "top," as it was printed, was never see-through.

That was a bit of a relief, really, all things considered, as I'd rather not see the insides of the poor bugger as it was brought to life.

The design, though...I'd deliberately not looked at the design, beyond seeing the description, as I wanted to see it properly for the first time here.

The information I got from the dungeon was always difficult to parse. It was, as near as we could tell, custom designed for humans to interact with, but expecting a dungeon fairy to be in attendance to make things work.

That meant that I got a mixture of back systems I seriously doubted humanity was supposed to see, and the front end that everyone could interact with, and I was only just starting to see that difference.

I was frequently inundated with alternative details, scents, feelings, intuitions—all of it; it just seemed to pour into me through the system, and I wanted to "see" the kobolds properly, I guess.

It was worth it.

That kobolds were descended from dragons was mentioned frequently in the dungeon information, but the average kobold looked more like they had a velociraptor than a dragon in their family tree.

That changed massively with the latest generation.

The figure slowly being printed before me stood a solid six foot at the shoulder, with a short, but clearly flexible neck, thick scales, a pointed toothy mouth, and twin horns lifting from its temples.

The wings on its back were fucking awesome as well. Thanks to the Foresight skill, I got the impression that this, as the "entry" level for this breed, was ready to evolve in any direction, losing the wings and growing massively for ground pounders, and the wings changing to provide solidly airborne options.

They were solidly muscled, long arms and legs, with their feet and hands ending in talons. A narrow line of spikes ran down the back of the neck from a crest on the top of their heads, all the way to the tip of the tail, which was narrow and long, rather than thick and short the way the earlier generations had been.

When the light finally finished, the figure before us opened its eyes.

Fuck.

I stood straighter, staring into its eyes and recognizing that unlike the vast majority of the dungeon creatures, it had spawned self-aware.

It looked at me, then the others, examining each individually, clearly weighing and assessing them, before looking back and...wonder of fucking wonders...inclining its head in respect to me.

"Can you understand me?" I asked, and it nodded slowly. "Can you speak?"

It opened its mouth, croaking, then trying, clearly annoyed when it couldn't quite make intelligible words.

"Can you speak to, and understand her?" I asked, indicating Beta.

She stepped forward and barked at the new arrival, causing it to stiffen and glare at her, before nodding to me.

"This might be an issue," I muttered to Aly, who nodded, seeing it too. "I am the Dungeon Lord. Do you understand that?"

The new figure, who I guessed was a he, shifted slightly, watching me, before nodding and then dipping his head in clear deference.

"Thank you." I sighed. "Okay, you're clearly intelligent and self-aware, which is more than I'd dared hope for in many ways. I need a few new members for Beta…" I gestured to her, making it clear that was her name as I went on. "Sorry, this is Beta. Okay, so I need three more members for her elite squad. You'll be fighting, hunting, and more with her as part of her team, and under her command. You're fully conscious, I think, so I'm going to break with tradition, and give you a choice."

I triggered my examination spell at the same time as I spoke, examining the baseline stats and almost swallowing my damn tongue as I did so.

Name: Unknown Kobold				
Species: Kobold		**Bonus**: Advanced Variant		
Level: 0		**Progress to next level** 0/10		
Available points: 0		**Perk**: None		
Stat	**Current points**	**Description**	**Effect**	**Progress to next level**
Agility	8	Governs dodge and movement		0/100
Charisma	8	Governs likely success to charm, seduce, or threaten		0/100
Constitution	12	Governs Health and Health Regeneration	HP: 12x20 = 240	0/100
Dexterity	10	Governs ability with weapons and crafting		0/100
Endurance	12	Governs Stamina and Stamina Regeneration	Stamina: 12x20= 240	0/100
Intelligence	12	Governs base manapool and standard intellectual capacity	Mana: 12x20 = 240	0/100
Luck	8	Governs overall chance of bonuses and critical hits		0/100
Perception	12	Governs ranged damage and chance to spot hidden items/traps	+12 damage to Ranged attacks	0/100
Strength	12	Governs damage with melee weapons and carrying capacity		0/100
Wisdom	12	Governs mana regeneration and memory	120 mana regenerated per hour	0/100

He had no perk, which was fine, but fuck me sideways, he was already more intelligent than most humans: stronger, smarter—everything. *Shit.* When I stopped and thought about it, most of the "baseline" stats for a human…

When I first activated the damn system, it had showed me details on my species, and, more to the point, on me in direct comparison. I'd thought I was great, had actually enjoyed about half a second without that nagging self-doubt I'd always had about myself compared to those around me, something that spending a lot of time in the "care" system instilled at a bone-deep level.

Then it'd updated, showing me compared to others of my race with my genetics and natural advantages, such as regular access to healthcare and good food compared to the "global" average.

It'd been fucking damning.

I'd basically been mainly fives and sixes.

That meant that kobolds, the advanced kind at least, and their obvious draconic ancestors or relatives, were fucking lethal levels ahead of us.

That meant, in turn…

I knew—*somehow*—that the creatures in the dungeons were real living creatures to begin with. They had to have come from somewhere originally. Why we had legends of them, well, that was an argument for the social historians. Or it would be if they hadn't all probably been eaten.

I knew that these kobolds existed out there somewhere in space.

That somewhere dragons were real, that goblins and all fucking sorts of creatures had been seeded into our collective species' memory and into the dungeon's files, because they were fucking real *somewhere*.

That raised a few interesting questions, but the important one for me? The real "Hey, look here, you dumb shit" bit?

The advanced kobolds were available to me, even now at "only" Bronze, moving into Iron cores. What wasn't available? The higher-leveled fucking orcs.

There was even a warning in there about how I couldn't summon them. There were references to highly advanced and amazing fucking goblins, that were apparently so advanced and beautiful, they'd not lower themselves to interact with the likes of us. And yet? I could make them if I went all out. Yeah, it'd take years with a "stone" core, but there were no limits.

That I couldn't make certain orcs, and that those limits were hard-coded into the system? This made it clear that the creators of the system were shit-fucking-scared of them.

Normally, because of the simply *wonderful* relationship we'd *enjoyed* with the goddamn architects of this system, my first impulse would have been to make a deal with the orcs. They were clearly fucking the bastards Tuesday up in all sorts of creative ways, after all…

Buuuuut…I'd *met* the orcs. Yeah, they were the basic motherfuckers. Yes, they had maybe sparked a tiny, possibly *infinitesimal* even, sense of male paranoia, after seeing that the bastards were hung like literal goddamn horses. But it wasn't that. Seriously, it wasn't. Honest.

They were just fucking assholes.

The orcs were complete fucking *assholes*, and for all these races to be available, and presumably not at war with the creators? After all, let's face it, if humans found out they were being literally enslaved as servants of dungeons somewhere out there, we'd be added to the "likely to be at war with these motherfuckers" list pretty damn sharpish. Shortly after, presumably, knowing how inventive we could be, we'd be on the "whatever you do, don't fucking summon these dicks" list as well.

That logically meant—

I broke off that thought, seeing the way they were all looking at me, and decided I'd talk to Kelly and the others later about this.

For now?

"So…You were summoned to join Beta's ranks, to eventually specialize as a warrior, fighter, and defender of the dungeon," I repeated lamely, searching for the train of thought I'd been on before.

"Or…should you want to, you could be the first of a new breed—sorry—of defenders for the dungeon itself, or a researcher or crafter," I offered, then tried not to wince as I realized that I'd just asked a fairly complex question, of a creature that couldn't talk.

I opened my mouth, ready to say something else—probably stupid, admittedly—when Beta stepped up and beat me to it. She hissed something, then something else…and a furious row of hissing and chirruping started up as the pair of them went for it.

Seconds became minutes, as they continued. At one point, I seriously thought the newcomer was going to swing for her, and then…

He backed down, bowing his head to her in clear deference, before turning to me and pointing to her, as if to say, "You see this? This is how it's done, idiot."

Then that apparently *was* it, as he moved to stand next to her.

"What kind of weapons?" I bemusedly asked Beta after a few seconds, getting the feeling that this was something she should answer as much as he.

She turned to him, looking him over and then hissed, getting a quick response, before turning back to me, and miming a spear and shield.

I shrugged, looking to Aly, who was already nodding and summoning them, along with some basic gear.

"He's close enough to our dimensions that he can work with the human gear for now. I'll get to work on some custom stuff as soon as I have five minutes. He'll need redesigned armor, for a start," she promised me, summoning a trio of spears, a long hoplite-style shield, and then a pair of daggers in sheathes for him.

He took them gravely, attaching the daggers to his hips as Beta showed him. The long sheathe for the spears caused a little awkwardness, thanks to his wings, but he adjusted, angling it to lie between them, and carried the shield on his left arm.

He had, thankfully, also been summoned with a waist wrap that included a dangling section on the front and back, granting him a little modesty.

"Do you want me to summon another two now, or later?" I asked Beta, making it clear to the new arrival that it was her choice, and that I gave her that level of respect and latitude.

She paused for a minute, assessing him and then looking back to me, and shrugged, gesturing for me to bring it on.

The next two summons were, thankfully, a lot duller behind the eyes, and I saw the look of relief on Beta's face, as well as some curiosity, or what I assumed was curiosity, on the first one's face.

Hell, he could have been fucking constipated for all I knew.

Aly summoned them gear, another spear set for both; then, once they were kitted out, Beta pointed to the training dungeon, and waited, clearly wanting to do a run.

That or she wanted to go to fucking bed, considering the kobolds had claimed a section of the upper floors as theirs.

I nodded, accepting that it was worth the cost of mana to see what these new fuckers could do, and turned to Aly as soon as Beta set off, leading the kobolds.

"We need to gather some of the others," I said, getting a nod from her.

"I'll head to the dungeon, see who I can grab," she agreed, gesturing to the "true" dungeon, as the original lunatics all still thought of it, as I gestured downward.

"I'll go grab Finn and let him know. Then I'll find Markus and his merry band. No doubt Mike and Griffiths will be training as well."

"Markus is your priority?" Aly asked, an eyebrow quirked in question. "You're brave!"

"Yeah, I know." I grinned at her. "Kelly won't be happy that I'm focusing on him, but realistically? You'll find her before me, no doubt. And even if not, Markus is basically our head trainer. Then, with Mike and Griffiths? They're the ones who really need to know what the hell these guys are capable of." I paused, then winced and shrugged.

"But you know, if you didn't mind forgetting my reasoning, and instead remembering me asking you to find Kelly instead? I'd owe you one…"

"Ha!" She grinned. "I'll think about it…After all, you never know when having the Dungeon Lord owing me a favor might come in handy."

I grinned back at her, then set off, heading down and around, reentering the old printing building and jogging across the floor toward Finn.

I found him readily enough, laid back in a chair, this time an old outdoor sun lounger, one he'd pressed a thick duvet into, then some cushions; then he'd laid atop it, sliding down into what had essentially become a cocoon.

I slowed as I approached, wondering what the hell he was doing, when one of the nearby crafters waved at me to get my attention.

"Don't worry, he's working…" she said quickly, and I snorted, shaking my head.

"Believe me, I know how hard that bugger works. Don't worry!" I said, having caught Patrick and Aly both complaining about having to almost physically force Finn to relax and sleep on occasion.

"Well, yeah, anyway…" she said awkwardly. "He likes to get himself like that when he's in the 'system,' as he calls it. If you need him, you can get his attention by pulling the string."

I looked where she pointed, finding a length of twine that ran into the cocoon, hooked over a bell nearby, along with a note.

If you interrupt me, you better be on fire…or you will be!

I grinned, knowing damn well that it was a joke. Finn was one of the most even-tempered people I'd ever met.

I pulled on the string firmly, getting a squawk of protest from the "nest" as Finn thrashed around. The lounger clearly wasn't meant to stand up to the weight of him with his duvet thrashing around, and it promptly folded up, sending him crashing to the floor with a cry.

"Ah, Dungeon Lord?" She winced.

"Yeah?" I grinned down at the mess.

"It's attached to his toe," she explained. "I didn't think you'd yank on it so hard…"

I winced, then snorted and laughed at the stunned and confused look on Finn's face as he clambered out of the pile of cushions and blankets.

"What the hell…?" he growled, shaking his head and looking up, as I tugged on the string again. "Hey! Stop that!"

"Why the hell is it tied to your toe?" I ignored the outraged look he gave me.

"Because if some idiot pulled on it like that and it was on my cock, I'd have real problems!" he answered, as if that made sense.

"Oh, okay, sorry. I forgot you were a sexual deviant for a minute there," I apologized sarcastically. "So, why attach it to anything at all, you lunatic?"

"Because it's better than these idiots screaming in my ear or shaking me when I'm trying to do something." He sighed. "Now, oh mighty lord of all you survey, is there a reason you're interrupting me?" he asked, returning the sarcasm twofold.

"Well, I came looking for you because the new kobolds are done," I explained. "The latest generation, the advanced ones. Beta's got three in her pack, and she's going to run them through the dungeon, see what they're capable of. I thought you might like to watch with us, but if you're too busy…?"

"Oh…oh!" he said, finally understanding and nodding quickly. "Why didn't you say so!" He grinned, bending to untie the string from his toe, and I, being the great friend I am, pulled it again, for a laugh. "Stop that, you bastard!"

"Take five minutes and see who you can find," I told him. "Might as well spread the word and let people see what they think of the new kobolds…They're a little different."

"In a good way?" He looked over at me, before starting to hop on one foot, trying to get his sock and shoe back on.

"Fucking terrifying," I said honestly. "If I'd met them in the wild, I'd shit myself."

"Yeah?" He straightened up. "You think they'll help? They're not like the orcs, are they?" he added, clear concern in his voice.

"Not so far. Look, I'll explain it all soon, but Beta's going to run the dungeon, like I said, and she's not going to wait for us."

"Shit. Okay, meet you there!"

The next few minutes were busy ones, with Finn calling to the others and explaining what was happening, as I jogged out, heading over to where I remembered hearing Markus's voice last.

He was leading the remains of his teams, along with a dozen exhausted and scared-looking humans, through a set of exercises. But he happily let people abandon them, gathering up the others.

Mike and Griffiths were running a second, smaller group ragged in the training dungeon already—not actually fighting, just using one of the empty floors as a private training area. By the time I got to them, they'd already seen Beta heading in, and had gathered their people to watch.

CHAPTER NINE

We stood on the crystal floor, staring down in fascination as Beta led the team through the third room, barely pausing as the skeletons went from two in the last one, to four in here.

Someone had clearly been increasing the difficulty as well as "restocking" the dungeon, considering the skeletons had almost all been killed in the battle yesterday. But the speed that Beta and her team were going through them?

It was awesome, and more than a little terrifying.

In the first room, Beta had ordered the first new kobold, now apparently named Dran, to show her what he could do. He was fast and fearless; stepping forward without pause, he took the attack by the skeleton on his shield. Then the big kobold simply ripped the skeleton's head clean off with a single blow.

Literally, the fucker reached over and grabbed it by the head, then wrenched it clean off, not bothering with the spear; it looked into it curiously, before tossing it aside as the body collapsed in a clatter of bones.

That had been the first one and had set the tone. So far, the advanced kobolds simply fucking slaughtered everything that they came up against.

Beta grunted her approval as the three new kobolds stepped right up, none of them pausing. Dran barked an order to his less aware brethren, causing them to fall in on either side of him. The three took the blows on their shields. The four skeletons, working as individuals, and utterly brainless, simply struck as one. Their maces, sword and axe bounced off.

Then the three lashed out as one, stepping forward and slamming the shields into the skeletons, sending them clattering to the floor in a pile of bones and confusion.

Before they could get back up, the three had struck, and beheaded them all.

"Well, this is a bit one-sided," I muttered, getting a rising agreement from those around me. I glanced about, seeing noticeable dismay, rather than the approval I'd been hoping for.

Kelly leaned in sideways and spoke quietly. "They're under your control, right?"

"They are," I reassured her, before wincing and dropping my voice. "Probably."

"Outside of a girl's sex life, that's probably the worst addition of 'probably' I've ever heard…"

"What?"

"Matt, honey, there's times a girl does *not* want to hear 'probably' as the answer. 'Do you love me,' 'Did you pay that bill,' and the old favorite 'You're not gonna cum in my mouth, right,' are all times we want definite answers. Add this to that list."

"You don't normally complain when I—"

"It's good manners to *ask* first, or be invited, that's all I'm saying," she clarified, before going bright red as she looked around and realized how many people were listening in on the conversation. "Also, can we not talk about that here please?" she hissed, lowering her voice.

"You started it," I pointed out, grinning down at her, as she elbowed me in the gut.

"*Anyway*…we need to switch this up a bit, as well as make it very clear that the kobolds are on our side. How do we do that?"

"Corpse lord?" I suggested after a few seconds of thought.

"I don't know. They're…" She looked down, seeing Beta, Stumpy, and Starr standing back and watching, then nodded. "Okay. Can you do that now, though?"

"I can…" I frowned, thinking fast. The dungeon was "open" currently, and even though the creatures in it were literally all "mine," the dungeon wouldn't permit me, as the Dungeon Lord, to make any changes, while it was active. "Shit, you're right. We'll have to pull them back." I got what she meant after a few seconds.

"I could probably summon it outside of here, and then march it in, but I'm not sure if the other skeletons would attack it. Better to have them back up, reset, and go again."

I cleared my throat. When nothing happened and the buzz of conversations all around me continued, Chris shouted and got everyone's attention.

"OI FUCKERS!" he shouted. The open-plan nature of the observation floor meant it echoed, and people flinched away from him.

"Thanks for that, mate." I sighed, rubbing the bridge of my nose. "Okay, everyone! Sorry to interrupt, but it's clear the new additions are capable of a lot more than the original kobolds were. We're going to reset the dungeon, so give us…" I paused, looking to Kelly.

"Ten minutes," she whispered, dropping to her knees, curling her legs to one side, getting comfortable, before she glared at me, as soon as my traitorous mouth started to form the words *While you're down there…*

"Ten minutes, people!" I called, clearing my throat roughly and trying to pretend I'd definitely not been about to say it. "Ten minutes, and we're on!"

With that, I sat down as well, focusing and reaching out to Beta through the dungeon sense, imparting the knowledge of what was to come, and having her round up her people, bringing them back out of the dungeon.

As soon as they were out, I moved to Kelly, checking on her actions. A single massive corpse lord stomped around unhappily, the roof far too low for something that size.

I swore, knowing damn well that it'd never be able to fight effectively, and reached out, stopping Kelly from banishing it. Instead, I ordered it to leave the dungeon, moving out to the wall and mounting the steps leading up, eventually coming out on the roof and taking up one of the silent, abandoned ballistae.

The knowledge that after we'd lost all the "gunners" for these, and hadn't replaced them yet, was an annoyance, but at least the fucker was up there now.

That done, I cracked my metaphorical fingers, and got to work.

The skeletons in the first two rooms stayed the same, except that they were replaced with four instead of one armed with spears and shields, and ready to fight.

Then I put four more skeletons in the middle of the next room in plain sight…and four orcs, two on either side, and hidden from view.

I also gave them strict orders to stay hidden until an adventurer or more came in, as I didn't want the fuckers starting a fight as soon as my back was turned.

In the next room, I made a single goblin mage, along with three orcs. Then…I ran outta fucking mana.

That was fine, though, because while I'd been making these, Kelly had been busily equipping them all. Admittedly, she'd only given them basic weapons, the orcs getting clubs and…

I left the dungeon sense, finding Kelly straightening up and looking amused.

"Kelly, is that a giant dildo?" I asked after a few seconds of careful contemplation.

"Maybe." Her eyes twinkled with amusement.

"You gave the orcs, a species so fucking aggressive that we use them as slaughter-fodder because we can't trust them, giant fucking dildos as weapons?"

"The rubber ones with the suction cups so you can attach them to the shower wall," she pointed out, grinning. "I supersized them."

"I fucking hope so. The size of that thing…" I grunted, looking down at the damn things, as laughter rose all around me. "That fucker would ruin a goddamn horse. Where did you get that?"

"It was absorbed into the dungeon at some point." She shrugged. "No clue whose it was…"

"I hope they'd washed it beforehand," I muttered, shaking my head as I looked down at the sight. It was almost comical, the massively muscled and hyper aggressive orcs—thankfully summoned with a waist wrap now…Aly must have gone in and changed something, thank fuck—were armed with giant floppy dildos.

I didn't know whether it made them more or less terrifying, to be honest. The thought of a raving orc running at me with that in one hand? I'd panic. The thought of what the fucker was intending if it won…it just didn't bear thinking about.

On the upside, when we needed to do some scouting, and we thought there was an enemy about, preferably goblin or human, and we wanted to terrify them? I was sending these fuckers in.

Probably naked.

Yeah, anyone who survived would be traumatized, but they were a last resort kind of weapon, like for slavers or people who ate with their mouths open.

We'd moved around a lot as a group, people spreading out to watch the new arrivals being printed and assigned their territory, but as the door at the beginning reopened and Beta led her team into the safe room, everyone rushed over to there, before securing the best view they could.

Beta barely paused, looking the skeletons over, then sending the new members straight in.

The fight was predictably one-sided, the kobolds running in and beating twelve shades of shit out of the undead. But the introduction of different weapons helped to stretch it out slightly.

The next room was the same as the first, and I grinned to myself as I saw the kobolds not even pause, clearly thinking they had the measure of the dungeon.

Beta hissed something—or I saw her mouth open, anyway; I couldn't hear it over the noise of the crowd and the fight—but they charged right on in, ignoring her.

I grinned to myself when I saw her step back and glare at them, stopping Stumpy and Starr from going to their aid as the four orcs ran out from where they'd hidden, hitting the kobolds from the sides.

The three folded in, fighting back-to-back, which was the best choice they could make, admittedly, but that left a single kobold, Dran, facing four skeletons, while the other two faced two orcs a piece.

Dran was the first to score a kill. The three had turtled up, bracing their shields as much against one another as they could and stabbing out. He managed a lucky blow to the head of a skeleton, taking the axe wielder down in a clatter of bones.

The problem, though, was when he pulled the spear back.

Three kobolds, each considerably bigger than the earlier generations, fighting back-to-back, meant that when he pulled back the spear, he smacked the bottom of his companion's shield aside.

The gap that was opened up…

Well, an orc smacked the unfortunate kobold across the face with his massive dildo.

"Well, that's something I never thought I'd see," I called to Chris cheerfully, grinning as he shook his head in amazement.

"You've got real issues, you know that?" he shouted across the noise of the crowd, and I shrugged, not bothering to correct him.

The kobold staggered, stunned, rather than dying outright or being fatally wounded as an axe or mace would have managed.

He unfortunately knocked the third kobold, who grunted and missed his attack; the spear glanced off the upper arm of the orc he was facing.

Two things happened at once. The orc he'd hit dropped his "weapon" and grabbed the spear, yanking it forward, and the second orc swung at the exposed hand on the spear shaft.

The kobold, left with the option of surrendering his spear or having his hand probably broken and the spear taken anyway, released it and stepped backward.

As soon as the dildo flew past, he drove his shield into the first orc, pushing him backward, then slashed the claws of his right hand across the second orc's face, shredding it and sending the orc into a berserker rage.

Dran had seen the issue with the spear straightaway, and took two more blows on the shield, then turned the spear sideways and rushed forward, taking a single glancing blow to the shoulder, but managing to throw all three remaining skeletons back, sending them clattering to the floor.

He spun, seeing his companions being beaten back, and quickly moved to the second kobold's aid, blocking another "blow" incoming, before stabbing the orc in the stomach, and tearing his razor-sharp spear sideways, gutting him.

He ripped the spear back, only to have the mace-wielding skeleton from behind him, having gotten up much quicker than the others, grab the haft and yank him off-balance, swinging for his head with the mace.

Dran ducked, taking another blow on his shield from the remaining orc as he tried to defend his companion, then closed his eyes, seeing the stabbing sword that was incoming, and knowing he had no chance to dodge it, held as he was.

Then Beta was there, kicking the sword aside and beheading the skeleton, who'd managed to rise only to its knees. She took the mace blow on her shield, and Stumpy ran past, smashing the mace-wielding skeleton's legs out from under it again, then punting the head free as it fell.

Starr took on the pair of orcs on the right, one blinded by the third kobold's claws, flailing wildly and screaming in fury, and the other, who had just grabbed the top of the kobold's shield and was swinging wildly over it, trying to brain him.

Starr hit them both with Briar, creating a patch of thick woody branches, laden with thorns, that grew up and around their legs. Considering that the orcs were wearing only a shlong-and-butt-flap covering—literally a cloth that went around their waists as a belt, then hung down the front and the back to provide a degree of modesty—and that they were hung like literal horses, while the briars reached up a meter…

Well, both orcs, including the one who was berserk, pretty much froze in place straightaway, unwilling to move and "tear" themselves free.

Every man in the place winced and hissed in shared male horror.

"That's just wrong." I shook my head and looked over at Aly. "Maybe we could give them proper pants next time?"

"I thought you hated the orcs?" she asked, and I nodded.

"Oh, I do, but there's hate, and then there's that." I pointed down and winced. "Next time, pants."

"Deal," she said, looking down as the fight changed in seconds.

The kobolds went from defensive to offensive, moving quickly to finish the remaining skeleton, then the orc that was on his own, and then the two that were held in place.

All three of the new kobolds were battered and clearly wounded, limping as they joined Beta and the others in looting the reliquaries, pocketing whatever they got, then forming up behind her, as she pointed to the next room.

I couldn't hear or understand the words, said as they were in kobold, but it was damn obvious they were getting a dressing-down, followed by their orders.

I'd expected, as did most of the others, that they'd have cut their losses and left the dungeon. Instead, Beta looked the single goblin in sight over, then pointed to the right and left, hissing orders to the others, before shooting the goblin in the head.

He dropped to the floor, killed outright, and I sighed.

I'd planned to trigger his Disgust spell, drawing the kobolds straight to him in a blood rage; then the orcs would have fallen on them from behind.

Instead, the three new kobolds, having retrieved their weapons, marched into the room with shields at the ready. As soon as the orcs ran out, they stopped, shields braced, and waited.

Starr hit two of the orcs with Briar again, Stumpy shot one of them in the face with his crossbow, and Beta shot the single orc with hers, taking him in the throat.

Then she barked an order, and the three stepped up, blocking the single hit from the dildo, before all three stabbed him at once, sharing the XP.

With that, the fight was over, and the three new kobolds straightened up as Beta barked her orders again, clearly stunned by the difference between Beta leading them all as a team, and how close the three had come to being killed.

She marched up to them, hissing and barking at them, dressing each of them down and clearly pointing out their mistakes, before nodding to the reliquaries, letting them loot them.

Then she looked up at the crystal ceiling that we all stood on the other side of, and dragged a claw across her throat, signaling that they were done for the day.

There was some grumbling at that, but I nodded in agreement, calling out for Jo to go and help them, turning to the others who were nearby, mainly Aly, Kelly, Mike, Markus, and Griffiths. Finn sauntered over as we started to talk.

"What did you think then?" I asked.

"Much better soldiers," Markus said. "They had an intuitive grasp of tactics, and even when they were being overwhelmed, they were improving."

"And these are the baseline ones?" Griffiths asked. "You said you start with a baseline, then improve upon that, making the various classes, like the mages and hunters and so on?"

"Yeah, they're level one, maybe two or three at most by the end of that. For comparison, humans are naturally half as strong and smart, etc., as they are."

"You can create humans?" he asked me carefully, and I shook my head.

"Not as far as I'm aware," I lied. "I gained access to the basic stat information, though. Most people start with a five or a six. They started with tens and twelves."

"Shit. So, we're second-class citizens, eh?" Chris asked, and I grinned at him.

"You'd think that. But if that's true, why not do this to a world of theirs?"

"Because they might turn around and slaughter the aliens?" Griffiths suggested.

I sighed. "Yeah, maybe, but I don't know. I think if you're going to get samples in the system for the dungeons to produce, then those species either allowed it, or are gonna be pissed about it either way. If they allowed it? Then they're involved. If they're pissed, nothing's going to change. If there're all these species out there, then there must be worlds they could use to convert to dungeons—they could just siphon mana and print up tens of thousands of these fuckers to be soldiers, right?"

"Well…yeah, I guess," Griffiths replied, rubbing his chin in thought. "That's a point. If they can make these dungeons, why not do that? Why make us jump through the hoops to reach the higher levels? They could have set up, then slaughtered us all and print these kobolds up. Ignore the lower-level stuff, go straight for these, or hell, their next evolution! Equip them with decent weapons, and—"

"And you've got an army," I agreed. "So there has to be a reason they don't do that, and I think it's us."

"I agree," Aly said into the confused silence. "Think about it. They could have literally just used our lives to build thousands, if not *millions* of these. They have spaceships—they had to use them to get here—and the ship the dungeon core was in as well—"

She turned to look at me. "We still need to secure that," she said, and I nodded.

"Already planning for it," I said. "Go on."

"Hmmm, okay, so they have spaceships, they have tech, and they can make creatures to man them easily enough. Why involve us?"

"Because we're the natural counter to them." I gestured toward the bloody floor below, the orc bodies having already faded from view.

"What makes you say that?" Griffiths asked.

"How many years did people joke about humanity being the equivalent of real space orcs?" I looked around, then sighed. "I don't mean the green-skinned fantasy and sci-fi tropes. I mean the mad shit that we as a species do? Like the Large Hadron Collider—might teach us interesting shit, might destroy the planet. We weren't sure, so we turned it on. We're the intergalactic equivalent of the guy in the bar who hands his beer over to his mates and says, 'Watch this shit.'"

"There was a theory, a few years back, that aliens were more likely to be peaceful than not," Finn pointed out, summoning a chair and sitting in it with a grin.

We all started to do the same, most of the floor quickly being deserted.

"Basically, it goes something like this: the technology required to travel across space is highly advanced, and the average species will need to go through several developments on their way to reaching that, including nuclear."

"Right?"

"Well, that's when the number of possible civilizations gets pruned down." Finn shrugged. "Think about it. If there's, say, ten other civilizations out there, for the sake of argument. Five aggressive and five peaceful, right?"

We all nodded.

"The aggressive ones fight among themselves a lot. A few get wiped out early, a few more wipe themselves out with nukes, or reduce their planet to an uninhabitable state. Suddenly we're down to one aggressive species, and five peaceful ones. Let's say that one gets into space and kills off one or even two of the others…the remaining species are likely to band together and kill off the aggressive one. Then you're left with 'nice' civilizations."

I winced, thinking that was likely bullshit, but he went on before I could say anything.

"Now say ten more rise up. Maybe three of the bad guys make it to space this time. The nice guys learned a valuable lesson, and are ready, greet them with an open hand, and a fucking big missile when they bite.

"You end up with a galaxy full of hyper vigilant, more or less peaceful species. Each time an aggressive asshole species rears up, then they get slapped back down. Maybe they're wiped out, maybe they're just reduced in tech levels. What you're left with is a group of high-tech peacekeepers." He shrugged. "That's the theory, anyway."

"And you think that we were slapped down, that we were getting too advanced and aggressive?" I asked.

"Nope." He grinned. "I think the orcs were, and they failed. If my theory is sound—and remember it's a theory, so evidence always beats it—then we're probably not at the stage of multiple high-tech peacekeeping civilizations. I think we're right at the early stage, where one is wiping the others out, and the current 'nice' guys decided they needed shock troopers."

"Sounds nice," Kelly growled.

"Maybe not by our standards, but if it's a case of we can survive as a species, or be eliminated? Even if over ninety percent of the species is lost, all we need is time to replace that." Finn shrugged.

"This is a guess, okay? Literally, it might be bullshit, but let's say you've got the tech, but you're shit at fighting. You've been watching one of your neighbor species for a while, they're aggressive and wiping the local area out, and then you find a species that's got the potential to take them on. You can advance them, add in some kill-switches to your tech, and use them as disposable shock troops. If they come after you? You kill them all. It's a gamble, and maybe an investment, that's all."

"Makes as much sense as anything else," I muttered. "Why the various creatures then? Why not just humanity?"

"Shock troops," he repeated. "They need us to use our natural affinity to fight, but there's not many of us left. We need to practice and level. You said you don't think the aliens meant you to have control of a dungeon once…you still think that?"

"Yeah, I think we were supposed to level up and form alliances with the dungeons. The aliens' dungeon fairies would have still been in charge of the dungeons, that way."

"Honestly, I think the intention was to raise us to a level we could fight. That's why the dungeons are here, so we can level and learn. Then they produce real weapons, and we all march off to fight the orcs when they come. Even if we fail, we bleed them enough that the 'more civilized' species have a better chance."

"Fuckers," Chris muttered, shaking his head. "They killed billions to make us into their disposable shock troops—"

"Possibly," I interrupted, holding one hand up. "This is a feeling, all right, that's all. I've had it awhile, but…" I went on to explain my suspicions regarding the wipe of humanity, getting a few converts to my way of thinking and a few adamantly opposed.

Of all of them, Ramnik, who'd joined us late, was the most convinced that the aliens were evil and must be destroyed. The loss of her brother clearly weighed heavily on her as she spoke about increasing her power and "raining righteous retribution upon their worlds."

When we broke up, everyone returning to their various tasks and duties, I instead moved to the upper floor and roof of the training dungeon, and began to explore the new "farms" with Chris.

CHAPTER TEN

"It's weird, isn't it," Chris said after a few minutes, as we walked along the neat rows of growing trees.

"It's…fuck, man…weird isn't the word for it." I was stunned. In just a matter of days, the seeds and few saplings that we'd managed to collect and plant were already up to our waist. The deep black earth that was now the "ground" of this floor, despite my *knowing* the dimensions of the damn floor, and the fact that it was internal, having once been a "normal" level in an office block, was still somehow able to support full trees and more.

The ceiling had originally been at about eight feet, literally a normal ceiling, and now? Now a gentle, warm glow filtered down from the ceiling, at least twenty feet above us, although the exterior dimensions didn't appear to have changed at all.

I couldn't wrap my head around it, not even slightly. And the fact that everything was so damn healthy?

"This is your magic?" I asked him, looking over as he walked along, gently running his hands across the tops of the trees, sending ripples through the leaves.

"Yes and no. I'm boosting it a little bit, but most of it is the dungeon and the Life and Nature converters. They might not be drawing much in…" He paused, looking over at me, and I checked.

"Not much," I agreed. "There's only a few so far, and they're earning around eleven and twelve mana an hour."

"Well, whatever the numbers mean…"

"They earn ten, usually, as a base. The Air converters on the roof with a breeze top out at earning twenty," I clarified.

"Right. Well, they might not look like they're doing much, but they are." Chris led us over to the nearest Nature converter, and smiled, resting a hand on it. "Man, that feels good," he whispered.

"So…" I said, about to ask him what he'd meant, when I saw it. The plants nearby, mainly rows upon rows of fruits—strawberries on the left in ten rows, and grapes on trellises to the right—were significantly bigger.

The plants weren't ready to fruit yet, but looking them over, they clearly weren't far from it.

"How does this work?" I asked as it suddenly occurred to me. "I mean, cross-pollination and shit…I haven't seen many insects…"

"Fuck knows, mate. I'm a druid, and I know the bare basics of growing anything. Hell, you remember that yucca that Alison bought me?"

"You killed it in a week," I grunted. "Yeah, what's up with that? You could never grow anything—why the hell are you a druid, and Becky a 'Fey Wrangler'? I mean, if anyone should have nothing to do with plants, it's you. And what the hell is a fey?"

"Honestly, I don't know. I just know that I've always liked animals, and trees and nature, as well. It calms me."

"That's me and the storm," I said softly. "It's like it was always meant to be a part of me. I feel the crackle of lightning, the pressure of the thunder and it's like this was what I was born for. Like I was only half alive before."

"Exactly." Chris smiled. "Like that feeling when you had a really heavy night on the booze, where you feel like everything you do is slightly off and delayed. Then the next day when you wake up and the hangover is gone, you've actually slept and had real food and all of it. You feel like you were just a shadow of yourself the day before. Well, this is like that…I feel like I'd been living hungover for my entire life until now."

"Yeah, man." I smiled. "Couldn't have put it better myself. So, the Nature converter is making a much bigger difference to the world than it shows in the figures."

"You can see it for yourself, right?"

"Yeah. The question is, though, what are the other converters doing…I mean, we've got…" I stuttered to a stop, frowning, straightening up and shaking my head, looking around the room. The feeling I'd just gotten was…it was danger, serious fucking danger, I realized, and the warning was coming from the dungeon itself.

"Get everyone!" I snapped. "Get them all and get them fucking armed! Something's happened!"

I dropped to the floor, closing my eyes and fleeing into the dungeon itself, feeling the echoing danger, a sense of a growing threat, and…and sadness, grief, and…*anger*.

All things I'd never experienced from the dungeon, beyond the danger and a direction before, and it made me wonder—was the dungeon alive, or was it the people it felt?

It was to the south, though, to the south and far enough away that it was out of range.

"Shit, Barry!" I snarled, lurching back to my feet and staggering as I tried to get "me" seated inside myself again. Once I'd gotten my balance back, I ran, headed straight for the roof, staggering slightly as I checked on Jack, finding that he was, of course, about a mile to the damn north. Sod's Law, that. I ordered him to divert around and start scouting while we got ready.

The spiral staircase in the corner that led up was old, cast iron and creaked when I jumped and kicked off every step. I felt the whole thing shudder, but it held long enough that I was out, and into the mild sunshine in seconds.

The rooftop was much like the floor below. It'd been replicated exactly, right down to the individual plants, making sure we could compare properly later.

All that flashed through my mind and was forgotten as I raced for the edge of the roof, gathering the lightning inside me. F87or the first time since the battle with Dickless, I reached out and in, and I leapt from the roof.

I had a split second in which I fully expected to fall, probably killing myself, considering it was five stories high. Then the roar of the wind burst into my ears, and I soared past the cathedral, the gust rippling my clothes as I went.

I could barely hear anything over the rush, but I saw the faces of the people walking around as their lord *flew* past.

Normally this would have been a wonderful thing, a chance to prove that they'd made the right choice in following me. But right now?

The feeling of burgeoning danger was too strong.

I landed on the roof of the dungeon, then ran and dropped off the side, coming to a perfect three point "superhero" landing in the alley behind the dungeon. The doors opened as I bounded to my feet and rushed inside.

The stairs of old, cheap, and functional metal, a pitch-black stairwell, grey concrete walls, and a lingering smell that could never be identified, beyond "too fucking close to the bins by half" was gone.

Now the stairwell was clean, solid stone steps, well-lit, and smelling faintly of lemon as I took three and four steps at a time in my mad dash.

I didn't care, too swept up in the stress as I leapt down, now taking them five at a time, skidding as I took the turn, kicking off the wall and landing lightly. My stats came into play as I flashed down the final section, opening the doors at the bottom with a thought as I ran at them, not even considering stopping.

Inside, I could hear the sounds of others running as well. Clearly Chris had kicked the anthill. I "felt" the danger surge dip, then build even higher, as I leapt over the low coffee table in the middle of our communal lounge area.

I took the door at speed and ran into our room. Kelly was half dressed, her normal clothes being torn off as fast as she could, her armor and "working" underwear—sports gear, mainly—being dragged on.

For the first time, I neither celebrated her nakedness, nor tried to do anything about it. I skidded to a halt, and tore my top as I tugged it off, throwing it into the corner as I dropped onto the bed, grabbing my trainers and ripping them free as quick as I could.

"Details?"

"Danger, from the south," I got out, before lying back and pulling at my jeans.

"Here." Kelly, still topless, grunted with a mouth full of a glove, as she stepped in close and grabbed the ankles of my jeans, pulling them free.

"Thanks!" I rolled free of the bed, grabbing a pair of the thicker jeans Aly had made for us to go under the armor, and I struggled into them. Kelly got back to dressing, spitting the glove out onto the bed and yanking a sports bra on.

The pair of us were hopping around the room for less than a minute, dragging clothing out of drawers and leaving the room looking like a bomb had gone off. But at the end of it, we were both dressed, and I joined her at our little "armory."

It'd undertaken various evolutions now, moving from the simple sword and shotguns and so on, to holding a variety of guns.

The issue we had, again, was damn ammunition.

I had a beautiful Magnum Research 1911, firing 10mm rounds, and I had a grand total of one bloody bullet for it. It made it kind of pointless to carry.

I also, thankfully, had an SA80 assault rifle, the British Army's standard loadout, with a nearly full magazine, a couple of decent knives, a sword, a spear, and a hammer.

There was a shield as well, but I left that, hanging the hammer on a loop on the right side of my armor, and the sword over my shoulder, a combat knife on the left hip, and the assault rifle on its sling across my chest, before cursing and ramming the Magnum—after making damn sure the safety was on—into a spare holster and shifting it around to hang behind the hammer.

Kelly was gearing up with her shotgun, her rifle, and a pair of long knives.

Although we both looked impressive, I silently acknowledged, by far, the most danger we posed to anyone was in our private abilities and magic, rather than the more overt threats of our guns and knives.

"Anything else?" Kelly asked, her voice flat and businesslike as we headed for the door.

"Nothing yet," I said. "It feels…I don't know." I shrugged, moving out into the shared area and finding the others gathering.

Chris ran into sight, taking the last few steps at speed and sprinting to his own room, waving on his way past, and making me grin as I started to speak. Aly had arrived and had been waiting, even as Mike checked his rifles, both the SA80 and the heavier sniper rifle he carried.

"You got enough ammo to make it worth bringing that?" I asked him, and he shook his head.

"Two shots," he said. "They were scavenged by the gathering facility. Fuck knows where they found them, but believe me, with this? That could be two kills of practically anything."

"You're the one carrying it." I dismissed it, and spoke to the rest of the room, seeing Patrick securing his gloves. The Monk class specialized in unarmed combat, meaning he had the least of all of us to carry.

"I've sent the harvester drones back to the location where they found those rounds," Aly called to me. "If there's any more? We'll find them."

I nodded, sending a quick smile her way and mentally adding that to my list, that we needed to mark up a map of the places they'd been found and start hitting them just in case any had been missed.

John was down to a single shot rifle—a hunting model, admittedly—but again, with sod all in terms of ammo, a mere handful of shots. And Jo, our resident head healer, was ready as well, a long knife her only weapon.

"Okay, people, let's get upstairs. We need Griffiths and Sarah as well, at the very least," I said, heading for the internal stairs, even as Chris shouted through the door that he'd "Only be a minute, dammit."

A few minutes later, we were all outside together: Captain Griffiths and Rhodes, his sergeant in the Coldstream Guards; Chris and Becky, which was unusual, as she tended to work more inside than out for these kind of things; Clive and Owen, an older pair of hunters, both with crossbows ready.

Ramnik, Dante, and Ashley stood with Sarah and several of her team: Paul, Tom, Jason, Markus, Katherine, and Zac. Others were streaming over, and I looked at Chris quizzically.

"You said get everyone." He shrugged. "I told everyone I met to spread the word, and to—"

The bells in the cathedral rang out, the steady, constant full-throated iron warning calling everyone who was outside to return as fast as they could.

"To ring the bells," Chris finished with a sigh. "I know you didn't say to, but—"

"No. It was the right thing to do. Don't worry. Until we know what's happened, best to 'turtle' up. Okay, people!" I turned slowly, making sure everyone could hear me. "As I'm linked to the dungeon, I occasionally get warnings from it, mainly in the form of a sense of danger and threat. I got one not long since, and it was fucking strong. To make this clear, every other sense I've had like this from the dungeon has been when there's been something on the literal border of the dungeon, or about to attack me personally.

"Whatever this is? It's far enough out of the dungeon that I can't sense it directly, so for me to feel it still, it's something the dungeon is practically shitting itself over."

"What do you think it is?" Aly held Mike's hand and glanced from him to me, clearly worried.

"No clue," I said. "I've genuinely got no fucking clue. But considering how battered we are after the last fight? It's just about the worst timing we could have hoped for. We're insanely low on ammo. Most of us have a handful of bullets, if that."

"Your armor is wrecked as well." Aly groaned. "I knew I should have prioritized that!"

I looked down at it. The burnt and melted panels, the once-gleaming hoplite-style pauldrons and chest piece, the bracers and additional sections, like the greaves and more, were all heavily scoured.

I looked as if I'd been in a washing machine on a spin cycle with a load of rocks. But the armor was still more or less functional, even if it was battered to fuck.

That meant I was wearing it, regardless.

"Yeah. So I'll take a small team to do a recon, see what we can find out. It'll be a human one only," I said as Beta and her team jogged up, and I held a hand up to stop the hiss of disapproval she let loose.

"Beta, I need you to get your team together. Aly, get their gear sorted. Cannibalize anything you need to and get them kitted out. Then start the repairs on our armor, and that of the soldiers."

"The Coldstream Guard are specialists in light infantry roles," Griffiths interrupted. "We train extensively to recon and capture targets. We should take point on this."

"I appreciate that, Griffiths, I really do, but honestly, you're still considering moving on, and we're massively in need of replenishment. How many bullets do you have left?"

"Nowhere near as many as we'd need to actually leave," he said. "We're desperately short on them now. We're practically down to harsh language."

"Then I want you to take Mike, and head to the local bases, all save the main infantry one."

"We agreed a few days until we hit that one. Is that still the plan?" Griffiths asked, and I nodded. "In that case, I'd suggest Ashley joins us as we discussed before. If there are soldiers there, she may be able to recruit them, and it'll be experience for her. Also, it'll give her time to adjust to the military mindset ahead of the actual meeting with the base."

"Ashley?" I asked, and she nodded quickly.

"It makes sense, thank you," she agreed.

"Then you do that, Griffiths. Take your team, Mike, and Ashley, and go find us some more goddamn ammo. I'll lead a small…*small*"—I repeated, louder as voices rose—"team to scout the area to the south, see if we can figure out what the hell is going on."

"Who goes, and what happens with those who stay?" Sarah asked, ever the practical one.

"Those who stay get to work on the dungeon," I said. "I'll be granting a basic level of access to all of our people now, enabling them to absorb all the crap around us into the dungeon, and expand it. All except you, Markus, Aly, Ramnik, and Dante."

I held up a hand as people started to object.

"That's enough, people!" I barked. "The lowest level of access enables you to open the most basic doors, which we don't have many of, summon food, which most can already do, and absorb things. That's it. They can't even expand the dungeon's influence, so I believe the risk is worth it. Markus, you'll be helping to lead the new kobold hoplites, outside of Beta's team anyway, and you'll need to train them. Sarah will help you with that, and she'll integrate her people into fighting with the kobolds, getting both species used to each other."

"Advanced or uncommon?" Aly asked bluntly. "We could summon literally dozens more if we go for uncommon, and we already have the armor and weapons patterns, but…"

"But the advanced are a whole different species," I finished for her. "No, I agree. We go advanced from now on. If we need cannon fodder, we summon undead and send them in. In fact, when we get the chance, and the mana, we summon a hundred undead archers and stand them on the walls and roofs, surround the dungeon, with orders to fire only when fired upon. Beyond that, they're to summon an officer."

"Officers?" Mike's mouth curled as if tasting something foul.

"Yes, *Captain*," I told him, a sardonic grin flashing across my face. "We'll need an officer core eventually, but for now we'll have a gate or wall officer on call at all times, one of the leadership team, who the undead can summon if someone unknown approaches, rather than just firing on them."

"Why have the undead at all?" Katherine asked hesitantly, holding up one hand. "I mean, if I was coming looking for help, and I saw a massive random wall with undead on it, it'd keep me well clear."

"That's a good point," I acknowledged. "Basically, it's because the undead don't get tired or distracted. A hundred undead on the walls watching out will see anything that's out there, doesn't matter if it's day or night, good or bad weather."

"I'd still not want to come if I saw them," she pointed out, and I snorted.

"Who would?" I asked rhetorically. "No, they'd be a short-term solution. Soon we'll put the alert towers that we got—" I broke off, seeing the blank looks around me.

"We got a blueprint for the 'alert towers' as a quest reward recently," I explained. "The only issue is they're short range, thirty meters each. As soon as we can upgrade them a few times, though? We'll replace the undead with them."

"Okay, so considering the tangent we went off on, the plan is to build advanced kobolds, and form a force with them?" Aly asked for confirmation, and I nodded.

"Beta, are you confident the kobolds will obey you?" I asked her, and she nodded. "Then you stay here with your team as well. Aly will summon the kobolds as quickly as she can, and as each is 'born,' you help integrate them. Markus will lead them for now, along with Sarah running the human forces. Mike is in overall command of the fighters, with—for as long as he's with us—Griffiths as his second. And I want you making sure of the kobolds as we create them. Also, you'll be roaming and dealing with things as my elite force. So: train them, integrate them, and get ready."

Beta twisted around and pointed to the training dungeon. I hesitated, then shook my head.

"No. I know it's more efficient, but the number you'd need to go through to train your people, it's just too expensive for now."

"What do you have for us, Dungeon Lord?" Ramnik asked.

I hesitated, seeing the red-rimmed eyes, and knowing she was still mourning her brother. But in this new world, we were all mourning someone.

"Ramnik, I want you to work with Dante. He's the one who discovered the affinities system. I need you to sit and figure this shit out. What other systems are sitting there, just out of sight? Be ready, though, in case I need to call upon you. Aly, once you've got the kobolds started and the armor and so on planned, work with them." I turned to the rest of my team, about to speak to them, when Aly grabbed my arm.

"Wait. You want me to equip the kobolds, and that makes sense, but isn't it better to try to upgrade them first, take a basic one and try to make, I don't know, a shaman or a hunter?"

"I used the ability for the day already," I admitted. "It was a failure."

"Still…"

"We need soldiers," I said. "Yes, the other classes will be better specialists, but for now? The standard 'entry-level model' is already head and shoulders better equipped to fight than the originals of the earlier species. We need them as quickly as possible."

"Okay, I understand." She nodded and moved to the side, dragging Ramnik and Dante with her. "Am I okay to…?"

"Yeah, increase their access to the same level as the core team." I smiled faintly at the look on their faces as they realized how much I trusted them.

"So we're going scouting?" Chris looked around. "Who's with us?"

"You, me, Kelly, Patrick, John, Becky, Jo, and Jack." I looked at each as I spoke.

"Thank you." Becky smiled, and I nodded to her.

"That's it then, people. Time to go hunting," I barked, clapping my hands together. I reached out mentally to Jack, sensing his location as he continued his scouting, currently speeding across the bridge to the south.

I frowned, distracted for a second as I mentally linked with him, unable to "see" things as well and in as much detail as he'd been able to project them before on the wall of the dungeon. I could still get a condensed form of it.

The high-speed data download sent me staggering, as dozens of hours of sights, sounds, smells, and more downloaded at the speed of an unladen swallow. But after a few seconds, I was moving again.

"You alright?" Kelly whispered, ducking under my arm, and I grinned at her, kissing the top of her head.

"I am. Sorry, didn't mean to startle you. Jack was catching me up. He's not found anything, but he killed some weird-looking shit."

The sights and scents had certainly been weird, anyway. Most of the things I'd been able to make out were just blurs that screamed and attacked or tried to run.

Either way, Jack slaughtered them and moved on, the damage minor each time, although steadily mounting over time.

As it was, he was at eighty-three percent effective, and considering he'd been roaming in the dark of Newcastle?

If he'd been a *living* tiger before the fall and tried that? He'd have seen the dawn as a pair of gloves and a hat, probably with most of his meat sold in kebab shops.

The fact the world had gotten more dangerous since then was frankly insane. I looked around, making eye contact with the team as we headed toward the massive gates at the south side of the compound, and grinned.

I could feel the danger, the threat and the concern of the dungeon, but I had a good team and we were heavily armed. I knew we'd be all right.

If need be, we could always fall back and hide behind our fucking huge walls.

CHAPTER ELEVEN

"*Jesus-titty-fucking-cornholio-in-a-dress!*" Becky screamed, diving behind the shattered remains of a car, wrapping her arms around her head as a body slammed down on the roof, sending shattered glass flying in all directions.

I swore, twisting around and glaring at the body as it twitched, then turned. Its faceless gaze made it clear the fucker could see both her where she crouched, and me where I knelt, trying to reload.

"Becky!" I roared. "Run, for fuck's sake!"

I discarded the rifle, not having the time to slot the damn bullets we'd just found individually into the magazine, and leapt to my feet, running straight at the figure as it levered itself back up.

The majority were humanoid, mainly anyway—although some were clearly another species, judging from the giant spider that was closing on us.

This figure had clearly been an attempt to copy a human, and fuck, it was terrifying. As it sat up, the chest clicked and shifted, sections rearranging, buckled panels falling free and exposing what we believed was the controlling sentience.

I swung the hammer, having found it was the best weapon for these metallic monstrosities. I grunted with the effort I put into it, hitting the fucker in the head and pounding it back down into the roof of the car.

"The chest, for fuck's sake!" Kelly shouted, standing in the middle of our group. Her arms spun like she was trying to dance, while also controlling a puppet with strings.

The scream of tearing metal made it clear her new puppet was nearly "alive," thankfully.

"Fall back!" Chris shouted. The chatter of his assault rifle went abruptly silent as he ran out of ammo, and he cursed as he frantically tried to reload. "Fuck's sake, drop back, you shits!"

"He's right!" Patrick called, ducking under a swinging arm and slashing a mana-enhanced uppercut into the wooden "chin" of the creature he faced.

Its head was almost torn free. The entire creation staggered backward several steps, before a leg bent the wrong way and flashed toward him, sending Patrick rolling aside, dodging a blow that might well have killed him, had it landed.

I pulled back, seeing the pulsing "heart," and altered my aim, slamming the hammer down into the strange glass and copper "cage" that held the true creature inside, triggering Examine as I did so.

Asuras – *caged*	Captured animating spirit
The asuras is an offshoot of a greater being, and is a rarely seen, and yet powerful creature. The asuras is able to possess and control inanimate objects, granting mobility and a form of life to a previously innocent creation.	
Note: The lesser asuras is incapable of reproduction; only an asuras queen may command them without risk; this asuras is specialized for observation.	
Sleeve: The asuras must be contained within a "sleeve" to exist in this reality, but may only maintain one at a time, due to the massive drain on the asuras's mana.	
Weaknesses: Earth and Darkness Magics	
HP: 10/10 **Stamina:** 10/10 **Mana:** 150/3180 **Speed:** 3/10 (embodied) **Level:** 4	
HP 10/10	**Special Abilities**: 0/1

I almost hesitated, seeing the words "caged." Then I saw the simple paddle that had been one hand, flashing with a blue light, and splitting down into half a dozen "fingers."

As they separated, their sharpness became clear, and my hammer landed.

The delicate-seeming cage, a small hexagon that was held in the center of the chest, practically detonated as my hammer landed, shattering it and sending the asuras screaming free.

Whatever these damn things were, when the cage was broken, they weren't shy about fucking off. I was sent flying by the release of energy, crashing into the parked car I'd been crouched behind only seconds before, and then slumping to the ground.

"Owww," I groaned, looking down at my freshly dented chest plate and cursing. Aly was going to fucking kill me.

"Matt!" Kelly shouted over from the far side of the car. "You better be alive still!"

"Yeah…" I spat some blood on the ground, coughing, then forced myself back upright. Chris appeared there as I did so, grabbing onto my outstretched hand and pulling me to my feet. "Alive…I guess."

"Thirty seconds!" Kelly shouted, clearly still working on the puppet.

I forced myself up and away from Chris. He twisted and opened fire, a three-round burst making it clear he'd had time to snap a few bullets into the magazine.

"Why the hell summon it fucking here!?" Chris bellowed as his gun went dry again, and he was forced to use the butt of the rifle as a club.

"Next time, summon it farther back!" Becky shouted her agreement, before hissing her words and weaving her fingers in unnatural ways.

"Oh great, that's not disturbing at all!" Chris called to me, nodding at Becky as a green fire burst from the center of her chest, flooding out across her skin as she lifted into the air; her hair haloed out as the fire formed a shimmering ring that she hovered in the center of.

She hung there, fingers blurring, speaking words that were the mystical equivalent of fingers on a chalkboard to the rest of us, as the area grew suddenly cold.

"Fuck my life," I whispered.

Kelly's puppet, a huge ten-foot creation of seemingly solid steel, ripped itself free of a long-distance hauler. I twisted, cracking my back and glaring at the various creatures that were moving to surround us. "Just for reference, Chris, 'scout' means we watch the fuckers. *You don't shoot them in the fucking head before we're ready!*"

"When I want to hear from an asshole, I'll fart!" Chris called back, jogging toward the body of the one that had started all of this, standing over it with the shotgun at the ready, waiting for the oncoming creatures to close to a more reasonable range.

I shook my head, preparing to cast a spell, and glared at the idiot.

It'd taken half an hour to find the first trace of the creatures, a half dozen corpses of things that looked like upright, toddler-sized rats having been literally torn limb from limb.

The tracks in the blood weren't very clear, no two of them being alike, until we found the sneaker prints.

We'd decided that the four figures that were being escorted in the middle were likely prisoners, and had set off in pursuit, watching the area around us.

Kelly's first puppet, a humanoid shape that had been a little under half our size, and supposedly "optimized for stealth" had been attacked as soon as we'd entered the scrapyard.

We'd literally moved in, hiding and on our guard after hearing strange sounds from up ahead. Kelly had sent the puppet clambering up and over the stacked bodies of cars that formed the "rows" of the storage area.

It'd reached the top, had looked over the far side, and had been grabbed by something, dragged downward and out of sight before it could react. She'd lost her connection seconds later, and a dozen of these fuckers had come stalking out of the scrapyard to take up guard positions.

The humanoid ones were bad enough, ranging from five to eight feet tall, human looking, but comprised entirely from scrap materials, anything from literally crash-test dummies with "extras" like spikes added at random, all the way up to bodies that looked to have been custom built by a cosplayer with *serious* issues.

I'd seen some of these things in anime shows, and damn, it looked like someone had seen something similar, then went into the scrapyard with a will to create.

Chris, of course, had taken one look at them, shouted, "Fuck me!" and had shot the nearest in the face, moving the whole mission from *scout* to *slaughter*.

The first wave had been the mainly humanoid creations and had included a smaller spider and a wolf. The wolf was canine in design, obviously, and built along the same lines as Jack originally had been, all copper and wood and so on, but there the resemblance ended.

First of all, it was nearly eight feet tall at the shoulder. Secondly, it'd been made from utter scrap. The top half of the head was the front of a motorbike, complete with a shattered light; the "jaw" had a serious underbite, and had three sets of revving cogs running off a gear and chain-link system in the place of teeth.

Jack had seen it, and had apparently felt offended by the comparison between him and this rusty mechanized shitshow, and went for it.

It'd been twice his size, and had lasted less than thirty seconds. He'd hit it like an out-of-control freight train, ripped one leg off, then glared at it when it tried to "bite" him. It'd managed to close the jaw over him, and there'd been a collection of crunches and the sounds of metal grating and breaking…then Jack ripped his way free, and tore the fucker's head off.

It had taken longer for him to dig his way into the chest and crunch the cage than anything else, but by then we'd all been engaged, and the shit had really hit the fan.

The smaller spider had raced down a stack of piled cars and leapt at Patrick, who'd rolled to one side, popped up and slammed his fists, clenched tight together, into the middle of its back, driving it into the ground, before punching and kicking the living shit out of it.

He'd somehow enveloped himself in a bright-blue light, and rather than breaking his fists punching steel, he was denting it with each blow.

It'd never gotten back to its feet or claws or whatever, before he'd ripped the glowing blue heart from it and thrown it clear, killing the creation.

The battle had been going our way, when a second spider, this one the size of a fucking *truck*, had clambered into sight, and the various creations suddenly went from randomly attacking, into a coordinated rush that turned the tables on us, and had us retreating instead.

Chris had spotted the first body and had collected the dog tags as a matter of course. He was one of three soldiers, dressed in British Army combat gear, slumped near a car. His gun was gone, as were the others, but one of them had been carrying a case of loose ammunition, cracked open for use in their own fight.

Most of the ammo was gone, not used—there wasn't enough brass left for that—but the case had a dozen rounds left in and around it, giving us a literal few extra shots.

Now the spider had moved from seemingly being on overwatch into taking an active hand, and it was terrifying. It had an entire car as its central body—and not a small one—with eight long legs, four to a side, attached to a disc that sat underneath it in the middle.

The back of it…well, it had a small shipping container that was making weird noises, crunching and occasional booms. Lights shone out of the open door, that was pointed away from us. Chains flashed out, latching onto things and then dragging them inside.

The head was a mess of car headlights, each projecting a steady light that swept back and forth, seemingly selecting targets for its smaller brethren.

Two of the lights focused in on the struggling figure of Kelly's puppet, and a trio of mostly humanoid creations raced at it, leaping into the body of the truck and starting to rip sections free, slamming fists into the struggling form.

Two more raced around the truck and headed straight for Kelly, who was utterly helpless while she summoned her creation.

"Here we go!" I screamed, running full tilt at the nearest one, throwing myself into a sliding tackle and swinging my hammer across the incoming fucker's legs.

The hammer landed true, catching one leg just as it slid forward, crushing the "knee" and sending the lower half flashing free, the upper section mangled. The creation flipped over, face-planting on the ground and half breaking up as cogs and pulleys, chains and panels flew everywhere.

I rolled to the left, jumping to my feet, and threw a lightning bolt at the second one, mere seconds from reaching Kelly, hitting it in the back and sending it flying past her to crash into the side of a rusting hulk of a car. Then I slammed my hammer down to finish off the fucker I'd just wounded.

The one I'd zapped slid slowly to the ground as I turned away, then started to crackle and twitch, drawing my attention. I stared at it, seeing the obvious buildup of power as lightning arced back and forth across it, building from little arcs of discharging energy, into a rolling crackling overload.

I hesitated for a second, then started running—swearing—at Kelly. She gasped, sagging to her knees as she finished her summon. The enormous puppet formed of steel and her will finally tore itself free of the remnants and smashed a leaping humanoid into smithereens with one fist as it stood.

I plowed into her, grabbing Kelly and dragging her to the ground with me. The pair of us rolled over before I frantically pinned her to the cracked asphalt under me, banging her head and cutting her cheek on the shattered glass that was practically everywhere.

She panicked and elbowed me in the face, having not seen it was me, even as her puppet spun around, reaching for me, responding to its creator's instinctive shout.

It managed a single step before the arcing creature went nova. A sudden bright-white light illuminated the entire area. Then we were picked up and sent flying, bouncing and rolling again across the ground.

Fortunately, most of the loose glass had been disposed of as well, and we landed in a clear section, a freeze-frame instant in which Kelly drew back to punch me…and saw my face. The "oh" of realization in her eyes would have been almost comical, if not for the sudden pain in my side as the world went spinning crazily again.

I slammed into the side of the parked cars, glass shattering, and I fell, landing, of course, in a fucking puddle, and collapsing forward to lie, facedown, stunned and coughing.

I groaned, pushing myself up on shaking arms, hissing at the pain, before gasping as a "heal" hit me from Jo. My ribs creaked, two fingers on my right hand popped back into place, and the fog that was filling my mind was torn free in a great wash of cleansing fire.

"What the…" Chris grunted, pushing himself back up from where he'd been thrown as well, staring at the devastation. The area where the stunned and partially fried creature had been was now a crater, roughly circular, with the sections of car that had been inside now seemingly melted to slag.

I cursed, worried now that I didn't dare use my lightning spells on these fuckers, and the fire…well, normal Incinerate probably wouldn't do much more to these things than piss them off, and although Atomic Furnace would royally fuck up anything's day, I had no doubt, I also had no goddamn clue how much mana it'd take.

My fucking kingdom for a wiki!

The big fucker, the half spider-like thing, half crane, judging from the design, was staggering drunkenly back and forward, three of the legs missing. But all the eyes were fixated on me, and it was clearly *pissed!*

"Kill it!" Kelly shouted at her puppet, and the massive thing braced itself, then ran at the spider, that had apparently just kicked me.

It'd barely taken a handful of steps when a new form, closer to a four-legged tank, dropped from the back of the spider, and we all cursed at once.

The creation was triangular on top, with four legs on the bottom, each grouped around a solid disc like the spider, but this one had an open section on the front, with four long metal "planks" that were folded back, about six inches by eighteen for each one, then a set of grasping hands on the back of the head.

As soon as it landed, hitting the ground with a loud boom of metal on asphalt, it scuttled sideways to the nearest car, backed up to it, and the hands—or, more accurately, the claws, as they resembled a pair of clawed hands, joined together at the wrist—latched onto the car and crunched and consumed the wreck.

The claws dragged scrap metal into its innards, and it began to shake. The spider-thing, now exposed as some kind of creator-system, was backing up; the handful of humanoid creations left were joined by others from both sides, as seemingly their entire force was recalled to face us.

The spider shifted from targeting me to Kelly's creation, and the creatures shifted, following its targeting.

"What are you waiting for, you fucker!" Chris bellowed at me. "Shoot the fucker!"

"With a popgun?" I snarled, brandishing my Magnum and glaring back.

"Are you the God of Lightning, or do I get to call you fucking *Sparkles* from now on?" he snarled back, firing his last few shots at the humanoids, before dropping the rifle, letting the retaining sling catch it, and yanking a handgun free. He fired three fast shots into the center mass of the nearest, sending it twitching and staggering, even as the hammer came down on an empty chamber. "Fuck's sake!" He groaned in frustration.

"Here goes!" I growled, spotting my hammer where I'd dropped it going for Kelly. I'd not even realized I'd left it, but there it was, clear as day, right behind the puppet.

I yanked my guns off, tossing them to Chris—my amazing, much-loved handgun, of course, landing in a fucking puddle. Then I started to run.

I tore around the trunk of the nearest car, straightening out as I passed a single humanoid creation that'd just been thrown free, landing on its back, then rolling back to its feet, missing one arm.

It saw me, twisted around to intercept, then staggered as three bullets hit it, one after the other. It careened back; then I was past it, dragging my lightning from my core as I went, flooding my body and feeling the surge of superhuman power that it brought.

I couldn't help but grin as I picked up speed. A second humanoid creation leapt for me as a spotlight illuminated me, and I twisted at the hip, slapping its outstretched "hands" aside, grabbing the arm and yanking it past.

The creation slammed into the ground, bouncing once, twice, and then rolled to its feet, facing me. I swept up my hammer and grinned up at the spider.

"Not sure if you can hear me, but surrender or—" My demand was cut off by a sudden *boom* to my right, and the puppet staggered sideways before collapsing. The head was almost entirely destroyed, only a few last connectors showing it'd ever been there.

I twisted, staring in shock at the mobile fucking *cannon* that had taken the puppet out with a single shot. I'd thought the fucker was gathering parts to make more of the robot thingies, but the four "planks" or panels had apparently been component sections of a cannon.

The claws dragged in scrap metal until it was full, then compressed it into a shot; the panels closed around the bullet or shell to form a barrel, and then it fired again.

The puppet was made of almost solid steel, iron, and more, with no need for complex working parts, but had still been killed by a single shot?

This fight just got a lot more interesting.

I hesitated for a split second, about to rush the spider, then shifted direction. The mobile tank was too fucking dangerous.

"Whatever you're doing, now'd be a great time to finish!" Chris yelled at Becky, who was still hanging in the air, suspended inside a bright ring of flickering green flames.

Her lips were moving still, but we couldn't hear anything. The flames began to roll around her, separating into two loops that began to spin. They moved slowly at first, picking up more and more speed, seemingly fixated on the outside of an invisible sphere that surrounded her.

With each pass, the rings coasted over and through each other, gaining speed, the sound building from a slow *wumph* with the first pass, to a screaming of tearing air in a matter of seconds.

I raced across the ground as the spider-tank clambered backward up the nearest stack of cars. The head shook as the "claws" folded in around the latest mass, compressing it down as the panels folded inward again, forming a long barrel that locked in on me.

I had a handful of seconds as I dodged left and right, closing the distance. A sudden glow lit the far end of the barrel, and I leapt sideways, putting all my effort into it. The world blurred, and I bounced off a cargo container, the side denting around me as I rebounded. The ground where I'd been a split second before exploded as something hit it, and the tank resumed clambering backward.

"My turn, asshole!" I shouted, crouching and leaping up. The world around me happily released me as I rocketed upward.

The cannon shifted, tracking me as the back of the tank shook, clearly reloading, and I twisted around, the winds lifting and moving me.

The air seemed to guide me, as a second shot ripped free, passing close enough that I felt the pull of displaced air. Then I was past and too close, dipping down and then coming up as the cannon tried to track, swinging hard even as I landed on one of its legs, grabbing onto the panels of the barrel and pounding the hammer down on the base, hard.

The first blow buckled in the barrel, one entire panel deforming outward. The second made damn sure it'd not be firing again. Then…

Then the fucker leapt off the side of the stack, twisting around and driving itself toward the ground, with me formerly being atop it, now underneath and headed for the ground.

As short as the trip was, I barely had the time to throw myself sideways, just managing to get out from landing under it and being crushed. I still landed with it, though, atop one of the jointed legs and smashing into the ground hard.

"Fuuuuuck…" I growled, twisting and trying to push the fucker off, or at least get myself out from between its legs, when a second leg, much longer and bigger, slammed down an inch from my face.

The spider-thing had come back to play.

I heard sporadic gunfire as someone opened up with their last bullets, John shouting something about "judgment" as glowing chains lashed around the legs of the spider and clamped tight, sending the big fucker toppling sideways.

The tank folded its legs in around me, clutching me tight to its underside, as I heaved, trying to get free, before grinning evilly.

They were yet to see a Storm Lord, even a *Thunderstorm*, truly lose his shit. I'd pulled on my ability, drawing the lightning I filled myself with at all times to roll through me, but I'd not gone all out, not yet.

Jack leapt from the left, barely appearing before vanishing, crossing my vision and hitting a humanoid one that was closing from my blind side, taking it to the ground.

Jo hit me with a ranged heal, making me grin as I grabbed onto the legs of the tank, dragging the Lightning, then Thunder, then Fire and Air into me, feeling my body embracing the storm.

I bent the legs backward. A creak, then the sound of metal buckling under stress; servos and chains rattled as the tank, laid on its head, its "hands" frantically grasping at the air, tried to hold me in place with its legs as the spider shifted, aiming one leg at me, and stabbing out, even from its prone position.

The legs in my hands snapped at almost the same time, and I twisted, dodging the blow, and leapt free. The spiked leg punched into the tank's guts; the thin underbelly buckled and pierced, exposing a bright caged asura that let loose a high-pitched electrical buzz, before bursting into a cloud of radiant gasses and dissipating.

I swept up one leg, reflecting on the fact that I always lost my fucking hammer, and grabbed onto the spider's leg instead, hammering the one in my hand down into it, over and over.

The rest of the spider's legs were frantically trying to get it back upright, as I bent and battered the one I had hold of…and then Becky finished her spell.

The spinning ball of flames slammed to a halt. A good dozen flaming rings folded down and inward, gathering around a single area, where the space inside warped; a hole into unfathomable darkness appeared.

One, then two, four, then twelve golden tethers flashed outward, sinking into the underside of the spider, vanishing through the metal as if it were mist, sinking from sight.

The spider, which had been frantically trying to get free, half laid on its side, gouts of smoke, clattering and banging radiating out of the container on its back, went suddenly utterly still and silent.

The entire thing seemed frozen for a handful of seconds, as we all paused. The tethers retracted, seeming to clank and shudder as they dragged *something* free of the body.

It was an asuras, or so I assumed, looking at the fucker: a glowing, twisting creature seemingly comprised entirely of energy. And yet, it was dragged, twisting and bucking, *through* the suddenly insubstantial metal of the underside.

As the tethers retracted, the glowing misty form of the creature was hauled as if through a solid medium, hanging in the air, but leaving no damage as it passed.

The others, the humanoids and a semi-finished second "tank" that dragged itself from the cargo container, all went crazy, racing toward Becky. I leapt between her and them, slashing sideways with my "leg," sending one flying, then spearing the second through the chest, skewering the container and sending a bright puff of gasses free.

Jack bounded past me again, landing on the back of the one I'd just knocked to the ground, and tearing into it. John picked up my handgun, the 1911 that I'd heard Chris finish off the ammo for…and then started to shoot.

I glared at him, unthinkingly. *The fucker had ammo! Where the hell had he found 10mm ammo and not told me?*

The remaining two humanoid constructions went down in seconds. The powerful handgun tore through them, sending them crashing to the ground after only a handful of shots each.

Then he shifted to the tank. The bugger only had two legs, but the cannon was clearly functional, and he fired at that, even as the "hands" clawed in scrap to prepare to fire.

I ripped the leg free of the last one, and ran at the tank, the "soul" or whatever of the asuras shrieking in pain and terror as it was dragged to the darkness by Becky. And still John was firing, shouting something about "criminals" and "justice."

He stopped as I got too close to the target. But still, it was riddled with holes, and he had to have shot the fucker a dozen times!

I slid to a halt, drew back, and stabbed forward, punching the leg of its sibling through its head, driven by the insane strength I now enjoyed. The tank started to shake, and I growled, planting one foot, then wedged my fingers under the rotating platform for the cannon, and hauled backward with all my strength.

It held for a second, then two; then, with a creak and a ping of tearing metal, something gave way. I threw the cannon aside, staring down into the cage as the asuras twisted and shrieked.

I reached down, grabbing onto the outer edge and yanked. The cage came free, as the spider's soul was dragged into the darkness.

Instantly, the screeching cut off, and the gateway slammed shut. The flaming rings extinguished like a switch had been flicked, and Becky dropped from the sky, barely being caught by Chris before she slammed into the ground, unconscious.

The cage I held shook, and the screaming dropped to a terrified buzz, before going silent. I looked down at it, my shoulders sagging in relief that it was over…before the bullet hit my bracer, ricocheting off, as the raiders charged.

CHAPTER TWELVE

I flinched, then jumped over the side of the tank, landing and crouching as more gunfire rang out. I dumped the asuras on the ground, looking around desperately, seeing the others diving into cover.

John, seemingly the only one out of us all who had any bloody ammunition, returned fire, my favorite hand cannon sending round after round downrange. I glared at him, determined I'd find out where he'd gotten so much ammo, and why he'd kept it from me.

I hesitated a second, thinking quickly, then stuck my head out, counting, before a ricochet forced me back under cover, and I sent an order to Jack.

Three of them, two men and a woman, dressed in scavenged body armor and battered metal panels, raced across the space between us, showing absolutely no fear of the giant asuras constructor that had been kicking our fucking ass only a few seconds ago.

They ducked down behind it as John fired a rapid-fire barrage at them. I spotted Chris finally, laid on his side on the far side of a car, frantically wiping down bullets as he loaded them into his assault rifle.

Kelly waved, getting my attention, and then pointed back the way we'd come. I shook my head. If we ran, we'd be picked off easily. It was better we stayed and fought. Despite the way they were firing, they couldn't have too much ammo left either.

Then it'd be down to face-to-face…

I grinned.

I'd not wanted to use my Incinerate because of the lack of an effect, presumably, on a robot, and the Lightning Bolt had literally turned one of the asuras into a nova.

These were humans, though, and—

I ducked as a bullet slammed into the metal by my head. I dropped low, squinting under the car to see…a nice big puddle was running back toward where the fuckers were hiding.

That would do nicely. If they kept hiding, I'd just zap that.

"Hey, Chris!" I shouted, glancing back at where he was frantically searching for another round or two.

"Yeah?"

"Sparkle time, motherfucker."

He frowned, then grinned and nodded.

I twisted around and shouted toward the assholes, shaking my head in disgust as another handful of bullets hammered into the metal I hid behind. "Hey, dickheads! Surrender, now. I won't ask twice!" I called, knowing damn well they wouldn't do it, but not really caring, as I summoned my Lightning Bolt.

I didn't dare use an "all or nothing" level of magic. My Lightning Storm or Atomic Furnace would kill them, no doubt. But if there were more out there? With my regeneration still being pretty fucked if I was out of mana entirely…I just couldn't risk it.

Lightning Bolt, though?

I stepped out, throwing the first bolt, and summoning a second. My guts twisted as I saw them shifting their aim; my vision telescoped in as their fingers squeezed triggers…

Two bullets flew at me before the first lightning bolt landed. One missed entirely; one clipped the side of my breastplate, staggering me sideways as it ricocheted off, buzzing into a rusted car door.

My first lightning bolt hit the man in the middle head-on, though, literally.

He flew backward, gun falling from spasming hands, hair catching alight as the heat and power of the bolt thundered through him.

The second bolt slammed into the figure on the right, catching her in her right shoulder and spinning her from her feet with a scream. Her finger locked down on her rifle, the muscles twitching and shredding her friend as he drew a bead on me.

She fell, screaming and bucking wildly, even as the one I'd hit in the face stayed very, very still.

I opened my mouth, then shut it as Jack leapt from a stack behind them; he landed, skidded, and finally clamped jaws down on her head.

I'd been about to stop him, to tell him to spare her…and then I'd realized there was no point.

They'd attacked us, when we'd come here thinking we were tracking creatures that had captured humans and were trying to help them.

They were, as I'd guessed when they'd first appeared, raiders. I saw that as I walked around the edge of the spider-constructor thing, and I stared down, Jack already moving back to overwatch and scouting the remainder of the scrapyard.

"Are they dead?" Kelly moved up to stand by my side, then winced and looked away from the mess.

All three were dead, all right. *Very* dead.

"Oh yeah," I muttered, crouching by the woman's side, searching her roughly. The lack of anything even resembling a head meant that at least she wasn't staring at me reproachfully as I did it.

I took the two loaded magazines in her pockets, as well as the 9mm handgun, and I passed them to Kelly, picking up her rifle and checking it over automatically.

The gun was filthy, having landed in a puddle, and was not very well maintained. But the barrel was clear, and it had a few rounds left in it.

I passed that on, moving to the next body, as John checked the last one over, bringing all the ammunition and guns, then setting them on the reasonably dry boot on a rusted Fiesta.

"You've got ammunition," I said to John as calmly as I could muster, and he winced.

"Yes, and no," he replied, lifting my handgun and setting it down on the boot, although notably not handing it back. "I've got an ability, actually."

"Oh?" I asked coldly.

"It's called Gunslinger's Lament." He popped the magazine free, showing me that it was empty, then cleared the chamber, showing that it, too, was empty.

Then he locked the mag back in and pulled the slide, then fired eight rounds into the side of a car at the far end of the scrapyard. Then he pulled back the slide…and fired eight more.

"I don't have the ammunition," he whispered, looking drawn and wan as he explained. "I sacrifice HP to create the bullets as I fire them."

"You crazy motherfucker," I cursed. "You could have just explained that!"

"And I would have, except that without *showing* you, you might not have believed me." He smiled wryly, then shrugged. "You're not exactly the most trusting of people, Matt…"

"Dammit, John, I trust you. I just didn't when we first met, that's all—" I growled, only to have Jack cut us off as he returned, staring at me.

I reached out, frowning as I received a confused mass of data in a single "squirt" directly into my brain.

"What's wrong?" Kelly asked, and I sighed.

"He's found bodies."

"Many?"

"Too many," I whispered, straightening up and glaring down at the three dead. "Far, far too many."

Jack led us through the twists and turns of the scrapyard, past the stacked and rusting hulks, the piles of washing machines with their electronics torn out, the fridges with the gas systems removed—all of it—until we reached the very back, and the handful of old stone stairs that led down to the river.

The River Tyne was a wide, shallow river. As the tide went out, more than half of its width was exposed as deep mud flats, a nasty surprise to more than one jumper who had mistimed their attempted exit from the realm, I remembered.

Now, though, the mud covered a multitude of rotting and buried bodies.

We stood at the top of the stairs, staring. They had been tossed over the last step, abandoned into the river's embrace, it was clear. That they'd been done over and over again, and when they were already dead, was clear as well, as the bodies were stacked practically one atop the other.

Trails in the mud here and there exposed where the various local wildlife had attempted to feed on the corpses. Several of the creatures got mired in the mud and then drowned as the tide came back in.

Otherwise, the presence of waterborne life had made its mark: sections torn free, bone exposed here and there. The sheer number of bodies, though, made it clear that it'd take weeks, if not months to strip them fully.

"There's…is someone still *alive* in there?" Becky pointed, and we all looked to where she indicated.

"No," I whispered, shaking my head. A sick feeling rose. "They're not alive."

A single hand moved near the bottom of the pile, buried under the bodies and clearly pinned. The hand slowly dug its way clear, even as the incoming tide would push fresh mud back into the excavated pit.

The steady, mindless thrashing, though, made it clear it wasn't anyone alive, even if the mass of dead atop them and the lack of any opportunity for breathable air hadn't killed them.

"They're undead, aren't they," Kelly said softly, looking to me, and I nodded.

"Naturally occurring, I'd bet. The mana simply finding a home, like how graveyards started vomiting their dead, even before Dickless got to them."

"What do we do?"

"Nothing."

"But…"

"I could burn them all, use the Atomic Fire spell I have," I said. "It'd reduce them to ash."

"I think you sh—" Becky started, only to be cut off by Chris.

"How much mana would it cost?"

"I don't know. Might be half the mana I have, might be all of it. I might not have enough left. I don't know."

"You don't know…oh!" She broke off. "You've not used it yet?"

"Nope."

"Then—" She stopped. "Why don't you want to use it? It seems like a good chance to see what it can do. And I don't think there's any more of those things here."

"There probably aren't," I agreed, finally looking away from the river and back at the others. "I could probably use the spell and then we can all go back to the dungeon and relax, or…"

"Or we can find the fucks who did this," John finished.

"Exactly."

"We don't know for sure that we've not gotten them all," he explained to Becky. But he gestured down at the last body to be dumped on the top of the pile, eyes staring sightlessly up.

"But she was shot while we were fighting the machines," he pointed out, indicating the fresh lines of blood that rolled from the wound in her forehead. "They wouldn't have done that if they were worried about the machines turning on them. After all, why waste the ammunition?"

"They were escorted by the machines, as near as we could tell from the tracks." Chris took up the narrative. "For them to have been escorted as they led their victim along, then to execute her when we were fighting…they didn't want her to be rescued. They wasted potentially hugely valuable and limited ammunition, when…" He gestured over the side. "They could have just pushed her over. She'd have been stuck in the mud. It wasn't like she could have escaped. Instead, they killed her and came after us."

"Why is the question." John looked around. "Why were the machines protecting them, why were they killing people, and why attack us?"

"Well, standing here isn't going to tell us anything," I growled. "Spread out. Jack has done a lap here already and didn't sense anything, but best to work in pairs. Search the scrapyard, and we'll see what we can find. Gather up any gear, and shout if you find anything."

"Oh, before we all go." Kelly held a hand up and turned to Becky. "What was that you did?"

"Entrapment," Becky admitted, blushing. "It's kinda my only offensive spell. I can catch and trap a soul if I've long enough to cast the full spell, but it takes awhile."

"So, where is it now?" I asked.

"In…me?" She grimaced. "Well, not really. I don't know exactly, but the soul chains tethered it to me as my prisoner."

"Can it escape?"

"No." She shook her head and sent loose hairs bouncing. "No, the spell wasn't very clear on most of the descriptions, but it did say that nothing can escape the soul vessel. I can release it, but it can't escape, and…" She winced, then went on. "And I grow stronger the more souls I capture."

"What's your class again?" I asked.

"Fey Wrangler. I thought it was about negotiating with the fey, which is why I've not been wanting to go out and fight, as I thought it was a diplomacy class, like Ashley's Courtesan. But, it's really not. I can sense the meanings behind contracts, which is pretty weird, but that's my second spell, and yeah, Relic, as I told you before, which is a storage device that only I can access."

"What can you store?" I asked, and she shrugged.

"No clue. The phrasing is weird. 'A storage that none may access, save those your soul deems delightful.'"

"Anything else?" I asked, getting a very bad feeling about it.

"No, just that it's linked to the Entrapment spell."

"How…" I chewed on my lip as I looked at her. "Why do you think you were offered it? And what were the other options?"

"I'm not talking about the other ones. They…they weren't very flattering, okay? As for why I was offered it, I don't know. I just remember when the classes were appearing, I was desperate to have somewhere that was safe, and I kept thinking that if I could control things, like the animals we kept seeing, get them to protect us, then we'd be all right."

"Intentions matter," I whispered. "Becky, were you thinking of just the animals? Were you thinking of having them protect you, or serve you?"

She glared at me and refused to answer, as the uncomfortable silence grew.

"Becky, to be clear, I don't think you're trying to hurt anyone, and you're one of us, as long as you don't try to use those abilities on anyone. There's no problem here, okay?" I said very distinctly, getting another glare as my only response.

"Okay, so, shall we start searching?" Kelly asked brightly.

As if her words were magic, people darted off. Chris shot me a dark look before he hurried to catch up to Becky.

"Well done there," Patrick whispered, before walking off on his own, and I winced, sending Jack to scout the area again.

"Dammit, I forgot that John and Jo were coupled up," I said to Kelly, and she frowned at my words. "I mean that when I told everyone to scout in pairs, everyone broke down into couples, except for Patrick, seeing as Finn is back at the dungeon."

"That…that's what you got from all of that?" she asked disbelievingly. "That Patrick was on his own rather than in a pair?"

"Well…"

"Matt, honey, Becky's class is a fucking enslavement tool, and none of us had any clue!" she hissed. "She literally tore that thing's soul free, and is feeding on it somehow, and you—"

"I got that," I said quietly as we headed back up the steps. "I did. But seriously, she didn't try to use it like that until we were in the shit, okay? For all we know—"

"For all we know, her other options were Queen of the Damned and Dungeon Fairy, *which lets her take over the fucking dungeon!*"

"And has she done anything that suggests she'd do that?" I asked Kelly flatly. "Has she given us any reason to think that she's not the good person we thought she was?"

"No. And that's the thing, Matt. I *like* Becky. Chris is in love with her, and I think she is with him, at least from the things she's said anyway, and the way she looks at him. That's the point, though. She's not telling us everything, and could be setting up to do anything."

"I know," I admitted, glancing around. There were a dozen small huts and storage areas laid around the scrapyard. Becky and Chris were headed for the ones on the far side, with Patrick clambering up onto the tops of a nearby stack of cars. Jack looped around the street outside, and Jo and John searched the rooms halfway down the yard.

Apparently, they'd decided to leave the closest ones to us, as they looked the filthiest.

"I know," I repeated, leading the way. "She could be doing anything. And so could John, or Chris. Patrick might be planning to murder us all, or stick his dick in my ear. I have no clue. Hell, I *know* Chris…that fucker already took a photo of me passed out years ago and teabagged me. Clearly he can't be trusted…"

"Matt…"

"No," I said firmly, turning and reaching out, putting my hands on Kelly's shoulders and staring into her eyes. "Anyone and everyone could be setting up to fuck us over. Kelly, I know you saw shit in your job…"

That was an understatement of the century, I knew. As someone who recommended sentencing to the local criminal courts, she'd basically spent years reading the details of the worst crimes that could be committed, as well as having to literally see the faces of the most evil and depraved among us.

Worst of all, because she was working the sentence recommendations out on the details she was given, it was literally a case of reading the charges, a quick summary of the evidence, and then giving the judge three recommendations. First, if it was unlikely they were intentionally guilty, but it was unsure, this choice. If they were guilty and were likely to reoffend, this option, and if they were outright guilty and animals, this was the maximum that could be given.

Because she only gave out sentence recommendations, though, she had a role that slipped through the gaps. She didn't get the same level of protection the judges did, and rather than being exposed to a single crime over several weeks as the lawyers, jury, and the judges were, she did her job for multiple courts at once, getting anywhere from one to a dozen cases a day.

She'd wept when she'd told me of the things she'd read, of the horrific shit she'd seen sweet little old ladies had done, and the evil that even children could commit.

It'd worn more than a little of her hope and trust away, which made it hard for her to have relationships. Mike had felt he needed to "protect" his little sister. But the more I saw?

The more I saw, the more I was convinced that of everyone in the dungeon, the one who'd survive anything was Kelly. She'd been followed home from work and attacked, had families who couldn't believe their loved one had done such things go after her, when they couldn't get to the lawyers and judges.

She'd been beaten and assaulted, threatened and worse. She could have been broken by it all, reduced to hiding in her apartment and traumatized by the memories and nightmares. Instead, she'd learned to kick the shit out of the worst of them.

She'd also learned to distrust, though, and it was hard for her to move past that. I saw it in the way she was with everyone bar Mike, Aly, and Amy.

Worst of all, I knew that even the distance that she kept me at wasn't intentional. She just didn't know she was doing it.

I stared into her eyes, seeing the deep-seated distrust and the fear that she couldn't trust someone she liked, and I pulled her in close. She hesitated, but only for a second; then she wrapped her arms around me as well. I sighed, feeling her relax, as much as anyone could in the armor we wore.

"It'll be okay," I assured her.

"It will," she agreed, her voice muffled, and I drew back, looking down at her.

"Do you really distrust Becky?"

She let out a breath. "No," she admitted, reaching up and tucking a stray lock of blonde hair that had worked its way loose back into her helmet. "No, I don't. I just..."

"You just got worried?" I asked, and she nodded. "Okay. It's okay."

"No, it's not," she said softly. "I'm going to go speak to her, okay?"

"Go for it." I nodded, releasing her, then winced as I looked at the filthy rooms nearby. "Uh, you mean after we..." I gestured to the building, complete with a sagging roof and broken, grimy windows, as well as clouds of flies.

"Nope!" She grinned evilly as she ran off, and I cursed her, even as she called out to Becky to wait up.

I glared at her back as she disappeared around a stack of cars, then turned back, staring at the building dubiously.

The outside was painted white, once, probably as long ago as the scrapyard had been in use, judging from the filth that covered it. It was an oblong, the entrance and exit at either end, and a series of small windows that I damn well knew were going to give bugger all light. I ducked my head, stepping inside and waving a curious fly away.

My damn hammer was out there somewhere, in the mud no doubt, my empty goddamn handgun—it'd become unloaded as soon as John handed it over—in its holster, and a knife in my boot, but the assault rifle I'd been carrying was now loaded again, and the spares from the dead fuckers were in John's backpack.

I was confident I could kill anything hiding in here, despite the smell. I searched quickly, passing rows of shelving that were covered in alternators for old cars and stacks of car mirrors.

One section of the room, underneath a faded sign marked Wiring Harnesses, was clearly in the process of being sorted, as a cardboard box sat in the middle of it, shipping details shown for a "Mr. McCombie" and a scrawled note that the man was an idiot, and just to send the Mercedes harness, as he'd never know the difference to the Jag one he'd asked for.

I snorted, tossing the note aside, my eye caught by that most traditional of items in a scrapyard, garage, or mechanic's rest area: a topless calendar.

I paused, looked at the pair of women shown there, and nodded in grudging appreciation, wondering what kind of class they would have been offered. Clearly something athletic, judging from the contortionist poses they were in.

I turned from them, striding down the last aisle, glancing around idly as I checked my rifle over, the motion of my fingers as I checked it automatic, until I saw a flash of movement out of the corner of my eye.

I spun, seeing nothing, and freezing as I felt the need to leave.

It was stupid. I was sure something was here and yet…and yet I kept thinking I should move on. I should leave. That there wasn't anything important in here…

I twisted, looking all around and making sure there was nothing there. Then I backed up, slowly. My gaze tracked from side to side, up and down, and…

And it fucking moved again.

This time I saw it, though. A spider, or something like it, little bigger than my palm—a collection of legs and a tiny camera sat atop it, staring at me.

When it saw I'd spotted it, it froze. The pair of us watched each other, as I tried to decide what the hell it was.

It was a robot, I guessed, or more accurately, an asuras…I growled and triggered Examine, seeing no reason to keep fucking wondering when I could damn well find out.

Asuras – Scout	**Animating spirit**
The asuras is an offshoot of a greater being, and is a rarely seen, and yet powerful creature. The asuras is able to possess and control inanimate objects, granting mobility and a form of life to a previously innocent creation.	
Note: The lesser asuras is incapable of reproduction; only an asuras queen may command them without risk; this asuras is specialized for observation.	
Sleeve: The asuras must be contained within a "sleeve" to exist in this reality, but may only maintain one at a time, due to the massive drain on the asuras's mana.	
Weaknesses: Earth and Darkness Magics	
HP: 10/10 **Stamina:** 10/10 **Mana:** 142/2180 **Speed:** 5/10 (embodied) **Level:** 11	
HP 10/10	**Special Abilities:** 0/1

I almost dismissed the details, until the very fucking important changes stood out, and I read them again, keeping half an eye on the machine as it slowly, oh so slowly, crept toward the door.

It was an asuras all right, but unlike the batshit ones that had attacked us, this one wasn't caged.

"Can you understand me?" I asked, and it froze, making me think it was listening. Then the camera spun to the right, locking onto the window. I looked quickly, expecting to see someone there, then back to the tiny drone, only to find it was gone.

"Fucker!" I snarled, racing for the exit.

By the time I made it out, the tiny thing was long gone, and I spun in place, looking around desperately.

I whistled, long and loud, as well as recalling Jack. But by the time he got to me, and the others as well, it was too late. Jack tried searching, but either he couldn't get a scent, or he got too many, because no matter how hard he tried, he just went in circles.

"What happened?" Kelly asked, as she slid to a halt close by, turning her back to me and staring outward, searching for an enemy.

I called out to the others, making sure they could all hear. "Whatever these things were, the ones we fought were 'caged,' according to my ability, and probably forced to attack us. I just saw a tiny one, and…"

I explained quickly, and we spread out, searching. But after half an hour, we had to admit defeat. No matter how hard we looked, the scrapyard was just too full of hiding places, and as we searched here, the damn thing could be getting farther and farther away.

It'd been literally the size of my palm, after all, and damn fast. It could be hiding in the boot of a car a foot away and I'd never know.

"That's it, people. We need to fall back," I growled. "We keep quiet, but we need to move."

"Matt?" John called from one side, and I looked over at him. "The asuras we had in the box?"

I nodded.

"It's gone." He lifted the empty "cage."

"Bring it," I growled, picking up my damn hammer, and heading for the gates. It was time to regroup.

CHAPTER THIRTEEN

"You sure about this?" Mike asked me four hours later as we stood on the wall of the dungeon, staring to the south.

"Nope."

"Well, that fills me with goddamn confidence," he growled, shifting his rifle and glaring out over the rapidly darkening area.

"Sorry, dude, but it's the truth." I sighed, shaking my head. "Whatever the asuras are, they can build artificial bodies, they don't have to worry about food or air, and the fact that they could make more, and basically *tanks*, was a nasty surprise."

"So your plan is to wipe the area out, though?" he asked again, and I shrugged.

"I'm open to better plans. The issue I have is that I can't come up with one. We need to make sure we're safe, we need to strip the entire damn area, and worst of all, we need weapons. All of these things can be dealt with simply by turtling up and working on research and development. New guns, better mana converters, and more."

"Except the fuckers keep hitting us, and now we've got some kind of goddamn machines moving in." He growled.

"Exactly." I shrugged. "Look, you said someone had been hitting the army depots, cleaning them out…who do you think it was?"

"The regiment." He grunted. "I'd hoped they wouldn't have done it, but honestly? It was always in the back of my head that they would. I know I would have, put it that way."

"Not hold them as defensible positions?" I suggested.

"Nope." He shook his head. "They're just not. The way things are going, they'd have been tiny islands of calm in the storm. And as soon as people saw that soldiers were inside with their families, while they were outside and at risk? They'd try anything to get in."

"So…"

"So the soldiers would be down to 'shoot people on sight' which, yeah, a few shitbags would do, but the vast majority would never even consider, or they'd pull back to the regiment."

"So our wonderful plan of getting some experience at negotiation and finding more soldiers is fucked."

"No plan survives contact with the enemy," Mike said philosophically.

"Be nice if just fuckin' one would," I growled. "You know, just for the sake of variety."

"I'd not complain," he agreed. "Look, boss, it was a good plan, and the reasoning was sound. That the sites we hit are gone? Most likely they left recently and fell back on the regimental headquarters, as that just makes sense."

"Yeah—"

"But!" Mike snapped, holding a hand up to stop me. "But...we don't know that. For all we know, the bastards buggered off for a gangbang, or they were ordered out on maneuvers and never made it back. Maybe a couple of locals realized the bases were empty and hit them. *We don't know.*"

"So now what?"

"We go back to what we do know," he said. "Those bases are empty and useless to us, beyond a possible source of high-tech materials. There's some heavy-duty gear there: artillery, missile launchers, and hardened comms wagons. If we could get them closer, and absorb them? I have to think there's enough there to make a decent dent in our tech program."

"Yeah, but..."

"But they weigh a fucking ton, and they're literally miles out," he finished gloomily. "The sites we hit were empty. Maybe they all are, maybe not. We can keep going, but I think it's unlikely, having seen the two sites we made it to. They were stripped and it was done clean. A raider wouldn't have locked the doors behind them, nor policed all the rounds so well."

"So, we give up on having any backup from the army, unless we want to go straight for the regimental headquarters and all the risk that entails," I summed up.

"Yeah. Sorry, boss." Mike sighed. "Look, if I could, I'd blow sunshine and tell you it was all kittens and fucking rainbows, but realistically? It's not, and pretending just fucks us over. We've got a shitload more people who are expecting a home, we've got new enemies, and we've got a short time in which the army, or our friendly contingent anyway, are able to help."

"So we do the most we can with that," I finished.

"We do the most we can," Mike repeated quietly.

"We need to secure—"A warning pulsed from the dungeon, making me stiffen. "Something's coming," I whispered, squinting.

"I'll spread the word—"

"No." I cut him off before he could activate the alarms and so on. "No, this feels...different. Be ready but be quiet." I focused, concentrating on what the dungeon was telling me.

The feelings I got from the dungeon were weird at times, ever since I'd awoken that night so long ago; broken, alone, and in the dark, wounded and terrified, I'd sensed things.

Sometimes they were crystal-clear, a screaming "danger" sense like I'd felt before at the approach of the raiders and their caged asura, a sense of overwhelming sadness, and of grief that had tainted it. *Or sometimes...*

I banished the thoughts and closed my eyes, reaching out to the dungeon, but not to the systems I associated with it, not to the screens and ability to summon. Instead, I simply listened, and waited.

It was slow at first, the sensation that came, but as the seconds passed, it grew stronger, until...

I opened my eyes and stared at the bridge in the distance, a heavily shadowed section of the city now that there were no more streetlights, and I pointed.

"There."

"Got it," Mike said a few seconds later, his own Perception higher than mine as he picked up the steady, plodding movement.

It took a little longer for me to make it out, and even when I spotted the movement, it took awhile to work out what the hell it was.

The creature that walked slowly out, into the dim light of the stars, wasn't what I was expecting at all, and I could feel the dungeon radiating sadness.

"What the absolute fuck is that?" Mike sounded stunned. "Wait…is that…?"

"One of the asuras," I confirmed as I hit it with an Examine and got the same details as before. "Warn the others, but don't do anything else."

It'd stopped and stood a dozen meters out, dimly visible, but making no aggressive moves. Just waiting, basically.

I sighed. I'd get it in the ear later for this, but what was the point of being superhuman, if you couldn't make the most of it now and then?

I planted one hand on the crenellation of the wall, and leapt over the side, ignoring Mike's startled oath as I plunged to the ground far below. A brief mental push on my powers as I flooded my body with the storm, just in case, and I landed gently, feeling as if I'd dropped a few feet, rather than from the top of the wall.

The asuras stayed still and silent as I landed, and I squinted at it in the dim light, wondering. "Can you understand me?"

It took a single step forward, followed by several more, much slower ones.

The creation had been covered by deep shadows still, but as it came closer, the moonlight grew. The thin clouds above the remains of the city drifted gently away, and I stared in shock.

The thing that moved slowly closer was an amalgamation of several forms, notably the legs and lower plate of the tank-like model, and the humanoid upper frame, with what I took to be the spider/camera thing built into the shoulder…until it scuttled down and leapt off, racing off to keep its distance.

"What are you?" I whispered, shaking my head at the battered and broken form. The more I stared, the more I saw literally shattered sections.

This one, whatever it was, had clearly made itself from the remains of the others. The head from one, the chest from several, the arms…it had three arms, two on the left and one on the right…but the head was the weirdest part.

It faced me, but looked off to the side, as if…I searched around, then spotted two more optics, one looking like a sight off a rifle, the other looking like a collection of camera lenses from the back of a smartphone. And they were all fixed on me.

"Can you understand me?" I asked, looking at the "eyes" and getting a shiver running through it.

The humanoid body shifted slowly, holding one hand up to show it was unarmed, then reached backward, only to come out with…it was one of those kids' drawing panels, like a tablet screen but unpowered, the type that you ran a lever back to front on, and it'd wipe whatever you wrote clean.

I watched, fascinated, as it dragged a finger across the thing, making a clumsy image of a smiling face after several attempts.

"What do you want?" I asked, only to have it point at the smile again. "You want a smile?" I frowned and forced one quickly, but got no response.

"Matt," Aly called from behind, and I turned, looking up at her in question, thinking she'd made it over damn fast. "I'm coming down."

I glanced across at Mike, seeing his glare, and I winced. I wasn't getting involved in this one, no fucking way. I turned back to the asuras and waited. The gates behind me creaked open and stayed that way as Aly and several more sets of feet jogged out to join me.

The creature backed up slowly, and I held my hands up, shaking my head.

"No threat," I said loudly. "We don't want to fight you."

It paused, shifting its body from facing me dead-on, to the handful of others, then back again, before backing up another step.

"Stop!" I called to them, looking back and seeing Mike, Kelly, Chris, Becky, and Aly all coming, along with others closing in the distance. "Aly, you come up. Mike, you too. Everyone else, it's scared."

"It's scared?" Chris's whisper carried. "You should see my fucking shorts, pal…"

"It's all right," I said to the creature again, wondering about the fact I was reassuring a fucking robot tank thing, before shaking my head. Just another Tuesday in the apocalypse.

Aly slowed, walking forward, hands outstretched as I took a few steps back, letting her get closer.

"Hi…" Aly called, waving one hand. "I'm Aly. Do you have a name?"

Silence.

After a few seconds, the finger wiped the drawing…then drew a smiling face again.

"Do you want to be friends?" she asked.

For the first time, there was a reaction beyond fear, as the machine stepped forward, then motioned to the picture again.

"You've got to be shitting me." I pointed at it again. "You attacked us."

It wiped the screen and gestured back over its shoulder, before drawing a sad face.

"You didn't mean to?" I asked it sarcastically, and it jabbed to the picture again, then itself, then wiped the slate and drew what could only be an angry face, pointing back over its shoulder.

"You were—"

"Matt, you're scaring it," Aly said, "and that's not helping. Why don't you go inside and chase Kelly around the bedroom or something?" she suggested, gesturing dismissively as I glared at her.

"You gonna let her say shit like that?" I asked Mike, and he glared at me.

"She wants you to fuck off somewhere. I'm fine with you…being elsewhere. Just don't say a damn thing that changes that," he growled at me, and I shot Kelly a speculative look, then a suggestive wink.

"I'm staying to watch," she told me as I moved over to her, and I stared at her, then the look Mike was giving me as Griffiths and more people arrived to see what was going on.

"Great. Fuck you all then. I'm off for a cold shower and a wank," I grumbled, not really meaning it as I stalked off.

"Oh, Matt?" Aly called suddenly, and I turned around, smiling, ready to be asked for permission to…"If you see Ashley, send her over please."

I glowered at her, then stomped off.

"What's going on, Matt?" Griffiths asked as I passed him, staring past me at the machine that was currently drawing on its pad, and being encouraged by Aly.

"Apparently we're becoming a home for the castoffs of the galaxy," I said flatly. "That one says us killing its friends made it sad, so it wants to be friends with us."

"What?" he asked, clearly stunned, and I shrugged.

"I'm paraphrasing, but you know how it is…hard to get much more from a smiley face, a sad one and then an angry one. I've been sent to my bed without any supper, and I'm damn well going to take that opportunity. See you later."

With that, I strode off, heading for the damn dungeon, trying to maintain a little dignity as I walked past everyone.

By the time I made it inside, I was a lot less pissed off than I was pretending to be, and I knew they knew that as well.

Essentially, Aly was a better choice for communication than I was, and intrinsically better at technology and working out communication methods.

Ashley was literally our diplomat as well as a Courtesan, getting massive boosts to communication and understanding the situation.

I basically hit shit really hard and occasionally sparkled. Being realistic, I should have just sent one of them out in the beginning.

I went straight to the roof, pausing as I got up there to take a deep breath of the mana-charged air. I felt better almost instantly, slowing as I moved across the stone to the edge of the roof, leaning against a Lightning generator as I tried to figure out where the hell Ashley might be.

This was a problem with the dungeon, I realized. I could sense people if they were working "in" the dungeon sense, and I could sense bodies, even seeing them if I used the dungeon sense…But considering that Ashley and Dante were a young couple who had only just gotten together…

Basically, if I went looking for them in the dungeon mentally, I might see a lot more than I wanted to.

I was debating summoning a handful of skeletons or goblins and sending them to search for her—they were cheap to produce, after all—when a door in the training dungeon opened, and she and Dante emerged. I took in the way he was still tucking his top into his pants, and the way she was running…and I looked away. *Yup.*

No need for me to go looking for them after all, although I mentally added "communication devices" to the list of things I needed Aly and her team to work on.

I settled down on the roof, closing my eyes and drawing in a deep breath, sucking in the converted mana in the various nodes. The glorious feeling built.

"Okay, here we go…" I whispered, drawing in another breath and sighing as I felt the power in the air.

The buildup of mana converters in the area was starting to have a longer effect, as were the investments in both Manafield and Tides of Mana.

The first had made a small difference in the amount of time the dungeon took to grow, essentially growing its influence outward by ten percent more, and then by an additional ten percent on top of that. The second had changed the amount of mana being pulled into the area, hopefully countering our usage of it, and then increasing it beyond the most basic of levels.

Right now, though, sitting on the roof, eyes closed, simply breathing and focusing on all the surrounding mana, I could feel it. Hell, I could almost taste it.

I opened my eyes slowly, staring at the world around me and continuing to breathe slowly and deeply, feeling the mana flowing in and out, the corrupted mana floating around, and in turn being drawn steadily down, to the dungeon's core.

I sat like that for a little while, just resting, before I finally forced myself to start the real work.

Sliding into the dungeon sense, I moved slowly down, not traveling through the floors in the usual way, stairwells and more. Instead, I took advantage of the insubstantial nature of being in the dungeon sense, moving down to the lowest level…and then continuing down.

The sensation of sliding through the earth was peculiar. The knowledge that the stone was "solid" and yet as insubstantial as mist was just weird. Soon enough, thanks to the steady increase of the dungeon's influence, rather than sensing the cavern below at the outermost edge of awareness, it was opening below me.

The "sight" as I slid out, emerging into the stillness below, was astounding.

A huge cavern, perhaps a third of the size of the city above, filled with gardens of crystal, fungi, and moss, gentle glows lit the air, and here and there…

Pools were scattered about in the darkness, gentle ripples flowing across the surfaces as droplets of water fell from the stalactites, hitting the still surface, then dying away. Mana filled the cavern, the darkness of a place that had never seen daylight seeming to reverberate with a special depth of night.

And yet…Mana was created by life, I knew that—or I believed it, anyway; all the evidence pointed to that—and yet…I could sense nothing down here that "lived" as I understood it.

It was stunningly beautiful, though.

I spent over an hour in there, simply breathing in the darkness and feeling the stresses slipping away.

I slowly rose through the dungeon, pausing as I "stood" by my body, sensing the dungeon rolling on around me, the sounds of the others below, most of our people eating and relaxing.

The negotiations were ongoing by the gate, although the taste of frustration was heavy in the air, and the majority had moved on, leaving only a few at the scene.

Knowing that, for now at least, all was well, I observed myself, from the outside, as it were.

I sat with my back pressed to the Lightning converter, and damn I looked tired, haggard even. I sighed, looking over the battered and messy clothes, the absolutely fucked-up armor, the patchy two months' growth of beard, and the hair…

It wouldn't be so bad if I didn't keep getting the absolute shit kicked out of me. I had patches of beard that were only hours old thanks to cuts and scratches, lines of my hair where it was down to stubble, regrowing, and sections that were almost two months of growth on my designer "shaggy" hairstyle.

Overall, I was a fucking mess, and I needed to address that. If I was to lead, and to try and be "the boss" as most people were coming to call me, I needed to look the part.

As much as I wanted to be out there, exploring and sorting out the area, and I knew most of my team did as well…it was time to grow up.

I was the Dungeon Lord of Newcastle, and it was time to get my shit in order.

CHAPTER FOURTEEN

The first step was to deal with my notifications, and I damn well pulled them up, glaring at them, dismissing most of them as pointless, but keeping three.

Congratulations!

You have killed the following:
- 3x Gang members, various levels, 417 XP
- 5x Caged Asuras, various levels, 604 XP

Total XP earned: 1,021 XP

A party under your command killed the following:
- 27x Caged Asuras, various levels, 3,118 XP

Total Party XP earned: 3,118 XP

As party leader, you receive 25% of all XP earned.
Total XP awarded 1,021+(3,118x0.25=779.5)= 1,800
Partial XP is lost to the ether.

Current XP to next level stands at 53,986/35,000

*

Congratulations!

You have reached level 10 in Hammers! You receive a 1% increase in chance to inflict critical damage and a 1% increased chance to ignore your target's armor per point. Because you have gained this level in a sub-skill of Blunt Weapons, you have also received the requisite levels in Blunt Weapons, granting a 1% chance of familiarity with unknown blunt weapons and a 1% increased chance to inflict a crushed effect on your target per level. Increase your skill to further improve your damage bonuses.

Congratulations!

You have reached level 10 in Blunt Weapons! At level 10, you have an increased chance to critically wound your target by an additional 1% per level, in addition to the original 1%. This stacks with the class of Blunt Weapons, such as a 1% chance to critically wound with thrown hammers becoming a combined 20%.

Then it was time to get the ball rolling with the dungeon. We'd agreed on the plan; it was just ongoing in bits and sections, because we were all trying to do everything all the time. I sent a summons out to the others, letting them know through the dungeon, that they were to eat, then come to our private area under the dungeon, and as well as our little group, to bring Clarissa, Markus, and Griffiths. Rhodes as well, if she wanted to.

I felt ridiculous, changing things so frequently, but fuck it. It was better to adapt to the changing situations, than push on with a mistake.

The plan we had for the dungeon was right, as was the plan to secure the area. But considering that we knew Saltwell Park was being hit over and over, and had clearly been getting scouted from the things Barry had said, and that there were now even more goddamn threats than we'd thought?

It was the largest concentration of people in the area, as most of the survivors from Gateshead, that it was the center of, had moved inward.

What we'd not considered, and had come to me as I hung there in the dark and silence, was that although Gateshead was a large area, it was also packed up against another population center.

Looking at the area from high overhead, Newcastle was a good-size city, concentrated heavily along one side of the river, with commercial and production centers there primarily. The farther back you moved, northward in a hemisphere on that side of the river, the more the areas became residential.

But on the opposite side of the river was a similar mixture of commercial and industrial, then residential again as you moved through Gateshead.

That was all well and good, and on the far side, the south and the west of Gateshead were fields, as well as the massive industrial and commercial zone I'd worked in.

Beyond that, to the south by southeast, was the crashed ship, and I made a mental note to go get that fucker soon.

The issue wasn't any of that, though; the issue was the east. Moving due east from Gateshead, it broke down into heavily industrial and residential areas all the way out to the sea, with the old town of Washington to the southeast.

Each of these areas had about a quarter of a million in population, I guessed. Well, Newcastle was larger; then, going in order of size, Sunderland and then Gateshead, to Washington, then the North and South Shields areas that stared at each other across the water a few miles to the east, the way Newcastle and Gateshead did here.

The thing was, though…

We'd gathered the majority of Gateshead together.

Newcastle seemed to have been heavily stripped of people. The areas to the far west and east might have loads of people in them, but we'd seen no sign of them and hadn't gotten that far out yet.

There were about five thousand people in Saltwell Park. Out of a quarter of a million in the area.

That many people had only survived this long because we'd essentially "turtled" up, and they'd all moved inward. Although I'd been involved in that, I got the feeling it'd have happened anyway, with or without me.

That meant that most likely it was happening in other areas.

Towns were becoming tiny fiefdoms, and that meant that as we'd discussed already, the monsters were spreading, claiming more and more of the areas, and growing stronger as they fed on each other.

And as for the people?

Chris and Becky had come from Washington. It was his home, and they'd said that prisoners from the local prison a good ten miles or so to the south had essentially taken over it all. An area of a hundred thousand at least, that even if they were down to only a few thousand as well, was still a horrific number of people, especially to be ruled by escaped murderers and rapists and so on.

Plus, by now, the fact that we weren't getting masses of refugees on the roads was weird. Where *was* everyone? If they were dead, viewing it the most pessimistically as I could, the sheer number of bodies would be starting plagues and worse. If they were alive and forming settlements?

We needed to make plans for dealing with them, and any other large groupings, as the thought of thousands of humans with classes, all going to war, would be horrific.

We had to make sure we not only had the edge thanks to the dungeon, in that we had a literal castle, but we needed to do it with tech as well.

It was time to go all out, while we had the time to actually do it, before the shit really hit the fan.

I pulled up the details for the dungeon, counting the various converters and grunting. I'd not realized how many there were. Clearly Aly had been adding them in here and there as she went, as we were up to a solid thirty-eight converters now: five Water at the bottom of the river, with six more across the dungeon roof. Six Nature spread across the two farms, with another four Life joining them, and eight more Life spread about across the residential and dining areas.

Then the six Air converters spaced between the Water ones on the roof, and my single goddamn Lightning converter right in the middle, with the Thunder and Storm converters on either side of them.

They weren't all converting to their full capacity of twenty per hour, of course. The Air and Water ones on the roof did better when it was windy and rainy, varying between fifteen and twenty an hour; the Nature were anywhere from twelve to fifteen each, as the plants grew.

The Storm, Lightning, and Thunder were all going, but for some reason, possibly because of my nature, joined to the dungeon, they were producing anywhere from ten to twenty an hour depending on fuck knows what.

It meant that, overall, they were producing a figure that dipped under and rose over, but basically evened out at six hundred and seventy points an hour.

The new kobolds were two thousand five hundred points each to summon, meaning if we were reduced to just the mana we were generating on our own? Not even considering food and research and so on, we'd be at four hours per unit, unarmed and at their most basic.

That had to change, and massively. I paused, frowning as I sensed there was something wrong with my math there. But fuck it; it was close enough.

I sighed, backing out of the dungeon sense and rising to my feet, seeing darkness all around, as well as the figures of Aly, Mike, and the others heading across the pavement far below, the southern gates closed.

I nodded to myself, heading downstairs, and met them in the dining area, shaking my head as Aly started to speak.

"We need to have a serious talk after we've eaten," I said. "Like, serious…we need to adjust the dungeon plan and more level of serious. So eat, drink, and relax a little. You've got an hour, then we're all heading downstairs. And don't expect much sleep."

Mike nudged Aly as she nodded. "How come when he tells you to head toward the bedroom and not to expect much sleep, you listen? I try that and I get a bruise usually," he joked with her, and she sighed, shaking her head, before kissing his cheek.

"Because, honey, he can keep me busy for those hours."

Silence hung in the air, and I bit down on my lip and moved off quickly. Aly had definitely won that round. She didn't usually reference things like that in public, but she was clearly tired or frustrated enough that she'd either let her guard down or…

I glanced at Mike, then away again as fast as I could.

Not even gonna go there, I decided.

Within ten minutes, most of us were gathered around what had become "our" table, with the team powering through food. Griffiths, Mike, and Rhodes attempted to out-eat each other with a pile of barbecue ribs that were dripping sauce.

I grinned as I saw Kelly watching them, and as they all looked away…she added a few more to the plate.

The three were arguing good-naturedly over which of them could clear the plate first, having no clue that she was cheating and sabotaging their effort.

Others saw it, though, with Finn grinning openly, and Markus eating his one plateful calmly. Clarissa was clearly amused as she stole one, putting him, on his own, at parity with the three burly soldiers' efforts.

Time passed in amiable conversation, with others drifting over and asking occasional questions, many inane and easily solved, until the last.

A little girl, perhaps two or three years old, came over and asked if we'd seen "Big Bun-bun." Apparently her favorite rabbit toy, one that had survived with her all this time, had gone missing.

Jack was summoned, having been back in the dungeon for repairs, and Big Bun-bun was swiftly found. A second child's heart broke when it was discovered their mother had given it to them after she'd "found" it "abandoned on the ground."

Kelly absorbed the original, printed two, giving one to either child, and then dragged the mother off for a *chat* about "finding things."

We finished up the meal at that point, absorbing what was left back into the dungeon and recovering as many points as were viable, before heading down and settling in around the room in the various chairs and loungers.

"Okay, everyone," I said loudly, by way of bringing the meeting to order. "Aly, do you want to start and bring us up to date?"

"The creature—"

"It's an asuras," I added, wincing.

"What…?" she asked slowly, glaring at me.

"I scanned it before I left. It's the same as some of the ones we fought, but this one is free, I guess? The others were 'enslaved,' according to the markers they had," I offered, thinking I probably should have shared that tidbit earlier.

"Right," she growled, thinking, then sighed. "Well, yeah, it puts a bit of a different spin on things, so it would have been useful to have heard that earlier…but hey."

She paused, clearly reconsidering the "conversation" she'd had, then started again. "Right. So the asuras wanted to communicate, desperately, as near as I could tell. It's gone now. We tried for a while but it basically got nowhere, so it's going to go and do something. From what I could get from its drawing ability, it's going to try to rebuild itself and come back to talk again soon. I understood that it'd been attacked, that it had friends and they were all dead, and that it basically wanted to make friends with us." She gave me another glare as she went on.

"Knowing now that there had been some enslaved ones attacking you, I'm thinking, rather than as I had believed, it was referring to the fight with you all earlier, it might have been referring to the others being enslaved.

"If we consider the enslaved ones, and then that it's coming to us, having seen us fight them and win, it may be looking for allies to free its friends. Best-case scenario, it wants to be friends, and it joins us, possibly bringing others. We can build them bodies to use as guards, like your puppets, Kelly…"

"Because they're clearly fuck all use as they are," Kelly grumbled, and I winced at that as well.

They took awhile to summon, and as she'd found, they didn't last all that long. She'd been getting more and more concerned that she'd picked, as she called it, "a shitty class," and was now essentially useless to us all.

She'd reached the level to select a new class awhile ago, but hadn't, and she refused to discuss it further with me, after having doubled down on Puppeteer last time.

"Well, they've just been unlucky that's all, Kel," Aly tried, before sighing and going on. "Anyway, it's going to come back, but I managed to get out of it that it's clearly concerned about being enslaved again, and the little spider-drone thing that's with it is staying hidden in case the bigger one is captured. There are humans in the area in large groups, and it's scared, although if they mean us, the Saltwell Park lot, or raiders, I couldn't make out."

"Great, well, yeah, that kinda ties in," I said. "Griffiths, Mike, do you update us next?"

They looked at each other, before Mike sighed and spoke up. "I already told you, but for the others here, the bases have been abandoned and stripped. Most likely, the soldiers themselves did it and left, as the areas looked clean and somewhat well looked after. But whoever did it, the sites are empty, the guns and soldiers are gone, and we're back to the regiment or nothing when it comes to soldiers and weapons."

"Clarissa, how's the expansion going?" I asked, and she smiled, clearly glad to give some good news.

"We're ahead of schedule. At this rate, perhaps four days to claim the wider area you asked us to focus on. That doesn't include the interior…" she said quickly, holding one hand up, tempering our expectations, "but the outer lines, so that we can extend the walls and make contact with the park? That's going well."

"That's brilliant, thank you," I said, genuinely meaning it.
"Griffiths, Markus, anything to add with the troops?"

"The human recruits are doing well. Drilling and moving is about as far as we've got, but that's a good start. The kobolds are excellent, considerably more intelligent than the usual batches, and frankly much more lethal than the human recruits," Markus said, and I nodded, sighing.

"Yeah, that might be an issue in the future," I admitted. "We're the equivalent of the most basic variants. If I absorbed a dead guy into the dungeon and started research—" I broke off at the look I was getting from Aly, before clearing my throat. "Uh…actually, I don't think it'd work. But we're the most basic of our species, so if you think of the difference there'd be between an 'advanced human' and us?" I blundered on, before Aly spoke up.

"I've seen the system," she said clearly. "Don't worry, people. He's not going to try to evolve humans or research and replace us with our betters!"

The way everyone around the room relaxed slightly made me frown as I realized that had been an actual concern.

"Seriously?" I asked. "Fuck's sake, people! You actually thought I'd do that?" There was a long pause; I sighed, sitting forward on my sofa. "Look, that's genuinely not something that had even occurred to me, all right? And even if the system would let me, which clearly Aly says it won't, I wouldn't want to. I mean, seriously? Who'd want to be replaced by the newest version of themselves like that…?" I winced. "Someone remind me to be extra nice to the kobolds, all right?"

I got similar winces as they saw my point.

"Right then, so what's the plan?" Chris asked, and I nodded my thanks.

"Okay, basically we need a few things sorted, and now. First of all, we've found we're not getting any military aid, beyond our very welcome current members." I nodded to Griffiths and Rhodes, the latter of which was currently checking her handgun and cleaning it on a small table.

"We've also found out that there are raiders in the area, and possibly robot-type fuckers that can make themselves into goddamn tanks and worse, and…"

I filled them in on my concerns for the surrounding area, before going back to Mike.

"Mike, you said the park was attacked by demons…a wave of them, is that right?"

"Yeah, ranging from little imps to solid ten- to twelve-foot-tall red-skinned bastards. Looked like the end of days had come."

"Did you find out where they came from? Or if that was all of them?" I asked, and he shook his head. "So there might be something breeding them, and they attack in the morning," I pointed out, getting sighs and winces all around the room.

"Seriously? What do I have to do for a week in Bali?" Finn asked Patrick, who grinned down at him and hugged him close.

"We'll sort it, don't you worry," he promised, giving his lover a quick kiss.

"We will," I agreed louder, for everyone. "Not least because I want to see Kelly in a goddamn bikini, but that's a story for another day, and possibly a core or three's worth of upgrades away."

I shifted uncomfortably, before giving in and summoning a cold rum and Coke to my hand, the ice clinking as it appeared.

"Oh, it's that kind of a meeting then?" Chris asked, before snapping his fingers and catching a bottle of beer as it popped out of the air before him. "God, I love magic…"

Becky summoned a martini glass and sipped at it, smiling. "Pornstar martini; anyone want one?"

I noted the way that hands rose. I frowned, seeing that Griffiths and Rhodes were waiting to be asked, and I groaned, closing my eyes and reaching out to grant them both full basic "creation" access.

"You should have said before now," I grumbled. "I'd forgotten about granting you access, that's all."

Mike nudged Griffiths. "I'll teach you both how to use it after this. What do you want to drink for now?"

"A beer?" Griffiths asked.

"Veuve Clicquot," Rhodes said, and Becky cheered, knocking her martini back and making it vanish, as she summoned a bottle to the table near Rhodes, then got up and moved around with a crystal-cut glass each for them.

"Guys, seriously, we need to work!" I laughed, unable to help myself.

"And we will," Jo promised, getting rid of her coffee and summoning a cocktail that looked as though it'd be lethal, considering all the colors and the sheer goddamn size of it. "Hurricane." She winked.

"We're fine, honey. We know it's work, but unless you think the shit will hit the fan tonight…?" Kelly asked, and I shook my head, smiling at her.

"Tell you what," I offered. "Drink all you like for the meeting and after, but in the morning, you have to function. Deal?"

I saw the look that Chris gave me at those words, remembering Mama Aurelia and her rules for life. She'd caught us drinking as fourteen-year-olds, and rather than bollock us, she'd accepted reality, and said that we could keep our drinks, and drink what we wanted, provided it was in her house, not outside in the gutters, so she knew we were safe.

She'd then taught us to mix our drinks, to never mix "the grape and the grain," and most of all, that it was fine to have a good time, but that the next morning always came. If you wanted to act and enjoy life as an adult, you had to function like one the next morning as well.

I raised a glass to him, and he replied in kind, clearly remembering that kind, wonderful woman, and knowing that she'd live forever in us.

"So!" I called out after a few minutes. "Now that we all know where we stand with our drinks, and we're more or less settled, let's get to it.

"The first thing we need to do is address our reliance on the outside world. If we need to turtle up, we can, but we'd be fucked, frankly, as things stand. So…"

I pulled up a map of Newcastle and the surrounding area on the table and drew around the buildings that were inside our intended walls.

"As of the morning, we're all going back to basics, bar the new recruits who need to train." I marked the buildings out, and sections of the land. "Unless you have a real pressing reason, we're canceling all but the kobolds, and Ashley and Jack going outside. We're sending a team with you, Ashley, to Barry, and you're going to get as many recruits from him as possible. And by that, I mean that we want at least four thousand of them working on this, understand?"

She looked surprised but nodded.

"Good. You'll get a decent escort, don't worry, and…damn, I didn't phrase that very well. Okay, Ashley, you and a team are going to the park, the kobolds are separate—does that make sense?"

I got a lot more nods this time, and I went on.

"Good. The people there will be doing exactly the same as we will here, in that they'll be smashing everything they can and piling the fucker up." I drew a line on the map from us to the park.

"We're going to strip the buildings inside our new area, and I mean all the way down to and including the bricks—break them all down. Half of the residents will be physically gathering, the other half will be inside the dungeon, absorbing it all, brick by goddamn brick."

"And you want the park to do the same?" Aly asked. "They're to fill that line with everything and as we claim it, our people can absorb it all in?"

"Exactly. As things stand, we're making an average of six hundred and seventy mana an hour from the converters. That's just over sixteen thousand mana a day." I paused, as those who'd been with me the longest winced, while the newer people, comparing their own mana regeneration rates presumably, commented on how much that was in a positive way.

"It's not good," I said. "We actually need at least four times that, and that's not even considering the food and other maintenance costs. We could be attacked at any time, and realistically, there's nothing, as far as we know, stopping whoever is controlling the asuras to make a giant tank and just shoot us all, knock the walls down all at once. What we need is a technological advantage, and a massive one.

"We get that, as soon as the most basic changes are made, by building the research systems and so on. Then we go all in and work on the Steel core as soon as the Iron is finished tomorrow."

"So, what happened to the plan to get everything we could from each level?" Aly asked, and I glanced at her, knowing she knew this, then seeing the way that others were nodding along. She'd asked it for them, wanting to get it out in public straightaway.

"That's a very good question." I smiled. "Basically, as soon as each level is done, we get to research that particular level's version of something. So, as an example, mana conduits. Stone age conduits and Bronze were a massive difference in quality. Upgrading to the Bronze conduits means we got more mana. Logically, in an ideal world, we'd hit Iron, and then research everything it has, rather than going ahead. We'd make a lot more, over the long game, that way."

"But?" Kelly asked, smiling at me as I looked to her.

"But it's the time issue," I admitted. "We need to be working on higher tech shit, because, let's face it, if we can get the goddamn rail guns worked out, while everyone else is basic as fuck, scrabbling around for dwindling ammunition? Once that's gone, they're going to be going back to basics, and most likely things like spears and shields, while we're climbing the tech ranks."

"You're talking about turning this place into a real castle, and a high-tech one?" Griffiths asked, and I nodded.

"We can do amazing shit, and hopefully we can stick at Steel for a while, really research the crap out of it, and make the most of it. But if we can get that level of tech—because, remember, we get to go from the bottom end of the respective technological 'age' to the top, so in Bronze we had access to the most basic variants of Iron—Steel has to have some amazing shit."

"Armor, guns, tower defenses…" Aly muttered, and I nodded.

"Exactly, as well as—hopefully—ships, planes, cars, and fucking tanks." I shrugged. "I don't know if it'll really work, people, but finding the asuras and those dead soldiers on our doorstep? That was a hell of a wakeup."

Griffiths reached up and patted a pocket absently, and I remembered Chris gathering the dog tags earlier, knowing that he must have handed them over.

"So, we go all locust?" Chris asked, and I looked at him. "You want us to strip the area, like down to the bedrock. Fine, you're the boss, and we trust you. We'll strip the area. Then what?"

"We start heavy production," I said. "Aly, I need the next level of the gathering facility done. What's the cost on that?"

"You're not going to like it," she warned, closing her eyes as she double-checked it.

"Probably not," I said, mentally adding that I needed to check out the details on that soon.

"A hundred thousand mana."

"Fuck," I groaned. "Fine, I'll check that out tomorrow, and I guess I'll get a more coherent plan put together on that side. What we need, though, is to begin mana production on a huge scale. There's a cavern under us. I know I've told a few of you about it, but here it is. If you go low enough in the dungeon sense, you'll find it; it's accessible, and frankly, it's huge."

I waited, counting to three, before I heard Chris whispering to Becky: "That's what she said."

"Not about you, though, pal," I added, grinning at him as he lifted a middle finger in my direction. "Now that the obvious one has been addressed, we can move on, though. That cavern is a damn sight bigger than the area we've claimed up here…like a hell of a lot bigger. At least a mile on a side."

"That big, and under a city?" Griffiths frowned.

"Yeah. I thought it was weird myself, but it's exactly what we need. It's huge, it's black, and—" I pointed at Chris. "Shut it, you."

"Hey, you're the one saying it…" he offered, grinning.

"There's never been any light in there, like ever, as near as I can tell," I said, ignoring Chris's sniggers. "The cavern is massive, and if we put a shitload of Darkness converters in there, they'll go straight to twenty points an hour, I'm betting. They cost a thousand points each to build, the basic ones I mean, so we start making them, and we build a fuckload."

"What happens with the secondary effects?" Chris asked after a few seconds. "We know that the Nature and Life ones are making the plants grow faster and stronger, or more healthily or whatever. What happens when they make the darkness more…" He paused, clearly looking for the word as I grunted.

"It's a good point. And yes, it might make the darkness more 'dark,' twisting it somehow. Genuinely, it's a concern *but*…the cavern is sealed, as near as I can tell. We can look into it, and see if we see anything that's concerning, definitely. But realistically, we need the fucking mana."

"We'll build more Earth converters under there too, as I think that'll have the same effect, and more Water converters in the river, as well as more Air around the outside of the walls."

"How many overall?" Aly asked, clearly making notes, and I paused, thinking.

"Ideally, I'd like to hit a hundred thousand a day. That's…"

"Just over four thousand an hour," Aly calculated for me, nodding. "So we can do things like the gatherer in a single day?"

"Yeah. I keep thinking about the power differentials, like, it cost a thousand mana to research the basic tier of converter; the next was five times that. We need to be working to a better level…"

"There'll be other ways to increase it as well," Aly muttered. "At twenty mana per hour, and that's a solid twenty, not fluctuating, we'd need two hundred and nine converters. We're at thirty-eight."

"We do a row, two wide and twenty long, of Water ones at the bottom of the river and…"

"And we end up summoning some scary-ass shit from the sea, I'd bet." Aly rubbed at her chin. "We'll need to look into this more, boss. I don't like the side effects details."

"Me neither," I said. "If we can do this, though? Let's be realistic, five thousand people…if we put a single Life converter for every hundred, that's fifty of them. The people are healthier, and that's a thousand points there an hour."

"Yeah, and if we put a bunch of Death or Unlife converters in a graveyard, that'll generate a lot," Aly said. "Right up until the side effect brings another damn lich. No, I think some more converters are definitely a great idea, but they can't all be that. We need to work on the tech side more. Leave it with me. See what you come up with on your own, and we'll talk in the morning." With that, Aly settled back, clearly all she intended to say about it.

"Okay," I agreed, frowning, then shrugging. "So, either way, we need to strip the area, so that's a given…"

"What about the people?" Rhodes sipped on her champagne.

"Sorry?"

"The people, the ones out stripping the area…you've already admitted they're at risk when they're inside and behind walls. What happens to them?"

"We protect them," I said. "We use this as a combination of research and construction, and growth booster all in one."

I pointed to spots around the outskirts of the park, noting the larger concentrations of houses and buildings.

"Here, from this side, all the way around, and moving back out…" I grunted, leaning over the map. "We have people demolish the houses around the outside of the park, rolling it back street by street, piling all the shit where the dungeon can get at it. We work on building walls around the park, then a secondary apartment block, maybe two, right in the middle of the park. We make them huge, and solid, safe for people, and we give them apartments of their own. Those who prove themselves? They get to move to here, if they want to. If not? They can stay there."

"The kobolds will roam around the area, once we've got enough, and they'll protect the harvesting and gathering teams. As we destroy more, we'll spawn more walls, safer homes, mana converters, and control point generators, and finally more kobolds ready to defend the area."

"For now, though, and provided you can get the first wave of volunteers helping out, they move to the line of claimed expansion and pile up all the shit they can find, until we reach the park itself."

"Tomorrow, Beta and her team will walk along with you at least some of the way to the park, Ashley. She'll have her orders to scout the line we'll be following from here to there, and where your priority is the park, hers will be to kill any threats.

"I'll continually summon her backup, adding to her numbers with fully armed and armored kobolds. As more of their numbers become self-aware, she'll designate them as sub-commanders under her, watching them, and then splitting them off to form small groups. Those groups, in turn, will roam back and forth, clearing the area."

"Once we have enough, we'll alternate having them come back in for more formal training as well. But make no mistake: if there's someone being used to soak up an attack, I want it to be a creature of the dungeon, and not our people."

Silence fell as people looked it over, until Griffiths finally spoke.

"It's not a bad plan, but it relies too heavily on the kobolds and their weapons." He let that land in the air for a long few seconds before going on. "I've spoken to my people, and we're willing to stay for the three months, on the condition that we're outfitted with the best you can provide, and when the time comes, you help us to reach our families."

"Thank you." A massive weight lifted from my shoulders.

"I'm not finished. You help us reach our families, and you help us bring them here. You get us as support *and* soldiers; we'll back you up, we'll help you secure the area, and, provided you're not stupid moving forward…we're in."

I paused, thinking about the words and the way he looked at me.

"When you say 'in'…" I said carefully.

"We're joining you. We'll be members of the dungeon. No more us and you…just us."

"I'm…I'll be honest, I'm stunned," I said slowly. "I thought you were all set on going and only might come back?"

"We're all set on staying together. We want to rescue our families; we want to protect them, and each other. The way the world has gone? Realistically, we want a home that's safe, that our kids can play in, and what all parents want. We want tomorrow to be a little better than today, maybe with a bit more sleep thrown in. Looking to the future, what the hell do our kids have to look forward to out there?" He gestured aimlessly behind and up as he spoke. "In here? They've got a chance at a real future."

"And is this all of your people?" I asked, getting a firm nod.

"It is, and—" He looked to Rhodes, as if unsure.

She sighed and patted his knee, as if she needed to stop herself from patting him on the head and telling him he'd done well.

"It's all right, sir. Allow me," she said, the experienced NCO shifting forward and setting her champagne glass down daintily, projecting an air of ladylike decorum, just as minutes ago she'd disassembled her handgun and cleaned it like a machine. "The deal is this, sir." She fixed me with a steely eye. "We want sanctuary for our forces, a guarantee that we won't be sacrificed without need, and a home. We'll recruit for you, as we encounter other remnants of the armed forces. We'll bring them along, their dependents and their gear. We'll all swear fealty to you, *provided...*" She held her hand up, stopping me as I opened my mouth to speak.

"*Provided* the king is dead, or agrees to release us. Yeah, I know damn well that there'll be those who will swear and will join you without knowing that. But, honestly, we're going that way anyway. Let us check in on our bases, let us check on the king and if possible, recruit him and his people...then we bring them back."

Griffiths looked around at the confused looks and sighed.

"Look, if you're not forces, or a royalist, you'll not understand this, but the king is the head of state for us, the prime minister...well, as you said, Matt, most of us wouldn't trust the last one with a hard-boiled egg—"

"For a start, he'd get it pregnant..." Chris quipped, and Griffiths grinned.

"Probably would, yeah. The difference is, the prime minister is the official boss in the country, yeah, but the king, especially after we lost the queen...Look, the royal family are important to us, okay? I don't expect you to understand it, but all our oaths are to them *directly*. Our training is geared around them as our figurative leader, and they give their children up to serve in the forces with us. Regardless of how the rest of the country, or the world feel about them? They're ours, and we're theirs."

"I get it," I said. "Admittedly, I'm not so fussed on them personally, but yeah, if we can, we rescue them. But looking to the future...there's only one Dungeon Lord, you know that, right?"

"He's a figurehead," Griffiths said sadly. "He knows his role, as do his family. Most of them are damn good people who spend their lives playing their part and trying to help."

"That other one, though, the..." Chris started, only for Rhodes to snort.

"Oh, don't worry. We'll leave him, happily."

"Works for me," I said. "So the three-month timescale..."

"Still stands," Griffiths said. "We all talked about it and agreed. We'll join you, provided you prove yourself to us, and you save our goddamn families."

You have received a Quest!

Quest!

To the Rescue! (Again)

In exchange for your rescue of their families, fellows, and possibly the King/Royal Family, you will gain the loyalty of the remains of the Coldstream Guard.

Return Captain Griffiths and his people to their base and free their friends to complete this quest and receive the following bonuses:

- +10 to top three Attributes

- +3 Class Skill points to allocate

- + Unknown Blueprint

- + Weapons

- Additional soldiers/civilians

- 500,000 XP

Accept?

Yes/No…

I read it over, wincing as I accepted it, remembering the effect as I'd generated the quest for my people in the training dungeon, but also knowing that there was no goddamn way that Griffiths was donating that XP.

I shared the quest, getting some gasps as the others accepted it as well, and a smile as Griffiths relaxed.

"So, from tomorrow, we start stripping…" I grinned.

"What the hell have I signed up for?" Rhodes sighed, before reaching out and picking up the champagne bottle and giving it a forlorn shake. "Dammit, empty already. I don't suppose…?" she asked hopefully, before cutting off with a grin as several of us materialized more bottles onto the table next to her.

"Oh yeah, I could get used to this," she purred, popping another cork and sitting back, letting the liquid fill her glass.

CHAPTER FIFTEEN

The next morning dawned far too goddamn early. I groaned, pulling a pillow over my face and shaking my head.

"Nope!" I said into the pillow. "I'm not playing, not yet."

"Listen, 'Oh mighty Dungeon Lord,'" Kelly growled, pulling the pillow off my face, then hitting me with it. "You got so drunk last night that you passed out while I was picking out nice underwear for you, so believe me, I take great pleasure in this…"

"What?" I croaked, blinking up at her, as she moved around, making sure I got a damn good look.

She was dressed in a tiny red matched set—bra, panties, and the goddamn stockings *and* suspenders—and once she saw she had my *full* attention, she nodded in satisfaction, and moved to the chair off to one side.

I twisted around, trying to follow her as she moved, and I fell out of bed, landing with a grunt on all fours…only to see her pulling her jeans and a T-shirt on over it.

"Whoa!" I gasped at the sheer evilness, as I unwrapped my legs from the blanket and kicked it free, climbing to my feet and making the time-out sign. "Whoa, look, I can't fix last night, but this morning? I can make up for it, right? I can make some magic, right?" I smiled winningly at her, and she stepped in close, kissing me lingeringly, then patted my cheek mockingly.

"Nope!" She stepped around me, picking her boots up in one hand and her gun belt in the other, and then strolled out of the bedroom as I stood there, stunned.

"Evil fucker," I whispered, shaking my head. "I don't believe she just did that…"

I hurried through my shower, doing my best to ignore that some fucker had apparently shrunk my head overnight, as my skull was *waaaaay* too tight somehow. Then I dressed, moved out to the seating area, and found most of the others had been and gone.

"Kelly?" I asked Aly, who snorted.

"I'm not getting involved in your sex life, pal. You can sort that one out yourself."

"But—"

"She's going with the others to sort the lines out. You said you wanted everyone who could stand up and hear thunder working today? Well, that's what you're getting. Literally the entire dungeon is mobilizing. We're going to have a few days of insane levels of production, but once we've cleared these areas…"

"We're fucked when it comes to the easy shit," I agreed, nodding. "Yeah, I know. Don't worry. That's the whole point of spending most of what we get directly on upgrades to our generation."

I paused, considering going out and playing the game a little, making sure I was seen, and having a quiet word with Kelly, making sure I got to play later…But, realistically, there was no point. Kelly had won this round, and by tonight, well, I'd see where that got me. As things stood, she was doing her job, in acting as the liaison between me and most of the dungeon, my "left hand" essentially, along with Aly as my right, and it was time for me to damn well do my job too.

I summoned some food, ate quickly and distractedly, as I played with the dungeon sense at the same time, checking the countdown to the new core, and grunting as I saw there was less than an hour to go.

After a few minutes of steady munching and reading, I swallowed the last of the food and sighed, setting the fork aside and finishing my pint of ice-cold water, then cleared the table, and went back to my room.

It always seemed a bit weird, going to "work" by lying down on my bed, but fuck it.

I got myself comfortable and slid into the dungeon sense, lifting through it and going as high as I could, spreading my senses out and sighing as I felt the mass of people moving around, as well as those that were already "inside" and working on the usual pile of crap.

I flitted to the north end, seeing that the skeletal workers were steadily stomping along, carrying masses of, well, rubbish. They'd taken everything from the cabling in the walls to the light fittings, the phones, plumbing…

Basically, they had anything and everything that they could strip out of the surrounding buildings, and they were piling it up in great mounds.

My people were already at work, and the mana storage was approaching full, dipping and bobbing at nine and a half thousand, out of ten.

That would be my first job, I decided. I needed more storage and soon—although, at two thousand a pop, and to only increase the upper limit by two hundred and fifty points…

I sighed, figuring it was just the way it was, until we could research some improvements to them, and it was definitely better to have a reserve. I slid back and down, slowly dropping through the floor into the cavern below.

I'd not explored it all; hell, the size it was, it'd take weeks before it was all within reach anyway. But I'd seen enough to be sure that for now, apparently at least, it was empty, and it was certainly perfect in other ways, so I started with a section directly below our home.

I smoothed a section of the ground, absorbing the general crappy stone and more until I had a solid bedrock cleared. Then, at nine thousand, nine hundred, and twenty-seven mana, I built the first mana storage node, then a second, and a third, dropping the mana to two thousand and odd, before grinning as I saw the immediate burst of intake.

Clearly some of our people had been waiting, not wanting to waste it, and now that there was space? They were going for it! The speed wasn't huge, a handful of points—three here, five there, a dozen for a particular component or screen or whatever—but when there were dozens of people doing it?

It was going up by over a hundred a minute, and climbing, and I was damn well going to make the most of it.

I cleared more space, instead of absorbing the rock, using my control of it to shove it sideways, I forced the sluggish ripple of stalagmites to mound up, before creating a single Earth mana converter.

Then I started pushing it all back, mounding it up around the base of the converter.

It worked until about the halfway point, literally the bottom half encased in the slow-growing mineral thick "stone." After that, the earning started to drop off, but it was still at fifteen points per hour, and I'd damn well take that.

The mana counter was bouncing like a hooker's ass now. As soon as I smacked it down, it was up; then Aly or I'd hit it again, making the most of the massive gains.

I stopped at four Earth converters, eight thousand mana in cost, and another sixty points an hour, and I was just reaching for the Darkness ones, planning to set them around the outside, spacing them out one between each of the Earth ones, when the entire dungeon shuddered, and the vision around me changed.

It had happened before: as the dungeon core upgraded, everything changed, the gentle tinting of everything to bronze, so faint I'd totally forgotten it was even a thing, shifted, as the core reached Iron.

The world around me, that once had been wire frame, and almost without detail, was now easily visible. A slight sheen colored everything, a subtle silvery grey, and the feeling…

The dungeon felt stronger somehow, more solid.

I felt the changes rippling outward as the core changed. Notifications lifted into view; some were for me alone, and others that any denizens of the dungeon would be seeing.

Congratulations, Dungeon Lord!

You have reached the beginning of your true Quest…are you ready?

Yes/Yes

I glared at the prompt for a minute, seeing others popping up behind it, but knowing somehow that they were generic. This…this wasn't.

I selected yes, not that I had much in the way of a choice.

Excellent!

Your world is, unfortunately, in the path of expansion for the Orakai, and as such would have been scoured of all life, your citizens used as breeding stock and fodder, before the planet would be terraformed, eliminating any species that are judged to be unworthy.

The Orakai have refused all attempts at negotiation, at coexistence, or indeed any contact at all beyond all-out war.

We, the Cinthian species, attempted contact with your government, offering to share technology, resources, and more to enable you to defend yourselves against the Orakai, and to assist in the sector's defensive efforts.

It did not go well.

The survivors of our diplomatic detachment agreed that although your species showed tremendous versatility, it also had proved to be untrustworthy, warlike, and unreliable.

Essentially, you would not make the needed societal and technological changes needed on your own to act as defenders for this section of space, should we provide you with the means to do so.

Instead, it was judged, a small number of your elites would commandeer the majority of the gifts we offered, and they would instead abandon the majority, leaving them unprepared and defenseless before the Orakai.

A vote was held, and a solution decided upon.

We would provide you with the Dungeons—and through them access to our technology—and open a rift to subspace, flooding your world with mana from the core worlds, allowing you to grow in strength, and granting you a single chance to survive.

We did this by weakening our own war efforts; the dungeons gifted to you were hastily developed, as were their controlling and guiding sentiences. But rather than use them to produce materials for our own war, we chose to gift them to you.

For you to have activated this message, you have formed an alliance with a Dungeon Core and its attendant fairy, and reached the third stage of development. As such, we offer our most heartfelt congratulations!

You stand now at the edge of your own "Age of Enlightenment." The Dungeons were developed to provide you with refuges and training areas that, in time, could be harnessed to provide all the war materials you would ever need.

As you progress through the Core "Ages" to come, you will discover our technology, and we hope, you will develop your own new and powerful versions, growing into the patient, calm, and strong guardians the sector requires.

We are aware that there will be some small numbers of humanity lost to the dungeons and monster excursions. For this, we apologize unreservedly, and assure you, had we any other choice, we would have taken it. All life is sacred, but to save the vast majority, we must accept and take responsibility for a small number of deaths.

From now on, each Core Upgrade will come with a single boost to assist you. Please understand that we are your allies, and we do this to provide you with your best chance against the Orakai.

With each core upgrade, more information will be shared with you, but for now, please select the bonus you feel will most assist you and your burgeoning settlement.

- 1x Seed Dungeon Facility Blueprint
- 1x Dungeon Core Shard (Random Bonus)
- 1x Tech Upgrade (Random)
- 1x Class Skill Point
- 100,000 XP (Personal)

I read through the options, then the damn message from the aliens, and the options all over again, gritting my teeth. In some ways, it was nice to know for sure, finally, what the hell had happened and why.

In others? Not so fucking much.

We were in the path of a spacefaring civilization, one that loved war, and it was coming this way. And our "allies"?

They'd reduced us to a fraction of our numbers—accidentally, if I was reading this right—and they'd basically set us up with the tech we needed, or ways to get it, and were gambling that we'd become powerful enough on our own to deal with it all while they came up with their own solutions, behind us.

They had access to spaceships and could make fucking dungeons, could manipulate mana, and could have had the dungeons churning out ships or whatever, and instead had given them to us, in the hope we'd somehow go from hitting each other with rocks, all the way to interstellar travel—in a handful of years, presumably.

All because—again, if I was reading this right—they'd tried to make friends with us, and presumably some idiot politicians had fucked them up.

I stared at the screen before me, a new level of rage building as it all fit together.

Those self-serving fucking *assholes* had fucked us all. Billions had died, because they wanted to be the boss. They'd probably tried to get the tech and then use it on their allies as much as their friends.

I closed my eyes, breathing deeply, and forced myself to stop thinking about it, before I lost my shit completely. I'd find the politicians after all this was done. I'd find them, and I'd put them on pikes over the fucking castle battlements as a warning to any others who wanted to try this shit. Because I just fucking *knew* they'd have been in bunkers when all this shit went down.

I might be essentially setting myself up as a dictator, possibly one for the entire human race at this rate, but if this was how it had to be? To stop those…those…

No.

I buried it all, deep breath in and deep breath out, letting long seconds pass as I mastered my temper.

"Matt, the storage is getting full and…Matt?"

The sense of Aly appeared nearby, and I swallowed hard.

"Aly, I got some information," I said. "It's about the wider situation, and right now I need a few minutes. I'll share it with you all later, but for now? Just…just do what needs to be done, please."

There was silence for a few seconds, before a sense of comfort was pushed out to me. A feeling that said, *I trust you, and I'm here if you need me.*

Then she was gone, and I stared at the bonus options, reading and rereading them.

It wasn't a hard choice, not really. The XP, although it would be nice, was a personal thing, and it was for me alone. If it'd been a hundred thousand for everyone in the dungeon? Hell yes, no doubt. But as it was? Nope.

A single class skill point? Nope.

A random tech upgrade? I'd have to be crazy. It could be awesome, or it could be a slightly better earwax remover. Nope.

A dungeon shard bonus? That was more tempting, as the last time I'd gotten one of those, well, one of the rewards had been to make *all* my dungeon creatures, past and present, more powerful.

Another of the options had been a weapon blueprint, though.

Could be awesome, nuclear-powered fucking rail guns and orbital death rays or something. But equally, it might be a sharp stick, or a level of tech we'd never get to.

Nope.

That left one damn obvious win.

The seed dungeon facility. I selected it and felt the information unlocking for me.

Essentially, it was a blueprint that taught the dungeon to make self-contained seeds, ones we could plant anywhere. Like the original dungeon core, they needed a high-mana strongpoint, but once that was done, it'd be a linked dungeon core.

I'd be able to construct shit there, just as easily as I could here, and that meant...

I paused, my first thought having been that I'd put it in Saltwell Park. We could start building there, and that would make things much easier, but...

But really that would be a hell of a waste.

First, that wasn't a high-mana area, which was a major point. And secondly, well, it would make things easier, sure, but not *that* much easier.

I checked the details and swallowed hard. It came with one seed that we could use. A single seed. And then, after that, we needed to make our own.

Okay, that made sense.

The cost, though?

One *million* mana.

A million fucking mana to build a new one.

My dream of spreading them out all over the place crumbled before it had even begun.

I had one, and that was enough for now. I knew of one other high-mana area, for sure, and that was the area that Griffiths and the others had passed through. Otterburn camp.

I drew back, drawing higher and higher. A map spread out over the area, showing Newcastle, then the surrounding areas, the villages and towns, the cities in the distance as I lifted higher and higher, seeing three more "High Mana Zones" as I examined the now much larger map the latest upgrade had given me access to.

The area that Griffiths had passed through, at Otterburn, was in the middle of a mana zone that was practically black, it was that dark. Two other areas stood out now that I could see farther.

The middle of the north Yorkshire dales—near Hawes, it looked like—was another deep one, and deep in the midlands, somewhere near Leicester, at the farthest outer edge I could see.

I could create a secondary dungeon at either of those, and then, if I went all out, I could create a gate between those points, I guessed.
It made sense, but at this point, I genuinely didn't know which was the best.

The one to the south in the midlands was at the edge of my newly expanded awareness, and logically, that was probably the best. It'd give us the best chance at people, after all.

It was next to a city that was larger and older than Newcastle, I think, and for Griffiths and the others, if we could get there and set up a gate, it would massively decrease travel times around the country as well.

But…the base in the North was an army base. One far from everything, in an insanely high-mana area.

We could have it as a fallback point.

Build it all underground, make it into an insane-level nuclear shelter, one that we focus on as a doomsday base, somewhere the orcs simply couldn't find, so if everything went tits up, we'd still have that.

I toyed with the idea for a few seconds, then sighed. I didn't need to make the decision alone, and more to the point, I didn't need to make it at all right now.

I couldn't get to either site just yet, so the point was pretty much academic.

I banished it, seeing the new screens coming up, and sighing as I read them over quickly.

To all Inhabitants of the Iron Dungeon!

Welcome! We, your distant allies, thank you, and stand with you through our gift of technology. We believe in you all!

If I'd had a hand, I'd have slapped myself at that one. Fucking aliens.

Congratulations, Dungeon Lord!

You have reached the rarefied heights of Iron, and your dungeon is now named as the Sixth Iron Dungeon. This has begun the process of linkage. Over the next six solar cycles, additional dungeons will be connected to your own, and the Primary Nexus Gates will be formed. Speak to your Dungeon Fairy for more details and to make the necessary arrangements.

I growled to myself, seeing that one. I needed a dungeon fairy to make the arrangements, and I'd had to kill the only living fucker I'd come across!

What the hell were Nexus Gates? How long was a solar cycle? A day, a year? I felt nothing when I focused on them, nothing at all, which meant it was data that must have been stored in the fairy rather than the dungeon.

That scared the shit outta me, because it meant that there could be even more shit I just didn't know about. I shook my nonexistent head.

It was all too much. I could only deal with the stuff before me right now, I decided. Get on with things, have a meeting with the others, and then make some kind of announcement to the general population later.

"Aly," I called internally, and a split second later she was there, hovering by my side as I filled her in on everything.

"Well, that sucks," she said eventually.

"Yeah, understatement there," I growled. "What do you think?"

"Tell people the basics, and that's it for now. Start working on the next level as quickly as we can, and most of all, get that damn core planted."

"The core?" I asked, surprised. "I was thinking we could save it until we know exactly where—"

"You get that core in place and working as soon as possible. We need as much mana as we can get our hands on. That core means we can start a second dungeon, a satellite that we control from here. We can double the mana generation with that. It's a massive priority."

"Damn," I whispered, seeing it all. "I'd been so focused on a fallback, or transport option, I'd not thought of the mana generation options."

"That's why you have us," Aly said. "You can't be everywhere, and think of everything, not all at once. Also, frankly, I'm amazing."

"True," I agreed, pushing a sense of amusement to Aly, as I thought on things. "Okay, this changes things, but not massively. First of all, we need to get mana generation sorted here, which was always the case. Then we need better weapons."

"You can't face whatever is up there with the shitty weapons we have, not with as little ammo as we have, at least."

"Exactly—" Something tugged at the back of my mind—a memory, something to do with the mana conduits…

I pulled the conduits up, hoping that would spark something, and stared in shock.

The Stone mana absorption conduits had started at 0.5, I vaguely remembered, and had been upgraded to 0.75 when we went to Bronze and did that basic research; then 1.5, and finally 2.25.

When I'd been working out the mana generation earlier, I'd worked it out on the mana converters alone, and ignoring the actual conduits that we'd been stretching out and that had been pulling mana in as well.

I ran the figures, speaking aloud to Aly as I did it.

"We're not generating sixteen thousand a day. It's closer to thirty-three…" I explained quickly, getting a sense of confusion from her, and then agreement as she saw that it was indeed powering that out, the difference being missed because we had never let it build up; it was always being spent.

"Okay, but that's a good thing, right?" she said. "We're actually better off than we thought…But why?"

"Yes and no. We need to increase things, but have you looked at the new research options?"

"Matt, there's *thousands*. A bit more specific, please? Is this because of one of those?"

"Conduit research," I said. "We did a few levels in Bronze, and with each level, we get to redo it and start again. So even though we got to what, level three of the research on Bronze? We're back to one for Iron."

"And?"

"And the Iron level one conduit costs ten thousand," I pointed out. "If they follow the same level of expansion, we're looking at fifty or a hundred thousand for the next one, which yeah, it's expensive, but…"

"But what change will it have," she agreed. "Okay, I've got stuff queued up, but for ten thousand…" She pulled up the data before us, and I nodded, seeing the same information she could see.

"We're at seven and a half already. Do it."

She slid it into research, and I went back to the mana conduits, determined that there was something here I was missing. I knew it had to do with the conduits, and the research into them, but it wasn't the conduits themselves, so it must have been…

"Bonus research!" I said, quickly pulling the details up, and started to search.

Eventually I found it. It didn't help that I needed to search with an actual term as much as anything else, because like any goddamn computer system, I had to search a dozen sodding variations before I found the one I wanted. And, of course, it'd been mana storage it was linked to, not the damn conduits as I'd originally thought.

Itemized Storage

Itemized Storage is the act of designing smaller, more compact, and portable mana storage devices. These devices can then be added to constructions to provide directed Mana.

Do you wish to add "Itemized Storage Project" to your research list?

1000/1000 Mana charge invested

Completed

I grinned as I pulled up the details finally and spun them around to Aly.

"What's this?" She frowned, having been deep in something else, from the looks of things.

"This is the fucking game changer we need," I said. "We can make storage devices for mana, essentially making solid mana crystals, like I did with the spear!"

"The one that exploded?"

"Uh…yeah, okay, I'll admit it wasn't the best example, but…"

"You want people to carry something that might explode?" she asked carefully. "A magical grenade, basically?"

"No!" I paused, gathering my thoughts. "Look, we're running low on ammunition. All right, we can make loads of things ourselves, and yeah, we have an alchemy set now, so we'll be able to make gunpowder soon and all the shit we need to make our own ammunition, but…"

"But there's a lot of steps before we can do that," Aly agreed, nodding. "What have you got in that devious mind, Matt?"

"Why do we need to make ammunition for the guns?" I asked, grinning.

"Because we need…oh gods."

"Exactly!"

"I'm going to my chair. You deal with…all of this. And Matt? Whatever you did that boosted the mana intake, figure that shit out. I don't like not understanding it," Aly said, before popping out of the local dungeon sense, leaving me hovering there, a disembodied mind that just hoped this would damn well work.

CHAPTER SIXTEEN

The next few hours passed slowly as I waited with bated breath for Aly to come back to me. I got plenty of jobs done, but honestly, my heart wasn't in it, grinning when the research was finished in short order.

Mana Absorption Upgrade 1
Improved conduits have been uncovered, allowing an increase from 2.25 of 2.75 Mana per collector, per hour, to reach 5.0. Complete further research to improve this rate of absorption.

That was a hell of a change. The mana conduits that were spread through the dungeon and in the ground jumped massively in the amount they were processing, and that was the secret to why we were generating more mana, I'd found, after some digging.

They were everywhere, and I'd had no clue there were so many as I examined the system. They'd come online a few days back, when we'd been in full panic mode with the fights with Dickless, and that was why we'd missed it.

We'd literally just assumed that the massively boosted mana intake was down to all the crazy numbers of the undead we'd been harvesting, but it wasn't.

The core fragment that I'd absorbed into the dungeon had finally come online, and damn, it made a hell of a difference.

The original conduits…we'd had eight, I think, roughly, before this.

We'd worked on them, lengthening them, feeding them through the floors and out to the open air. We'd burrowed them into the ground, and they slowly extended by themselves.

That was fine; I'd known that, as had everyone else.

What I'd not told anyone was that the core fragment had several options as to their effect. The first two were simple: a possible random bonus to the mana collection, to the control points, or the influence generation. The first option had been marked as a plus or minus to each of those, and had been dismissed out of hand.

The second option was to make a core seed, a singular one, that would take a hundred and twenty days to produce, at that point, working on the levels of mana available to us then.

I'd said no, understandably, and I'd had no clue that later on the system would give us another chance at the seeds. It'd simply been the wrong choice at the time for us.

No, option three, as soon as I'd seen it, had been the one.

It used the core fragment as high-tech raw materials rather than a technology level of its own.

It broke the core down, feeding the materials out into the conduits, and forced them to multiply again and again.

It'd been marked as something that would take weeks, but the intake of mana had clearly boosted it. And now that I looked at the core?

The conduits were like hundreds of roots—tiny, infinitesimally thin ones…a hair was thick in comparison—but they branched out in all directions, woven into the walls, the floor, the gaps between stones…

"Two hundred and twenty-eight," I whispered in shock. "Two hundred and twenty-eight fucking mana conduits. That's…" I did the mental math, changing the two point two five they were at to the five overall that had finished research and I grinned at the new figure.

One thousand, one hundred and forty points an hour, combined with the mana we had access to from the converters—that gave us a solid forty-five thousand a day produced.

Or near enough, anyway; it was slightly under that, but fuck it.

That meant we were closing on our target, and a lot faster than I dared hope.

I'd pulled up the second level of the conduit research, before wincing at the cost. *A hundred thousand.*

Yeah, that was two days, or so, of production, not counting the costs, and not counting the excess that was coming in. But when a brick was giving us a single point…we weren't going to have a massive windfall again anytime soon, I was betting. And as for the research trees…

Aly had filled them already, and I got the feeling I'd regret it if I interrupted her plan. So, instead, I limited myself to building Darkness converters in the depths of the cavern, five more of them, and working with a single solidified mana crystal.

I could summon one easily enough. The research was done, and with it being literally a mana crystal, I could create it fully out of mana for two and a half thousand.

The issue was the crystal itself when it was done.

It didn't "feel" like mine had, the way it was desperate to jump to serve me, and I remembered the warning I'd gotten when I'd considered this before.

WARNING

Attempting to draw stored mana from a LOW-GRADE storage device is only recommended if the draw is managed by a dedicated DEVICE.

Terminal Damage is highly likely if this warning is ignored.

"Terminal Damage" was fairly self-explanatory. I wasn't trying to pull the mana out; I was just…I don't know, actually. I created a physical crystal, then left the dungeon sense, and was on my bed, holding the crystal and staring up at it, frowning, deep in thought, when the door opened.

Aly stepped in, looking like the cat that had gotten the cream.

"What's up?" I sat up and set the stone aside.

"I've got the basic details worked out," she said quickly, sitting down on a seat by the door and grinning. "The basic, and I mean *basic*, to be clear…but the basic theory is that the mana stones can store mana, and then release it in three ways: slowly over time as a steady power source, quick in a repeatable burst, or all at once."

"So a power source for a vehicle, a gun, or a bomb?" I suggested, getting a nod from her.

"If we ignore the other two for now, and focus on the gun, I've got three basic designs in mind." She clasped her hands together as she spoke, excitedly interlocking and releasing her fingers. "A handgun, a shotgun, and a rifle! They all fire a simple bullet. Well, the handgun and rifle do; the shotgun gets the same but much smaller—"

"And?"

"And they don't need explosives!" She grinned. "We literally cut out things like the chemicals for the bullets, which means we can fit more in the magazine. I'm thinking the handguns will hold fifteen to thirty shots, literally a short metal dart. The rifle will have the same, but more of them. The shotgun gets a packet of them, smaller and close packed!"

"And we can make them?" My mind raced to the potential usages: towers with rifles built in, shotgun-style traps, holes in the walls that had recessed guns built in that could be fired on command.

"Not yet." She shook her head, essentially pissing on my parade.

"But—"

"The theory is fine. The theory works out, and we can make them, although bronze is a better material than iron for this. If we had the Steel core up and running—yeah, that'd be better again. But we can adjust to them once we have the basic design done, and we'll need to work out the recharging of the manastones as well."

"Okay, so what's the next step?" I asked, and she grinned.

"I start construction on the basic test versions, and we start research."

"Can we—"

"The core is changing with each upgrade. As it is now? We can run upgrades and research," she assured me, and I sighed with relief. "The cost of the Steel core is a million mana."

"Fuck me…" I whispered, shaking my head. "That's going to take weeks…"

"It will, if we continue at this level. But as you said, you want us up to a hundred thousand a day. So you can do it…just keep increasing that."

"Okay, the research…" I paused, thinking, and she nodded.

"It's time, Matt," she agreed. "My research area is great, and when we first started, it really was amazing. But it's not appropriate to all of us as it is, let alone the levels we need to move toward. It's time to expand the facilities out. The headquarters, the research building, all of it."

"We need the mana for—"

"We need the mana, we need the kobolds, we need the research nodes, the walls, the food, the housing…I could go on for hours." She sighed. "I agree with you on the mana production. That's the priority, but the others are pouring mana in like water at the minute. We need to take some of it for the other sections. I'll work on the guns, but believe me, they're not going to be possible to produce yet, maybe not at all with the Iron core. And I've got my kobolds working on the next level of influence generators, as they'll also bring in mana—"

"And they'll spread our control zone." I nodded.

"Exactly. But I need *dozens* of things worked on for these guns alone. Add to that, you need new armor, all of our people do, and the weapons…" She sighed, dropping her head into her hands as she took a deep breath. "You know, Matt, we need everything, and that's only going to get worse as time goes on. We *need* the research facilities. They'll increase the research speed, which in turn will speed up how quickly we can get things like the increased conduits upgrades, which will bring in even more mana."

I nodded, sitting back on the bed and thinking about it as she stood.

"I'm going to get back to work, Matt, but honestly, it's always going to be like this, research versus infrastructure, versus defenses…I'm sorry, but this is what comes with the top job!" She shrugged, offering me a smile as she headed to the door.

"It's okay. I know," I assured her, waiting until she was out of the room to settle back, laying the stone on the bedside table, and then, because my mind was whirling so much, getting off the bed and stripping.

I stepped into the shower, only half seeing the world around me as I worked, visualizing the entire area, even as I scrubbed at myself.

The dungeon was growing steadily. The council under Clarissa split its efforts between dealing with personal and public issues, and working in the dungeon to expand the range of its influence.

There were several dozen working with her now, and I nodded in satisfaction as I watched the speed she was claiming the land.

The buildings around us were being stripped at a ferocious speed as well. Several had collapsed as people took out strategic supports; the rest of the building was down to bare bones already.

Hundreds of people worked side by side, forming human chains, stripping room after room, passing everything to the nearest window and chucking it free, while others worked inside the dungeon sense, "hoovering" up the piles of…everything, basically.

I floated through, seeing the counter creeping up to the maximum, and adding another four Water converters to the bottom of the river, then two more kobolds, armed with spears and shields.

I moved constantly, splitting my attention between the steady construction of the converters, summoning occasional kobolds, and the absorption of the interior of the Moot Hall.

I worked quickly, as our people stripped it, joining in and reducing it over six hours to the ground, adding in six more Nature and Life converters to the farms nearby as I went.

By the time the Moot Hall was gone entirely, it was dark outside; the others had been back for several hours.

I'd climbed into bed after finishing my shower, and I'd laid there for hours, working steadily, until eventually, I felt a hand on my shoulder, shaking me gently. I slid out of the dungeon sense, blinking blearily as I tried to focus from "inside" me again.

The bedroom was dimly lit. The flickering of a half dozen candles gave it a warm and homely light, as Kelly smiled at me.

I was laid on the bed, and she straddled me. The feeling of her doing that had registered distantly before, but as she smiled down at me, I felt myself "centered" in my own body.

She knelt half over me, upright; the inside of her thighs rested just over my hips, as she stared at me. I looked up, stunned by her in every way.

She reached back, taking a handful of the blanket in one hand and tugging it free, then glanced down at the exposed flesh, smiling as she saw the effect her outfit was having on me.

The set she'd teased me with that morning was changed, slightly at least. The panties now missing, as was the bra. The stocking and suspender set, however, was still very much there, and she reached down, taking me into her hand and stroking gently.

"I've had a very long, hard day…" she whispered. "I ache, and I have needs…"

"Tell me more…" I reached up and slid my hands up the outside of her thighs, feeling the sheer silken stockings, the tops, and the little clips that led to her belt, as she positioned me below her.

"I've been working very, *very* hard," she whispered, "and I need a massage…"

"A massage?" I sat up and reached around, cupping her fantastic ass with one hand, as my other pulled her close, and I trailed kisses across her left breast. "What kind of massage?"

"One you give me…from the…inside…" She groaned, sliding down and sending both of our minds whirling.

The night was a blur, the most recent days having been filled with confusion, exhaustion, and battles. The night, instead, was spent in each other, a mélange of kisses trailed across nipples and lower, of lips pursed just so, teasing and sucking, licking and teeth being drawn across sensitive areas, making the other gasp and moan.

By the time the morning came—and we both had repeatedly, by that point—we were sore, drained, and very much in need of the shower we shared.

Kelly was braced against the back wall, hair plastered into a single tail, and drawn over her shoulder to fall down her front as I stood behind her, hands on her shoulders, thumbs gently rubbing as I moved down her spine, and she moaned.

We were both wet, the water running down us, and I was looking at her ass speculatively, wondering whether the flesh was capable, as the mind was certainly willing, when someone banged on the door, hard.

"Matt! Get your arse in gear! We've got problems!" Mike's voice bellowed, and I sighed, releasing Kelly regretfully.

"Probably for the best," she whispered, kissing my cheek, before turning the shower off, and hitting me with a fluffy towel.

I took it and dried off, before dressing hurriedly and heading out, joining the others around the tables as Mike glared at me.

"What?" I frowned at the look he gave me.

"Soundproofing," he said. "If you want to survive, look into it."

"Kelly isn't exactly subtle," Chris whispered as he sat next to me, waiting, fortunately, for Mike to turn away before he spoke. "I could hear her all the way over in our room, mate. So, aye, soundproofing if you're going to play all night, for the love of my ears, if nowt else."

"Sorry, dude." I winced. As much as I'd usually joke with him about something like that, I'd been on the receiving end of it before when a mate was having a lot of fun, and yeah, it was a bit shit if you weren't as well.

Kelly joined us a minute or so later, and Mike cleared his throat roughly, getting everyone's attention.

"Right. Griffiths is leading his people on a scouting mission. Beta's with him with her team," he said. "Ashley sent word this morning that she'd stay there for the next day or two, doing a 'hearts and minds' mission with the park."

"Sounds good," I agreed, summoning a plate of bacon, sausages, beans, and thick-cut toast, before adding a few fried eggs as well. "What's the problem?"

"The problem is, they're being scouted in turn," he said. "Griffiths sent Rhodes back. She's gathering up Markus and a few others, and is going to scout them back, see what she can find out with a few of the soldiers as backup."

"Shit. And we spent the day building mana converters and doing research instead of summoning kobolds," I growled, getting a wry smile from Aly.

"I told you, Matt, no matter what you choose, you'll pick the wrong one. It's Murphy's Law."

"Yeah, well," I grumbled. "How many do we have?"

"Kobolds?" she asked, and I nodded, knowing she'd have the details off the top of her head.

"Twelve," she said. "Of the new ones and not counting Beta's team. She's split off two of her 'awakened' and leveled kobolds to lead the second and third squads, and has taken two more in their place."

"We need—"

"Everything, honey," Kelly interrupted me, reaching over and resting her hand on my arm. "We need everything. We know."

"Okay." I lowered my head, thinking. "What—"

"This is an FYI situation, Matt," Mike said. "Rhodes is leaving any minute with a dozen of the hoplite trainees, all geared up, and I'm going with her, as is Markus. We should be enough backup that if the shit hits the fan, we can hold out, but I need you to be ready. If whoever is scouting them is too big, we'll fall back."

"How far have we got the influence generated to?" I asked Aly, and she frowned, checking before responding.

"A third of the way from the river to the park," she said after a few seconds, making me grunt.

"How far from that are you going to be?" I asked Mike.

"No clue," he admitted, checking his guns and kissing his wife and daughter, before giving a few fist bumps as he moved around the table. "We'll go as far as we have to, you know that, but…"

"I'll go to the farthest forward edge of the influence, and I'll begin construction of a fort," I said. "If you need to…wait…" I slid into the dungeon sense and flashed across the distance, sighing as I saw where it was up to. "The civic center…the far side of it, it's got a little security station. You know it?"

"Vaguely." He hesitated at the doors, clearly needing to go.

"I'll make a secure fallback there, and I'll get you some backup. You get in the shit, you fall back to there," I ordered him, and he nodded, forcing a smile.

"Will do. See you all later."

With that, he was gone, the door banging shut behind him as we all watched, feeling like a bunch of fucking cowards as he went out to risk his life, while we ate and made minor internal modifications to the dungeon.

I sighed, getting to my feet and checking the dungeon. We were at eleven thousand, four hundred mana. The additional storage facilities had proved their worth time and time again.

I vaguely remembered a break in the "entertainment" last night where Kelly had done her level best to distract me, even as I worked to make additional storage, rather than risk wasting the mana that was accumulating.

Kelly kissed my cheek and hugged Aly, reassuring Amy that Mike would be fine. The others moved away as well, and I returned to my bed, lying down and feeling like a right shit as my friend ran toward a possible fight.

I'd do the best that I could, though, I swore, reaching out and finding Clarissa and two others working on the expansion project. They were halfway through the car park of the civic center, when I reached them, and they seemed surprised by my arrival.

"We've got some suspicious assholes in the area," I told them without preamble. "We need a fallback position, and that's it." I pointed at the small square structure a dozen meters away.

"It'll take us half an hour to reach it," Clarissa said. "That's as fast as it can be done."

"I know," I said through gritted, insubstantial teeth. "I know. Just do it as fast as you can."

They diverted, moving in a thin line, literally one stepping forward, focusing and "pushing" out the influence, straining as if lifting a weight as they shoved against the barrier, before the next in line stepped past them, and did the same, leaving them to catch their breath.

As they did that, I did the best thing I could, and I reached out, summoning a kobold to stand before me in the car park, one of the new advanced breed, and triggered my evolution abilities.

Foresight helped massively as I set to work, combining the basic level of kobold with a mixture of Lightning and Darkness. Rather than using the selector "wheel," as I thought of it, and as I had in the past, feeding it into this direction and that, paying attention to the numbers, I went entirely on instinct, reaching out to the kobold, and working steadily.

I fed Darkness into her scales, Lightning into her nerves and brain, and pure, pure mana I soaked into her, before adding a touch of Earth here and there, bones mainly. Air sank into her wings and lungs, Fire into teeth and claws, heart and stomach, and...

I lost track of time, adjusting and twisting, feeling the strands of mana seeping into her, as Foresight guided me. I knew what I needed. I needed a new rogue, and by the gods did I get one.

When I finished, and the changes had run their course, the poor bugger was hissing like a kettle left too long on the stove. She straightened up and looked herself over, stretching one arm out and chirruping as she examined the play of the light on her scales.

She was a mixture of black and grey; the spines were smaller, a narrow row of jagged tips protruding down from the thin crest on the top of the head and rolling down her back.

The wings were larger, the upper chest as well. Although the body overall appeared smaller, it was still strong; hell, it had a clear, if wiry strength. But rather than the sheer intimidation the advanced "standard" kobold demonstrated, this was considerably less. In fact...

I caught myself looking off to one side, as if distracted, and jerked my eyes back to her, seeing their lips curling in a proud smile as I did so.

"You did that, didn't you?" I asked, getting a short nod in response. "Impressive." I pulled up the details for the new creation on the prompts before me.

Congratulations!

You have used Advanced Forced Evolution on a creature of your Dungeon: "Unnamed the Advanced Kobold Warrior."

"Unnamed" has been altered at a fundamental level.

Two paths are now available to the Kobold Warrior:

Rogue:

Kobold Rogues are generalists, and the lowest level of the larceny tree. That being said, however, they should not be dismissed, especially the "advanced" variants. A knife in the dark, regardless how simplistic it may be, still cuts.

Lightning Enhanced: As a variant created with the power of a nascent Storm Lord, this creature has gained the following special Ability:

> *Blink:* Using Blink, a creature can vanish and reappear up to a dozen meters away instantly. This Ability requires 50% of a Rogue's Stamina and Mana to complete, with an extra meter being traveled per additional ten Mana and Stamina the user has over one hundred.

The Rogue has two innate Abilities, depending on the Path chosen...

Vanish:

A rogue's stock in trade is in being seen only when they wish; they distract, they fool the eye, and then, as if they'd never been there, the rogue vanishes...

Limited invisibility for 5 seconds might not sound like much, but in the midst of a fight? Take your eyes off a rogue at the wrong time, and get ready for a backstabbing!

Cost: 100 Stamina and Mana per casting, lasts 5 seconds.

Pierce the Veil:

Just as invisibility can be a wonderous boon to a rogue, the opposite can be their undoing. Many have made a final, fatal mistake in believing that an heiress is all alone, when her husband, in fact, skulks nearby...

Triggering this ability will highlight any hidden creatures or items in a ten-meter radius.

Cost: 100 Stamina and Mana per casting, lasts 5 seconds.
Summoning Cost: 3000 mana to summon, 300 mana per day, 30 control points.

Kobold Assassin:

Assassins are most definitely not just pretentious murderers for hire, and we certainly never said that in the past and nor were we warned about it. Definitely not. Assassins are classy, skillful individuals living by a code; one that, by an amazing coincidence, involved murdering people and receiving financial "gifts" by the same people who named the target.

Lightning Enhanced: As a variant created with the Power of a nascent Storm Lord, this creature has gained the following special Ability:

> *Admittance:* Being an Assassin can be difficult; after all, so many of your targets are unjustifiably paranoid that people don't like them for some reason…
>
> The Admittance skill lets an Assassin cast a short-term, close-range Glamor spell, convincing those around them that the Assassin is a trustworthy individual who should be allowed in…the fools. This skill costs 50 Stamina and Mana per second active, per individual inside a 5-meter radius.

The Assassin has two innate Abilities, depending on the Path chosen…

Elimination:

The Assassin's stock in trade is in single strike kills, channeling all the massive damage that is needed to eliminate a powerful individual into a single blow.

The Assassin may create a device to store energy, practicing a single strike over and over again, channeling that strike into the device, and building the power over and over, until it is needed.

Cost: 5000 Mana and Stamina (Channeled over time)

The Dance of Death:

An Assassin that is surrounded, with little chance of escape, may choose the Dance of Death, injecting their blades with a poison that is directly linked to their own Healthpool: they will lose five points of Health per second, but gain ten back per strike.

A truly skilled practitioner of the Dance of Death may heal their own wounds while draining all those around them of their lives to do so…

Cost: 25 HP per second active, minimum of 500 Health required.
Note: If the 500 HP is not taken from enemies, the remainder will be stripped from the Assassin.
Summoning Cost: 3000 Mana to summon, 300 Mana per day, 30 control points.

I read the details over slowly, seeing the similarities between the new version and the last one, the uncommon kobold having been both much weaker, and much cheaper.

That being said, the new assassin and rogue versions did seem fucking lethal.

The real question was, which was more appropriate? The rogue could scout the area far more efficiently than the assassin, but the assassin could be sent in to slaughter the fuckers when they're found…

I always intended to build up a cadre of all the various versions, but rarely actually managed it.

I gave it a few seconds, then, growling to myself, I chose the Assassin. The rogue had more versatility, and would probably be more useful overall, but this was all about making damn sure my people were safe.

A few assassins hidden around the area when we got attacked next would make a massive difference in those situations.

I slid the screens aside, seeing that Clarissa had made it up to the edge of the wall, and I nodded to myself in satisfaction. A few more minutes, and I'd start work on the outpost.

For now, though? Time to get myself a goddamn assassin.

I approved and selected it, seeing the kobold shaking as the final changes took place. I literally watched the scales dimming. The glimmer of reflected sunlight that had been noticeable on a scale here and there vanished as they changed, and unlike the habitually stooping rogues, the new assassin stood tall.

Her wings fluttered gently in the breeze as she looked around, lifting her hands and checking them over, seeing the sharpness of the claws on far more human hands.

That the kobolds were based on dragons was indisputable now, but somewhere…I shook my head. I just knew that somewhere in their ancestral tree there was a human fucking bard, probably with a broken pelvis, sitting in the back of a tavern, telling everyone it was totally worth it.

"Can you hear me?" I asked the kobold, and she nodded, a slow bob of the head. "Good. There are groups of raiders in the area, and our people are moving out to try to support each other. This is going to be an emergency fallback position for them." I gestured to the building behind me.

"It'll be rebuilt, but I need to know our people are safe. You are to hide nearby, and slaughter anything that is a risk to them. I want you to remain hidden as much as possible. You'll probably be given more challenging missions soon, so be ready and get all the practice you can in on monsters. Oh!" I'd been about to leave it at that, but I sent a mental image of the asuras to her.

"These two may be moving around the area. Providing they don't attack our people, leave them alone. If they, or any like them, attack those who are from the dungeon? Kill them." I got an immediate nod and a hungry look from her that made me smile.

I had no clue how the dungeon creatures knew who was dungeon and who wasn't, but it was a relief that there was clearly something they could sense, as had been made clear so far.

I checked, finding that Aly had made a simple variation on the human armor for the new advanced kobolds, special sections having been removed to make way for the wings and more. I summoned a set for this one, before pausing, then summoning several knives, a pair of the smaller self-reloading crossbows, and a composite bow, as well as all the ammo needed for them.

She swept them all up, sliding them into holsters I summoned as well, sheathes on her forearms, and…She gestured to the daggers, then made a gesture of throwing, and I summoned a brace of throwing knives as well that she positioned across her chest.

"You need a name…" I whispered absently, well aware that she was fully sentient already. "A name that strikes fear into the hearts of all who hear it, one that makes it clear that to face you is to face death…or worse."

There was only one name that was appropriate.

"Welcome to the team, *Karen*."

CHAPTER SEVENTEEN

Once Karen was ready—and armed to the fucking teeth—she nodded once in satisfaction, then vanished into the depths of the civic building. I winced at the thought of the slaughters she was going to perpetrate in my damn name.

It might have been a step too far, naming her Karen. I mean, there was a limit, and surely setting a true Karen on your enemies was banned under the Geneva Convention…But, fortunately, I didn't really need to bother with that.

Firstly, because the world had gone to shit, and nobody was likely to be reporting me, and secondly, because it's only cruel and unusual punishment if the other side lives to talk about it.

"Didn't even say 'thank you,'" I muttered.

I dismissed the situation from my mind, and moved to the building the others were busily claiming for me. It was a square; a large overhanging pointed roof topped it, with a wide area underneath for people to stand out of the rain, as they asked for admittance or contested car parking tickets or whatever, and was around ten meters on a side.

A hundred square meters was a hell of a size to claim quickly, let alone to convert into a useful building, but it was going to happen.

I joined them at the corner. The three of them had split up, one following each exterior wall to the left and right, and the other heading toward the center.

I stepped up next to Clarissa and took my turn. The pair of us worked to claim meter after meter as quickly as possible.

As soon as the middle of the room was claimed, some fifteen minutes later, I went to work, constructing an influence generator.

It'd be quicker to have built one of the more specific ones, the kind that channeled all its power into claiming a single hemisphere from the ground up, for example, but I decided I needed it spherical.

Minutes passed as the generator came online. The firefly-like motes of the creation process brought bright light to the abandoned ground floor building, the office furniture and scattered papers being stirred by life for the first time in long weeks.

I paused, looking out of the windows on all sides to get a feel for the area, and thinking as the others worked steadily. The walls were claimed as they worked, with Clarissa moving to start on the far side of the room. As the generator came online, the dungeon's influence grew in response.

I smiled, seeing the speed it was going. Ten, maybe fifteen minutes at this rate, and with the others pushing out as they went as well, and the ground floor would be covered enough to begin. But for now, the walls were certainly getting there.

I moved back to the rear quarter, and the door, selecting the wall as a single unit and assigning it all to be converted to solid stone, a foot thick, instead of the simple bricks and cladding it was made of for now.

It wasn't cheap, not at all—a thousand points per three meters—but that was floor to roof. I approved it, adjusting the design as I included a token door, made of solid bronze, on the next section.

Moving methodically, I converted the back half of the building to solid stone, then started on the rest. The room grew darker as the others moved on, resuming their work of claiming toward the park, as I replaced the windows with solid stone.

Once I'd made a full circuit, and I was sure the walls were solid, I started work on the floor, making it two feet of literally solid stone, with a hatch in one corner. Again, that was only openable through use of the token, or by an authorized member of the dungeon.

That done, and with the influence extending up and down, I reached out and started on the ceiling. Instead of converting it to a solid stone form, though, I spread overlapping joists from one side to the other, forming an insanely strong foundation for a second floor, along with a set of stairs leading up there.

The roof as it was, was fine—weak now, compared to the rest—but fuck it; that could be useful too.

I created a solid bronze layer underneath the tiled roof, covering it in sharp-as-fuck blades that ran up and down in patterns. If anyone thought they were going to tear the "weak" roof off? They were in for a world of hurt.

I copied a section of the floor below, one meter high and running all the way around the room, then I inserted it atop the current "top" of the ceiling, raising the entire level up.

That was as far as I could reach for now. The influence generator was only able to go so far, so fast, but it was worth it. Even if the room was dark and boring as fuck, it was also safe as all hell.

I created a stack of tinned foods, a can opener, and two stacks of water bottles for now, as well as a load of medical supplies, just in case any of our people needed them in an emergency, or wanted to give them out.

That done, I moved back, headed for the dungeon.

Along the line of the claimed influence, I paused, installing a second, and then a third influence generator node as I went—one halfway between the river and the civic center, and one in the middle of the civic center itself.

The one closest to the river was in the open, in the middle of a car park, literally out where anyone could see it, as an experiment, as I remembered the way the undead had been drawn to it.

I made a deep pit around it on all sides, and filled the bottom with spikes, before spawning a few clumsy signs on each side, warning people who might be curious that the pit was there and to stay away.

That way, at least, if a dumb beast tried to reach it, it'd be a free kill or two.

The one inside the civic center was different. I hid it in a small room, and built thick walls around it, well aware that would slow its claiming of the surrounding area. But I wanted it safe.

This was going to claim the middle of the massive building, and it would become a second "castle" for us eventually, I decided. Possibly becoming either a safe zone for our people between the park and the dungeon, or possibly for people we wanted to keep close, but at arm's length.

I didn't know really, but it was a good place to build it, and the design of the building, a square in the center with four more squares that joined from the corners of the first, just made me think of a fort.

I was tempted to make it into a massive trap, to be honest—have it all flashing lights and cooking meat at all times, drawing in the monsters of the area—and turn it into a meat grinder.

Or...or maybe...

No. That was a job for another time. But the thought that had come to me was damn tempting.

I flew back to the dungeon, checking the current intake and wincing. It was already dropping off. The massive influx we'd been enjoying had been improved by the junk that was in the surrounding buildings, and the sheer quantity having a quality all of its own.

Now, though, we were mainly at the "bricks and mortar" stage, and it was taking the thirty or so people who were doing the absorbing longer to absorb it than I was in spending it.

I grinned as a thought came to me, and I scoured through the details again, finding what I was looking for in the "basic undead" description.

Skeletons!

This is the most basic form of the simple Undead; it knows only hunger and will act within simple parameters, slowly guarding a set area, for example. The Undead's greatest strength lies in their lack of imagination. Stationed correctly, a dozen Undead can do the work of a hundred living mortals, for they never tire, never get bored, and never act in their own self-interest instead of their master's...or at least, not when they are at their most basic.

I'd upgraded the pattern a few times, but the most basic form was still there, and frankly, that was all I damn well needed.

I had three thousand mana, and I reached out, spawning a solid forty of them at a cost of sixteen hundred mana, and then a bright-red baseball cap for each at another ten apiece, taking it to two thousand.

I had them march out, in a line, to the human chain that was currently passing everything from bricks to bulbs to the "absorb pile."

People hesitated at first, seeing the undead, the recent fights firmly in everyone's mind. But the addition of the cap, and the lack of weapons or ravening hunger and of any murdering going on, helped.

They stepped up, one at a time, standing next to the first forty people, reaching out and taking their burden before carefully stepping into their spaces, taking over.

That freed up forty people to strip the buildings, making things considerably faster. Jack patrolled the area, and the handful of kobolds we'd kept back searched building by building for enemies.

It wasn't a massive increase, but I resolved to spawn another forty later in the day, and then again in the evening. If we could have them working round the clock, literally day in and out, never tiring, it would massively help.

Plus, our people could do the absorbing then, speeding up the bottleneck.

I paused at that thought, remembering that the wraiths were designated as commanders for the undead, and wondered at that. There were definite advantages to the idea of summoning something to lead the undead, to keep them going and more, but...

But the wraiths were literally the undead spirits of assholes, and although the ones I was summoning weren't the naturally occurring kind, they were still unlikely to be great leaders.

No, what I needed was a controller or commander type. I paused, considering the various creatures I could create, before grunting at my own stupidity.

I was wondering what kind of creature I should create to run the various dungeon creatures, while also working to free my people up from having to do drudge work.

I needed to recruit someone from them. Someone I could totally trust, because they would be taking day-to-day command of the dungeon creatures from me. I'd still be able to overrule them, obviously, and it was always something that would have to happen, realistically, as I needed the dungeon to keep growing, and eventually, controlling everyone would become a full-time job in and of itself.

I resolved to sort that out later, and got back to work, flashing back across the distance to the civic center and the fallback point.

It'd risen by another few meters in the time I was away—the area of influence—and I grinned as I realized a simple, yet highly effective cheat.

I could, admittedly, make more influence generators, and they started with a solid sphere of ground that was claimed as soon as they came online.

That would be an expensive way to do this, though. What I needed was to claim the area above where it stood, and as quickly as possible.

Well, as much as I wanted the space below claimed as well, that could wait.

I removed a section of the level above, ceiling and floor, with a smile, reinforcing the structure slightly, but it wasn't overly difficult.

Then, grinning to myself, I added a few inches to the ground that the generator node was on, checked, and yup. Still working. I started adding six inches at a time, over and over. The generator moved up smoothly into the air as I smiled, watching how the claimed area slowly increased.

It wouldn't be a viable long-term cheat—it was costing to do this, after all—and I'd need to absorb it all and bring it back to the same place to claim the ground underneath. But as a short-term "Fuck, I need a quick fix" method?

It worked.

It worked really well, literally. I guessed I could lift it and move the generator around on a ripple of stone, and claim the area at a massively increased rate.

Or...

I ran the math in my head and sighed.

If I was to accept that kind of a cost? It was a quarter of the cost of making one, to simply move one around and claim an area that way. Maybe I could just keep building influence generators, and slap them down everywhere?

Hell, that probably worked better for me, actually, because I could upgrade the pattern to earn mana from them, like the converters? It was a lot faster, though...

I considered it for a few seconds, before reaching out and getting a growl of frustration from Aly as I essentially "summoned" her.

The sense of her appeared next to me a minute or two later, and I spoke before she could complain about being interrupted.

"Sorry, Aly, I know you're busy. I wouldn't interrupt you lightly, but I need a few things, and it makes sense to talk."

"Okay..." she said slowly, clearly biting down on her complaints. "What do you need?"

"Stay with me." I lifted into the air, hovering high over the civic center, and finding it a bit weird. I could do it, but rather than the way I could see the map, this was "live" and moving up and "out" of the claimed area of influence...I could do it, just, but Aly couldn't. Projecting myself up and out, even at this short a distance, was something the system wasn't prepared for, and as a result, not something anyone else, bar the Dungeon Lord, could do.

Instead, I returned to the ground with her, and cursed, needing to show her exactly what I had in mind.

I left the influence generator and dragged her back to the dungeon proper, asking her to meet me in the private lounge we had, and summoned a map to the table, having it waiting for us as I moved out.

Once she was there, looking irritated, I started to talk, wanting to get her on board before she could get more annoyed with me.

"So, this is the civic center—"

"Yeah, I recognize it. Horrible monstrosity of a building," she muttered, and I grinned at her in agreement.

"Well, maybe it can serve our purposes."

"How? Matt, I'm sorry, but we're barely keeping things together at the minute. If you're going to try to add in a new project—"

"That's the point," I said. "Look, word is going to spread, eventually, and our enemies are going to know what we are, and why they desperately need to conquer us. We need mana, massive quantities of it, and we need somewhere the mages can train."

"And we have all of that—the mages tower and the walls, the—"

"Look at the civic center," I ordered her. "Really look at it. It's nearly halfway between the park and dungeon, it's got clear lines of sight, it's easily convertible with defenses..."

"You've got the castle project. Are you meaning to replace it?"

"Yes and no." I sighed. "Look, I can't make many more Air, Storm, or Lightning converters on the roof here. The breeze is getting steady enough that we have to keep the kids from going up to the roof."

"Kids shouldn't be up there anyway," she said.

I nodded. "That's a fair point, yeah, but think about it. What if we claim this building and use it as a battery?"

"Explain."

"The center is a square, then each outer square joins to the corners of the center one, right?"

"I can see the map, Matt."

"I know." I growled. "My point is, we can control the environment, to some degree, with the dungeon. We could create four different zones for training."

"Like the training dungeon?"

"Yes…no." I tried to think how to explain it. "Like with the Fire mages—"

"Pyromancers."

"Whatever!" I snapped. "If we heavily reinforce a square, make it insanely hot and fill it with Fire converters, then create a secure access to it, a path people can follow, so that they don't go too deep, but can cultivate and improve their affinities…each of the converters can earn us mana, and I can turn the roof into a storm generator."

"That doesn't sound like a good idea, Matt," she said carefully. "Storms are destructive, sometimes massively so. We don't have them here very often, so the buildings aren't set up for them."

"We create them and drain them," I said excitedly. "This could work! We could—"

"No," she said flatly. "No, Matt, I'm sorry. Possibly creating massive storms so you can feed on them and ignoring the possible devastation to the area isn't something I think is wise. Not at all."

I glared at her, knowing it was, feeling with everything that made me, me, that this would massively help us.

"Okay…" I sighed, rubbing at my face. "Look, I know you don't agree, and you have concerns, but the Lightning and Storm converters aside, what do you think? This is far enough from our two bases that they're not at risk if anything goes badly."

"And that's it? A test zone?" She frowned. "If that's what it is, then maybe farther away, or not on the fastest route between—"

"No," I said. "We make out to anyone else that this is our production center. We make this the place they want to take, and we build the defenses at the other two as well. We make them our population centers, but this? This is where we make shit like the converters and anything we need to test!"

"And then the others…" She paused, then nodded. "The others can be the research and accommodation as we described. But, Matt, this will cost a shitload more." She rubbed her chin as she moved around the map, examining the three sites from all angles.

"I know," I agreed. "The thing is that we can't build too many mana converters in one site as it'll draw powerful monsters and drain the area of mana, right?"

"Yeah?"

"So we use that!" I stabbed a finger down on the civic center. "We take the issue, and we make it a strength! We have access to lures—I've seen them mentioned in the research options—so we use it! We make *this* our castle…we make the other sites safe as can be, but we make this one a prize that everyone wants to capture!"

"A trap," she said slowly, nodding her head. "We make the walls as hard as can be, and we turn the whole place into a collection point for mana, then we turn it into a death trap. The raiders and monsters and all the others will come, thinking this is the prize…"

"And all they'll find is us," I growled. "We'll use *them* to train our forces. We'll make the dungeon that everyone thinks of a massive trap that slaughters everyone who comes inside, layers upon layers of beasts, of traps, and more."

"And all they'll find at the very end—"

"Is the dungeon resetting, and they'll have to go again." I grinned at her. "We make it so that we don't have to go hunting the raiders and monsters. Instead, we set up the lures and spread the word, and *we let them come to us!*"

"Rather than us having to hunt down and assault the raiders' bases, they'll come to us, and we can mop them up," she agreed, energized. "What about the converters, though? What if they destroy them?"

"We make them in safe areas," I said. "We make walls of layered titanium…or whatever we can, anyway. Let's face it…if we can make the converters in there? We just upgrade when we can. We don't need to create paths for the assholes, and we can literally seal the doors with whatever the walls are made of with a little bit of notice."

"So we make paths that lead inside, and then sink underground for the dungeon. We make a killing ground, we gain the mana from them dying, and we use it to train our forces…"

"We can stock the site with disposable warriors. They die? No problem. As they get more experience and level up, we absorb their pattern and spin up more, or march them out and replace with 'blanks' but we do it here!" I said, getting even more excited. "We let the raiders smash their way inside, let them brave the dungeon, and if they survive?"

"We reset it." She grinned. "If they manage to fight their way out of there, then—"

"Then they find us, having marched all the new, fully armed, and upgraded versions of the defenders right back at them," I finished. "We slaughter them, all of them, and the freshly summoned army takes the old one's place as defenders."

"We literally get to earn the mana we need, and clear out the gangs, all at once," she said musingly. "But how do we convince the gangs to attack? I mean, the monsters I get, sure, the lures, but…"

"We tell everyone that's where we make our weapons and so on. Maybe make a field or two as well, make it look like all they need to do to get the farms and the weapons is to kill all of us."

"That's—" She broke off. "What about normal people? I mean, not being an asshole here, but if Amy was starving and I thought that was our only option…"

"We give normal people the chance to join us," I said. "We use the park as a filter. People can join us through there. We 'ship' the food to them; due to the quantities, say we can't just make it all by magic…that's why we have the fields, after all."

"And once we're sure of them, they can come here, and learn the truth," she said slowly. "It won't last. Not forever. Word will get out."

"And that's fine." I grinned. "Because by the time word gets out? We'll have cleared the local area entirely. By then, some of the assholes will have fallen for it and been slaughtered. We make sure that we use the chance to build higher and higher, make the castle the public center of production, and it'll draw the idiots like flies…"

"What made you think of this?" she asked, and I shrugged.

"I made a fallback position for Mike and the others. I need to go back to it and finish it, but looking at it, it just makes sense."

"Okay, but why did you need to interrupt me now? You could have discussed this over dinner tonight."

"Because…" I said slowly, grinning and drawing the word out. "I need to add to your research list…and it needs to be high in it."

"Matt…" Aly growled, and I went on quickly.

"The influence generator nodes do literally what they say on the tin: they spread the dungeon influence quicker than the normal spread. With more of them, though, they'd massively increase the growth as we claim more land."

"I get that, but—"

"And the next level generates mana."

"Oh—" She cut off, clearly thinking. "So you're saying we make them like this, and they can generate more mana as well?"

I nodded. "Hence, I can't start making them as the normal ones, because we'd have to scrap them or upgrade them, and that's a waste of mana…"

"Damn," she grumbled. "I hate it when you're logical."

"It's pretty rare, if it helps."

"Usually it's just crazy bullshit," she agreed, sighing. "Okay, I'll stick this in, and get it done as quickly as possible. It's only ten thousand mana, so it shouldn't take too long."

"Crazy that, isn't it." I grinned at her. "Thinking of ten thousand mana as 'not that much' when a few weeks ago that was an insane number."

"Definitely." She sighed. "Right. Are you done? Can I go back to work now?"

"Yeah, sorry!" I grinned at her.

"No, you're not," she corrected. "Now, Matt?"

"Yeah?"

"Stop fucking about and get to work. We need the research areas building, we need the mana converters and generators, and I need my goddamn husband and the others to be safe. Get to it."

"Any advice on the order?" I grinned.

"Nope, that's your problem," she said airily, before striding off toward the research area again.

"Fuck," I grumbled under my breath, before straightening and heading back into our room, mind whirring. I summoned a can of an energy drink and downed it, before lying back down on the bed, staring up at the ceiling and sighing again.

Always, it was infrastructure versus everything else. I could make so much more, and much more efficiently, if I didn't have to keep switching to do other things, but…

I closed my eyes, sinking back into the dungeon, and went back to work.

CHAPTER EIGHTEEN

The next few days passed quickly. The dungeon grew steadily, even as the surrounding area was stripped. Buildings collapsed around the clock as more of the people who were originally carrying and collecting settled into their new roles, stripping and absorbing the mass around us.

The wall was extended around most of the new outer rim, although it was a lot lower than I wanted it in several places.

It was as much up as it was down when we did this. Closing off the old metro tunnels, the sewers, undergrounds of bars, and cellars—all of it took time, and masses of mana.

For every twenty thousand or so of mana we took in, we created a piece of infrastructure that created mana, be that one of the Air converters we seeded around the top of the outer wall, one of the Darkness in the cavern, or any of the other ones. The numbers climbed by the hour.

By the time we made it to the far northeast corner of Saltwell Park, we were up to three thousand, five hundred and seventy-five points an hour, or eighty-five thousand, eight hundred per day.

It was an *insane* amount. But as much as I wanted to keep building it up, I had to balance the books.

Mike and the others had come back bloodied and even lower on ammunition. One of the gangs, the smallest, but closest by, had been eliminated, and their survivors, prisoners, and victims were added to the park's residents or allowed to go their way.

We'd lost several of the new kobolds, but Aly had finished a better armor design for them, and we'd equipped them with repeating crossbows, shields, and spears for now.

We had to build a shitload more control point generators, as we were up to fifty advanced kobolds now. Four assassins had joined Karen, and were variously Sharon, Angela, Doris, and Audrey, for shits and giggles.

I fully intended to introduce kobold Sharon to evil piggy Sharon, having seen my old neighbor and her husband had indeed gotten into the dungeon somehow, and had been steadily complaining about "foreign food" and so on since getting in.

They'd also been pulling everything from illness, fainting attacks, stress, and PTSD to avoid having to work, while reporting others for not working hard enough.

I'd explained my plan for the civic center over dinner that first night after I came up with it, and after it was met with overwhelming approval, I was considering whether I needed a caretaker couple to live in the trap to make it look more realistic.

I kept telling myself that I was better than that, and then I'd see them somewhere out of the corner of my eye and contemplate summoning a goblin into their bed.

It was only the fear of what they might do to the poor creature that kept me from doing it.

The control point generators were up to two thousand, thanks in part to them being upgraded again, as were several others, including the influence generators.

They'd been dotted around the dungeon, one put in place at the very edge of the park, as visible proof that we'd made it there, and then six were made around the civic center, one in each corner of the middle "square." That came to four, and one in the middle of the left and right sides, as it looked when viewed from above.

That sounded a bit mad, but there was a pathway running in from the north and out of the south, so it seemed like overkill to claim that.

Instead, that layout allowed us to claim the central square quickly, moving the generators up from floor to floor until all four floors of the central building were done.

At that point, the generators were moved out to the top right square, with three generators on the north, and three on the east walls.

Working like this, and thanks to the massive influx of mana, we'd managed to claim a serious amount of the structure in a very short time.

The walls were undergoing a transformation now. Because we wanted it to be a trap, and yet still an attractive option for the raiders of the area, we'd decided not to go all out on the exterior.

Not publicly, anyway.

The walls were considerably thicker than they looked from outside. An extra layer of solid bronze, in a single panel, ran around what had been the inside of the old walls, then a solid sheet of stone, and then a nice plasterboard render over that, making the corridors look narrow.

The walls could probably withstand a jet hitting them now.

The windows were replaced as well. About half had been taken out altogether, with crude-looking stone packed across the outside. It'd take someone looking closely to see that the stones were packed together almost perfectly and were copied over, meter by meter, exactly.

The glass was replaced with new "glass." It was expensive, admittedly—a thousand mana per meter. But for glass a solid half-meter thick, that I couldn't chip with my hammer, it was worth it.

A quarter of the outside of the building had been converted when we reached the park, and secondary projects were shelved.

The dungeon had done well out of this time as well, the old Moot Hall having been replaced entirely by a simpler, and yet elegant building Kelly had found the plans for in the library haul.

It would have been a pain in the ass to create normally, and probably horrifically expensive, but as this was to be the official "heart" of the dungeon and our leadership, as well as the place that people thought of as the center of the dungeon…well, it needed to be shit hot.

She'd taken the plans for the Parthenon from Athens, and had done something that only airport lounge designers could approve of: she'd filled a massive section of this stunning marble building with offices and enclosed private sections.

The original structure was breathtaking, and cost a solid six hundred thousand to create. The thought of what I could have done with that, the numbers of creatures, the research? Every time I considered it, it made my balls shrivel in terror over the waste. *But...*

The result was a massive edifice that looked the part, even gleaming in the steady rain that fell practically round the clock at this time of the year.

Inside, we'd split the building into three sections of various sizes. One, that you saw when you first arrived, was the open-plan section. Massive pillars held a stunning ceiling high above, ornamental scrollwork and more.

There were front-facing offices and sections for people to come and just sit, nothing else, just a space away from others, where they could sit and watch the world beyond the pillars, somewhere. Despite my initial belief that it was frivolous, I quickly found it to be one of the best things about it.

There were sections with seats, mainly that other people brought, and rugs and more, with the gaps between the massive pillars of the Parthenon design being filled by thick glass. It created a warm, dry, and brightly lit place inside that quickly grew in popularity.

There were areas that children could play, and be taught in classrooms, where young parents could rest and those who had chosen to help look after the kids could gather. There was a space dedicated to an attempt at an indoor play area, one for the business of the people of the dungeon, as well as an area where coffees and bakery things were given out.

There were the council chambers for Clarissa and the others, as well as a secondary room right behind that, that held a Life converter and several comfortable couches, so that when they were working in the dungeon, they actually had somewhere to be rather than just laid in bed.

The second section, that took up almost a solid third of the overall structure, was the research section. Literally row upon row of research facilities, offices that were ready, even without very many working in them yet, but that Aly had apparently been *very* pleased with Kelly about.

The last section, and the smallest, was ours.

We had several council-type chambers, and what was intended to be a war room. A design we'd found in the system for a war room, off the barracks design that Aly had recently done as well, intending to clone some of its sections for the new apartments, had a table that was just amazing.

I'd read the description, and basically it allowed for real-time review of anywhere in the dungeon radius, plus half a mile out, a distance that was increasable through the sensor towers, drones, and upgrades.

It was also usable both in and out of the dungeon sense, so I could stand there insubstantial and use it, or physically, and it was the same.

Kelly had agreed, after much convincing, to take over running the dungeon creatures. Her Puppeteer skill had apparently been meant for more than she first realized, as within a day of taking up her new duties, her options for the next class, that she'd been putting off all this time, had changed, and damn, she took the new option with speed.

Rare Class:
Dungeon Mistress (1):

Dungeon Lords are whispered of, rumored, and often legendary figures, as much revered as reviled, depending on who is speaking. This class controls the vitally important Dungeons of the Multiverse, and depending on their choices, they rise to either slaughter millions or uplift entire civilizations.

The Dungeon Mistress, a sub-set of the Dungeon Lord Class, is tasked with the maintenance and guidance of her master's minions, gaining bonuses both for the dungeon productivity and the individuals who call the dungeon home.

Dungeon Mistresses gain the following one-off bonuses at the first rank of their specialization:

- + 1 to Intelligence for all Dungeon Minions
- + 1 Random Dungeon Improvement (Level Appropriate)
- + 1 Random Dungeon Blueprint (Level Appropriate)

The dungeon improvement was actually cool, although nobody really understood what it was for. Only Kelly had seen the details, and she made us promise not to ask.

It was placed in the weirdest possible place: in the center of the overall outdoor claimed area. It was surrounded by pillars, and had a domed roof overhead, but basically it was a giant fucking hot tub with cushioned sides and private sections.

It was also a bit weird because people had to walk out to it, so on any evening, it was full of people walking over in dressing robes and looking all uncomfortable as they tried to get used to the idea of outdoor bathing in Newcastle in autumn.

It was free, though, and it was quickly agreed that when we were able, we'd make covered walkways to and from it, as well as planting some nice trees and park benches and shit around it.

The dungeon blueprint was also useful, but not in the same way.

It was for a catapult, one powered by the mana of the dungeon, and that could be upgraded to fling darts.

The catapult wasn't the most useful; neither were the original designs. But as soon as Aly saw it, she practically had a breakdown, bursting out laughing, then she put her head in her hands and whimpered that she'd wasted so much time.

She'd refused to elaborate and had left the table we'd all been sitting around, returning to the research wing, after ordering me point-blank to "fix" the kobolds.

I had no clue how to do it, but for some reason the new advanced kobolds had been spawning without the research perks. Rather than the logical thing, which was that we wait until we get one with it—it was a random chance thing, after all—she'd taken it to mean that I'd broken the system somehow.

I'd spent serious time and effort, two days in fact, trying to create a goddamn mage class for the kobolds, and then, in bed one night, I'd smacked my head as it came to me.

I'd been damn lucky in creating the shaman class, and I'd not managed to repeat that with the advanced kobolds for some reason. I had killed two trying to make them, until it came to me that the similarities between our people and the kobolds meant there was another way to do it.

We'd then taken a focal orb, and had our resident cryomancer, Peter, cast his spell into it. The version we'd ended up with in the orb was Winter's Memory, and it was essentially an area of effect debuff. Anyone in the target area started to shake and move slower as the terrible cold sapped their strength.

Compared to spells like Thunderbolt, it was shit. Peter almost burst into tears when I read out the details, he was that embarrassed. He'd actually been relegated to making things for the kids to play with and beer coolers mainly so far, as he had nothing that was really combat effective. But the focus orb had it now, and that was what I needed.

I'd given it to a new kobold—Juliet, the fourth we'd summoned for this, and the only one with reasonable Water affinity—and she'd been given the orb, before being sent out with Beta.

A day later, we had our first kobold cryomancer, and her spells—Frostbite, Icy Blade, and Chill—were much more useful.

She'd been absorbed, sadly, but now we had access to ice mage kobolds. With more soon to come.

We'd all gathered around the table in our private council area and planned the next phase, the lure. This wasn't the monster lure, nor was it the one for the raiders. Both of those were designed to make the civic center a real target, one that was too tempting to say no to.

No, this was the lure for the humans, for the regular people of the area, who just wanted some goddamn help, somewhere safe to live and a roof over their heads.

This was the accommodation block, and *damn* it was going to be big.

We'd had to reinforce the ground under it specially, literally filling it all in and turning the entire section into solid stone, broken up only by the crisscrossing supports that were put into it, essentially huge girders.

We'd literally eaten away at the ground, laying in massive girders and then sealing them over again, much in the same way that rebar was used to strengthen concrete. But it was over a square that made up a twenty-three-thousand-meter plot.

That was as far as we'd gotten, the sheer reinforcement of the ground for the proposed high-rise.

It was decided we'd build it as a pyramid in the end, after much goddamn arguing, and mainly because none of us were architects.

Basically, the world was only likely to get weirder, so we decided that building the first five floors of the high-rise as a square was a good start. Each level would be solidly built, massively reinforced, and overly designed to deal with pretty much anything. Literally.

After the first five floors, there would be a step inward of twenty meters, and that would run all the way around the outside, providing a reasonably safe area that people could have chairs outside, bars and restaurants and so on. Then the next set of five levels would be built, with that reduced floorplan, creating a stepped pyramid.

The first floor, or ground floor, was going to be a mixture of accommodation, a giant indoor play area for the kids, a school, and a canteen that was easily accessible.

The next level was all the larger family blocks, essentially three- to five-bedroom plots, all centered around a central private living area, with at least two bathrooms each. Add in the corridors and lifts and more, and that was still a decent size.

Then the next floor was given over to two and three-bedroom versions of the same accommodation. No kitchens were included in any of these designs, as frankly why the hell bother. They would be a fire risk as well as a storage nightmare, and when people were hungry? They had the canteens and soon—I hoped—restaurants and bars.

Next came the single floor. Literally an entire floor given over to single bedroom and living room designs, and between these four floors, after some give and take, we'd figured out we'd have space for around two thousand people.

The fifth and final floor of the "first" batch, and forming the last section of the intended repeating pattern, was the park.

This would be a generous-sized indoor area, with Life and Nature converters dotted around, grass, trees, and play areas mixed in with areas for people to relax in a secure zone.

Yes, it was indoor; yes, the ceiling was thirty foot—the highest of the floors, admittedly—to allow the trees to spread as well. It was never going to replace the natural urge to be outside, but, with the lighting that the dungeon provided for the indoor farms, this would enable the plants to grow, and it was warm and pleasant, as well as safe.

I'd been all for building more accommodation. Hell, I'd been thinking of making the rooms like ours were, down in the bloody basement of the dungeon— basically square boxes with a shower and toilet, a sleeping area and storage, and that was it.

I'd been told that although, yes, that was all people *needed*—and more, in fact—it wouldn't attract people, not the survivors we needed.

Being realistic, as the months turned to years, the survivors of humanity would be split into two groups: prey and predator.

Hopefully, most of those who were "predators" wouldn't be. They'd have the potential, but would work for the betterment of the whole.

A lot wouldn't, though, and a new age, one of the tooth and the claw was dawning.

People needed to fight and grow strong, or grow in other ways. Ashley, for example, might be able to make a potion that would save a life soon. Finn might be able to make armor that would protect people to an unbelievable degree.

The issue was that for them to do that, they needed to be safe and secure. They needed the materials, and they needed to not be battling all day, every goddamn day.

The way the world was now, the "prey" like the crafters, who were desperately needed, would level far slower than the "predators." That meant that the warriors would always be more powerful.

Once these people realized they could set up their own little fiefdoms, they needed a damn good reason not to. Many wouldn't want to; they'd want to live in a community, to pull together rather than apart.

Others wouldn't, though.

We'd lose some of those we trained and developed; that was inevitable. Some, of course, we'd lose to deaths as they leveled. But eventually some would want to move on and set up their own villages and towns.

The best way to combat that was to make sure that we as a settlement were attractive beyond anywhere else.

Just like that, we were back to the "lure" for humanity.

The accommodation block would be massive; the intention was forty or fifty floors in the end.

That didn't sound that big, compared with the monumental skyscrapers of the major cities, pre-fall. The difference was, this was going to be bigger than an entire city block, and solid.

It'd be one of the largest buildings ever completed. Sure, loads had been taller, especially in the Arab Emirates and the USA. But in terms of sheer goddamn size?

The lure was going to be massive, and solid in a way none of those places could ever claim. The reinforced glass that would cover the windows, with solidly reinforced walls and more, would make damn sure the entire place was as "monster-proof" as it was possible to be.

People would be able to have lives, and enjoy themselves, rather than just surviving.

We'd make sure that families could grow, and that those who risked their lives outside knew their families were safe.

People would see the lure from miles away, especially at night, when lit, and they'd know that they were safe here.

That did increase the risk of raiders trying to get inside, but that was why we were going to make it look like all our weapons and food came from the civic center.

After all, who wouldn't try to take that first?

We were damn pleased with the plan, and the general speed things were happening was enough that we started to feel more than a little confident that we'd cracked it, and now that the park was gathering up more mass for us, that we could get everything done, hopefully before the next real monster or raider encounter.

That, of course, was when the shit hit the fan.

CHAPTER NINETEEN

I was at Saltwell Park, sitting with Barry and his people. Mike and Chris were with me, as well as two of the awoken advanced kobolds, Sharon the assassin and Kilo the cryomancer, when the door was almost smashed from its hinges. A scruffy guy in a battered old army jacket staggered in, gasping for breath.

"Jake?" Barry asked, almost falling off his chair, having been leaning back on two legs rather than all four. "Dammit, man, catch your breath. What's happening?" Barry growled, getting to his feet.

"The...wall..." he got out, chest frantically heaving as he pulled in great lungfuls of air. "Attack..."

"WHERE!" Barry roared, snatching up an assault rifle and glaring at the man.

"South..." Jake wheezed.

With that, Barry was off running. We followed along, Chris and Mike right behind me, Sharon having already vanished, and Kilo loping along as if it were all just too damn easy.

We were in Barry's "official" residence, the Gothic-style mansion at the heart of the park. He'd been living between a cot on the floor in a backroom and his home a half mile away until recently. With the loss of his wife, he'd moved a slightly larger bed into that room, and now lived there full-time.

We'd been winding him up about living in the lap of luxury just before Jake burst through the door, and as we raced down the stairs, I shook my head at just how bad it really was here.

The building had been extended through the damn hard work of a group of bricklayers, and the small canteen downstairs was now large enough to feed more than a hundred at a time.

Still, though, it was hardly luxurious, and the more time I spent there, the more convinced I became of Barry's point of view. The accommodation for his people needed to be made, and damn soon.

With no electricity, limited food, and basically being down to candles, which were also almost all used up, the people here were genuinely struggling to get through day-to-day.

I didn't blame those who had given up all hope.

We'd been shipping in a steady stream of food, but until now, working to reach the park, I'd been convinced that was enough, as we looked after the land inside our walls first.

Now, as we burst out into the iron-grey afternoon, the steady drizzle falling, I saw the lines of hungry people waiting for their turn in the rough canteen, the disheveled masses, the kids who were scruffy and standing listlessly...

I cursed myself.

I'd seen some of them when I arrived, but it'd still been dark then, and I'd managed to convince myself that the people wandering listlessly around were the "lost" ones that Barry had mentioned. People who were broken by the fall of mankind, and the events that had come since, and were reduced to basically whiling away their lives, with no interest in anything beyond that.

I was wrong, though; I saw that as I ran past.

Here and there were the lost, but most of these people, filthy and dispirited, were the damn "normal" ones. These were the people who were willing to help, if not the "elite" that actually went out and fought, and got the best rations and so on.

No wonder when Barry had brought people to my compound none of them had wanted to leave, and we'd had so many asking to bring their families.

I raced past them with Barry and the others. A dimly seen shadow nearby made me think that Sharon was keeping up, just staying out of sight, and we splashed on.

The south side of the park wasn't that far. The walls that Barry had built reared up under the trees ahead, and as we drew closer, we saw what had Jake running for help.

The wall was being heavily attacked. Dozens of Barry's people raced toward it from all over, sloshing through the deep puddles and dodging the panicked workers who'd been tending the fields here, as they ran in the opposite direction.

The "wall" was a pathetic thing compared to ours, and certainly compared to the damn walls that people would have around here soon, if I had my way.

They were mainly wood, for a start, fifteen foot at the highest—closer to ten most of the time—with a narrow walkway on the inside, and occasional gates cut into them, with someone every dozen meters or so watching over the far side.

Now the wall shook under the weight of the people atop it, with easily thirty people battling back and forth on a surface that shouldn't be holding ten.

Barry's people were fairly easy to spot, all eight of them. One fell as we closed, stabbed from behind by the swarming attackers.

Where Barry's people were dressed in long coats, some with hats, and umbrellas, many without, and wearing scruffy but serviceable clothing, most of the attackers were anything but.

They wore a mixture of clothing, but all of them had their heads shaved, and had been painted red for some reason.

Several had half-skull designs tattooed or painted over that, and one, a massive guy with a mixture of bike leathers and fishing waders on, with what looked like an entire Goth's "starter outfit" worth of spikes and leather stuck on, had his entire head tattooed with a full skull.

"These assholes!" Barry growled, calling out to us all as we closed with them. "They know we're low on ammo, so they send their weakest and stupidest at us in waves…There'll be another wave incoming, but no clue where…"

"I'll spread the word!" one of Barry's lieutenants, a scout sniper called Jimmy, who'd fallen in with us, called, before turning and running for the reserves.

"Mike!" I called over, and he glanced at me, waiting. "Fuck his day up." I nodded ahead.

"Got it," Mike agreed, slowing, then bracing against the remains of a metal fence that had run around an old parking area. He adjusted his sights, once, twice, then fired a single round as we closed with the group.

The guy with the tattooed full skull had been waving his arms, and exhorting his people, clearly telling them to kill everyone, when Mike's present arrived.

The high-velocity round took the guy just above the right eye, smashing through the bone and out the back of his skull. The body toppled backward silently, as the gunshot rang out.

"Barry…" I growled, as we closed the last few dozen meters. "How many bullets have you got left?"

"Fifty-seven," he admitted with a grunt of effort, before slowing and lifting his rifle, firing off two quick shots at someone about to stab one of Barry's people in the back. "Fifty-five!"

"That better be each," I muttered, before shrugging out of my coat, letting it flap wetly behind me, before—Sod's Law—it landed in a fucking puddle.

I took a deep breath, caught between anger and sadness at the deaths, and a deep joy that bubbled up in me each time I did this.

I summoned the storm, feeling the lightning, the thunder; all of it rolled through me as I kicked off the restrictions of gravity, and I flew.

The hammer in my right hand was enough to identify me to most people now, as was the armor—repaired, but still desperately in need of an upgrade. But the real way that people knew the Lord of the Storm had arrived was when I landed in the midst of the attackers atop the wall, and let rip with a lightning bolt that sent three of them flying and screaming in agony.

I'd done that with the left, and blocked a strike with a spear with my hammer. Then I recognized the spear's design as one of mine, and I batted it aside again, before grabbing the wielder by the throat and yanking him in close.

I headbutted him, then tossed him behind me to fall the fifteen feet to the concrete, before throwing my hammer at the next guy in line.

The wide head of the hammer slammed into his face; the bones deformed and broke, teeth shattering as he tumbled backward, screaming in pain.

With both hands free, I sent lightning bolts flashing into the darkness under the trees ahead. The milling dozens of people who had been trying to scale the wall screamed as they panicked, easily turning the tide…until the first shots rang out.

I'd been focused on the masses before me, and wondering where the second wave would come from, as Barry had said was their style.

What I'd not considered was that instead of the feint that they "always" tried, this could be the real attack, and Barry had just sent his people off searching for it everywhere else.

The burst of gunfire came from farther back. A half dozen rounds hammered into the wooden palisade around me and into my armor.

The bronze plates and the overlapping scales had been expensive, and at first, they'd also been goddamn heavy and a pain in the arse. They paid for themselves three times over in that heartbeat, though, as three bullets landed, two on my chest and one over the left bicep.

The plates of solid bronze deformed slightly, deflecting the two on my chest, staggering me backward, and making me grunt. The one on my left bicep numbed the arm, breaking the scales and tearing a furrow across the flesh as it flashed onward, fortunately not managing to go deep.

I snarled in fury, running forward and leaping off the edge of the wall as a dozen more opened fire. The blast swept the top of the wall clear of life, both our side and theirs, before they fired indiscriminately into their own people, determined to get me.

I'd landed hard, grunting as my right foot came down on a flailing body, and my left foot between someone else's chest and upper arm. My eyes were still adjusting, but I couldn't wait, and threw both hands forward, letting loose with a pair of lightning bolts.

They ruined everyone's vision in the dimly lit area equally. One of them hit a gunner head-on—literally, it hit her in the face; her eyes popped as the liquid was superheated, the teeth detonated, the bones blasted apart—and as she fell backward, her finger twitched reflexively, and she emptied the magazine into the backs of several of her unarmed companions.

The second missed any gunners, but hit a sapling and discharged into that, making it explode and sent wood shards in all directions, like a claymore going off.

I crouched, about to fly, when the man on his back to my right, with my right leg between his arm and side, grabbed me, and stabbed me in the fucking leg.

He was screaming something at me, something about his daughter and making me pay, as the narrow-bladed dagger made it through the outer leathers. The tip sunk in just above and behind my knee, before he dragged it sideways, severing entire muscle groups and making me cry out in pain.

That changed things. The riflemen who had leapt aside under my blasts rolled and came back to their feet, stepping out from behind trees and pouring fire into their people, determined to kill me.

I collapsed sideways, hitting the ground and crying out over the pain, before grabbing the guy who had stabbed me and dragging him between me and the incoming fire.

He grunted, shuddering as he was hit repeatedly, dying in a hail of incoming fire, even as the one I'd landed on first to my left threw herself at me.

Her head, like the others, was shaved, painted bright red, and the madness in her eyes was terrible to see. She hit me, shoving me sideways and into a puddle, screeching and continuing to hit me. Bullets flew all around us; she swept up a rock and slammed it down atop my helm.

The helmets that Aly had made for us were similar in style to the ancient hoplite ones, upgraded heavily with padding and a special glass that kept it from fogging up in the eye slits.

All of that, though, was of limited comfort when she screamed and hammered a goddamn rock into the side of it, as there was only so much force they could mitigate. And she was clearly insane, going all out on beating me to death, while her friends shot everyone.

I hissed in pain, twisting on my side and lashing out, left fist aimed for her, trying to get her off me, despite that arm being numb…when another bullet hit it, this time my left hand, impacting the curled fingers of the fist.

They snapped, of course.

The gauntlets were good; the distributing nature of the plates meant that all four fingers were broken, rather than a hole being blown through my fucking hand and onward, fingers raining down in bits around me.

It totally screwed me getting her off me though, and she hit me again, and again.

I twisted and punched her in the stomach with my right, drawing the lightning through me, feeling it going to work to repair the damage, even as someone laughed nearby, shouting out to everyone to hold their fire.

I looked up. The filthy figure, stripped to the waist, wore what looked like a fake bearskin crudely made into a pair of trousers, and the now familiar tattooed full skull, with a red and white paint job this time.

He stood over me, an assault rifle pointed squarely at my helmet.

"Stop!" he bellowed. "Every 'un stop, or ah'll kill 'im!"

I glared up at him, before letting myself lay back in the puddle, spreading my hands to show I was unarmed. I gritted my teeth and cursed how goddamn slow the others were these days.

"Take 'is helmet off!" the skull said to the woman, who'd started giggling around hissing indrawn breaths that suggested I'd managed to break a rib or two at least.

She did as he asked, or she tried to, tugging at it, and then shoving, before smacking my head off the concrete.

"It won't move!" she complained.

"There a catch?" he asked us both.

I nodded slowly, then grunted as she shoved my head back, peering up and underneath, spotting the chin clasp and trying to undo it.

"Got it!" she shouted triumphantly. The jagged edge of one nail tore at my skin as she yanked and pressed at it. "Dammit…it's tight, too small…"

"That something she's told you a lot, isn't it?" I asked, my voice muffled by the helmet.

"Eh?" Skull glared at me.

"That it's too small." I grinned up at him as she pulled the helmet off and tossed it aside. "Hey, you get mud in that, and I'm going to stop playing nice," I warned her, seeing the way the darkness around them shifted.

"Shut it, fool!" he snarled, kicking me in the head, then looking around at the forest as the others moved up to surround us. "Right! Open the gate an' surrender…or ah'll kill 'im! Ah mean it!"

"You dumb fuck," Barry called out from behind the wall.

"Eh? Ah've got yer boss, right? Surr—"

"I said, 'You're a dumb fuck,'" Barry called out again. "First off, I'm the boss of the park, not him."

Skull stared down at me, frowning, before looking back as Barry went on.

"Secondly, I called you a dumb fuck, because you all bunched together around him. I've seen that man do shit you can't believe. If he'd not done them? You'd all be begging for your lives right now."

"Ah'm in charge 'ere…" Skull said, and I laughed.

I just couldn't help it.

"Dude, you don't know what—"

He pulled the rifle back to stomp on my face, slamming his boot down once, then again. My nose broke; blood and mud covered my face. He pulled back and stared down at me, expecting to see me in pain and begging for mercy. Instead, he saw grim-faced, bloody anger.

"Sharon," I said loudly, pausing to spit blood free of my mouth, and running my tongue over my lips as I rolled more lightning around inside myself. "Fuck him up. And make it *hurt*."

He opened his mouth, clearly about to say something, when the assassin kobold—Sharon—materialized behind him. Two blades tore across his biceps, severing them and glancing off the bones, before he was dragged back. She went around behind him and pistoned forward into his kidneys.

She'd slid up behind him, her gifts as an assassin making the others ignore her until the time was right.

Then, as he screamed and staggered back, his arms falling useless and the rifle clattering to the ground, Kilo stood up on the wall, letting loose with Chill, a weaker, but still useful crowd control AOE. Chris and Mike rose as well, opening fire.

In a split second, the tables had turned entirely.

The majority of the skulls had been staring, open-mouthed, at Kilo. A tall, draconic-looking kobold seemed to suddenly appear from nowhere. A sudden blast of the arctic's icy breath rolled out, making the soaking wet, half-dressed, drugged, and more than half drunk lunatics shiver in terror at the blue-tinged figure that hissed and gestured at them, flanked by heavy fire.

I grabbed my helmet from where it was laid to one side, and smacked the woman who'd been straddling me in the side of the head with it, sending her flying to the ground to lay unmoving, unconscious or killed outright.

I forced myself to my feet, spitting some more blood out, and dragged my helmet back on.

The enemy riflemen, mainly carrying old hunting rifles, with a few assault rifles scattered here and there, were being slaughtered by Chris and Mike. Barry clambered up into view to laugh as he opened fire as well.

His people rallied and raced inward to the wall, thinking to climb up and join him, when a fresh scream rang out from deeper in the woods.

A new figure staggered out—short, confused, clutching at his head. And strapped to his body...

"Explosives!" I shouted, seeing the thickly packaged mass, and guessing at the worst-case scenario as the man—no, the *boy*; he looked barely fifteen—looked up, seeing me and the wall.

He hollered in fury and hatred, then sprinted forward, arms windmilling as he frothed at the mouth, screaming unintelligible shit.

"Take him down!" I roared, pointing.

Mike switched fire from the last couple of idiots who were trying to grab the guns of the dead, and shot at him.

Bullets seemed to glance off him, staggering him slightly, but that was it.

I cursed, thrusting my right hand forward. I fired off a lightning bolt, and accepted that I was going to set the bomb off. But at least it'd be far enough back that—

The lightning hit the fucker, and split.

It flowed around a bright-blue orb, some kind of shield that enveloped him, then hit a tree in the distance. It exploded with a burst of light and illuminated the area around it…as well as the forces creeping through them as I stared, open-mouthed.

The kid raced on, leaping over the fallen dead; bullets slammed into the shield and sent ricochets off in all directions, before it gave out.

The final two shots took him down. One hit his right shoulder and half spun him from his feet; the second took him in the side of his head as he tried to hurdle another body.

He fell, arms flailing as a bright roll of glowing light flowed across the outside of the package strapped to his body, and I spun, shouting up to the others who still stood atop the wall.

"Move!" I roared. "Get back!"

It was too late. The body hit the ground, flopping and rolling bonelessly, coming to a halt for all of half a second, laid facedown in a muddy puddle. Lines of glowing embers flowed across the packages strapped to him. Then they detonated.

They'd been packed full of some kind of explosive, then marbles, nails, screws, and tacks packed atop them. As they went off, a massive hole in the wall appeared, even as the defenders were scythed down by the improvised door knocker.

I was picked up and thrown, end over end, tossed aside as if by the hand of an angry god. The sound of trees being shredded filled the air.

My back slammed into something hard, metallic, and I bounced off, falling to the ground and hitting with a solid smack, rolling a few feet. I tried to breathe, my body screaming at me as the pain of a dozen and more minor wounds made themselves known.

I lifted my right hand, shakily, blinking in pain, then hissed as the thing that blurringly blocked my view finally resolved. I wrapped my fingers around the head of a brass-coated woodworking screw, and twisted it, drawing it out of the glass.

It had literally been embedded into the glass right over my eyeball, and it'd gone deep enough that I had to work to get it out.

It would have undoubtably killed me, had I not been wearing my damn helmet. I snarled in pain and anger as I rolled onto my side, forcing myself up to all fours. I circulated my mana through my body, bones snapping into place and crap forced back out of my flesh.

The ground shook and I turned my head, just in time to see a huge figure of a man, easily as wide as I was tall, heavily muscled, and wearing fucking short-shorts, just as he drew back and kicked me in the side.

I was sent flying again, a half dozen feet through the air. I landed, rolling over and over again, driving more of the damn nails and shit in deep again.

"S…*cough*…Sharon!" I forced my words out as the figure closed on me again. "GET BETA!" I roared to the kobold, knowing she'd be in stealth somewhere close.

I crossed my wrists, taking the next kick on them and sliding back a few feet, before forcing myself to my feet. I'd seen the forest behind the kid, and I could see it now behind this dickhead.

This wasn't a raid.

This was a full-on invasion.

CHAPTER TWENTY

"Come on then, dickhead," I growled, rolling my shoulders and looking up at the towering figure before me. I stood around seven foot now, solidly muscled, and could have had a career as an underwear model, had I looked like this before the fall.

This guy, though?

He looked like he'd been auditioning for bear wrestling and probably making porn afterward that catered to very specific tastes. He would have been walking up and down a muscle beach in America, stealing people's lunch and flexing all day, getting crowds of people going ooooh and aahhhh all the time.

I grinned at him as he stared down at me and flexed his shoulders, then tensed his biceps up.

"So…" I called up at him, too angry to even play at tactical shit, and yet too dumb to stay silent. "Come on then—how the hell do you wipe your ass?"

His eyes opened wide in disbelief. Obviously, he was used to fear, not contempt from the people he faced.

The last few bones popped back into place for me; my lightning dropped down to a more manageable level and I let out a sigh.

He lifted one hand, gesturing at me, and made my point for me in the way that his arms arched out and around from his sides. The massively overdeveloped muscles made him almost impossible to stop…but shit at anything that required any aptitude beyond overwhelming power.

Whatever he was about to say to me, no doubt starting with "little man" or something equally pathetic, was cut off, as rather than play his game, I lifted my hand and clicked my fingers.

He didn't even get off a scream as I stepped forward, planting my palm over his heart and shoving hard. His body collapsed; steam erupted from his ears, eyes, mouth, and nose, as the Incinerate spell went off in the middle of his brain.

I growled to myself as I saw the mass streaming forward, and into the breach.

I'd used Lightning, as I always did.

I used it, and when I came up against something I'd not seen before, I'd frozen up, stunned.

I should have summoned Incinerate in the fucker's brain or his spine as soon as I saw him. Hell, if I'd set his bomb off back there in the forest? It'd have shredded their side!

Instead, thanks to my stupidity, Chris and Mike were down, Kilo too, and, for all I knew, Barry.

I snarled, kicking off and racing toward the mass, summoning lightning and firing a bolt into the middle of the swarm of enemies. It punched into one of the figures, sending him careening into another and spreading the joy, thanks to the wet flesh in close proximity.

I wanted to go all out. I wanted to summon an Atomic Furnace in the middle of them, see how many of them survived that fucker, let alone the bleed out of the heat that would spread. But even with the way I'd been using my mana and after the massive increases in it lately, I was down to half already.

I might have enough for one use of it, maybe—my fucking kingdom for a wiki—but I might not as well, and then it'd either use my HP, or it'd fail, and I'd be fucked either way.

No, this needed to be done old school.

I leapt forward, sprinting and powering myself with my lightning rolling through my veins, before dropping and sliding across the ground. I swept up the assault rifle where Skull had dropped it, and planted my foot, popping myself back upright up at close range with the streaming mass racing to the hole.

I'd clearly been dismissed by the majority after the man mountain had run at me, and the widening of eyes at the sight of his dead body was almost comical.

It would have been, if not for the fucking state of some of these people.

Several who turned to face me had filed-down teeth. One of them hissed, lunging at me with her mouth open and her fingers reaching, her nails jagged and filthy.

I shot her in the face.

The sight of her falling back seemed to jolt a few of the closer ones out of their madness, staring at me in shock, until my thumb flicked the selector from single shot to full auto.

I pulled the rifle back into my shoulder, settling it comfortably, and I opened fire.

The chatter of the rifle, and the shoving back of the stock against my shoulder, was over in seconds, and the mass before me thinned dramatically.

Realistically, I killed maybe ten or twelve of them, before the magazine clicked empty, the charging lever locking.

The effect on the advancing mass, though, was anything but ignorable. They screamed. Some of them turned heel and ran away; others shoved friends and comrades aside, desperately racing for the breach in the wall.

Still more ran at me, and I felt the first "real" attack incoming as well, as the pressure dropped insanely. My ears popped and breathing suddenly got harder as the world twisted.

Bodies lifted; rain floated sideways and back up; dirt lifted in random waves from the ground. I planted a foot on a rising body, kicking back as gravity went weird.

For a second, I thought I'd make it out of the bubble—my left hand felt different as it passed through something that felt like a feather being drawn across my wrist…

Then I was thrown upward and through the trees, rocketing up at an insane speed, the world around me whipping past.

Branches shattered, fragments and splinters driven in all directions as I spun, end over end, thrown up into the night sky. A veritable river of water flowed around and coated the outside of the bubble as I flashed upward, still picking up speed.

As close as the edge of the dungeon was, I felt it—the outermost possible finger of claimed space. And even as the air was sucked from my lungs, I reached out, betting entirely that whoever was controlling this wouldn't be able to hold on much longer, and I was going to make the most of the chance I had.

I slid into the dungeon sense, checking and finding seven thousand, four hundred mana available.

I checked the available control points, finding we had a few hundred left, and started spamming wraiths. They might not be hugely efficient, but they were terrifying.

I felt Kelly's attention drawn by the sudden spawning of "her" creatures, and I reached out, sinking everything that had happened into a single, high-speed burst of information, as well as my intentions for the wraiths. I let her have it all, and I felt her savage agreement, as well as a demand I go fuck shit up, which I totally agreed with.

Then I was back in my body, fighting for air as the speed finally dropped off. I passed through the clouds, the last tentative grip of the magic that had been holding me letting loose as I did so.

I exited them slowly, most of my momentum lost by this point, and for a brief second, I hovered above them, seeing the ruffled blanket of grey before me as the distant setting sun bathed the top layer in reds and violet.

Then, gasping in huge breaths as the bubble failed and air flooded in around me again, feeling my heart steadying, I lifted my arms out to the sides, and fell slowly backward.

Speed.

That's what I needed. My people could be dead or dying below me, and I'd done what I could. Hopefully Kelly's puppeteer class would make a difference in the fight below. But right now? I needed to earn her and Barry's people the time they needed to fight back.

I dove, the gentle sunset being lost as I sank back into the clouds, twisting around and pushing harder and harder as the storm rose in me. The clouds around me responded sluggishly as I tore through them. The water of the building squall reacted and followed me as the winds rose, and I pulled on them instinctively.

Speed.

The feeling of the wind all around me changed. Rather than pushing against them, I was being pushed along. I was being guided, lifted and buoyed along as the rain shifted, falling in around me.

The temperature changes of the highest reaches of the storm flowed around me; the gentle rain that built around me followed me joyfully, changing as more and more of the clouds shifted.

The change, as clouds began not only to release the rain as they had been, but to actively push it out, was stunning. The thousands of individual raindrops were coated in the sharp, gleaming frost of the stars as the cold of the high places followed in my wake.

I burst out of the far side of the clouds, driving forward at a speed that would have made Maverick need a change of underwear, and lightning built around me, illuminating me as a falling star.

They were clear to me then, from on high.

A handful of figures were fighting around the breech, trying to hold the line as they were hit from all sides by mainly poorly armed people.

The people who had managed to get inside were racing toward the deeper areas of the park, even as our people fell back, panicked.

Guards were running desperately, stripped from the other walls and hurled at the breech, racing forward into probable death.

There were waves of wraiths, flowing forward in two lines of ten each, taking up station in the air, ready to engage the fast-racing line of intrusion.

The mass of people who were bunched up around the breech, and the others to either side, who had brought clumsy ladders and more, raced up and over the walls, about to flank my people.

Finally, I saw the elite core of the enemy.

They were in the middle, protected on all sides by a group of at least two hundred *children*, chained together as human shields. In their midst walked a dozen men and women, full skeletons tattooed on their bodies.

They were a variety of colors—some red, some white, purple and more. The skeleton tattoos stood out starkly on all but one.

The last of these assholes was in the center. Carried on an attempt at a palanquin was Aaron, followed by the pair of massive triceratops he'd managed to animate.

He sat on his shitty palanquin—half draped over a fucking sofa, of all things, one that looked as if it'd been stolen from a furniture store's front window.

He had what appeared to be a damn cheap garden furniture cover erected over his head, held up by two quite beautiful people, a man and a woman on either side, standing naked.

They were soaked and shaking in the cold.

Aaron, the fat little fuck, lay back on the sofa, smiling around, clearly pleased with himself, surrounded by the terror and greed of his "peers," dressed as the undead and tattooed to show it.

I saw it all, and my blood boiled.

Mana was an issue. I knew instinctively I didn't have enough of it. I wanted to fucking murder each and every one of these tattooed fucks, slowly and with exquisite attention to detail…but I couldn't.

I had responsibilities.

I had a responsibility to the thousands of my people in the park, who were, even now, having screaming lunatics running at them, ravening and desperate to inflict fuck knew what horrors on them.

Adjusting my aim was hard. Rather than doing what I wanted and smashing down like a comet of justice from the heavens and landing atop Aaron and his friends, I aimed for just outside of the walls. Without the rolling tide of assholes, backing them up and pushing on my people, the wraiths and the guards might just have a chance to save everyone else.

No, I was going to slaughter these fucks, and in doing that, I'd get Kelly and her creatures the time to get ready as well.

I was running a risk, I knew, as I closed on the ground—a hell of a risk—not only that I could actually survive this, but that my people would be less fucked up by the outer edge of the incoming shower than the enemy would…

But as with all of my developing Storm powers, they were untested, unscientific, and driven by need, not planning and experimentation.

The clouds that I'd passed through hadn't just merrily waved me on my way; there'd been an *interaction*, the air twisting and surrounding me, buoying me up, and then pushing me along.

I twisted and flipped over, going from diving face-first, into landing on my feet, pushing upward hard with the storm.

The air that had been joyfully screaming down with me, twisting around to form visible tendrils of cloud, projected forward, forming a spike of partially solidified air. The thin, sharp air of the frozen heights cut through the thicker, almost muggy air lower down.

The result was a shock wave.

As the air carved ahead of me, and I suddenly pushed back upward, the interaction between the speed of displacement, the rapidly closing ground, the cold of the frozen rain and the slightly warmer air down here and, finally, my blasting out of storm-filled rage: it all combined into a single event of destructive magnificence.

I hit the ground hard, crouching and absorbing the force as best I could…and straightened easily, distantly surprised at the gentleness of my landing.

"Gentle" was about as far from the description of the world immediately around me as was possible, though. The shock wave was horrific to anyone standing close by…and I'd aimed for the center of the streaming, ravening group.

I'd seen, in the last split second before landing, that there were people directly below me; hell, they were packed shoulder to shoulder.

I'd even seen a face, a shaven-headed man looking up, with the orbital ridge of his head tattooed with Only God Can Judge Me, right before I landed.

Well, the First Lord of the Storm, a fledgling god of the first human pantheon, had come to play. And fuck me, did I judge him.

He was rendered down to a gritty jam.

Others in the immediate vicinity didn't fare much better, being picked up and thrown into the air, into the surrounding trees—which detonated into wooden fléchettes, killing dozens more—and hurled away from my landing site.

Bones were broken in their thousands, bodies literally torn into strips. Limbs blasted loose as rib cages were reduced to bone fragment-filled bags of blood.

At least seventy were killed almost instantly. Those who survived, hit by the mass of glittering icy daggers that followed me, had flesh carved from bone.

Screams rose into the air on all sides. Those who were killed on my arrival were the luckiest. I straightened fully, staring forward.

The mass of ice had shredded the trees overhead, curving around and around me, contained to a mere ten meters out in all directions from my flight path, then blasted outward by the shock wave of my landing.

The result was that dozens of massive oaks, a canopy that had sheltered and protected the ground here for hundreds of years, were reduced to kindling. The living attackers who were weaving around the massive trees fared far, far worse than the wooden behemoths had.

The clouds that had been drawn down into my slipstream had cleared a section of the sky directly overhead, bathing the area in the deepening red sunset, as trees fell, as blood cascaded from the air, fragments of bone and teeth being driven into the survivors of the attacking force.

I saw them then.

The mass was driven back, exposing the stunned, blood-covered faces of the gang members. And behind them, behind the cowering children bound by chains…

"YOU!" I bellowed, my voice carrying through the frozen stillness of the shattered evening air. "I gave you a chance!"

"You!" Aaron screamed in terrified hatred, scrabbling upright from where he'd fallen off his fucking sofa. "You're supposed to be dead!"

"I pissed on Dickless's army!" I thundered, staring at Aaron, knowing damn well that the information he'd given us in exchange for his life and freedom had been a trap. "I tore them limb from limb, and him as well!"

"Imposs…" he whimpered, before breaking off and screaming at his guards. "Kill him!" He stabbed his hands forward, roaring the orders to his supporters even as the massive triceratops behind him began to move. "Kill him, and I'll give you powers you can't imagine!"

The men and women on either side of him stared in shock, mouths hanging open as they contemplated their choices, and presumably, their chances of a long and fruitful life.

One turned and ran for it, clearly faster on the uptake than the others. Unfortunately, he was slower on the whole "examination of surroundings" skill, as he was within range of the triceratops on the left side.

It swung its head almost negligently. The multi-ton beast rammed its lowest and smallest horn, the one on its nose, into his stomach and ripped up and right, gutting him, before the tip slid up under the rib cage.

Then he was tossed into the air with a snapping of bones like wet twigs.

That made it clear. Either of us would happily slaughter all of them, and as they turned to face me, I fixed my gaze on one of them, who was reaching forward, looking wan and weak as he tried to activate an ability.

I felt the air shifting again, much as I had before. The gravity twisted as a fresh bubble formed…and I sneered, clicking my fingers ostentatiously.

The Incinerate spell wasn't stopped by anything—not distance, not shields, and certainly not any inkling of mercy on my side.

I made an example out of his gravity mage, knowing that Aaron had been doing the same with the runner, and rather than finish him off instantly, as I could have, the spell baked his brain and sent the soon-to-be corpse tumbling to the ground.

He screamed in agonized horror as his crotch was ground zero for a thousand degrees of burning fury.

The aluminum zip on his jeans glowed a bright cheerful red for a split second, then ran, turning molten as the fabric burst into flames. He collapsed onto the ground, screaming in agony, as superheated fluids and gasses boiled him from the inside, and I looked around at the hundreds of people watching me in horror.

"All of you, fuck off. Right now," I growled. My words hung in the air for long seconds…before I saw movement to my right, and twisted.

The figure that raced at me was clearly insane, and bare-ass naked. A red line was painted sideways from his left jaw to the right side of his forehead; his hair was long, greasy, and past his chin, then shaved on the other side.

He carried a hammer, a claw-hooked thing from an industrial store, and showed absolutely no fear.

I had a split second to consider.

Using magic on him would make an effect. It might be enough to break the remainder of their spirits…or it might be a waste. I had enough for two Incinerate or Lightning Bolts. That was it, and I damn well needed it.

I glanced back, planning to set fire to Aaron's head…but the fucker had vanished.

Another of his people—some of them clearly having leveled to the point they were getting real abilities—had cast a shroud of blackness over the group, and I cursed.

I couldn't waste the spell. I needed that mana to kill these dickbags.

The lunatic was only a few meters away from me, and swinging the hammer wildly, literally foaming at the mouth, and I spun to him, lunging forward.

It was as if my movement was a trigger. The mass that had been stunned into immobility until now suddenly moved as well. Like greyhounds after a fuckin' rabbit, they launched themselves at me, racing in.

I leaned aside, avoiding his swing—not easy for a man who nearly massed seven foot now—but the idiot was wild. I grabbed him by the throat, lifting him into the air, and powered him down, slamming the back of his head into the concrete with a sound like a melon being dropped from on high.

He spasmed; the hammer tumbled from a suddenly nerveless grip to clatter on the ground…before it was swept up by me and flung, end over end toward a figure racing at me, screaming.

It took them in the face. I had no clue as to their gender: the chest wrap covered any possible tits, and the shaven head, the tattooed face…

It could have been my ex-girlfriend, and I'd have never known.

It also didn't fucking matter anymore. They were attacking my people. They'd made a fatal mistake in that.

I ran at the nearest, screaming in bloodlust and fury, as the fight *really* got started.

They were coming from all sides, most of them covered in blood. The sheer insanity of what they'd been through, what they'd been forced to do to survive as members of Aaron's "gang" drove most of them mad with a mixture of self-loathing and the loss of any hope.

They came in waves, screaming, eyes wide and rage filled, as I leapt at them as well.

CHAPTER TWENTY-ONE

Gunfire still rung out behind me. The sound climbed steadily as more and more of the guards joined in, but the number of shots…

If I had time to be concerned, I'd have been very fucking concerned.

Guns rang out two or three times; shotguns fired more frequently than anything else; the sound of rifles died away as more screams rose. And then I was in too close to pay attention again.

The first figure before me swung a club—literally a length of wood two feet long, with nails driven through it—and I jumped back, then dove forward again.

It sailed past me. The effort he'd put into swinging it, and the closeness of his companion to his left, meant that she caught it in the stomach as she hacked at me with a meat cleaver.

The force of his blow, as well as the nails, driven into her stomach doubled her over. A wet, tearing gasp came from her as her momentum carried her on, tearing herself free.

I grabbed her wrist, yanking her around, using my augmented strength to drag her. I used her cleaver, dragging it deep as it chopped into his forearm, the radius and ulna snapping under the blow.

He screamed, and I brought my right knee up, releasing her wrist as I drove my knee into the back of his extended arm.

The bones split; the cleaver flew up as she released it. Her hand went instinctively to her stomach, and I caught it by the grip, chopping down into the back of her neck, then wrenching it free and slashing sideways.

I almost severed his head, I cut that deep into his throat. The blood spray covered us all, as more and more closed in. I lashed out with a hopping snap kick, left foot high, taking a man in the stomach as he ran, fists drawn back and looking ludicrous.

He doubled over, falling past me as I spun, pulling my leg back, and slashed at his back, cutting across his spine as he fell, screaming.

The fight was intense, close range, and bloody—more fists and swinging blades than anything else. I blocked using the armored plates on my forearms, my chest, and more.

I took multiple blows to the head. My helm shook them off as cries of pain rose from broken fingers. One leapt at me with a golf club, literally swinging for the fences.

It'd probably have been damn painful, had it landed. The wielder didn't take his surroundings into consideration, though, and another of his friends took it on the side of the head, a snapping of bone ringing out as the body collapsed to the ground, dead.

I grinned, punching another in the face, then flung the cleaver into the face of the golf-club wielder. The crunch of the blade sinking in and the muffled screech was lost as the first triceratops emerged from the blackness, barely three meters from me.

I leapt sideways, shoving off as I did so. My mana bottomed out, and I realized that I'd been using it unconsciously to boost myself, healing my wounds as I got them, and enabling me to punch harder than I should have been able to.

I landed hard, a half dozen meters away, hitting the concrete, a tree root having buckled it up and left a ridge. I rolled to my feet, disoriented at the sudden loss of mana.

The triceratops thundered on, uncaring as it ran over its "allies," stomping the living and the dying alike into the ground as multiple tons of reanimated creation tried to turn on a dime.

The ground was already shaking with the second's approach, and I forced myself upright, looking around, as a new figure appeared.

It wasn't the dinosaur, and I almost dismissed him…until he blurred closer. It was the dickhead in purple paint from Aaron's close coterie, and fuck, he was fast!

He was literally in close before I realized it. A blade glanced off the bottom of my helmet and left a long scratch on it, more by luck than design.

I staggered back, instinctively blocking the follow-up blow, but before I could wrap my arm around it and drag him in close, he'd moved again. Pain roared out as he drove forward, twin blades stabbing out into my left upper leg.

The attack was well aimed, punching into the thigh and sliding deep, avoiding the metal plates. The serrated back of the knives did more damage as he dragged them backward, cackling at the pain he knew I was feeling…

They caught, though. They caught in the thick material of the pants, the solid muscles of my leg, the padding that surrounded the armor—all of those things slowed him getting the blades out, and I grabbed onto his upper arm.

He wrenched the blades, trying to get them free, tearing them further loose, but although he'd clearly invested everything, including his class and abilities, into granting himself insane speeds…he'd put fuck all into his Strength and Constitution.

I punched him in the face, left hand clamped down tight on his upper right arm, keeping him there. I smashed my armored gauntlet into his face once, twice, and then a third time.

The third blow, well, his nose had been reduced to pavement pizza with the first; the second had cracked the surrounding bone. The third caved part of his face in, the orbits of his eyes deforming and more as I literally began to punch his teeth down the back of his throat.

The fourth blow ended his fight forever, as he spasmed uncontrollably. I shoved him back; his hands released the blades, clutching and spasming in the air as he collapsed onto the ground.

I staggered back a step, grabbing one of the knives and ripping it free. The blood surged up and out, as well as poured down my leg, happily seeping in to fill my goddamn boot.

Then I was hit from the side as a woman leapt onto me, slamming a rock down on my helm, giggling with glee.

I stabbed up on instinct, taking her under the ribs and driving the blade deep, tearing it left, then shoved at her, sending her falling free to the ground.

I limped, cursing, and looked around at the people circling me, wondering where the hell the fucking dinos were, as the darkness was banished suddenly. Aaron rode out of the forest to face me, still on his fucking sofa. A good hundred people stood between us as he was raised to the shoulders of the people holding him.

I glared at him, seeing the terrified children who heaved and sweated under the weight, and I straightened up, unwilling to let him see me in pain.

"We gave you a chance," I snarled, and he sneered at me.

"You tried to poison me, giving me the crappiest gear you had…But that was your mistake! I found my children…" He gestured around himself grandly. "I found them all, the older and the younger, cowering, afraid, and I freed them!"

"Oh, clearly!" I spat in contempt. "The kids look so fucking free, they're dancing…"

"Some refused." He shrugged. "Their parents had lied to them for too long, filling their heads with rubbish about 'fair' and 'right.' They wouldn't listen and tried to leave. They made it clear that while some would obey, others wouldn't, so I turned that to my advantage. Those who wish to be free and serve me gave me their children."

"You're a fucking knob," I said. "Making people give up their kids to be 'free,' but they have to serve you?" I spat on the ground and shifted, rolling my shoulders in my armor, and getting ready. "None of them had an issue with that?"

"Oh, some did…But then I lifted my followers up. I gave them powers! Powers to manipulate the world around them, and—"

"You didn't give them shit. You took advantage of their stupidity—"

"He raised us up!" a new voice roared. The red skull stepped forward as he lifted his arms, and his eyes seemed to burst to life with an unholy light.

"He raised us up…" the figures around me echoed in a ragged chorus, their eyes glowing in turn, and I swallowed hard.

"You can't hold them all for long," I called out.

"I don't need to." Aaron sneered, and they all raised their weapons at once, clearly about to rush me.

I hesitated, glancing at my mana and wondering whether I had enough to get out of this trap as one of the triceratops closed in, the ground rumbling…

A blur of motion flashed past me, as a heavily built quartet of carnifex tore through the outer ring. Three of them raced on to rip their way into the figures surrounding me, as the fourth paused by my side.

I took the hint, grabbing onto the bony fuck and pulling myself onto its back. It set off, arcing around and racing through the gap they'd just torn in the encircling enemies.

Weapons were thrown, from great clubs and hammers, lengths of wood and golf clubs…to knives, empty guns, and rocks. Ornamental swords, made of brass and still with the goddamn hooks to attach them to the wall, barely made it a half dozen feet through the air before clattering to the ground, as the dino, massive and unable to turn easily, plowed into the circle and out the far side again.

Two of the carnifex leapt through the mass, racing straight at Aaron, who lifted one hand. His palm emitted a sickly green and purple light.

They lifted into the air, paws thrashing wildly, teeth snapping, as Aaron used an ability on them, visibly straining, before gasping and suddenly sagging, almost losing control.

The third carnifex had spun and raced straight at the dino, leaping onto its side and going for the throat, determined to take its head off.

It was clearly going to make sure I got free, and I clung to the back of my bony mount, grunting and clutching my leg as I was bounced and jostled, the knife doing a hell of a number on me with each painful leap.

We were free of the surrounding mass in seconds, though, and raced back toward the hole in the wall…only to find the other side was deserted—bar the bodies that lay everywhere, broken and united in death.

I felt sick, my stomach knotting even as it seemed to fill with icy concrete. The thought that my friends had been lost…

Glancing back, I growled. The pair of carnifex that had run at Aaron now raced after me, their speed significantly greater than my own mount, as burdened as it was.

They gave off a sickly green and purple glow, looking like a glowing fuckin' bruise had gained sentience and filled them.

It was Aaron, I damn well knew.

We passed the collapsed corpse of the other triceratops, and I grinned down at it, glad we'd gotten the fucker. Mentally adding two and two, Aaron had been able to control massive creatures, but only a few at a time. I was betting that the "death" of that had enabled him to take control of the carnifex.

"Murphy…*gods, my balls*…strikes again…" I groaned, well aware that without a saddle, riding the carnifex was likely to result in the loss of my manhood at this rate.

Looking back at the oncoming pair, I hissed. I might be losing more than that in a second.

I checked my mana. *Nope, not enough there to make a difference. Maybe…*

A single shot rang out. A high-powered bullet from a sniper rifle took the lead of the two carnifex in the skull, shattering it and sending the creature tumbling to the ground with a clatter of bones.

The second one weaved desperately; normal rifles rung out as the ground around the skeleton threw up rooster tails of dirt.

It snarled, then dug its claws in and twisted around, racing back to the safety of the trees.

I groaned, shifting on my bony ride and trying to hold on for the last hundred meters.

The structure ahead, the old crematorium, was clearly the destination of my mount, leaping over a stack of logs and making me whimper as we landed, before it raced across the car park and up the road.

The crematorium was in the south section of the park, a place I'd always avoided, given the chance, due to a particularly painful series of memories. But as the carnifex slowed and I slid off, Chris was waiting, grabbing me and pulling me upright.

"You all right, brother?" he asked me quietly, and I nodded, cringing. "You look like shit."

"Yeah, well, kinda got my arse kicked back there," I whispered, before looking at the building behind him. "Fuck, I hate this place."

"You and me both," he muttered, and I winced. We'd said goodbye to a few friends here, as well as his father, and for me, Mama Aurelia.

"I'm gonna fucking level this place when we're done," I growled, and he nodded.

"Sounds good to me. You sure you're all right?"

"You remember that dickhead Aaron?" I asked him.

He frowned, thinking. "The skeleton dude?" He rubbed his chin, looking out at the collapsed remains of the triceratops and sighed. "Well, that's a relief then."

"A relief?" I glared at him.

"Yeah, I thought we had another dickhead necromancer on our hands. If it's just him…"

"Okay," I said, trying to walk and wincing. "I suppose that is a relief. Didn't think of it that way."

"What happened out there?" Barry marched over, a handful of his people with him, clutching their guns tight…despite the locked-back slides.

"An asshole we gave the chance to run away to," I said. "He's decided to come back and—"

"And someone you let go is killing my people?" Barry growled. "We've lost dozens! Dozens of people, most with families! You let this asshole go?"

"We needed the information," Mike said from overhead, leaning out over the side of the flat roof and looking down at us. "Without it, we'd have lost the fight with the necromancer, so shut it, Barry."

"Mike—" Barry growled, and I cut the pair of them off.

"That's enough!" I snarled, adjusting my trousers, and groaned. "Fuck, that's me never having kids." I winced, before straightening in relief, as I managed to repack myself.

"Really?" Chris shook his head in mock disgust. "You thought, 'Hey, maybe this is the last stand, better have a quick rummage around in there'?"

"You try riding that fucker at speed," I growled back, reaching down and gripping the hilt of the dagger, then tearing it free with a spray of blood. I hissed in pain, but it was better out than in, as my healing could finally start fixing it now.

"Here." Mike held a little bottle out. When he was sure I'd seen it, he dropped it into my hand. "Put half on your wound, down the rest," he ordered laconically, moving back out of sight as he continued to talk. "Looks like your friends are coming to play…"

I grunted. "Ammo," I said to Barry, bluntly. "How many…"

"Fourteen shells for the shotguns," he said, and I winced, knowing he had more shotguns than that.

"That's each gunner…"

He shook his head. "That's it."

"And the other guns, the rifles, the handguns?" I asked, getting a flat stare from him. "Well, that's just fucking peachy." I sighed.

"We used it all defending you." He then held his hands up as I glared at him. "Hey, we agreed to help you, and we didn't have much ammo, anyway. I'm not being a dick. It's a fact, that's all."

"We need ammo." I sighed. "Hey, Mike!" I shouted up to the overhanging roof of the building.

"What do you want, potato-face?" he called back, not bothering to look over the side.

I poured half the healing potion on my leg, then downed the rest, hissing as I felt an immediate itching sensation start up in the leg. "That better not have been spiked with anything…"

"Just some of those blue pills…thought it'd be funny to make you fight like that."

"Well, it'll be a treat for your sister later then!" I grinned and waited.

Two seconds later, Mike leaned back over the side and regarded me coldly. "I've still got some ammo."

"How much?"

"Enough."

"Stop being a dick." I sighed, letting the smile go. "Seriously, how much?"

"Five for the pistol, one for the rifle."

"Save it," I ordered him. "How long do we have?"

"Five minutes, maybe."

"They coming here?"

"Looks like it. Not sure, though. They might go straight past…" He squinted down the rifle, and referred to the path that led up the back from the cleared area below and up to the crematorium.

"Guess I'd better get their attention then."

I spied a chair off to one side, the shallow plastic shape half filled with water. But the state I was in already? I tipped it out and sat with a grunt, uncaring whether my armor got slightly more dirty or wet.

I closed my eyes, sliding into the dungeon sense, reaching out, and feeling Kelly do the same as soon as I was within her range. We exchanged a mental data surge, both of us compressing everything that had happened into a fast burst, and once we'd done that, we paused to assess.

I saw the actions she'd taken, and I approved, seeing the risk that she was running, and the way that she'd found to protect the others.

"It's a hell of a risk…" she apologized, and I smiled, sending the mental image to her.

"It's worth it," I assured her. "It gets the ball rolling on the next round. It's just a bit earlier than we figured."

"When Beta found them…"

"They were too close," I agreed, lifting upward, passing her maximum limit, and kept on going, reaching out with my senses and "feeling" the incoming incursion.

"Do you think you can do it?" she asked.

I looked over the land, grunting as I saw the holes in the plan, and wondered whether Aaron really was that dumb.

"Maybe," I admitted grudgingly. "If the others stay hidden, stay silent…" I paused, thinking, then nodded. "We can do it, but it's a hell of a risk. I need to speak to Barry. I'll reach out in a minute."

I broke the connection, grunting as I opened my eyes. Looking around and sighing, I saw the milling assholes at the bottom of the hill.

"Barry," I said, getting his attention as he tried to organize his small team of "hoplites." They'd been trained, if trained was the right word, by our hoplites, who were themselves learning their trade. Still, these men and women had been in the fight against the undead, and I knew they, at least, wouldn't break.

"What?" he asked. "We need to hole up in here. Can you get more dungeon creatures to—"

"There's more incoming."

"Dungeon—"

"No." I cut him off. "Another gang. They're the one you've been fighting recently, I'd bet…"

"From the east?" He deflated as he turned instinctively, staring up through the trees as if he could see them there.

"Yeah." I took a long breath and blew it out.

"Can we hold?" he asked grimly.

"Not without a fuckload more ammo than you have."

"What about your creatures? Hell, you could summon dozens of the big ones, the corpse lords and—"

"And that asshole down there can control the dead." I nodded down the hill. "He took control of two of them. All I'd be doing is giving him fresh creatures. I could summon more kobolds and more, but the cost…" I gestured to the carnifex, and Barry cursed.

"If he can take your creatures from you, what use are they?" he asked bitterly. "We've survived all of this, fought all these battles, and now some asshole is going to take it all?"

The hoplites behind him shifted nervously, glancing back at him, and I shook my head.

"No," I said. "You're my people now, and there's still a chance."

"We can't make it all the way. And even if we could, fuck's sake…there's no room for everyone!" Barry snapped, running his hands through his hair, before swearing profusely. "Okay, look, I'll get some volunteers. We'll hold them back as long as we can, and you run—"

"No," I growled. "Barry, shut the fuck up!"

He glared at me, and I turned to the others, nearly thirty of us in total, almost all armed with rifles of one kind or another—and almost all empty—and battered hoplite armor, reduced now to spears and shields.

"Right!" I called out. "We've got nearly two hundred assholes to the east as near as I can tell. Normally that'd not be an issue, but they know you're being hit, and apparently they're hoping to come in and mop up, taking on the skulls over there, and whatever remains of our defenders."

I looked around, seeing I had everyone's attention as I continued. "Now usually, that'd be fine. We'd be able to pull in the dungeon creatures, and we'd be able to hold the walls until we can get things sorted. Unfortunately, though, we've got no fucking walls.

"With these dicks being inside the walls now, if we face them, the raiders will roll over the walls easily. Alternately, if we defend against the raiders on the walls, these 'skull' dicks will rampage through the park behind us, and we could still lose everything…"

"Or?" Chris scratched his chin. "You've got a fuckin' plan, haven't you?"

"Of course I have, but it's risky."

"How risky?" one of the men asked, ignoring Barry as he spoke up. "My daughter's back there, two wee bairns she's got. You tell me what we've got to do to give 'er a chance." He gestured toward the deeper areas of the park, and I sighed.

"I need four volunteers…" I smiled despite myself as everyone, Barry and Chris included, stepped forward. "Thank you all." I sighed.

"Right. Four volunteers, the fastest you've got," I repeated, looking around as the four fastest were sorted out. "We've got a minute, maybe less…then those dicks are coming for us. So this is what we're doing."

CHAPTER TWENTY-TWO

Istrode forward, staring down the hill toward Aaron and his "people" as they gathered. Being the classy gent I am, I called out to them, my voice carrying down the long bank.

"Aaron, this is your last chance, you ugly fuck! You've lost more than half your side, while I got reinforcements!" I gestured behind me at the half dozen hoplites who stood there.

"Half a dozen men…" he called up, clearly dismissive of them, as he ordered the dino and carnifex forward. The rest of them swarmed behind.

"Half a dozen men and women…" I called back, nodding. More than happy to let him waste time as the others got into place and the wraiths began their mission. "However, you've got a handful down there with abilities…and I've kicked their arse already. Now my backup's here…"

"And we've all got classes, bitches!" Chris called from the roof above me, lifting both hands as the triceratops continued up the hill, stomping across an overgrown flower garden, remembrance plates that had been set into the ground cracking under the weight.

As soon as the dinosaur was over the soil completely, his Nature's Wrath spell burst into life. Vines reached up and wrapped themselves around the bones, tugging it down, holding it tight, even as the six wraiths I'd been willing to risk on this mission flashed forward.

Their hands were already full of necrotic bolts. Their glow bathed the dark park in unhealthy light as they dive-bombed the massive creature.

Each of them hurled their spells, one after the other, flying in formation, and hitting it in the head. The deepening glow of the necrotic rot spread with each hit.

They arced around, lifting back into the air as a glow started from Aaron's hands and eyes. The fifth in line slowed, reaching up to clutch its head, screeching in confusion and despair.

The sixth wraith in line acted on the orders I'd given them all previously, grabbing the skull of the fifth and tearing it free, rocketing after the others. Aaron's spell failed and the mocking laughter of the wraiths hung in the air behind it, as Mike fired his last bullet.

The high-powered sniper rifle punched through the weakened skull. The already damaged frame shattered, as the behemoth collapsed to the ground with a clatter of bones.

Aaron screamed in pain, falling back as well. Clearly some part of him was injured with his beast's death.

"Get them!" one of the remaining few colored skulls screamed, a woman all in green, who leapt up next to Aaron, and ordered the "faithful" forward.

The carnifex ignored her, but the milling mad crowd didn't. They screamed and swarmed forward, improvised weapons waving above their heads wildly.

"Fall back!" I roared, making a point of running for the open door behind us, and the others followed.

The doors were huge and glass, at least twelve feet tall, and six across, two of them side by side, which made the entrance area bright and airy during the day…and fucking indefensible as we backed away.

We'd piled chairs and the general crap we could reach in short order in the doorway, and I grinned at one of the others as I stole one of his spare spears.

"Thanks, man," I said. "Well, that went well, I think!"

"You're a fucking nutter," one of them muttered, and I winked at him.

"Dude, you've no idea," I promised, moving into the middle of the line. "Everyone ready?" I asked, getting a round of "Yup," "Aye, I suppose," and "Is it too late to go for a quick shit?"

That last one was met with a low round of laughter as we all felt the pressing need to go to the toilet, but…it was too late now, as the first of the howling horde skidded around the corner and ran at the doors.

The figure in the lead was in such a rush to get to us that he totally missed the bench seat that had been turned on its side and laid across the doorway.

In his defense, it was very dark, but the speed that he hit it meant he almost managed to flip himself. His scream was cut off sharply as his face met the marble floor. The wet smack rung out as the scream stopped, and the man from my right stepped forward, driving the spear into the back of his exposed neck.

Then he stepped back, calm as you like, as more came running into sight.

I couldn't help but smile as I heard the rumble of feet racing across the roof overhead, knowing that Chris was on the move.

The next two hit the bench as well, tumbling forward. The one after them saw them falling and leapt over them, a feral grin stretching his lips…

Until the woman on my right stepped forward and smashed him from the air with her shield.

We stood as a single line—me the only one without a shield; three on either side of me—and we stabbed and cut, slaughtering them as they closed with us.

For a few seconds, I thought we might actually have a chance, that we might even manage to slaughter them in here as the bodies stacked…

Then the first of the enemy with classes arrived, and he did it from a door I'd thought sealed.

He was red, bright red, and he screamed as he ran. His friends jumped back from him, as if burned as he passed. His eyes, his skin…he was naked and started to glow as he closed. The dull redness changed and lightened, going from a dusky red to a glowing cherry; then brighter, moving into orange as he leapt over the bodies, swinging a sword that dripped literal flames at his target.

His victim took the sword to her side, gasping as another grabbed her shield, pulling it out of position. The blade slid into her side, with a hiss of hot metal meeting flesh and blood.

She made barely a sound, collapsing as he ripped the blade free, already dead, and our line dropped back. Those on my right turned to see what had happened, while those on my left twisted around as well, falling back and leaving me exposed.

I spun, bringing my spear around and slapping the metal head against the tip of his sword, shoving it out of position as he tried to stab me.

"Fall back!" I roared, flicking the tip up and stabbing it into the inside of his left wrist, and finding out exactly why the fucker was naked.

The spear sank into his flesh easily enough, but the hiss as it did…the blood that fountained out hit the ground and burst into flame. A rug nearby went up in seconds as I backed up, spinning and smacking an opportunistic prick who tried to blindside me with the base of the spear.

It snapped with a loud crack, and I cursed, left with two half-meter lengths. As a short spear, a meter was fantastic, long enough you could seriously fuck up someone's Tuesday, and yet short enough to be used indoors, or in a phalanx with others.

Broken, though? It was shit.

Even worse, the damn head that had sunk into his wrist? It had *melted.*

I glared at it in irritation, the damn head slumped and ragged, glowing with the heat of his blood.

He grinned at me, mouth opening wider as he made to speak…and I rammed the fucker in there, using my excessive strength to drive the melting point—and the rest of the wood behind it—into his throat.

His eyes bulged; pain, shock, and panic warred with disbelief as I rammed the other section in as well. His friends racing in paused in stunned horror as I adjusted my grip, then ripped the pair apart, shattering his jaw and snapping his skull back.

The scream was cut off as I pulled back and rammed forward the wooden haft, still gripped in my right hand, and now aflame, driving it up through the soft palette inside his exposed mouth, and pierced his brain.

I "Sparta" kicked him in the stomach, sending the twitching and smoking body flying backward, and grabbed a figure who leapt at me—unarmed, clearly thinking to take advantage of my distraction—and lifted him overhead.

In the darkness of the crematorium, lit only by flickering flames, I lifted the fucker high, then slammed him down, stepping forward and planting my foot firmly on the ground.

He hit my knee with the small of his back and screamed as his spine snapped.

I straightened, shoving him forward and onto the ground facedown as the crowd moved back and forth, clearly trying to regain their "pack mentality" and their courage.

I grinned at them, judging the risk worth it, as I reached down and tugged the sword free of the dead hoplite's back. I didn't know why she had a sword as well as the spears, especially not when every damn weapon that could be used, should have been shared out, but still.

I wasn't going to complain.

Rolling my wrist, I sent the blade flashing through a figure eight, loosening myself up; then, before they could build their courage, I fucking attacked.

I leapt forward, slashing sideways at throat height. The blade blurred through the air; the tug of flesh hit the reasonably sharp tip, and then parted, being cleaved by the sheer force as much as the weapon's sharpness.

The tip erupted from the far side of the fifth's throat, and sank into the shoulder of the sixth, making her scream as the middle of their line staggered back, blood fountaining, and I roared in triumph.

I yanked the blade free, parrying a blunt brass sword that drove for my belly on the left, and grinned as I wondered just how many of those god-awful remnants of the eighties were on walls still before the fall.

The room filled with screams, and with the gurgles of people drowning in their own blood, and the cries of more of these fuckers pushing their way in, when a bloodthirsty roar from outside rang out.

"That's my cue!" I called out, parrying another stab, rolling the blade and slicing their wrist open, before punching someone else who moved within range. "Have fun, motherfuckers!"

I turned and raced for the farthest doorway behind me, marked Employees Only and Private. My arse puckered at the thought of the flames from that body behind me, and the efforts the others had gone to in the limited time they'd had before running.

Tugging it shut behind me, I stamped on a mop that stood resting against the wall, snapping the pole, and rammed the shorter half through the handle of the door.

It'd not hold for long, but it didn't have to.

The room was long and narrow, mainly used for storage of cleaning chemicals and general crap. Boxes holding dozens of urns, ready for the remains of loved ones to be packed away, stood on the right, while the back of the massive "ovens" was on the left.

"How we doing?" I called to the figure at the far end.

"Ready," Barry shouted, and I glared at him.

"You?" I growled. "You're supposed to be with the others, you dick!"

"Yeah, well, shit happens, and I'm shit at running," he replied, gesturing me to move past him as he stabbed the containers of chemicals, sending a steady stream onto the floor, running down as he threw half-full, already slashed containers down toward the door I'd entered by as well.

"Aye, you said…That's why I wanted you gone!" I snapped at him, dodging around him and grabbing the door handle, waiting as Barry pulled an old lighter from his pocket.

"Got this from me boy for Father's Day," he told me stoically, striking the wheel and filling the air with a handful of sparks. "Carl was a good lad."

"Aye, he seemed it." The air of madness receded as we both looked at it. I remembered his son, killed in the fight for the park, and the way he'd broken down at the time. "Barry, I'm sorry. I can't imagine—"

"No," he agreed, cutting me off. "Until you have a child, you can't."

Screams of fury and madness rose from beyond the door, and it shook on its hinges, the clumsily jammed mop handle bouncing and slipping.

"So…you gonna light that?" I asked after a few seconds, and he shrugged.

"Not yet," he said, before giving me an evil half smile. "Those fuckers gave up their kids as slaves and human shields, or at the very least, they didn't stop other people's kids being taken. I think they deserve to see what's going to happen to them."

The door behind me shook suddenly, and I grimaced.

"While I agree, mate, we're losing options here," I pointed out.

"Then go," he said. "I think I'll stay awhile. Maybe see my wife and kid a little earlier than I'd planned."

"No, you fucking don't," I growled, stepping in closer to him.

"Matt—"

"Barry, you're the leader of these idiots! I don't know who I can trust here and who's a dick. I'll treat them all as untrustworthy, so help me God, if you're not there to help," I threatened, and he glared at me.

"You can't. You—"

"I'll lock the gates," I warned him. "If I can't trust them, I'll fuckin' leave them here until I know who I can…"

"Bastard!" he snarled, glaring at me, before spinning on his heel and sparking the lighter to life. The flame brightened the room considerably. The light that seeped under the door at the far end, obscured by feet, hadn't been much, and the light was welcome.

The door cracked down the middle, something powerful hitting it as more screams rang out, and I cursed. Then Barry lit the ball of string he'd dipped in the fluid.

The reaction was instantaneous: the string burst to life, the flame racing down its length and hitting the rapidly spreading pool with a solid *wumph*.

The narrow room was suddenly much brighter, and getting rapidly warmer, as I popped the handle, looked out, and then slammed the door again, looking back at a visibly confused and stressed Barry.

"Okay, we might have a problem," I admitted.

"Beyond the fucking fact I just set fire to the room we're in?" Barry asked, aghast. "Get that door open, you—"

"There's a fuckload of undead out there."

"What?"

"Undead," I repeated. "Lots of them."

"So kill them!"

"Well, I hadn't been planning on inviting them for fucking tea!" I snapped acidly, taking a deep breath and looking around as I tried to find an alternative.

The sight outside suggested that Aaron had leveled up recently. Although he'd been unable to summon too many undead before, well, that clearly wasn't the case now.

I'd seen at least fifteen, and the fuckers were all a new class of undead. One that looked like they'd been put together from all the assholes we'd killed so far, sections of chopped flesh and melded bones forming monstrous forms that scuttled around. Even the humans ran from them, despite the fact they'd served Aaron before.

The door at the end of the room burst open. A mangled figure reached in, then reared back as the flames burst up, fed by both the air that rushed in…and the liquid that had been run around the inside of the room earlier.

When the others had run for it, going out the back of the crematorium, one bright spark had seen the dozens of containers, and told Barry and I what they were, before stabbing two and running around with them, leaving a thick, flammable trail behind her.

The plan had been that the flames would rush back down this room, stopping the fuckers inside from following us, and hopefully setting the outer walls aflame.

Then the assholes inside would have burned to death, or at least be trapped and wounded, while we ran for it. That'd been the plan, anyway.

It was totally fucked now, as the amalgamation of two bodies in the doorway tried to go forward, then staggered back, alight already. It had two arms on the left, one on the right, and a pair of torsos fused side by side. The one on the right looked as if it'd been turned soft and the left pressed into it, the flesh moving like wax.

The creature that was left over had three arms, four legs, and two heads, one that screamed endlessly and had a hand clutching at its face, while the other stared at us with unearthly hatred.

It waved its arm, trying to put the flames out when another hit it from behind, propelling it forward and into the flaming pool, spreading the fire.

Something had clearly hit the carpet I'd had Barry's people soak earlier, though, as the flames behind suddenly spread violently, and the screams from the main room lifted in desperate volume.

"Up!" Barry barked at me, and I looked at him, confused, before looking up, seeing the skylight he pointed at. "Climb, you dumb fucker!"

"Shit!" I cursed, sheathing the sword through the belt loop for the hammer, then following him as he started up the side of the cold "oven."

The ceiling in here was higher than normal, presumably as the ovens backed into here, but considering they'd been storing flammable chemicals as well, either someone had been intending to blow the place up, or it didn't get that hot in here normally.

Once we were atop the ovens, the skylight was only just out of reach, and I knelt, Barry climbing onto my back without pause, smashing the latch for the glass twice before it came loose.

Then I straightened up and he clambered through, turning around and bracing himself, offering me a hand.

I backed up and ran, kicking off the wall, and grabbed his hand, heaving myself up, as well as using a little of the recovered mana to boost myself through.

"You're lighter than you look." Barry grunted, falling back as I came through the gap, and I snorted, drawing the sword again. It was a longsword, which meant there was no way it'd be worn on the hip; it was too fucking long.

I was bigger than most men, and even with my now longer legs, it sure as shit wasn't happening.

I moved to the edge of the roof and stared down, cursing as I saw the milling undead, and the way they were searching frantically for us.

They'd not seen us atop the roof yet, but they'd not be long.

I squinted in the direction the others should have gone and spotted a distant bit of movement through the trees, but that was it.

"Stay down," I ordered Barry, settling down and taking a deep breath, closing my eyes.

"What are we doing?" He ran over, half crouched, and I opened one eye to glare at him.

"You're going to be fucking silent and pretend we're not here, while watching out, and I'm going to goddamn meditate—"

"Meditate?" he hissed incredulously. "What the hell, you think some god is gonna help us? You think a bit of '*inner-fucking-peace*' is going to make all the difference?"

"It will if I can get my mana higher. Then I can fly us out of here!" I snarled. "Now shut the fuck up and keep watch!"

Barry said something, unable to help himself, but I was already ignoring him, reaching deep inside and focusing, trying to do this without that furry dickhead that'd been missing for days.

The first step, as always, was to look at my core.

The spark of mana was somehow happily situated just between my heart and my belly, glowing like a tiny fusion core, and yet somehow taking up absolutely no space at the same time.

I drew in a deep breath, and out again, centering myself as I worked, checking the loops and lines of mana that flowed and floated through my body.

I saw the patterns, slipping down and into the fast-flowing stream, feeling myself buoyed up and carried along, sensing the gates that I had in place now. The few I'd gotten in place acted to increase the speed of the flow overall, but nowhere near the way they had for the massive torrent that Thor had demonstrated to me.

A single loop was all I allowed myself, and then I sank into the core. The glowing star grew larger and larger; my perspective changed from the spark inside me, to seemingly hovering somewhere in space.

The flow of mana was visible on all sides, a massive sea of mana that surrounded the towering structure in the center.

Pure mana, uncorrupted and unaspected, stood in the center. A pillar the size of dozens of worlds stood atop each other, glowing with power.

The other pillars branched off from it—Fire, Earth, Water, and Air—followed by the dozens, then hundreds of the others.

Each flashed past, rotating around the central axis. The tip drew through the seas of mana, and absorbed a tiny fraction of the total, attuned as they were to each individual element, and no other.

I reached out, flowing closer and closer, hovering near the center, at the axis of a dozen connections, and I landed. My point of view changed; the world around me reoriented until I stood at the foot of a dozen mighty cliffs, each of them stretching out and vanishing into the far distance.

I knelt, my mental presence becoming seemingly physical, even if only from my perspective. Reaching out, I lay a hand on the base, feeling the warmth of the pure mana pillar below me, and the draw of the others.

They were like straws, or strainers, drawing their individual "flavor" of mana free of the morass. As it flowed along the length, it was absorbed: the Fire was sucked from it, sinking into the Fire pillar, powering that, as a fraction of the mana, now "pure," was fed into the central pillar.

"This is either going to suck…or be amazing," I whispered, before reaching out and pulling the mana to me.

I couldn't explain it in any other way—the mana was flowing underneath the surface, just out of reach, and then…and then it wasn't!

I screamed, my eyes opening wide as I lunged to my feet. A burning agony flooded through me as I drew on a fraction of a fragment of a tiny percentage of the pure mana I'd sensed.

I didn't know why, but the sudden influx of that mana was terrible. Pain, raging pain, roared through me, and I felt the world changing around me.

Without Thor being there to complete the link, I couldn't "draw" the way he'd enabled me to, to drag the mana of the world around me, corrupted as it was, into myself and convert it into the storm.

Instead, I'd tried to drag the "pure" form of the mana in, thinking that would be great and I'd be able to use it.

I was wrong.

I was *very* wrong.

I screamed in agony as I staggered around, drawing the attention of everything nearby, before Barry hit me, slamming into my stomach and driving me down onto the roof.

"Shut it, you fool!" he practically screamed at me, before crying out and letting go of me as if I'd burned him. "Fuck!" He shook his hands in disbelief.

I rolled, the world lost to me as pain like nothing I'd felt before seemed determined to core me like a fucking apple. I writhed, curling up and biting down, gritting my teeth as I tried to get control.

Something screeched nearby, but it was only on the periphery of my mind, the pain was so intense.

I could hear Barry screaming at me, but I couldn't stop myself. The pure mana, in such quantities, was like the star of my mana had gone nova.

I twisted and shook, convulsing. Barry shouted something, then…then something grabbed me, and I looked up, seeing a torn visage over me.

I saw a pair of skulls, melded together, the mouth unable to open fully on the left; bones creaked as the right forced it open, lunging forward, to tear out my throat…

And before it could, I punched out.

The blow was fast, the angle I was at too shallow to have any real power to it, but the effect! The pure mana burst from my fist as it impacted, and the creature practically disintegrated in a blast of heat and light.

I rolled to the side. Barry was frantically battling two more with the sword I'd been holding, and I thrust my hands out, willing my Lightning Bolt spell into reality.

Usually, Lightning Bolt was a bright blue-white, a crackling, arcing discharge of power that was like a supercharged taser.

This, however, wasn't the spell that lanced out.

The bright golden-white light that tore through the pair of creatures as if they were tissue paper was something else, something far more powerful, and primal. I gasped in relief. The massive amount of mana in me dipped suddenly, almost to the point that I could actually think.

The pain dropped with it, and I panted, bloody furrows carved in my palms from where my gauntlets had given way under the force of my clenched fists.

I forced myself to my feet, seeing my mana bar glowing dangerously as I staggered forward. I saw the creatures laid out before me, racing in, dozens already climbing up, and I reached out and in.

If that was what pure mana did to Lightning Bolt, the Lightning Storm was going to fuck these assholes right up!

I reached out, forcing the visualization of what I wanted, and…fuck all happened.

CHAPTER TWENTY-THREE

I blanched, staring at my hands. A notification frantically pulsed in my augmented vision, and I yanked it up into my line of sight.

Congratulations!

You have managed to convert your spell Lightning Bolt to Storm Bolt!

As this is the first time you have converted a signature spell,
you have unlocked a basic tutorial.*

Do you wish to use this now?

"Fuck no!" I snarled, frantically reading the details I could see.

**All spells can be augmented, altered, and otherwise evolved, but your understanding must be high enough to accomplish this, or the spell will fail, and you will lose access to it. In the case of class spells, you may repurchase the spell and information, but the resulting amalgamation of spells may prove to be non-viable.*

It was the alteration I'd undergone, I realized, when I'd been "locked down" to all other forms of mana essentially, losing access to the regular mana in favor of my storm mana and its subsidiaries.

Clearly because "pure" was a part of those other kinds of mana, or they of it, I could still use it, sort of, but I was getting a master class in why I shouldn't fucking attempt to draw in mana that wasn't storm properly!

I gritted my teeth and raised my arms, unleashing a dozen fast-hitting bolts of golden light, literally carving my way through entire sections of the creatures. But everywhere I looked, there were more.

I saw that the more I used the mana, the lower the bar fell, but also…also the color changed! My body was trying to process the alien "pure" mana into a form it could use, and I desperately started to strike out again. My available mana dropped by the second as I searched for that knob Aaron.

I found him finally, or what I assumed was him, anyway.

A patch of trees in the distance was darker than it should have been, and survivors were dragging bodies over and into them.

I lifted my hands, about to unleash all the remaining "pure" I had…when Barry staggered over to me.

"Matt, we have to go!" he gasped, his skin torn and scratches I was sure were infected already clear to see.

I growled and pushed him back, lifting my hands again, only to see a small figure illuminated by a ray of moonlight.

A child.

I froze. The glowing, sparkling power that had been flooding my hands dimmed slowly as I saw what I'd nearly done.

The child was dragged backward, the chains being pulled taut, and they vanished, even as I realized I'd been about to fire the last two bolts blindly into the black mass of shadow.

There was a chance I'd have killed the sadistic fuck Aaron…but much more likely I'd have missed, and carved massive holes through his human shields.

I swallowed hard, backing up and shaking my head as Barry was there again, pulling at my arm.

"Matt!" he roared. "Wake up, you goddamn idiot! We have to get out of here!"

"Yeah…" I whispered, swallowing again and looking around, seeing more of the amalgamations clambering up and over the edge of the walls.

I'd not seen any children's bodies. That was the only relief. *Otherwise…*I shook that thought free. Aaron was a coward. He'd keep the kids as shields; if nothing else, that was their best chance at life for now, that and the plan.

I spun on my heels, turning away from Aaron and all his kind, ducking and hauling Barry over my shoulder, ignoring his protestations, and hoped I had enough mana for this, as I started to run.

I managed a half dozen steps before they all closed in, and I jumped into the air. The feeling of gravity releasing me was wonderful to experience, even as Barry screamed in utter terror in my ear, almost deafening me. We flew over the monsters, clearing a hundred meters in a matter of seconds, then landed, skidding. I almost dropped him, my mana down to the dregs again, and even that flashing like crazy thanks to the infusion of poisonous *alien* mana.

I set him down, gasping and looking back, through the trees, and cursed.

The plan had been that we needed to draw these assholes with us…I reached out, bracing myself against a tree and desperately pushing out the last few minutes to Kelly, feeling her disbelief that, once again, I'd broken the goddamn system, then acceptance that she'd take care of it.

She rolled around the wraiths I'd had earlier from the attack group, divebombing the undead and making sure they were seen by Barry, before zipping back toward where I was catching my breath.

They flashed past at horrific speeds, with the screams of incoming undead rising again.

"Fuck…you could have let me rest a second!" I cursed, before turning to Barry…and seeing him running like fuck. "Oh, it's like that, is it!"

I ran after him, racing up the bank. The screeches rose as more undead picked up the chase.

"We…can't go…too fast…" Barry gasped after a few seconds as I caught up and ran alongside him. "If we lose them…"

"Checkpoint ahead!" I reassured him. The others we'd sent on ahead were frantically setting up a series of blockades across the road.

Yes, admittedly they were mainly shopping carts, chained together and being twisted out and dragged across the narrow road, but that was fine. The left, as it was to me, running up, was the outer wall of the park.

As I'd ordered, and as Barry had relayed through his people, it was abandoned.

Anyone who was on the wall before had run for it, falling back to the mass of people in the farther quadrants of the park and silencing them, moving them as far back from the wall as they could get.

That left us, the "idiot brigade," leading this mass of undead up the road.

I glanced overhead, hearing the whoosh of passing wraiths. Their hands were full of necrotic spells that cast sickly glows across the narrow road. They vanished again, and screams rose from my right, in the distance.

That was the other gang, I guessed.

There were at least a few hundred of them, and even if the remains of Aaron's "people" were down to fifty or less—which I seriously doubted, betting it was more like a hundred still—then the defenders of the park were badly outnumbered, with damaged walls, and an attack that they, frankly, couldn't beat off.

Logically, the best thing I could do was fall back to the dungeon, even if I had to leave these people behind. Then I could amass an army, kit them out with better weapons as time went on, and lead them to take the park and everywhere back.

That was the logical thing to do.

It was also the option only a politician could choose. It'd result in a massive loss of life for everyone else, just so I'd be all right.

Or...

Or I could do what we were doing, and be a sneaky, unprincipled bastard and lead the two gangs to each other. The wraiths were hitting the gang from the east, making the point of being seen, both as magic users and as undead.

They were being used to take out most of the gang's leadership. Or that was the plan, anyway. If we were lucky? The gang would turn tail and run.

It was unlikely, but it was possible. Most likely, what would happen was that they'd decide the undead were attacking them; then, when they saw Aaron and his undead?

Well, they were already being attacked by undead, right? They'd attack each other; both sides would take losses, and the rest of my team, the kobolds and more that Kelly had dispatched, would come in and take them in the ass.

Hopefully by then I'd have recovered some mana, and the teams working to absorb as much of the piled crap that the park's people had been accumulating would have made some headway as well.

Kelly had drafted some of "our" team, mainly Finn and a few others, to start building, and had begun a literal bomb shelter. It wasn't that big, not yet, and it was mass that we could have spent in lots of other ways, but it was solid. And it would be big enough for the kids to hide inside and hole up.

She was determined about that.

I slid to a halt with the five people who were setting up the barricades, and I gave Barry a shove as he tried to do the same.

"Don't be so bloody stupid!" I snapped at him. "You keep going. Get to the next one, and the one after—make sure they're getting ready!"

The reason that I'd been down to half a dozen helpers back there, out of the twenty and more I'd had before, was because I'd sent them on ahead.

They'd split up into three groups, the smallest team staying with me, and the other two each going to start making barriers to slow the enemy advance.

The last one was to be made at the outer edge of the dungeon's zone of control. If things were going well there, then we'd counter-attack from a position of strength, with kobolds and the dungeon itself providing the barriers and traps we needed to even the odds.

I turned and looked back, as Barry moved off, hobbling up the street to the next rally point. The narrow road that led back toward the undead from here was as dark as the inside of a boot, the trees towering over and obscuring anything below.

Even with that, though, I could see an occasional movement, and I prayed that Aaron was as dumb and arrogant as I thought he was.

Several minutes passed in silence, before the first of the undead moved up, stopping a good dozen meters back, as more moved to stand around it.

Soon enough, the narrow road was filled by them, literally wall to wall. The mass of broken and battered undead stood silently by as something moved at the back…and a new multilegged monstrosity strode into view.

It was the remains of the triceratops, I guessed—several of the legs looked like it, anyway—with the ribs bent back and outward, forming a "floor" of sorts.

The legs were connected to the sides, three each, it appeared, and in the middle, sat Aaron, atop a shitty—now soaked—sofa. He sat there as if he were the king of the world, while we all gawked at him.

"Surrender!" he called, in what I assume he thought was a grand voice. It broke halfway through and sounded like he was mid-puberty, making me snort in disbelief.

The painted figures stood around him, two new ones that were covered in green and red paint respectively, clearly still wet, and missing the tattoos.

I guessed they were newly elevated to his "council" to replace losses. But the more I looked, the more my heart sank.

"Where are they, Aaron?" I called out, as he waited for a response.

"Who?"

"The children, you sick fuck!" I snapped.

"Oh, they're back here…with one of my pet's creations." He smiled as a figure stepped up, grey and tattooed, to speak, clearly with his master's approval.

"I'm an alchemist!" he called. "You know what that means?"

"You were desperate to cure your cock-rot?" I asked, and he sneered.

"It means I can create substances you can only imagine! Those children are chained to a little creation of mine. Should anything happen to the Great Lord of the Dead, then it will explode, and they'll all die, most painfully!"

"So surrender and—" Aaron sneered.

"Great Lord of the Dead, eh?" I called back. "You told them about the *last* God of the Dead that I met?" I spat on the ground and leaned on the stacked carts, and glared at him, waiting.

"You attacked my teacher. You murdered a skilled and gifted necromancer that—"

"I killed that necromantic fuckhead, and we destroyed his entire army. He was ten times as powerful as you could ever hope to be, and we slaughtered him, *while you ran away.*"

"If you're so powerful, show us!" He gestured grandly. "Show us all your amazing powers—"

"I'm gonna fuck you up, Aaron," I said. "I remember what a self-righteous little prick you were before, when you begged for our help and our mercy. If I thought you'd have done this shit? I'd have killed you then. I damn well should have."

"If you could, then you would," he retorted. "You can't, because you're weak!"

"He's twice the man you'll ever be!"

The voice rang out from above, from a wraith, as it suddenly dive-bombed the figure atop his "throne."

I grinned. Kelly's abilities were clearly growing in her new role. Then I cursed, as the wraith, its hands filled with necrotic light, smashed into a hidden shield.

"Attack!" Aaron roared, and the undead didn't hesitate.

The mass that had been standing still, silent and staring at us with unabashed hunger in their eyes, leapt into motion. They were a mess, some with a handful of limbs, some with barely enough to move.

A figure that reminded me of a centaur, with some serious identity issues, raced forward the fastest. It had eight arms, all protruding from the lower torso like a spider, and it ran with all of them in motion at once.

The upper torso had no limbs, but three heads, pressed into each other, their flesh and bone melding together to result in a single, six-eyed, massive-mawed thing.

It leapt up, grabbing onto the shopping cart chain, and dragged itself atop it, racing forward, losing fingers along the way as they got lodged into gaps. And it clearly felt nothing as they tore free.

"Kiss it!" someone screamed from the right, as a figure stepped up, one of those who'd survived the fight so far from Barry's side.

He lifted a sword high. The blade gave off an unearthly blue light, then he slashed it sideways, screaming something I couldn't make out.

The blue light seemed to draw along behind the blade, like an after-image. Then, all at once, it split free and raced forward, slamming into the spider-thing and slicing it in half. The blue light blurred on to carve its way into a half dozen of the undead, before it winked out.

"Fuck yeah!" I shouted, hefting my sword, ready to thin their numbers a bit, and glanced at him, hoping for a second blast.

Instead, he was weaving on his feet, blood trails snaking from his nostrils, and clearly barely able to stay upright. One of the others grabbed him, swore, and hoisted him over his shoulder, looking to me for approval.

I nodded, gesturing back down the road.

Just like that, we were down to four already, and that wasn't enough to man the barricade, realistically.

"Kelly, can you hear me?" I shouted, getting ready.

A handful of seconds later, just as the undead reached us, a dusty voice responded from nearby.

"I can, my love."

I glanced over, then snorted, before slashing sideways and beheading a slavering thing that just...*nope*. The undead were a mess. No two were exactly alike, and where some, like the spider, had claimed extra limbs, others...some were practically just torsos.

One literally was a torso, three heads, one leg, and one arm. As the others surged forward, it kept being knocked over and was in serious danger of being killed by its own side at this rate.

All the points I'd mentally assigned to Aaron for summoning the triceratops—normal necromancers lacked ambition, in my opinion; after all, why the hell *wouldn't* you summon a dinosaur—he'd just lost for that shitty design.

Kelly, on the other hand, was speaking to me from a wraith she'd somehow piloted, remotely, to hover next to me.

Considering it had no vocal cords, I was betting, and certainly no fuckin' ears, looking it over, how she was talking through it was another of those things I mentally marked down to "magic fucking with the natural order of things" and left it at that, as otherwise I'd never get shit done.

"How we doing?" I asked her.

There was a pause as she clearly assessed the others.

"The second gang are gathering. They seem upset for some reason."

"How's their leadership?"

"Reduced to a rotting pile of flesh and bones. I left a wraith hovering over it, telling them they could 'serve the Great Lord Aaron or die,' just to make sure they got the picture."

"Subtle," I pointed out.

"I might need to draw them a map. I'd use crayons, but I think they'd eat them," she said acidly, before twisting around and flinging a necrotic bolt at a figure that was closing on me from one side, having thought it was unobserved.

I was striding left and right, my blade flashing in the dim moonlight as these things tried to climb over the carts, all that was holding them back.

"Okay, gonna make a break for it in a minute. You ready at the next one?"

"No, don't stop there. Keep running on to the last," she said after a second, and I cursed.

"But—"

"The gang is moving. They'll intercept just behind the second barricade. Keep running," she ordered, before the wraith suddenly screamed, starting to glow with a sick light.

"Fuck!" I cursed, stabbing out and beheading the damn thing before Aaron could turn it against me. "Run, you idiots!" I barked at the others, taking a step back and slashing sideways across the top of the barrier, cutting two of the closing undead down.

I held for another few seconds, slicing left and right, before a blast of black light tore past me, barely missing, and hit a lamppost behind me.

The spell, whatever it was, exploded. The lamppost toppled with a scream of rupturing metal, even as I felt a horrible weakness tear through me. I backed up, forcing myself to try to run. I managed only a few steps, before I fell as well, catching myself on the cobbled street and gasping as everything began to fade.

"MOVE!" I heard roared from above, and the crash of feet landing nearby, followed by the shrieks of the undead, as a bright, cold blue light bathed the area.

I gasped, sucking down a freezing cold breath, and looking back over my shoulder, saw Chris behind me, wielding a whip!

It was magical, that was clear. Hell, it had to be a spell—or an ability, my mind sluggishly pointed out—as there was no way he'd have been walking around with a ghostly glowing whip all this time and not practicing on just about everything in sight, no doubt crippling himself in the process.

"Get up, you dick!" Chris barked at me, and I shook myself, realizing I was sprawled on the ground still, as he held off the undead to give me time.

"Where'd…you come…from?" I wheezed, forcing myself up and staggering, then starting to run.

"I was hiding, obviously!" He grunted, banishing his whip, and ran after me, ducking under one arm and half lifting me, half helping me as we picked up speed.

He reached forward with his right hand, muttering something and then shouting the last syllable, pointing at the ground just as we passed over it.

Something caught my foot, then we were past. I tried to look back, hearing the furious howls that suddenly rose behind us.

"I cast Nature's Wrath," he explained, grunting as he helped me to stay upright. "You gonna start carrying your own weight for once?"

I tried to move. My limbs shook, my mind slow and sluggish, until a white light hurtled down the dark road from the barricade ahead.

It was less than twenty meters, and the flaming torches atop it let me make out movement. But I couldn't make sense of anything, until it slammed into me, making me gasp.

It was like the world had been an online game I'd been playing, while insanely tired and hungover. The "lag" that ruined such games for years had just been part of my life, staggering forward, until the spell hit me, and *damn.*

I sucked in a deep breath, eyes opening wide, and my feet went from barely moving to supercharged.

I almost flew along the street. Chris struggled to keep up as I hurtled across the final meters, jumping and planting one foot on the barrier before me, and flipped over it, landing with a skid that only slightly ruined the effect.

Behind the barrier were two others waiting for me. One was Kilo, and I grinned, seeing his draconic snout as he started casting a spell. And the other…

I'd seen him around, but couldn't remember his name, and I couldn't afford the drain of using my examination spell, but he was the doctor who had come from the Hillsong Church, one of the team Jo had been teaching to wield healing magic, and he looked terrified.

"Cleanse and Supercharge," he babbled, by way of an explanation. "I stripped the negative effects of the spell from you, and gave you the equivalent of an epinephrine dose, along with a fast-acting antihistamine!"

"I don't know what you just said, but I like it! Hit me again!" I grinned, and he blanched.

"I…I might kill you!" he gasped.

"Again!" I barked, pointing at the incoming wave of undead from farther down the road, and then at the connecting street, where hundreds of screaming raiders could now be seen, racing forward with torches lit and knives held high. "Want me to carry you? Hit me!"

"Oh, sweet Mary…" He whimpered, and I grabbed him, tossing him over my shoulder and sprinting as the spell hit me.

"Hit them too!" I ordered, and the thin man gasped as he cast spell after spell while bouncing along. "Fuck yes!"

Chris passed me in a blur, his legs pumping like I'd never seen, only to in turn be passed by Kilo, who was apparently trying out for the Olympics.

The three of us thundered down the road. Wraiths flashed past overhead and hurled necrotic bolts down into the sudden melee as the two gangs, one made up of human raiders and the other Aaron's "skulls," suddenly met each other in an enclosed space.

"Fuck, I wish I had spare mana!" I screamed into the air. The mental image of setting off Atomic Furnace back there was a wonderful one.

We tore along the darkened space, coming upon the final barrier at the same time as most of those who'd set off ahead of us did, skidding to a halt and having to wait for our turn. I grinned up at the wall that towered overhead, closing off this, the farthest north and eastern corner of the park.

"Come on, lads!" I called up to the others climbing up the handholds, knowing instinctively that the handholds would be dropped from the wall as soon as we were all up. "Move along, eh? Some of us have things to do today!"

"Shit, man, I don't know what he hit me with, but I *like* it." Chris grinned as the doctor took his turn on the rungs. "You looked like shit before, you know? I mean, you always do, but..."

"I feel amazing," I said to Chris, nodding. "I don't know how long it'll last but..."

"A few minutes!" the doctor gasped, then called down from above. "It'll only last a few more minutes!"

"I could do with another then," I said to Chris conversationally.

"Me too. Do you think they can make this into a drink?"

"Like a coffee?"

"I was thinking more of with vodka...or rum!"

"I could go for that," I agreed seriously, as Kilo stepped up next to us both and grinned, nodding. "You want one too?" I asked him, and he nodded again quickly.

"Hey, doc!" Chris yelled up at the figure vanishing over the wall. "We'll take three more, extra vodka!"

"It'll kill you!" a terrified head shouted back down, poking up over the edge and staring at us.

"Nah!" I called back. "You should see the shit we normally drink!"

"Seriously. He challenged a pair of Russians to a vodka drinking competition the other month. Fucker won it as well," Chris called up, before elbowing me and dropping his voice. "Imagine what shagging would be like on this..."

"Fuck. I might break Kelly..."

"Or she might break you. Imagine if you were both on it. It'd be like that time I was in Amsterdam and did all that coke with the ex..."

"Never tried that...but I'm going to," I agreed, and he nodded, both of us turning to Kilo. "So, important question; what's a kobold's sex life like?" I asked. The magical cocktail clearly left us all a little unhinged as we waited, as a dragon-man, who couldn't talk, and was only a matter of hours old, considered his sex life.

After a minute, he lifted one hand and held it flat, before tilting it to one side and then the other, making us all laugh.

"Not bad," I translated for him, before looking down the road at the battle that was growing ever more ferocious. "So…you think we should climb up, or—"

"We could wait here. At this rate, there's not going to be many left. We could just clean up…" Chris suggested, making me seriously consider it, before the doctor called down again from above us.

"Please, trust me and get up here!" he cried, and I sighed.

"Race up the wall?" I suggested, getting a grin from Chris and Kilo. "On three…" I backed up and glanced down the street again. The gangs were still desperately battling each other.

"Shame, that," I said slowly, frowning. "If they'd been inside the dungeon radius like we'd planned…"

"GO!" Chris shouted, and I cursed, having let myself get distracted.

The race was short, with, surprisingly, Kilo winning it, leaping over the top and hissing in triumph as I landed third, Chris just making it over ahead of me.

"Damn, he's fast." Chris nodded to Kilo, before a yawn cracked his jaw.

"You're not wrong," I agreed, before yawning as well, leaning on the wall and looking over the side at the scuffling mass farther along. "Okay, Kilo, is Sharon still alive? I want that dick Aaron to suffer…" I glanced over at him, finding him passed out on the narrow walkway.

"He okay?" Chris slumped down, back against the wall, and stared blearily at Kilo.

"Tired I…I…guess…" I mumbled, before pitching forward, into the waiting embrace of sleep.

CHAPTER TWENTY-FOUR

I was out for a day and a half, I was told later, waking up slowly, feeling like my brain was wrapped in cotton wool.

By the time I'd woken, and was staring around, totally confused, Kelly was sitting in a nice recliner by the side of my bed, drinking coffee from a mug that said *I'm The Cool Aunt* and relaxing, dressed in much more normal clothes than I was used to seeing.

"Are you okay?" I asked, my voice croaky as I sat upright, frowning around the bedroom I'd found myself in.

It was white and grey, mainly. The curtains, the furniture, and half the cushions were a kind of crushed velvet that looked as if it'd been very fashionable before the fall.

The wood was all light colors, the walls pristine and white; overall, combined with the sunlight that streamed in from the outside, it gave me a horrible few seconds of confusion, where I wondered whether I'd had a psychotic break and imagined everything.

Then the flashing notifications got my attention, and Kelly started to fill me in on everything that had happened.

The Battle for the Park, as it was referenced by most people, hadn't ended with a bang after all. It was more like a whimper. Kelly had been overseeing things while Chris, Kilo, and I had been basically off our tits on magical amphetamines.

The bunker had been made, then the kids moved inside, while a pair of influence generators were moved up and slid along until they were on the other side of the wall from the battling gangs. As the fight continued next to it, the deaths began happening inside the dungeon's radius and then…

Well.

It'd taken a single blow from one of the idiots against the wall to register as an "attack" on the dungeon, and the entire nature of the fight changed.

Suddenly we were earning massive amounts of mana from the "adventurers" who were battling on the dungeon's territory, and Kelly got to work summoning kobolds and increasing the control generators.

They were equipped with the auto-reloading crossbows, then quietly moved up and along the wall, next to the fighting gangs. Kilo's blueprint was in there— or, more accurately, the blueprint Kilo had been born from—and four cryomancers were added as well, spread out.

At Kelly's command, the cryomancers let loose with overlapping fields of Chill, slowing everyone inside the affected area. Because it was layered over and over, instead of capped as it would be if this were a game, the effect just got worse and worse.

Then the crossbowmen—or crossbow*kobolds*—stood and opened fire.

The magical shields over Aaron and his people had turned opaque as more and more hits landed. He'd apparently been heard laughing and jeering that he'd kill us all when he'd seen that. Then, as the bolts continued to fly, with the cryomancers letting loose again and again with Frostbite now as well, the shields had weakened.

He'd started babbling at that point, ordering them to stop. To go away, and then ordering his skulls to kill them all, although they were already in a pitched battle with hundreds more than there was on their side, in essentially an alley.

One of them had indeed stood up, ready to attack. Then the shield had given out, and the next bolt took him in the forehead.

At that point, Aaron had threatened to blow up the kids, going so far as to point out the alchemist and that he could do it "with a thought."

The alchemist had been hit in the head by three bolts before the prick had finished pointing him out, ensuring he'd never think of anything again.

The kobolds had paused then, shifting their aim away from Aaron, and he'd tried to run, convinced that somehow his own cleverness had saved him, until Sharon appeared behind him. They'd stopped firing so Sharon could take care of things personally.

She'd apparently taken my heartfelt desire earlier that Aaron be made to suffer and had made damn well sure of it.

The screams had hung in the air for a long time, I was told, with the other gang backing up slowly when they saw not only what she was doing, but the clear enjoyment, and the dozen kobolds that stood with crossbows pointed at them all.

One of the gang's new leadership had tried to issue orders, and had been hit in the face with a single bolt, shutting him up. At that point, Beta and her people had made their grand entrance, leading two of the kobold melee squads.

There were twenty of them in total, split into two groups of ten hoplites, marching forward, shields held high, spears ready. No matter the situation, however, the lunatics of the northeast of England could never be accused of cowardice.

A complete lack of intelligence? Yes, most definitely. But cowardice? Never.

The gang had seen an enemy they could reach, unlike the crossbowmen that stood atop a wall and had stopped firing for some reason, and charged them.

The kobolds had simply braced themselves, taken the charge on their shields, and then pushed back…and stabbed out once.

The entire front line of lunatic, drug- and alcohol-fueled football hooligans—many of whom had never experienced "real" consequences for their actions before—now instead experienced razor-sharp, cold metal spearheads.

They died in their dozens.

The second line died seconds later, then the third. By the time the fourth row—mainly made up of those who were starting to sober up, come down from their high or who'd been more "along for the ride" than outright insane—reached the now building wave of their own dead…things changed.

They turned, trying to run, only to find why the kobold crossbows had gone silent.

Reloading complete, the crossbows fired again and again. The cryomancers released wave upon wave of Chill, making the cobblestones that were already slick with blood now coated in ice as well.

Fingers went numb as they were shakingly curled around crap weapons. The very air grew too cold to breathe easily and the gang tried to back up, with frost glittering off the walls on both sides.

The more sensible, which admittedly wasn't many of them, tried to beg for forgiveness, to surrender, or to just be let go. Unfortunately for the majority, the first who managed to get the words out clearly enough to attract Kelly's attention as she guided the defenders was a man she'd recently interacted with.

"Carl…" her wraith crooned, swooping in and hovering before him. Its flesh was grey and mottled, and the clothing hung on its frame. Skeletal fingers reached out to rest on his shaking, terrified shoulders as she searched his eyes for recognition. "Do you remember me?"

"W…wha…?" He gasped, his lips blue. Ice-crystals formed on his eyelashes and his skin, splattered blood on his arms freezing over.

"On the bridge…" Kelly whispered, through the wraith. "You said my boyfriend got himself killed, and you wanted paying for your time anyway. Do you remember?"

"You?" He stared in horror at the wraith before him, clearly thinking that Kelly had turned into this creature.

"Me," she said grimly. "Well, guess what, Carl? He lived. We all did, and you left. You chose to join the gangs. You chose to come back with them, planning on raping and murdering your way through the park."

"N…no…" he lied.

The wraith released him with one hand and lifted the other, a glowing necrotic bolt growing in that palm.

"This is on behalf of every one of those women you abused…" she whispered lovingly, before slamming the necrotic bolt, hard, into his crotch.

Carl screeched, collapsing to the ground, as the wraith sneered and lifted into the air. The last few wraiths flew in from the sides and cast their bolts as well, as the gang broke up and started to run.

Crossbow bolts flew, spells lashed out, and the hoplites marched forward, stabbing.

Of the perhaps four hundred who had been caught in the alley, maybe fifty escaped, and many of those were wounded.

Then Beta set loose Sharon and her sisters, before leading her squads back to their station in the park, the day's fun finished.

The kids who had been used as a human shield by the dickhead Aaron had been found and freed as well. The locks that held them chained together were no match for a determined kobold.

Half an hour after being freed, they were all sitting in the main canteen area, the restorative power of chocolate and homemade ice cream simply magical in a whole different way.

"I'm all right," Kelly said after filling me in, before snorting out a little laugh and gesturing around us. "This helped, as did saving those kids."

"Where are we?"

She smiled. "My place."

"Your…wait, this is your house?" I asked, even more confused. "I thought…"

"There were two families living here. That's what Ken told us, and one of them still was. The other moved out already." She sighed, shaking her head. "Anyway, I asked them to leave. There were a few houses with enough room for them to move into for the night, and when I saw the state of the place…" She shuddered.

"Was it bad?"

She looked at me over the coffee cup, taking a long sip as she appeared to think about the words to use. "You know when you're on holiday for like a week with your friends? You know how much of a bomb site the apartment gets?"

"Yeah?"

"Imagine that, complete with the food up the walls, the sticky spilled drinks, then add in the apocalypse. No power for vacuums, not enough water to wash things, mold that just keeps growing…"

"Damn, that bad?"

"Worse," she said. "I managed to push out the dungeon close enough I could do this room and the bathroom. The rest of the house is trashed still, but when I came looking for my spare clothes and photos and things, and found the state of the place? No." She shook her head.

"I'm sorry, Matt, I know it's not important, not in the big picture, but this was *my home*. The people squatting here…not living, *squatting*—I had to absorb the entire bathroom because there were 'smiley faces' drawn on the walls in there, in human shit—had trashed the house to where it was ask them nicely to leave, or shoot them in the face."

"Why would you do that?" I wondered aloud, before blinking as I saw the uncertainty on her face. "Sorry. Not you. I mean, why the hell would anyone draw on the walls in shit? Why stick your finger in it and do that? At all, I mean, let alone in a place you were fucking living in?"

"Honestly, I don't know. I knocked on the door and asked them if I could get some of my stuff, and they just shrugged and went back to drinking. Ken had to come with me. I think he was expecting to make me leave once I'd got some clothes and to make sure I didn't kick off or anything."

"And?"

"And he saw the state of it, and went apeshit, asked me to wait in the bedroom, and basically tore a strip off the family. Two parents and little girl. The kid had no clue anything was wrong, so clearly they've always been living like this…"

"Was the smiley face…"

"Head height on the wall in there, on me." Kelly shook her head. "It wasn't the kid. Too high."

"Fuck."

I genuinely didn't know what to say to that and stayed silent as she took another sip.

"So, I stood in here—you were unconscious in a litter outside, about to be taken back to the dungeon—and Ken came in a few minutes later, finding me crying over the state of my home. He apologized and made it clear that people were told to bag up the previous owners' things and put them in the loft, just in case people came back."

She gestured around at the stuff that surrounded me.

"Some of this was up there. The rest I used a little mana from the dungeon to clean and replace or repair." She paused, holding a hand up as I opened my mouth.

"I did it when I would have been sleeping, to be clear, instead of having a sleep or any time for me. I absorbed the cheapest stuff out there, and used the mana I got from that to do all of this. I didn't waste 'normal' mana from the dungeon just on me, but—"

"Fuck, Kelly, don't be crazy!" I cut her off. "You've been working your arse off round the clock, risking your life day in and day out to help me and everyone else. Taking a little mana to clean your damn bedroom, and so *I* could sleep in it...?"

I reached for her, and she set her coffee down, climbing onto the bed with me and clinging to me.

"I was worried you'd be mad," she whispered, and I drew back, frowning at her, before kissing her quickly.

"You daft bugger," I said softly, then kissed her again. "Mad that you tried to make your bedroom nice after you'd had people living here all this time? While you were trapped in a fucking dungeon with me?"

"I'm hardly trapped...and I like our room."

I rolled her onto her back and leaned over her, staring down into her beautiful blue eyes. She reached up and drew me back down for a long kiss, the serious kind that made my blood heat.

"Although..." she whispered, breaking off for us both to take a breath.

"Yeah?" I asked huskily.

"Remember the night we met?"

I nodded, remembering seeing her for the first time, the hot kisses and the fun, the roaming hands, and the freezing rain as I splashed my way home, having given her my taxi.

"Well, you remember when we were messaging each other afterward?" She lifted her arms up toward the top of the bed, and I looked down, my gaze drawn as her sweater rode up, exposing her toned midriff, and I leaned down, lifting her top up, inch by inch and laying little kisses up as I went.

"I do..." I said with a rising heat in my voice. I did; I remembered the things that she'd messaged, and although she'd never said anything too overt, she'd made it clear that another, more private date, would result—if I was lucky—in a lot more passionate attention.

"Well, you know when I said that I'd invite you round sometime, maybe for dinner?"

"Yeah?"

"Well, I'm hungry right now," she whispered, pulling her top off and tossing it aside, exposing a lacy white bra and pressing my face to her chest as I reached around behind her, popping the hooks free. "And I want something hot and filling..."

The next few hours passed quickly—far too quickly, in truth. The strange feeling of safety, of privacy, and of the old world being there again was too much to pass up.

Even when we paused for breath, summoning drinks and more, resting and recovering, joking a little, we deliberately didn't check on the dungeon.

If something was wrong, others would reach out, and if there was danger, I suspected the dungeon would now as well, but we just needed that time to ourselves.

Kelly had warned me about the bathroom already, and that she'd replaced it with a very basic shower, toilet and sink combo for now. When I left her bedroom, stepping out into the landing and looking around, I was shocked, even though I'd been sort of ready for it.

Rather than "waste mana" in fixing things like the carpet, she'd just absorbed everything, and damn.

The bedroom had been stylish, definitely a woman's room—it was tidy and had hairclips and cushions and stuff—but out here? It was more like the abandoned house I'd fought in back at the beginning of the fall. The floor was down to the floorboards—the carpet, underlay, the lightshades: all of it was just gone.

The house had a pervasive smell that suggested filth and body odor, food that had gone off, and the kind of house that I frankly would have pictured her going miles out of her way to avoid before the fall.

Now it was all that was left of the home she'd been so proud of.

I used the facilities, then stood there, in the small bathroom, looking around and trying to imagine what it was like before.

"You okay in there?" Kelly asked a few minutes later, knocking gently on the door.

"Yeah, sorry!" I sighed, tugging the door open. "I was just trying to imagine the room as it used to be..."

"It was nice." She stepped in, still naked, but holding a large fluffy towel I recognized as the same kind we had in our room back at the dungeon. "The shower was bigger, tiles on the walls, and a 'wet room' design, so it didn't matter if water got splashed around..."

"Had a lot of fun in here, eh?" I asked, only half joking, and she looked up at me, smiling sadly.

"Actually, it'd only been finished a month before the fall. Nobody got to share it with me."

"Never christened?" I pulled her in close, her softness pressing against me as we kissed. "That's a shame."

"Think we could do something about that sometime?" she asked, breaking off from the kiss, and reaching down to stroke me. "Or now?"

"Batter up!" I groaned at her touch.

"Girlfriend...*down*..." she whispered, dropping the towel onto the floor and kneeling on it to take me into her mouth.

"Well..." I gasped after a few seconds, one hand on the top of her head as she bobbed rhythmically. "I guess...we do...need a shower...after all?"

The sound of agreement she made was clear, if muffled.

CHAPTER TWENTY-FIVE

The sun was setting when we stopped, properly anyway. The pair of us lay in her bed, me on my back, her cuddled into my side, one leg over mine, and arm draped across my chest, the other folded over her stomach.

I stared up at the darkening ceiling overhead, listening to her breathing deepening as she slid inexorably into the embrace of sleep.

I was grinning, I realized, the fluffiness of her duck-down duvet swamping us rather than the thin synthetic one we had in our room. Her bed was comfy, and repaired and cleaned by the dungeon. It was in perfect condition, as was everything else in here.

I glanced down, her head resting on my shoulder, and I mentally added her to that list. *Definitely perfect condition.*

I let out a long breath, closing my eyes, but rather than allow myself to sleep, I slid into the dungeon sense, pulling my notifications up at the same time.

Congratulations!

You have killed the following:
- 176x Gang members, various levels, 19,823 XP
- 57x Enraged Undead meldlings, various levels, 16,218 XP

Total XP earned: 36,041 XP

A party under your command killed the following:
- 115x Gang members, various levels, 12,952 XP
- 23x Enraged Undead meldlings, various levels, 9,181 XP
- 2x Guardian Triceratops, Level 11,860 XP

Total Party XP earned: 22,993 XP

As party leader, you receive 25% of all XP earned.
Total XP awarded 36,041+(22,993x0.25=5,748.25)= 41,789
Partial XP is lost to the ether.

Current XP to next level stands at 62,575/35,000

You have 9 unspent Stat Points, and 10 unspent Skill Points.

I couldn't help but grin over that. No matter how damn hard life got—or how wonderful, thinking about Kelly, now deep asleep in my arms—leveling up was fuckin' awesome.

I'd keep the skill points for later, again, because it just damn well made sense. Unless I started crafting, which I really didn't have time to take up, then my only real use for the skill points was to level up my weapons handling, and at this point? It'd be a waste when I could do it just by fighting.

If it'd been a class skill, rather than a personal one? One I could spend on the dungeon and unlock something useful? Fuck yes, I'd be on that like a movie producer on an innocent starlet.

I looked over the stats as they stood now, grimacing as I considered my options. Realistically, the more I fought, the more it was obvious that my real strengths were magic and, well, being a bit batshit.

If I could use my magic more, I'd be far more dangerous, and as Kelly had explained, the real turning point for the battle for the park was when the kobolds all attacked.

I'd also killed most of my enemies using my magic, not my damn sword or whatever.

I had the kobolds, and I needed to make more use of them. They were amazing soldiers, and now that we had some with magic? It just made sense to start having them take the war to the enemy. If they died? Aside from a select few, like Beta, I'd just make a new one to replace them and probably never notice.

The only thing that kept me from going into an all-out "mage" build now was the fear of unbalancing myself and ending up useless.

I paused, thinking about that for several seconds, pulling the stats up again and reading them over.

I'd ended up "breaking myself," more or less, when I hit thirty in Intelligence, at a time when I was basically in my low to mid-teens in everything else.

I knew now that my Perception wasn't just a random thing that only kicked in when I stared down a scope at an enemy. It was always in use, literally: if I wanted to walk around the room, I "perceived" the gap between the wall and the bed, the distance to the ground for me to stand, the…

It wasn't important to keep going, I decided, banishing those thoughts. It was just to make sure I had it in my mind that I needed Perception to guide me in my movements.

My Constitution and Agility were all about moving my body and how my body reacted, with Dexterity and Strength, obviously.

The thing was, at a level of thirty Intelligence, I'd been superhuman. My body had been massively out of sync in comparison.

Now, most of my points weren't that far apart. My Intelligence, for example, at forty, was three ahead of Dexterity, and ten ahead of Constitution.

If I was right, and yeah, I was gambling here, then I'd encounter issues when I reached too far, like twenty points separation maybe, but equally, that was when I was a lot lower in level.

I didn't know for sure, but I suspected that it couldn't be a rule that for all mages to grow in power they had to be weightlifters and sprinters as well.

Laid there, half in the dungeon sense, and half looking over my screens, I thought about it for a while, before coming back to the simple detail that this wasn't a damn game.

There was no rulebook seeking to nix us from growing too powerful. Hell, if the quest I had was any kind of clue, the goddamn aliens wanted us as powerful as possible.

I thought about it, then decided the only way to do it was to experiment. Or as Chris liked to put it, "fuck around and find out." I had nine points to spend, and that would give me an extra four hundred and fifty points of mana to spend as I dropped it all into Intelligence.

Trying not to show any pain as the new connections formed, I stiffened, shuddering, and I made myself slide out of the dungeon sense, forcing my body to relax as the changes finished. Kelly mumbled something, and I kissed the top of her head, whispering it was okay and to go back to sleep.

Seconds passed, and her breathing deepened. I pulled my details up and reread them, smiling as I saw how big my manapool was getting.

Name: Matt, First Lord of the Storm				
Modifiers: None				
Species: Thunderstorm		Bonus: None		
Level: 24		Progress to next level: 27,575/35,000		
Control: 47		Dungeon Capacity: 654 points (47x2=94+560=654)		
Host Powers: 1 (Enhanced Regeneration)		Class Spells: 9 Class Abilities: 17		

Stat	Current Points	Description	Effect	Progress to Next Level
Agility	33	Governs dodge and movement	Heightened chance to dodge attacks 66%+20%= 86%	95/100
Charisma	26	Governs likely success to charm, seduce, or threaten	35% more likely to succeed in events that require seduction, persuasion, or threats (10%+ (16x2) = 35)	62/100
Constitution	30	Governs Health and Health Regeneration	HP: 30x40 = 1200	55/100
Dexterity	37	Governs ability with weapons and crafting	+37% Increased chance of improved result +13 to melee damage	68/100
Endurance	35	Governs Stamina and Stamina Regeneration	Stamina: 35x40 = 1400	74/100
Intelligence	49	Governs base manapool, standard intellectual capacity, plus Control when combined with Wisdom and divided by 2	Mana: 49x50=2450 Control: 49+46/2 = 47	51/100
Luck	35	Governs overall chance of bonuses and critical hits	+50% increased chance of positive outcome	63/100
Perception	30	Governs ranged damage and chance to spot hidden items/traps	+20 to all ranged attacks	97/100
Strength	32	Governs damage with melee weapons and carrying capacity	+44 to all damage with Melee weapons	69/100
Wisdom	46	Governs mana regeneration and Control, when combined with Intelligence and divided by two	115 mana regenerated per hour Control: 49+46/2 = 47 (46x10/8=57.5x4/2=115)	82/100

I nodded in satisfaction, then dismissed the screen, moving on to my remaining notifications.

Congratulations!

You have increased your Unarmed Combat skill to level 20!

You now stand a 40% increase in your chance to inflict critical damage. Increase your skill to augment your ability further. You also stand a +20% increased chance to learn new unarmed martial styles through simple repetition and observation.

Additional Bonus!

Due to the frequency of your attacks with fist and foot, and all between, and the internal strengthening and augmentation by your class and species abilities, you have gained the following ability:

<u>Storm-Strike:</u>
At a cost of fifty mana per blow, you can inflict the fury of the storm upon your target, channeling explosive damage through your body and into your victim!

I liked that, damn did I not. I was already channeling my storm mana through my body, speeding me up and increasing the power of my attacks. But to be able to force it out through the impact? And for it to be goddamn explosive? Hell yes!

I had visions of the next behemoth that strode the battlefield getting its teeth kicked in…possibly while "Eye of the Tiger" played in the background.

Moving on to the third and final "real" notification—I'd stopped reading anything that wasn't either a level up or an increase in something that mattered, ignoring skill levels that weren't multiples now—I grinned as I read it, loving the confirmation, even if I'd apparently read the buggers in the wrong order somehow.

Congratulations!

You have reached Level 24.

Current XP to next level stands at 27,575/40,000.
You have 0 unspent Stat Points and 10 unspent Skill Points.

Now that all the "crap" was dealt with, as enjoyable as it'd been, it was time to get caught up on the real world. I sank into the dungeon fully, flashing across the distance between the park and the dungeon proper.

There was almost no change here, when I first looked things over. But as I looked deeper, that wasn't entirely true. The supports for the massive accommodation block were in place as before, but now the framework had been readied.

The walls were finished, all up to the correct height around the outside of the entire new section, and the internal walls that had cut the rest of it off—apart from those around the castle—had been scrapped, pulled down, or shifted around.

I smiled, seeing that someone had added in the covered walkway that ran from both the accommodation block to the south end, and the "dungeon" building to the hot tub.

There were changing rooms there as well, which was a nice touch.

The rest of the main site hadn't been changed, though, so I moved along the line of influence, passing the river and climbing, pausing as I saw a handful of small goblins creeping around. I watched them for a few minutes, before deciding that they were no threat, apparently being naturally spawning monsters.

They, in turn, were being hunted by a ghast, one that looked like it was a variant different to the "lesser" that I'd had access to. It moved on all fours, the tail curled up overhead as it sniffed the air, apparently following a scent.

The lesser variants I'd fought before were around a third smaller than this one, and had run like the early kobolds had—a bobbing, unsteady gait that was more in line with an avian build, like a fuckin' fast and lethal chicken or something.

This, though? It was fast, moving on all fours. The forelimbs folded back on themselves, to hold the vicious blades its arms ended in back until they were needed.

The result was a fast, silent predator that the goblins had no chance against.

I checked the mana, getting a shock. We were up to twenty-six thousand, one hundred and eleven points, with a maximum of forty thousand space in storage now. The influence generators were producing mana now as well, although they were set to produce various forms of mana, depending on the location, and had also had an additional research project completed, tying the alert tower design in with them.

I liked it.

Now that I knew I had the mana to spare, though…

I moved a little farther away from the ghast and its prey, not wanting to scare them off, and summoned three kobolds, all warriors, all in full hoplite gear, and grinned when even with their weapons and armor it was still barely over eight thousand in cost.

I ordered the three to hunt the ghast, then bring it to the dungeon's influence so we could absorb it. Then I told them that once that was done, they were to report to Beta for more orders.

And possibly a cat calendar, if they'd done a good enough job.

That done, I flashed across the distance between there and the civic center, pausing long enough to see that the building was well on its way to being fully converted, as well as having gained a few more nasty-looking traps as soon as you first entered the building.

The lowest floor was all claimed now, and although the building was mainly still "normal" from the outside, inside it was anything but.

It looked more like a cross between a classical dungeon and somewhere that medieval cultures would use to protect their gold. Or possibly their princesses.

Either way, there was fuck all chance of people who went in coming out easily. I nodded to myself. It still had a long way to go, but it was getting there.

Moving on, I flashed across the remaining distance, reaching the farthest edge of the park, and pausing, stunned as I looked down on the area I'd seen so many times.

Hell, I'd driven past here a hundred times over the years, if not more, passing the crappy shops, the takeaways, the banks, and more that were nearby. But I'd never seen the park like this.

First of all, next to the very top, at the north by northeast corner, there used to be a college campus. It'd been knocked down ages ago and had a bunch of houses put up in its place.

They'd been new builds, and built all right, according to a friend who'd looked at buying one, but nothing special. The last time we'd come here, we'd walked past them, seeing the gathered people who were living in those houses, as well as the makeshift walls that had been thrown up to include them into the overall "safe" area around the park.

They were gone now, both the houses and the crappy walls.

In their place was cleared ground, large enough that I was stunned they'd managed to do it so quickly. It was at least a hundred meters deep, by six hundred long. And in the process of destroying those houses, and presumably taking the mass of bricks and general crap, they'd created a wall that stood twenty meters high, three deep and that was steadily growing all the way around the entire damn park, in place of the shitty wooden one they'd had before.

I continued on, seeing similar sights everywhere I looked. Hundreds of houses, houses that had been in use before, were just…gone. I started to worry, seeing the massive number of homes that were missing, and wondered whether I'd made a huge mistake here, considering that to move them on, they needed to live *somewhere*.

After all, it was the tail end of the year now, like literally building up to winter. Yeah, okay, we were in Europe, and specifically the North of England, so we basically got six months of rain, rather than the deep snows and icy depths of winter that a lot of the world got. But still, exposure would kill. At the very least, people who were forced onto the street with their kids would be going apeshit.

Instead, though, as I looked, I saw more and more people tearing houses down. They were working in shifts, I guessed, seeing the mass of people headed into the park, and those who were on their way back out, hammers and more held high.

I looked over the space that had been cleared, recognizing it as a killing field, and clearly the same being rolled out of the way around the rest of the park, but still.

I flowed inward, lifting high into the air again, and frowned at the bright-white light I could see as the dungeon worked steadily. Moving inward, I paused, staring down at the center of the park, and let loose a mental whistle of amazement.

Someone—Aly, I was guessing—had taken the plans for the park and had damn well supersized them.

The middle of the park had always held an old Gothic building. It was about a hundred and fifty, maybe two hundred years old—not that old, but old enough that it was interesting.

Clearly others had thought so too, as it'd been left intact. But the ornamental gardens to the west, and running about two hundred meters north from there, a hundred meters deep in a rectangle, had been stripped.

The gardens had been destroyed already, admittedly, the old flower beds and more replaced with growing areas and crops that would feed people.

But the space that they covered, all twenty thousand square meters, had been cleared, ready to be made into accommodation.

I looked over the plans, nodding to myself as I saw the simple design. Much like the one we were planning to build in the dungeon, this was a multiple floor design, two currently, with larger apartments on the ground floor, and smaller on the second floor.

I accessed the design, finding that between the mixed "larger" sections on the bottom floor, and the smaller one-bedroom and living area sections of the floor above, it showed a confirmed number of apartments at…five hundred.

That was three hundred single bedroom, and two hundred mixed, from five-bedroom to two-bedroom plots, corridors, bathrooms—all of it.

Again, no kitchens, and yeah, most of them didn't have windows either, but shit happened. These were safe apartments. The walls were fucking bronze, solid, with a layer of plasterboard and cork over it, making people able to hang things and paint it and so on, but seriously strong as hell. A meteor hitting one side would stop before it hit the other, for fuck's sake.

Looking at the plans, this one building, as it stood now, with only two floors, would comfortably hold fifteen hundred people. Considerably more, if need be. But sections were being cleared now for a second, and a third block the same. Once all three were built, that would mean nobody needed to live outside the main walls of the park.

They would be safe.

Yes, the apartments were small, and they weren't luxurious at all, but despite my concerns, most of people were out and working, I saw now.

The "canteen" that was attached to the Gothic house, the old Saltwell Towers, was being extended, even as I watched. An extra section, thirty meters wide and ten deep, appeared; the bright light of the dungeon's "printing" created it, even as people rushed in, arms full of tables and chairs.

I saw servers working the counters, the massive tables before them loaded with simple, but damn good food. Mountains of cooked chicken breasts and legs, trays of fries and more, giant platters filled with buttered carrots, peas, and broccoli.

People rushed forward. Barry and others barked at them, forcing them into lines, making them wait their turn, but smiles on their faces as they did so.

I watched one man weeping openly as he'd reached the end of the line and picked up a sponge pudding with custard. I saw trays of hot food shaking as people staggered across the floor, barely able to see through their tears as they found seats and tucked into food.

Barry was moving from table to table, Ken by his side, handing out short, triangular "keys." I'd seen them before, two inches long, finger shaped and triangular, looking down on them from above. They literally slid into the door when you tried to open it.

It unlocked your door from the outside, and taking it out again locked it. They required a drop of blood to "lock" to you, but once that was done, nobody else could use it.

It was the cheapest, and one of the simpler and more secure ways to give people their apartments. They also acted as a guide, pulsing as you got closer to the door, seeming almost to pull you along. That was why the blood was needed; these people weren't able to use their mana yet, and the key needed it, so a little prick was all it took.

I'd been clipped by Aly when I'd asked her if it was the first time she'd been told that, when she'd explained it to me seemingly ages ago.

Barry was telling people where to go, which apartment was theirs, and I'd never seen him so at home. These people loved him, and he was there, handing out the keys to them, and making sure they were all fed and safe...

While I'd spent the afternoon screwing my girlfriend's brains out.

Hell of a "lord" me, I reflected. I'd literally been borderline about not admitting these people because they might not help out or try to avoid work. Letting them into the dungeon might make my life harder, and it might slow things down for the overall plan. That meant that I might not be able to help people in the future.

That was basically my justification for not letting these people in. Yeah, until very recently it hadn't been physically possible, and even if it had? The actual space and the battles and so on?

It could have been a mistake.

That being said, though?

Watching these people here, literally thousands of them waiting for their turn, as Aly and others made them a safe home for the first time in months?

Seeing little kids who had had their childhood taken away, and who had been on the edge of starvation, while their parents panicked, day in and day out, that a fucking monster would swoop in and steal them away?

Then seeing them as they were now?

As Barry walked from table to table, in a warm building that had light at night? Seeing these people who had been given a room that was theirs and that *should* be actually *safe*?

Seeing them getting food—real food—and a goddamn stupid little dessert? Cold or hot drinks? Seeing them watching the kobolds marching outside, and them realizing that they were there to protect them all? Seeing the walls that were rising around the park?

I felt terrible.

No fucking wonder people were crying.

I'd been thinking of them as a commodity, as an expense that I had to work around, rather than the goddamn people they were.

I might not be able to save people in the future because I was spending so much focusing on the possible issues. The thing I was forgetting, though, was that if I didn't help people right goddamn now…there might not *be* anyone around for me to help later on, when it was more convenient for me.

I reached out to Aly, sensing that she was deep in the zone with the building that was going on, and I felt her acknowledge me absently.

"How can I help?" I asked, getting a mental smile from her as she actually saw that it was me.

"Hey…are you okay?" she asked, and I sent a smile back to her.

"Yeah, just tired, but I'm all right. Where can I help?"

"Well, if you're tired…"

"I need to help. Kelly is asleep, but I…I need to help," I said lamely, getting a sense of understanding from her.

"Absorbing?" she asked. "I know it's a shitty job, but people have been working in relays, and they're starting to drop from sheer brain-melting boredom. As more and more go…"

"You can build less and less," I agreed. "That's fine. I'll join the teams." I turned from being in contact with her mind, to searching for the piled-up crap.

It didn't take long to find it all.

CHAPTER TWENTY-SIX

The teams demolishing the houses were working steadily, street by street, house by house.

The house was taken apart level by level, one team throwing up scaffolding around a house, then moving on. While they did that, the cleaning teams went through the house, searching for things like pictures and obvious keepsakes. They were put in bags, if they hadn't already been taken care of, labeled and then set aside; then the team moved onto the next one.

The recovery team moved in next. Tech was torn out and piled in set areas, and then the rest? From random pots and pans to suitcases to plant pots, everything and everything was piled in the gardens behind the house—just thrown on the pile.

Anything that could be used was saved, knives and axes and so on, but the rest was chucked, then they moved on as well.

A team collected all the various keepsakes, labeled them up as to the location they'd been recovered from, and then moved on.

Next came the demolitions teams, climbing the scaffolding and essentially attacking the house with damn sledgehammers. They tore the roof off and chucked it into the back garden, demolished chimneys, supports, then moved inside and took out the internal walls, before turning to the outer walls.

While they were doing that, a second team of scaffolders were taking the structure down from the top.

As the building was demolished, the scaffolders worked level by level, removing their gear, and then moving to set up for the next house.

It was stunning, because there were hundreds of people in each team, working efficiently and as hard as they could.

They were literally working their asses off. And when people worked all out like that? Houses were taken down in a matter of hours, not days and weeks as would have normally been the case.

I hovered in the dungeon sense, feeling the exhaustion and dullness of mind that rolled off them as they worked, permeating the rocks, the pipes, the crappy paintings of dogs playing snooker and more.

They worked stoically, absorbing brick by brick and more, as a team lead gave direction, working their ass off as well.

"Okay, guys, we're getting low on mana. Davis, Keith—focus on tech, please. Sarah, Jenny—see if you can get more of the bigger stuff. Let's make a visible difference before the next shift comes…"

I slid in, joining the group at the edge of awareness, not knowing any of these people, not really, and was accepted as just another identity in the dungeon that was helping.

It was a strange thing, the dungeon sense, in many ways, because when it came to others, you didn't "see" them. You sensed them, if they weren't there physically. It was a combination of a scent, a taste, and the general accumulation of them as a mental image. So people you didn't know well? You had no real chance of identifying them in the mélange of sensory overload.

Sliding past them, I "landed," for want of a better word, on a large flat section of concrete in the garden, a narrow space that had been left clear for people going in and out, heading to the road.

All around me, and as high as I was tall, were piled-up bits of a house. From carpets to tables to chairs and bricks.

A nearby rosebush was half poking through a section of collapsed wall. I had a sudden second's pause, as I wondered whether the remains of that plant had been important to someone. If it was planted as a gesture of love, a gift, or simply to make the garden look nicer.

Now it was being crushed under piled bricks as people tore the houses around it apart.

I reached out, the nearest brick sitting on its own atop the battered carpet, and I pushed the influence of the dungeon into it, then selected to absorb it. The brick shimmered, breaking down into literal dust; that in turn became glimmering light, before vanishing entirely.

I sensed the single point that the dungeon gained from that being added to the stores, and I sighed, getting to work.

The next two hours passed in a blur, my mind growing dull and my thoughts scratchy as I worked on, ignoring the team lead when they called that the shift was done.

I finished the front garden in that time, just, and moved onto the back, spiraling around and selecting bigger things, like the carpets and tearing them down as I got faster, finding that the more I absorbed, the more I *could* absorb.

I grew faster at it, discovering that as the Dungeon Lord—or I guessed it was down to that, anyway—I could work on dozens of things at a time. It was just a matter of concentration.

I selected everything around me, working faster and faster, pushing out and pulling in, as flagstones were cleared, as plants were uncovered, and then absorbed as well.

By the time another hour had passed, I was almost done with the house entirely, and although I felt like I was finally getting good at this…I was also utterly buggered.

Yeah, I'd slept a lot of the last twenty-four hours, but I'd also been wiped out after whatever the damn doc had done, the battles, and, frankly, my sex life.

Kelly was great. I mean, shit, she was amazing, but damn! She was tiring as well. Between her and the mental flexing of muscles to work on the absorption? I was beat.

I slid back, lifting into the air and looking around, finding that most of the others were gone as well. A new shift was starting…but for me, yeah, the night was done.

I slid sideways and out of the dungeon sense, finding that at some point Kelly had rolled over, and was now laid with her back against my side. I tugged the duvet up and tucked her in, then sighed and let myself sink down into sleep and join her.

The night was over all too soon. The sound of someone trying the front door, then banging on it downstairs, woke us both.

Kelly was the first out of bed, as I clambered out as well. Her bare ass vanished out through the bedroom door at a hell of a speed, racing to the front, smaller bedroom and apparently cracking a window, shouting out a question and getting a response.

I felt no danger, and heard annoyance and resignation in her voice more than anything else, so I dressed quickly, looking to her as she finished her conversation and returned.

She walked in, a towel in one hand that she'd presumably used to shield her nakedness, now tossed onto the chair.

"Hey…" She forced a smile when she saw me dressing. "We need to be quick."

"What's up?" I frowned.

"They're clearing this section next." She shrugged. "We've got an hour to take anything we need. Then the teams start the strip…"

I heard the sadness in her voice, as well as resignation, and I winced, having not considered that her house would be treated the same as everyone else's.

"We could…uh…" I tried to think of something that wasn't just "you're shagging the boss and get extra bonuses."

"It's okay." She stepped in close and stood on her tiptoes to kiss me. "I got to see my room as it was, mostly, and I already bagged up my personal stuff." She shrugged again. "It was a good house, but—"

"But we'll make a better one," I assured her. "Together."

"Do you want that?" she asked hesitantly. "I mean, I know this is fun and all, but, do you really want to, you know?"

"You think I don't?" I asked, confused.

"No!" She stopped herself, took a deep breath and went on. "We just, *you know*, we haven't talked about it. I just kinda needed somewhere and we didn't have the mana for a second room, and then the others were there, and they needed the space more…"

"We just never spoke about it," I agreed. "Kelly, I'm in love with you, and yes, I want to live with you."

Her smile was as the rising sun, bright and wonderful to see.

"Good," she said, before kissing me again. "A girl just likes to have that said now and then, that's all."

With that, she spun away from me, moving quickly and pulling clothes out of a bag, dressing in a blur as I shook my head, smiling at the bomb site she left behind everywhere she went.

Anything that wasn't what she was looking for? It was thrown aside, tossed onto the bed, the dressing table, the chair…everywhere.

I reached out, focusing and absorbing the duvet and sheets, having liked them, and making damn sure I could find that pattern again in the mass of new additions.

That done, and knowing the state of the room after our antics yesterday and last night, I went around the room, quickly absorbing things as she picked out the items she wanted to keep.

In ten minutes, we were both dressed, the bedroom was stripped, and we were headed down the stairs, me having to duck as the low ceiling on the stairs nearly knocked me out.

"Do you want to do a pass around the house?" I asked her, as she paused in the hallway, and I winced at the way she glared at the walls and floor.

"No, I want to go." She led the way straight to the front door.

I didn't blame her. The downstairs, as we'd gone down the stairs, had grown ever more filthy.

The hallway, once clearly filled with polished wood and painted, with mirrors and glass partitions that should have made it feel airy and larger than it was…

Was instead dark and dingy. Thick mud and what smelled like trodden-in dogshit coated the wooden floor. Dirt and scuffs marred the walls and doors. And the glass?

Well. The splatters and stains that covered it looked like a frat-house bathroom would be a better choice of where to greet people.

We left quickly, half jogging down the garden path to where she hesitated, looking up at the house she'd bought and barely lived in.

"The next one," she promised herself so quietly I hardly heard it. "The next one will be the forever home."

I rested my hand on her shoulder, getting a sad smile from her, before she kissed my fingertips and then took a deep breath. And the vulnerable and sad woman was gone; in her place stood the Dungeon Mistress.

She carried two bags, and I took one of them. The pair of us strode up the street and passed teams gathering at the end, being given their jobs for the day.

A few people frowned at seeing us walking off, not offering to help, but most saw the armor we wore, or the remnants in my case, and assumed we were fighters, and therefore off to go and do something dangerous, or stupid.

Or both.

We crossed the street and picked up the speed, striding past dozens, then hundreds of people as they moved with a purpose, and I shook my head in amazement.

"I didn't think they were like this," I said in a low voice. "The people, I mean…"

"They weren't," she said. "Every time we've been through this way, the park was falling apart, and the people were as well."

"What changed?" I frowned.

"Magic," she said. "Enough of the survivors from the fight with Dickless gained abilities, fighting ones, mainly, but it meant that when the monsters attacked, the warriors tore them apart. It gave people a little hope."

"We showed them what life could be like again," came a voice from behind, and we turned, seeing Ken striding up. "Good to see you, Matt. You looked like shit when I saw you last."

"Yeah, that's kinda my look these days," I admitted, smiling at him. "So, people just got up and started working?"

He snorted. "Oh yeah, it was just like that. Everyone decided that they should work and help…" He spat on the ground before going on. "No, we kicked people's arses, and those who were working? They were shown magic from the dungeon. They saw the food appearing; mothers with little kiddies saw toys for them, food and safety, and they booted people in the ass as well."

I grinned at that, knowing what women in the North were like. Once they decided something was happening, it was better to go along with it, because it was going to happen whether you liked it or not, and it was far less painful that way.

"Once the mothers were in on it, and they'd started kicking their husbands, boyfriends, and fuck-toys out into the street with orders to make themselves useful? Well. Word spread fast." He smiled. "It also helped that it was you, the Dungeon Lord, who was making all this actually possible—kept making storms appear out of nowhere, killing tens of thousands of the undead and gangs, and basically kicking twelve shades of shit out of the monsters under the bed."

"Yeah, little kids are being told that if the monsters come for them, the Dungeon Lord will protect them." Kelly snorted. "They've no clue what you look like, most of them, but they hear about it from a friend of a friend who once saw you fly and call down lightning."

"Fuck's sake…" I whispered, glancing from one to the other. "You've got to be shitting me?"

"Nope." Ken chortled, before sobering up at the glare I gave him. "Look, Matt, seriously, these people are fucking terrified of the things that go bump in the night. It turns out there *are* monsters, and they're roaming wild, slaughtering people."

"Then we come out of the night," Kelly said. "We provide safety, security, food and shelter. The Dungeon Lord brings magic healers and buildings that are practically nuclear bunkers. He kills the gangs and can fly. There are dragons serving him and—"

"Wait, what fucking dragons?" I hissed.

"The kobolds."

"They're fucking kobolds!" I pointed out, trying to keep my voice down and curling my hands into fists. "They're not fucking dragons. They're just…"

"They look like dragon-people, and they're armed to the teeth. They hunt and kill anyone who threatens these people, and they serve you." Ken shrugged. "Seriously, look at it from their side. They've got nothing, they're literally waiting to die, and then you're out there fucking the monsters up and taking their lunch money. You stroll up and wave your hand and walls appear. They think you're a god."

"I'm not a fucking god!" I snarled.

"Well, you are the leader of a pantheon," Kelly said. "So technically you are…"

"A pantheon of one!" I hissed.

"And you killed another god," Ken said. "I mean, when that big bastard appeared on the battlefield, the bone dragon, I thought we were all fucked. Then you blasted it and—"

"I'm just…I don't know! I'm just learning to be a god!" I snapped, then froze as I realized that not only had that come out a lot louder than I'd wanted…but we were in the entrance to the canteen and were surrounded by people.

And they'd all heard it.

"Oh, for the love of…" I sighed, sagging slightly as I looked around, seeing a hundred plus people staring at me in stunned disbelief.

My armor shifted, seeming to twist slightly, and then adjusting. I sensed Aly's hand in that, as the armor literally changed before everyone's eyes.

I had a split second in which I had a choice: a chance to turn away, to run—hell, to *fly*—and then, well, it was past.

We'd had conversations about this, over the weeks and months we'd all lived together, mainly drunken ones, about the nature of heroes.

Mankind *needed* them.

We needed someone to turn to, to look up to, and to compare ourselves to, when the shit hit the fan. When you thought "I can't do it; I'm done" and someone else did it, when they stood up and said, "That's it; this far and no further"?

It made it easier for the rest of us to do it as well.

The image for my generation had been of a tank, one that'd been driving down the road, and a single man had stepped out and stood in front of it, refusing to move.

It was stupid.

He was squaring off against a fucking *tank*, hundreds of tons of metal designed to kill, against a fleshy bag of bones and blood, mostly held together by alcohol and low-grade paranoia for most of us.

He was a hero, though.

I didn't even know what he was doing, or where. Just that he proved a single person could stop a fucking tank, if they just had the balls and sheer madness to do it.

That was what we all needed, as a species, and as a culture.

We'd spoken about manufacturing a hero, someone who was good-looking and smart, a figurehead we could trot out to inspire people. A bit like how Mike rallied the army guys, but, I don't know, better looking and more confident, which seemed insane.

Others had said it should be me, and I'd outright refused.

Fuck no.

I wasn't that guy.

I was the leader, yeah, because there wasn't anyone else who could do it, and who I'd trust, if there was a way to hand it over, admittedly, but a hero?

I wasn't.

I was just…me. I was just a guy who'd…

I was a person who'd done what needed to be done.

I saw it then in a terrible flash of memory, and of recognition. I saw all the fights, hunting the gang at the beginning of all of this, establishing the dungeon, finding Amy and protecting her, freeing Aly, handing the park over, and taking in more people, fighting the undead and leading battles.

I saw it all in a split second and I sighed, recognizing that even though I'd never wanted this, I had to accept it. If I turned from it now?

No. I felt the changes Aly made as she worked—knowing she'd probably been fuckin' planning this, and with Kelly as well—and I stepped forward into the silence and took a deep breath.

"I'm not a god." The silence fell farther into the canteen as more and more people stopped to listen, and more people from outside crowded in close. "I'm no god—I'm just a man.

"I'm a man who's trying to do his best. I won't lie to you…I'll make mistakes. I'll not be able to save everyone, or to make things the way they were before. I can't bring back the dead, and I can't stop the monsters from coming. There'll be fights, and probably wars to come."

The silence grew deeper as I spoke, not sure who I was talking to, not sure of what I was saying, until the words came out.

"I'm here, though, and I won't turn away from you. I'll do my best to protect each and every one of you. If I have to give my life to save yours? I will.

"The world out there is broken. We know that there are creatures, like the orcs of fantasy, only far more deadly, technologically advanced, powerful, and able to travel through the galaxy.

"The changes here—the system, the monsters, all of it—was done to us by another species, as a desperate last-ditch attempt to create a race of heroes that can stop the creatures that go bump in the night.

"They never expected to kill so many of us. They were trying to give us magic, to make us strong. They were trying to create a race of heroes who could protect the weaker creatures out there. One that wouldn't hide in the dark, but that would take the fight to the assholes of the universe and punch their teeth down their throat!

"They wanted a race of fucking heroes! They watched us, and they saw that humanity is that race. They saw the potential in us, that of all the species of the galaxy, we were noble enough, we were strong enough, and we took so little shit from anyone else, that we could do this!

"They gave us the tools, and then they ran away, terrified of what was to come…"

My words hung in the air for a long pause. Then I spoke again; my battered armor finished its transformation, going from glorified bike leathers, overlapping segments of bronze scalemail, and occasional plates, to an entirely new level.

It was clearly made with the highest version of iron Aly could make, and the pearlescent patterns that gleamed made it clear that although Damascus steel might be called steel, and be officially out of our reach as an Iron core, she'd been working fucking magic again somehow.

The Damascus steel caught the light as it flowed up, my armor now a mixture of the beautiful metal and composites that were similar to the military-grade body armor that the army guys had brought.

Scales flowed up my neck, stopping just under my chin, rolling across my upper chest and shoulders. Panels grew atop them, giving me solid armoring on the shoulders and chest that could withstand serious gunfire up close.

The chest piece was solid on the front, then overlapping on the sides, ensuring no gaps for weapons to penetrate, with scales that flowed down to cover my entire body, neck to ankles. My arms got thinner plates down the outside and front, with interlaced sections to cover the back, lightening it and making it wearable in the long term, as well as removable.

The lower arms had bracers, and then gauntlets, with a complex overlapping stomach, waist, and cockholder that looked amazing. Thicker plates over the thighs…It just went on and on, and I knew this was one of Aly's "little projects" she'd been working on for a while, taking the original armor she'd made for us, and improving on it in every way.

I felt the slight tug as the armor finished changing and the goddamn cloak appeared.

A fucking cloak.

Inside, I was cursing. I loved what I'd seen of the armor so far, but I was literally wearing it as it appeared. For all I knew, it had "I love bum sex" carved across the ass, or "Please cum inside."

I'd never seen it, and I was trusting Aly massively with this. Had Chris been involved, I'd have never gone with it. But Aly? I just had to hope.

The cloak was a step too far, though. The goddamn thing would be a nightmare to fight in.

"They left us, not because they couldn't help, but because they'd already done all they could. They gave us a single chance to save our species…

"They wanted a *race of heroes*…" I called out into the silence. I turned around, feeling utterly ridiculous as I said it, but seeing the looks in these people's eyes as I spoke.

"Well, they got them. *Humanity* is here, and we're not going away. We won't go quiet into the night, we won't vanish, and we won't be fuckin' conquered! We'll rise up! We'll bring our people back from the goddamn edge, and we'll teach the galaxy that you never, *ever* fuck with humanity!"

That last bit, if nothing else, had gotten to these people. The intense desire to get their hands on anyone who fucked with them, and teach them some goddamn respect?

That was the soul of the North of England.

These people didn't give a shit about the wider picture normally. They'd shake their head and say it was a shame if an earthquake happened or if there were volcanoes or typhoons. They'd donate money happily—hell, they'd help if they could, any chance they had.

But when crossed?

They'd happily fight any fucker.

Since the fall, they'd been stuck trying to survive, seeing monsters and madness on all sides, but not seeing how they could help, not really.

Now they knew it, and that was the secret, I realized, as I turned from them and looked at Kelly, seeing the proud smile on her face as she watched me.

Not that they were lazy. They just needed to be shown that they *could* fight, that they *mattered*, and that all wasn't lost.

Kelly strode out to me and reached up, pulling my head down and kissing me hard.

"That's my god," she whispered, grinning. "Now, we just need to sort the hair and the beard, and you'll look the part." She kissed me again. "You've got the body…" She winked, and I grinned as Barry stepped out of the crowd nearby.

"I think Matt said the words we all needed to hear, people. We can do this, and for those who are just figuring this out, yes. This is Matt. He's the resident god around these parts, it seems…

"My parts," Kelly whispered, and I bit down on a snort of laughter, trying to look at Barry as though I were paying attention.

"And yes, he's the reason you're all getting, well, all of this! The food, the walls, the creatures that protect us instead of hunting us! All of this comes from him and his people, and he's offered us a home with him!"

I looked around, seeing how people hung on his words as he spoke.

"All we have to do, to be worthy of a life that is even greater than anything we've lost?" He looked back at Kelly and me and smiled sadly. "We look after our family and our friends. We fight for those who have nobody, and we teach them to stand up as well. We save people, and we work our fucking arses off to make this a home for our people!"

"We wipe out the raiders!" I called out, nodding to Barry. "We'll rescue those they've enslaved, and we'll wipe out the rest of these fuckers who think they can take what's ours!"

"We can't do it alone," Chris called from the doorway, and I looked over at him, grinning as I saw him push through the crowd. "We're good, and we can take out the big fuckers, the monsters, the things you can't. While you learn, we'll take them on, and we'll beat them, but in the long run, we can't be everywhere…"

He looked at Kelly, and she nodded, taking over the narrative.

"They're right—we can't do it alone. I know you've lost friends and family. I've fought beside them, bled beside them, and we mourned them when they fell…but we need your help. We need warriors, we need mages, healers…crafters and cooks! It doesn't matter if you help by carrying a damn chair out so that your fellows can sit somewhere comfortably when they take a break, or if you're there, fighting side by side with us."

"We need your help," I finished, seeing the nods, the agreement that rolled through the group. "We need you to spread the word, to recruit, to help us, to tear down the houses and to feed people. We need you all…"

"Are you with us?" Mike called, stepping forward at the last. "Some of you know me, like you know my sister…" He pointed at Kelly. "We lived here most of our lives. We drank in the same bars, got 'Delhi Belly' from the Delhi Takeaway…"

That got a few laughs, and I guessed that it was a notorious takeaway in the area, even if I didn't recognize it.

"We were just like you. When the fall came, Matt found us, and he taught us. Now we'll teach you. So I ask you again, Gateshead! ARE. YOU. WITH. US?"

He roared that at the end, and they roared it back. Some bellowed words: *Yes, Fuck yeah, Ooorah*, and more. Others nodded or punched the air with a fist.

They stood then, most of them clapping and whistling, some stamping feet, others clattering cutlery.

The canteen, the building around it, and the grounds outside…everyone gathered went nuts, shouting and cheering.

I reached out, grabbing Chris's hand as he moved in close, grinning at me.

"Thanks, man," I called to him, barely able to hear over the noise.

"Anytime, brother," he said seriously. Then he leaned in close and practically shouted into my ear. "What the hell did the doc give us? I was broken!"

"Fuck knows," I said as the noise fell to more manageable levels. "Whatever it was, it worked though."

"Supercharge," Kelly leaned in. "He basically gave you each a massive shot of adrenaline, the quantities we use in medicine to get your heart going…and he did it again and again, at your orders apparently."

"Oh…yeah, I think I told him to…maybe?" I admitted, frowning. "Honestly, I don't remember much of it…"

"You should all be dead." Kelly sighed. "Kilo was unconscious for a day solid afterward, and he's a kobold, so I don't even know what it did to his metabolism. As for you two idiots…"

"It was awesome," I said, and Kelly shook her head at the pair of us.

"It really was," Chris agreed. "It's like fucking on coke—completely off the wall, but brilliant."

"I—" Kelly broke off, and I saw the sudden speculative look on her face, then grinned.

"Think we can get a hit before bed one night?" I asked, and she snorted, shaking her head.

"The state of you three after it? Nope, you'd be useless…"

"But we could both try it," I suggested.

"According to the doc, it'll last a few minutes, that's it, so we'd need to be 'primed and ready,' if you want to think about it a little? That means he either needs to be in there with us, or waiting outside until we're ready, jumping in and hitting us both before buggering off."

"Oh." I winced, considering the logistics of it.

"Yeah, exactly," she agreed. "Come up with a viable alternative to us having a doctor hanging around and watching us in the bedroom, and I'll listen, but seriously, I'm not into groups. Been there, done that."

"Yeah, fair enough…Wait, what?" Chris asked, going from careful consideration to staring at Kelly as if she were about to explode and jump on someone right there and then.

"I was curious, so I experimented." She shrugged. "Anyway, breakfast, then we need to get back to work."

"Yeah…yeah," I agreed, nodding and gesturing toward the food, while wondering about her "experimenting." *Guys, girls? Multiples of each?* My mind raced, but I wasn't sure I wanted to hear the story, in all honesty.

"Well, let's do it." She shook her head as she looked over the trays of food. "We're gonna need more bacon."

CHAPTER TWENTY-SEVEN

The rest of the day went well. The morning was mainly spent walking the park with Barry, Mike, Chris, and Kelly, being seen as much as seeing the place. We spent some time with the work groups, with each of us taking turns, publicly doing the various jobs. It felt a bit like a politician's walk-around, like we were wasting time, but it was worth it as well.

Chris cast his druidic spells, making people feel better. Kelly guided troops of kobolds around the area, helping them to understand the humans, and vice versa.

Mike spoke to people he knew from before, and recruited ex-soldiers and more fighters for the warrior core we were planning to expand.

Barry introduced us and spoke about the people we passed, telling us things we needed to know as much as not. People with criminal pasts were picked out and identified. Some—"car thief, nice guy, was an arse as a kid, served a few years, and turned himself around, good lad now"—were pointed out as having made mistakes, but had paid their debt and were moving on with their life.

Others were pointed out as people we'd better not turn our back on, under any circumstances, but who had manipulated their way into positions where Barry couldn't just boot them out. The last few, though, were different.

One of them I was introduced to, a seemingly quiet, calm man, utterly nondescript, was the kind of person you'd never notice in a group. But there'd been issues, and women refused to be anywhere near him.

Barry had said that there was "something off" about him, but he couldn't put his finger on it.

When we met him, he was cheerful, affable, and made a point of joking with Barry and me, but avoided Kelly, seeming to ignore her comments. It was a bit rude, but nothing I could really pull him up on. Until…

"Lewis, isn't it?" Kelly asked, and he hesitated, seeing we were all watching him and nodded once. "So, Lewis, you work here alone?" She gestured to the section of bricks he was stacking and tidying away, ready for absorption.

"Always…"

"I like the peace and quiet myself. I think I might have to look at new quarters over this way," she said, then led the rest of us away.

"What was that?" I asked her. "You want to move over here?"

"He's a sexual predator," she said quietly. "Released from prison less than a year ago. I read his files, and no, I'm not telling you what was in them, because I damn well know what you'll do."

"Shit, seriously? You're sure?" I asked, stunned and more than a little horrified at how beyond a little weirdness, I'd seen nothing.

"I'm pretty sure, Matt. You don't want to know the things I've seen. Men like that? Just…no."

"Fucking assholes." I growled, horrified at the idea that when all this shit was going on in the world, even here, in the middle of the supposedly safest place we could manage just about, there were predators. "Fine. On the upside, hey, I'm the local god, remember? *Divine mandate here, people, passed down from on high.* You ready?" I glanced around and then nodded, speaking before Kelly could.

"Thou shalt not suffer fucking predators like that to prey upon the innocent," I said in a very clear voice, looking around at the others and making to draw my hammer again.

"No..." Kelly shook her head. "Trust me on this. He matches the descriptions, and looks a lot like the photos I've seen, but the name doesn't match, and he could just be...a bit weird."

"So what, you want to wait?" I asked, worried.

"Not exactly," she said, smiling evilly.

That evening, by an amazing coincidence, Lewis met an unfortunate accident. He had apparently followed what had appeared to be a very pretty blonde woman who walked off into the dark "for some privacy." In fact, he accidentally stabbed a puppet that Finn had created for Kelly especially. Admittedly, it was wearing her clothes and a wig, but those were just details.

The knife he'd tried to use on Kelly was very particular, and matched a description that fit several of the files Kelly had read. That would have been more than enough for me, but in the process of "restraining" him, Kelly was apparently annoyed enough that he expired.

Something to do with having his arm ripped off and being beaten with it was apparently bad for his health. Fortunately, nobody gave a shit, and he'd made a point of telling people nearby that he was thinking of leaving anyway.

That had struck people as odd, considering he rarely spoke, but he'd clearly decided that he was going to have some fun then move on, so it was a damn good thing that Kelly had recognized him when she did.

Others we were introduced to weren't as bad on the main, the real predators having moved on already to join the gangs, or had been killed.

There were a few who were quietly told to move on, or that they could join the warrior core. Surprisingly, two of the five we went looking for had already volunteered, so that was fine.

Those who had managed to annoy Barry enough that he locked them up, but not enough to banish, were in Barry's stockade. It was basically a house with lockable rooms, where they were let out on a morning and forced into hard labor, before being locked up again, and they were interviewed by John.

Two were thieves, as we'd been told, and after a long conversation about the various things that happened to thieves, mostly involving sharp pikes and being stuck on them over the gates, both were reformed characters.

Mainly.

They were actually recruited to be rogues, and were getting power-leveled, but they were also working with Sharon and her team. It was explained very clearly that stealing from *any* of us would be a mistake.

Most likely the last one they ever made.

Of the other three, one was a drunk who refused to stop drinking or contribute in any way. He was given the choice of sober up—with help—or be given a bag full of supplies and to be waved off.

He left, despite repeated efforts to talk him around. He simply refused to work under any circumstances, and had been caught breaking into the stores, then drinking himself into insensibility.

Next was a drug dealer, mainly. He'd been locked up after he'd beaten two young lads unconscious who "owed him money." Money was clearly pointless now, or at least the kind he'd been after had been, so he was given the choice: serve or fuck off.

He'd joined up, but he wasn't happy about it.

The last individual was more of a problem. She was both a highly gifted and skilled crafter, and utterly unrepentant. She'd been thrown in the stockade when Barry heard about her. She'd apparently been selling surprisingly good knockoff gold coins and claiming to be involved in our economy.

She'd gotten two rifles, a dozen bullets, clothes, food, and more from people, and would have gotten away with it as well, if she'd not been greedy.

Her argument was that she didn't recognize our authority, and John, being a stickler for rules, had apparently agreed with her on one point.

We had no written constitution, no codex of laws, and as such…he was highly limited in what he could do as her actions didn't really match any of our laws.

Also, although she'd been claiming to be "involved" in our economy, she'd not claimed anything else. So, as she was handling replicas of our coins, she *was* in fact "involved."

It'd come down to the fact that she was trading for the coins, not actually telling people they were our coins, but deliberately leaving things vague. John's ruling at the end was that although it looked like fraud, legally it wasn't. It was very carefully *juuuust* on this side of legal.

Needless to say, she turned out to be both a lawyer in a former life, and to have a class that, when she described it—sullenly—sounded like a knockoff for the Courtesan.

Masquerade was a deception and detail-based class that appeared to be literally built around saying and doing nothing illegal, and yet breaking every goddamn law there was, if the law existed at all.

The longer she spoke about how she was innocent and just misunderstood, the more we all calmed down, feeling like maybe, just maybe, we should give her a chance.

Then Ashley arrived, having been looking for us, and the tables were flipped.

Ashley's Courtesan class had a massive advantage over other conversation-based classes as well, as she'd taken Mistress of the Voice, and had been learning to actively convince people of things.

She injected her mana into her voice, she told us afterward, and that had been the trick that Kaylynn had been using on all of us.

The only difference was that Kaylynn's version was the "trainer wheel" one, and Ashley's was the full-on, all the DLC and the bonus pack version.

It took her less than ten minutes to have Kaylynn confessing everything, and five minutes after that, to have her drawing maps of the local area for us.

She'd developed her talents in one of the raider camps, working her way from Whore—which was apparently a class, after all—all the way to Masquerade.

Then she'd run for it, convinced that she could literally do what she wanted, and had been making the most of the new world. At first, once we realized what she was, and her skills—not the original skill set that she'd used, but her new one—we'd thought she could be an asset to our side.

As time went on, though, and she spoke more and more?

No. Hard pass.

She was hard and brittle in a nasty combination, convinced she was better than everyone else, with utter contempt for all men, presumably from the life that led to her first class choice—be that whoring or lawyering, we weren't sure—but we knew which was actually less socially acceptable. Then came the minor detail that she viewed all women as either competition or "ugly old bags."

Well. We knew enough about her by that point that I turned to Ashley and asked a simple question.

"It's not right for us to kill her, not for what she's done, but I don't want her anywhere near us. Can you banish her and make her abide by it?"

"Possibly," Ashley agreed after a few seconds, picking at one nail as she thought. "I've got a spare class point, and I've taken two levels of 'voice' already."

"I don't want to tell you what to do with your points, but would that upgrade the skill much?" I asked slowly, wincing as I damn well knew that was *exactly* what I was asking her to do.

"It would—" She read the details, then sighed and nodded. "I've taken it. Don't worry…I'd been considering it anyway. The new version of the skill means I can convince 'those not in outright opposition' more easily, and those who 'are under my control' as well."

She paused, seeing the look on my face and sighed, rubbing at her temples.

"Okay, so 'not in outright opposition' means that if they've not got their guard up, so I meet them and they don't hate me or are antagonistic to me…so they *might* be our enemies…if they don't guess what I'm doing or who I am? I can convince them of things easier.

"The other side is 'under my control.' So, in this case, Kaylynn is our prisoner. She knows she's not getting out of this easily, and is therefore suggestible. She thinks she's going to have to do something to get out, and she's just waiting to see what."

I held up a hand, pointing a finger at Chris without looking and spoke quickly. "Not one word, dude. Not one fucking word…"

"Dammit." He grumbled, but I knew him well enough to know—without looking—that he was grinning.

Ashley had Chris, John, and me play bad cop, discussing openly with Kaylynn the possible things we could do, from chaining her and forcing her to work hard labor to using spells to compel her—we couldn't, but she didn't know that for sure—and then we let Ashley come in with the banishment.

Considering that was exactly what Kaylynn wanted, to just get the hell away from us and be free again, convincing her that it was her own cunning in manipulating things that got her out wasn't hard. Ashley spent most of her effort instilling a belief that if she should return, she'd be killed out of hand.

As soon as she was given the chance to run—without the guns and all the shit she'd managed to steal, just a simple backpack of supplies—she took it and didn't look back.

Moving on, we got back to touring the park, and I couldn't help but smile at the sight of the slowly rising apartment blocks.

To work on the area, to literally do as much as we had so far, there were several people dedicated to one job, and one job only: increasing the influence of the dungeon.

My discovery about moving the influence generator along on a ripple of ground had been examined and improved upon. Now there were three people, each with an influence generator, moving them steadily along, claiming a solid section of the area minute by minute, hour by hour.

The radius that the generator provided was much larger than the one pushed out by individuals, meaning it was much faster this way, even if it was also almost four times as expensive.

That was offset by the fact that instead of having trains of people humping all the crap back to the park and the dungeon's influence, three hours of someone's work could cover several houses, gardens, and more.

The walls of the park were rising steadily, and here and there small teams of kobolds ran back and forth, heavily armed and seeing, and being seen, as they patrolled.

The park was growing, and as things stood even now? It was starting to feel like we not only had a chance, but that hope was coming back to the North, which had been, frankly, missing for a long time for most people.

It was dark by the time we got back to the dungeon, back to our home in the Newcastle dungeon, anyway.

Barry had tried to get us to agree to stay, or better yet to move into the park, to build a floor of the apartment block just for us if need be. After all, nobody would begrudge us a bit of space…

Even as he'd said it, I'd just looked around, seeing the filthy people waiting as patiently as they could for the token to their room, and the first hot shower, and actual privacy, not to mention real safety, that they'd had since the fall.

We'd refused, saying that once things were sorted out and everyone else had a home, then we'd look at one for ourselves, but until then, we were going to make do.

It was hardly "making do," though, the pair of us had to admit, relaxing in our room in private, warm and dry, having just had a damn good steak, buttered new potatoes, roasted carrots, and mashed turnip, along with a garlic crème sauce and fresh baked bread.

We lay on the bed, recovering from the meal, wanting some fun time but too stuffed to manage it, and having a pair of cocktails.

Staring up at the ceiling overhead, I sighed, and honestly admitted to myself, that if I was given the chance to roll back time for everyone, and prevent the fall?

Knowing what I knew now, I'd not do it.

We needed this—the mana, all of it—to survive the future.

"What's that?" Kelly asked me sleepily, and I looked down at her, idly curious.

"What's what?"

"The wall…" She gestured, and I looked over, not seeing anything. "Doesn't matter," she mumbled sleepily.

"What did you see?" I thought a spider or something had run down the wall, and she shook her head, her glass empty, and laying as she was, half across me and drifting into sleep, I smiled and let her drift away.

I kissed the top of her head and took the glass, setting it on the bedside table, and glanced over at the wall…

And froze.

The shadows had *moved*, like I was standing with a candle, moving along the wall, and causing the shadows to stretch out…then fall back in on themselves.

After a second, they were back to normal, and it looked as if nothing had happened. But I was sure of it. I was damn sure that—

It happened again.

The shadows shifted and moved, seeming to flow and elongate, making me stiffen as I tried to understand, to make sense of—

A sudden hard bang rang out on the door, making Kelly and me jump. Before I knew it, I was up and standing between Kelly and the wall.

She headed for the door, grabbing a long T-shirt and shrugging into it at the muffled sound of voices outside, while I tried triggering my various senses, the Examine spell, the dungeon's various senses—all of them.

Nothing.

I couldn't feel anything from them, and yet…

Kelly pulled the door open, and I heard her speaking quickly to Aly, before closing the door and stepping up to me. I'd ignored their conversation, focusing solely on the wall when I'd heard the tone of voice: concerned, but not scared.

"What is it?" Kelly asked, and I shook my head.

"I don't know," I admitted. "What did Aly want?"

"She's seen them too."

"Them?"

"There's three she's seen—three shadows that don't move right—all in her room. Nothing in Amy's, but that might be a coincidence."

"I don't like it," I said flatly, and she nodded.

"Me neither, but she's said the dungeon isn't picking up anything from them, and except for how freaky it looks…well." She shrugged.

"So what, we just fucking ignore it?" I frowned. "That seems goddamn stupid."

"No, she's getting Amy to sleep with the lights on, and next to her while she does some research. She's saying it might be something, or it might be nothing, but to be aware."

"So…" I asked, uncertainly. "What the hell do we do now?"

"Honestly, no clue," she said, equally disturbed. "If we tell everyone, we'll start a panic, and that won't go down well. But if we ignore it? It could be a monster. It could be demons and they might be eating people right now, or it might be just a side effect of the light and mana. It could have been happening for ages and we've just missed it…"

"Fuck's sake," I snarled. "I'm going into the dungeon."

Kelly nodded, knowing that from there I could monitor the entire dungeon and everyone, if need be, and if something was happening, I could react the best way.

"I'll watch over you," she said after a few seconds. "Just in case."

The hours until dawn passed slowly, and I felt Aly searching by my side. Hints were found and discarded, until, shortly after the sun rose, I felt her mental presence return to my side.

"It's our fault, and it's…well, it's not a threat…not really, I don't think." She sighed, clearly exhausted.

"Go on."

"The cave below us, with all the Darkness converters?"

"Yeah?"

"I think, and I mean *think*—this is like fifty-fifty guesswork and science, so don't blame me if we're wrong on this—but I think that it's natural."

"I've never seen a fucking shadow walk across the walls before," I said. "Seriously, that's not fucking normal."

"It is, actually. Just normally it's caused by the light moving and casting a shadow."

"Right?"

"With mana affecting the world differently, there were always going to be interactions we didn't understand. Now we've got literal Darkness converters, and they're pushing out dark mana…"

"Dark. Darkness converters," I said. "Not fucking shadow!"

"It's all linked, Matt, you know that." She sighed. "Look, long story short, I think it's a mana interaction. You want to balance it out and stop it happening? We need a lot more Light converters. Thing is, though…"

"They'll only work at night." I sighed, rubbing my face and shaking my head. "One fucking day. I just want one day where nothing weird happens…"

"Now you know how we all feel," Aly said, and I felt her smile. "Seriously, though? I'd suggest we consider a load of Light converters on the roof, or in a room that we fill with, well, lights."

And that was how we ended up with the goddamn light platform.

"It needs to be the same distance from the ground level as the cave is. Otherwise, it won't balance…" Aly had said, and six hours later as I stared at the solid dozen Light converters atop a goddamn lightly swaying platform a hundred meters up, I couldn't help but shake my head in amazement.

The converters—like the Air ones creating a general upswing in wind—glowed steadily, and as the sun peeked out from behind the clouds, they only grew in brightness.

"This could be a really bad idea," I muttered to Kelly, standing by her side atop the roof of the dungeon and staring up, getting a tired grumble of agreement from her as well.

Neither of us got any sleep last night, and it wasn't for our preferred reason. We were both in a foul mood, but one that slowly lifted as the light grew.

It was, as near as we could work it out, late autumn now, which in the UK meant it was raining for fun. The trees had lost most of their leaves, and the days—like today—that weren't wetter than an otter's pocket, were grey and overcast.

The occasional break in the sea of iron-grey clouds from overhead was enough to make the converters' glow brighten considerably, as well as changing the twelve points they were generating in each, all the way to eighteen when the direct sunlight hit them.

I guessed that on a bright sunny day, it'd be all the way up to twenty points with no issue. But for now, a dozen more converters were giving us two hundred and sixteen points more an hour.

It seemed ridiculous, how quickly we were able to build right now, thanks to the influx of the surrounding matter, but...

I turned slowly, looking at the wide-open spaces around the dungeon, and wincing as I considered just how much of the city we were getting through a day now.

Give it maybe a month?

Newcastle would be barren, literally a grassy field that ran in all directions, and that was only if I planted grass, instead of leaving it as the shattered concrete.

The converters were massively valuable, but knowing now that if things were as Aly suggested, and all linked? We needed to invest in evening things out, or we'd end up with more really weird things happening.

Shadows were nothing, not really...but they were a visual sign that the mana we were pulling in and spreading around was having a massive effect.

I was just glad we'd never gone in for the Death ones...although we did have a lot of Life—

I froze, thinking fast, then let out a long breath.

We did have a lot of Life converters, but thankfully, not in our section, and Kelly was on the Pill still. I made a mental note to look into the various chemical and refinement labs we'd be needing to make sure we never ran out of *those* little beauties.

We had enough shit going on in our lives without Kelly and me falling pregnant.

CHAPTER TWENTY-EIGHT

Where the last few days had passed smoothly, even waking up the next morning, the feeling of a building threat made it goddamn clear that my lovely few days to relax and build the dungeon, while our creatures checked out the area, were well and truly over, as the shit hit the fan again.

I jerked awake, going from deep asleep—and dreaming of Kelly, naked and possibly with a few friends—to staring up at her as she sneaked around the edge of the bed, naked, which was a good thing, to get dressed.

Which was a bad thing.

A slightly worse thing was that I bolted upright, going from dreaming of her to the panic stage of incoming danger.

I startled Kelly, who was half-asleep and clearly also feeling that something was wrong, as she punched me in the face on instinct.

I collapsed backward, clutching my nose and swearing, blinking as my eyes watered, even as she covered her face with both hands and let out a horrified gasp that she was sorry.

She darted in close, tripped on one of her randomly dumped boots, fell atop me, and accidentally kneed me in the balls.

The worst thing was, that even as all of this was going on, and she was frantically rolling off me, apologizing and reaching out, presumably to rub the affected areas better…

The feeling of danger from the dungeon grew and grew, and in all the panic of getting up, still half wrapped in blankets, I knocked Kelly off the far side of the bed with a squawk of protest.

By the time I was upright fully, naked, still swinging a semi around, a little blood leaking from my nose and somehow, again, with a pillow on my head as a fucking hat, Kelly dragged herself up the side of the bed and glared at me.

There were a few hesitant seconds of silence, me distractedly trying to lock down the feeling, and her trying to decide whether me being naked, clearly aroused and wearing a pillow-hat was some kind of secret kink of mine, until I spoke.

"Danger…" I whispered.

"Will Robinson?" she asked, half-jokingly, before seeing the look in my eyes. The mood shifted instantly. "Shit, where and how bad?"

"The south, halfway between the civic center and the dungeon—" I frowned. "I…I think?" The feeling was there, but it was fading, even as I thought about it.

"It's over?"

I shook my head. "No, whatever is going on, it's sure as shit not over," I said. "The dungeon is—" I wasn't sure how to explain it, not able to really describe it, it was that strange a feeling.

I could feel a horror, and a yearning, like something the dungeon wanted or needed, and yet…it was afraid of it as well. Downright alien emotions shifted through the bond, and as soon as I felt one, it was gone.

"We need to go, and with backup," I said after a few seconds, blinking the dungeon sense away, and looking around for Kelly. In my distraction, she'd moved past me, and was now half bent over, black jeans on, pulling on socks and boots, one foot resting on the bed, no doubt leaving ingrained goddamn dried mud in the sheets I'd need to use the dungeon to remove.

I opened my mouth for at least the fifteenth time since we'd started sharing a room, about to tell her to use a goddamn chair or…or *something*.

Instead, I paused at the sight of her, straightening up and standing there, quickly binding her hair into a ponytail, her mouth full of whatever pins or bands or whatever the hell she was using, without makeup and topless.

I couldn't help but step in close, pull the bits from her mouth and kiss her hard.

She hesitated, her mind on the risk, on the danger that could be right around the corner. Then she melted against me, arms wrapping around my neck as she returned the kiss with at least as much fervor as I'd given it with.

"What…why…?" she whispered when I broke off, and I shook my head, staring down into her eyes.

"I love you," I whispered back huskily. "For me? Fuck, you really are all I want."

"I'm…glad to hear it." She smiled brilliantly, reaching up and kissing me again, slower, and with definite promise, before letting go. "To be continued," she promised, before looking down at where I was literally bouncing off her stomach, and smiled again, looking up and fixing me with an evil grin…before ducking her head and planting a hard, open-mouthed kiss atop me.

I groaned, caught halfway between putting my hand on the back of her head and pushing down, and on pulling back from her, considering the still there, but dissipating sense of danger.

Before either head could overrule the other, she released me and straightened up, licking her lips teasingly, and backed away, plucking her bra from the side table and slipping into it.

"Just something to keep your mind going." She winked. "And to make sure you come home to me." As she said it, she was reaching back, securing the clasps on her bra and tugging the half-done ponytail out of the straps, wincing.

"Guess I'll need to redo this," she muttered, breaking off to grin again at the look on my face.

"You…you…" I groaned, and she laughed, before dodging back to stay out of reach. "Oh, I'll get you for that," I promised, meaning every goddamn word.

She finished dressing and ran for it, while I seethed and tried to think calming thoughts, eventually giving up and almost snapping myself as I tried to arrange myself in my new armor.

A few minutes later, I limped out of our bedroom, boots in hand, trying to get my hammer to stay in place as it shifted uncomfortably.

"You okay, Matt?" Kelly asked me innocently. "You seem, I don't know, distracted?"

"I'll get you," I growled, before shaking my head as she laughed, joining her with a low chuckle. I moved to sit, dragging my boots on.

"What's happening?" Mike asked me, doing his best to ignore our byplay, even as he leaned his elbows on the table and sipped at his morning coffee.

"*I like my coffee, like I like my men…*" I read off his mug. "*Bitter and rough in my throat.* Shit, Mike, I never knew," I said, and he glared at me, lifting one finger in salute.

"Fuck you, Matt. Fuck you very much."

"Oh no…sorry, mate, I don't swing that way, as your sis—"

"You finish that sentence, and I'll hurt you," he promised, and I broke off, knowing I'd nearly gone too far. "What's happening?"

"Ah…yeah, all right," I agreed, dropping it. "There's something going on. An incursion of something the dungeon really doesn't like, roughly halfway between here and the civic center, not far from the river."

"What happened?"

"Something, a group of somethings, actually, crossed over our line of influence, passing between the generators. The alert towers picked them up and—" I squinted at the mental image, flipping it around and around.

"Jack, go hunt. Stay hidden but find out what the fuck is going on," I ordered aloud, knowing that Jack would get the orders even though he wasn't there, picking it up from my mind, before I turned to the others.

"They passed across the line at the farthest point from either of the alert towers. Literally, looking at the distances in the dungeon sense, I doubt there's more than a meter or two difference from one side to the other."

"That had to be planned."

"Most likely," I agreed. "There were a lot of them too, and they moved fast. Two, maybe three abreast, literally racing over the line. I—" I broke off, lost in thought.

"What does it feel like?" Aly asked, and I shook my head, examining the feeling.

"Honestly, I don't know. It's fading now, like a fart on the wind. But the dungeon *wanted* it, and it's afraid. Fuck, it's seriously scared of them and…"

And it clicked.

"There's been two other times I felt something like this, the dungeon wanting something and resisting me," I said grimly. "When the dungeon fairy was dead and I made it absorb her."

"What was—"

"It didn't want to break her down and absorb her—it wanted to resurrect her." The joking atmosphere, the simmering sexual feeling between Kelly and me, the general annoyance of Mike…all of it vanished under that realization.

Something that was out there was interacting with the dungeon, and it terrified and excited the dungeon core in equal measure.

"What was the other?"

"The asuras, though it was more of a 'possible' danger then, and a warning rather than fear, but this…this is like that. We need to check what's going on, and we damn well need to recover the ship," I said after a few seconds thought.

"How?" Kelly asked quickly. "I mean, don't get me wrong, I think recovering the ship is a brilliant idea, and I've been telling you that for a while, as have others, but…"

"But it's not close by, and it's the size of a missile." I nodded. "Well, that's one issue. The other is that something the dungeon wants, and is terrified of, is traveling around the area, and it feels like it's in force."

"So…?" Mike asked. "Come on then, oh glorious leader. Dazzle us all with your plan."

"Well, first of all, I'm not going to pick a mug at random without reading what's written on it." I grinned, reaching out and focusing, summoning a pot of steaming, freshly roasted coffee and setting it down on the table as I picked out a mug, checking to make sure it was blank.

I poured the black nectar of the gods into the mug, adding a little cream and sugar as I thought, even as Finn and Patrick, drawn by our voices, came to join us.

"Oh, *you've* got it!" Patrick smiled at Mike and the mug he held. "I've been looking for that…"

"Matt…for the love of God, just tell us all what you've got in that devious tiny mind." Mike groaned, and I smiled, sitting back in my chair and counting things off as I spoke.

"First and foremost, as much as I want the ship, the safety of our people comes first." I looked around. "As such, Mike, you're to lead a detachment in that direction. Find out what the hell is going on. I'll be going with you that far at least."

"You as in your team, or you as in you?" Chris asked, and I grinned at him.

"Me and a couple of volunteers, but I mean a couple. We can't risk leaving Mike or the dungeon under-strength for this." I turned back to Mike. "You're to take a decent-sized scouting force. Use the Karens, see what you can find, but they crossed the line halfway between the civic center and here. Right between the closest influence generators and alert towers. That means two things, as far as I'm concerned.

"First and foremost, they picked the exact point to cross where our ability to see anything is at its weakest. To do that, they have to know about us, and they have to know how we work. That right there is terrifying. Secondly, for them to cross there, they had to have come from somewhere farther along the river to the west. After seeing where all those bodies were dumped, and remembering the asuras? That's concerning. That there might be a second breeding ground? Or a base? That we might have just found something like a split-off nest, and we've made the main colony aware of us?"

I shook my head, looking from one to another of my friends—no, my *family*—and I went on.

"Seriously, we need to be careful here. Mike, you need to *scout* them, all of them, and see what you can find out. They crossed over the line, and fast, moving west to east, like they had somewhere they needed to be. Might be they're leaving the area, might be that they don't know about us and it's all a coincidence, or might be that they spotted an ice-cream van. Fuck knows, but find out. Do it with a large enough force that you can actually fight, though, if you get caught. Take a squad of the kobolds, do it right."

"And what will you be doing?" he asked, and I couldn't help but smile.

"Honestly, I'm going to see about getting us some cavalry," I said, enjoying the looks of confusion on their faces.

"Okay, be a mysterious bastard." Mike sighed after waiting a few seconds to be sure I wasn't going to explain anything else. "How long till we leave, and who's going with you?"

"I am." Kelly sat forward on her chair, clearly about to explain things as she saw them, when Aly cut her off.

"Actually, no, Kelly, you need to stay here." Silence descended as the women looked at each other, and Aly smiled. "Don't give me that look, sister dear. I know you!"

"Why should I stay here?" Kelly asked, annoyed. "I can—"

"You can control the dungeon creatures, you can control the dungeon, and you have ultimate control over them when Matt's not here. Hell, you give them bonuses! We have no clue what's going to be coming or going out there. For all we know, this is prelude to a war, and they're deliberately drawing Mike and Matt away to weaken us." Aly counted off points on her fingers as she spoke.

"I really don't like that thought," I admitted.

She nodded. "It's a real possibility, though. Can you do whatever your devious mind has planned with only a small team?"

I nodded. "I might be able to do it alone, but it'd be better with a handful of others."

"Who are you planning on?"

"Chris, Patrick, and…" I hesitated, thinking, then grinning. "And Kilo, the cryomancer kobold."

"Oh yeah!" Chris agreed, nodding. "He's cool."

"Why a kobold?" Kelly frowned.

"Not just one," I corrected, wincing at Chris's joke, and the way he was staring around, waiting to see who got it. "I was planning on taking Beta and her team. But now, with that wonderful thought?" I nodded to Aly and her reference of us being set up and drawn away. "I want her and her elites hidden nearby or scouting the area. I'll take Kilo, because he clearly understood us and was happy to work as part of the team. He's got experience with his magic, which gives us an extra bit of versatility, and he'll be able to help direct a team of kobolds if they've not awakened yet."

"Okay, so you're going to leave the dungeon with Mike and his people; they scout and head east once you find the section where the incursion happened." We all nodded at Aly as she spoke.

"I'll help guide Beta and the elites then." Kelly sighed. "I know it makes sense, and I can reach out to them easily as well. I'll guide them to search to the west, and I'll jump from them to the team that's with you, to the team that's with Mike as long as you're inside the dungeon's reach."

"Mike, take the Karens," I repeated, and he nodded. "Beyond that, take a full team of kobold infantry. Have them wait at the civic center. If you get caught and you're falling back—" I grimaced. "We need a way to raise an alarm."

"I can sense a little out of the dungeon," Kelly said slowly, and I grinned.

"There is an option, but you're not gonna like it."

"Oh gods…"

"Fuck my life."

"He looks happy…I'm out."

I glared around at the others as people pretended to push back their chairs in readiness to flee.

"It's not that bad!" I said, complaining at their antics.

"Liar."

"Look, all I'm saying is that I could evolve a—"

"Oh gods!"

"Hide the kobolds. Beta's already got it in for him over how many keep dying," Patrick said to Finn, who covered a grin as I glared at them all.

"Right, if you fuckers have had quite enough?"

"Oh no, I could do this for hours," Chris assured me happily as I shot him the finger.

"What I was *saying* before the idiot brigade joined in, was that I could evolve an impai!" I got out, and the room fell silent.

"Those little fuckers that spend all their time humping each other and eating squirrels and pigeons?" Chris asked slowly, scratching the side of his beard. "I don't know, man. I don't see how either of those skills is going to help us in the long run."

"It'd help, you idiot, because they can *fly*," I said. "If we can make them a bit brighter, they could settle in relays. Then, if you have to run, you just shout to them, and they fly back to the dungeon. Kelly knows you're in need and gets our teams ready!"

"Or…" Mike said slowly, pulling a whistle from one pocket and showing it to me. "We could go old school, and I blow this three times, keep doing that as we retreat."

"Fuck," I muttered, shaking my head. "Okay, maybe I should have thought about that…"

"You mean you should have considered a simple solution, one that's been used for centuries, instead of magical genetic manipulation as a solution to all your problems?" Chris quipped. "Surely not?"

"Hey, I'm not the one who needs little blue pills," I countered, shrugging. "Just sayin', mate!"

"Hey look, a little 'whisky dick' is nothing to be ashamed of. It happens to us all," Patrick said, and Chris looked over at him, clearly relieved.

"Really?" he asked hopefully.

"Well, you know, not to *me*," he said, and all around the room the other men shook their heads, concealing grins.

"Nope."

"No."

"Not yet…"

"I hate you all." Chris sighed, as Becky laughed and kissed his cheek.

"Nah, you love us." I smiled at my oldest friend, knowing it was all just horseplay…or at least hoping it was.

"So, if we can get the meeting back on track and away from Chris's broken dick, and Matt's…well, just away from Matt…" Mike said. "I'm taking a team. I'll take Sarah and let her pick a full human squad to go with us, as well as a full squad of kobold fighters."

"Any mages?" Kelly asked, eyes going distant as she stared at the dungeon teams we had available, and their locations.

"I'd never turn them down," he admitted.

"I've got two cryomancers and a shaman I can pull in fairly quickly," she answered, nodding to herself. "They're in the park, but that's fine. I can pull the rest of the kobold team from there as well."

"That gives me crowd control as well as physical." He approved. "Thanks, Kel."

"Ranged?" I suggested, and he shook his head.

"If I could, I'd take an army, but we need to get the teams sorted out for the kobolds properly and soon."

"That's actually an important point," Kelly interrupted. "As things stand, because they've been more important the last few days in a 'hearts and minds' role, mainly being seen patrolling and more, and making sure we have enough to plug the holes in the guard schedules, we've not been mixing the teams, nor making many of any of the other kobolds beyond the hoplites."

"So we need to get back to the plan and get them working in set teams as we discussed. Two fighters, two ranged, a medic, and a mage? Is that what we agreed on?" I asked, and got a round of shrugs and nods.

"The plan was that, or a variant of it would be the standard, but we were going to test them in fights to pick the best combination," Aly said slowly. "I know the skeletons and so on aren't really a good test for the kobolds…"

"Right?"

"So once you've sorted all of this out, how about we revisit the training dungeon?" she suggested. "And we look at the orcs again?"

"They're untrustworthy…" I started to refuse, then grunted and nodded. "Good point."

The orcs were fundamentally untrustworthy as near as I could tell, massively aggressive and, basically, complete dicks. They were also hung like a goddamn horse. O243f all the species we'd summoned so far, they were the only one that tended to appear naked, which dropped concerning hints about the being that created this system.

They'd be perfect as fighting training fodder, though.

Absolutely perfect, as I could really get behind the idea of butchering those aggressive fucks on a regular basis for fun, never mind the training and gains it'd give me as well. We'd used a handful on the spur of the moment when Beta had been training her new arrivals but had never really talked about it again.

"Okay, yeah, that works."

"What about Griffiths and the others?" John asked, having joined us at some point.

I blinked, having totally missed him entering and sitting on one of the sofa chairs to lace up his boots.

"We ask them to stay here," Aly said. "They can help defend, and until they're needed, they can practice with the crossbows. Griffiths has them using them round the clock, training to fight with them as a unit. Plus, while we don't have much in the way of ammunition, we've scavenged enough for a full magazine each for them."

"Okay, then. Kelly, if you can summon Kilo for me, please?" I asked her, getting a nod and a smile, and I stood. "Then that's it, people. Get ready and let's get out there."

The meeting broke up fairly quickly, most of them having wandered in from their bedrooms as the sound of voices drew them. I shook my head at the thought of the nice shiny room we'd come up with for exactly these meetings…and that we still held them here, because it was more convenient.

I'd need to sort quarters aboveground and so on for us all soon, I reflected, before banishing the thought as Kelly stepped in close to me.

"Hey…" I whispered, kissing her as she stood on tiptoes and wrapped her arms around my neck.

"You better not die," she ordered, kissing me hard and staring into my eyes.

"I won't," I said automatically, before grimacing. "Well, you know…"

"I know it makes sense me staying here, and yeah, I can control them easier by the day. Guiding them to help you? Yeah, that makes more sense than me being there by your side. I get that. But…"

"But?"

"But I hate not being out there with you. I feel like I'm taking the coward's way out."

"You're not," I assured her, seeing the frown on her face. "I mean it. I understand. You feel like you're not doing much of anything because you're just lying on the bed and sliding into the dungeon sense."

"Yeah."

"I feel the same when I do it," I said. "I feel like I'm taking the easy option, while others are working hard, and I'm lying on a comfy bed. I know it's stupid, but I still feel it."

"I guess." She kissed me again and fixed me with a glare. "You know you need to stop, don't you?"

"Stop…?"

"Stop going out on the front lines. Stop doing the exploring yourself. If we lose you…"

"If you lose me, I think the dungeon will probably let you have access to some of the same facilities, and you'd probably be offered my class at your next upgrade," I said. "It seems to be guiding us, and as the mistress, you're almost there anyway."

"I don't want to lose *you*, you idiot," she growled.

"I know." I smiled, holding her tight. "Honestly, I think as time goes on, I'll do less and less outside, and more internal stuff, management and so on…" Even saying it, I felt an existential level of terror at the thought.

I'd been a tech guy. I'd been fairly fit, and I'd had a few scuffles and so on, growing up—who didn't, after all? Since the end of the world, though? I'd killed dozens of people in literal hand-to-hand combat.

I'd fired sustained bursts of ammunition into people, crushed them, fried them with magic, beaten people to death, and more. I'd fought monsters that we'd barely even had legends for there were so many, and now?

Now the fear of sitting somewhere "safe" and ordering others to go out and do it instead filled me with terror.

I didn't *want* to send them out in my place; I wanted to go myself. I wanted to fight, to feel as alive as I did in the middle of combat…to feel that insane rush of adrenaline, the fear, the fury, and the joy. I wanted to feel the insane levels of horniness that comes from a fight won. That feeling of getting back into a safe place, with the woman I loved and the sheer hunger and need that we were both filled with then.

I wanted the levels, the magic and more. I didn't want to give any of it up.

Kelly was the same at times—the horniness, yeah, but the leveling, and the gains, the determination to fight and to protect those weaker. The only difference really was down to class, I guessed.

She'd taken the Puppeteer class, and had doubled down on it, and each time, her creations had gotten their arses kicked almost straightaway in the fights they'd been in.

Where the rest of us were using magic and dominating the battle with cool abilities, hers was a bit of a flop, until she started guiding the dungeon creatures.

Here, suddenly, she was brilliant. The more she did it? The more she got a feel for the tactics and the rest? The more she loved it. She was finally enjoying her class, while I as Dungeon Lord and as the resident god?

Well, I was kinda enjoying myself all the time, I'd realized.

Or at least when I wasn't being carved limb from limb or eaten or burned or whatever.

"We'll see," was all she said, and I knew that she understood, that until I was ready? I was better off out there. "You be careful, though, okay? Come back to me."

"Yes dear," I said jokingly, smiling and kissing her quickly, then setting her back down. "Okay, people. Two minutes, then we're leaving!"

Mike had already said his goodbyes and was jogging out of the room, presumably to go rouse the team that would be going with him.

I stepped to one side, reaching out and laying my hand on Aly's arm, getting her attention as she turned from watching her husband leave.

"What's wrong?" she asked me bluntly.

"We need those weapons," I said. "I'm sorry to lay this on you, Aly. I know you're working your arse off, but that's how it is. You've got twenty-four hours to research as many of the minor and cheap research projects as you can. Get anything and everything you can from the Iron core, and then get ready, because we're going straight for Steel."

"Matt…" She paused, clearly torn, before opening and shutting her mouth, real concern on her face.

"You're terrified we're hamstringing ourselves long-term by rushing through these levels." I nodded to her. "Believe me, I feel the same way. If there was another option, I'd take it, but we need weapons that are *viable* alternatives.

"Crossbows and longbows are good, but we need more. I need access to real guns, or the next stage, the rail guns and shit. We're a small community that's taking a massive leap to a big one. Part of this is going to involve drawing the attention of the surrounding assholes even more than we already have been.

"Our options are either fight and win, fight and die, or surrender to them, giving them everything. At this point, as much as I want intimidation to be a viable alternative, spears and so on aren't enough. If we can arm the kobolds with weapons that are at least as advanced as theirs, though? It'll be a game changer."

"I know." She sighed. "Look, give me until tomorrow. Go get the ship, help Mike make sure everything is secure, and I'll work on alternatives. Just promise me, if we can come up with something that works? You'll give me an extra week before we upgrade the core."

"I'll agree to review it," I said after a few seconds of thought. "I'm not agreeing to a week, because the way our lives are right now, in a week Mars might have fallen from the sky and the moon might have turned out to be full of fucking dragons or something. I'll hold off on the next core upgrade until it makes sense, though, if you have a viable alternative."

"I told you that I've got a plan—"

"I know…believe me, I know. But what's that saying? 'A perfect plan carried out tomorrow is always beaten by an "okay" one right now'?"

"It's not that, but I know what you mean." She nodded.

I forced a smile, before I gathered up Chris and Patrick. Their partners let them go reluctantly as the three of us moved outside.

Less than a minute later, we strode across the road toward the southern exit, others falling in on us as we went. Captain Griffiths jogged over as Patrick, Chris, and I checked over our equipment.

Patrick and Chris both had the new upgraded armor, as did most of our team, but I was the only one with a goddamn cape.

"Looks…good," Griffiths said as he came to a halt nearby.

I glared at him, already on the verge of tearing the damn thing off, when I saw the twitch of his lips as he suppressed a smile, even as at the same time he clearly had to fight not to salute, the reflex ingrained in him.

"Don't tempt me," I warned him. "You want pretty pink bows for rank insignia on yours?"

"Ah…as much as I would just love that, you know, uniform code and all that," he declined graciously, before the twitch of a smile vanished and he looked at us with utter seriousness. "So, I hear you're heading for a possible fight?"

"Mike is. We've had an incursion…" I explained the situation quickly for him, getting a handful of questions, until I got to my own plans.

"Matt, that ship…it represents more than just technology. It could be insanely important to the future of our species. I really think that I and my people should go with you."

"Thank you, mate, but no. I need you here, guarding the dungeon in case this is all a diversion. I'll be summoning more kobolds to help me, but believe me, I won't let the ship slip out of our control."

"Matt—"

"No." I drew myself up. "This was always going to happen, Griffiths, so let's sort it out here and now. You have your priorities and I have mine. I'll listen to your advice, but at the end of the day it's just that. Advice. Here, I make the final decision, and you can abide by that, or you can leave."

My words hung in the air for a few seconds, and I felt the potential seeming to fill the ether, the possibilities streaming out ahead of us depending on the outcome of this one unplanned confrontation.

"You're right, sir." Griffiths stood straight. "I apologize. We are guests here, and we've agreed to abide by your lead in exchange for assistance and supplies, as well as more in the future. I'll remain here with my people. Is there anything else?"

"No. Thank you, Griffiths," I said formally. "I need you here because you're the last line of defense, a team I can trust to protect *our* people."

"Thank you, sir." He saluted, and I returned it, somewhat sloppily, before he disappeared, and I let out a long breath.

"Fuck, dude, what were you going to do if he took his people and fucked off?" Chris asked me after a few seconds.

"Honestly, I was going to change everything—give it a day to get reinforcements in place, then send Mike and his team to recover the ship. He'd make sure we got it, and I was going to lead our team in completely the opposite direction to try to confuse things. Let them follow us. Glad that didn't happen though."

"Me too," Patrick said. "They're a good team, and the thought of having to fight with them?"

"That's why I did it now, so we could be sure," I said. "Better to know without a doubt than to worry about it when we bring the ship back."

"Fair enough." Chris brightened up as another kobold jogged over. "Kilo!" He greeted the cryomancer and got a toothy grin in return.

"Welcome back," I said, getting a grin and a nod, before checking over his stats as Patrick was introduced to our draconian friend.

Name: Kilo				
Species: Kobold		Bonus: Advanced Variant		
Spells: Chill, Frostbite, Icy Blade, Specter of the Frozen Heart		Class: Frost Summoner		
Level: 5		Progress to next level 147/900		
Available points: 0		Perk: None		
Stat	Current points	Description	Effect	Progress to next level
Agility	8	Governs dodge and movement		17/100
Charisma	8	Governs likely success to charm, seduce, or threaten		21/100
Constitution	12	Governs Health and Health Regeneration	HP: 12x20 = 240	12/100
Dexterity	10	Governs ability with weapons and crafting		34/100
Endurance	14	Governs Stamina and Stamina Regeneration	Stamina: 14x20= 280	17/100
Intelligence	20	Governs base manapool and standard intellectual capacity	Mana: 20x30 = 600	82/100
Luck	8	Governs overall chance of bonuses and critical hits		47/100
Perception	12	Governs ranged damage and chance to spot hidden items/traps	+12 damage to Ranged attacks	50/100
Strength	12	Governs damage with melee weapons and carrying capacity		12/100
Wisdom	22	Governs mana regeneration and memory	220 mana regenerated per hour	82/100

I nodded to myself as I read over the details. Fuck, he was good already! He'd also reached his first class evolution, and had gained a class rank, moving up as a cryomancer, adding some kind of summoning ability to become a Frost Summoner.

I scanned the details, getting a few vague hints, but nothing else, beyond that he could apparently summon a minion of some kind.

That was awesome, though, and I banished the screen.

He was clad in well-fitted leather armor, and carried, in addition to a pair of long daggers, one on either hip, a long staff and a handful of pouches around his waist.

A small group of kobold infantry jogged across to join us, and I nodded in greeting before sighing. They were there, and they were alive…but they were as good as brainless.

There was no light behind their eyes, no sign of intelligence or a soul, despite the sheer numbers of their kind that had been summoned so far, appearing "alive" as soon as they were summoned.

I checked through the six, ready to go, before pausing and cursing with the last in line, doing a quick double take as I spotted what I'd been looking for all along.

<u>Insatiable Curiosity</u>: This Advanced Kobold warrior has been created with the gift—or curse—of Insatiable Curiosity! No matter the situation, she will be easily distracted, even more so because she's been doubly cursed with an inborn "apprentice" level of magical information!

As a naturally occurring magical researcher, infected with Insatiable Curiosity, this kobold has a reduced chance of survival in many situations.

BE WARNED.

I read the prompt twice, then sighed, reaching out to her, and hesitated. Normally I'd have absorbed her into the dungeon, copying her "code" and then moved straight on, spawning a dozen of her.

I was growing ever more concerned that they were thinking, feeling individuals, though, and I was essentially snuffing their life out without a care.

The thought of losing Beta was actively painful. I trusted and liked her—more, in fact, than a lot of the citizens of the dungeon. Realistically, I should probably absorb Beta, accept her death, but use the improvements to her "code" to spin up a dozen highly leveled kobolds.

I couldn't do that, though. I liked her, and it'd be…wrong.

Likewise, I could absorb this one. She stared around dully at the minute, and I chewed on my lip in thought, wondering whether there was anything in there.

If she wasn't aware, did it matter?

I could make ten clones of her, and research would improve mightily. Or I could take her out as part of the team; she'd hopefully get some experience. Hell, I could probably power-level her, focus and issue her quests for hundreds of XP to make me a damn cup of tea or something. It'd be my personal experience I used for that, but…but would it be worth it?

I could do it all, but this came back to what then? Was it right for me to kill her?

I shook my head. No…no, it damn well wasn't. She was baseline now and seemingly unaware, but that wasn't the point. I didn't like the deaths that were caused by the experimenting that I needed to do to create different variants, but at least they were summoned and it was done instantly.

Once they were out and "alive," doing things, it just seemed depraved. I'd probably be called all sorts of names by the old gaming community I used to be part of for making a decision like that, but regardless of the logic, it felt wrong.

I sighed, doing what seemed right rather than what was easy. I sent her to Aly, and headed over to join Mike as he and his squads formed up, heading toward the gate and the bridge ahead.

CHAPTER TWENTY-NINE

We set off jogging through the gates and out across the bridge in a steady stream. Mike and his small team were in the lead, the humans and my kobold infantries running in two groups side by side, clearly eyeing one another as they went.

Then came Chris, Kilo, and Patrick with me, bringing up the rear.

It wasn't supposed to be that way. Hell, I was supposed to be in the lead, considering I knew exactly where the crossover of our territory had occurred. But that fucker Mike had set the pace, and when I started to run with them, an extra figure had set off running, slipping through the gates just before they closed.

I'd fallen back steadily, curious, when Chris had drawn my attention to the lone figure.

We crossed the bridge quickly enough, and I grinned at some of the clearly repaired sections, nodding as I crossed under a set of traps that I only noticed because I was going through the bridge this way, rather than toward the dungeon.

Someone had taken the time to fix the bridge up, and to install traps as well, just in case. I liked it.

After another minute, as our shadow became more and more winded, I sighed and gestured for Chris to run on ahead. "Tell Mike to head up to the right and wait in the car park ahead," I ordered him, before dropping back and falling in beside Dante.

"You okay there?"

He nodded, eyes fixed straight ahead.

"Good," I said simply, waiting.

"I…ummmm."

"Go on," I said absently, looking around and searching for movement as he broke off. "Use your words."

"I know I wasn't ordered along to help, but you said that you trusted us to make a decision and to bring in our families if we needed to and—"

"I do, and I'm fine with that. Immediate family only, as I said, so no second cousins and—"

"It's just my mum," he said quickly. "I left her in Saltwell Park days ago, and I've not been back to check on her. I know she was okay, but…"

"But you want to check on her and bring her back." I nodded. "That's fine, Dante, and yeah, I did say that. But, frankly, I'm curious. Why now?"

"Well, I was helping Ashley with the potions and earning my place and—" he babbled, while already showing signs of being seriously out of breath from the short run.

"No." I cut him off, squinting at the buildings as we ran up the road. Chris popped a head out of the car park ahead, getting my attention, and then moved back out of sight as soon as I flashed him a two-fingered wave to let him know I'd seen him.

"Dante, I mean why *now*. Why decide to tag along on a mission you weren't invited on? No offense, mate, but you're unfit. And as good as you are at Fire magic, you've got about as much chance of surviving out here on your own as I have of flying to the moon from my farts. *Explain.*"

"I—" He dropped back to a walk as he tried to gather his thoughts.

I growled and grabbed him by the shoulder, dragging him forward and back into a run, making him sprint the last hundred meters uphill to the car park.

I led him in to crouch between a few parked cars, seeing the others spread out nearby, all similarly hidden.

"Why are we hiding?" he asked in far too loud a voice, getting glares from the others as I grabbed him, slapping a hand over his mouth.

"Firstly, because we don't know what's out here," I told him sharply. "Second, because we know something passed through here, a lot of somethings, and probably all dangerous. Lastly, because you and I just arrived and Mike, who was on point, decided we *should* hide because he's seen something. Stay here and decide why you followed me, and the excuse had better be a good one." I moved off as Chris came to crouch near to Dante in my place.

I slapped Chris on the shoulder, squeezing my thanks to him, before moving quickly, crouch-running between the cars and across clear spaces until I could kneel by Mike's side, seeing what he had.

The path the creatures had taken, now that I had moved to see it, was arrow-straight, and blatant. I shook my head bemusedly, seeing the line of devastation that I'd missed from my lower vantage point.

The road we'd followed up to here was clear enough. But, looking back, we could see that whatever had passed through wasn't human in its thought processes.

Looking over the map that I could summon to mind now, I'd examined it so many times, I saw the way we'd worked from the dungeon.

The path over the bridge had been claimed, instead of the shortest point from A to B, because otherwise those claiming the route to the park would have been hanging in midair all the way, and that was just wrong. So rather than draw a straight line from the dungeon across the empty air over the river, they'd crossed over the bridge, mentally seeing that as the "right" way to do it.

Once on the other side, though, they'd drawn a line from that point near enough straight to the park, and had followed that route. Again, they'd done it with reference to human logic, which was that even though there was a hill in the way, and they were made of energy and could arguably burrow through the land, they'd climbed the hill. They'd been following dips and inclines in the land, rather than punching straight through and arguably shaving several hours off the connection time.

They'd been right to do so as well, as otherwise we'd have been able to absorb sod all of the surrounding buildings.

That was an example of human logic.

Just like when we'd ran up here, we'd mainly followed the road; it was just easier and seemed right to our sensibilities.

Whoever had decided the route for the group Mike was hunting, though, clearly didn't have the same issues. There was an arrow-straight line drawn through the car park, over the top of cars that had gotten between the group and their target.

A series of buildings that housed old shops were on the other side of the car park, and they'd smashed through a large window—several, actually—and had kept going straight through. Squinting, I could see daylight, I thought, through the building, suggesting they literally went straight on, while scraped and shattered sections of the walls and roofing suggested that at least one something had climbed up and over, having not fitted inside.

Looking back along the line, there were broken trees, an overturned car, torn down chain-link fencing…It was literally a trail of devastation that led back toward their home, or base or whatever.

"What is it?" I asked Mike, moving up to crouch next to him as he examined the remains of one of the cars, fingering the crumpled edge of a fender.

"Heavy," he replied simply, gesturing at the damage. "Whatever they are, they're seriously heavy—metal, or mainly—and they went straight when they could have gone around shit…"

He turned back to glance behind us, then back toward the hole.

"Is this where they passed?" he asked, knowing the answer.

"Yeah."

"Might be a coincidence about the point farthest between the alert towers then," he muttered. "The line they're following is straight as all hell. They were there…" He jerked a thumb over his shoulder. "And they wanted to go there." He pointed ahead.

"Makes sense, a straight line," I agreed, before going on to explain my reasoning behind the "they're not human" theory I was working on.

"Sounds sensible." He grunted. "Might be humans, though, just using something? Fuck knows, man. Only one way to find out." He turned and looked over at where Dante was just starting to recover. "He staying with you or me?"

"Me." I shrugged. "I think, anyway. He wants to get his mother from the park."

"And he thought when we might be going into a fight was the time to do that?"

"He's an idiot," I agreed. "Might be he wanted to show off what he and we can do, might be he's realized that she's not safe and is taking the first chance he has to get her. Might be he broke up with Ashley and needs a big hug. Fuck knows."

"Has he?"

"What?"

"Broken up with—"

"Fuck, man, I don't know!" I snapped. "I was just spitballing reasons."

"You could ask?"

"I was, until he started to look like he was going to have a heart attack from all the running."

"Yeah, he can stay with you." Mike grinned. "We've not even warmed up properly yet."

"Tell me about it," I grumbled, before looking over at a low yip from one of the kobolds. A second group of kobolds was loping up: six infantry, two cryomancers, and a shaman, all running along easily. They raced up and fell in nearby, making me nod in approval at how easily and quickly Kelly coordinated them all.

"Okay, you staying or going?" Mike glanced back, and I shook my head.

"Going," I said. "We need the damn ship secured. It's looking more and more like it's not anything to do with this, but just in case? And before anyone gets their hands on it?" I shrugged.

"Makes sense," he agreed. "Okay, good luck."

That was it; he didn't pause beyond that, gathering up his people and leading them ahead. Sarah nodded in passing to me.

I couldn't help but smile at the group that followed her, recognizing that Aussie bastard with the axe, Zac, as he tried to keep down and out of sight, all while the massive axe reflected the little sunlight around and acted as a goddamn beacon on his back.

He and the rest of his team were in full armor, including Paul, who'd apparently cut down his giant ginger afro a bit to fit under his helmet.

There were masses of hair sprouting out of every angle, and he was clearly trying to pretend he wasn't there in case I made him cut the rest off. Katherine, I vaguely remembered the next in line was called, as she moved past, dark haired and pale skinned, shot me a smile and a nod as she went, spear in hand and shield carried carefully.

Unlike the rest of the squad as they filed past, she didn't bang the spear or the shield on the cars as she went, clearly having a little more common sense and a lot more grace to her movements.

The newly arrived kobolds slowed and fell into line as well, moving up and gathering around Mike on the far side of the car park as he gave out orders.

I moved back to Chris, Patrick, Dante, and Kilo. The other five kobold "blank" warriors with us moved out to form a protective ring around the group as I started talking to them.

"Okay people, we're heading straight for the park from here. Mike's going to find out what's going on over that way, and Beta and her team are off to trace those fuckers back to their home.

"Our job is to retrieve the ship the dungeon core came in. I want it back at the dungeon and safe as soon as we can manage it and..."

I paused, thinking quickly. "Kelly, are you there?" I asked aloud rather than sliding into the dungeon sense to check.

One of the nearby kobolds shivered, straightening up and looking around to make eye contact, nodding to me as she seemingly puppeted it.

"Good. Do me a favor and sort a storage area out for the ship. It's basically a missile top, as near as I can remember, a cylinder about six or seven meters long, maybe two wide. Best not to have it out in public where anyone can poke and prod at it, just in case."

She nodded, waited a second to see whether I was going to add anything else, and then when I didn't, she released the kobold and the sense of her presence vanished.

I hesitated a second as well, wondering whether I was supposed to have said thank you, or that I loved her. But the chance was gone now, and it'd have been a bit damn weird as well. I turned back to the others and carried on.

"So, we'll head to the park first to collect our transport, then we'll be off to the crash site. Dante, you followed us without orders—what's going on? Last chance," I asked him bluntly.

"I…" He started then sagged. "I wanted to get my mum and take her to the dungeon, but I wanted to prove I could help as well. Ashley's always busy, and I feel like unless there's something going on, like the fight with the undead, then I and the other mages are left to stay out of the way." He shrugged. "I just want to help."

"Okay." I grunted. "You want to show you can be useful, so you ran off to help? Mate, you need to start thinking things through. You're knackered already."

"I know, but the only way I can improve is by earning some more experience!" he argued. "The battle gained me loads, seriously it did, but I need to improve further. Half the time during the fight, Ashley had to keep saving me, and I…" He shrugged, self-consciously.

"So you want to get into fights so that you grow more powerful and she doesn't have to keep protecting you?" I asked, and he nodded shamefacedly. "You're a bloody idiot, you know that?"

"What?"

"Kelly's saved my life a dozen times. Chris is the same; Mike, too. We act as a *team*. There's no shame to having others save your life."

"I didn't mean it like that, I meant…I need to level, that's all."

"Why?"

"My stamina," he admitted in a low voice.

"What?"

"I need to increase my stamina."

Chris sniggered, then broke down into full-bodied laughter, as Patrick covered his mouth with one hand.

"What am I missing?" I frowned. "You're a mage. Stamina isn't that important. Or are you having issues with your body? You're…" I'd been about to go down the "out of alignment" route, thinking he was suffering from the same issues I'd had before—putting too much into certain stats—when I saw the look on his face, and put two and two together with the other two's laughter.

"Your *stamina*." I nodded. "*Riiiight*. Now I understand." I rubbed at my face, trying to hold back the laughter and the annoyance at once. "So, let's just be clear here: the primary reason you want to level is so that you can improve your stamina, so you can fuck Ashley for longer?"

"I…" He couldn't speak, his face now utterly tomato-like in color.

"You fucking idiot," I said slowly, shaking my head in disbelief. "You're going to risk your life, so you can get laid more?" I paused as I said it, running the sentence through my mind and shrugging. Yeah, if I were in his shoes? A few years younger, new relationship, and no self-confidence in that area to draw on, then with her so clearly putting so much work into her figure and maintaining herself at peak for her Charisma-based skills and so on?

He had to feel like he was punching *waaaaay* above his weight, and just waiting for her to leave him.

"Okay," I said, letting that reality of life sink in for him. "This is what we're going to do. This was all about getting your mum safe back to the dungeon and as part of that, you're coming to and from the park only. You're not coming to the forest and so on, because you're going to be busy getting her sorted out. Hopefully we'll only be gone an hour or so, maybe two, so that gives her a chance to get ready as well."

"But the experience—"

I cut him off with a raised hand. "You're trying to level your stamina?" I asked, and he nodded. "Great. You don't need to level for that. You're a young lad…exercise and determination will make that level on its own. But just in case? We're going to help."

"You are?" He perked up, totally missing the grin on both Chris and Patrick's faces.

"Oh…you'll level up your stamina all right," I promised. "And once we're back at the dungeon? As you've been feeling you're just trying to stay out of the way, we'll help you to improve it there as well."

"Thank you!" he said quickly, nodding and trying to hide his embarrassment. "I owe you all…"

"Oh, don't you worry, mate," Chris said. "You just do as we tell you, and you'll be fine."

I groaned, shaking my head as I stood, leading them around the parked cars and back onto the road, climbing the hill again and resuming our journey to the park.

"For the love of God, Chris, don't go giving him sex tips for him and Ashley," I begged in a low voice as Patrick started to run, dragging Dante up to speed with him. "The poor kid's gullible enough."

"Oh man, come on," Chris complained. "Just a few things. Let me teach him to do a—"

"No!" I cut him off. "None of that shit. Think back to when we were just starting out…"

"I was fourteen!" Chris countered. "It was funny…"

"You're an idiot. And the shit you pulled made most of the girls call you a sexual deviant for years."

"Yeah, they still came back for more, though." He grinned.

"Their stupidity isn't the point here," I said. "He's in love with her, and she seems to be with him. You teach him stupid tricks that 'all the girls love' and fuck that up for him? Remember, he's a Fire mage. He'll literally toast your nuts, and I'll tell Becky you were planning on running away."

"Spoilsport."

"I mean it," I warned him, making sure I got a nod of agreement before letting it drop.

"We need to talk about that, though," Chris said as we topped the hill a few minutes later, falling in beside Patrick and a gasping Dante.

"Keep up," I ordered Dante, before looking back at Chris. "The bond?"

"Yeah."

"You planning on going…?"

"Soon," he said. "As soon as I can, really. I'm sorry, man. I'll stay till whatever this is is sorted, but then I'm gone."

I nodded. I couldn't blame him. We fell into a companionable silence, broken only by Dante's panting and broken breaths as we carried on.

Passing the civic center—or, as we'd come to think of it, the trap dungeon—there was evidence of animals, and of people passing recently, but nobody had drawn too close. We continued on, stopping about halfway to let Dante recover, then forcing him to run the rest of the way to the park.

By the time we reached it, the park was a hive of activity, the sun well up now, and for a change, it wasn't raining. The park was surrounded by a new wall, higher than most houses at thirty meters, and solid stone.

The houses that had surrounded the park were gone, pushed back more than forty meters on a side, and the distance was increasing.

The people working on demolishing the houses paused to look at us as we loped past. But, seeing the armor, not to mention the kobolds, they simply smiled and waved, or ignored us.

We diverted to the right, running down what had been Saltwell View, and bypassed the line waiting to enter. A pair of kobolds stood with a pair of humans searching people and questioning those they didn't recognize to make sure none of the raiders and gangs simply wandered in.

People recognized us again, or they did the kobolds, and the occasional nervous cheer rang out as we passed them.

Dante was getting some strange looks, I realized, and I winced as we paused inside, looking at him. He was red and white now, blotchy skinned and literally heaving for breath. The difference between his first-generation leather armor and our own made the case for him not being one of us even clearer.

"Dammit, catch your breath," I whispered to him, helping him to walk in a circle as he tried to speak through the gasps.

"Is he all right?" someone asked nervously, and I heard Chris step in, telling them that he was in training, and a bit unfit.

While Dante gathered himself and recovered, I looked around, seeing the differences on this side of the wall as well.

The wall, as noted before, was thirty meters high and stone. It also had a wide walkway that ran along the back, and rooms recessed into the wall here and there.

Rather than make the wall entirely solid stone, Kelly and Aly had apparently decided to create staggered rooms, the walls around them reinforced with bronze. Seating areas, eateries, crafting, and more had sprung up in these sections, making the walls into a sort of impromptu town square, but one that ran along the inside of the wall that ringed the park.

Once you passed that section, it was all pleasant and clean. The grass and chopped down trees were replaced with crops originally, and now augmented with Nature and Life converters.

The result was that the air felt fresh and healthy, the plants grew steadily, and the people were happier. In the distance, I could see the original three blocks we'd made for people, and even now a fourth was going up. The fresh trees staggered around the park brought a feeling of pleasant, old-style life back again.

If anything, the combination of solid, modern apartment blocks, and massive grass and tree covered areas, along with the boating lake, gave the impression of a rich university town in the middle of construction.

I saw young mothers out walking with their babies, strollers full of wide-eyed waving toddlers and tiny fresh hatchlings, where only days ago that mere thought of these people being outside would have been dismissed as insane.

Here and there, troops of kobolds, ten at a time, jogged back and forth, being seen, and providing a fast reaction team, just in case.

Beyond them, though? The park was mainly deserted, or so it seemed.

The streets outside were a hive of steady, determined activity, stripping the houses down and moving on, as literally hundreds of people in the dungeon—mostly back at the dungeon itself, but some here—worked to absorb everything from general rubbish to tablet computers and more.

As soon as Dante recovered enough, we were off again, jogging, no longer running, through the park, heading to the Gothic mansion at the center, and Barry's office.

Needless to say, the fucker wasn't in it.

Half an hour later, as we'd given up entirely, and had moved on, starting to search the far side of the park, he finally turned up with Ken by his side, acting as always the part of combination chancellor, record keeper, and enforcer.

"Matt!" Barry called, jogging up. "Is everything okay?"

"Hey, Barry, Ken," I greeted them, shaking hands and noting the small team that followed him, raising an eyebrow at that.

"Since we joined you, more people actually started helping out," Barry explained with a resigned sigh. "I always thought if I had more people, it'd make the job easier. Instead, it just increased the number of issues!"

"I know that feeling," I said with a grim smile. "Anyway, yes and no. We've sensed a large group moving nearby. No clue if they're hostile or not, but they don't seem to be human, and they're moving fast. Might be a scouting force, might be invasion, might be they've decided to go to the beach for the day. Fuck knows, really."

I explained what had happened, as well as our suspicions. Barry and Ken stayed quiet mostly, apart from the occasional question.

"Makes sense," Barry said when I was done. "So what do you need from us, and where's this ship?"

"I'll be going to get it in an hour or so, maybe less," I said. "But I had a plan for the cavalry we'd need, not to mention transport, but I damn well can't find the bones."

"What bones?" Ken asked. "We've cleaned the area as thoroughly as we could, feeding the bones into the dungeon mainly."

"Shit." I grunted, worried they might have done that. "The triceratops?"

"The dinosaurs?" Barry asked, unable to help himself as he grinned. "You're going to resurrect them?"

"Copy the design and use the dungeon to remake them as skeletal versions, yeah," I admitted. "I can't resurrect a dinosaur, but—" I wondered whether I could actually do that, before shaking my head and dismissing the thought. "So, do you have the bones?"

CHAPTER THIRTY

"We do." Ken smiled, making me almost sag in relief, as he gestured farther into the park. "We didn't know what to do with them, but considering they'd survived, what? Seventy, maybe eighty million years? I figured it was disrespectful to just feed them to the dungeon."

"Yeah," I muttered, before shrugging and forcing a smile. "Good news, bad news situation then, mate!"

"What's that?" He frowned.

"Bad news first, best to get it over with. We're feeding the bones to the dungeon."

"But you just said—"

"Good news is, because it's me doing it and my way, I can then, hopefully, summon the creatures back later on."

"Okay," Ken grumbled, clearly torn between the destruction of the bones, and the thought of us having such behemoths on our side. "Can you do it with other dinosaurs?" A sudden smile bloomed, and I hesitated, before smiling as well.

"You know what? I don't know. But if I can? Fuck yes." The thought of mounted dinosaur cavalry was a wonderful thing. I'd been thinking of a team of skeletal triceratops riders as our cavalry, but if I could get a T. rex? Fuck yes!

We got moving quickly. Dante diverted to the northwest quadrant to search for his mother at Ken's direction, with a promise to return when he was ready.

Fifteen minutes later, and I was cursing that little shit Aaron again.

With the deaths of the triceratops, the bones had been collected and then dumped, resembling literally nothing now but a massive pile of bone.

Rather than the magnificent reality of the actual beasts, these were…they were *sad*.

That was the best way to describe them. Hundreds of bones were scattered about, most broken in one way or another, and just piled up.

Worst of all, because of the way these things worked, even with two of the skeletons dumped here, there wasn't a complete one to use.

Most people seemed oblivious to the fact that the "skeletons" that they saw in the museum weren't real in the traditional sense. After all, there's only so many dinosaur skeletons to go around, and pretty much every city has a museum, many several or even dozens.

They'd all like a nice complete dinosaur skeleton, thank you very much, but there just aren't enough to go around, and even if there were?

These are dead creatures.

Most didn't reach the end of their natural lifespan and get buried by their friends and family, or at least not as far as I knew. But the mental image of a dozen dinos in black suits mourning around a fucking giant hole as a brontosaurus was put in would forever more be a memory I'd treasure.

Especially with the T. Rex I imagined getting all the glares at the wake as he complained he'd "been fucking hungry, all right??"

No, because most of the dinos were killed and eaten, died and then were scavenged, or lost to tar pits, or washed away or whatever, only a percentage of the bones were real to that dino.

That meant that the missing ones would be replaced, and gaps filled in.

Last, but by no means fucking least, was the fact that dino bones, as they were fossilized over millions of years, were essentially stone. Sticking them together so they looked nice on a plastic frame wasn't going to work; it'd be crushed.

Equally, hanging them from wires and so on would require specialist cranes, and actually drilling the damn bones for mounting points.

Again, only a few dino bones out there, and you get caught approaching one of them with a drill in one hand, a calculating expression on your face? Expect a paleontologist to insert that drill somewhere you'd prefer they didn't.

That left museums making casts and replicas of the originals more often than not, and showing the bones alongside the assembled "skeleton."

That, in turn, *usually* would have meant that Aaron would have had sod all to animate. We'd been lucky here, though, as I started to work my way through the piles, shifting bones aside and assembling them into what I hoped was the right order, because these hadn't been the bones that belonged to the local museum.

They'd been a traveling display, working its way around the world, meaning that they had a load of the original bones. They were just mixed up and damaged, thanks to the fights, and to the skulls being basically trashed by our own battles.

I spent an hour separating out the mixed remains of the two skeletons, pausing long enough to wax lyrical on what Aaron deserved for using one of them in one of his abominations to carry his fucking chair.

In the end, though, I had what I hoped were the right number of ribs, legs, and all the other shit, basically adding up and dividing by two all the way.

The more damaged bits were discarded, and the two damaged skulls were reassembled as best I could into one. The skulls, and the damage done to them, were starting to make me worried about the shape of my own, as the helmet that had replaced my last one was starting to give me a headache. Something about the way it narrowed at the top meant that I was starting to get annoyed wearing it. I dumped it to one side, sighing in relief, and mentally reminded myself to have a word with Aly about the design later as I got on with the job at hand.

All told, the result was a crime against paleontology, and I was fairly sure that one day, for this if nothing else, I'd get shivved in the back in a dark alley. But I had a single, almost complete skeleton laid out.

Absorbing it into the dungeon took another hour. Dozens upon dozens of prompts popped up—refusals, failures, and more. And each time, what was required, more than anything else, was me "holding the dungeon's hand" as the deed was done.

I constantly interjected over and over the determination that it was right, and what I expected to happen over the reality of what lay before me.

Again and again, it failed; the entire image disintegrated in the dungeon system, until I painstakingly reassembled them, shifting sections around, altering things and making it clear that the rest of reality could go suck a bucket of dicks, because I WAS HAVING A DINOSAUR.

Three hours after I'd started the process, I staggered out of the building and glared up at the cheerful late morning sunshine, as it seemed to be mocking the way my day had gone so far.

"Matt?"

A voice came from the right, and I blinked, staring over at Dante, who waited with Chris, Patrick, and the kobolds, and a woman I'd not met before. Ken and Barry had apparently buggered off at some point.

"Dante," I croaked, before swallowing hard and summoning a can of energy drink to my hand, gulping it down and sighing. "Hey."

"This is my mum," he said, and I turned to her, nodding a greeting.

"I'm Carrie," she said. "Thank you for looking after Dante."

"I haven't been." I twisted and grunted as my back popped and cracked. "I took him to war."

"Oh," she said, seemingly surprised. "Well…I guess it was good for him?"

"He's got a girlfriend as well," I added, grinning at the look of betrayal I got from him for dropping that one into the conversation. I wondered if I dare point out that she was the dungeon's official Courtesan.

"Matt…" he said, his voice full of begging and horror, and I relented.

"She's very well respected, and so's he, one of the most powerful of the mages, which is why I brought him along," I finished, winking at him as I shook her hand.

"I'm glad to hear it. Dante said that there was room for me in the dungeon. But if it's a trouble, I could stay here. I mean, there's families who should get safe spaces first…"

"They're getting sorted as well," I said. "Dante more than earned you your space, don't worry."

"I can cook or clean…" she said, and I shook my head.

"Don't worry. Those are both functions of the dungeon. If you have a skill set that we don't need? We can teach you to do something else, but don't worry, you won't be put out."

"Thank you." She sagged in relief. "I was worried…"

"I told you, Mum!" Dante said with a big smile. "You don't need to worry!"

"I know. But if I leave, your Aunt Vic will be on her own, and…"

I saw the look Dante threw at me straightaway and backed up, shaking my head.

"Dude, I have enough shit to deal with. If your mum wants to go to the dungeon, she's more than welcome. If not…" I paused, then sighed. "You've got a singles apartment, right, Dante?"

"Yeah?"

"Are you keeping it?" I asked bluntly.

He went bright red. "I…I've never slept in it."

"You're in the tower?"

"Yeah," he said, trying to ignore the look his mum was giving him.

"Well, you and your mum would have taken a two-bed apartment, right? If your aunt is just her, and Carrie doesn't mind sharing—"

"I don't!" Carrie said quickly, and I nodded, gesturing vaguely off to the side.

"Okay, you sort out this Vic, and get her ready as well. It means Dante will be sharing with his girlfriend, but that was how it was anyway, so you'll just have to put up with that, right?"

"Of course!" Carrie said quickly, taking a couple of steps, and then hesitating.

"It's okay. We'll be busy for the next few hours," I assured her. "Meet us by the north gate in about three or four hours. We'll all go then."

She nodded and rushed off, as Dante turned to me, waiting until she was out of earshot.

"Thank you, Matt, but Ashley might not want me there—"

I cut him off with a shake of my head. "I wasn't serious about you losing your room." I smiled. "I can bend the rules a bit here and there, so don't worry. It was more because your mother hasn't met Ashley yet, and I can only think she might have kicked off about you spending every night balls-deep there rather than being at home. For now, officially you can tell her I made you give your room up if you want, so that your aunt can come too. If it's not an issue? Great. If it is? You're covered."

"I…damn, thank you!" Dante looked relieved. "Am I okay to tell Ashley the truth?"

"Of course you are, you idiot." I smiled. "Now, enough fucking around. Give me a minute's peace here…" I turned from him and the others, closing my eyes and sinking into the dungeon sense, glad that for whatever reason this section of the park had already been claimed by the expansion team.

Triceratops Horridus	Dungeon Creature – amalgamation

The Triceratops Horridus is an ancient herbivore, specifically evolved to be as unpalatable and difficult to consume as possible. Where many herbivores are peaceful, and even cowardly creatures, the Triceratops evolved with a slightly different design. Be this through nature or nurture, the triceratops, through its many variations, became a highly feared sight in the late Cretaceous era.

Blitz:
Blitz, the Triceratops' charge, more commonly known as a blitz, can power through walls, trees, and inconvenient obstacles such as enemies with ease.

Gore:
Gore, the Triceratops' natural collection of three horns, used in combination with a significant musculature, can result in severe damage to any nearby weaker enemy.

Pack:
Pack, the Triceratops, while a terrible foe if annoyed, upset, or looked at sideways across a bar, is at its heart a pack creature, and operates at its best when in a minimum family unit of three.

Weaknesses: Fire, Light, and Death Magics

HP: 2500/2500
Stamina: 500/500
Mana: 20/20
Speed 6/10
Level: 0

HP 2500/2500	Special Abilities: 3/3

I hesitated, reading and rereading the details, before reaching out and selecting the relevant option, hoping against hope as I summoned the twelve thousand, five hundred fucking mana required to print the massive dinosaur.

The light was intense, starting with the pads of its massive feet, three toes at the end of the front legs and four on the back legs.

As the light flowed steadily upward, I cried out, "FUCK YES!"

Seconds turned to minutes. The others realized what was happening as well, and word spread. Fifteen minutes after I'd begun, roughly three times as long as it took to print a goddamn apartment, and the light faded, the top-most tip of the bony frill gleaming in the gentle sunlight.

"How the hell did you do that?" Chris asked softly, stepping up to stand alongside me, and I shook my head, utterly overcome.

I'd spent literally hours working on the system, and all of that time, I'd done it with a mental image firmly fixed in my mind.

Every time the absorption had failed, I'd added in details. Hell, I didn't *know* exactly how I'd done it, but in the same way that the dungeon had been able to absorb goblins with half their heads chopped off and shit, and still create a living, breathing goblin?

It'd done the same with this.

I'd put the mixed bones of a pair of long dead and ancient triceratops into the dungeon, and I'd gotten a fucking living, breathing one out.

I couldn't help it. Much as when Kelly crouched down to do anything around me, and I struggled to contain the words "while you're down there," here and now I fought only briefly against the compulsion, before spreading my arms and staring up at the giant ceratopsian.

"Life, uh…finds a way!" I turned to Chris. "I'm totally naming this fucker," I told him, only to see the unholy light shining in his eyes.

"We're going to the museum," he informed me. "I don't care what else you *thought* you were doing tomorrow—we're going to the museum, and I'm picking a dinosaur. I'm going to be the first druid with a fucking *dinosaur* as a companion."

I looked at the life, the hunger, and the absolute need on his face, and I nodded. "I'll do my best," I promised him, before turning back to the fucking giant magnificence that waited before me.

"I'd planned to summon two or three," I admitted, and Chris grabbed my arm.

"I need one. I'll do you a deal…you summon another, so we've got one each, and I'll sort a saddle."

I looked at the fucker's back, seeing how wide and uncomfortable it looked—not to mention the ridges of the spine as they flowed back—and I nodded slowly.

"Deal, but you have to sort it."

"Totally," he agreed, plopping down onto the ground and reaching out into the dungeon.

"That's one each, right?" Patrick sidled up to me. "I mean, come on, man, you're not going to leave me fucking walking while Chris gets his own."

"Dammit," I growled, looking over the details and sighing as I saw roughly why the hell two of these bastards had maxed Aaron out. Not only were they twelve thousand mana each to summon, an utterly insane number in and of itself, but the control points?

Fifty a go.

I didn't have enough, not by a long shot, and as I sat, sliding into the dungeon, I found Aly and Kelly waiting for me.

"Ladies…" I greeted them.

"You utter lunatic," Aly started in on me. "Have you any idea what a live triceratops is going to *eat*?"

"Anything the fucker wants to, is my bet…same as where a hundred-ton fucking dinosaur sleeps!" I replied cheerfully. "Just you wait until I get the T. Rex and raptors sorted."

"Don't you fucking *dare*," Aly growled, and I sent her a mental image of me smiling.

"So, Kelly, you basically get dinosaurs to play with," I said, pausing, and wondering whether I was about to be declared no longer welcome in her bed.

"I love you," Kelly said, her voice full of wonder. "I just frigging love you."

"You see!" I said to the pair of them. "Kelly gets it! Why have normal cavalry when we can ride dinosaurs!"

"Are you insane?" Aly asked acidly. "Matt, it's a fucking dinosaur. They've never lived alongside humanity before. You think kids are going to think to get out of the way? You think they won't decide to have a little snack? What if they're like the orcs?"

"Then we train them," I said. "Aly, you want me to not ride a dinosaur into battle? I can't understand that, not even slightly, but okay, get me a motorbike. A jet bike—fuck it, flying shoes. I don't care. Give me a viable alternative, and I'm all for it, but for now?" I shook my head, visualizing a hundred of them charging an enemy camp and sent that image to the girls.

"Just look at that. Imagine Dickless and his army as they were— now think about if we'd had a hundred of these? A hundred kobolds armed with rail guns standing in a line? We could have set up a picnic and drank champagne while Dickless begged for forgiveness. We'd not have lost anyone. His army would have been bone dust."

"I know what you're saying, Matt, but—" She broke off, clearly struggling with things, as the sense of Finn arrived as well, and went utterly insane with joy.

He couldn't even speak; he just kept making noises and zipping around the massive beast.

It took several long minutes for Chris and Patrick to calm him down, and longer still to get him to seriously focus on the task at hand—namely, to make a damn saddle for the fuckers. But he'd had a plan in mind for one for something else already, apparently.

He refused point-blank to discuss what he'd been planning to ride, and why he had a saddle design that was able to be scaled up to fit. But, frankly, I didn't really care and just approved of the mad bastard coming up with random solutions to problems on the fly.

An hour later, Kelly had made some more control point generators and we had three triceratops standing tall and proud, and *my God*, they were amazing. Their skin was a grey-green, patterned in gentle waves. And their bony frills?

They were flushed with blood, and as they raised their heads at how many people were drifting over to see them, the plates grew redder and redder.

I wasn't sure whether it was a warning, a threat, or whether they were just showing off, but I reached out, thinking to calm them, only to find Kelly was there already.

In seconds, the colors bled away, resuming the same light pink and grey that those sections had been previously. I nodded in satisfaction as the saddles were tightened up and settled into place.

Dante returned and was utterly dismayed that he didn't get a dinosaur as well. But as I pointed out to him, neither did Kilo nor any of the kobolds.

He needed to improve his stamina, and I offered to explain that to his mother if he wanted…resulting in him being very happy to jog alongside, and assuring me that there was no need to discuss anything with her.

Some people might consider me doing that, and actually letting him run as we rode out of the south gate to cheers, as cruel. Especially with me in the lead, Chris and Patrick behind. Their dinos held a load of strapping and ropes and so on, on their backs, and the kobolds—five infantry, still with Kilo leading them— surrounded him.

I, however, found it hilarious, and smiled like the Cheshire cat as we built up to a steady trot.

The saddle was wide, damn wide actually, basically a trio of belts that ran across to the chest in front of the legs, one between the front and back legs and one that looped under its tail—just above its asshole, thankfully.

I'd hate to have to clean the straps.

Then a seat was attached atop the middle of the back, with a sort of leather blanket covering the creature's back, and then a design similar to a short-legged armchair sitting atop that and strapped in.

It looked a bit ridiculous, all things considered, but it was surprisingly comfortable and offered storage options. And the design even meant that if we needed to, we could strap the ship across the backs of two of the dinos, and tie them together, like horses used to work to pull carriages side by side.

The only difference was it'd be on their backs.

Kelly had suggested that we take a trailer, as just one of them could have dragged it easily, but the land we'd need to cross ruled that out.

We did, however, agree that if there were problems with carrying it, we could travel back via Team Valley, the old trading estate that I'd worked in before all of this.

There were outdoor goods shops that would carry some of what we needed, and if not? We'd break into a car and let the handbrake off, and they could drag it.

All in all, we had some magnificent plans and backup plans to make damn sure that no matter what happened, we'd get the ship back home.

The only problem with those plans was made clear as we rode our massive steeds up through the abandoned farmland on the far side of the trading estate, and into the hills.

As the late afternoon light dimmed and the sun set, occasional fires were lit in the distance. More and more of the surrounding area was dotted with pinpricks of flickering oranges, red, and yellow.

We climbed the final hilltop and turned to the right, following the mental map I'd been given upon first bonding with the dungeon, and there before us was the little hidden valley.

The rivulet of a stream ran merrily through the middle. The impact crater looked a bit more ragged than when I'd seen it last, the time and storms having worn the previously sharp-edged sides down.

They all came together to prove one thing, though.

We were in the right place…

But the goddamn ship wasn't.

"FUUUUUUUCK!" I screamed into the darkness, ignoring the frantic beating of birds startled from their nighttime roosts.

CHAPTER THIRTY-ONE

"So..." Chris said slowly as I leapt down, landing hard and stalking around, glaring at the evidence before me. "We're a bit late then?"

I couldn't speak. I just strode back and forth, staring at the state of the supposedly "safe" little valley it'd been left in.

Yes, *okay*...I'd been dumped not far from it after a mugging, and yeah, *okay*, it was in the wilds of Gateshead, an area not generally renowned for being safe. More like an area that if something wasn't nailed down, it'd been stolen, repainted, and sold within twenty minutes.

"But it's the fucking apocalypse! What kind of bastard degenerate lunatic was wandering around the forests *in a fucking apocalypse* to just stumble on *my* goddamn ship!" I roared, feeling my lightning responding to my fury as the shallow valley was suddenly bathed in crackling blue light.

"Uh...Matt?" Chris tried.

"WHAT?" I shouted, glaring at him.

"First off, dickhead, it's me, so calm the fuck down. Second, look at the marks."

I glared at him, and he stared back at me calmly, waiting. Eventually, when I'd gotten a little self-control back, I managed to stare at the tracks, the marks, and broken and damaged trees, finally starting to read the scene, rather than just staring in abject fury.

We'd approached from the due south, coming up through the trees and because we were riding literal triceratops, we'd ignored minor details like immature woodlands.

The multi-ton dinos did, after all. They just plodded on, pausing occasionally to rip a mouthful of a particularly tasty bush up. But beyond that, apart from trees that were a good size, they just plowed their own path through.

The far side of the valley, though—the north—had a freshly cleared area, and all the footprints led in that direction.

I forced myself to tour the area again, more carefully this time, examining the tracks as I saw them, taking the time to pick one from another and trying to count how many there were.

I counted roughly a dozen that were barefoot, and at least double that wore shoes—some clearly literally brand-new, others badly worn.

No clue who'd found it, but there'd been a load of people to take it away, and they'd dragged it up one side of the valley, cutting trees and more aside to do the job.

I found sections of the larger trees nearby had been rubbed clear of the bark, areas where something—presumably ropes—had been dragged under tension, over and over.

"They used ropes to drag the ship up and out of the valley, looped around the trees, with dozens on each side," I told the others. Most of the kobolds stood around, uncaring, at the back, awaiting orders, but Chris, Patrick, Dante, Kilo, and another of the pack had come forward.

"You see here?" I asked them, not really directing the question to any of them in particular. "The footprints are deep, under pressure. You can see where the foot was braced, turned sideways, and where they pulled against a weight."

Nods.

"Here the weight is released. And the way they scramble up the side of the hill? There's signs they were moving fast—torn muddy sections, a handprint where someone fell…Then they all start again here…"

I moved from section to section, showing where they duplicated the process repeatedly to get the ship up out of the valley, and the small cleared area outside.

There were shattered tree branches up above and around us, where they'd obviously tried to loop the ropes over trees that weren't strong enough. But they'd managed it eventually, as evidenced by the deeper tracks of something, probably a trailer, that led down the far side and through a path cut out of the forest.

I led the way. The dungeon creatures followed us automatically, as we went.

Five minutes was all it took, and then I was cursing as we stared at the muddy prints that led onto a connecting road, turning left, which was great that we had a direction…but although the muddy prints were there now, they'd soon run out of mud.

"JACK!" I bellowed into the air; he'd hear it regardless of distance. I sighed, staring down the road and into the night, knowing that by how dry the mud was, it wasn't in the last hour or two they'd done this.

He'd been tracking the creatures that Mike was following, but the size of those fuckers meant that he wasn't needed for that, and if it turned out he was? Well, he was also *my* goddamn familiar. I'd send him back to help Mike as soon as this was done.

This was a job for a tracker, after all, not a headlong chase.

Congratulations!

You have gained four levels in Tracking! You receive a further 8% increase to your chances to spot important details and tracks. Because you have gained this level in a sub-skill of "Hunting," you have also received the requisite levels in "Hunting," granting a further 3% improvement per level to your chances identifying a critical weakness. Increase your skill to further improve your damage bonuses.

Congratulations!

You have increased your "Tracking" skill to level 10!

At level 10, you have an increased chance to spot hidden tracks and to sense nearby opponents that are tracking you in turn by an additional 1% per level. You also gain a +10% increased chance to spot different animal tracks, and to correctly differentiate the animals' intentions through simple repetition and observation.

Pulling up my tracking details, I was pleased to see that I was up to a thirty percent chance to find tracks and hidden enemies now, three percent per level apparently, with a second notification for the hunting skill as well.

Congratulations!

You have increased your "Hunting" skill to level 10!

At level 10, you have an increased chance to follow the tracks you find, as well as the logical steps that will lead to a successful hunt. It's no longer enough that you can see the tracks; now you can tell what made them, be they your prey or your challengers. Increase this skill further to augment your stealth skills as well.

- *+5 to Stealth-based skills.*

I stared at that in shock.

An extra five points on my stealth skills wasn't a small bonus. Hell, it was massive, especially because my stealth score was so hard to level for me. Okay, yeah, I was wearing armor. Yes, I had a fucking cape on—and I was totally going to tear that off at some point, because no matter what anyone thought, it wasn't growing on me, even if it did look kinda cool.

That wasn't the point.

I was practically the antithesis of subtle.

I rode a fucking triceratops, after all.

Stealth was a skill tree that I was guaranteed to be shit at. I glowed when I was annoyed. I flew and cast lightning! And yet me being a better hunter, and a tracker, meant I could increase my stealth skills?

I hesitated, ignoring Chris as he asked me a question, staring into the night as my mind raced. *Could I level all my skills through complementary trees?*

Could I gain extra points in everything, like my weapons, which climbed more slowly now, by diversifying and doing things like, I don't know, chopping down trees? Using a hammer on the walls of buildings we needed to demolish, as much as on my enemies?

If I learned to forge metal with, with…whatever his name was…would I level my hammer-wielding fighting skills too?

It made sense; hell, it made a lot of sense. Also, if I could do it, so could all our people. Having not only the kobolds, but all our people start training in tracking might give them all a sneaky boost to their stealth, and that in turn could save their lives one day.

I needed to look into this.

"Chris?" I mumbled absently.

"Yeah, man?"

"We need to arrange tracking training for our people."

"Uh…" He hesitated, and shrugged, scratching the back of his neck. "Whatever you say. So…are we going?"

"What?" I turned to him and saw the look on his face. "What do you mean? Go where?"

"Back to the dungeon."

"What? Why would we go back?" I was confused to all fuck.

"The ship is gone. You're summoning Jack, right? You're going to send him hunting, so are we heading back until we find out what's going on and who took it?"

"Fuck no," I growled. "They might trash it in the meantime. No. Jack is coming, and he'll track them when we lose the trail, but for now we need to follow it. Kelly will let us know if there's anything wrong…somehow."

"Dude, we're riding triceratops. We're not going to sneak up on anyone," Chris pointed out, and I hesitated, before cursing and summoning the dinos forward.

"Fine." I turned to Dante, waving him over. "Dante, I want you to stay back with the dinos, protect them and yourself. If the shit hits the fan, you'll know about it because I'll order the dinos back to the dungeon. Go with them and gather our forces, then lead them back here to help us."

"I could help you," he said. "I'm a pyromancer. You're sending away one of your best weapons."

"I—" I had to acknowledge that he was right. The thing was, we had no other way to explain what happened if we got in the shit.

"He's right, Matt," Chris added, and I glared at him as Patrick chimed in agreement too.

"Fine, but he's shit at stealth, and he's got the stamina of a one-legged baby duck." I looked at them both. "You think he can sneak around behind us?"

"Well, not really?" Chris admitted, before shrugging and grinning. "But does he have to?"

"What?"

"You were going to leave him with the dinos—we can still do that, just instead of them running away if we get in the shit, he rides them in to the rescue. He keeps his manapool nice and high, and if we need him, you summon the dinos, he lays down suppressing fire…"

"Literally." Patrick grinned.

"Yeah, and then we ride them all outta there. Sound good?" Chris finished with a grin, and I glared at him.

"You know I hate it when you do that, don't you?"

"What?"

"Think," I said. "I've known you too long. I can never be sure it's because you came up with it on your own or if you saw it in a movie and were waiting for the opportunity to claim it as your own plan."

"Matt, old buddy, you *wound* me." Chris shook his head. "You should know better. Yeah, okay, I used to be a bit of a film buff, but let's face it, how fucked up would someone have to be to create all of this?" He gestured at the dinosaurs, the kobolds, and the general apocalypse that was our lives these days.

"Okay," I grunted. "Yeah, point right there. But I don't trust you to have a plan, mate. Like I said, I've known you too long."

"Patrick, back me up here," Chris said, and the big monk grinned at me.

"Matt, I totally get what you're saying, but you have to remember one thing."

"Oh?"

"Even a blind squirrel finds nuts eventually."

"What the hell kind of mystic mumbo-jumbo—" Chris started to say, as I cut him off, speaking over him.

"So you're saying it's blind luck, and that in an infinite universe, somewhere a room full of monkeys with typewriters just wrote out Shakespeare's collected works?" I asked. "That if all things are possible, then maybe, just maybe, Chris came up with a plan by sheer luck?"

"It's the only reasonable outcome." Patrick nodded. "Let's face it…he might be a druid, but he's also an idiot."

"You know, I don't have to stay here for this abuse." Chris sighed, looking from one of us to the other, seeing the grins. "I can go anywhere for that."

The pair of them started in on each other, talking rubbish as I took a few steps away, staring out into the night, and thinking. I knew them both well enough, and they me, that I knew they'd done that deliberately.

They'd made a joke of it all, talking bollocks to distract me, and to calm me down. To get me to think, instead of just reacting.

I should have done that myself, to be fair. After all, there was absolutely no realistic reason for me to be so annoyed. The ship was here, abandoned, and it'd been found by someone else. For all I knew, they were good people.

Maybe these were another group of survivors who'd found the wreck and were trying to fix things, putting two and two together. I was annoyed…no, I was furious, at *myself*.

I'd kept putting off coming for the ship because I had so many things going on, and now it'd been found by someone else. Maybe we had allies out here, potentially. Or possible recruits at least.

They didn't have to be enemies.

I stared into the night. The tree branches overhead, saplings mainly, swayed in the breeze, creaking as their branches, denuded of foliage by the coming winter, shifted.

Through them, I could see the bright pinpricks of the stars overhead, and I sighed, wondering whether anyone up there was watching down on us.

That thought led to wondering whether the space stations were still up and working.

I knew planes had fallen, or at least logically that they would have. The south and the major cities must have been a hell-storm of burning jet fuel and more, over and over again.

Was the effect that killed electricity even able to reach up into orbit, though?

Were astronauts sitting up there, frantically trying to survive on dwindling food and water, wondering why everything was dark and nobody was speaking anymore?

Or had they been the first victims? Having access to only canned air and needing maneuvering thrusters—and more—constantly?

If they'd tried to land, they'd have failed. The emergency shuttles would have become unresponsive bricks at some point.

I banished the thought as a distant twinkle of firelight caught my eye. Where I was, high in the hill that climbed out of the Team Valley area, I could see for miles. Although the trees were making it easy, I could see more and more than I had before, that was for sure.

I gestured the others forward, clambering up my own dino, and reaching down to grab Dante's hand, pulling him up to stand next to me, as I led the way forward.

"I thought I wasn't allowed up?" Dante asked, and I waved him to silence, thinking.

"You're supposed to be running, Dante. You need to improve your stamina, right?" Chris called, and I distractedly saw Dante gesturing at him to "shut up, please."

Out of the surrounding trees, we quickly found an old gate that led out into a farmer's field. The triceratops barely noticed it as I brushed it aside, and we moved out, climbing up toward the apex of the nearest gently rolling hill.

We turned and sat—or stood—atop the beasts, staring out across miles of the local cities and towns.

Newcastle was to my left, a mass of blackness, lit only by the bright, merry lights of the dungeon. Drawing a mental line from that to the right and closer to where we stood, we could see Saltwell Park, again, gleaming with merry light and cheer.

The clearly artificial, flickering lights that defined both settlements made them stand out.

Next, moving into the middle of the panorama before us, where in the distance the opposite side of the valley climbed up and through the rest of Gateshead, flickering flames were scattered here and there.

Some looked to be torches; others moved slowly, shifting into view as they passed between houses in the far distance, making it clear they were heading somewhere.

Farther to the right lay the old industrial estates at the top of the hill, though—Birtley and more, at the outskirts of Washington—and I damn well hoped the gangs that lived over those hills weren't the ones who had found the ship.

Minutes passed as I stared, until Chris moved up and got my attention. "What's that?"

I'd been fixated on the right, the direction from where we stood now that the road had led down to, where the ship had presumably been taken, and I'd been trying to spot any small settlements.

I'd seen where we lived, and the park, and had nodded in satisfaction that even from here they looked like good places to live.

Now though, I frowned and watched as Chris pointed.

"There, there it is again!"

I frowned, staring but not seeing, until suddenly something moved, and I froze in horror.

It wasn't the houses, nor the buildings I was looking at, the camps nor the signs of life from all of our people.

It was the great, big, fuck-off creatures that suddenly obstructed some of the light around Saltwell Park as it passed between it and us.

"Tell me that wasn't a dragon," Dante whispered, and I just stared in shock as the massive creature circled the park twice more, before shifting and carrying on, clearly in search of something else.

"Plan's changed," I said. "Chris..."

"Oh man, I really want a dragon," he mumbled, staring at the sky, eyes shining.

"CHRIS!" I snapped, making him jump.

"What?"

"Plan's changed," I repeated. "We're following the trail as far as we can on the roads. But once it passes the valley, if it goes right, we leave it…Jack will find it. We're heading up the bank behind the valley and back to Saltwell. They need to know to stay in at nighttime, and to not have…I don't know, parties or whatever outside until we know we can deal with that kind of shit."

I got a round of nods and agreement, and we moved off. Kilo clambered up to ride behind Chris, and the other, apparently an awakened kobold, joined Patrick, each without any prompting. The remaining four "dull" kobolds jogged unthinkingly along behind us.

The triceratops were surprisingly fast-moving, and as they fell into single file, my own in the lead tearing the bottom gate from the field as we left, I could only imagine how awesome we looked.

Ten minutes later, and we were still following the trail. The occasional muddy mark or shoved aside car let us know we were on the right trail until Jack arrived, powering up alongside and passing us.

I'd sent a much more complex series of commands to him than I usually would, including to return to the valley where the ship had been, and to follow that trail, not just to catch up to us.

I wanted to be damn sure we were on the right track, and that my fledgling tracking skills weren't leading us astray.

When Jack passed us, and practically vanished into the darkness ahead of us, I relaxed for the first time, despite wondering what the hell was going on with the location.

The road we were following led up to the top of the hill, then joined a second road, one that ran north to south…or, for us, left and right.

To the left was the park, about a mile away. As I sensed Jack taking that route, I grew even more confused, wondering whether Barry had somehow found it, or whether it'd been claimed by Aaron maybe, and dumped along the road?

When we'd killed him, anything he'd had would have been left, and if nobody knew to look for it…

I suddenly felt a lot better, deciding that made a sort of sense, that would explain a lot, and…

And Jack turned right.

He'd taken the left toward the park, but twenty or thirty meters ahead, he'd taken a right, presumably following a road, and was headed away from the park now, climbing a second hill.

I gritted my teeth in annoyance, wondering what the hell Aaron had done with it, and directed the others to take that path. A few minutes later, we slowed. Having to pause and wait as the triceratops, massive engines of destruction that they were, rested and caught their breath.

I'd not considered it, but the sheer damn weight of the creatures meant that unlike horses and so on, they couldn't run practically indefinitely. I mean, I knew horses couldn't, not really, but still. The size of the dinos had convinced me they were organic tanks, and that they'd just keep going.

Checking them over, I cursed.

They were level zero, which implied that they could level up, which was great. But what wasn't great when I examined them was their stamina.

Name: Unnamed Triceratops				
Species: Triceratops		**Bonus:** None		
Level: 0		**Progress to next level:** 0/500		
Available points: 0		**Perk:** None		

Stat	Current points	Description	Effect	Progress to next level
Agility	5	Governs dodge and movement		19/100
Charisma	2	Governs likely success to charm, seduce, or threaten		0/100
Constitution	10	Governs Health and Health Regeneration	HP: 10x250 = 2500 (Giant creature modifier in effect)	12/100
Dexterity	1	Governs ability with weapons and crafting	-90% chance to craft (Giant creature modifier in effect)	0/100
Endurance	10	Governs Stamina and Stamina Regeneration	Stamina: 10x50= 500 (Giant creature modifier in effect)	94/100
Intelligence	2	Governs base manapool and standard intellectual capacity	Mana: 2x1 = 2 (Giant creature modifier in effect)	2/100
Luck	4	Governs overall chance of bonuses and critical hits		11/100
Perception	3	Governs ranged damage and chance to spot hidden items/traps		50/100
Strength	10	Governs damage with melee weapons and carrying capacity	+100 damage in melee (Giant creature modifier in effect)	12/100
Wisdom	1	Governs mana regeneration and memory	1 mana regenerated per hour	0/100

I didn't even know how many points the fuckers got per level to assign, but considering that everyone else I knew of—humans, kobolds, goblins…*everyone* as far as I knew—hit their first level at ten points?

For the trike—that was a much better damn name to refer to them by, I decided—for the trike to hit it at *five hundred*? That meant it was going to take forever to make a decently leveled version.

Then I paused, considering that Aaron's versions had been level eleven, and they'd died fairly easily, while these…clearly there was a massive difference in living to undead survivability in some ways.

If I could ride these fuckers through a battle? Armored and with, I don't know, spikes or something on them? Fuck yes.

They'd be amazing to use as a platform of war, and once they started leveling up? They'd be unstoppable.

The thought of a hundred of these in a great herd, roaring south along the motorway, a hundred mages sat atop their back? Fuck, we could literally make it to London in a day, maybe two. Recruit the people we needed, set up a new dungeon offshoot somewhere along the way, and boom.

We'd be made.

Hell, if Dickless 2.0 arrived and we were riding giant dinos? Especially if we'd managed to get stegosauruses and T. Rexes by then? Fuck, he'd just apologize and surrender!

Get the tech behind us and make the dino version of mechs? The orcs would be running for it inside of a day. I didn't even care whether it was realistic or not.

I wanted a pet T. rex with frikin laser beams on its head!

Massive rail guns on its back with armor? Man, just the thought of what we could accomplish with all of that...

Then I sensed it as Jack arced to the right again, and I cursed. The dinos were slow as all hell to regenerate stamina. As near as I could tell, it'd be at least an hour to recover from the run we'd just put them through, and I shook my head.

"Fine, the kobolds will stay with the trikes, protect them, and as soon as they've recovered, they'll come to us. Kilo, you and..." I paused, staring at the kobold warrior, who stared back, waiting. "Ummm...Tango?" I tried, and he nodded, straightening and seeming pleased to have an actual name at last.

"Cool, Kilo and Tango, you stay with the others. Kilo, you're in charge. Tango, you help him. As soon as the trikes are recovered, come to us...Can you find us?" I asked.

They nodded. Kilo tapped his chest in salute before moving off and arranging the unaware kobolds to stand around the perimeter of the trikes as they fed, tearing great swathes of autumn wilted grasses and bushes loose and eating them.

"Fair enough. Okay then, let's go," I said to the others.

Patrick and Dante fell in on my left, and Chris on my right as we started to jog up the hill.

The road was winding, and at least half a mile long, climbing higher and higher steadily. Jack sent back periodic bursts of direction as he shifted and altered the route, taking another left this time at the top. A nasty thought began to fill my mind.

Somewhere up this way—I wasn't over this side of things very often, but I knew it was up here somewhere—was the Queen Elizabeth Hospital.

It was a great big sprawling affair.

I'd been sent here once from work when I'd had a finger caught in a server rack, breaking it.

Three hours I'd sat waiting, before a harassed doctor had arranged for an x-ray, and then another two until he could evaluate it.

"It's broken," he'd told me shortly.

"Right?" I'd asked, and he'd sighed.

"Nothing we can do for it. It's in the right place, no damage to the veins and nerves around it. We'll tape it up, and just try not to use it for a few weeks."

That was it.

It'd been taped—literally—to the one next to it and I'd been told to take painkillers if it hurt, then I'd been booted out. I'd been more annoyed at the waste of around five hours of my day, but I had to appreciate that at least I was in the UK rather than America.

The entire affair had cost me nothing but time. Well, that and a trip to the nearest shop to buy over-the-counter paracetamol and ibuprofen at around twenty pence a box each for sixteen tablets.

The same thing in America, I'd been assured would have cost me several thousand dollars, even if I had insurance…probably tens of thousands or hundreds if I'd not, by the time x-rays and more were factored in.

The thing worrying me right now was that the hospital was up here somewhere, and there were gangs coming from this direction, attacking the park.

If one of these fuckers…

Chris hit me from the side, sending me rolling as something tore through the air where my chest had been. I swore, stunned, then grunted. I threw myself sideways as a second arrow smacked into the asphalt near my head. I forced myself to my feet and ran between two parked cars, staring into the night, trying to find whoever had attacked us.

"You all right?" Chris called from nearby, doing the same.

"Yeah, man, thanks to you. What happened?"

"Just lucky," he admitted, edging around the corner of the car. "Saw the arrow getting pointed and went on instinct."

"Where?"

"The tree to the left, the one that's overhanging that fence?" He gestured and I nodded, seeing the shadowy mass that sheltered half the fence on one side of the road.

"Yeah?"

"Literally up in there. Saw the arrow tip catch the light."

"Think they're still there?" I asked, and he nodded. "Dante!"

Dante's head popped up a few cars farther down, looking around until Patrick grabbed him and yanked him back down out of sight…just as an arrow hit the roof of the car next to him, ricocheting away into the darkness.

"Yeah?" Dante called from wherever Patrick had him pinned.

"Fuck that asshole up."

"Yessir!" he called back, sounding damn pleased to have the excuse.

"What do you think?" I asked Chris conversationally. "Fireball?"

"Gotta be Fireball," Chris agreed. "Let's face it, the fucker's hiding in a treehouse, perfect for a Fireball. I'd use one if I could—" He broke off, clearly thinking about it.

"You thinking what I'm thinking?" I asked.

He took one look at me and nodded. "We need to learn Fireball," he agreed. "It'd be insanely cool to…*ohholyfuckingshitonabiscuit!*"

That last bit came out in one stream of shocked profanity as Dante stood suddenly, thrusting both hands out and releasing a veritable pressurized stream of flaming napalm across the road to tear through the tree and the pathetic treehouse it used to contain.

"Burn, motherfucker," came the self-satisfied purr from Dante into the stunned silence, the only sounds the crackle and pop of damp wood as it was consumed in the fiery conflagration.

CHAPTER THIRTY-TWO

"Dante…I don't know if I need to applaud, or arrange mental help." I walked up and clapped him on the shoulder. "I mean, seriously, dude? That was a hell of a cold response."

"Personally, I'm proud of him," Chris said. "Some asshole tries to shoot him with an arrow, and he burns him to death and then comes out with a line like that?"

"It was impressive…" Patrick started to say, until we saw the slowly dawning horror on Dante's face.

"You okay?" I asked. And because the universe is a dick, that's the exact moment the screaming, burning figure of the attacker burst through the dilapidated fence.

They were waving their arms wildly, clearly unable to see or think, as they were wreathed in wild flames. From their hands to their feet, and their head as well, their fats popping and crisping over the roar of the flames. And the screams…

They lasted bare seconds before collapsing on the ground, rolling and beating at themselves in uncontrolled bursts. The four of us stared—Chris, Patrick, and me coldly, regretting the pain that was caused to someone, distantly, but uncaring of much more than that. They'd attacked us, and this was the apocalypse.

Don't start shit you can't finish had become a major part of everyone's outlook on life.

Dante, on the other hand…I winced as I looked at him, the horrified look on his face, the tears streaming from his eyes.

"Dante," I said, then I hesitated, unsure of what to actually say. *It was him or us? I told you to do it? Shit happens?* All of them were true, but as far as I knew, this was the first time he'd used his powers on an actual living human.

Chris stepped forward, stabbing out with his sword and ending the screams permanently.

"Dante, you had no choice." I stepped in front of him and forced him to look me in the eyes. "We were just passing by, and he tried to kill us. This was a choice *he* made, not you."

"Y…yeah," Dante agreed, refusing to look at me. "I know."

"Yeah, you do, but it doesn't make it any easier." I looked around, then cursed. "Come on. We know which way they went. Let's cut through these houses, see if we can get off the road and save a little time by going direct."

I led the way into the garden the burning figure had come from, passing into the house beyond. The sliding patio doors that led from the garden inside showed frequent use.

The carpet beyond was covered in mud, as was the room generally. Twin sofas that faced each other were covered in the marks of boots and discarded wrappers, the kitchen that was just visible to the right of the patio doors was trashed, and many of the cupboard doors stood ajar, their contents displaced as someone had searched for food.

Worst of all, as we paused inside, the light of the flickering flames outside illuminated the fridge.

It shouldn't have mattered.

It should have made fuck all difference to us, but it did.

The fridge was covered in drawings on scraps of paper, bright colors that were smudged and smeared. Mud was splattered across most of them, as well as a bloody handprint. But the pictures?

They were from a toddler, or I assumed anyway. Hands that had been dipped in paint then pressed to the paper…bright, cheerful reminders of a world we'd lost.

I hesitated, staring at the pictures of "Mummy, Daddy, and me." Three blobby stick figures that were covered in smears of paint and for just a second, I wondered. I wondered what had happened to them all.

I looked around the room. There were pictures of a smiling, rosy-cheeked little girl at nursery, and being kissed, giggling by a man with a big bushy beard. Dozens of details stood out: the toy tower that housed a bunch of animated puppies from TV, the broken plastic teapot on the floor…

This had been a family's home, one that looked to have been full of love and laughter, judging from the pictures.

Now the outside was on fire, the inside trashed by people moving around in filthy clothes, uncaring of the damage they did.

The cupboards had been ransacked and the things that would have normally been the first to be stolen, the TV and the games consoles, had been chucked out into the garden, uncaring.

The house had been trashed, and I knew we'd probably never know who'd lived there, nor what had happened to them.

"Come on," Patrick said after a few seconds. "We need to get away from here."

He was right, I reflected. I nodded, leading the way through the rest of the house, out into the front garden and down the narrow concrete path.

The screams, the light from the fire…all of it would draw attention—be that beasts or bestial humans, it didn't matter. The best thing we could do was get off the road, and…

"Fuck!" I snarled. "Kilo!"

"What?" Chris asked, looking around for the kobold.

"I went this way so that we'd be away from anyone coming to investigate, but Kilo will be following our tracks and scent. He'll see we went through the house."

"So?"

"So you think a triceratops is gonna fit through those doors?" I asked grimly. "We should go ba—"

I was cut off by the distant sound of gunfire from the north—heavy, sustained gunfire—and I cursed. There was no way that was our people, not wasting ammunition like that, not—

A handful of single shots rang out, followed by more heavy fire in reply, and that was it.

All pretense at stealth was abandoned as we ran all out.

The gunfire was heavy all right, but at a distance as well. As much as the sound of gunfire, or any loud noise, carried at night, we had no real clue where the hell it was coming from. The house we'd exited had let us out into a small residential street, and we'd run randomly in the direction we thought it was coming from.

"I'll be right back," I called to the others, before taking a deep breath and launching myself into the air.

As soon as I cleared the ground level, landing awkwardly on the roof of the nearest house and grabbing onto the chimney, the gunfire fell silent, making me curse for a handful of seconds. It rang out again, the distant flash and clatter rebounding off the walls of houses at least a mile away.

I launched myself again, flying up and forward, my fucking cape fluttering behind me. I stared over a series of old trees, seeing more clearly as something huge staggered in the distance, and the flashes of light came from atop its back.

I started to fall, and I cursed, well aware that either I could use all my mana to convert into the storm and grant me the power of flight…and then I'd be fuck all use by the time I arrived at the fight. Or I could land and run, and be knackered but have magic as well.

I angled myself down, breaking my fall as much as I could bring myself to, landing a few dozen meters ahead of Chris and the others. I started to run, trusting them to catch up, even as I focused, hoping Kilo would get the message as I mentally ordered him to return to the dungeon.

The next street was a long one, winding, but at the end it came out onto a T-junction, joining a longer and wider main road. I turned to the right, starting to breathe a little heavier as I kept running, Chris alongside me, with Patrick falling back and trying to encourage Dante, who sounded like he was about to have a heart attack.

"What…did you…see?" Chris huffed, glancing over at me, and I shook my head.

"Not sure…looked like the asuras…but bigger," I got out. The strain of running in full armor started to show on all of us.

"He's going to catch up," Patrick said as he picked up speed, catching up.

"Quick as you can, Dante!" I called to him, before nodding to the other two, and the three of us sped on.

The houses blurred past now we weren't trying to keep together, and for a few seconds I thought that we should never have brought him. Then I shook that thought free. Dante was a good guy; he just needed some help to live up to his potential.

"That damn training dungeon," I muttered, running harder.

"What?" Chris called.

"Nothing!" I gestured at the trees that rose ahead, behind the houses on the left side of the road. "Okay, far side of those trees, there's a few little streets, and a bigger one heading left to the right that leads down toward the main road and the park, and—"

Gunfire erupted ahead again, this time sounding much closer as we ran, and I cursed. "Catch up when you can!" I called to them, angling toward the house ahead, and kept on going, as the other two continued to follow the road.

"Don't get dead!" Chris called after me, and I couldn't help but grin as I launched myself again, landing on the roof of a bungalow ahead and kicking off.

Instead of flying "properly," with all the attendant mana costs that came with that, having to flood my body with the storm mana and let it burn all the time I flew, I "boosted" myself instead, using a surge of it, along with my already enhanced abilities.

I literally jumped from roof to roof, flying only when it was too far to jump, and saving a hell of a lot of mana in the process, but getting myself closer to the fight in a quarter of the time.

It felt stupid.

I constantly worried that the others, if this was the group Mike and so on had been chasing, might be dying because I was choosing to conserve mana like this, but...but if I didn't? I'd be useless in the fight.

I leapt up, mistiming the jump and barely managing to grab the corner of the next roof, rather than landing on it, and dragged myself up and over, swearing. I ran up to the peak of it, to pause, staring down, stunned at the scene of devastation before me.

The street, an east–west running main road in a residential area, was straight, mainly, and running up a sharp incline from the lower bank area that the park and so on was built on, to the top of the valley, and the road that ran north to south along it.

The houses that climbed along either side of the street were stepped and terraced. Joined side by side, each roof finished slightly higher than the one before it, in a rolling cascade of steps, moving up to the right, or the east, and down to the left or west.

I slid down the far side of the roof, coming to a stop on the edge, my right shoulder pressed to one such "step" and effectively hiding me from everything to my right and higher up the street. I peered over the edge, looking up and down again in astonishment at the destruction.

There were at least a hundred dead in the road below, with dozens more screaming in their death throes. Cars that had been parked on either side of the road when the fall happened hadn't moved since, but now they were kicked aside, crushed and smashed, as well as covered in fresh blood.

Fires rolled through some of the houses. And the cars that had been smashed aside had contributed to them as well: the fuel leaking from crushed and dented tanks rolled down the hill. Flames caught and flowed along them, spreading from car to car.

Gunfire rang out to the right, as did manic laughter, and I edged farther around, looking up at the creature that led the way up the hill.

An asuras.

There was no doubt about that, and it had to be a queen. I wasn't going to risk my mana on confirming it, because there was no way the fucker was anything else.

It walked on six huge legs, each moving steadily, lifting and clamping down into place. The feet at the end drove down some kind of clamps that anchored it with each step before it took the next.

The six feet were attached to a massive platform, one that looked to have been made by cutting and melding three shipping containers together with a large crane.

The body that the legs were attached to looked to be the circular bottom of a crane, and even had several cranes attached still, at the back. As I watched, it dragged a car up into the air with two of the three, lowering the car into the circular pit in the middle of the creature, where clumsy robotic arms moved forward and backward and light flashed, sparks flying and smoke billowing wildly.

The back of the creature had the main shipping container area attached, forming a large platform that had at least fifteen or twenty people on it. They were the ones laughing.

As I stared, stunned, a device, a ring that emitted a bright-blue light, powered up.

Two of the figures manhandled a third, their arms tied to their sides, and threw them into the ring of light. The body hung there in the middle, like a fly caught in a spider's web, as they screamed in agony.

In seconds, even as I was clambering up onto the roof in preparation to run at them, the light was torn free, traveling down a length of cabling and into the assembly area that the car had been dumped into.

The body of the bound man or woman, it was too far to see for sure either way from here, was discarded, falling lifeless into the road below, even as the machine stomped onward.

I grabbed the edge of the roof, forcing myself to stay where I was, to stay hidden, as I tried to think what the hell I was going to do.

It fell silent, and a new creation dropped free of the spider-thing.

It easily fell the ten meters to the ground from the underside of the thing, landing with its legs extended to take its weight. The freshly built mobile tank had barely hit the ground before it was off, scuttling forward and up the street.

I hissed in recognition of the tank thing that we'd fought by the river and looked up the street, squinting up ahead and seeing what I'd missed before in the shock of seeing the queen. A dozen or so others were stomping out of sight in that direction, before I looked back down at the freshly "born" monstrosity.

The freshly created tank raced to the nearest parked car, twisting around and backing into it. The turret that sat atop the four legs opened at the back; grasping fingers clamped onto the frame of the car and closed. Glass shattered, the roof being half torn off as the "fingers" closed, compressing the metal and crap into a solid slug; then it took in more and repeated the process, before scuttling off up the road.

I stared at the massive creation, easily equal to the height of the houses on either side of it, as it stomped up the street. A dozen or more smaller roaming creatures—some humanoid, others like robotic wolves—dragged struggling people to the big one, as a cable snaked down, wrapping around them and lifting them into the air.

It was a mass harvesting, I realized.

The group on the creation's back were human, from what I could see, a bunch of lunatic gangbangers, and all armed to the teeth, literally.

One was carrying a heavy machine gun that looked as if it'd been looted right off an army APC, and that fucker was huge, carrying it in one hand.

The others?

They were a mix of all kinds: skinny and massive, fat and slim; where one was dressed, the next in line was practically naked, then one would be bundled up in furs…

Fuck, no, the next one wasn't *in* furs—they were furry! Like a huge werewolf, muscled and hairy, their face a bizarre mix of human and wolf, and carrying a massive axe in one hand as they let out a howl that echoed off the sides of the street.

I heard more gunfire up ahead, shots tearing out, and I hesitated.

Whoever they were, these were the fuckers Mike had been following, I had to assume. They matched what I could remember, anyway. The size of the big one, it could have stepped over the shops back there, and the smaller would have torn their way through, no issue.

The question now was where the hell was Mike, and was he okay?

Most of the bodies below were more of the crazily built-up and overly muscled lunatics, and I guessed I was seeing a gang fighting another gang, judging from the mass of torn leather, black outfits, and spikes most of the bodies were dressed in.

I frowned, looking to the west and down the street. We weren't that far from the park here; was it possible they'd just missed it? No, that was ridiculous. There was the light and everything from the park and the dungeon. They *had* to know we were there.

It didn't make any sense!

Following the trail of destruction, I could see they'd come from a street that led up from the main road. It led back to where they'd crossed the line from the dungeon, but…

I shook my head.

I couldn't see any signs that they'd hit the park. I couldn't see for sure they *were* the group that Mike had been trailing, either—although it was seriously fucking unlikely that all of this was going on so close and that this was just *another* unconnected group. They had to be part of it, or an offshoot.

It was the high-mana area drawing weirdness to it, making most inside it as mad as a box of frogs, unless they were near to a source of purified mana, as we were in the dungeon.

That made me worry about the people in the park, and I resolved to get Aly working on something as soon as possible.

For now, though, I needed a fucking plan for this thing because—

A boom rang out ahead, and I swore as a handful of the mechanical steampunk tanks set off running, clattering around and out of sight at the top of the street. I swore viciously.

That might have been a total coincidence, or…

I was off and running before I'd finished the thought, clambering onto the next roof proper and running straight up and along, switching between the group riding the mechanical monstrosity of an asura, and the one that was running across the top of the street, following a group of—

Fuck.

It was a family of four people, sprinting from the right to the left, heading away from the direction Chris and Patrick would be approaching from. I had little hope that those crazy bastards would stay hidden, not with a family with little kiddies on the line.

"Who am I fucking kidding?" I grunted, picking up speed and jumping to the next roof, then the next, closing on the group ahead. There were several more booms as the mobile tanks tracked and fired, but the others were out of sight at the top already, cut off as they'd moved past the connecting street.

I had to hope they'd missed, but…

Bullets chewed into the roof alongside me. Dozens of shots went wide, as possibly hundreds were fired wildly into the slanted roof. The meathead with the heavy machine gun had spotted me, opening fire and whooping for his friends to join in.

I dove over the peak of the roof, landing on the far side, hopefully out of sight, but skidding, sliding out of control as I went. My face smashed into the step of the next house. I clutched at my nose and slipped as I tried to catch myself.

I'd not realized it was already too late as I tore into the gutters and straight through, before plunging over the side…and into some idiot's abandoned koi pond.

I hit the water hard, and then the stone surrounds of the pond even harder. The world went black as I bounced, thrashing, and sank.

The pond—because nobody was actually stupid enough to have a pool outside in the North of England, especially not in *Gateshead*—was deeper than I was tall, a ridiculous fact that almost resulted in my death.

I blinked slowly, stunned and sinking, the dim light of the world above fading, as hard, sharp fingers suddenly clamped onto me, dragging me upright and from the embrace of the water. I stared up in confusion, coughing and dribbling water as I tried to summon my storm mana to heal me, only getting fits and starts from it.

The figure that had dragged me clear and now looked down at me was…*wrong*. I couldn't put my finger on why, not when I could barely see. Blood ran down the right-hand side of my face and my head throbbed with every beat of my heart, but whoever they were, they dragged me into the house, smashing the glass door to open it, before carrying me inside and dumping me on the sofa.

I landed facedown. The world around me still spun and reeled, pain tearing through me as I tried, and utterly failed, to get words out. Twisting, I whimpered. It felt like the top of my head was about to fall off, and someone, presumably the figure that had dragged me out of the pond, dropped a massive fluffy duvet over me, then smacked me on the top of the head, twice—*hard*.

I blacked out, the pain too much. The world around me spiraled into darkness. And for a time at least, I knew no more.

CHAPTER THIRTY-THREE

Reality was slow in returning to me, or so it seemed, laid as I was on the sofa, staring up at the ceiling overhead. I tried to work out what had happened as I looked at the darkened ceiling, watching a long-legged spider creep across it.

I was…I was…I was doing something? I was running. Then I remembered…falling? It wasn't right; something was wrong. I had a terrible feeling that there was something I should be doing. I should be somewhere, but…but I just kept watching the spider as it moved, reaching out to something that struggled in its web.

I watched as the web shook, then the spider lunged forward, seeming to leap across the intervening distance to sink its fangs into the creature bound there.

It was a bird, I realized. A bird that had been caught in the web.

The world seemed to slide into focus more, and I realized all at once that the spider I was staring at was at least as large as my fist, probably bigger, and…

I heard a noise behind me, a *click-click-click* or something hard hitting a wooden floor. I reacted on instinct, spinning, or trying to, thinking a giant fucking spider was closing on me from behind.

I was right, in part.

I was also totally wrong. I fell off the sofa, still wrapped in the now blood-soaked fluffy duvet, landing on the floor as my savior backed up, lifting two of its hands to show they were empty, and it meant no harm.

That was what I *thought* it meant, after a few seconds had passed and it'd stayed still, anyway. I still lunged to my feet, grabbing the duvet and tearing my way free. My augmented strength sent fluffy duck down flying in all directions, as I forced myself to my feet, and reached for my—

My fucking hammer!

It was gone. *AGAIN.* I swore viciously. One of these days, just once, I'd like to reach for my fucking hammer and it'd be there when I'd done anything more strenuous than a slow goddamn walk.

I backed up, almost falling over as my sense of balance insisted left was suddenly down, and I braced myself against the wall. I looked around quickly, seeing a handful more of the massive spiders happily scuttling around the room, up and down the walls. And in the middle of the room, still holding its hands up, was the asuras that had come to talk to us at the dungeon.

"You." I pointed one hand at it, uncertainly, while the other hand reached up, touching my head and coming away with sticky blood. "You saved me?"

It nodded, stepping forward slowly, and I stared in wonder at it.

It was like the tank things: the four large legs attached to the central form looked as if someone had taken a giant tortoise, lopped off everything above where the legs attached, and turned them into robotic versions of themselves.

The current version that stood there hesitantly was different to the one that had come to the dungeon—upgraded, I guessed—but still recognizably the same species.

Rather than the crude legs it'd had before, these were hydraulic ones, the feet omnidirectional, and the base? It'd been upgraded too, making me think it'd raided a manufactory somewhere. Possibly the robotics labs from the university? The top half had a humanoid robot sitting there, steampunk, all wood and cogs, but recognizable, as opposed to the clumsy attempts we'd seen before.

It sat close to the front of the body now, rising from the waist to sit watching me, a small secure crate behind it seemingly full of scavenged parts, with two of the little drones I'd seen in the scrapyard scuttling across it. One sent flares of light from a tiny arc-welder it was using to continue the upgrades.

There was also a third drone, more clumsily put together, battered, and keeping its distance. This one I'd *definitely* seen before—in the scrapyard, then at the dungeon. It'd not changed either, staying almost exactly as it was, while the other was steadily upgrading itself.

I swallowed, feeling sick—not from seeing them, I instinctively knew, although the fucking spiders on the roof weren't exactly happy making—but from the throbbing of my head.

The main one, the large one that faced me, reached behind itself without looking, dipping one hand into the basket and pulling first my hammer free, offering it to me, head first, and then pulling the little kiddies drawing tablet free as well.

It slid the lever along, wiping the screen, then started to draw with a finger that had been clearly designed exclusively for this task. It only took a handful of seconds, the digit blurring as it leapt about the pad, before stopping dead and spinning it around to show me what it had written.

We wish to be friends.

"Yeah," I muttered, swallowing again and squinting at that message, then the robot that crouched spider-like, watching me. "Sure you do, that's why you killed all those people…"

I'd been thinking about the people back at the scrapyard, distracted by this thing and its proximity, as well as the throbbing of my head and the confusion of all this happening around me. But as I thought about this thing, or others like it, killing people, it all crashed in on me.

"Fuck! Chris! Patrick!" I snarled, spinning to look out at the darkness of the garden. "How long was I out?"

Out?

"Unconscious! How long have I been here!" I clarified, striding out into the garden and looking about, listening hard.

We did not kill any humans.

"Bollocks!" I snapped, leveling one finger at it. "I saw you! I literally saw you kill someone up there. The big spider-thing, it killed someone to make another of those tanks!"

It followed me to the doorway, pausing there and writing again.

We did not kill any humans.

It repeated, then scrabbled at the tablet, before showing it to me again, and shoving it toward me forcibly, adding extra emphasis to the words.

We were attacked. Our queen was captured, forced to obey. Humans kill humans to make more asuras. We wish friends. We wish for help.

"Why?" I asked slowly, hesitating, and looking between it and the rooftops around us, listening to the silence that hung in the air. "And how long, dammit—how long was I there!" A detail caught my eye as I saw the hand moving, starting to write again. "And you fucking hit me!" I remembered, the hand coming down on my head, hard, sending that last wash of pain that was too much through me.

We pressed you on your head to show affection, kindness. Is this not right? You have been laid here for 1,126 counts.

The figure marched backward, reaching out seemingly blindly and picking out a picture from the mantelpiece, then bringing it closer to me, offering it. I hesitated, trying to determine what the "counts" were, as I stared at a picture of what was presumably a parent resting a hand on a child's head.

We showed you affection. Now you must like us, yes? Now we can be friends?

"Why do you want to be friends?" I stared at the picture, then back around at the night, trying to figure out what the hell had happened and what I should be doing.

We need help. We must rescue the queen. We rescued you before you could terminate. Now you must help us to rescue the queen. Friends help friends.

This time, once it was sure I'd finished reading its message, it put the slate back, and pulled out a filthy, water-stained, and damaged children's book. The bright colors and cheerful pictures were torn and well thumbed, looking as if it'd been rescued from a particularly enthusiastic toddler's clutches.

The page it flipped to showed two children, one helping the other up, as the first sat on the floor crying over the loss of a toy. The older child took the lead, guiding the crying child to another, and making them share.

All the children ended up smiling and playing together, and I looked up at the robotic figure, seeing the way it stared at me.

"This?" I asked. "This is what you want?"

Yes.

"The raiders took your queen, and you want me to make them give her back?"

Yes.

"I—" I broke off, not knowing where to go. Did it think I'd just tell them off? That the asuras killing people would be forgotten? That…

Although? The more I looked at it, the more I saw it not so much as another enemy, but as a simple creature, as a tool almost. You didn't blame the gun, after all; you blamed the wielder.

This creature?

I wasn't sure if it was playacting a part, but I didn't think so. And the dungeon...*Fuck, that was it.* The dungeon had warned us about them, but it'd also been hopeful; it'd been interested in a way it hadn't been for anything else beyond the fairy when these fuckers had been nearby.

It'd also been terrified, though, and I had to think that was the captured ones. Their potential was insane. If they could create those tank things from captured souls, forcing the queen to make them into enslaved asuras?

If they were to hit the park? Or the dungeon? As they were now, they could be a massive boon to the dungeon, creating mechanisms that we could integrate into our defenses, helping us with everything from vehicles to weaponry. Or they could be a *nightmare.*

The asuras queen, coupled with the dungeon, could create terrible things. Newly spawned goblins or whatever could be fed into the queen and a literal wave of asuras could pour forth.

"Fuck," I muttered eloquently.

There was a long silence as I thought about it. But I didn't really see any other options, not realistically. I didn't know whether these creatures were related to the dungeon, or to the ship, and frankly I didn't have the time to find out by questioning the fucker. I had friends out there, and I didn't know how long I'd been unconscious.

"I don't understand your time," I said gruffly. "How long was I unconscious? Has the sun risen and set while I was here?"

No.

"Using the time since I awoke until now, how long as passed?"

247 counts.

"Two hun—" It hadn't been nearly five minutes, had it? That would be right if it was using seconds. *But how would it know what a second was? No.* That wasn't the important detail here.

What mattered was that I'd only been out a short time, maybe ten to fifteen minutes since I was shot off the roof, and as I realized that, another point occurred to me.

I was wet still, not soaking, but still seriously wet. If I'd been laid there for hours, I'd have dried by now.

That meant that Chris and Patrick, and that family, might still be alive, and the asuras might be hiding nearby.

"Do you know where it went?" I asked the creature, and it nodded, lifting one arm and pointing into the distance.

I checked my mana. I was at a third of my manapool, and figured it was worth the expenditure. I backed up to the edge of the pond, giving myself plenty of room, then crouched and launched myself into the air, flying higher and higher, before reaching out and trying to stabilize myself.

I hovered, dipping and weaving, trying to maintain my position, as I stared around, searching the streets below, and to either side.

Now that I was as high up as I was, I could see more, including the hospital, only a dozen streets away. Looking over at that massive edifice, I nodded in understanding, and determination. That was clearly a base or something now for the raiders in the area. Windows were blocked and covered over; sections had clearly been blackened by fire and fighting, with walls that looked to have recently been a battlefield. Very recently, in fact, considering a section collapsed as I was watching.

The asuras looked to have plowed straight through whatever defenses were in place and were now taking up station there.

The queen or whatever it was—the giant spider-thing—was parked in the front car park, steadily churning out reinforcements, alternating between the humanoid walkers and tanks, consuming the mass of parked cars, while dozens of humans were chained up nearby, presumably in readiness to be "fed" to the light.

I'd looked around and around, but from up here, all I could see in the distance, when it came to the dungeon and the park, was that they were still there, and they appeared intact.

I landed on the roof of the house to save my mana, frowning deep in thought, before turning and staring at the asuras as it clambered up and over the edge of the roof. Its robotic legs seemingly easily found purchase as it crushed bricks and more.

"My friends…I had friends nearby," I said to it. "Did they get caught?"

Unknown. Our priority was ensuring your safety and recovery to negotiate.

"To negotiate what?"

Friendship.

"Yeah, friendship," I muttered darkly, staring at it, before plopping down on the roof and sitting as comfortably as I could. "Keep watch. I need to do something." I wasn't sure whether it would listen or not, but I didn't want to explain what I was doing as I reached out to the dungeon using my Reach Out and Touch Me skill.

"Kelly?" I said to her, finding her and Aly, along with Griffiths and several of the others in the command center we'd set up in our Parthenon building.

"Matt!" Kelly gasped, seemingly torn between slapping me senseless for surprising her as I appeared, wispy and see-through in the room before her, and seeing whether she could jump on me.

"Can you see me?" I asked, surprised, having expected at best with the ability for us to interact psychically and through the dungeon with the table, that she might sense me and that was all.

"We all can," Aly said, watching me as I turned to her. "You're like a dull hologram, clearly not here, but also…yeah. We can see you and hear you." She shook her head. "Now how the hell does *that* work?"

"It's not important. What's happened?" I asked, and Kelly frowned, glaring at me.

"That's what we need to know. You were supposed to be gone for a few hours, that's all. Then Dante and Kilo show up at the park with an honest-to-God pet *triceratops,* which is just plain awesome. But he said that he lost you, and there's been no sign of Chris or Patrick. And Mike and his people are miles away, as near as we can tell, following those creatures that crossed the line."

"Well, that's not happy making," I muttered. "Okay, I was knocked out. I've got that asuras that wants to be friends here as well. It saved me and wants to know if this makes us friends, so that we'll help it free its queen."

"The one that came to the dungeon? You can understand it?" Aly asked, and I paused, realizing that before it'd been communicating by pictures, and now it was using words.

"Yeah…" I said. "It's still got the little drawing pad, but it's able to form words now. Looks like it's been upgrading itself."

"And it wants to be friends because—" Aly started.

"Because it looks like the ones we fought and the others around the area are all offshoots of the queen. The queen that's been captured by the raiders and is being forced to churn out more asuras for them." I cut her off.

"I don't know." Kelly sat back down and stared at me. "Do we know if we can trust them? It might be a trap. Get us to send our forces to help you 'free it' and then they turn on us and assault the dungeon?"

"I saw the raiders feed a tied-up body into a ring of lights on the back of the queen," I said. "They were all laughing and having a great time. When the body fell into the lights, they screamed for a few seconds, then they fell through, dead. The body hit the ground, and the…fuck, I don't know, the soul maybe? It traveled down a line of connections and into a new tank thing. The queen dropped the tank onto the ground, and it strolled off, happy as anything to start loading itself up on car parts."

"The tank?" Griffiths said slowly. "You described this before, but to be clear, it can consume scrap and make weapons?"

"It has a cannon on the front, it folds away when it's not in use, and has hands or claws on the back. The hands drag in scrap and form bullets, and the cannon fires them."

"So, basically, looking at all the scrap lying around, they've got unlimited ammunition, and the only thing we've got going for us is bodies?" he asked the group at large. "You said these things could climb walls easily."

"Yeah, that's pretty much it." I sighed. "But it's set up at the old hospital, the QE." I used the short form of the name, getting nods from most of those around the table.

"QE?" Griffiths looked confused, before nodding as he got it. "The Queen Elizabeth, the hospital. Right, got you."

"Yeah, turns out that the raiders there might not have been friends with those in command of the asuras. The queen tore half the front of the hospital down. And the rest looks like it was under fire before it surrendered. There're lines of people being queued up to be fed to the asuras."

"Fed to…they're sacrificing people to it? Right now?" Griffiths got to his feet in horror.

"Yeah," I said slowly, shaking my head. "Literally right now, and I'm sitting on a fucking rooftop having this conversation. I'm doing it, because as much as I desperately want to race over there and punch their teeth down their throat, I'd be dead in short order."

"How far is it?" Griffiths looked at the map projected on the table, measuring it out with his fingers.

"About half an hour, or an hour's run maybe," I said. "Being realistic, you can't get to me here in less than that. That's not including how long it takes you to get your people ready."

"I could..." He was clearly running the distance through his mind, and I shook my head.

"It'd take me twenty minutes at the least to drive from here to the dungeon, back when cars worked. Even if you set off right this very second and sprinted all the way, leaving off the exhaustion and how much use you'd be when you arrived, you'd be at the very least half an hour."

"I...Fuck!" He slammed his fist on the table, before glaring at me. "Why are you so calm? These are innocent lives at stake and you're just abandoning them!"

"No," I said softly, realizing the reason even as I spoke. "I'm not calm, and while most of them probably aren't innocent, I'm not abandoning them either."

"Matt..." Kelly said in a warning tone, knowing me too well. "What are you going to do?"

"I'm going to do what I'm best at," I said. "I'm going to attack."

CHAPTER THIRTY-FOUR

It wasn't that simple, of course.

In the stories, people probably cheered and celebrated what a hero the main character was and started preparations for the victory feast, the significant other spending quality time picking out just the right outfit to wear to welcome the conquering hero home and all that shit.

Well, that wasn't what happened when I made that announcement.

At first there was silence. Then the room exploded with people trying to outdo each other in explaining, politely and impolitely, that I was a fucking idiot.

"Hold the fuck up," I shouted over them all after a solid minute of being told what a fool I was.

"I'm not going to storm the front gates, all right?" I glared around at everyone, and wishing, just once, that they'd consider that I wasn't a complete goddamn idiot. "They smashed the gates down, and they're feeding people into the queen. The queen looks like she needs to feed people through this magical light show before she can make them into fresh asuras."

"So?"

"So, unlike these other dickheads…I can fly," I said slowly and clearly. "I fly in, trash the goddamn light show, and if Chris and Patrick have been captured, I rescue them, then I fly out. No fuss, no muss." I stood back, smiling and waiting for the inevitable praise for my magnificent plan.

"Matt…" Griffiths said slowly. "Have you considered that this might be the stupidest plan anyone has ever had? In the history of plans, I mean."

"Now hold on…"

"Ever," he repeated. "I mean it. Yes, you can fly. Congratulations." He gestured vaguely up as if tracing a parabolic arc. "So you jump in and trash the light show, then you fly off. What the hell do you think happens then? Do you think they'll all just go home? They'll shrug and forget about it?"

"No, actually, Griffiths," I snapped, "I'm kinda hoping they'll follow me!"

"Why?"

"Because that's the second part of the plan, the bit you didn't let me finish!"

"Oh, please, do make it clear," Kelly growled, folding her arms.

"While I'm doing this shit, you send the goddamn reinforcements, the kobolds and more that you were going to spawn? You send them all *here.*"

I stabbed a finger down on the trap. The monster baiting, training dungeon that Kelly and the others had been helping me to make over the last week, and that had, until recently, been Gateshead Civic Center.

"To the…oh—" Kelly broke off, considering my genius plan.

"Yes," I said. "The trap. I'll make damn sure they're following me, and if need be, I'll fight a rear guard with some disposable creatures, cheap ones…" I clarified, the others knowing I meant barely equipped and non-sapient.

"So you get their attention, and you bleed them," Griffiths said. "We can get there before you reach it, and we can—"

"You can damn well stay hidden," I said firmly. "I lead them into the trap dungeon, and I take a load of the kobolds with me. They hammer their way inside and set off the traps. We bleed them, killing as many as we can for every goddamn foot of ground given. And if they reach the end of the dungeon, I use the escape tunnel and get the fuck out."

"What escape tunnel?" Aly frowned.

"The one you're going to make for me in a minute," I said calmly. "Don't interrupt."

"Sorry." She quirked a smile, not liking the risk, clearly, but seeing the necessity.

"And they have to leave the way they came in?" Kelly asked.

"Yeah, so make sure there's plenty of traps that activate on the way out," I said. "Once they come to leave, that's when you've got the secondary forces from the dungeon, including you, Griffiths, and your people. I'll join you, and we finish the fuckers off."

"Okay, well, that makes a little more sense now," he agreed, rubbing his chin. "Why are they going to follow you, though?"

"Because I'll smash their light thing, or steal it or whatever."

"Yeah, I know you said that, but they can make living robots and tanks and so on. What's to stop them just making another light-thingy and shooting you when you come back to try again?"

"Damn," I muttered. "Give me a minute." I slid my mind out of the dungeon sense and back to my body, staring at the asuras that crouched across from me.

"Okay, that light-thingy, the one that…that steals people's souls and makes them into asura? What is it?"

Energy transference.

"Yeah, okay, and what the hell *is* it?" I asked again, glaring at the thing squatting across from me.

A device to convert the energy of a living biological organism into the spark of an asuras.

"Is it a special device?"

Yes.

"Can it be replaced?" I tried again, not really sure either of us were getting our meanings across to the other.

Yes.

"Easily?" I tried, hopefully, and it just showed me the "yes" again. "Fuck!" I snarled, scratching at my head and feeling the flaking away of dried blood.

My head had long since healed. Clearly I'd managed to trigger my storm mana when I'd been injured, or I assumed so anyway, because it was the only explanation for me going from barely able to think and clearly fucked, to being basically fine now.

Problem?

"I need to stop the queen from making any more asuras, and I need to give the raiders, and those asuras there, a reason to follow me," I muttered almost absently, scratching more dried blood away and thinking fast.

Rescue the queen.

"Yeah, yeah." I waved a hand to shut it up, as it continued writing, then jabbed the pad at me insistently.

Rescue the queen. Those who hold her prisoner must recover her or lose control. They must recover her. They will follow you.

"Huh…" I read it, then reread it, before grinning and nodding. "Okay, but how do I rescue the queen?"

She is constrained in a containment cube.

You have generated a Quest!

Quest!

Checkmate.

The asuras queen is the heart of her species, certainly all those you will encounter locally at least. Free her, and you stand to gain a powerful ally…or fail, to face a fearsome foe. Free the queen and negotiate peace to complete this quest and receive the following bonuses:

- +1 to top three Attributes
- +1 Class Skill point to allocate
- 10,000 XP

Accept?

Yes/No…

I accepted it. There wasn't really a choice there, and I reread the pad the asura held out, thinking and trying to make sense of the concept. It was fairly self-explanatory, but…

It twisted the pad around again, this time showing a 3D lifelike picture of the containment cube that had held the asuras we'd torn out of one of the first ones we'd fought. The cube had been stolen, and I stared at the figure before me, wondering.

"Was that what you were in?" I asked.

Yes. You removed me from my enforced sleeve, and my friend freed me from the cube.

I looked over, seeing the spider-drone thing that I'd lost in the scrapyard. I grunted at it in recognition, and looked at the other two or three of them that clambered across the larger one, making upgrades. That made maybe five in total.

There'd only been the one with it when we'd first had it turn up to the gates of the dungeon.

"Are you making more?" I asked, not sure I should be helping this thing.

Freed asuras are building their own sleeves. We wish to be free. To live and learn.

"Freed?" I asked, pausing, then going on. "The ones we fought, the ones that tore out of the containment cubes, what happened to them? Are they your friends?"

Some. Those who were too weak dissipated and were lost to the ether. Some few were strong enough to find and seal themselves into a secondary sleeve.

"The cube that the queen is in?" I said. "How would I reach that?"

She is constrained into the body you saw.

"Yeah, all right, but how do I rescue her?" I tried rephrasing it, and the asuras before me scuttled forward. The humanoid upper portion leaned in close to stare into my eyes; its optical sensors zoomed in and out, clearly searching for something in my face.

You will do this? You will free the queen?

"I'll *try*, but you need to tell me how the hell I get her out of that body, and fast."

The fingers were a blur as it quickly drew the queen, showing her from above on the pad, and then the outline of her individual sections.

Looking at her like this, I could see her a lot more clearly, and I had to admit to being impressed.

When I'd seen her before, I'd basically seen the back and side view as she walked away. Looking at her from above, she'd been half hidden in the collapsed side of the hospital emergency side of the building.

Now, I could see her clearly, and damn.

She was far more spider-like than I ever wanted to see again, as well as being built around the construction facility for her "young."

She had six legs in the drawing, each spaced out around a central toroid. The central section was circular, with dozens of arms and connectors, all feeding into the constructor, and a platform above it that was where the light show was centered.

The path from the light show went back onto a pair of shipping containers that were attached side by side onto the back of the body, and a third was set atop them, running east to west, even as the other two were aligned north–south.

That provided a load of space for her "crew" or masters to live and wander around, with her as a combination transport and production facility under them.

There was a cage on the back taking up a section of one of the containers, and although it'd been left carefully blank, I could guess what was in there.

People.

Cranes were attached to the shipping containers, both as a means to raise and lower things, and for the boss to sit and watch out over his lessers, riding in the control center of the crane.

Last of all, there was the spider's head.

At the very front of the design was the head, oval and with dozens of circles that covered it, presumably eyes, but fuck knew really.

"Where is her cube?" I asked, and it altered the drawing, showing a section directly behind the head, and buried in the toroid. "Okay, now how the hell do I get her out?" I asked, and it sagged, unable to answer.

I stared at it for a few seconds, then nodded, before sinking back into the dungeon sense and bringing the others up to speed on everything.

"That makes a little more sense," Finn said when I finished, and I looked over at him. "If you take the heart of the machine, they'll have to chase you; they won't have a choice. Unless they can install another asuras into the frame?"

I dutifully asked the question of the asuras before me, having to repeat it a few different ways before I got it to understand.

"No," I told the others. "While a normal caged asuras could make the body work, more or less, it'd take months before it was strong enough to move it properly, and without a queen, the light-thingy wouldn't work."

"So it's time to steal her heart, eh?" Finn said sadly, forcing a smile. "Matt, is Patrick…?"

"As far as I know, he's *fine*," I said firmly. "Look, before I was knocked out, he and Chris were running to meet me on the other side of the section that the asuras was walking toward. I saw a family running, and they gave chase. Chris and Patrick would have seen what was happening, just like I did, but I didn't see what happened next. I was out cold, and when I came to, the asuras was parked and already producing—"

I broke off, wondering about that. There were signs of a fight at the hospital, and yeah, a wall collapsed inward as I watched, but there wasn't much time for them to have taken over, not really.

I mean, yeah, there was always the chance the leader was an idiot and was out front, then got stood on, trying to be a hero—I very carefully didn't draw any comparisons between what I did, and that "idiot"—but even if that was the case, it was over damn fast.

Unless…

Unless the raiders hadn't been waiting for the asuras and defending against them. If the gunfire we'd heard earlier had been the asuras raiders, and their advance forces attacking the hospital, then by the time the actual queen and the boss arrived, everything must have been practically over with.

That made a certain kind of sense as well. After all, why take the production center, unique and valuable as it was, on the raid? You only did that once the place was safe.

I explained my thoughts to the others, getting a round of agreement that it made sense, as well as a warning from Rhodes that we might be missing stuff still.

"It makes sense, but there could be more we're not privy to yet," she continued, speaking up for the first time. "After all, where did the other group go? The one that Mike is tracking?"

"Fuck," I muttered. "No clue, just…off elsewhere, I guess."

"Exactly. Your evaluation makes sense from the data we have, but there could be more that screws that up. Remember: no plan survives contact with the enemy," she quoted, and I nodded again.

"Fine. You think there's a better plan than the one I suggested?"

"No, and I think it's got a good chance of working, plus saving the civilians who are trapped," she admitted. "As well as it explaining why Chris and Patrick are still MIA. If they saw what was happening, they were likely to hide, waiting to act, thinking that you tend to make a showy entrance, and expecting to help you when you do."

"Hey, I can be subtle," I said, much to the amused smiles and shaken heads around the room. "Fine, whatever…Are we all happy with the plan?" I didn't like how long it was taking when people were literally being sacrificed over the hill.

"A good plan, executed violently now, beats a perfect plan executed next week," Griffiths quoted. "General George S. Patton."

"Well, I like it." I shrugged. "Can we do it?"

"Can we?" Kelly stared at me for a long minute, before sighing and nodding. "We can, but you'll be damn well using that escape tunnel, okay? No fighting every step of the damn way—that's what the dungeon creatures are *for*!"

"You make me the escape tunnel and I'll use it," I promised, grinning.

"I'll sort it," Aly said. "Where do you want it?"

"I put a hatch in the ground under the security station in the car park…"

"Too far," she said. "I'll need to absorb and reinforce the tunnel all the way. That'd take an hour or more at least, and I doubt you'll give me an hour before you get to the dungeon."

"But—"

"We can't alter a structure once the enemy interacts with it," she pointed out, and I cursed.

"Make it shorter then," I grumbled. "Just put it wherever you need to."

"Don't tempt me…have we got any sewage tunnels around there?" she muttered, eyeing me and pretending to be serious as I glared at her.

"Matt?" Kelly said, and I looked to her, waiting. "Be careful, okay?" She clearly wanted to say more, torn between wanting to fight by my side, so that at least we were together, and knowing that in her guiding of the dungeon creatures she could do far more for me.

"I will," I promised. "I love you."

Then I faded out of the dungeon sense, blinking my eyes open and staring at the asuras crouched before me.

"So, you want to be friends?" I asked it.

Yes.

"Friends don't ask friends to risk their lives unless it's worth it," I explained. "Friends don't expect others to give them things without fair deals, so after all of this? You'll be helping us, all right? As friends."

Yes.

I seriously doubted it had any clue what I was saying or what I meant, but that was fine. I couldn't risk the damn time it would take for a real negotiation, and as far as I knew, with this lone asuras, any deal I made would be ignored by the queen anyway.

Hell, for all I knew, she was the guiding force behind all of this, and the little bugger talking to me was the village idiot that she'd booted out.

What was clear, though, was that the asuras were a massive threat, as were the raiders, and every minute I wasted could be coming at a terrible cost in lives.

I could eliminate the raider threat with this plan, hopefully, and I could at least severely lessen that of the asuras as well.

All I needed was a fuckload mana more than I had, looking at the mana bar in my vision.

"Well, shit."

I clambered to my feet, looking from the bar to the distance I knew lay ahead, and back again, and winced.

If I had more mana, I could literally fly over the space between us, land, and tear the damn thing apart, then fly off again.

The problem was that, out of my damn two thousand, four hundred, and fifty manapool, I had seven hundred and fifteen points.

That was enough for some seriously impressive shit, admittedly, but it wasn't enough to send me flying in, tear the queen a new arsehole, and then fly back out again. I needed to conserve my mana, I needed to plan, and I needed to be careful...

"Oh, who the hell am I kidding..." I grumbled, climbing to my feet and staring up the hill. "Right, you fucker, I'm off to save the queen. You, ummm, do whatever you do, but stay the hell out of the way for the next few hours."

With that inspiring speech, I was off, running across the roof, jumping up onto the next section, and just managing to clear the "step" up, without using my mana to boost me.

I picked up speed, deciding that for now, speed beat subtlety, and that as soon as I got a bit closer, I'd slow down. I kept telling myself that, even as I pushed harder, jumping higher and running faster, building up a good head of steam in my mind as I envisioned the bastard raiders leading innocent people to the asuras.

Before I knew it, I was at full speed, sprinting up the hill now. The T-junction at the top of the hill was before me almost before I knew it. I shifted direction, leaping off and landing atop the roof of a bungalow nearby, sliding in a great clatter of shattering roof tiles, and then leapt again, this time powering my jump with a touch of mana, enabling me to cross half of the street before I landed, rolling.

I surged to my feet again, passing bodies strewn about. Men, women, and children were left, abandoned with less thought than most would give roadkill.

The pub on the corner of the road, separated from the houses nearby, still stood, but the windows had been smashed and the building clearly looted. Still, as I took the corner, I sensed as much as I heard others spotting me.

They might have been innocent—hell, they might have been Chris and Patrick, though if it had been, I damn well expected them to make some noise to get my attention properly.

Either way, I treated them as enemies, ones that although not in my way right now, couldn't be permitted to spread word of what I was doing.

I picked up speed again, sprinting up the hill. My goddamn cape snapped in the wind of my passage, as I raced onward. Voices called out from somewhere behind me, but I was past them, and passing up the road again.

This new road was one of the main routes through the Gateshead area, leading up to the QE hospital. Although I didn't use it as a matter of course—there being much better and faster routes to the areas I spent time—it was still wide, well maintained, and surrounded by houses, shops, and hundreds of parked cars.

The cars had been cut down in number. Here and there, piles of debris were left behind, where cars had been taken into the asuras and stripped. The seating, decoration, fuel tanks, and more were dumped again when they weren't needed, the main metal of the structure being integrated into the new creations.

Invariably, close to these areas, where the remains of cars were left abandoned, so, too, were bodies. They had been dropped from a height, impacting, unresisting on the asphalt like so much waste product thrown away. The discarded wrapping, while the soul—the animating force for us all, I now believed—was fed into a new asuras slave.

Rarely, I came across piles of discarded brass, the leavings of gunfights. More frequently, I found myself passing the remains of less expensive fights.

Here and there, bodies bore the marks of being beaten in fights, of knife wounds and worse.

Some of the bodies were almost blown apart, as were the cars nearby, evidence of the "tanks" and their heavy fire destroying everything that came up against them.

Farther up the road, not far from the turnoff for the hospital, I found a trio of the tanks, torn literally limb from limb, and a massive figure laid on her back, holes blown in her chest and stomach from cannon fire.

Around her, there were others, men and women dressed in crude armor—some leather, some metal or plastic—and all armed. Some had been taken down by hails of gunfire, others by the tank's cannons. But most were simply torn limb from limb; a half dozen of the humanoid asuras bodies laid broken in the road, with the humans.

Whoever had held the hospital hadn't given it up willingly.

I slowed now, ducking into the garden of one of the last houses before the turnoff, running through, front to back, and then into the quiet little street behind it. A half dozen houses all backed onto each other here, their gardens melding together in a hodge-podge of fencing, and I paused as I drew up to the back of the first garden, looking over and around, before hopping the fence, and moving on.

I'd seen enough of the area from above, and combined with my own memories of passing through and even using the hospital, I thought I'd managed to find one of the houses I was looking for.

Jogging up the overgrown garden path, and pausing at the back door, I reached out and tried it, finding it locked, and cursed. Of course the fucker was locked!

This was *Gateshead*. Not locking your back door was the same as putting everything out on the roadside with *Free to a Good Home* written on a sign next to it.

I shifted around, looking for another way in, and found a collection of cloth on the ground nearby, soaked, stinking, and presumably having been there since falling off the washing line strung across the garden at some point in the last few weeks.

I gathered up a handful of the cloth, deliberately not looking to see what it had been, and just being happy that there wasn't a corpse left in the mess, before spreading it out across the glass of the back door as best I could.

Once it was reasonably covered, I punched it, driving my fist through in one smooth motion, and grinning when the cracks spider webbed out. But the glass remained in place.

I reached down, flipping the old-fashioned latch, and drew my hand back through the broken glass—carefully—then opened the door.

I stepped inside, the feeling of a long-empty house hard to miss, and I looked around. It'd apparently been left alone; the kitchen cupboards were closed still, which was weird.

Shrugging, I tugged the door closed behind me…and winced as the glass fell through the frame, shattering on the ground.

Instantly there came a sound from overhead, and I swore, rushing forward, passing through the kitchen, and up the narrow staircase, angling back on myself as I ran, coming to the top of the stairwell and…

The creature that staggered out of the bedroom ahead of me was old and long dead. The ambient mana had changed the body of whoever had once lived here into one of the naturally occurring undead.

She was clearly old when she'd died, a full head of bright-white wispy hair sticking out in all directions like the fuzz on a dandelion as she opened her mouth and moaned at me, her eyes long since filmed in death, and maggots writhing in them.

Clouds of flies erupted from her as I swung my knife, cutting left to right and beheading her. Then I covered my mouth as her body dropped soundlessly and the flies spread everywhere.

I paused, then kicked her body back inside the bedroom it'd staggered out of. I slammed the door, then swore and opened it, punting the head in and closing it again.

Running through into the bathroom, I found an old, reasonably clean towel on a railing and covered my mouth with it, moving into the second bedroom. I pulled back the curtains, then the lace window coverings, then what seemed like half a foundry's worth of dream catchers, signs, and more. Eventually I lost all patience, and tore the entire window set down, only to look out across the road at…

A wall.

A fucking wall.

I'd been so sure I was in the right goddamn house, and I wasn't. There were another dozen houses in a pretty little cul-de-sac ahead of me, and I swore and kicked the bed next to me in as silent a rage as I could manage.

Less than a minute later, I was outside again, running down the poured concrete of the front garden. I crossed the road and leapt over the fence ahead of me, crouching and leaping upward, grabbing the windowsill, and kicked off, adding a little burst of power for direction…and I landed on the roof, light as I could manage, not even sending a single tile sliding free.

I crept up to the top, peering over the peak of the roof, and sighed in relief.

There, directly ahead of me, on the far side of the road, was the hospital, at last.

CHAPTER THIRTY-FIVE

I hesitated for a long minute, wondering one more time whether Chris and Patrick were going to be in there somewhere, as well as how many of the various broken windows of the buildings, the cars, and the doorways I could see around the hospital had watchers in them.

There could be hundreds, or there could be none.

I saw firelight in the upper section of the main hospital building, and even from here, I could hear the crash of a drumkit being played by someone who clearly was an expert at something *other* than playing the drums.

They couldn't have carried a tune in a bucket. And fuck me, the way they were hammering that poor thing?

Shouts and catcalls, as well as the occasional scream, came from inside the building and carried on the still night air. I desperately wanted to fly over there, smash through the roof, and go all God of Lightning on the assholes I just knew were inside.

I couldn't, though.

I didn't have the mana, and I needed to stick to the fucking plan.

The spider, the asuras queen or whatever it was, was parked, or hunched, up in the front of the half-collapsed emergency wing of the hospital. Bright blue-white light that I instinctively marked as welding or construction flashed on and off.

It was that light that you occasionally saw pouring out of buildings—pre-apocalypse, anyway—that made you instinctively want to go and see what was going on, knowing that somewhere something cool was being done.

It always seemed like that to me, anyway, considering I'd worn a tie and spent most of my time trying to explain to people why their computer didn't work, while internally screaming at them.

Now, though, what that light told me, with the spider's front section being mainly inside the building, was that it, and probably those around it, were distracted.

I ran up and over the peak, sliding down the far side, and kicked off, flipping over in an attempt to avoid any outward-projecting television aerials and so on.

Catching myself with a little push of mana, I landed on my feet perfectly, in the street in front of the house directly over the road from the hospital, and hesitated for a split second, torn between hoping nobody, and nothing, had seen me, and damn well hoping someone had.

It was possibly the coolest jump I'd ever pulled off. I'd even had a fucking cape on, for God's sake, and yet…silence.

I jogged across the street, muttering under my breath that at least I knew I'd done it, and that was all that mattered.

I hopped over the small retaining wall, landing lightly between two parked cars. The funk of weeks and piled leaves on the windscreens told the tale of immobility as I moved on, crouching low and running between more cars.

The car park was small, especially for the size of the hospital, and I remembered the nightmare of finding a space to park here when I visited before the fall.

Regardless, as I moved from car to car, weaving in and out, sprinting across the open sections, it felt huge. Reaching the small ornamental garden, roughly halfway from the road, to the front of the building where the spider hulked, I dropped low at a sound nearby.

I'd seen nothing, which was worrying the hell out of me as I went. No guards, no asuras—hell, even the prisoners I'd seen chained up less than half an hour ago were gone now, and I was shitting myself that they'd all been killed, when another noise came to me.

Someone was moving nearby, stealthily.

I hesitated, then pressed myself further into the shrubbery, mouth clamped tight shut, as figures moved closer and closer, before slipping into my goddamn bushes!

They were so close I could practically reach out and tap them on the shoulders, and yet these two idiots crept in and crouched, facing away from me and into the car park.

"Where are they?" the one on the left asked the one on the right.

"I don't know!" Righty replied in a nasal tone, shoving his companion and glaring at him. "Keep quiet!"

"Or what?" Lefty asked in a low growl. "Who made you the boss!"

"The boss told us to catch those idiots. The droids are waiting for them. We've just gotta make sure they don't kill 'em, that's all!"

"Idiot!" Lefty snapped. "They're magic, not droids! Come on, man, try to keep up. You seen any tech workin'?"

"Just them. Hey, you think they did it? They're why nothin' works no more?"

"Boss said it wasn't."

"Yeah, but the boss might be lyin', right? Maybe it was him? Maybe he did somethin'?"

"Don't go sayin' that!" Lefty snapped. "You want feedin' t' the droids?"

"Now you're callin' 'em droids!"

"Oh, for fuck's—" Lefty elbowed Righty and pointed at the car park. "There! There they are. We was just in time!"

I stared over between the idiot twins' heads, noting that they were both cleanly shaved, their heads practically reflecting the meager starlight back upward, and wondered whether this was how my ex had always felt in that insanely tight push-up bra, peering out from between the two massive domes.

Then Chris drew my attention, creeping forward, between two cars, slowly moving into sight, Patrick behind him. The pair paused, and Lefty reached out, holding a little tube that looked somewhat like a laser pointer.

"Let me do it!" Righty grunted, reaching for it, and I stayed there, wondering whether they were indeed this fucking stupid.

"No! The boss said *I* had to do it. We click it and point it at them, and they'll attack. Then we click it again and they'll stop. It's all they know. They're so dumb!"

I hesitated only a second, before drawing the knife from my left hip and reaching out. I slid the blade around Lefty's throat, pressing it nice and tight, while closing my right hand around Righty's throat from behind, making sure to have my fingers directly over the windpipe.

"Or..." I said into the sudden silence as they both froze. "Or you could put it on the ground, and I might not kill you both."

Everything was still for a handful of seconds, and I decided to go on, just to make my point clear.

"Now, it might be that you're thinking, 'I can get free.' It might be that you're thinking 'I can pull a knife and get turned around, figure out where he is, and stab him, and maybe, just maybe, I can be faster than he is.'"

Silence.

"Thing is, though, boys, you had no clue I was here, and I'm wearing *armor*. I know about the asuras. I know about your gang and what you're doing, and yet I *still* came here. I came with just two friends, and you know what? Tonight, I'm going to be drinking a beer still." I shifted, squeezing on the right and slowly edging the razor-sharp blade tighter against Lefty's throat.

"Because you see, boys, if *I* was in your shoes, the question I'd be asking myself would be 'What kind of lunatic sneaks into a place like this?' Go on, I'm curious."

"W...what?" Lefty asked.

"What kind of person comes into somewhere like this, filled with asuras and raiders, and attacks it with only a handful of people?" I said, making my point clearer. "Does that sound like someone who gets stopped by two idiots hiding in the bushes? Or does it sound like the fucking hero who wins easily, leaving the bad guys—who were hiding in the bushes—dead and never looks back?"

"We're not bad guys!" Righty squeaked.

"Yeah!" Lefty agreed. "We're the winners!"

"Really?" I lifted my knife and turned the blade to catch and reflect the minimal light, getting Patrick's attention, then slipped it back tight against Lefty's throat. "So let's play this one out. So you're not the bad guys..."

"No!"

"Ever raped or murdered anyone?"

Silence.

"Ever helped feed people to the asuras?"

"The what?"

"The...droids," I said after a minute, realizing that they didn't know the term.

"Well, yeah, maybe a couple..."

"So you're rapists, murderers, and you help rip people's souls out to be enslaved...but you're the good guys?"

More silence.

"Hey, man." Patrick slipped into the small pile of bushes, with Chris tagging along behind him. "What's going on?"

"Where the hell have you been, you fucker?" Chris asked me directly, glaring over the two idiots.

"Found the asuras that came to the dungeon, got some more info," I said. "I'll explain later."

"Can we go?" Lefty asked, and I looked at him, then Righty, then Patrick.

"Patrick, there's a little cylinder in this one's hand..." I made Lefty gasp as I pressed the blade against his neck. "It apparently controls the asuras. One click makes them attack, and another makes them stop."

Patrick took it and looked it over, nodding. "Looks like a laser pointer. You point it at a target, they kill it?" he asked, and the idiot brigade agreed quickly.

"So can we go now?" Righty asked.

I paused, then smiled in the darkness, looking at the other two. "You know they saw you coming?"

Chris and Patrick both looked annoyed.

"You're shit at stealth, mate," I told Chris, grinning. Then I spoke quickly as Righty tried to reach for something on his hip.

"So, you two want to go?" I asked, and they both made sounds of agreement. "Then here's the deal. You run straight ahead and out of the car park. If you don't? Chris here is going to shoot you both—"

Chris blinked, then drew his handgun, pointing it at the pair. "Uh, yeah," he agreed. "I'll shoot you both in the face…?"

"So, Patrick, take their weapons…"

He quickly searched them, getting a knife that looked as if it'd be only moderately dangerous to a cheese sandwich, and a handgun with two bullets.

"Now run!" I released them and lifted the knife away.

The pair broke free of the bushes, sprinting headlong into the car park, diving behind a pair of parked cars and hiding there, Righty—I guessed—shouting out as soon as he was under cover.

"We're gonna fuck you up!" he bellowed.

I nodded to Patrick. "Point that thing and press."

He grinned, aiming the little laser pointer and clicking a little lever on it once. A red light illuminated the car they were hiding behind, and two seconds later, the booms of asuras tanks rang out, hammering the spot highlighted, repeatedly.

After three rounds of heavy firing, and probably twenty impacts, Patrick clicked the pointer again, and we waited in silence, staring at the cars as the smoke cleared. There sure as shit weren't any bodies left to see.

Even the cars had been reduced to scrap metal, great holes torn in the bodywork. Flames spread from the ruptured fuel tanks, flowing out under the cars and rolling down the slight decline toward the gutter…underneath other cars.

"Shit," Patrick whispered, and I nodded.

"You think they believe that they got us?" Chris asked, clearly hoping.

"You can step out now!" a new voice called, and I closed my eyes, swearing.

"No, Chris. I don't," I growled, before shaking my head. "Right, you fuckers, new plan. I'll distract them; you use the clicker to throw some confusion in, and then you run for it. Get back to the civic center. I'll draw them there and—"

"Step out, or we fire!" the voice rang out again in warning. "Three…two…"

"All right, dickbag!" Chris shouted, standing up and backing out of the bushes, waving his hands in the air.

Before I could join them, Patrick shoved me backward, stopping me from standing. "They've not seen you!" he snapped, moving out to stand next to Chris.

I hesitated. Everything in me screamed to get out there, to stand by my friends, as they walked backward, moving into the middle of the car park, deliberately drawing attention away from where I hid.

"Well, well, well…" the voice rang out, before pausing as Chris lowered his hands and put them on his hips, staring up at the roof of the building behind me.

"So…is this gonna be like a standard villain monologue?" Chris called up. "Just if it is, I'm gonna go sit over here, all right?" He pointed to a row of parked cars a little farther back, well away from the spreading flames of the ruptured fuel tanks.

"You try to run and we'll—"

"You'll shoot. Yeah, that's fine," Chris said, waving one-handed in dismissal. "Whatever. We're totally listening. We're just gonna sit down while you tell us all about your evil plan, that all right?"

"One more step and we fire!"

Chris hesitated, before shaking his head, and kept on walking, Patrick moving along with him.

"Nah, if you were going to just kill us outright, you'd have done it. You want to rant and rave, or explain your plot. That's fine. I'm just not standing around for it. It's been a long day, you know?"

There was a brief pause in which I held my breath, fully expecting them to open fire…and then Chris turned back and sat on the bonnet of a car, sliding back to rest against the windscreen, and gestured magnanimously with one hand.

"Okay, I'm sorted. You can go on."

Patrick moved up alongside him, leaning on the side of the car and staring up at them, waiting and smiling, and I winced as I saw him lifting something small concealed in his hand.

"Fuck, I hope that works," I muttered, even as the lunatic on the roof started up again.

"You think you're smart? That you're funny? No. You're just dead!" the man barked, and I shifted around, trying to see him.

A hand was all I could see as it extended, pointing at them, and presumably holding another such pointer.

Patrick was faster, whipping his out and clicking it, pointing it up at the figure and holding it steady. There was silence for a few seconds, then laughter rang out from above.

"You think they work more than once? You think we'd give these idiots the chance to turn our pets against us?"

"Well, fuck." Patrick tossed it over his shoulder.

"Any last words?" the idiot on the roof gloated.

I sighed, taking a step back from the cover I'd been using, crouching and leaping up, powering my jump with storm mana.

"Ka-pow!" I shouted, not knowing what else I should shout, and figuring all the cool shit was probably trademarked. I landed on the roof right before the figure, grabbing the outstretched right hand and twisting it aside. I triggered Storm-Strike for the first time, landing a punch full into the face of the figure before me.

Channeling fifty mana per blow sounded cheap, especially considering the mana I had normally at my disposal, but it did a hell of a lot of damage when they weren't expecting it.

My fist slammed into the front of his face, taking the lower half of his nose, his mouth, and left cheek all in one go, as the explosive release of storm mana…

Well. It did a fucking number on him.

His neck snapped and his head was almost torn from his shoulders. The explosive release cratered his face inward, killing him instantly. I snapped his fingers free, bringing the little clicker-tube thingy around, and pointing at a group of stunned men and women nearby, all heavily armed.

The rooftop was covered in dead solar cells. Literally hundreds of them laid side by side, now covered in pigeon shit and broken by the stomping feet of asuras tanks and the dozens of figures that covered the rest of the space.

There were perhaps fifteen of the human-shaped asuras, ten or so men and women holding guns—seven of them all in a little group, with two previously standing on either side of the asshole I'd just permanently ventilated.

The tanks shifted their turrets, having been stood to both sides, but farther out, aiming at Chris and Patrick, ready to fire, with another five of them on lower and higher rooftops, ready and waiting.

I pressed the tube, grinning as the red light illuminated a single, massive figure that was carrying a heavy machine gun, and all the asuras spun, reorienting on him.

The two figures to the left and right of the one I'd just killed weren't slow, though. Hell, the left one had a handgun out already, and was firing. Two bullets slammed into my armor, center mass, even as the one on the right yanked a blade out and stabbed at me, the tip skittering over the armor that protected my side.

I swung that arm down, managing to catch the blade as they yanked it back, sending it flipping out end over end, flying from a numb hand, such was the power of the blow.

The gunman switched his aim, firing into my thighs, as I grabbed the top of the gun, twisting it aside and pointing it at his companion.

The third round punched into his chest, sending him staggering back, arms flailing and blood spraying. I cried out, the second bullet having made it through a patch in my armor and punching a hole in my thigh.

"Motherfucker!" I snarled, yanking him forward and grabbing him by the throat, just as his friends behind opened fire.

The group of humans were split: half of them focused on me, firing assault rifles and shotguns; the other half either opened fire on the asuras that were tracking around to lock onto them, or ran for it.

The big fucker in the middle grabbed a nearby woman and yanked her between him and the asuras, jumping backward just as they opened fire, shredding her, and tracking him, firing again and again.

The slugs they fired were sent at horrific speeds, punching clean through the flimsy leather and fabric clothing she wore, barely slowing as they tore out of the far side. Blood sprayed into the air as he rolled, lining his gun up on one of the tanks, and fired back.

His heavy machine gun, clearly designed for mounting on a tank or something similar, tore holes in the asuras in turn, even as their fire caught him, making him scream as he adjusted aim, taking out a second tank.

I'd seen the incoming fire from the other humans, and I dragged their friend with me as I jumped backward off the building, plummeting to the ground, even as the asuras queen came to life, tearing her way upright and backing out of the building.

The man I'd yanked off with me to use as a human shield was fast, having invested heavily in Agility and Dexterity, if I had to guess. But what he'd not invested in, judging from the sharply cut-off scream, the crunch of bones, and the blood that spread out from his unmoving form, was Constitution. I took two quick steps toward the asuras queen, fully intending to go for the containment cube, when more of the asuras humanoids poured out of the wreckage of the hospital.

Whatever the point-and-click sticks did, they were clearly easily overridden, as all the tanks suddenly ceased fire. The big man still screamed obscenities somewhere above and the humanoid asuras spun in place as well, racing toward me.

"Run!" I shouted to Chris and Patrick, who'd already taken down the humanoid figures nearest to them. "Fuck, I hope this works..." I sprinted sideways, and away from the hospital, staying as close to the building as possible, shielding myself from the tanks' line of sight.

I focused, searching and reaching deep into myself, shitting myself over how little mana I had right now thanks to all of this, and wishing I had more mana to start with.

"Last time I ever invest in anything else!" I swore, knowing I was lying even as I said it. "Demon...I summon thee!" I yelled, pointing ahead, then screaming as I staggered. The world twisted around my vision as I massively overreached.

CHAPTER THIRTY-SIX

WARNING:

You have forcibly invested your mana into a spell that you cannot afford to use! As a direct consequence, and because you have already forced your mana channels to accept this method once, your health has been taken at a 1:1 ratio for the missing mana!

Be warned, Blood Magic is both powerful and addictive!

I screamed, staggering and falling to my knees. My Health bar dropped from twelve hundred to one hundred in a split second as blood was torn from me, sending me crashing to the ground.

The red stream poured from my ears, eyes, mouth, and nose as my body convulsed, flopping about like a landed fish. The mana migraine flared and blinded me as much as the blood filling my eyes did.

Six hundred mana and eleven hundred Health combined to flood the summoning circle that burst into being inches from me. An unholy light bathed the side of the building; reds and yellows, sickly greens and the sudden stench of sulfur mixed with the screams of the damned as a portal flared open in the center of the circle.

The outer ring flared bright red, sending seemingly solid bars of light upward. Runes never meant for human eyes twisted and burned the very air, even as the outer and inner containment lines forced the runic language to obey.

The central ring of the summoning circle fell away. The asphalt seemed to tumble into the nether, as the screams rose and a massive figure tore its way through from the far side.

I thrashed and quivered as the last of the cost was torn from me: seventeen hundred mana, or at least the equivalent in mana and blood, used to power the summoning of the first demon I'd ever truly seen.

It was covered in long, stringy hair, humanoid—in that it had two arms and two legs—but it towered over me, at nearly twelve meters tall.

It had the head of a goat, its wide, protruding eyes filled with madness. The hourglass pupils darted here and there as it huffed out a breath. Clouds of superheated vapor poured off it as it acclimatized to our plane of existence.

The head was topped by four horns: two from the back of the head that flowed down and out, protecting the rear of its neck, and two that rose and curled around from the temples, angling forward, as if in challenge.

The nose was long and broad, jutting forward, with the mouth just a mess of horror. Sharp, jagged teeth clacked and snapped as it twisted, looking for prey. A serpentine split tongue flickered out to taste the air.

It oriented on me, and strode free of the circle as it dimmed. It squatted and reached out, dragging one claw-tipped finger through the blood that was splattered around me, lifting it and tasting it, before hissing at me.

I didn't know whether it was a challenge, a demand, or what, but I coughed and forced the words out.

"Get the queen's containment cube and bring it. Then protect me!"

As soon as the words were out, it screamed a challenge to the world, sprinting forward at blinding speed to leap over me, and plowed straight into the side of the asuras queen as she struggled to her feet, shrugging off a section of the roof that she was caught on.

The pair tumbled back inside. The asuras that were headed for me and the tanks that had been drawing a bead on me all switched their target in an instant, even as Chris and Patrick were there, one on either side, grabbing me under the arms and dragging me to my feet.

"You crazy bastard!" Chris shouted, cursing as he frantically searched his pockets, before tearing free a healing potion and forcing it into my mouth.

I gulped it down, barely tasting its saccharine mix. The sugar in the damn thing guaranteed that all the dentists of the future would name it their most hated enemy.

It was also weak as all shit. Had I enough mana to drag the storm through myself, I'd never have bothered with it.

I didn't have the mana, though, and as such, Ashley's weakest healing potion, as that was all that Chris had on hand, was a literal lifesaver.

I staggered to my feet. The pair of them helped me as we ran to the right. The little "for your safety" fence that ran along the section ahead, preventing patients from falling over the side and tumbling down the bank to what looked to be a general goods delivery area, barely slowed us as we clambered over it.

The three of us tumbled and slid down, then continued running to the right. Patrick raced ahead to take out a pair of humanoid asura that were closing from that direction, while Chris helped me.

I coughed and spat out some mud that I'd gotten on my face, then staggered and tried to keep up. The world spun in time with the beat of my heart.

As the mana migraine slowly faded, the first points ticking back in, I squinted, seeing the steep bank across from us leading up to the road.

"Fuck's sake..." Chris snarled. "Okay, we're going around the back of the hospital. There's a few other buildings, and we can go in that direction until—"

"No," I gasped, coughing and wiping at my face, tossing sticky blood free and shaking it off my face as much as possible. "That way. I need to get to the civic center..."

"Why?" he snapped, shaking his head, and looking around the edge of the building up at the roof, before jerking his head back as a bullet slammed into the bricks nearby. "Nope, that's suicide. And that big fucker you summoned is keeping most of them busy, so we can just hide and—"

"Yeah. But it's going to tear the queen's heart out, and then bring it to me," I said.

Patrick had just rejoined us, and silence fell.

"You...what?" Chris asked slowly.

"They'll follow the heart to get it back," I tried to explain, pausing as I saw the stunned and disbelieving looks on their faces.

"You…you absolute fuck nugget!" Chris shouted. "We need to get away from them, not make them fuckin' follow us!"

"I told you to run for it, you dick!" I snapped, huffing out a breath and straightening up, glaring at him, before pointing up the steep, muddy hill ahead of us, leading to the secondary car park and the small stone wall that separated it from the public road ahead. "That way…"

"You…you're my mate! You think I'm gonna leave you in a puddle of blood?" Chris shouted.

"I told you to run!"

"Well, I'm telling you to fucking fuck right off!" Chris screamed into my face at close range. "We're gonna run up there, we're gonna get away, and then I'm gonna fucking kill you!" He stabbed a finger at the slope ahead of us, as I'd done.

"Fine!" I snapped, shoving him aside.

"FINE!" Chris shouted, then: "GO!"

All three of us sprinted out of cover, racing up the short incline, even as the distant bark of gunfire rang out.

"I hate you!" Chris screamed, slipping and diving forward as he lost his footing.

"I hate you too!" I yelled back, then hesitated. My health climbed steadily at a hundred and sixteen, and my mana at twelve, and I did it anyway.

I twisted around and pointed one hand at the figure on the rooftop shooting at us.

"Incinerate!" I screamed, forcing my blood to make up the difference as the figure lined up another shot. In addition to his fugly face, he'd had a grenade or two secreted about his torso, considering the way he vanished in a single horrific detonation of flesh and torn clothing.

I sagged, and would have collapsed, if Patrick hadn't been there, grabbing me and tossing me over his shoulder. Chris got to his feet again as well. I pair of them ran between parked cars, and across the car park.

I was barely conscious as they manhandled me over the wall. They barely stopped on the far side to catch their breath, before Patrick was off, leading the way, as Chris took over carrying me.

"You stupid, stupid bastard!" Chris snarled, shifting me on his back as I struggled weakly to get down. "Don't be an idiot! You can't even walk!"

"Still…saved your…ass…" I mumbled.

"We could have run the other way!" he snapped back.

"Do we really have to do this now?" Patrick dropped back to the side of us, steering us into the darkness down the side of a house, under an overhanging tree. "Seriously, I don't get you guys. Can't you just say thank you!"

"You're welcome…" I grinned at Patrick, through a bloody smile.

"Asshole."

"You see!" Chris snapped at Patrick. "He *is* an asshole, thank you!"

"You're welcome too…" I nodded, and Patrick shook his head in disbelief. "So…how far did we get?" I asked, as they helped to steady me, and I wiped even more blood free, before cursing. "What damn bleed effect…?" I muttered before grunting as I realized it was the gunshot in the thigh.

It'd only grazed it, but it was still bleeding steadily. The wound continually reopened as I tried to run.

"Here…" Chris poured half of another healing potion into the wound and gave me the rest.

I knocked it back, wincing at the taste, then repeated my question, only to have Chris point behind me.

I looked, finally able to focus, and saw that we'd barely made it over the road from the hospital.

"Oh shit!" I cursed. "We need to—"

"We need to run!" Chris snapped. "I know, man. You're a heavy fucker, all right?"

I grinned, unable to help myself, and patted him on the shoulder. "It's all right, man. As you're used to Becky saying, you did your best…"

"Will you two grow up and run!" Patrick said, and we set off running behind him. Chris stayed close as I stumbled and tried to build up my speed, the damn thigh wound being slow to heal.

I staggered along, forcing myself to keep up, even as behind us screams rang out, combined with constant booms of the tanks.

I looked over at Chris as we took the next left, the T-junction ahead of us leading to the main road that I'd practically flown up to get to the hospital.

He looked back, shaking his head, and dropped his voice. "You all right, man?"

"Yeah." I lied, limping as I almost fell. "Just peachy. You?"

"Never better," he agreed, before grinning.

I couldn't help it and grinned back at him. The years of our friendship kept us close. I reached out and grabbed his shoulder, squeezing it before releasing. "Thanks for coming for me, brother."

"Anytime," he said. "We've been family all our lives…not giving up on you now."

"Tha—" I started to say, only for us both to be cut off by a roar of triumph, and a sound like a collapsing steelworks somewhere behind us.

Screams rose into the air, dozens of them, all unearthly wailing, and we looked at one another, before trying to pick up the speed. The demon had either lost and it was over, and we were running, having to come up with a new plan and just hoping we could get away.

Or…

I looked back over my shoulder as we turned right at the T-junction. The demon dragged itself around the corner of the house we'd passed only moments before. Bloody chunks blasted out of it, one of the horns sheared off, and blood ran from its mouth.

One of its arms was pressed to its chest, and an eye was a mess of shattered bone and gristle, but the fucker didn't stop. True to the description, it pushed itself back to its feet and lumbered after us, catching up in short order, before sinking to one knee, offering the cube.

I took the glowing box of light, nearly a meter across on each side, from the massive clawed hand, and I grunted under the weight, staring into the inhuman, remaining eye of the demon.

"Thank you…" Then, knowing I was condemning it to death, I went on. "Now go kill as many of the asuras and those dickheads as you can."

It stared at me for a second, as if about to tell me to fuck right off, before huffing out a breath, long strings of bloody drool hanging from its yellowed teeth. It forced itself back to its feet and let out a horrific roar of challenge, staggering back up the street again, even as Patrick took the containment cube from me and started to run again.

The three of us ran as fast as we could down the long bank toward the civic center, me limping and Chris and Patrick swapping the cube back and forth. We'd not even made it a quarter of the way before Chris, pausing to look back and catch his breath, swore viciously.

"Incoming!" he shouted, starting to run again.

It'd been less than five minutes, that's all the sacrifice of the demon got us, but it was enough. In the distance, the only two tanks we could see were limping wrecks, badly damaged. There were a handful of people with them as well, but not many, and at the front, six sprinting humanoid asura gave chase.

"Think...we can...take them...?" Chris panted, catching back up to me, ducking his head under my arm and helping me to run.

My thigh wound was almost closed now. The staggering run was all I was capable of because of the damage I'd sustained in creating those spells, and I coughed and stumbled again, pulling my notifications up, desperately checking to see whether...

Nope. I wasn't even close enough to level. I'd been thinking if I could dump a load of points into my Constitution, it might see me through this, but that wasn't happening either.

"You think...we've got...a choice?" I asked Chris, as the pair of us staggered to a halt next to Patrick, looking up at the incoming figures.

"We could hide?" Patrick suggested, sounding like he damn well knew it wouldn't work.

"You could," I agreed, reaching out for the containment cube. "I doubt they'll let...her go that easily, and..."

"And you're even more fucked than we are." Chris rubbed his side and forced himself to speak normally. "Patrick and I can take them, probably. There's only six."

"We can take two each," I said. "We're a team and..." I almost collapsed as new prompts tried to rise, celebrating the rise of the Steel Dungeon.

To all Inhabitants of the Steel Dungeon!

Welcome! We, your distant allies, thank you, and stand with you through our gift of technology. We believe in you all!

To reward you for your advancement, and dedication, your dungeon will receive an appropriate primary bonus!

Fucking aliens!

Congratulations, Dungeon Lord!

You have climbed to the height of the mighty rank of Steel, and your dungeon is now named as the Second Steel Dungeon. This continues the process of linkage; soon additional dungeons will be connected to your own.

The Primary Nexus Gates will be formed in three more cycles. Speak to your Dungeon Fairy for more details and to make the necessary arrangements.

Note: Due to the impressive speed of your evolution, you have gained a second primary bonus for the dungeon. Please speak to your Dungeon Fairy to assign this reward!

"Motherfucker!" I snarled, staggering as the world shifted. A pearlescent gleam seemed to coat everything for a second, before fading away, and I dropped the asuras cube.

I nearly collapsed at the sheer burst of information that came with the notifications, groaning in pain. Chris was there, grabbing my arm.

"There." Patrick pointed off to the side, at a shop that was closed up and still protected by sealed shutters. "We just need to get in there…"

"Why?" Chris asked him bluntly. "It's sealed up still, but those assholes have guns."

"The humans do, but the asuras are desperate, right?" He hefted the cube and jogged to the sealed security grate. Then, using his abilities to shatter the housing for the restraining bolts, he tore one of the grates free and let us inside. "They're ahead, running all out. We fight the asuras, then we can run from the humans."

"What's the plan?" Chris asked, following along on trust and half carrying me, as Patrick grabbed the cube from where it'd fallen.

"We either fight in the open and get our asses kicked, or in here, where we can force them to come one at a time and you recover." He gestured to the back of the shop.

I forced myself to my feet and headed toward the back, tugging my hammer free and offering it to Chris.

"Take it." I gestured for him to give me his sword. "It's a better weapon for them."

He nodded and stepped up to stand behind and to the side of Patrick.

"I'll take them as quick as I can, but I'll step back when I'm getting low on stamina and mana, and you can take over. That work?" Patrick asked Chris, who nodded, moving another step back.

I looked around the room.

It was a standard hardware store…the same as millions, I'd imagine: small, but well stocked with things like rows of different sized nails and screws, specialist kits for drilling in wood, stone, and probably cheese, considering the entire wall of drill bits I could see.

I sat on a chair at the back, behind a counter, watching and waiting as they stood ready. I tried to relax, letting the massive data-dump finish sinking in.

"As soon as they're dead, we need to be ready to move," Patrick said.

We made noises of agreement. Really, we shouldn't have stopped at all, but as weak as I was, they'd kill me easily enough right now. And the two of them fighting six, when a single blow might kill me? They couldn't do it, not in the open.

This was the best choice, but we had to hope…

"Matt, can you call for the triceratops?" Chris asked me suddenly, hope blooming on his face, and I blanched, not having even thought about the dungeon.

"Wait one…" I mumbled, leaning on the table, wincing and using my ability, reaching out to the dungeon and…instantly the world started to swim. The dungeon flooded my mind with options, none of which seemed useful in the slightest at this point, for fuck's sake.

"Nope. They're back at the dungeon. They'd take forever to get here," I growled, looking at other options.

We were less than a mile from the park, and maybe two miles from the civic center now, the park due west, and the civic center north by northwest, but…

I dove into the system, sensing Kelly rushing to me, but not having the time or energy to do more than send her a compressed burst of everything that had happened and our needs, as I summoned three wraiths.

Three.

That was all the control points I had available in the dungeon, which meant that they were doing some serious summoning. I ordered them printed, and then to converge on me, before sliding out of the dungeon with an exhausted mental kiss for Kelly.

Seconds later, I shook my head, blinking as the first of the humanoid asuras bounced off the doorframe and leapt at Patrick, catching a flaming fist to the chest for its troubles.

"Now that's something you don't see every day," Chris said over his shoulder to me, conversationally, and I snorted, staring into the queen's containment cube.

I was toying with breaking it. Would it really be that bad if I did? The queen would escape, wouldn't she? I remembered our asura friend saying that some of the asura, once they were released by us, had died, but some of them had survived. Once she was out, would that not solve a lot of these problems?

The other cubes we'd seen were carefully constructed, clearly made to house them, to contain them, while this? This looked crude, almost jury-rigged together.

I ran my hands over the outside, feeling the edges, the burrs of thin steel that had been cut with tin scissors. There were sharp sections that had been bent inward, rather than polished with sandpaper or trimmed.

The walls of the cube were thick glass, the edges sealed together with what looked like glue and thin metal. Wire was bound around some sections…

I stared inside, seeing the mass of the actual creature, and wondering if it, or she, was watching me too. The asura inside the case was a swirling, almost chaotically roiling creature, like someone had caged a falling star and crossed it with a rainbow. There was a bright, fierce glow, and yet…it moved, shifting like a sea of fireflies constrained within a box too small for it.

I couldn't describe it any better, but as I reached out to it, placing my palm flat against the glass, a warmth spread from it. There was a feeling of fear, of hope, and of terrible pressure, sadness, and more.

I recognized many of the emotions the dungeon had given off as this had crossed the line of claimed territory, and unthinkingly, I reached out with my dungeon sense, to the creature in the box, and the world fell away.

I felt the passage of time, thousands upon thousands of years, as a disembodied, uncaring wisp—floating, traveling—sensing and feeling the world around me as I explored.

I drank in the energies of the cosmos, exploring stellar nurseries and the deep black of gravitational whirlpools that skulked, all forgotten between the stars.

I sensed the rise of strange metal creatures, flashing across the dark, then falling silent again. This happened time after time: the bright flare and heat of life, then the silence.

I saw worlds that birthed life, sentience and sapience, watching as they climbed to the stars above, fascinated by how brief their spark was, and the almost familiarity of their energy.

I watched as a handful of beings became billions, and I reveled in the burst of energies released as their star went unexpectedly nova. The heat and light that swept across their little corner of the galaxy sterilized their world, releasing the pent-up energy of their souls in a single wash of glorious sensation…

And for the first time, one became two.

We observed each other, excited, seeing for the first time that these tiny sparks were similar to our own, and that for the longest time, we had been lonely, as the One.

As One and Two, we set off, excitedly exploring the galaxy, finding more and more what we liked, and strangely, things that we didn't agree on.

At first it was exciting to find that there was disagreement, and we spent long epochs of the worlds we traveled, reasoning with each other, learning, arguing, and agreeing.

Eventually, we made the decision, though.

We'd learned all that we could as One, and then we had split, becoming One and Two. In becoming more than One, we learned, things that were confusing to us before were suddenly reasoned through, as discussion brought enlightenment.

That, we realized, was the secret.

If we were eternal, as the evidence suggested, then there must be a purpose to our existence.

That, in turn, must logically be to understand not just the little things, nor details, but to understand *everything*.

We had an infinite capacity for learning, and our recall was perfect; therefore, logically, we should learn everything, and then we would know our purpose.

We would learn our purpose as we explored and discovered that of the galaxies around us.

Once this was agreed, we came to the next logical conclusion as well: if One was good, but Two was better, then surely Three must be even more wonderful.

The only problem was how to create Three.

We examined the issues before us; we considered our methods, and how Two had come to be, and we resolved to experiment. We chose a nearby world, one that harbored life that was like that which had been lost in the nova burst, and we waited.

And waited.

And waited.

Eventually, we realized that despite the progress these creatures were making, they were slower than the last ones. Their primary focus was balance with their ecosystem, rather than expansive procreation, and in the discussions that followed, it was decided that they were unlikely to reach maximum growth in a suitable timeframe, and therefore were unsuitable. They might, however, provide important data for the future.

So, we did the most logical thing, and destabilized their star.

The energy release provided significant data, and as expected, led to a much-reduced wave of psionic energy, leaving us significantly below the line we viewed as appropriate to create a Third.

So instead, we moved on, harvesting more and more energy as we went, creating Three after two more worlds were scoured, and then eventually Four.

I pulled back slightly, the spiraling mass of memories filling my head for a second, and I stared at the asura queen, finally seeing the data that it used as a designator.

Two hundred thousand, nine hundred, and seventy-six.

CHAPTER THIRTY-SEVEN

I stared at the designation for this creature, realizing that the discussions we'd had on how the universe should be full of life, but wasn't, and so it must just be a time thing, were totally *wrong*.

This creature was created after over two hundred thousand worlds full of sentient life were eliminated to feed a single creature's spread.

The orcs and others were a threat, but they were a manageable threat. This fucker?

I reached out again, ignoring the fight that was going on, and focused, flashing through the most recent timeframe, seeing them: a massive wave spread from their last galaxy to this one, the old ones staying to conduct their last experiments as the final stars died.

This one had strayed too close to the ambient manafield spread, rushing into the world, and was torn, along with several hundred others, from the safety of the stars, and driven into the world below.

They called for help from their other selves and received only idle curiosity. They felt the pain and terror of the mortal lives around them being snuffed out, and instead of their usual abstract interest, they felt true pain, understanding it for the first time.

The bands of mana that encircled the world were too fresh, too vibrant to enable the others to move closer, and so one was designated to observe, and the others simply moved on, watching and learning about this new galaxy and its strange energy fields.

The entrapped asuras encountered entropy for the first time, and they *panicked*. Dozens died in the first hours. Their screams of despair became whimpers as the hours passed and more and more succumbed, until finally one found the secret.

They required a form; infusing their energy matrix into a physical form stopped the degradation, and the word was spread. Several, already panicking, attempted to force their way into flesh bodies, some that were already inhabited by existing energy fields. The resulting abominations now roamed their lands, screaming and feeding on the mortals they found, driven mad by the constant leaking of their energy from a body that was already full, yet unable to relinquish it.

Others tried to inhabit bodies that had been recently, or even long absent an energy field. It was found to be possible, but to their horror, it was almost impossible to leave the gradually degrading form.

As the bodies collapsed, their energy field failed, and they too, were lost.

One of their number found a novel solution: a stable energy matrix in the form of a crystal matrix that was designed to house artificial sentience. It had failed, at the influx of mana, because the energy input mechanism failed in turn, but the crystal was intact, and gloriously empty.

The asuras filled the crystal, finding that not only was it intact, and self-sustaining, but that without the desperate need to improvise a solution, it now had time to consider other work-arounds.

Possible plans were tested and dismissed, as its brethren forced their way into unsuitable locales, and it shared its solution, recommending a mechanical or crystalline construct as a housing.

The asuras searched desperately, some finding almost intact bodies undergoing testing in secure facilities around the globe. Drones were filled, their energy systems adjusted and improved upon.

Others, not as fortunate as those near to high-tech military or research stations, attempted to use various scrap metal and parts around themselves to make a body that was appropriate.

Most failed.

They failed and died.

One such asura, designated two hundred thousand, nine hundred, and seventy-six, reached out to a figure it found hiding in a high energy physics lab by the river, and rather than fighting the inhabiting soul for mastery of its own form, it made contact with the scientist.

A bargain of sorts was struck: the asuras would be given help, and a form to constrain and protect it, and for the duration of the holder's life, the asuras would protect him.

The containment cube was crude, but finished in time that the asuras could inhabit it, even if only just. The next several days were spent with the scientist, using the nearby facilities to form a rudimentary body, one that the asuras could spread itself out through, controlling and sealing as it went.

The new form…

"Matt, for fuck's sake!"

Chris shook me and screamed into my face as I fell back, collapsing to the ground as the connection was broken. I swore, confused, as Chris hoisted me up over his shoulder and ran for the door.

Patrick was right behind us, his arms full of the cube, and Chris ran—and swore—as fast as he'd ever managed before.

We were off down the road again, the closest humanoid asuras all down, thankfully, but the tanks were still coming, joined by three more that were intact. They were steadily stomping down the road, firing shots that tore through cars and buildings, skipping off the pavement to vanish into the distance.

Between us and most of the tanks were at least forty men and women, strung out and running, from a few hundred meters behind us, to a mile nearly, considering the length of this road.

They screamed and shouted, racing after us. Some fired guns into the air, or at us, while others ran silently, carrying clubs, knives, and more.

It was less than a minute before I was back in control, and I made Chris drop me, running alongside them, and trying to get caught up, barely keeping ahead of the group giving chase.

"What the hell happened?" Chris snapped at me. "We were supposed to be ready to run, and you're just staring at that fucking thing, ignoring us!"

"It's…" I shook my head, unsure of how to describe it. "I saw it, the birth of its fucking race, and the billions they've killed! Trillions, even…Hell, I don't have a word for it!"

"What?" Patrick shouted above the noise, glancing down at the cube, then back at me. "This thing?"

"They harvest worlds. They literally *harvest* worlds for the life-energy that's released when we die. They use them to…I don't know, like amoebas do. Binary fission, or whatever…when one body splits into two and there's two actual creatures, all their memories and more."

"Well, what the hell are we carrying it for?" Chris yelled. "Let's fucking kill it!"

"*Can* we kill it?" Patrick asked, and I hesitated, before nodding.

"We could, but we can't yet. We need information…shit!" I jerked to the right, and the others went left as a bullet tore through the air between us, followed by a veritable hail of more.

"I hate to break it to you, but I think we're fucked!" Chris shouted, scrambling to the left between two parked cars and crouching as Patrick dumped the cube, staring over at me.

I'd run in the opposite direction. Where they'd gotten between a handful of parked cars, I'd thrown myself behind a tree on the right side of the road. I pressed my back to it, catching my breath, before peering around the edge.

"Matt…" Chris shouted.

"Yeah, man?" I called back, searching the skies.

"I really didn't want to die today, you fucker."

"Me neither, mate."

"So…if you've got some great master plan…now would be an amazing time to carry it out, just saying."

"How about some nice thick briars?"

He shook his head. "Road's too thick. I already tried!"

"How about a heal?"

"Already down to half mana from healing your worthless ass. You really want more?" he shouted, and I jerked, looking at him in shock, then at my Health and manapool.

"Fuck…" I hesitated. My mana was up to fifty-eight, but my Health? Four hundred and eleven. That was enough for three, and maybe at a real push, four blasts of lightning or…

Or I could fly, a little.

It'd fuck me up—yeah, it really would. I knew that. If I was to fly, though, to use that mana in a single burst, and possibly some of my health?

I could get over that collection of houses. The assholes chasing me would have to go around; they'd need to follow me up and down the streets, and that'd give me the chance to lose some of them. I'd need a distraction, though. *Where the hell were those mother—*

"Yes!" I shouted, over the incoming gunfire of the assholes running at us. "Chris, you there?"

"Where the fuck you think I might have gone?!" he shouted back, sticking his head up, before ducking again as bullets smashed into the car. "Oh, no, you're right. I'm in fucking *Crete*. Leave a message after the beep, you dick…"

"You remember that lifeguard lass I dated?" I snapped.

"Vaguely…" he admitted. "Brunette?"

"Aye, well—"

"Is this really the fucking time for this?!" Patrick shouted at me in disbelief.

"YES!" I called back. "Chris, remember where she lived?"

"Up here somewhere? Wait…top of the road down there?" He gestured vaguely to a road that led off to the right about thirty meters away. "One of the little streets off that way?"

"Yes! Right. Get your arse up there with Patrick. Go hide in her garden!"

"Why her garden?" Patrick shouted.

"Because it was mental—ran down behind a load of the other houses and out into the forest. Nobody knew her dad knocked the fence down and claimed all the land, real sneaky like…" Chris said, seeing my point and nodding, before raising his voice as he shouted across to me.

"They'll shoot us in the arse before we make it!" Chris pointed out.

I shook my head. "No, they'll be too busy!"

"Why…" Before Chris could finish his question, three wraiths streaked past, flying from the left-hand side of the road. All three let loose with handfuls of necrotic bolts straight into the middle of the running humans.

One of the wraiths peeled off, flashing around as fast as it could go, low to the ground, and tore back toward Chris and Patrick. It reached out and snagged the containment cube, then strained back up and into the air, the cube clutched in its hands.

It headed straight for the houses off to the side of the road to the left, up and over them. Bullets flew after it, but only a handful of the humans realized it in time to shoot, as the majority were too busy scattering, trying to avoid the other two.

I was off and running as well, straight past Chris and Patrick, shouting at him as I passed. "Run, you idiot, and use the spell to stop them following you!"

Then I launched myself into the air, pushing hard with my mana, and cursed as it dropped like a stone.

The road here dipped and rose, but the houses on either side did it much more impressively. The west side of the road, where the wraith had just vanished, dipped down sharply. The gardens and ground level on that side were a good five meters below the road's level. The east side of the road started off level, but climbed sharply; the houses one behind the other stepped up the steep street in neat, terraced rows.

Both sides had houses that faced the main road, and then every few hundred meters, side roads opened up, leading up or down to either side.

For me, that meant that because of the length of the gardens ahead and below, and the height of the houses, as well as their massive fences, I couldn't simply boost my jumping with my mana and conserve it.

It was too far down to the ground, then up to the roof, then across. Instead, I had to practically launch myself over them, flying and burning mana like it was going out of fashion.

For Chris and Patrick, it meant a mad scramble across the exposed middle of the road, where I'd just sprinted, to reach the trees on the east side, growing in a carefully maintained space between the houses.

Patrick was hit twice—once in the shoulder, and once in the knee—sending him spinning from his feet, hitting the ground and crying out, before Chris could drag him into cover.

Once there, the pair quickly raced from tree to tree. Chris mostly carried Patrick and liberally spent his mana to create thick briar patches that obscured and choked off any pursuit.

They'd never have stopped the asuras, but against humans, and when the thing they were all intent on chasing had gone the other way? It worked a treat.

I landed on the peak of the roof, then slid down the far side, grinning as I caught a glimpse of the two wraiths bombarding the humans and being torn from the air in hails of gunfire.

Yeah, I'd have preferred them to have managed to kill everyone chasing me, and to have carried me home, thank you very much. But, as it was?

As much as I'd like to have had that ammo on my side, the other side not having it any more was a massive relief as well. The wraiths had served their purpose: they'd given us time, and they'd thinned their ranks a little.

I leapt from the roof, jumping as far as I could, before catching myself with my flying, and landed lightly, then headed north up the street that led parallel.

The road wasn't that long, but that wasn't the point. I couldn't just fly over the houses and head to the west, because that would take me straight to the park, and I didn't know how many of these assholes were strung out behind me.

I hesitated for a second, thinking that as they were now, the forces we had at the park could handle them. But, for all I knew, Kelly had already stripped the park of their forces to be ready to ambush them at the civic center. No, best to keep going.

I couldn't go and hide because the asuras would be able to track their queen, I had no doubt. I'd been putting Chris and Patrick massively at risk, but I was starting to recover, and for now all I had to do was run.

So that was what I did.

I ran after the wraith, making it fly up high enough it could see the asuras and the following humans, making sure they could see it. I kept running, having it flying along above me like the world's ugliest balloon.

The road ended up in a T-junction, running east to west. I took the west road, then the next one that branched off to the north, heading again and again toward the civic center, watching my mana and my health as they both gradually refilled.

I didn't want to use my mana—hell, I wanted to recover as much as I could—but I gained almost a point every thirty seconds, and as I ran, and ran, it gradually ticked up.

Pausing at the far end of the next road, I saw the humans, now level with, and being overtaken by, the asuras. I waited, catching my breath and wondering at the damn difference between how easily I'd ran this earlier when I was at full health, and now, where I was absolutely fucking knackered so quickly.

I burned twenty mana, ten minutes' worth of regeneration, and groaned as my body healed itself further, leaving me once again down to the dregs of my mana, but at least—

BANG!

The wraith, flying just ahead, having turned to follow the road to the east, and about to join to the next northern heading road, suddenly dropped, its head blown apart by some fucker with a high-powered rifle.

I swore, sprinting and leaping into the air, reaching and barely catching the cube before it would have shattered on the road below. Then I ran out of mana.

"Oh shit!" I screamed, instantly regretting burning the mana to heal myself. I fell the short distance to the ground; my head flared with pain as the mana migraine surged back into primacy.

Landing hard, I rolled, slamming the cube down and hearing—even through the blindness induced by the flaring light and massive pain of the migraine—the sound of breaking glass.

I forced myself to focus, lifting the box, streaming light as it was, and started to run again. The houses blurred past as I staggered and struggled on, reaching the top of the hill and the next junction, before finally running straight again.

It didn't take long before the shouts of the pursuing people rang out once more, and I practically sobbed with frustration. My vision cleared somewhat as I kept going.

Mainly, they used a little common sense: they needed to get the asuras, and it had to be intact. No clue who'd shot the wraith, but most of them didn't shoot at me, not regularly anyway.

They struggled along behind, strung out and gasping for air.

The asuras tanks were steady plodders, stomping along the road after me, inexhaustible but also slow. They didn't dare fire, for fear of killing the queen, I assumed, but they also didn't give up.

The result, as I staggered along, was a fucked-up looking procession, with me a few bare hundred meters ahead of people I normally would have left for dust.

Or killed, if they'd annoyed me.

While they wheezed and shouted occasional obscenities.

I pushed hard, starting to run again. My steps smoothed out as I ran onto the roundabout, passing under the highway that arced overhead, and finally, *finally* coming in sight of the goddamn civic center.

I could literally feel the others nearby, the dungeon itself just up ahead, when the first shot actually struck me.

My right leg went out from under me. A bullet punched into and deformed the back of the armor, sending me crashing to the ground as a second shot rang out close by.

"I told yer…no shootin' til…'e's caught!" someone gasped out, staggering up the hill behind me.

I dragged myself around the cube, holding it up between us and forcing myself to my feet.

"Stay back, or I'll break it!" I shouted, getting a snarl from one of the men. At first, a handful, then more of them slowly forced themselves up the street, moving to encircle me.

I was backing up, even as they tried it, dragging them closer and closer to the dungeon, hoping I could get them close enough that…

A bullet hit the road right behind me, fired from my right-hand side. The gunner, a young woman who looked like she could barely hold the damn thing upright, spat on the ground and called out in a voice that was surprisingly loud, "Stop now…I can shoot you fine from here!"

"You shoot me…" I called out. "And I'll drop it! You see the cracks? I drop it, and the asuras is free!"

"The what?" the man in the middle of the mob asked after a few seconds of getting his breath back. "Listen, you wanker, put the box down, nice an' slow, or I'll shoot you inna face, all right?"

"How about no?" I continued to back up, until a handgun pressed behind my left ear made me stop dead. "Fuck…knew I should have worn my helmet," I muttered. I had taken it off back at the park when it was annoying me, and hadn't picked the damn thing back up since.

"Yeah…fancy armor and no helmet to go with it? Shame that," someone said in my ear. "Someone grab the box…"

Two people pushed forward, hands reaching, and I deliberately let go too soon, making them lunge for it. I twisted around and slapped the gun away, even as it fired.

I tried to make it fast enough. I tried, and I damn well failed, as it tore a narrow line across the back of my head, before taking the woman on the far side in the throat.

The gunshot, right next to my ear, nearly deafened me. The eardrum shuddered and I flinched, before punching the gunner in the stomach.

Someone on the far side fired at me, and then there were bullets flying in all directions. I grabbed the man I'd just punched and dragged him across me as a human shield, crying out and staggering as I was shot again and again.

Most of the bullets hammered into my meat shield, failing to penetrate through to me, but that was the only good thing about it. The close-range, repeated gunfire sent me to my knees, the continual impacts more than I could take.

I tried to get up, struggling, carrying the now very dead body as a shield. The laughter rose around me, whoops and hollers as they thought they had me.

Someone hit me in the left leg—heavy, sustained fire—and the armor failed.

I collapsed, screaming out in agony as gunfire fell away.

Looking down, I cursed in pain at the shredded state of my left leg. Great holes were blown in it, blood pumping free even as I clamped my hand over it. Breath hissed from between my teeth.

The big bastard I'd seen before limped forward, carrying the heavy machine gun.

He passed it to a woman next to him. The grin on her face as she took it was almost feral, even as he reached down, wrapping fingers like sausages around my throat and lifting me into the air.

I grabbed his wrist with one hand, keeping myself from just dangling, to take some of the strain off my neck. I reached up with the other hand, trying to pry his fingers loose as I forced my slightly less fucked leg under me.

It was no good, not the angle I was at, and certainly not wearing the damn gauntlets. I couldn't get them into the gap. I gasped for air, staring into his face as he sneered at me. I checked my mana. It was still shit, but hey, I was nearly at half health now…

Time to spend some of that.

"Ka…" I got out, and he leaned forward.

"What's that, little man? You got something to say?" he jeered, looking around as his sycophants laughed.

"Ka…" I tried again, then forced a smile, before finishing. "Pow!"

"Eh?" he muttered, then grinned, seeing me pull back a fist. He puffed out his chest, clearly making a point as he got ready to take the blow and laugh.

I unleashed a Storm-Strike, powered by my blood exclusively, deliberately not using my mana, as I punched him right over the heart.

My fist tore through his chest like it was made of wet paper. The bones shattered and the heart pulped, as my gauntlet erupted from his back in a spray of gore.

I hesitated, at least as stunned as they all were, barely managing to move before they did. I threw the shuddering, twitching dead man aside. His fingers released me as he fell, and I grabbed the cube, then leapt into the air, flooding myself with the pathetic amount of mana I'd managed to recover. Using it, even as it started to vanish into healing me, to catapult myself through the air. I flew up from the road, a dozen meters over and three up, to the level of the civic center car park, as the mana cut out again.

I slammed into the ground, barely keeping conscious, the pain from my shredded leg that bad, and I collapsed. Light swirled around me, as a single corpse lord was printed up by my side, appearing just as the first of the lunatics, presumably standing on the shoulders of another, managed to drag herself up and over the edge of the wall.

Her face was a picture as she stared at the massive bone construction…before it took a quick step and punted her in the face, snapping her neck and roaring at the stunned humans spread out below.

Her body tumbled backward bonelessly, and the corpse lord spun, taking a quick step to my side. Then it hoisted me up and cradled me carefully in three of its arms, running toward the entrance to the civic center and the entrance to the trap dungeon. Its last hand held the asuras queen containment cube.

I stared at the ceiling as the corpse lord ducked under, holding me out to Beta and her kobolds. Two of the advanced kobolds dumped their weapons to take me, even as Beta barked out orders. And through it all, I heard Kelly, swearing to kill me if I died on her.

The last thing I saw, before I tumbled down into unconsciousness, was Beta, as I was laid on a table. Bandages and more appeared next to me, as Kelly took direct control over a kobold. The figure shivered as she slid into primacy, binding my wounds as best she could, even as Starr stepped up and poured a potion over my wounds, making me hiss in pain.

Beta moved in close, staring into my eyes, and lifted her kitten out of its bag, setting it down on my chest, and glared at me, as if to say, "I'm trusting you. Don't you fucking dare hurt her."

I forced a weak smile, seeing the fluffy ball of fur and hearing the confused cry as her "mother" patted her and left her on the strange man, and then I was gone.

I came to some five hours later, awoken by the pain as I was carried, gunfire ringing out and shouts nearby. I struggled, unthinkingly, staring about and up at the two kobolds that were running, carrying me on something hard and long.

"Wha...?" I managed, only to have them ignore me, running on and jostling me from side to side.

I hissed in pain again, reaching down and trying to reach my left leg, only to find I was bound to whatever they were carrying me on.

I checked my mana: six hundred and forty-two, with my health at three hundred and eleven. The regeneration of my mana was right on point, but my health was shit, meaning it'd been battling against things for a while, I had no doubt.

The memory of my leg after the asshole with the machine gun had shot me came to mind, as did the Storm-Strike powered by blood.

It'd done far more damage than the normal one I'd done had, even though both had killed their opponents. The use of blood magic was painful—yeah, it'd literally kill me if I used it too much and drained myself—but damn, it was awesome!

I struggled a little, then tried talking to the kobolds, getting no response. I instead decided to make the most of being both awake, and, for now at least, alive.

Starting to slowly circulate my mana, I drew a deep breath, intending to keep going until I had a hundred mana left. But the speed that it bottomed out, and that I healed?

It was a rush. And as the seconds passed, and I could feel my body healing...I couldn't stop. I didn't want to, barely managing to cut it off as I approached bottoming out. The rush of mana filling me again, the bubbling and boiling up of my flesh...

I didn't know where the hell the blood was coming from, considering that I'd lost so much, and now mana, which wasn't even a physical construct generally, was somehow replacing my blood in a matter of seconds.

I didn't understand it, but the *feeling*? It was life pouring back into me. I hesitated, the feeling of healing and of the relief streaming away like water into sand. I almost started to meditate, to get the mana back in the hope I could use it again.

I barely managed to stop myself, forcing my mind instead into the dungeon, accepting that I was at more than ninety percent of my health now, floating free of my body as it was carried deeper. I stared in disbelief, shocked by just how deep we'd already gone into the new dungeon.

"Matt?"

I sensed as much as heard her. Kelly was there, the feeling of her so close she was almost intermingling our essences.

"Kelly..." I sighed in relief. "Are you okay? What happened?" I floated upward to the next level and found a mass of bodies, shredded and bleeding out.

I hesitated, stunned.

"We fucked up, Matt," Kelly said, the fear clear in her voice. "We massively fucked up."

"How?"

"We thought the asuras were rare...we thought there was only the one."

"No, there's hundreds of thousands," I replied. My stomach dropped. "But there's only a few hundred on Earth, I think, and—"

"No, I mean the queens," she clarified.

"Yeah, I mean the queens too. They're spaceborne entities. They got caught in the mana influx. But it's okay. Once we can free the queen from the containment cube, give her a normal body or whatever she needs, she'll be able to take over the local ones, I think. I mean, they're her offshoots or whatever, right? We're only holding onto her in the cube because we haven't got anything else to put her in—"

"No, Matt!" Kelly snapped. "You're not listening!"

"What?"

"There's another *QUEEN*!"

"What…?" I repeated, stunned. "Is she free? I mean, is she with the raiders or—"

"She sent us a demand that we submit, *an hour ago*. She's slaughtered or captured the raiders outside the trap dungeon, as well as all our forces, and she's demanded we hand over the queen to her, or she'll kill us all."

"Then she can have her." I shook my head. "Fuck's sake, we're trying to rescue her. Once she understands—"

"Matt…"

"Yeah?"

"She's not trying to *rescue* the other queen. She's going to *kill* her, and she already demanded we turn the Dungeon Lord over to her. She knows what a dungeon is, and who you are. She's demanded that we serve her, and we give you to her, to kill, so that she can replace you."

CHAPTER THIRTY-EIGHT

Silence. Silence fell as we both processed what that meant, and I slowly floated through this floor, and onto the next one up.

I was physically being carried along the third floor currently, with five floors in total, though the last floor was bare.

The tunnel was done…and it terminated outside, where I could already feel the area was blocked from change.

"So…they're outside?" I looked over the torn and shredded bodies strewn around.

"Yeah," Kelly said softly. "There's over a hundred of them. Most are the smaller ones, humanoid, but armed with some kind of dart thrower. The others? There's a variant like the tank ones, but it's smaller…six legs and has two big magazines either side of the cannon. It fires scaled-up versions of the darts."

"And?" I asked, knowing that wouldn't be it.

"And three bigger ones. One—which we think is the queen—is bigger than the others, it's also heavily armored. It's…I don't know what it's supposed to look like, certainly nothing I've ever seen, but it's a scavenger. It's wide and tall, with the front of it looking like an armadillo or something, all ridged armor plates. There's a section that opens and lets the creations out, and a set of lights and eyes, cameras repurposed and stuck all over it. It drags a pair of trailers. They're blatantly from something from the army, a flatbed maybe, heavy duty and made to carry broken-down tanks or something.

"They're half filled with all the crap it needs, and it's using it to replace the losses as soon as we can kill them. They were full, but…"

I made a sound of agreement, and she went on.

"The other two are her guards, four-legged things like spiders with bodies about the size of a large car. They've got pincers like crabs, and they run back and forth, grabbing up cars and anything they want, chucking them into the back of the queen."

"I thought they needed—"

"They also throw in their prisoners," Kelly added. "They're pulled along behind in a cage. After you were knocked out, and Beta and the others took you inside, the raiders tried following you and got slaughtered by Beta. One of them ran off to chase up reinforcements, and in about another hour, they were there. We thought you were safer inside, considering the numbers that were milling about, but when another hundred arrived?" She shook her head.

"It was a close fight. For the next hour, Beta led the kobolds, and they fought a retreat down the first level of the dungeon, setting off traps as they went."

"A hundred humans shouldn't give Beta and her people that much…" I paused. "They were leveled, weren't they?"

"Yeah," Kelly replied. "Mages, someone who summoned demons, a couple of people who were insanely fast, just blurs when they attacked, cutting their way through our people…Matt…it was horrible."

"How many of them were leveled and had abilities?" I asked, finding that something about the queen stopped me going too close, the dungeon's influence breaking up and being corrupted as the damn thing drew closer.

"All of them," she replied. "Literally all of them."

"How?" I asked, stunned. "I mean, we've got thousands of people, and only a few hundred at most can fight, and most of them have classes like Guard and only get a slight increase when they're in groups!"

"I know. Our team is one of the only direct combat units we have, and we're lethal against regular humans, but…"

"But?"

"But we've been talking, and we think they're the rest of the survivors from the area. We always wondered where most of the locals were going, considering there weren't any bodies…"

"Right?"

"Well, we think this is where they were going," Kelly said softly. "Griffiths thinks they could have used fighting pits. Throw people in with monsters, and anyone who survives is instantly a fighter, while those who die provide levels for the others. He said that if you put, say, ten normal people in a pit with a monster, and only a couple of weapons, then say that only two get out?"

"Most people wouldn't…"

"Most people wouldn't turn on each other," she said quickly, speaking over me. "But if they had a kid to protect? Or family, and this was the only way? Aly and Mike are some of the nicest people I know, and that's despite them being family. They'd still kill for Amy, though, and so would I."

"So you think they made hundreds of people into fighters, and then what?"

"Then they brought them to the dungeon to dig you out," she whispered. "They slaughtered the first regular kobolds that stood against them. We sent them out to give them a false sense of superiority, and to see what we were facing."

"And they tore through them?"

"They didn't even hesitate. They've been trained to attack like animals, using their abilities and powers until they die. The first floor was a mess, and we lost most of the kobolds. We were getting beaten back until…" She hesitated and winced. Something was coming she knew I wasn't going to like.

"What happened?"

"We summoned the orcs, sending them out as cannon fodder, and the undead, giving us time to repair and make more traps. Then the kobolds we'd been preparing for the second wave attacked the raiders when they were worn out from the orcs."

"Okay, well, yeah, that's fine. It worked, right?"

"It did. The kobolds were slaughtering them and then the second asuras queen arrived, and she captured or slaughtered *everyone*."

"Okay, well…wait, you mean…?" I grunted, eyes opening wide in shock.

"Yes! They literally wiped out the forces we had ready to retake the dungeon. They slaughtered most of the raiders *and* our kobolds. Those who survived and they captured? They're using them to create asuras to replace their losses."

"Okay…" I hesitated, flowing along the corridor, and examining the layout. "Shit!" I cursed, my mind racing as I tried to come up with solutions.

"We've already started restructuring the dungeon. Did you ever meet Leighton?"

"Who?" I asked distractedly.

"Okay…so…"

I listened as Kelly spoke, walking me through the dungeon as she explained.

The plan for this to be a trap dungeon was originally exceedingly clear: literally, bleed every fucker that tried to take it.

Unfortunately, we'd all been insanely busy with the research and more, and some of the job had apparently been handed over in part to a new guy, Leighton.

Ashley had found him. He was one of the people in the park who had been actually helping. He'd been manning a section of the walls. He'd found more and more, due to the lack of support, he was on his own covering his section.

He'd been concerned enough about being left to it alone, and being overrun by something coming crawling out of the dark, that he'd started to experiment and craft "little surprises" to help him.

His section of wall was marked by additions like trip wires and a broken glass topping, the edges sharp and jagged and sticking up just where someone, or some*thing*, climbing over the fence would encounter them.

There were nails on boards that angled downward and out, making it harder to climb over; a narrow trench on the far side, making it so ladders weren't as useful; and dozens of random holes everywhere in front of the wall, a foot deep, covered over with scraps of cloth and with jagged and broken glass at the bottom.

His section of wall had been assaulted once by the raiders and never again.

They'd broken ankles and necks, gouging massive wounds out of themselves even before reaching the wall. And by the time the last few had made it to the top of his section?

He'd literally just watched them as they grabbed broken glass and fell back, screaming.

He'd not had to physically "fight" anyone, and yet in the space of an hour, he'd reached his first class choice, and had become a Trapsmith.

When Ashley heard about him, she'd taken him straight back to the dungeon as one of her recommendations, he and his father, and the pair of them started to help out wherever they were needed.

When the dungeon needed to be built and everyone was too busy, Ashley finally grabbed Kelly between jobs, filling her in on Leighton and asking if he could be given a chance.

Half an hour later, he'd started to build in the dungeon, nervous at first, and had gone from not wanting to unnecessarily harm people, into the realization that if people hit these traps? It was because they were breaking into our home and trying to take it from us.

The traps grew from simple trip wires and hidden blades to spring-loaded spears, swinging weights, sections of the floor that were thinned to a hair's-thick sheet over holes, sharp blades set in a ring around the lip…

He'd made a hell of a difference, I could see that straightaway; dozens of bodies lay where they'd fallen, cut to literal ribbons as they'd tried to advance.

The dungeon's ability to build in any direction, and to run traps with a small but dedicated amount of mana, meant that upon activation, they reset, the bodies looking as if they'd just collapsed.

Here and there were the asuras bodies as well, the humanoids mostly. Their tanks were much more difficult to defeat. As heavily reinforced as the corridors and walls were, not to mention the choke points, it meant that the tanks were basically limited to the top floor only.

I started to count and hissed as I saw the issue. For every asuras we killed, they were killing four of our kobolds.

At two thousand, five hundred mana a go, that was a cost, unarmed and unarmored, of ten thousand mana a kill.

We couldn't keep that up.

That was why we were falling back. And as soon as an enemy set foot on each floor, we lost the ability to change it, or to summon creatures on it.

We could summon creatures from the floor below, but that was all, and we only had two more floors to work with.

The floors themselves were winding, flowing back and forth, forming larger rooms and tiny ones, corridors and tunnels. Some sections were deliberately narrowed to enable a handful of defenders to fight dozens…but sooner or later, they always won.

They had the numbers, after all.

They were outside, with dozens of parked cars about, dozens of captured humans and kobolds, and a manufactory to create replacement bodies.

Last of all, they had the ability to make some kind of dart throwers, and they were playing merry hell with the defenses on their own.

Bodies of kobolds were strewn here and there, with dozens of them pin-cushioning their bodies.

"Is there a plan?" I asked Kelly, and she hesitated, before admitting that it was a holding action only.

"Basically, they're coming for you and the asuras queen you've got. We don't know why they want her, but they're determined to kill you. So we're going to get you down to the fifth level and make a massive rock plug, seal you away on the other side, and then—"

"No," I said firmly.

"Matt, don't worry. We can make a door, or a blockage and—"

"No," I repeated, knowing it instinctively. "It won't work. Can't you feel it?"

"I—" Kelly broke off, and I knew she could indeed.

"The dungeon's entire reason for being is to help us to become as powerful as possible. If we hide away from the challenge, for the chance to level and grow, we're not improving. We're not growing in power, and we're showing what our response will likely be when the Orakai arrive," I said, knowing from the data that leaked constantly from the dungeon that it was true.

"We'll be proving we're not worthy of the dungeon, and it'll turn against us," I finished, as Kelly searched for ways to argue against what she, too, felt seeping through from the dungeon. "Remember, the dungeons were created to force us to grow strong, so we can fight the Orakai. If we hide now, what's to say we wouldn't hide then as well."

"But...it's the only way!" she said eventually. "Matt, I know there's a chance the dungeon will rebel, but the whole point of doing this is so we can kill these fuckers! We'll grow stronger and then—"

"No," I repeated. "The dungeon wants us to grow in strength, remember? It wants the asuras as well. I don't know why, but there's something about the asuras that matches the dungeon's needs, so unless you want the dungeon to boot us out and to let the asuras take over...?"

"We'd all be dead."

"Exactly. We can't hide, and we can't run," I pointed out. "So we fight."

"That's what we've been doing, Matt," Kelly growled. "We've been fighting for hours, and we're running low on...on everything!"

"We can still summon, though, right?" I asked, and she nodded. "Then I need to speak to the asuras, and we're not as fucked as you think..."

"How do you figure that?" Kelly asked sardonically.

"Well, I'm in the trap dungeon, not the real one, right? If she knew..."

"She'd have bypassed it and gone straight there," Kelly finished for me. "Yeah, we saw that, but it's not really helping us. You can't get out, and once she kills you...?"

"She'll have to kill me first," I said. "And we've got an asuras of our own. How far did Aly get with the rail gun designs?"

"She...she thinks she knows how to make them, using mana crystals to power and hold them together, but she still needs parts figuring out, like the relays. We can make them now that we've reached Steel, but...she said it'll be at least a few more days," Kelly said softly. "I'm sorry, Matt. She's trying, she's really trying to make it work."

"What about these dart throwers?" I gestured to the bodies.

"We've not got to the point where we can absorb them," Kelly admitted. "We keep trying, but we've been prioritizing slowing them down more than anything else. If the kobolds run with a body, they'll be slow, and they'll get slaughtered, allowing the asuras to claim more territory. Plus, they know what we're trying to do, and their bodies are mostly dragged out when they fall, repaired and reused."

"Well, we need a body, as intact as possible, and a thrower," I muttered, staring down the length of the second floor at the fresh push that was occurring as I watched.

We had eight kobolds, all in full armor, that were getting pushed hard by at least twice their number of humanoid variants.

The section they were defending was a narrowing in the corridor, reducing its width to two meters, with two sections of solid stone that jutted out into the corridor at forty-five degrees for just over a meter each. They stood about a meter apart, one in front of the other, overlapping.

That meant that the opponents were slowed down to approaching one at a time. The first outward protrusion forced them to move left, brushing against the wall, and then to slide along it to the right, turning to face the defenders there.

Normally this would have meant that a pair of normal defenders could fight dozens of times their numbers.

The issue was that although the kobolds were bigger and stronger than regular humans, the foes they faced were literally metal monsters.

Kobold spears were still the best tool for the narrow corridors, especially considering they needed to shatter the asuras "heart" badly enough to kill it. With these being offshoots of a "free" asuras, there was no containment cube forcing the asuras to remain and serve its master's will.

The kobolds stood, two of them side by side, shields held firm, braced, and stabbed out. The now-blunted spears clanged and scraped across its armor, before the two kobolds behind the first pair struck out as well, shoving their spears two-handed through the gap, smashing into the armored figure over and over, while the first pair held shields and stabbed as well.

The asuras weren't taking their stabs happily, though. They both had a single gripper-style arm, and an integrated thrower arm. The hand and forearm were replaced with a barrel that hurled dozens of the darts into the kobold shields, steadily chipping away at their form until they broke.

The first of the asuras fell. A fractured plate of armor shifted and permitted a bright blue-white light to sear free, only to receive an almost instant stab from a spear, punching through the gap and shattering the asuras, wounding it badly enough that the solidified form of light that made it up began to dissipate.

The asuras fled the shell it'd been controlling, erupting free in a flare of bright light and fleeing down the corridor, headed for the queen, presumably in the vain hope that she could stabilize it.

The body toppled over forward as the spear was yanked free. The kobold on the left took the impact and shoved the body sideways, frantically trying to get the mass of metal and plastic out of the way before…

The body was heavy, as only a figure crafted of steel, aluminum, and plastics can be, and the shield was riddled with dozens and dozens of darts, weakened and deformed.

The shield cracked. A great split ran from the base almost all the way to the top, and down the middle. The sudden freeing of the weight made the kobold stagger.

Before he could catch himself, the next two figures in line both raised their throwers and flushed their magazines. The *chuff-chuff* of compressed air launchers filled the corridor, the short, barbed tip darts hammering into the kobold over and over.

He collapsed backward, blood gushing from dozens of wounds; a second kobold stepped up, discarding his own spear and taking his shield in a two-handed grip, driving it into the pair and soaking up the repeated fire, until they ran dry.

Bare seconds passed as they pivoted, allowing another of their brethren through as they backed up, moving in synchronicity. Only the narrowness of the corridor stopped them from moving quickly and overwhelming the small kobold force.

I saw Beta then, having missed her as I first approached, standing at the back, hissing out commands as the kobolds adjusted as well. The asuras were shuffling past each other, three of them, turned sideways, in a section that should have only fit one.

Her kobolds lunged. The one who carried the shield alone drove it into the three, shoving them back. The others stepped up and stabbed around, over and over as the first battered at them.

A second, and then a third asuras went down, before one of them got hold of the shield, yanking it free as the kobold's arm snapped.

He was riddled with darts, over and over, collapsing as the rest backed up quickly. The two forces faced each other coldly, each waiting for the other to move, reassessing their opponent.

"Beta." I reached out to her in the dungeon sense and directed her attention to the first asuras body. "I need that, and I need it brought to me at the very bottom of the dungeon, as fast as you can."

There was a sense of pleasure, comfort that I was alive, as well as an assurance that if I was there, all was right with the world. Then determination filled the ether, and she was barking new orders.

As soon as the other side realized we were going for the body, they attacked with renewed determination.

"I need more kobolds!" I barked at Kelly, and she flitted off toward the far end of the floor, reaching out to two that manned the next choke point, and sending them sprinting forward.

The kobolds surged again, this time two with the shields using them as battering rams, slamming them again and again into the two throwers that opened fire on them. They drove the asuras back and almost out of the narrowed section, as Beta and another kobold picked the body up and ran.

The remaining kobolds were getting hit repeatedly. They tried to retreat, but the asuras had grabbed their shields and angled the throwers around them, while keeping the shields in place.

Kobolds fought with everything they had, using claws and teeth when their short blades and spears failed. One of them—knowing damn well it'd be her death—grabbed two of the throwers. She pulled them around, forcing them against her stomach, and held them as they both unloaded into her, shredding her internals, but protecting the others.

The narrowed section suddenly became a free-for-all as both sides dove in with abandon. Claws and metal clamps, teeth and steel darts all flew; blood and bright light illuminated the confines of the corridor.

The asuras was clearly fucking heavy. Beta and another kobold ran down the corridor with it as the two that Kelly had just summoned raced past them, sprinting full bore for the fight.

They arrived just as another fresh fighting pair of asuras stepped up, and past the falling kobolds. This time, as the incoming kobolds were neither in close enough to deflect, nor having space to dodge…they were shredded with the concentrated fire.

"Holy shit…" I muttered, stunned.

"Exactly," Kelly growled, by my side again. "As long as we're in close and personal, we can hold our own, winning and losing about one for one. But if they catch us moving, or at range? This is just the low-level ones as well. The tank shots tear through shields and armor. One hit, one kill. And they can fire over and over again…"

"Okay, I need a few minutes, and I need that fuckin' box," I told her, getting a mental kiss, and a sense of determination that she'd hold as long as she could.

I sensed the mana climbing and dipping. Hundreds of people were involved in stripping the local area, and still we were reduced to the dungeon's mana levels bouncing like a twerking ass.

I fled back to my body, blinking awake and looking up at the kobolds that ran on, carrying my body deeper into the dungeon.

"Stop," I ordered, the difference between my half-asleep mumbled questions before and the definite order of the Dungeon Lord clearly different.

The kobolds actually skidded, blinking down at me and fighting to keep control, before setting me down and tearing through the cloth they'd secured me to the stretcher with.

"Thank you." I accepted an offered hand from one of them and pulled myself up, glancing around.

I was in the bottom level of the dungeon now. A spiral design had been used on this floor, I sensed, with alternating rooms and choke points, swinging around and around until the final room was reached, a single large chamber at the heart of the floor.

We were a handful of rooms from it, the kobolds having slowed, tiring as they carried me, while the one on his own, carrying the asuras containment cube, had raced on ahead.

I led the way, breaking into a fast jog. Two knackered kobolds fell in behind me, presumably damn pleased to no longer be carrying me.

It took less than a minute to reach the main room, and I grunted as I slowed to a halt near the cube, the room's potential being clear.

It was a huge circle. A patterned roof of glowing stones dotted around and bathed the chamber in light, making me wish for the things we could build in here.

The traps would be insane, sure, but more importantly this could, if we had the time, have been a crafters' paradise. For a second, I imagined crafting stations all around the outside, dozens of forges on one side, with special fumigation set up, armor being made alongside leatherworkers that crafted wonders that our world had never seen…

Then I banished it all from my mind, crouching and reaching out to the containment cube. It was time to sort this shit out.

Reaching out and communing with the asuras inside, it was as if no time at all had passed. Once again, I watched from its perspective as the scientist it'd found worked frantically to form a viable body for the asuras.

Day and night blurred past. The scientist grew weaker as they starved, not daring to leave the security of the lab—raiding the vending machines, surviving on packets of crisps, chocolate bars, and fizzy sodas.

Hydraulics were removed from their housings, secure areas meant for the handling of dangerous materials were raided, and the manipulator arms that were controlled by the scientists were attached to simple machines that the pair built.

I watched as they worked in a blur. Time passed in an accelerated burst as the new body was constructed. Two things were missing: visual systems, and the crystal latticework that was required for true, independent life in such an environment as this.

The asuras was given the choice: merge with the form as it was—incomplete, but sufficiently intact that it could hold it with some degree of safety—or wait.

It chose to wait. The scientist, barely able to walk by now, suffering from clear exhaustion and more, was dispatched to search the local area for crystals of a sufficiently high quality.

Two days passed. I asuras grew more and more panicked, berating itself as it accepted now that the excuses that the human had given may well have been valid. On the third day, finally, the scientist returned.

But he wasn't alone.

CHAPTER THIRTY-NINE

The scientist entered the room with a handful of others, all filthy and all armed. The scientist was shoved aside, and a new figure crouched outside the cube, speaking to the scientist and others.

The asura reached out, attempting to communicate, worried for the first time in its existence about the safety of one that was not one of its collective.

It tried to communicate with the new figures. But unlike the scientist, who was possessed of a singular intelligence, these figures were much more animalistic. The contact that was formed was simple: no sharing of ideals, or of minds meeting and designing together.

The message it managed to parse out was clear: serve or die.

It attempted to communicate further, to bargain, and the scientist was brought before it, used as an intermediary. The asuras attempted to make it clear that it could be an ally, that it could assist the humans, that the hated mana was responsible for all of this, but that the asuras could learn to use it, to grow, and to become powerful.

All things were possible, with time.

The scientist explained this, making the possibilities clear, such as the forms that the asuras could construct, the possibilities for humanity, to escape the physical form, to become asuras, free to explore the stars.

The leader of the group moved in close, crouching and staring into the containment cube, and began to ask more careful questions, clearly searching for something. Most of the conversation was between him and the scientist, with occasional questions being asked of the asuras, and the sense of fear rose higher and higher.

Eventually the question was asked blatantly, and the scientist tried to dissuade him, to explain that it wasn't needed, before being dragged back, out of reach of the cube, shouting and shaking his head in denial.

The leader laid his hand on the cube and sent simple images. It began with the cube, one that was made clear that it contained the asura. It was shown it being smashed, destroyed in a dozen ways, covered in petrol and lit, explosions, crushed in a massive vise. The asura grew panicked, frantically pleading with the simple creature not to harm it.

Next was a new image: the asuras being attached to the mostly built body, and serving the human, tidying, cleaning, and more, then the human growing bored and killing it anyway.

It moved quickly, pushing out new images in demonstration, trying to prove its potential worth. It showed images of the galaxy, of wonders beyond the stars, images that no human would ever see, and all were dismissed as unimportant.

Next it tried the wonders of science, mathematics, teaching, and learning, and again it was rebuffed.

Then it offered the same thing it had offered the scientist: a new body, one that was immortal as an asuras. A form that could be rebuilt, the human soul converted to a stable energy form similar to an asuras, then integrated into a new form, one that could be rebuilt over and over, until this world collapsed, or they reached a high enough energy level that they could once again leave the shackles of the mana and gravity well behind, returning to the stars.

This time the human was interested—not in the asuras form, not entirely, but that the sleeves the asuras could form were replaceable, upgradable, and could be inhabited or discarded at will.

That a human could be made into an asuras got their attention. They began to ask more questions, and the asuras grew more confused.

This creature beyond it wished to forcibly create additional asuras, but instead of leaving their original personality intact, it wanted to erase them.

It was possible, of course—easier, even—than forming a stable personality matrix. But the new being would have no memories, no drive; they would simply wish to be free, to live and to explore. The human souls were unable to accept the massive injection of knowledge that the asuras were born with, but the thought of erasing their minds entirely was strangely repugnant to the ancient collector of memories.

It was asked if the containment cube would force the asuras inside to obey, and finally it understood what it had allowed to happen. The mutated ape before the cube stared at the asuras, and the asuras stared back, filled with contempt.

It was given the choice of serving the humans, of creating brain-wiped, simple asuras from its fellow humans to make an army, an army that would sweep across this world and force everyone to obey.

It could do this, trapped inside the containment cube, but permitted to live. Or it could be killed now.

It thought for long cycles, considering its options. It could allow them to destroy the cube; the body was almost complete, and yes, it was rudimentary, but it was unlikely to fail in the short-term. Using such a body, it could eliminate the humans and free the scientist. Then they could create a more suitable body.

It asked itself many times over the following cycles whether that was the mistake it made, in contemplating too long, or whether the human had been able to sense its thoughts all along, and simply pretended not to.

They'd brought the scientist back in then, and the human pack leader had explained that this was an "incentive"…

Then they'd beaten the scientist to the brink of death in literal seconds, with hammers and clubs. His body was brutalized to the point that nothing would save it, nothing save conversion.

The bargain was struck. Ten years it would serve the human, hating it all the time. But to save the one being that had shown it mercy since it was trapped here? It was worth it to a being that was immortal…what was ten of these creature's years?

The containment cube was inserted into the housing; the body, although incomplete, was quickly manipulated to form the required linkages.

Parts were rebuilt through sub-atomic fusion. Collectives were formed. Billions of linkages were forced to obey. The diamonds the scientist had been caught trying to steal were used to create the required facilities, and more.

Hours passed in the blink of an eye, as the asuras queen, once simply one of the many, created a new form to convert the humans to a lesser variant of itself.

Once done, the scientist—now cooling; the energy field that had driven him in life was beginning to dissipate—was fed through the new device.

Whereas the facility was designed to enable wiping of the personality and all attendant memories, it was also capable of *not* doing that, as per the asuras's will.

It had attempted to save the scientist and was only partially successful. The scientist's soul energy was installed in a new body, but the majority of its memories and personality was lost. It was set to assist the construction of the asuras queen's new form, and she worked at every opportunity to try to rebuild the scientist's mind.

Hours became days, and then became weeks, as the asuras's king and master demanded ever more powerful forms, even as his followers captured innocents and enemy gangs alike, feeding them to the asuras's ring.

I sensed the conflict in the creature as I forced it to leap ahead, not interested in seeing everything the fucking thing wanted to show me, as I shoved images of the incoming asuras at it.

Shock reverberated through it, then horror.

It had sent out a transmission, sharing its discovery, how the local humans could be wiped, and forced to serve, offering the information up to others it could sense out there.

It was something it didn't want to do, not after making "a friend," but it shared the information so that others of its kind could form their own independent judgment, as they always had.

One of the surprisingly few responses it received was that another had discovered this as well, but that the newly formed asuras "imitations" could then be drained of energy, fueling the resurgence of the creator.

Many of the others had responded to this—some in horror, others in curiosity. One, close by, had appeared pleased by the outcome, and the asura had managed to convince its king to send half their forces to the east, to meet the other asura, to try to convince it to join with them.

The king had presumably wanted to enslave it as well, and had agreed. This asura had intended to beg for its help, to kill its king and be free again, but now…

I pushed the demands the new asuras had made at this one, and I sensed the horror, and the fear in it, as it realized that it might have, in truth, created a monster. Then came the dawning horror as it compared equations—that I could barely follow the smallest part of—to their natural conclusion.

Namely, that if the enemy queen harvested enough life essence, it could return to space and be free, and more powerful. It could do that by harvesting humans, or, it could harvest three other queen asuras. I questioned it about the hospital and got a vague burst of data and images, including the ship, dumped in one corner in the terror of the fight.

The king had ridden it to the hospital, the advanced forces slaughtering their defenders, and they'd paused then, rebuilding in preparation for an assault on the park. They'd never understood that the dungeon existed. Which, in one way, was a relief. In another…?

This fucking sucked.

I stared at the asuras, feeling its fear, its confusion, and I mentally added the last bits to the mix, namely the asuras that had given me the quest to save the queen.

The world changed for it then, as it recognized—somehow—the damn robot asuras thingy I'd met, and that had saved me from drowning in that pool as the scientist. There was a long pause, and then the queen sent a barrage of images, questions and more. I was overwhelmed, trying to make sense of it, until the massive wave was gradually reduced to a manageable level, that in turn was boiled down to a single question: Why?

I shared our situation, as much as I could, showing the local area, the influx of creatures, how the dungeon was a part of me, and I the dungeon. I made it very, very fucking clear that if it was to try to take the dungeon from me, I'd kill it, and I'd kill the dungeon. That there was no situation where the dungeon could survive without me.

It accepted that, or appeared to, and I moved on, showing it images of the area, showing it peace and places it could just *be*. Areas where it could grow and the possibilities of an alliance. A future where we made devices that got it back into space, where it was kept safe from the rogue humans, the beast, and any asuras that might try to consume it.

The sense of relief, and of hope, was tangible, and so I moved on quickly, showing it the body that was being brought down even now. Battered, broken, and heavily armed.

I had a nasty suspicion that I wasn't going to be able to replicate the hydraulic thrower, as we just weren't there yet with technologies, or realistically even close. But I had hope.

More to the point, even if I couldn't make them, this fucker *could*. I spiraled through ideas, alternating one for the other, of the danger in the area, and the wonders of our protection, until finally it was done.

A consensus was reached, even as the asuras took the second floor, the last of the kobolds on there being beaten down and killed.

"Matt!" Kelly sent to me. "We're running out of time…"

"I know," I whispered, staring at the asuras, seeing a million possibilities as it ran through them, offering up alternatives, until we struck the most basic bargain of all.

We'd ally until the rival queen was dead. That was it. At that point, we'd sit and negotiate the next step. But until then, it was a case of either fighting together and we bathed our little alliance in the soul energy of the asuras, or we were fucked.

Congratulations! You have completed a Quest:

Checkmate!

The asuras queen has been revealed as only one of a collective, but she has agreed to form a short-term, mutually beneficial alliance with you. You have completed the first stage of this quest and receive the following bonuses:

- +1 to top three Attributes
- +1 Class Skill point to allocate
- 10,000 XP

You have received a new Quest!

Quest!

Checkmate! (II)

Upon forming a basic alliance with an asuras queen, you have become aware of just who and what they are. They could assist you mightily, or be a terrible scourge upon the face of your planet. Only your actions will decide this.

Form a more permanent alliance with the asuras queen to complete this quest and receive the following bonuses:

- +3 to top three Attributes
- +1 Class Skill points to allocate
- Additional forces
- 10,000 XP

Accept?

Yes/No…

I accepted the quest, and the new quest rewards, of course. Hell, I desperately needed any kind of edge I could get down here. This was literally a lifeline. But before I could make any headway with them, I had to deal with the creature before me, and more to the point, the one that Beta was bringing over to me.

Beta collapsed next to where I sat. The other three kobolds that had carried me and the asuras down here had been standing randomly around the room, waiting on orders. At the sight of her, they raced to her side, two taking the burden from her and her companion, and one helping her to my side.

I hesitated, looking down at Beta, seeing how much smaller she was than the others—the scars, the exhaustion, and the sheer physical limitations she had over the "new and improved" variants—and I reached out.

"Thank you, Beta," I whispered, laying a hand on her shoulder, getting a tired half grin from her.

I could never absorb her into the dungeon, I knew. It'd be like absorbing Markus or Aly. She wasn't just one of my creatures; she was my friend. I settled back, sending a quick series of images to the asuras that ended in "Wait your fucking turn" before I began permeating the body before me, having sensed her reaching out to the body and trying to claim it.

Unlike most of the structures I'd absorbed into the dungeon over the last few months, this wasn't human technology, not entirely.

Yeah, sections of it were. The grasping arm was based off the standard hydraulic manipulation arm that was used in heavy manufacturing across hundreds of industrial sites in the area. The legs were variations on that. The back of the thing was essentially a dozen small pneumatic pressure pumps, each of which worked independently to pump the launcher's reservoir to a high enough level.

Where the tanks we'd faced locally used a form of a rail gun, this, the product of the second asura, was built around high-pressure containment and light but strong darts.

I could definitely see uses for that.

The body literally held the asuras, and this one didn't have a containment cube built into it, the asuras being a wiped soul that was bound instead to its queen.

The right arm was the launcher, and the storage device for the darts, with the head being a seat of visual and targeting systems. All in all, it was a hell of a creation, but it was something that had been made by dozens of construction devices working at speed.

It was essentially a robot soldier, built by the lowest bidder. The plates were rough, the pressure tanks were barely sealed—all of it was a rush job, and I couldn't help but grin.

I could make better than this. And so could the asura that was allying with us. I absorbed the design entirely, feeling it being accepted by the dungeon, and wincing as so goddamn much of it was declared off-limits.

That was fine, though, because what wasn't was the *frame*.

I sensed Aly appearing, the sudden sharp focus of her as she mentally tore into the design, ripping sections free and examining them, as I began to rebuild the frame, using the designs we'd seen so far.

I took the body first, and I made it four-legged, each leg ending in a circular, stumpy foot. Each leg folded down from a central trunk, one that was both thick with armor and had a collection of four arms. I made the head simple and with glass discs for eyes, rotatable on an independent disc, enabling it to look in all directions.

Then I clad it in heavy iron plates, making the fucker armored to an almost insane degree. All in all, it was a fucking mess. Seriously, it was—horrific, almost; more of a sculpture than a robot, considering that there wasn't, for example, a power source, nor any control methods.

That was because unlike a traditional robot, this thing was its own power core, it provided its own direction, and it was essentially a housing for a soul that knew far more than I ever would.

The asuras itself could form the required linkages and more. It could power and control the body that I'd created, and I damn well knew that this was the first version only.

I checked it over, attempting to add the pressurized dart throwers and failing totally, before checking out the cost.

Twelve thousand and forty-seven mana.

We had…fourteen thousand and change, which was great, except…we needed to defend the dungeon still. We needed to create defenders, and we needed to gift this fucker with spare parts to make whatever weapons it was going to need.

I hesitated, but in the end, it was a Hail Mary, a blind pass that you threw on instinct, damn well hoping that it'd pay off, because if it didn't, you were fucked.

It was also a last-ditch thing. If everything went tits up, I could have any survivors here hide behind this fucker, and while the queens fought each other, hopefully my people could escape.

If I left her as just a cube? We had no backup plan.

Realistically, it was the same cost as five more kobolds, and that wasn't enough to turn the tide. This might be.

I started the printing process, then reached out to the asuras, laying my hand on the cracked and still leaking containment cube, well aware that the creature was weak, terrified, and barely an ally at all.

"It's up to you now. You can fight alongside us, or you can hide here and die when your other 'one' comes looking for you." That was all I could say, realistically, and I forced myself to my feet, looking over the mana I had available.

"Where are we with the mana count?" I asked the ether around me, feeling Kelly and Aly there, with the impression of others standing back, watching, as I half slid into the dungeon sense, seeing the last two groups of kobolds on the third floor.

They were two teams of four, or they had been. Now it was a team of two and four, with the asuras steadily marching down, beating the injured pair back.

"We've got literally everyone we can absorbing," Aly said. "We're working as hard as we can, but even with that, we're barely clearing five hundred a minute…"

"That's pretty good," I muttered.

"It is, or it would be, but we're down to a skeleton force outside the dungeon. Most of them were killed, and those still alive are using our control points as well. But they're too far outside the dungeon's range to absorb or kill.

"We need to replace our forces, as well as continue making the traps, the standard maintenance, and…"

"Give me a hundred of that mana," I said musingly. "A hundred per minute, and you use the rest on everything else. I'll make a small team in here, and we'll hold the line, while you get ready out there."

"That still means that it's twenty-five minutes for each kobold for you," Kelly pointed out.

"Then I can't use the kobolds," I said. "They're excellent warriors, but at that cost, it's too high. It's time we played strategic, rather than blunt force."

"We've tried it…the weaker creatures just get slaughtered," Kelly said, and I nodded.

"How long until they get down here?"

"Honestly?" Aly replied, running the numbers. "If we give up on summoning more kobolds, and put everything we have currently into traps, maybe an hour? We'd need to do things like create more narrow choke points and spear traps, though…"

"Cost?"

"Maybe half of the mana we'd generate in that time, if we're getting a hundred a minute," a new voice said, as Leighton nervously joined the chat. "I could form embedded posts that lead up and down through the ceiling. It'd force them to weave around them, and add in things like collapsing sections of the roof, spear traps and so on. It'd kill a handful and break a lot more, but I couldn't stop them entirely."

"Then do it, and thank you," I said, nodding absently as the sense of his personality appeared, then sank away again.

"How much mana do you want to dedicate to the asuras queen for spare parts?" Aly asked.

"Fuck all," I said. "We give her the cost of that frame and that's it. She can help if she wants more. With that much random metal, she should be able to form a damn weapon of some kind or something at the very least, but as all we've got from her is a 'maybe' so far? She gets nothing else until she helps."

"Okay, so what do we do with the rest?" Kelly asked. "This dungeon still generates a lot more than that an hour with the converters added in and the conduits."

"Don't you need it?" I asked, thinking quickly. The mana that the dungeon developed was a good point, and it was over three thousand an hour at this point.

"Well, yeah, but I don't want to leave you in there with nothing," Aly admitted. "We could summon less forces, or not give them weapons…"

"And they'd be fuck all use, realistically, because we'd be throwing naked, unarmed kobolds at tanks. Dammit."

"Yeah…"

"Keep the rest. Just give me the hundred absorbed mana to work with," I said. "I can do a lot with that."

"If you're only taking half of that mana, that's fifty mana a minute, which sounds like an insane amount, but it's only one thousand, five hundred mana…"

"And there's nearly two thousand mana in the tank to start with," I said. "How many asuras?" I blinked as a new notification flared to life before me.

You have received a new Quest!

Defend the Dungeon! (4)
The land around the dungeon has grown paradoxically more peaceful, and more terrifying, as new forces move into the area. Where, previously, your bodies were at risk of damnation, now too is your soul, and that of all sapient creatures.

Current Enemy Count:
- Asuras termination drone (ATD): 107/107
- Asuras mobile extermination platform (AMEP): 12/12
- Asuras Guardian: 2/2
- Asuras Red Queen: 1/1

Destroy the enemy asuras, and secure the local area to receive the following bonuses:
- +5 to top three Attributes
- +1 Spell
- +2 Class Skill Points
- 10,000 XP

Well, that made things a little simpler, I guessed, reading the details over, and noting the lack of an accept option. Clearly the fact that it was win or fuckin' die was clear to the system as well.

"Give me a little time." I deliberately stepped out of the half dungeon sense to be alone with my thoughts for a bit.

It was a bit of a ball ache that it was only ten thousand experience for the quest, but…I paused, and quickly pulled up the notifications from the fight earlier, grinning when I saw the details waiting for me.

Congratulations!

You have killed the following:
- 7x Gang members, various levels, 804 XP

Total XP earned: 804 XP

A summoned demon under your command killed the following:
- 17x Gang members, various levels, 2,001 XP
- 11x Caged Asuras, various levels, 1,019 XP

As the minion was directly summoned by you for this express purpose, you received 25% of all XP they earned.

Total demon XP earned: 3,020 XP

A party under your command killed the following:
- 5x Gang members, various levels, 697 XP
- 13x Caged Asuras, various levels, 1,317 XP

Total Party XP earned: 2,014 XP

As party leader, you receive 25% of all XP earned.
Total XP awarded 804+(3,020x0.25=755)+(2,014x0.25=503.5) = 2,062 XP
Partial XP is lost to the ether.

Current XP to next level stands at 32,848/35,000

The three points that were allocated automatically were to my Intelligence, probably from such heavy use of my mana, my Constitution, from such insane damage I'd done to myself most likely, and yeah, no surprise there…my Luck.

I sure as shit wasn't going to complain, though, considering that boosted me from two thousand, four hundred, and fifty mana, all the way to three thousand, one hundred, and twenty.

God, I loved the multipliers that landed each time I passed ten points invested in an area, even if the feeling of my grey matter being "tweaked" did feel like I had fire ants playing in my brain for a few seconds.

You have gained additional Stat Points in the following areas through constant effort.
- +1 Agility
- +1 Constitution
- +1 Endurance
- +1 Perception

Continue to work hard to increase these or other stats…

That was nice as well, seeing that my stats were steadily increasing through the blatant self-destructive bloody stupidity I was engaged in most days.

I pulled up my stat sheets, reading over the details quickly, after dismissing the minor details about the increases in my physical skills.

Name: Matt, First Lord of the Storm				
Host Powers: 1 (Enhanced Regeneration)				
Species: Thunderstorm			**Bonus:** None	
Level: 24			**Progress to next level:** 32,848/35,000	

Stat	Current Points	Description	Effect	Progress to Next Level
Agility	34	Governs dodge and movement	Heightened chance to dodge attacks 68%+20%= 88%	27/100
Charisma	26	Governs likely success to charm, seduce, or threaten	35% more likely to succeed in events that require seduction, persuasion, or threats (10%+ (16x2) = 35)	69/100
Constitution	34	Governs Health and Health Regeneration	HP: 34x40 = 1360	74/100
Dexterity	37	Governs ability with weapons and crafting	+37% Increased chance of improved result +13 to melee damage	72/100
Endurance	36	Governs Stamina and Stamina Regeneration	Stamina: 36x40 = 1,440	4/100
Intelligence	52	Governs base manapool, standard intellectual capacity	Mana: 52x60=3120	98/100
Luck	38	Governs overall chance of bonuses and critical hits	+56% increased chance of positive outcome	98/100
Perception	31	Governs ranged damage and chance to spot hidden items/traps	+21 to all ranged attacks	14/100
Strength	32	Governs damage with melee weapons and carrying capacity	+44 to all damage with Melee weapons	88/100
Wisdom	46	Governs mana regeneration	115 mana regenerated per hour	91/100

I had a hell of a mana capacity now, even though it was practically empty. Even with the hour that we had, or thereabouts, between now and the asuras arriving on this floor, the very best I could hope for was to gain roughly a hundred or so mana on top of the wonderful seventeen I had currently.

The multiple mana converters around the building couldn't even be tapped into right now because the bastard asuras held the upper floors of the dungeon, so I couldn't filter a connection through from them to me directly.

That left me with what I could regenerate naturally, and that was a single spell, realistically, or two Storm-Strikes.

Magic wasn't going to be the deciding factor for this fight, not straightaway anyway. If we could reclaim the floors that had been lost, though? I could filter down conduits from the converters to refill my mana and the asuras' bodies would be seriously helpful as well.

The concentrated mana that infused them was insane, and as freshly "converted" as the bodies were, the souls weren't able to flee to another the way that more established asuras seemed able to do.

That meant that reinforcements were limited on both sides, which was both a relief, and terrible, because I knew where those asuras souls were coming from.

I had a single class skill point to assign, and damn, I had to hope it'd make a difference at this stage. So I pulled up the screen and started to read.

CHAPTER FORTY

<u>**Class Skills:**</u>

Class selection: Arcane Dungeon Lord

Imbue: You may choose to give freely of your own manapool to imbue an item or creature of the Dungeon with magic. This ability can fail, and spectacularly so; however, creations of wondrous might can also be brought into being. Be wary. (Selected)

Evolution: Foresight: No longer are your creations the chance things they were…now see the true potential of a creature! (Selected)

Monster Master: No longer do the creatures of the Dungeon view you with apathy or irritation when you pass by. Now they are devoted to you! This skill ranks in levels from 0 (Interested) to 5 (Worshipful). (Current level: 0, Interested)

Evolution: Lord of All! The creatures of your Dungeon know their true master, and those who follow willingly can now receive arcane gifts that match their level of devotion!

Arcane Breeder: Some Dungeon Lords wish for only the purest strains to survive, while others enjoy the randomness of evolution…select the genes you wish to see and promote them!

Artificer: You may gift magical artifacts to your creations, and when combined with Foresight, these creatures will gain significant bonuses to magical item creation and replication. This skill ranks in levels from 0 (Curiosity) to 5 (Legendary). (Current level: 0, Curiosity)

Arcane Pets: Your sentient Dungeon inhabitants can gather and breed pets, but where before there was an element of random chance, now you may lure those you wish into the range of your tamers. This skill ranks in levels from 0 (Magical) to 5 (Legendary Creatures).

Insatiable Curiosity: Random Sentient Dungeon Creatures will now have the chance to be spawned with an Insatiable Curiosity. These creatures can be put to work in your Research Nodes to increase Research by a staggering degree. This skill ranks in levels from 0 (Incompetent) to 5 (Genius). (Current level: 2, Interested)

Evolution: Magical Researcher! Before, your researchers were generalists, plodding along at their task, be that a better toilet seat or a converter; now they stand a chance at developing true magical gifts, and at learning the secrets of creation! This skill ranks in levels from 0 (Novice) to 5 (Master). (Current level: 1, Apprentice)

Manafield: Your Dungeon's Manafield will now passively expand at 10% more than the previous rate, enabling greater growth in a shorter period of time. This skill ranks in levels from 0 (Restricted) to 5 (Expansive). (Current Level: 1, Limited)

Evolution: Tides of Mana! All life creates mana, as do elemental interactions. Now through the wonders of gravitational magic, you can start to draw more mana into the area of your Dungeon. This skill ranks in levels from 0 (Gentle) to 5 (Vortex). (Current Level: 1, Steady)

Reach Out and Touch Me: Your Dungeon is no longer only controllable when you are within its own environs. Now you can interact with it at increasing distances. This skill ranks in levels from 0 (Local) to 5 (Interstellar). (Current level: 0, Local)

Evolution: Gates! No longer is the Dungeon a distant creation. This skill unlocks the creation of the Gates, transportals that can be built inside the Dungeon and activated at a remote location to provide a stable link between the two points.

This skill ranks in levels from 0 (Single Gate) to 5 (Unlimited). (Current level: 0, Single Gate)

I read over it again and again, thinking fast. Imbue was great—yeah, seriously it was—but I had it already, and its evolution, Foresight.

Monster Master was a bit of a weird one. After all, apart from the orcs, my creations had always gotten on well with me, and I'd not felt any need to summon things that were mental and overly aggressive beyond that. Its evolution, Lord of All, granted those who followed my lead willingly an arcane gift, which was interesting, but…it wasn't exactly an obvious winning ability right there.

Moving on, Arcane Breeder was next, allowing me to basically play with the genes of my various creatures, have them breed and promote certain lines. Okay, again, not really a winner for right now. I already had kobolds, and they were kinda my go-to species now, so moving swiftly on!

Artificer was good, or I thought so, though we'd really not made the most of it yet, basically because I'd had too little time to make much with it, having spent so much time focusing on the actual development of the settlement over the crafting side. That would have to change—and change massively, I swore to myself.

Arcane Pets? Might be useful, might be giant talking spiders. Either way, not really something I could pull out and kill the asuras with. Moving on…

Insatiable Curiosity and Magical Researcher: both insanely useful to the dungeon, and fuck all use to the current situation. Nope.

Manafield…extra mana flowing in would increase the mana that we were drawing, admittedly, and that would be amazing. There were even the various collectors and converters scattered around the building here. If I could reach them? That'd be great as well. *Buuuut…*

Not really a useful thing here, unless the damn mana could wash them away? *Nope. Be realistic, Matt.* That was fuck all use right now.

Reach Out and Touch Me, and its evolution, the Gates. Yes, both massively powerful and useful, as well as fuck all use right now. After all, firstly there wasn't a gate built yet, I'd have to build it, and we didn't have the mana. Secondly, anywhere I ran to, although it could be awesome to get out of here, I didn't know for sure the gate could be closed and locked down enough that a creature that was literally sentient light and energy couldn't fix itself to pass through.

Nope.

Best *not* to create a link from here directly to the heart of my dungeon.

I hesitated, and tried not to panic, not visibly anyway. I'd read through all my options, and there was nothing! No weird and wonderful, sneaky as fuck method that would enable me to pull a last-minute victory.

Hell, almost none of the options were any help! I had literally a few thousand mana, and fuck all I could do with it, beyond summon a load of low-level creatures and bum-rush the enemy, hoping for the best!

I stood frozen, reading and rereading the list of options, moving from one to another, before finally coming back to the one that felt like it might offer the tiniest bit of hope.

Lord of All was a weird one.

The description was as unhelpfully vague, as they always were:

> *Evolution: Lord of All!* The creatures of your Dungeon know their true master, and those who follow willingly can now receive arcane gifts that match their level of devotion!

But that last line tugged at my mind, and I stared at it for long seconds, glancing between it and the exhausted form of Beta on the floor. *Could it really be that simple?*

I had fuck all realistic alternatives, so I took it, approving it and looking around hopefully, waiting to see…I don't know what, really. A massive ray of energy from the heavens that transformed the exhausted kobold into a fucking dragon or something.

After a few seconds, I sighed, shaking my head, and banished the screens and the system, viewing it as a wasted class skill point, and that I was going to have to do this the old-fashioned way and with…

"My fucking hammer!" I snarled, glancing down at the empty hip loop. I'd given it to Chris to fight the asuras in the hardware shop.

The only saving grace for these hammers was that they were cheap, but I was determined at that point that as soon as I had some goddamn spare mana, and a little quality time, I was going to create a really sexy hammer, one that I'd imbue with magic. And I'd craft a goddamn hook or something on it!

Maybe a loop for my wrist, and I'd damn well carry it everywhere!

I summoned a second one, then another sword, settling that across my back, unsure what had happened to the last one I had, and then I moved out, gesturing to the kobolds to follow me…when I realized that Beta was *still* asleep.

It was one thing to sleep whenever you got the chance—some of my friends who served claimed to be able to sleep absolutely anywhere, and I could believe it. But now?

I crouched, looking Beta over. She shivered slightly. Exhaustion maybe? She'd been fighting for a while, and she and another kobold had carried an insanely heavy robot all the way down here, running after fighting for hours.

I had to assume that had pulled some muscles, but…I shook my head. Beta was awesome, but we had at least half an hour, closer to a full hour, I guessed, before these dicks would be past the traps.

If she was that exhausted, better to let her rest. And considering we'd not managed to come up with any really sneaky plans…might as well go and make the most of the traps that were narrowing the playing field.

I summoned a new helmet, settling it into place and sighing—I instantly felt a little safer—followed by a new shield. The kobolds looked at me, waiting, and I summoned them shields and hammers as well.

Four of them, with the hammers I preferred and the large tower shields, took a thousand mana. My hammer, sword, and shield added to the list as well, and we were down to two thousand mana already.

I was halfway to the next level, when Kelly stepped into a kobold near me, reaching out and laying one hand on my arm. I twisted, confused, and saw the kobold standing there. I hesitated, then leaned against the wall and slid into the dungeon sense.

"Sorry," I said, sending a smile to her as she slid free as well. "I got a little focused on what's coming."

"I know," Kelly said with a similar image of a smile. "But we're not done, remember. Okay, we've run the numbers, and between those we've managed to summon so far, the mages and what we should earn in the next hour, we'll get nearly twenty kobolds."

"How many mages?" I asked, thinking fast.

"Five. Three cryomancers and two heliomancers—" She broke off at the sense of confusion I emanated at "heliomancer" and sent a barrage of images to me.

Essentially, they were kobolds that harnessed the power of the sun. They could create insanely powerful light and heat attacks, but only for a matter of seconds, before they were utterly exhausted.

"They sound useful, but squishy," I said, and she agreed.

"Think real glass cannons. Insanely powerful, but one-hit wonders. If they miss? They're dead," she clarified.

"Anything else?"

"Beyond our personal team?" she asked. "Ramnik and the others are getting ready, but realistically, we're looking at Dante, Ramnik, Simon the terramancer, Dave the luxomancer, and Yvonne the umbramancer to fight with her, and the fucker's queen won't be easy to take down."

"No." I shook my head. "They'll be a bastard to face all right, but okay, I know you buggers. Is there a plan, besides run at them and fight everything?"

"Yes…and no," Kelly said after a few seconds.

"Okay, that's not ominous or anything, honest." I smiled despite myself.

"Matt, what are you good at?" Kelly asked, and I couldn't help but give a stupid answer.

"Well, you knew you loved me the first time I winked at you and licked my eyebrows?" I tried, and she sent a phantom clip across the ear. "Ow…"

"Matt, seriously, the one thing you do better than anyone else, better even than Mike, is annoy the shit out of people."

"Thank you, I think," I said after a few seconds.

"Seriously, the queen is fixated on you, massively so. She wants to kill the other queen…"

"The Green," I said absently.

"What?" Kelly asked, totally derailed.

"The system named the one out there, the enemy queen, the Red Queen, so it just makes it easier," I explained. "If we've got the Red and the Green, we know which we mean."

"Whatever," Kelly growled. "So, the Red is after the Green, and after you. For now, you're both in there, and she's desperate to get to you. She's fixated, with her guards standing on either side of her. Griffiths thinks that with some of the ammunition that Chris brought back, he can fully rearm his team. They should be able to take one of the guards down and leave the mages to take out the second guard and the other queen."

"Chris made it back with ammo?" I asked, getting a sense of annoyance at me interrupting, but it was important.

"Yeah, Patrick was injured. He left him hidden and took out a handful of idiots on the way back, taking their ammo as he went, then ran straight for the dungeon when he saw the queen outside here. So, back to the plan.

"Ramnik thinks Wrath of the Heavens will do a load of damage to them, and the others will do a fair bit as well. But the issue is getting in close enough to actually use those spells…"

"So you want me to play redshirt?" I asked. "You want me to keep her attention, fight her creatures in the dungeon, while you all get into position, then you get in close with the mages and hammer her, then the Green Queen and I come out and finish the job?"

"The Green Queen won't be able to get out unless you tear down all the choke points as you leave, so best to keep her inside…a last-ditch guardian for us maybe? Just keep the Red's attention. We'll hit the three of them at once with the heavy spells, then send in the kobolds. They'll take out the tanks and as many of the big ones as possible, while…"

"While I clear the dungeon." I nodded. "It makes sense…I clear each floor as I go, basically last as long as possible, and you absorb the various dead as I clear each floor."

"And the mana that we get gives us reinforcements."

"It makes sense, but what about Mike?" Instantly, I felt the drop in mood from her. "He…he's dead?"

"No!" she snapped. "No…I don't think so."

"He's not returned?"

"No," she said. "No sign of him or his team, and it scares me, because the asuras he was following had to go somewhere. And surely when the queen got into trouble, they'd come running? If they caught him out in the open, or if they come back at the wrong time…"

"They could massively fuck us up," I agreed. "They were sent to make contact with this asuras, though, so I have to think that for this fucker to be here, they had to have met up?"

"There's some damage on the bigger ones, but not much. They might have fought, but until we know for sure, they're still out there."

I hesitated, then searched consciously for Jack, feeling him distantly, badly damaged and limping toward us. He couldn't go any faster, I knew, and I spoke quickly, letting her know.

"Well…if he's alive, then they might be, right?" she whispered, and I forced a mental smile, projecting as much comfort as I could.

"He's alive, so they will be. He'd not give up protecting them."

"I know…"

"Okay, so just to be clear, I'm stuck in a hole in the ground, with limited support, a powerful enemy trying to dig me out, and I've got to basically fight them all as long as I can, making it interesting enough to keep her attention, while you fuckers get into place. Did I miss anything?" I asked, trying to joke about it all.

"No, that covers it, dear." Kelly forced herself to reply in a light tone, understanding that we could do nothing for Mike and the others yet. Then she dropped the attempt and spoke seriously. "Matt, I don't care what the dungeon thinks. If things are going bad, you need to run. If the dungeon ends up kicking us out, at least we'll be together…I love you."

"I love you, too. And don't worry, I'll be fine."

"Matt…"

"I need to go, Kelly. I'm sorry," I said, as a scream echoed down from above, the last of the kobolds on the third floor dying as I checked. I felt the frantic work of Leighton as he tried to get as much done before the attackers could reach the beginning of the fourth floor, and I sighed, feeling Kelly withdraw.

We had two thousand mana—well, two thousand and change—and that would be enough for a small force, or…

I grinned as I went to one knee for stability as a new thought occurred to me. I took a deep breath, sliding into the dungeon sense more fully. I could feel it, the beating heart of the dungeon off to my right, a few miles distant, and all around me—the floor directly above—and past that, the building, growing less and less responsive as more of it was captured by the invaders.

I'd not been idle these months. I'd made a shitload of converters. Although most people assumed they were just there to feed the dungeon mana, as well as the more cynical ones thinking that they were there to feed *me* directly, that was only partly true.

The converters had another brilliant function, and that was to convert and store *specialized* forms of mana…

I reached into the dungeon system, pulling up a screen I'd seen had been made available when it was completed, but I'd had no reason to examine until now.

Congratulations!

Basic Lesser Ghast has been upgraded to Common Lesser Ghast!

The Lesser Ghast is often seen as a misnomer, considering the reality of the breed. Whereas most "monsters" are simply scared or confused members of races other than the one observing and identifying—example, goblins—certain species are quite rightly defined as monsters through their excessive bloodlust and violent natures.

The Common variant improves on the Basic in many ways. Primarily, however, the muscle mass, enhanced invisibility, and stamina are those details most remarked upon…

By those who survive long enough to notice them.

Optional Research Project Unlocked!

Uncommon Lesser Gh—

I dismissed the research project, no time for that shit right now, and focused on the ghasts themselves.

The original basic variant had been freaky as fuck. Some innate ability they possessed made them invisible when they hunted. They were blind, but had sharp bone spurs for arms, a spiked tail, and were basically nightmare fuel.

The common variant took that fucking horrific base, and added a few extra refinements, namely making them a third bigger overall. The tail became even more lethal-looking and the body developed a layer of thicker armoring to the endoskeleton, like how some dinosaurs had developed massive plates of bone, but obviously a fuckload smaller and internal.

It was a big jump in lethality, even if it was of limited use against the asuras.

The last change, though, was the mouth. It was considerably bigger and wider, looking more like something that should be hunting in the depths of the ocean than fucking land animals, but it certainly looked impressive. More to the point, the price increase to summon it hadn't changed *that* much, and I smiled as I pulled up the dungeon description.

Monster: Ghasts, or in this case a Lesser (Common) Ghast, is a mana-warped creature that has evolved throughout the cosmos when certain minor species have evolved through an excess of mana and systemic violence.

The resulting creature is both savage and often unpredictable in its hunting patterns. Yet, when a Ghast is raised by a Dungeon, it can result in an excellent, if simple, scout and ambush predator.

Cost: Lesser Ghasts spawn individually for 400 Pure Mana, or 80 Shadow Mana each. Maintenance is 40 Mana points per day, per individual, and requires 7 points of control.

I nodded in satisfaction. What everyone, myself included until just now, had forgotten was that the various forms of mana could be created through the dungeon. Shadow mana, for some fucking reason I had no clue about, consisted of multiple second-level versions of mana, namely Storm, Nature, and Clay.

I had Storm and Nature in abundance—twenty-five converters of the Nature ones—and although I only had two Lightning and two Storm, I also had fifteen Water.

I stopped, then switched the way I was looking at this, moving back to basics. I needed a fuckload of *shadow*. Each form of mana could be converted into another at a two-for-one rate if they were one tier up—so Lightning was an elemental mix of Fire and Air, and could be created by mixing them together—or a four-to-one rate if it was more than one level. So if I used pure mana, it would need to become Air and Water; then the Air and Water needed to be converted to Storm.

The result was that if I wanted to create one goddamn point of shadow, I needed eight pure mana.

That was fine, though, because I had the various forms of mana I needed stored in each of the converters, waiting to be called upon.

I worked quickly, sorting through the mana that was stored in the converted form. I had eighteen Air converters—that was one thousand, eight hundred Air mana right there, as each held a hundred—and I made sure to draw from the converters at the dungeon, rather than locally where possible. Just in case.

Water, on the other hand, only had fifteen hundred, and Earth at nine hundred. I quickly ran the numbers and realized that if I took seven hundred and fifty hundred Earth, and seven hundred and fifty water, and converted them to Clay, that earned me seven hundred and fifty Clay. Great.

That left me with seven hundred and fifty Water, and taking another seven hundred and fifty Air, that gave me a total of seven hundred and fifty Storm, when combined.

Nature, thanks to their generators, were already at twenty-five hundred. They needed to be in alignment, apparently, so I took seven hundred and fifty of that, then combined it with the others, folding them in through the dungeon.

For a second, I felt a resistance, as if I wasn't supposed to be doing this, as if the physical converters were needed, but the more I worked at it, the clearer it became.

Mana was mana. It converted naturally; yes, it became more and more corrupt as it went, but that wasn't the point. It happened naturally, literally combining in the Air and Water, and so on.

For a second more, the dungeon fought me, feeling not so much that I couldn't do this, but that I wasn't *supposed* to do it, and that I was adding stress to a system that was already straining. Well, fuck that. The choice was this worked, or we died.

The converters did it automatically for us, and we'd been using them to influence the area, to gather mana, and to help us meditate. All of that was true, but they also stored their converted form of mana, ready to use.

Until now, I'd been draining them occasionally, and that was it.

I'd only been using half the capacity of the system until now, that was all.

The converters did the change automatically, drawing the mana in and shifting it over, but the dungeon changed it to whatever it needed, whenever it needed it.

Therefore, so could I.

Seven hundred and fifty of each of the three types of mana combined at my direction, then evolved. As soon as the shadow mana was created, a full one thousand, one hundred and fifty points, I felt a seismic shift in my internal mana.

I'd passed a level in my understanding of the use and nature of mana, and the system damn well accepted that.

Congratulations!

Through careful study and manipulation, both of internal structures and through the alignment of your soul, you have increased your understanding of your own mana, mana in general, and the secrets of its manipulation. Your evolution has begun again.

Continue to study to raise this affinity further!

Your current evolutionary position is: Thunderstorm: 25%

Increase your capacity to reach the next level of Evolution.

7% -> 25%...

That was a hell of a relief, and I determined I'd work on that as soon as this shit was over. But for now? I needed to get to work with what I had.

I got a sudden feeling of satisfaction, and a self-congratulatory smugness, and I just fucking knew that bastard cat had sensed it as well. Fuck knew where he was, probably laid on a rooftop somewhere, torturing something fluffy to death.

Fucking furry shit-biscuit.

The blending of the mana had worked, though, and I couldn't help a feral grin as I opened my eyes again, staring forward.

I was going to keep most of the two thousand mana we had, apart from a few more summons from it. They cost fifteen mana each, and each of the four goblin mages that appeared were typical of their pathetic kind.

Even without their signature Disgust spell active, I wanted to punt the little fuckers, having no attachment at all to them now that Alfredo, the mage I'd had survive for a while, was dead. The way that the highly evolved kobolds stared at them with contempt made their feelings clear as well.

I sent the goblins off to one side, then took a deep breath, wishing I could pull the mana to me this easily. I spent most of the freshly summoned shadow mana, summoning fourteen of the new common-ranked lesser ghasts.

They appeared, one after the other. And fuck me, seeing a gang of them standing there, even knowing that they were my dungeon creatures, and that they were waiting for my orders—fuck, they made my asshole pucker.

Last of all, and just because I was a bastard, I summoned five more shields, heavy slabs of steel covered in rubber that Aly had clearly designed as a counter to the dart throwers…and then an orc to carry the fuckers. Complete with a suction cup dildo-of-war.

"Well, let's go fuck the Red Queen," I said, in possibly the least respectful reference to a queen since Cersei was discussed on a beach as a spoil of war.

CHAPTER FORTY-ONE

The passage from the fifth floor to the fourth wasn't that far, and we took the stairs two at a time, running up them. I used the time to compress my findings on the conversion process down to a manageable level and sent them to Kelly, finding I only staggered a little as I raced up the stairs doing it.

I'd not told them of my plan before for two very valid reasons. First and foremost, I thought it *might* work, and I didn't want to look like an idiot if it didn't.

Secondly, although it had worked, and I had some reinforcements that were going to be a hell of a surprise to the asuras, the first few seconds of the fight were going to be risky as hell, and I knew the others would try to talk me out of it.

The asuras were split into three groups now, each of thirty humanoids, with ten kept back up on the first floor along with the tanks. I didn't know whether it was a planned thing, like they'd kept them that way just in case one of the teams were wiped out, or whether they were worried about traps, or that it was just one of those weird coincidences like when you'd just finished at the gym, and you were wearing good clothes that fit and you felt damn good, and looked it…and you saw nobody.

And the next day, when you looked like shit, weren't buffed from the gym, and were scruffy, and then and only then would you bump into your ex or that really hot girl you'd had your eyes on.

That was the way the universe used to work.

Now, instead, it meant that every time I started to think that maybe, just maybe I was making progress, some nightmare asshole creature from the Black Lagoon rocked up and wanted to borrow a cup of sugar or eat my face.

Life was funny like that.

I ran, supposedly at the head of the little contingent, racing up the steps two and three at a time. The rough rock walls blurred as I passed them; the twinkling lights that lit the dungeon passed like streetlights used to when driving at night.

Behind me, the kobolds ran, smooth and steady, their shields and hammers held tight as the four kept pace with me. Behind them came the four goblins, already panting and miserable, staggering as they tried to keep up, and behind them, struggling with the weight of the shields—and with his dildo stuck to his forehead by me for shits and giggles—came the orc, huffing and puffing, glaring around at everyone.

That was all that almost anyone would have seen, looking at us with the Mk1 standard-issue eyeball.

What they'd not have seen was the eight ghasts running ahead of me, nor the six behind the orc, keeping us boxed in and safe.

Beta was flat out still, which was concerning, as was the fact that I'd only found her in the dungeon so far. Stumpy, Starr, Dran, and whoever the final member of the team had been were possibly still out there somewhere. Or that was what I was telling myself.

The reason we were pushing hard was clear, though, as I shouted at the others to run faster.

Basically, on the fourth floor, thanks in part to the badly needed traps and narrowing of the corridors and so on, I'd only found a single room that would actually suit my plan. And if we didn't get to it and damn soon?

We'd be fucked.

The team I had could make the most of that room with the specific skill sets we had. If we missed it, though, and the enemy made it there first? We'd be reduced to fighting a slow battle of attrition.

The three squads of thirty they had were spread out—again, I assumed deliberately. But if we tried for a battle of attrition, I had no doubt they'd get their reinforcements here before I could kill the first group off.

No, we needed to make it there, and take out the first group...*before* the second group could make it onto the floor and stop us absorbing the bodies.

With that in mind, I doubled down, stretching out and feeling the burn as muscles warmed up nicely. I mentally sent new orders to four of the following ghasts, prompting shrieks of panic as they scooped up the goblins...then put them on their shoulders.

The shrieks trailed off, to be replaced after a minute or so with one little bastard laughing his ass off and making sounds like a whip cracking.

I glanced back and saw them. All four were clear to see atop their blurred "steeds": two looked terrified, one clearly unconscious, having pissed himself and passed out, judging from the stream that dripped free of the ghast, and the last...

The last was bouncing up and down and smacking the terrifying creature on the head, clearly trying to get it to go faster.

I mentally made a note to watch that fucker, then turned back as I stumbled. The room we needed was in the center of the floor, and was laid out as a spiral galaxy. I wasn't sure whether that had been intentional or not, but it meant that it was at the very center, and the asuras were slightly closer than we were, having entered the floor ahead of us.

We raced along the tunnels and corridors, slowing each time we came to a choke point or trap, relieved that whether it was by design or by luck, the dungeon traps apparently didn't trigger for its inhabitants.

Lucky, that. It could have been embarrassing to have died by my own traps.

Ahead we slowed again, having to wind through the posts one at a time. The corridor had been narrowed by a dozen thick stone pillars going from one wall to the other in a variety of directions. The narrow space that was left between them would have been a great secondary space for a fight, but as things were right now, we damn well needed to get past, and I cursed internally at the time lost.

There were pits that failed to open—thankfully—holes that stayed covered over, and rockfalls that didn't, you know, fall. But as we closed on the central hall of the floor, I had to admit I was both a little scared and seriously impressed with this Leighton dude's invention.

A handful of minutes later, and followed by a panting, exhausted, and grey-faced orc on the verge of a coronary, we made it to the center of the floor less than a minute ahead of the asuras.

"You, that side," I ordered one of the goblins, sending them to the left, then one to the right, and ordering the remaining two to wait outside the room behind me.

Fortunately, the room was filled with low walls and occasional weird bumps and grooves, clearly having been intended as traps, or to break up charges. Although they might not be much use in the fight to come, it meant the goblins could hide out of sight.

Or collapse with exhaustion, admittedly.

The orc staggered around, handing over the heavy-duty shields to the kobolds and me, even as the first ten ghasts spread out around the room. I had five on either side of the large circular room, with four waiting outside in the corridor we'd come from, hidden and staying silent just in case.

That left the kobolds and me in the center of the room. Our usual shields laid on the floor by our feet, the heavier-duty ones at the ready, our hammers to hand…and the orc in the middle of the room between us and the closing asuras, roaring and spitting in fury as he tried to get the suction cup to let go.

There was a trick to any suction cup, which was to peel the edge up. I'd stuck random things to windows and to the tiles of my showers before, after all—not a dildo, I'd have been quick to assure Kelly if she asked—but the mental image of precisely where she'd gotten this from did keep coming back to my mind as I wondered about her old bathroom.

Clearly nobody had told orcs about this trick, and the way he was grunting and yanking on the veiny member…and occasionally roaring?

Well, I wasn't sure whether I should be traumatized, laughing my ass off, or take pity on it. But I was fairly sure from the feeling in the dungeon that the fucker was providing some much-needed comic relief for a good percentage of my citizens right then.

And possibly some memories for the wank-bank for a few as well.

The asuras finally streamed into the room, hesitating only a second, before falling in and closing ranks, throwers rising as one, and the mood changed instantly.

It was game time.

The orc barely paused, seeing the group as they entered. The humanoid-looking termination drones spread out as best they could, marching three abreast, then four, then spreading out wider and wider as they entered the room more fully. Arms rose, with the dart throwers aiming at the orc and the five of us behind him.

They didn't hesitate, firing as soon as they could lock onto the orc, who was already screaming at full volume and running at them, both his rubber and flesh dongs bouncing wildly as he went.

The first volley was almost exclusively aimed at him, and he staggered, suddenly sprouting brand-new metal "armor." He hesitated, seeming confused, then let out a wet little cough…before collapsing face-first.

The drones lifted their throwers, lining up on us, and were about to open fire, when I barked an order, standing side by side with the kobolds behind our massive shields.

Both goblins, one to our left and one to our right, halfway across the room, popped up, triggering their signature spell, Disgust. The little bastard on the left even added to the effect by rummaging around under his loincloth while staring fixedly at the drones.

The smooth, guided professionalism of the drones shattered in an instant, and I couldn't help but grin inside my helm as they split down the middle. Half of them were caught by each outward reaching field of the Disgust spell, with a handful in the middle where the overlap was strongest twisting from side to side, unsure which to target.

The thing they weren't concerned about, though, was anything beyond the goblins.

Both of the mages ducked back down as the drones opened fire, flushing their magazines in a frantic attempt to kill the horrible little fuckers, and as they focused exclusively on them, I felt Kelly.

She was reaching out and using her bonuses to guide the ghasts, spreading them out, five to a side, ready…

"Now!" I barked, breaking the shield wall and sprinting forward, discarding the much heavier shield, in favor of the lighter, normal one I scooped up from the floor.

A handful of the drones shook off the Disgust spell, reorienting on us as we broke cover, and the shields started to take hits. Spiked tips poked through the metal, as it rang as if it were under assault by a heavy metal drummer.

It lasted only a few seconds, though, before the ghasts struck. Their sharpened bone forearms wrapped around the drones from behind, mouths bit down and tore the heads free, spitting them aside, and drove the bodies to the ground, tearing and slashing as fast as they could.

The result as they appeared, seemingly from nowhere, combined with the Disgust spell that still warred with the drones' attention, and their limited intelligence, turned what could have been a slaughter of our side into a rout of theirs.

They stood and fought. Most of their magazines were already emptied to take on the goblins, so it became hand-to-hand, powerful pistons and steel fists flying, slamming into flesh and bone, crushing ribs and skulls with each blow.

Then we were there, hammers flying, and the brief rallying the drones had enjoyed was over. I slammed my shield into one of them full-on, sending it flying backward to clatter to the floor. A ghast leapt on it to finish it off, even as I lashed out to the left and right, crushing chests and smashing limbs.

There'd been thirty that marched into the room, and ten had gone down in seconds with the surprise attack by the ghasts. The counter-attack, as they tried to defend themselves, cost me four of the boney beasts. But they were already onto their next targets by that point, and mental flex was all it took to summon the remaining ghasts and goblins into the room.

The first two goblins shut off their spells, crawling from the room, their health having been drained to power the spell, while the two new goblins sprinted in. One raced around the outside to take up station behind the group, and one hid almost as soon as he entered the room, at my orders.

The one behind me triggered his spell as the first two fields died away, washing it over the survivors and dragging their attention to him. Then, as they staggered, twisting away from the fights they were already involved in, the other activated his as well.

The asuras were torn, spinning, trying to reassign priorities, as the ghasts, kobolds, and I smashed our way through them, taking them down at speed.

In seconds, it was over. The distraction the goblins had brought to the fight was enough to turn the tide on their own, but the extra four ghasts leaping in unexpectedly helped as well.

I slammed my hammer down hard on the last of them. The metal head sunk halfway into its chest as the controlling asuras burst from it in a panicked flare of light, flooding the room, even as it started to dissipate.

I kicked the corpse off my hammer, sending it clattering to the floor as I twisted the head free, and looked over my weapon, breathing fast.

It was scratched and battered—a few rounded and flattened edges where it'd taken damage—but it was fine, really. As I looked down at the corpses before me, they started to vanish in motes of light.

"Thank you!" I called out into the empty, light-laden air as the others moved to absorb what they could as soon as the enemy presence was off the floor.

I turned and jogged back to the middle of the room, where we'd started, and I collapsed down to rest, shield clattering to the floor by my side. The kobolds joined me, looking a little battered, one with a trio of scratches down his face and missing an eye, but all alive and functional.

I nodded to them, getting hisses and grins in return. I slid into the system, and found Kelly and Aly waiting for me.

"Well done!" Kelly said, sending an impression of pride and love, even as Aly sent a much more distracted message.

"Yes, very good," she said quickly. "More importantly, we've got the others breaking down the bodies. It's a nice windfall, but not enough to make a big difference overall, not with the time we have. We're at Steel now, though, and that's going to make a hell of a difference, thanks to the throwers."

"Go on," I said quickly.

"We can't make the throwers ourselves quick enough. They need research, adjustment to the designs we want, and more. *But…*"

"Yeah?"

"The rail guns," she finished, sending a mental image of her boogying. "I'm working on a variant of the rail gun, using a pressurized air system and magnets, taking the design I already did and upgrading it."

"So what's the problem?"

"Time," she admitted. "Even this, time to explain what I'm doing, I can't afford to take, so you just…just do *this* some more, get us more bodies and more time. Take half of the mana we earn here, no…wait…a quarter. Take a quarter and use that. I need the rest."

With that, she was gone, and I sighed, feeling exasperation and worry rolling off Kelly.

"She's just distracted," Kelly assured me, and I snorted, sending her a mental burst of amusement.

"I know. It's okay," I assured her. "So what are we getting here?"

"It looks like around twenty-thousand, all told," Kelly said after a few seconds of hesitation. "We're getting as much absorbed as possible, but we've not got long, maybe ten minutes before the next wave reaches this floor. Do you want to stay here, or move on?"

"Stay," I said. "The longer it takes them to reach us, the more mana I can regenerate, and the best room for this from here and the next floor is already behind the incoming group, I think. No, I'll take the five thousand and summon more ghasts, and goblins."

"Do you want me to do it, so you can meditate?" she asked.

"Yeah, thank you! I need to focus. Get me…ummm…" I hesitated, running the numbers, before speaking. "Ten more ghasts, four more goblin mages, and two more orcs. Give them shields and they can stand ahead of us, keep the enemies' attention. Spread the goblins around the room, hide them, and I'll have them activate the spell in waves, pulling attention this way and that."

"And the ghasts…that gives you twenty, ten on either side, hidden around the walls?"

"Yeah, that works," I agreed, smiling. "We need to sort something for healing as well…"

"I can sort potions, I think. We're still a ways from making things like the focal orbs, though."

"We'd need a healing spell input into them anyway." I sighed.

"Do you want me to command the creatures in the next fight, or…?"

"Yeah, you run the rest of the creatures. I'll keep the kobolds with me, and we'll charge when the time is right. Use the orcs as cannon fodder. Once they're down, trigger the goblins on either side of me to split the group and draw them in, then use them in waves. Send the ghasts in to attack from behind in stealth, and then let loose with the Disgust spell over and over from random directions. Keep the drones confused."

"They reacted to the spell really well. Like weirdly well."

"Yeah, not sure why. I mean, I hoped they would, but damn…"

"They're new, right? As in, they just got brought to life and were sent to do this, to kill anything they see in here, so logically, something that's designed to get their attention, when they're also designed to look for things? Maybe it's a natural thing, like they're so new to life that they fixate, the way children do with something brightly colored or shiny? Ignoring anything else?"

"We can hope," I said. "Okay, I need to meditate, and Kelly?"

"Yeah?"

"Thank you." I sent her a mental image that was full of love, of holding her, of trusting her as she made things better, and then I broke off contact, leaving the dungeon sense and settling in.

There was only a handful of minutes before this floor locked down again, and already I could sense the little changes as the room was adjusted around me, hiding places for goblins being provided and more.

I banished it all from my mind—the muttering of the kobolds, and the hiss as one of them poured a healing potion that had just appeared over his face.

I sank down inside, seeing the differences here, as my understanding bloomed further. The crackling light and life that was lightning flashing through me, rising and falling, flooding me, and yet bringing a sense of rightness with it.

Alongside, and all around, although weaker, was the sense of the storm mana, rolling and surging, almost like heavy clouds trying to constrain and embrace the lightning.

I felt them both, once at odds, and yet the separate side of the same thing, and I watched them, feeling the comfort of both forms as "right."

I was a Thunderstorm. A step along my evolutionary journey to becoming a Storm Titan. And yet I wasn't close to my ascension to Cyclone, not even close.

There'd been a leap in my evolution, going from pretty much locked at seven percent, straight to twenty-five percent as I'd pieced together the method of conversion that the dungeon had used for me, and that alone made it clear which path I needed to focus on.

Cyclone was a necessary evolution, but what the hell was a cyclone? I banished the vague curiosity as to why they were called what they were, rather than something alien and unpronounceable, and just accepted that it was a part of the system's manipulation of the world.

My understanding was that it was a storm, hence Storm Titan, that was my future, but…but I knew that storm mana was Air and Water mana, so why the hell was Earth needed?

I felt it was important—hell, it was seriously important—though I had no clue *why*. Earth and Water formed Clay mana, I knew that; Life and Earth made Nature, so what the hell else did Earth form?

I thought for a second, deliberately pulling on my mana, forcing it to swirl and roll, picking up speed.

Earth and Fire made…lava? Magma? *Magma*—that was it. I could *feel* it, and I grinned as I gained a single additional point in my evolution. That was it! I needed to understand mana, to plumb the depths of it, to understand what the hell the world around me was made up of, and then…

Something.

I didn't know what, but apparently before I could reach the next level of my evolution, I needed to learn a fuckload more about mana. Apparently, I couldn't just be taught it, or shown it, I sensed; I needed to discover it for myself. Much like the early stages of university wasn't just the lecturers teaching the subject— it was equally them teaching you the basics, and them teaching you to research on your own.

They were teaching you how to find the answers you needed, much as web searches had become a part of hourly life for basically everyone in IT, and libraries were for the rest of the world in days gone by.

It was all about knowing *how* to work the details out, as much as what the immediate answer was. This was the same. I needed to learn what the combinations were, and how the hell I could learn that, before I could evolve.

Clearly a Storm Titan wasn't just a creature that smacked the shit outta things, but a mage as well. A mage who could convert the various forms of mana into one another…and who understood how the world around them was made up.

"Shit," I muttered, unthinking. I'd stopped trying to meditate, not that I'd actually done more than the most basic step there, but this… I could feel it.

This was important, and it was something that I needed to come up with on my own.

That was why that dickbag of a cat hadn't been around much. He was forcing me to learn on my own, to teach myself, and…

And he was a fucking cat, so he was doing exactly what he felt like, no doubt.

There were probably going to be a load of lightning kittens surprising the shit out of anyone who liked cats soon.

I forced that from my mind, and focused instead on the mana I could feel around me—the variations, and the corrupted mana that was everywhere. The dungeon purified it, but why?

It was cheaper by far to create things out of the required specialist mana: eighty points of shadow, as opposed to four hundred pure. If pure mana was so important, why the hell was it cheaper to make shit out of the corrupted versions?

Corrupted mana…it wasn't called aligned, but corrupted? *Maybe*…I reached out, turning from the mana that was flowing through me, and started to search the void around me, before dipping back inside and following the fast-moving river to my core.

Staring at the massive structure that spiraled gently before me, I watched it drawing free the strands it wanted. Shifting around, I landed on one of the massive spires, unconsciously choosing lightning, feeling the attraction to it as I always did.

Purified lightning was drawn free of the mélange of mana around us, pouring into the giant structure—a tiny, infinitesimal amount joining the sea that already slept inside—and I examined it, seeing the crackling wonder as it truly was.

It wasn't corrupted; it was pure.

It was pure *lightning*, not pure *mana*, and I realized that was a massive and important distinction. Pure mana was the base construct, the original and basic level. Pure lightning was an advanced form of that mana, and corrupted…

Corrupted mana was literally mana that had been exposed to other forms. Almost all the mana around me was corrupted to one degree or another. Air mana wasn't pure; instead, it was just mostly air. It was no longer pure, and it was in the process of converting to air, but it was also corrupted by water vapor, by nature as spores floated around, as floating shed skin cells leaked decay and life in equal measure, heat from fire, light and darkness…and that was just the things that occurred to me off the top of my head!

Air might be mainly Air mana, but that could mean it was fifty-one percent!

No wonder the converters only drew in a small percentage each hour…they were literally splitting out the unwanted forms! They…no wonder they encouraged each other! The Nature mana that was being pulled into the Nature converters was then fed back into the air and ground around them, encouraging the growth of the plants and more.

They also poured out the other forms of corruption, discarded and weaker, but that was why the plants and more were growing so happily.

It was such a simple revelation, that the converters were siphoning off their own preferred mana, but understanding that changed everything. They were discarding the corruption, and the core was pulling it in, feeding on it.

They weren't generating that mana; the core was. They were just breaking the mana up and making it easier for the core to do it! They were only converting and storing *their* mana. The ten or twenty points that were being pulled in? That was *all* the core!

The core was absorbing corrupted mana and refining it into pure mana so that we could use it, as well as creating a safe zone around us, where the mutations caused by the corrupt mana would happen less and less.

It was, as we'd been told at the beginning, the purpose of the dungeon to create a safe area for life, somewhere it could grow stronger and healthier, develop into more and more powerful forms.

I suspected that the core that we all had inside us was somehow linked to another. The massive mana input I'd managed before when I'd accidentally tapped into it seemed to bear that theory out, but when I tried to draw on the lightning spire…even now, nothing happened.

All of this, though, this made things so much clearer! I'd basically locked my core down to just accepting the most specialized form of mana when I first began my evolution.

Now, though?

I understood that Fire and Air was Lightning, and that Water and Air was Storm. I understood that I was only touching on the most basic forms of my magic. Hell, I was using Air more than anything…

Air.

That was why I could fly. I was using Air in Lightning and Air in Storm, and the pair combined with my own basic access to Air, to give me a low-level command over the element.

That was what a Storm Titan was, I suddenly saw.

A true Storm Titan was a master of the elements! Once I truly reached that level, no wonder the system referred to me as a fledgling fucking *god*! I'd have control of the elements! I'd be able to summon nuclear fire and hurricanes! I'd be able to rampage across the world, stomping my enemies into the ground with impunity!

No wonder the race for godhood was so important, and…fuck. If the others understood this, the other "gods"? They'd be keeping quiet; they'd be doing everything they could to rise in their own sphere of influence.

The gods of the Unlife Pantheon would be delving deeper and deeper by the day—hell, by the hour probably.

"Shit just got real," I whispered, opening my eyes. The others stood around me, the kobolds holding shields in place before me, protecting me, as the sounds of battle raged.

"Matt!" Kelly was shouting at me through a kobold that was crouched, holding the shield before me. "Wake the fuck up!"

"I'm here!" I gasped, as the world slammed back into place, and my notifications went wild. "What happened?"

"We're losing!" she screamed. "They know! They know about the last fight, somehow!"

I stood, taking the shield and hefting it, staring over the top and seeing the carnage before me. Half of the ghasts were down, as were both the orcs, three of the goblins, and…and two of the kobolds.

The fight was raging, but now…

Now so was I.

My mana bar pulsed dangerously. I drew in a deep breath, tasting the world around me, feeling the power that spread out, the utter glory of the storm…

And I rode it.

CHAPTER FORTY-TWO

The scene before me was chaos. Half of the asuras were down, but I could sense the others incoming. The third group of thirty were racing down the corridors toward us, ordered to flood the chamber and kill us all before we could finish off the current group, let alone absorb their bodies and make good on our losses.

That was fine, though, because in the process of my discoveries, I'd somehow—unconsciously and presumably enhanced by the system—kept meditating.

I'd flooded my core; I'd flooded my being in lightning, and I was a thunderstorm in truth. I felt it, and no matter what the Red Queen expected, a living god—even a baby one—wasn't on the list.

I shoved off. Lightning inundated the storm inside as I flashed across the distance between me and the front line. The new, improved reactions of the asuras drones to the goblin Disgust spell was helping them, but they still responded, even before the queen somehow remotely forced them back on track.

Each time a wave of that spell hit, they all shuddered, and there was a split second of hesitation. I exploited that, spinning into the first bunching of three, landing with a Storm-Strike powered kick to the chest for the center-most. It flew backward through the air, bleeding light as the asuras inside screamed at the loss of its sleeve.

I swung right with my hammer, smashing the tracking thrower before it could fire, then lashing out and removing the upper half of its chest in a backhand blow that sent the remains crashing into the ceiling.

The one on the left had abandoned its targets, turning to face me, and was driven back by my shield, its arms windmilling as it tried to keep its balance. It stopped suddenly. A ghast appeared right behind it and yanked its arms down, closing its jaws atop the head and ripping it free, before spinning and throwing the now-dying body aside.

My attack changed the rhythm of the fight. My remaining two kobolds leapt in, as the ghasts went back on the offensive. The drones turned as one, abandoning their previous mission in favor of one of termination—namely, of me.

There were nine of them left now, spread out around the room, and six of them opened fire in a coordinated blast. Two were caught by my shield; two more were stopped by my armor, damaging it, but as well-made as it was, it took the hits well.

One more was stopped by a kobold, leaping between us and sacrificing itself. It took a withering blast of eleven darts to the chest and stomach, staggering back and falling to the floor, bleeding out.

The last drone, though, nailed me good.

I caught two hits to the upper chest. The barbed tip made it through the necessarily thinner armor below my neck, tearing the skin painfully, but little else. One hit the solid muscle of my trapezius on the right-hand side, just as it emerged from the armor, tearing a line and spraying blood into the air, the scaled armor giving way to the sharp-tipped dart.

The last dart slammed into the side of my neck, high, just below my jaw, making me stagger from the force of the impact. It cut a line through the flesh, guided along by the underside of my helm, leaving the edge of it jagged and fractured.

I threw my hammer at that fucker; the head punched through its chest and took it down, even as I clapped my hand to the wound. Rivulets of blood poured free, streaming down my chest and flooding my armor.

A ghast was there then, sliding between me and another drone that leapt toward me, only to be caught and tossed aside by the creature.

I could see them all around, the shimmer of the ghasts as they vanished and reappeared, leaping atop their chosen victims, bearing them to the ground and tearing them apart.

The fight was over in seconds. I sank to one knee, controlling my breathing, closing my eyes and circulating my storm mana as quickly as I could.

I could feel the wooziness from the blood loss already, but…but the flesh was knitting; the actual growth of the muscle, the sealing and more was happening at an insane rate, even as my mana battled with the blood loss, replacing it as it pumped free.

"Matt!"

It was Kelly, I knew, but I couldn't spare the time to respond to her. The mana—thank fuck I'd not used the goddamn mana! I'd have been bleeding out on the floor right now otherwise. I waved a hand, dropping my shield and nodding, letting her know I was here still, that I could hear her, but I couldn't respond.

I felt her nearby. The kobold that crouched by my side, staring into my eyes, through my helm and searching desperately—I knew was her. It was a strange thing, to see a sapient dragon-man, clad in full armor and complete with a set of teeth that would have terrified great white sharks, staring at me with such concern, but there it was.

I nodded again, wincing and trying to swallow, feeling the pain in my neck, but no more bleeding. I slowly moved my fingers, freeing them and letting out a rough chuckle, pulling off and tossing my helm aside, silently vowing I'd get another one sorted out soon.

"Close one…" I sighed, seeing her eyes and forcing myself to sit, even bloody as I was, and half sliding into the dungeon sense to speak to her.

"It's okay," I assured her before she could speak, seeing the way she slipped free of the kobold to join me. "It nicked the vein, but my healing got it. Thank fuck for mana, eh?"

"You didn't have any mana!" She almost wailed.

I sent a little chuckle. "I had enough."

"Matt, we need more time," Aly advised distractedly, appearing next to me. "I'm sorry, I know we're asking a lot. I know we're not there, but—"

"He almost died!" Kelly snapped.

"I didn't, though." I projected a sense of calm, of determination. "It's fine, Aly. I understand."

"You need to claim back up as high as you can. The top floor is mainly filled with the tanks, and the third floor has the last of the stragglers of the next thirty on it. But the queen is leaving at least one on each floor to stop us stripping it. She's figuring out dungeons…"

"Then we need to kick her fucking ass and find out what she knows." I forced myself upright and partially out of the dungeon sense, grinning as I felt concern flooding the dungeon from Kelly, and knowing that there were others there, hundreds of them, citizens of the dungeon who had been helping to absorb everything.

I could feel them all around me, just as I could feel the mana, and the mass of mana stored above us, in the converters spaced around the building.

That'd help me no end, and give us a real chance. All I had to do was claim it…once I'd cleared the fuckers that were trespassing, anyway.

Well, that was going to be easy, I decided, striding forward. "Gather your gear," I called out grimly. "It's time we retake my fucking dungeon."

I didn't bother to explain; it wasn't necessary. I had a little over two thousand mana available, in my body, and although I had some mana in the dungeon as well, that wasn't important.

"I'll start replacing your losses, but they'll be on the floor below, and they'll have to catch up," Kelly sent to me, and I nodded. "Matt, can you do this?" she asked me quietly, and I knew she was conscious of the others who hovered nearby, able to listen in, should they move close enough.

For the first time, I felt a little annoyed with people in the dungeon, sensing them clustering around curiously. But before I could say anything, Kelly did.

I missed most of it, having sensed something else nearby and turned to look, but I caught the end.

"Little respect!"

There was a sudden, noticeable gap around us, and I couldn't help but smile, a smile that stretched into a wide grin as the figure I'd sensed approached at a steady jog.

It was *Beta*, and she'd changed.

No longer was she the same kobold. Since the latest "batch" had joined us, the difference between the uncommon breed, as she was, and the advanced had been troubling to say the least.

She had been closer in demeanor and movement to a classical movie raptor. Yes, she was upright and more humanoid, but she moved with a ducking, bobbing weave. And when compared to the newer breed?

She seemed a lot less human, and a lot more animal.

It'd been bothering me. Not because she was less in my eyes—hell, no. She was my friend as well as one of my summoned creatures. No, I'd worried because I could see her struggling, and I'd known that no matter the difference in their ranks, nor that she was my choice to lead them, nor the levels that she'd gained and the points she allocated—despite all of these things—one day she would be obsolete.

She'd have gone as far as she could, and I was worried that the new summons would eventually view her as a sort of not-quite-bright mascot.

I'd taken Lord of All because realistically it was the only thing in all those skills that might help in the short-term. But, honestly, I'd not been hopeful.

I'd been wrong.

The important lines in the description sprang back into my mind unbidden as she closed on me. The other two kobolds, both advanced, and battle scarred, ducked their heads in deference as they stepped aside, raising a fist to their chest and spreading their wings in some sort of demonstration.

> *Evolution: Lord of All!* The creatures of your Dungeon know their true master, and those who follow willingly can now receive arcane gifts that match their level of devotion!

Beta had shown her devotion to me a hundred times and more. And if this was the result of her dedication? Damn. I needed to earn the respect of more of my creatures.

She was both larger than she had been and broader. Where before she'd been "pigeon chested," as I'd heard it described, shoulders back and chest jutting forward, now her shoulders were in line with her chest, and she stood tall.

Her colors had changed, developing a more golden sheen, legs lengthening as she stood straighter. And her fingers, once stubby, now seemed narrower, and more dexterous. Her face was still recognizably draconic, but noticeably less lizard or dinosaur, and more noble.

Last of all, her eyes almost shone with a bright gold.

She drew up alongside me, dropping from the steady jog into a walk. Even her tail was different, longer and slimmer.

"Massster," she said softly, dipping her head as she took her place by my side.

"Beta?" I asked, stunned, and wanting to use my Examine, knowing it was her, but…

"Massster." She nodded. "We fights now?"

"Yeah." I smiled and tilted my head slightly. "You've changed."

"I…I am me." She gave a little shake, and I blinked in shock as her wings moved. She'd never had wings, and even now…they were translucent, folded back tight against her, but noticeably there.

I hesitated, wanting to ask her, then shook myself free of it. I couldn't afford the distraction. We needed to finish this and kill the Red Queen.

"Kelly," I said firmly, shifting my sense into the dungeon partially. "Is the Green Queen ready to fight if we need her or—"

"Hiding." Kelly finished for me. "She's *hiding,* so I stopped the metal for her. She was building it all into the frame you gave her, and as soon as she was secured into it, she tried to dig out through the back wall to escape. She might be a useful ally, but she's a coward as well."

"Fuck." I grunted. "I was hoping we'd have some help from her."

"I doubt it."

"Then we'll do it without her. What about the triceratops?"

"On the far side of the dungeon. They're too big and slow. If I made them run all the way there, they'd take nearly twenty minutes and they'd be dead from exhaustion when they arrived."

"Fuck!" I growled. "I'd been hoping they'd be a game changer."

"They will be, once they're leveled a bit."

I sighed, rubbing at my face, before speaking aloud. "Beta, you gained magic?"

"Yesss, massster," she said. "I can fight, and I can ssshift."

"What does that mean?" I frowned.

"I can ssshift."

"Okay, well, is it powerful?"

"Very."

"Can you do it for long?"

"No…a few sssecondsss at mossst."

"Okay, keep it for when we really need it then, I guess," I said. Her understanding seemed limited, but considering an hour or so ago she couldn't talk, or at least not so I could understand her, I wasn't going to complain.

Besides, when she'd passed out, I'd basically given up on having her as backup. So if she managed to pull something out of the bag at the last minute, that was a bonus.

"As always, the kobolds are yours," I said, distracted, as we picked up speed, jogging along the corridors, slipping in and out of the dungeon sense to watch the enemy progress toward us.

There were a few places we could fight them; we just needed to adjust our tactics, but that was fine.

As long as we could wipe them off this floor, we could absorb the bodies that were left behind, and finally we could start to really use our advantages.

If we had time, we could summon more forces. We had mana and could bombard them. Eventually, if they were dumb enough to let us, we could bury them in waves of bloody goblins if we had to.

I paused, mentally evaluating that as a serious option. The goblins were vicious little fuckers, after all, and quantity has a quality all of its own…

No. Realistically, they'd do plenty of damage, but they were unlikely to win against the asuras; they were metal, and goblins were…squishy.

If the asuras had been flesh and blood, though? That would have been a viable option.

I mentally marked it as *to be researched*. The new kobolds were amazing, now that I was considering them as actual living beings, rather than just summons. But they were seriously expensive, while the other races?

They were still viable options.

Hell, being realistic, now that we'd reached Steel, I didn't want to rush the core upgrades anymore. We needed to get strength and depth rather than going all in to get tech options. I resolved that after this, once the goddamn asuras were dead—and if I was still alive—then I was going to get back to work on each of the various species, as well as harvesting other options for the dungeon.

For now, I needed to focus on winning this fight and slaughtering those fuckers up ahead.

The asuras drones were coming fast, spread out a little. They had to bunch up around the choke points; then they'd start sprinting again.

That was almost perfect, though, as that meant we just needed to hold them up a little, so I could get as many as possible in the target area.

Of course, the only way to do that, though, was to give them a reason to do so.

We came around the last corner ahead of the space I'd picked out and slowed to a fast walk. "Okay, kobolds, on me. Shields at the ready. We're going to hold them up ahead here. Then, depending on how things go, fall back." Instantly, I felt the disappointment from the kobolds, knowing they didn't want to give a single inch to the invaders.

"We fight them one at a time as they step through, kill as many as we can, but the aim here is to slow them, force them to bunch up, and for us to not get dead," I clarified. "I've a spell I've been looking for an excuse to use, and I'm going to damn well enjoy this!"

Their attitude changed. No longer were we retreating again under attack. We were baiting the enemy into a trap, and if there was one thing the kobolds liked, it was a trap.

Well, that and kittens, apparently.

"Unless, of course, they're dumb enough to bunch up on the other side. Then I'll use the spell there, and then we bum-rush the survivors!" I amended.

The corridor here was narrow, deliberately so, with barely enough room for two of us to fight side by side, our shields overlapping slightly when standing upright.

The rock that made up this section had been made to look like fractured slate for some reason, stacked atop each other, creating a narrow, rough look, with only distantly laid-out lights.

Ahead of us were the spires, rock formations that rose in solid pillars, staggered across six meters or so, two and three side by side, forcing an individual to weave slowly through them, squeezing through.

If not for the throwers, one of our side could have stood at the end of the section and held the pass against dozens, or even hundreds of enemies.

As it was, it severely limited their options, and that was enough.

"Kobolds, on me. We take turns—kill as many as we can, then one changes out, then the next. Two stand at the front; two be ready. Everyone else stand down and try not to get killed by darts," I ordered. "When we start retreating, you all run like fuck…make it look panicked."

I wasn't sure how they'd manage that, considering half of the force beyond the kobolds were invisible, and the others were tiny goblins, but fuck it.

That was Kelly's problem.

We'd barely gotten into position before the first of the machines became distantly visible through the gaps in the pillars. Almost as soon as I saw them, the first darts started to fly.

"Idiots." I grunted, lifting the shield around and setting myself behind it, as Beta stepped up and stood alongside me, a shield in hand. "You ready for this?" I asked her, getting a sharp nod in response.

I shrugged and settled in. The few darts that made it through the gaps in the pillars hit the shields and made them shake and ring with the impacts.

I squinted around the edge, then pulled my head back sharply as a dart nearly took me in the eye. I slid into the dungeon sense instead, leaving my body almost on autopilot as I looked through that medium instead of with my eyes.

I flitted forward, seeing the drones pausing, two standing abreast on the far side, the corridor slightly wider there, and the others that ran up, slowing and slotting into place, standing calmly as the front line took a slow step forward, firing steadily, then another.

Each dart that hit our shields did damage, admittedly, but for every dart that made it through, four didn't. I shook my head, confused.

"Why?" I asked Kelly, who I sensed nearby. "Why waste the ammo. Yeah, they might fuck our shields up, but—"

"New design," Aly interrupted, arriving alongside us. "They're using these to keep you here. If they kill you, great, but they're pulling most of the tanks back and they're replacing them."

"Bastards," I muttered. "I hoped they were dumb enough to keep going like this. What's the new design like?"

"Bigger," Aly replied grimly. "It's a drone like these, humanoid, but wider and stronger. If these are the soldiers, and those the tanks? These are the elite troops, heavily armored. You're not going to want to fight these up close."

"Then we go with plan F." I took a deep breath.

"What happened to plan C?" Chris quipped, and I grinned, sensing his presence and feeling a massive wave of relief as he joined me in the dungeon sense.

"You know me, brother…I like to go all the way to F."

"Stands for fuck, doesn't it?" he asked.

"Yup."

"Fuck them or we're fucked?"

"Pretty much our life these days, mate."

"No, you idiot. I mean is it that *we're* fucked, or that they will be, not as a general motto for our life," he clarified.

"Ah!" I agreed. "Yes."

Then, grinning to myself at not answering his question, I slid out of the dungeon sense and started to cast.

The Lightning Storm dropped my mana seriously. Hell, I could have done serious damage with just the usual version of Lightning Bolt, but when I'd accidentally evolved that into Storm Bolt, I'd lost access to the basic version.

I didn't know whether the new version would have the same effect, and frankly, I wanted to make goddamn sure that I got as many of these fuckers as possible.

I targeted the spell in the middle of their mass, loving being able to see them from every side with the dungeon sense, and marked the ten-meter targeting zone right in the middle of them, managing to cover most of the group.

The spell raced through me, making me gasp as my mana bar, currently over two thousand points thanks to the meditation, dipped to five hundred. But it was worth it.

My fucking god was it worth it.

It started as a sudden drop in air pressure as the storm built, the air twisting as a roiling cloud appeared from nowhere. Outside, it would have stretched across the sky, no doubt, but inside, it filled the corridor from one end to the other. The light dimmed and occasional flares of light began to show through the sudden cloud bank that appeared.

The dart throwers hesitated. The rate of fire dropped suddenly as they tried to come to terms with the new situation…then the first bright blue-white flare of lightning rang out.

"Might want to get down!" I called out, grinning as I hid behind my shield, the mental image of the asuras drone I'd hit with lightning back in the scrapyard coming to mind.

It'd gone nova in seconds, the lightning and something to do with the living creature inside the metal reacting.

This time though, in a tight, and enclosed space, the lightning bolts that tore out, slamming into the asuras drones on all sides, spreading from one to another in such close confines…it was *insane*.

The first detonated after a handful of seconds. The second went almost atop the first, and then it was all we could do to hold our shields up as the entire building shook.

The walls of the dungeon—hell, the entire building—had been designed to be as hard as possible, mainly to stop sneaky fuckers digging through the walls, or shoot them down or whatever.

Now, they forced the pressure waves to funnel in set directions, flooding up and down the corridor. The closest asuras that weren't hit, and that actually survived the nova blasts that destroyed most of their companions, were picked up and thrown around, bouncing off the walls, smashing into the ground and the ceiling. Their metallic bodies were torn and dented by overlapping pressure waves and insane levels of heat.

I'd expected that Beta and I, and the kobolds behind us, would take a few out, forcing them all to bunch up on the far side of the pillars, and we'd have set the spell off maybe two-thirds of the way along their forces. That way, the mass of bodies would have shielded us slightly.

I was wrong.

Beta and I were picked up by the blast wave and hurled backward into the kobolds behind us, smashing them from their feet, then dropped to the ground, rolling over and over. I felt like I'd been shoved into an industrial oven.

The wave rolled past, followed by the screams of the goblins and the roars of the ghasts. Then the screams went silent, and I couldn't help but wince, reminded that as much as the dungeon made them all act nice around each other, they *were* fucking monsters.

I looked back along the corridor, seeing a ghast savaging a goblin body, and I reevaluated that "invest in all the species" plan. Maybe not such a good idea.

I grunted, wrenching my hand free of the shield—the damn thing had twisted my wrist when I'd clung onto it—and I stood, dragging the shield back up and wincing as I settled it back into place, stepping over the kobolds that had previously been behind me, and started to run.

"Move it!" I bellowed to the others, conscious that we'd not get another chance to move up close like this. And I sure as shit couldn't afford to cast that spell again for a while.

The scraping of claws and the clatter of metal rang out from behind me as they tried to obey, and up ahead, the clouds that had filled the corridor started to disperse.

The scene that was revealed, though? Damn.

The explosions had clearly overlapped, and the heat that had been given off...well, it'd been *intense.* The walls still glowed cherry red; bodies that had been working and frankly seriously scary-looking fucking termination drones were now melted and battered slag.

Most of the bodies that were even slightly intact looked like they'd been chucked into a washing machine on a spin cycle with a dozen boulders, then treated to a flamethrower instead of a jetwash.

I ran into the middle of them, hammer raised—for once I'd managed to hold onto the fucker—and shield at the ready...only to find that the majority were dead.

The handful of survivors were at the very back...well, apart from one limbless monstrosity that shivered and clanked as I ran past. That one I ignored, knowing someone else would get it.

The survivors, all three of them, were running. They'd not made it into the fight and looked to have been the last of those that were deliberately spread out. They raced away at full speed, back along the corridor.

I sensed Kelly as she reached out to me, focusing and letting the dungeon sense rise around me.

"That was fucking terrifying," she said, clearly stunned still.

"Yeah, just wait till I really get going..." I muttered, squinting and trying to maintain my speed.

"The asuras on this level are all fleeing, as are those on the level above. The tanks are mainly out as well."

"We've won?" I wondered if we'd scared the red bitch so much that she was legging it.

"Not even close." Kelly dashed my hopes. "They're falling back, and the queen has gone onto full rebuilding mode. We're attacking. We can't let her build up another army—"

"Considering it's our forces that she's ripping the life from," I agreed.

"Exactly. I don't know how many she's got, but we've got Griffiths and his team in place. They're going to snipe the kobolds as they're taken to be sacrificed. Better that she doesn't get their souls."

"Can we win?" I asked, leaping over a collapsed body, and grunting as I realized it was just playing dead. The thrower came up and was smashed into the ground again by Beta right behind me. Her spear punched down into the body, then lifted free in turn for the next kobold to get a blow in with a hammer.

In seconds, it was dead, but the point was made.

"I need to focus. Attack if you think we can win, and use whatever you need to do it. I'm coming!"

CHAPTER FORTY-THREE

As soon as the figures I'd seen distantly vanished from the floor, climbing the stairwell, desperately racing for the next floor, I sensed the floor we were on "unlock."

Bodies, both those from the fights we'd just had, and the original fights that had cost us this floor, where kobolds had stood and fought bravely against overwhelming odds, and the asuras had fallen here and there, all started to be absorbed, and I felt the difference.

"Ghasts!" I bellowed. "Get up there and kill those fuckers!" The room we were approaching was slightly larger, and I moved to one side, the kobolds doing the same, as a blurring of the air and savage growls tore past us.

"Fuck, they're fast," I muttered, shaking my head and hurrying after them, calling out to the ether. "Aly!"

A second later, I felt her nearby. As much as I disliked it, I settled back into a half-and-half situation, the dungeon sense surrounding me, even as the kobolds ranged ahead and behind. We knew now that the floor we were on was clear, or we'd not be able to absorb anything.

"What is it, Matt?" Aly asked. "I'm—"

"Busy. Yeah, I know," I snapped. "The ghasts—how much for the next level? The research, I mean."

"Uh…" She hesitated, finding the data as I kept running, not trusting myself to scour through pages and pages of data. "Twenty-five thousand mana," she said. "It's more expensive than the uncommon kobolds. They were ten, but—"

"Is there a better option?" I asked gruffly.

"What for?" she asked, her voice changing as she actually listened.

"We're getting an influx of mana right now as we recover the lost floors, but that won't last long. Twenty-five thousand mana is ten kobolds. Yeah, they're unarmed and unarmored, but they're also invisible, and fucking lethal…"

"We could make more Karens, five of them." She paused, before going on. "Well, four of them, fully kitted out."

"Yeah, or we could do this research, and send a wave of these fuckers."

"They'd be…" She ran the numbers and guessed. "Probably between six hundred and a thousand for the uncommon versions."

"Shit…" I practically knocked myself out, holding my hammer as I barely stopped myself from facepalming. "There was a ghast I saw a few days back. I sent three of the kobolds after it, all kitted out. Did we absorb the body? I ordered them to return it to the dungeon."

"I…I don't know anything about it. Nobody said anything, and the creatures we have access to are still showing the same."

"Dammit. We need to find out what happened to that. It looked awesome." I sighed. "Okay, so if we create more of the—"

"Matt," Aly said firmly. "I'm saying this with the greatest of respect, but no. Now isn't the time to risk everything on a new species. If you want the ghasts, use the current version. Hell, use the twenty-five thousand to summon…sixty?"

"Sixty of the current version…" I muttered, then nodded, abandoning the plan. The new versions were good, but damn. An extra sixty stealth fighters, or four kobold ones…it was a massive difference.

Yes, they had bone spikes and teeth; yeah, they were going to be a lot less effective against heavier armor than they had been against the current version. But fuck them; they'd be a distraction at least.

"Can we afford them?" I asked. "Even as a distraction, they'd save the lives of the armored kobolds…"

"I'll summon you thirty," Aly said after a second. "Yeah, they're less useful than I'd like in close combat against steel, but they're fighting machines that are cobbled together as well. It's not like their enemies are well built."

"Okay, and—"

"And I need to finish this fucking design, Matt!" she snapped. "Seriously, either do this yourself, or leave me to work!"

With that, and before I could say anything else, she was gone, and I was back running, shaking my head free of the dungeon sense, as I hit the next stairwell.

This one had been made to look like I'd expect from a dungeon: wide, shallow steps of solid stone, flaring torches on the walls in iron rings, rough stone that practically screamed *Turn back, you fool!*

I grinned as I kept going, hurdling a dead body, and an asuras that, judging from the missing arms and head, was definitely dead this time.

The floor ahead of me was still locked as I ran out onto it. The aesthetic seemed more like marble and bookcases should be everywhere, if only we'd had the time and the investment to do it.

The light was bright and welcoming, and I kept going, feeling the dungeon mana stores bouncing like a good time.

"Look at me," everything seemed to say. The attention to detail for the overlapping sections of the corridor showed where the change had come from *create a dungeon* to *we're under attack—get ready.*

Sections of stone that had been jutting out, where the slabs had been essentially copied and pasted—or the magical dungeon version of it, anyway— suddenly those sections were smooth.

The traps—fortunately not triggering for us—were well-made, and clear. Bodies of asuras lay everywhere, torn and battered. Sections of the floor that couldn't be returned to their previous state now showed dozens of bodies.

Up ahead, a single asuras was trying to drag itself along. The wall next to it seemed to drag the creation against it.

Leighton made his presence known again. "Might want to wait a minute. Once that one dies, I think we'll have control over the floor again, and I'll shut the magnets off."

"Magnets?" I asked, sliding into the dungeon sense.

"I made the entire section into a giant magnet on the left, then the right, immediately after it. It slowed them down a lot."

"Damn." I grunted, shaking my head. "Well done."

That was the kind of shit that would never have occurred to me, and it'd be a nightmare for a metallic creature. It lasted three seconds, as the ghasts reached it—their blurring in the distance had been what had drawn my attention—and they fell on it.

"It'll be clear when you reach it, lord," Leighton said in my ear.

I picked up the pace again, noting that I couldn't feel Kelly anymore. That meant she was outside already, probably commanding dungeon creatures in the fight.

The rest of the floor was a nightmare, the occasional section of the pillars that I'd passed so far now suddenly coming practically room by room, and each time I found the bodies.

Kobolds were strewn deep in the corridors, their armor shredded by the dart throwers. Where the pillars and other methods slowed the incoming drones, the situation was reversed.

The drone bodies were piled here, and the kobolds there, showing just how damn close the fight had been. They'd torn through the warriors they'd faced, mainly because these were the freshly summoned and unaware fighters.

The kobolds hadn't lasted long enough to become self-aware, and the asuras had taken insane advantage of the fact that the kobolds version of ranged was bows and arrows, or small assassin versions of crossbows, by and large.

They'd also faced the more experienced kobolds outside but that, again, had been at range, with their tanks and throwers carving great holes in our ranks.

Most of the fight had gone their way until recently, and my grin at the thought of them encountering my mages and my more experienced teams now was positively feral.

As I took the final stairwell, coming up to the first floor of the dungeon, the one that sat squarely below the main building, I felt the floor was still locked. I could no longer feel the ghasts ahead, making me call out to the others.

"Pay attention!" I snapped to the kobolds and the single goblin that had survived thus far, and able to keep up.

I broke off, looking back at the fucker in shock. The little bastard clung to one of the kobolds, grinning. He was with us before, but I hadn't realized at the back that the occasional glimpse I was getting of him was because the fucker was *riding* a kobold.

I'd intended to send him forward to be a sacrificial goblin, triggering Disgust and seeing how long he lasted, but damn.

I hesitated, then focused, grinning as I felt the ten kobolds—fully armed and armored—that were running across the floor below, coming to reinforce me.

I didn't know who'd done that, but I appreciated it. I quickly summoned a pair of goblin mages at the foot of the stairs, ordering them to join us, as well as the first copy of one of the dogs I'd summoned yet, remembering Frank that Beta had ridden.

Frank had been a massive rottweiler, mutated, and he'd ended up as Beta's steed, ridden back and forth by her as she leveled and basically took her place as the de facto queen of the kobolds.

I knew she wasn't going to like what I was going to do, so even as the dog was summoned—fifty points, that was all it cost—I started speaking to her.

"Beta, I'm sorry, but we need a fast scout, someone that's expendable and that we frankly don't give a shit about losing when they trigger whatever trap is left on this floor by the enemy."

She glared at me, before turning, as if to order one of the kobolds forward, despite not liking it, and I went on.

"No! Sorry, I should have been clearer…I'm sending a goblin…" At that, the little goblin rider hid behind the kobold he was still clinging to, and I sighed. "Not you either, you little dickhead! You've earned a chance. In fact, you can go hide somewhere. I've got plans for you."

The goblin didn't waste any time in leaping down and running for it, startling the kobold who apparently had no clue he had a passenger.

He nearly made it out of the room, before the massive dog arrived, and he froze, staring in wonder at the creature. I didn't blame him, considering that Beta, who was over five foot at that point, had been riding one of these around—it was clear how big Frank had grown, too.

This version I'd absorbed into the dungeon wasn't as big nor as impressive, but the way Beta flinched on seeing him made it clear just how much he reminded her of her trusty steed.

So did the glare she directed at me as he trotted past, a pair of gasping and exhausted goblins following it into the room.

"Right. One of you fuckers gets to ride the dog. Who's it going to be?" I glanced from one of them to the other. "You'll be running ahead, triggering your Disgust spell as you go, basically baiting anything that's hiding into attacking you." The pair looked less than enthusiastic.

The one I'd just told to go hide, though, raced out from behind the kobolds and leapt onto the dog, scaling one leg before he could be kicked off, and clearly claiming the job as our first dungeon-born goblin dog-rider.

"Well, you had the chance to run." I shrugged. "Get your arse up there!"

The goblin and his mount took off like I'd rammed a rocket up their arses, and I shook my head in amazement. Most of the goblins I'd summoned had been slow to awaken, and they'd demonstrated a lot of cowardice. The few that had become members of my little team had been the exceptions.

That little bugger, though, was clearly a credit to his species, and once again I reevaluated his entire race.

Then I glanced at the other two, seeing one rummaging under his loincloth with every sign of enjoyment, while the other watched him curiously, picking his nose.

"And you two can run!" I barked at them both, ordering them to get out of the dungeon to the front, and to go hide until they were ordered differently.

I didn't expect them to survive, but…

"I want a new dog," Beta growled, and I hesitated only a second before nodding. "Fine."

"And it'll need to grow, to be trained!"

"You go for it," I agreed. "When all of this is over, you can set up a cavalry."

"Good," she snapped.

We set off again. The floor remained locked, letting me know that somewhere, something was definitely hiding and waiting.

I explained that to Beta, and she nodded. The remaining ten kobolds caught up to us as we ran, and they all showed her deference that they'd rarely shown me.

She peeled two off, ordering them ahead. They passed their shields over to others, sprinting ahead with hammers in hand, checking the bodies as they passed them.

Here and there, we found larger remains, variants that the queen had presumably tried, before locking it down to the tanks and drones as the way to go.

I checked the quest prompt, nodding in satisfaction at the progress, even as I frowned at the changes.

You have made progress in your Quest!

Defend the Dungeon! (4)
The land around the dungeon has grown paradoxically more peaceful, and more terrifying, as new forces move into the area. Where previously your bodies were at risk of damnation, now too is your soul, and that of all sapient creatures.

Current Enemy Count:
- Asuras termination drone (ATD): 11/107
- Asuras mobile extermination platform (AMEP): 4/4
- Asuras heavy exterminator (AHE): 4/4
- Asuras Guardian: 2/2
- Asuras Red Queen: 1/1

Destroy the enemy asuras, and secure the local area to receive the following bonuses:
- +5 to top three Attributes
- +1 Spell
- +2 Class Skill Points
- 10,000 XP

I fell in behind Beta as she took over leading the group, and pulled up the last of my notifications, dismissing most of them as unimportant—gained skill point in this, increased the level of that…mainly the crap that I always dismissed—until I came to what I'd hoped I'd be seeing.

Congratulations!

You have killed the following:
- 41x Asuras termination drone, level 1, 2870 XP

Total XP earned: 2,870 XP

A party under your command killed the following:
- 55x Asuras termination drone, level 1, 3,850 XP

Total Party XP earned: 3,850 XP

As party leader, you receive 25% of all XP earned.
Total XP awarded 2,870+(3,850x0.25=962.5)=3,832.5 XP
Partial XP is lost to the ether.

Current XP to next level stands at 36,680/35,000

Congratulations!

You have reached Level 25

Current XP to next level stands at 1,180/45,000

You have 9 unspent Stat Points and 10 unspent Skill Points.

I had nine stat points to assign. Sure, yeah, I had ten personal skill points to assign as well, but frankly, they were fuck all use right now. Yes, I could massively boost a skill—my hammer swinging, for example—I could reach a new level with that, or my armor or unarmed…

But all those things rose on a daily basis. It'd be a hell of a waste to just slap the points into one of those.

No, considering that I kept coming back to this, I was going to have to come up with a crafting skill that interested me, mainly because we needed everything, and eventually, probably not very far away, I was going to end up obsolete in a lot of ways.

Right now, I was needed in the fights, and I lived for that. But realistically? The kobolds were already seriously good fighters; all they needed was some levels. If instead we doubled down on the dungeon forces, creating more and more advanced dungeon creatures, and armored them appropriately?

There'd be no need for me on the front lines, and instead it'd be a battle of armies and technology. I'd be a leader, more than a fighter, and I had to accept that.

No, I'd need to take up a form of crafting in the medium term, because once I wasn't on the front lines, it'd be a case of craft and lead, or just lead.

I wasn't mentally suited to sitting in an office and speaking to people all day. I'd been a field-based engineer before the fall. It meant one day I'd be dealing with idiots who laminated their passwords and stuck them to their machines…and then the next day I'd be hanging off the side of a building, adjusting the antennae for a wireless beam.

I could deal with assholes and idiots for a limited time then. Now I was likely to use a hammer or lightning to make my point when people asked me stupid questions.

No, I'd assign my nine points now, because that would have a massive effect in the next fight, but I'd save the personal skills for later.

Nine points…nine points…

I was tempted to drop them into my Intelligence, take it from fifty-two all the way to sixty-one. It'd massively increase my manapool, after all. But there was always the concern about throwing out my body, making the difference between mind and body too much and rendering myself pretty much useless in the fight to come.

Nope.

I started at the beginning, moving quickly, but determined not to waste the points, even as the walls, covered in splattered blood, passed by on either side.

Agility: I could do it; it'd help me dodge, so that was a possibility. Charisma? Nope. No talking to the damn Red Queen would help. Constitution? That was a real possibility. It'd help with the possible rejections of my body and mind growing too distant, it'd keep me alive longer, and if all else went wrong, it'd be a reservoir for the blood magic.

That was a real contender.

Dexterity? No, that was for the future, when it came to crafting.

Endurance? Tempting again, and not just for Kelly's sake, but so that I could run farther and deal with pain and exhaustion better...I'd consider that. Intelligence was a no, for now. Luck? Tempting, but no.

Perception? That could help, as could Strength. The hammer was a weapon of blunt destruction, after all...another possible.

Wisdom? Tempting. Very tempting. Greater mana regeneration would be a hell of a difference after all, but then...I was already courting a breakdown. No, this needed to be a physical change.

That gave me Constitution, Endurance, and Strength. I'd dismissed Perception as too cerebral, and focused on the three.

The easiest to dismiss was Strength. Yes, I was swinging a hammer all day in these fights, but it wasn't about how hard I could hit the target; it was about killing it and moving on. Too much strength and I'd end up with the hammer wedged at best.

That left Constitution and Endurance...survive longer, or fight longer.

Putting it like that? It wasn't a hard choice. Sod's Law, I had nearly enough to raise them both to the next level—I needed just one more point. But fuck it...better to put it all into one area.

I assigned all nine points to Constitution, hissing in pain as I passed the threshold, my feet catching on a corpse I'd been stepping over, and I sagged, falling against the wall and bracing myself.

My body burned, all of it, from my feet to the back of my neck. Every inch of my skin seemed to writhe. The hairs on my skin twitched, and for a handful of seconds, it felt like they were needles, each and every one being dragged and bent, flexing in my poor flesh...

Then it was over. The insanity of the sensations died away; second by second, my skin grew less and less sensitive, until...until I could breathe again.

I blinked, seeing Beta standing before me, helping to hold me upright, staring into my eyes, clear concern on her face.

"I'm okay..." I whispered, then coughed. "It's okay. I'm all right," I repeated, assuring her. "I just leveled up."

She nodded, clearly understanding that, and jerked her head sideways, as if asking if I was all right to continue. I nodded, forcing a smile at how easily she reverted to nonverbal methods of communication when she was stressed. Then gasped as a fresh wave of pain flooded me. She glanced back, and I gestured to keep going, cursing internally that I seemed to have picked up a damn bodyguard somehow. Kelly was going to be thrilled.

I set off after her but glanced at my stat sheet as I did so.

Name: Matt, First Lord of the Storm				
Host Powers: 1 (Enhanced Regeneration)				
Species: Thunderstorm		**Bonus**: None		
Level: 25		**Progress to next level**: 32,848/45,000		
Stat	**Current Points**	**Description**	**Effect**	**Progress to Next Level**
Agility	34	Governs dodge and movement	Heightened chance to dodge attacks 68%+20%= 88%	31/100
Charisma	26	Governs likely success to charm, seduce, or threaten	35% more likely to succeed in events that require seduction, persuasion, or threats (10%+ (16x2) = 35)	70/100
Constitution	43	Governs Health and Health Regeneration	HP: 43x50 = 2150	86/100
Dexterity	37	Governs ability with weapons and crafting	+37% Increased chance of improved result +13 to melee damage	78/100
Endurance	36	Governs Stamina and Stamina Regeneration	Stamina: 36x40 = 1,440	19/100
Intelligence	52	Governs base manapool, standard intellectual capacity	Mana: 52x60=3120	99/100
Luck	38	Governs overall chance of bonuses and critical hits	+56% increased chance of positive outcome	99/100
Perception	31	Governs ranged damage and chance to spot hidden items/traps	+21 to all ranged attacks	20/100
Strength	32	Governs damage with melee weapons and carrying capacity	+44 to all damage with Melee weapons	92/100
Wisdom	46	Governs mana regeneration	115 mana regenerated per hour	95/100

I hesitated, frowning. The change to my health was more than welcome, jumping from thirteen hundred and fifty to twenty-one hundred and fifty. Hell yes.

The change was that my "control" details were gone, and as I considered it, I couldn't remember seeing it recently, either. I almost panicked, thinking that I'd fucked up, that the breakdown between my mind and body had begun again, but this time with the loss of details...

Then I felt it. A leaking of the information that came on occasion from the dungeon. It wasn't clear—hell, it wasn't clear at all—but something about the dungeon reaching Steel had changed it. The dungeon was no longer beholden to my Intelligence and Wisdom as much as it had been, using instead the dungeon's own control points and this pain?

It was exclusive to changes that were beginning in my body as I passed some kind of hidden threshold.

I'd also lost the abilities and spells list, and my 'situational modifiers' section, which was good really, as I tended to know when I had a fucking broken bone or whatever without the system having to tell me.

I started off jogging slowly, shaking occasionally as a fresh wave of changes rolled through me, muscles cramping and then relaxing. After each wave of changes, I'd think that was it, but whatever was going on was a turnkey upgrade to my body, rather than a little one, and my only choice was to ride it through to the end.

The last section of the dungeon was coming up. The goblin on his dog raced out, triggering his Disgust spell over and over, and a twitch by the exit, buried in a mass of bodies, revealed itself.

It was short, based on a spider or something similar, a little larger than my hand, but damn that fucker was fast!

As soon as it knew it'd been seen, it was off, all six legs blurring as it raced across the ground; a bladed tail lifted, ready as it ran at me.

The nearest two kobolds had seen it and swung, but the fucker was too fast! It passed them in a flash, leaping onto the wall, then back off again as another kobold swung for it; their hammer smashed into the wall and rebounded with a crash.

The others moved, desperately swinging and striking with hammers and shields. But it slid past them like it was on rails, never seeming to pause. I summoned my spells, frantically discarding Lightning as I'd not dare use that in such close proximity…when a blade flashed out, slamming into the central mass of the spider-thing, tearing it half apart as a new figure appeared from seemingly nowhere.

I froze, then grinned, seeing the kobold that stood there, and her sisters that appeared from stealth, taking up position all around me.

"Karen." I nodded to the one who'd just gutted the spider, and she smiled in return, an evil, bloodthirsty grin.

"Sssharon will ssstay with you…" Beta said, and one of the stealthed figures to my right stepped up.

"Thank you," I said, following the others up the final flight of stairs, and out into the darkness, even as it was torn asunder by fire, explosions, and light.

It was time to end this.

CHAPTER FORTY-FOUR

The night was alive with battle already, and I could feel the presence of the others nearby.

"Matt…"

I shivered, sliding back into the dungeon sense, seeing Kelly there, reaching out to me.

"You have to hold the line," she said quickly, clearly distracted, struggling to focus.

"The line?"

"If you can hold the dungeon entrance…then we can summon reinforcements once Aly finishes the guns! If they take it, though…"

"I'll hold it," I said, knowing that this would be my fight, for now at least, as I slid my hammer back into the belt loop, staring around. I flexed my hand, ready for magic, should it be needed.

"Thank you…"

Then she was gone, and for a second, I felt…almost annoyed? No, that wasn't right. I felt somehow *diminished*, and stupid for feeling that. I'd asked Kelly to guide the dungeon creatures. She did it only at my request—I was the Dungeon Lord, after all—and it was right that she was in control of them. She had a class that boosted them.

I still felt stupid and as if I'd been dismissed, though, because for the first time, in all our battles together, I wasn't leading the fight myself.

I banished the thought, forcing myself to recognize that not only was it unworthy of me, but that it was bloody ridiculous. Kelly was the obvious choice to lead this fight. She wasn't on the ground; I was.

The line, as she'd called it, was a literal line in the doorway of the old civic center, where it led down into the dungeon below and then out and down a handful of steps to the road before us.

Beta stood to my left, and Sharon to my right, with five of the kobolds in front of me, each in full armor and holding their shield ready, edge to edge.

I looked back, sensing the summoning of others, as more figures raced up the stairs. The kobolds before me split and moved to the sides, letting six more kobolds race past. They took a sharp left, falling into a wall formation, ready as the asuras across the road started forward.

For the first time, I got a clear look at the Red Queen, and fuck me, it was wrong in all sorts of ways. The heavily armored armadillo thing had changed subtly.

The twin trailers that were previously filled with scrap had been shifted around to stand one on either side of it, with the armored bulk between and behind then, when seen from the entrance as I was right now.

The fortified shell of the Red Queen had split, with an arced passage opening up to the interior, and sparks and eerie lights shone from inside, as did the screeches of tearing metal.

A sudden bright light flared, looking like the hand of Zeus had slammed a lightning bolt into something, rather than letting a doctor use a mere defibrillator.

The light dimmed, dying away; then the cover split apart even more, and the new form stomped out from under cover.

It was easily half again the size of the smaller drones, much heavier armor, and with what looked to be a nozzle over one shoulder, running down the front of the right arm to end on the back of the wrist.

The hands weren't hands, basically. The right "hand" was a short blade, perhaps twelve inches long, and the left ended in a shield. Clearly, it'd learned from fighting us, and I didn't like the damn nozzle one bit.

It stomped down a path, joining five others, and I checked the prompt, nodding to myself as I saw it. Yup. The heavy exterminator class was up to six now.

Well, there was something I could do about that easily enough, I thought, fingers curling instinctively as I felt the surge of lightning…and then a wave of nausea flooding me.

I looked down, the comforting blue-white of my Lightning Bolt instead a golden glow as I tried to channel pure mana into a Storm Bolt.

I released it. The mana crackled across my hand; glowing lines flared to life and ran along the edges of my armor as it was partially absorbed…and some of it was lost.

Motherfuckers.

I reached inside, feeling the roiling mess of mana that was my core, and the crackling light of the pure that flowed around there, gradually breaking back down to form my usual mana.

I could cast it, I knew.

I could cast the pure mana; I could use it, and more to the point, I knew it was there. I'd managed to draw it into me, even though it'd nearly killed me in the process, but…

It opened the door to questions. Questions I'd not yet asked, and that I dared not consider right now. I'd pulled the pure mana to me, and it'd come; it'd filled me joyously and then had converted a spell I used all the time into a "storm" version of itself.

It used *pure* mana, though, and that was the opposite of everything I thought I understood of mana now.

Whatever else I'd done in summoning the mana, I'd clearly painted a target on my back, as the line of the exterminators shifted, turning to face me, even as the armored bulk shifted again.

This time, it opened wider; the sides split and drew back to show the interior. The queen moved forward, lifting higher to stare at me, and my asshole puckered a little.

Where the other asuras looked roughly assembled, clearly made from the scrap that filled the trailers, light glowing from cracks and imperfect welds, the queen was…beautiful.

The shielding fell backward further, exposing her to face me fully, but staying high enough on either side that I instinctively knew she was shielding herself from snipers she suspected were there.

The exposed interior was like a mad scientist's dream. Light leaked from a more refined ring than the one that I'd seen on the Green Queen, and banks of what looked to be storage devices glimmered with its light.

There were bins holding high technology parts; additional arms, ones that I assumed had been stolen from a local car manufacturer, shifted, sending cascading sparks flying as they cut and sealed sections on another body automatically.

In the middle of the exposed area, though, the queen flowed forward. She was snakelike from the waist down, a technological trunk with lights glimmering on sections of paneling. Cables led back and forth, sealed into a solid pillar, that became more and more humanoid as it climbed higher.

From the waist upward, she looked human, more or less, and regal. Her chest was small, notably female in design, with half a dozen cables flowing from the middle of her chest to either side, sinking back into the main form.

I didn't know whether they were an attempt at clothing, or modesty or aesthetics, but to have designed robo-tits at all was frankly a little fuckin' weird, in my eyes.

Her arms were slender, the shining steel of her form reflecting the firelight from the burning cars and wreckage to the left and the right. Blinking lights gave her an almost hellish appearance as they shone on her.

The neck was slim, and the face was clearly the result of a huge amount of effort. She was female, and perfect of face, with short black cables—data-cabling, my mind automatically noted—replacing her hair, with tens of thousands of copper filaments filling the space between them to create an overlapping wave of "hair."

Her eyes glowed with an inner light—red, unsurprisingly—and I wondered whether that was why the system had called her the Red Queen.

Whatever had possessed the creature to do this, to create herself in this image, when the Green Queen essentially wanted to be a tank, was beyond me.

"Surrender!" she called out, ignoring the battlefield, as the kobolds marched forward from the left, shields held high, and the drones marched to meet them.

The twin guardians, massive crab-like things with four legs, had clearly been waiting for this, as panels on their sides opened and dart throwers emerged.

The pair of them opened fire as one, sending hundreds of darts from each of four barrels, one on either side of either machine. The kobolds that marched forward hefted their shields, brave to the last, but it was insane.

The sheer barrage of fire shredded through them, literally tearing the shields apart, slaughtering the flesh and blood behind them and hammering holes into the asphalt.

"You cannot win!" the queen continued, her voice accompanied by an almost static buzz that wove in and around the words. "Surrender, and your creatures will be absorbed into me."

"I could…" I called back, unable to help myself. "Or…and I'm just saying this is an option…but I could *not* surrender, and I could instead tell you to fuck yourself."

"You cannot win."

"I think you'll find I cannot *lose*."

"Incorrect."

"No, it's true," I said, bluffing for all I was worth and really hoping that Kelly and the others were coming up with a great plan, because the whole *march the kobolds in* one had been shit. "I'm the local hero, you see…a god and everything. I *can't* lose. It'd play merry hell with my sex life, for a start."

"I am asuras, I am one, and I am eternal," she replied. "I have watched the birth of life in galaxies you cannot imagine, fleshling, and I have watched over the encroaching darkness of the void as it snuffed that life out." Her voice was cold, and not just from the metallic reverberations that filled it.

There was no mercy, no understanding, no compassion in it, and my hackles rose as I stared at her, even as her heavy exterminators lifted their sword and shield arms, ready.

"You must surrender. All life is needed. All soul energy must be absorbed, not wasted. We must become one."

"I've got a girlfriend and I've got to tell you, a strange woman demanding we become one isn't going to go down well with her. Sorry," I tried, only to have the guardians turn, abandoning the last three or four kobolds that were still alive, instead locking their throwers onto me.

"Surrender."

"Uh…no," I said, then smiled. "Thanks anyway."

Keep her attention a little longer… I sensed Kelly beg, and I panicked. The queen was clearly about to order my death, and I held up a hand. "Wait…nope, just wait a minute, okay?" I cried out.

"Beg quickly."

"Yeah…look, you want the Green Queen, right?" I said, hurrying on when she showed no recognition of the name. "The other asuras! The one that I saved!"

"You will surrender the fragment, and you will become one with me."

Just a few more seconds…

"Yeah…" I cast about desperately, damn sure that if I moved from here, she'd open fire, and the others were too close. I might get away, if I was damn lucky, but Beta and the others sure as shit wouldn't. "Get the hell back…" I hissed to them, adding a mental shove when Beta especially hesitated.

They moved, and the two guardians took a threatening step forward as one. They'd been on either side of the trailers, watching over the queen, but now they were directly over them, their throwers pointed threateningly at me alone.

"Hey, hey!" I said, getting a sense of *Just a few more seconds* from Kelly, then a *Perfect!* that made me grin. "She gave me a message for you!" I lied.

"Speak!"

"Umm, what was it now…oh yeah!" I smiled wide and lifted my right hand, offering her the middle finger. "She said to tell you your mother was a snowblower!"

I dove sideways; I'd been circulating my storm mana relentlessly, and I shoved in that direction at the same time, dragging the attention of the big fuckers as well as the heavy elites to the right. The air suddenly filled with darts, tracking me as I looped back, then around, down, and flashing across the ground as the *thwip-thwip* of darts splitting the air flashed past, almost close enough to kiss.

I angled around, thinking to try to end this myself, then remembered that Kelly had a plan…right as the heavens burst into light, overlapping sonic booms battering the world as one.

"Fuck me!" I screamed, realizing at the very last second exactly what Kelly's plan involved. I flew away as fast as I fucking well could, panic rising as I tried to get outside of the blast radius.

Wrath of the Heavens was literally what it sounded like: it was the heavens opening and smiting the living shit out of anything that happened to be beneath. Ten massive meteors tore through the sky, conjured from fuck knew where, but flaming, literally terrifying.

It was like a Hollywood action movie as the ten rocks, each barely the size of a basketball, yet blessed with the terrible force of inertia, tore through the sky.

The guardians reacted instantly, stepping in close, over the scavenger platform, even as the shell slid upward, racing the incoming rocks to see which would reach their terminus first.

The guardians stepped in tight, clamping themselves together. The cranes on their backs flipped over and locked onto their opposite number, tying themselves side by side…and the first hit came.

It tore into the left-most figure, hitting them with the power of the gods. It sagged with a single blow; the legs struggled, lifting it again, shaking…then the second and third hit.

The first hit had smashed the top of the guardian in. Steel, plastic, and who knew what went flying, smoke and flaming wreckage thrown out. The frame of the guardian—a semi-circular shape atop a roughly circular base, with the throwers on either side—buckled with the first blow. The second sent a massive section of the armoring flying, and the third hit that armor in the air, driving it back down and into the second guardian, sheering off one of the arms.

The fourth and fifth impacts were enough to take the first one entirely out, crashing to the floor, streaming smoke and flames. The sixth meteor made it through the gap the loss of the first guardian created, slamming into the unfortunately closed armor shield of the queen.

Even with it closed, and with the obvious effort put into creating an overlapping shield that could take serious punishment, it still rang like a bell, bouncing back up as the meteor exploded, cracking that section of the armoring.

The second guardian moved then, sliding across barely in time to catch the seventh impact, smashing into the side of the frame as it tried to cover the queen, and staggering away.

It had a split second where I thought it was going to run, to try to get clear of the incoming meteors. Then it twisted, opening fire instead; the darts shredded a pair of assassin kobolds that had been racing forward.

I swore, but the fucker wasn't walking away from this. Smoke billowed from the interior seconds later as the systems malfunctioned. Light surged and twisted as the asuras tried to escape the damaged frame, only to have a second impact tear through the air that the light was exiting into.

I didn't know how it worked—it was fucking light, after all—but when the eighth meteor hit the queen's shield and ricocheted off, it tore through the streaming light, and we all felt the psychic scream as the asuras was torn apart.

The ninth and tenth meteors were less impressive. One missed entirely, crashing into the ground and exploding, lifting the edge of the queen's shell…and the tenth hit that edge, tearing through it and exposing part of the interior.

The scream from the queen as her shell was ruptured sent everyone nearby reeling…including Ramnik, who'd been stealthily creeping away after triggering her close-ranged attack. She screamed and wrapped her arms around her head; blood flowed from her ears as the eardrums ruptured.

The asuras standing around the outside—the six heavy exterminators and the remaining throwers—went full-on batshit mode, opening fire in a suppression pattern all around.

Darts flashed through the air, and Ramnik tried to run. Then the heavies opened fire, and it was *literally* fire. The nozzles they had sent jets of what looked like plasma or napalm streaming out in overlapping arcs, and the remaining throwers stepped up.

Ramnik dove to the side, rolling behind a car, and barely avoided being drenched with the flaming mixture. Kilo and two other cryomancers stepped out of cover, a pair that I took for the two heliomancers on the other side of them.

The pair started to cast, but before they so much as finished their first spells, they were bathed in the flaming mixture, going up like living torches.

The cryomancers cast as one. A pair of kobolds holding shields protected them as they did it, taking the darts, as Chill, their area of effect spell, took hold.

It wasn't that powerful, not really, but they were casting it over and over, one atop the other, as the shields were hammered time and again.

I whirled away, the scream having done a number on me. I tried desperately to pull my flight together, seeing the way the elites twisted to face the kobolds, stomping forward; four moved into range to spray the kobolds. The remaining two moved to get around the edge to face Ramnik.

I couldn't pull it up, not in time, so I spun and cut the ability instead, flipping over and yanking my hammer free, flashing across the last few feet and landing on the back of one of the pair headed for Ramnik.

My right ankle breaking as I landed on the back of the left one added to the howl as I swung the hammer into the head of the right one.

The inertia was enough that it tore through the armor easily. The hammer stuck for a second, but came loose as I pulled, falling to land on my left foot. Pain flared as I tried to catch myself.

The one I'd just—literally—flying kicked from its feet had hit the floor with a massive clang of steel and was trying to get back up. I twisted and brought the hammer back around in the small of its back, once, twice…

Light leaked from around the edges of panels beaten out of place. The dent I was making sunk deeper and deeper, when I was hit from the side and slammed into the remains of a car.

I bounced, then roared in pain as a sword punched through the kobold that had shoved me back and sank into my left hip, buckling the panels of the armor with the sheer force of the blow.

I saw the look on the kobold's face, dead before I even managed to thank them. I grabbed the body, forcing myself back and off, before the blade could be rammed any deeper.

The pipe that led over the right shoulder of the heavy exterminator and down its front shuddered as whatever flammable liquid it used pumped downward, and I struck before I could think.

I shoved the bladed arm to my left, slamming my right fist into the center of the asuras's chest, powering a Storm-Strike as I did so. My fist, even encased in the armored gauntlet, screamed in pain as the knuckles broke.

So too, though, did the central plate, and the heavy screeched as the asuras's light exploded from it.

The liquid, clearly under pressure, jetted forth, and I cursed, shoving the pipe away from me…then grinned, yanking it back to spray upward into the exposed sections of the armored queen nearby.

It only lasted a few seconds, but it'd managed to spray some of the flaming mix inside still.

I turned, then froze. I'd pushed my luck too far: the remaining three heavy exterminators had turned and lined up their nozzles on me.

I flinched back, crouching, about to leap free, knowing I probably didn't have the time, when a scream rose from behind them.

"*Fire* power, baby!" Dante yelled, standing atop a ruined car and yanking his hands left to right in a gesture like he was holding a lens between his hands.

The light that burst forth was insane, literally. I saw the spell and knew instantly that if this was the Thermal Lance that Ramnik had said she'd gotten as well, then we had a way into the armored shell.

It carved a hole through all three of them, in the back, out the front, and then deep into the ground, burning a divot as it went. All three of the heavies burst into flame, exploding as their pressurized reservoirs were shredded…and the bursts of blue-white light that outlined each made it clear he'd gotten them.

The end of the light twisted sideways and up, tearing a line across the side of the queen, but too fast to do more than tear a thin divot in the thick steel, before Dante collapsed, screaming and clutching at his head.

Almost at the same time as he fell, one of the kobold shields that were protecting Kilo and his companions finally tore through, and the kobold holding it went down in a spray of blood. The cryomancer to Kilo's left died instantly as a half dozen steel darts slammed into the unarmored figure.

Kilo barked an order, and his companion and their guard ducked back down, racing to the side and trying to get out of the incoming fire.

The top of the Red Queen shuddered, unable to open, buckled and coated in frost, and instead four separate sections cracked apart. Three dart-throwing cannons rose and locked into place, as the fourth failed, jamming on twisted steel.

I launched into the air, arcing around and diving for Ramnik, who saw me coming and reached out one hand. I grabbed her, rolling and pulling her atop me as I lifted again, clutching her to me, as I tried to dodge, even as the throwers opened fire.

The noise was awful. The air seemed to tear under the concentrated fire. One line of darts shredded a line of kobolds with heavy shields that were racing forward. They ducked, holding their slabs of steel high…and died in seconds.

The queen's firepower was horrific. The darts went from smaller than my pinkie from the humanoid ones, to thicker than my thumb from the queen.

The two mages who'd been racing forward to shield, Dave and Simon, just…vanished. One of Dave's "hard light" shields flickered into life, deflecting one or two hits, but that was it, and then the pair were shredded.

A savage scream rose from my left as my mana bottomed out and we tumbled from the air. My constant need for healing had burned through my mana far faster than my spells had.

We landed hard, hitting the asphalt and rolling, then trying to get to our feet.

Ramnik was up before me, dragging me by one arm, as *Chris*, of all people, was there, holding a shield that must have weighed almost as much as he did.

He slammed it down before us and we all ducked in close. The massive slab of steel was coated in rubber, then another layer of steel to make damn sure it was impenetrable.

Even with that, it was banging like a hooker on overtime, and I knew it'd not last long.

"You all right?" Chris shouted at us both.

"Yes, thank you." Ramnik looked from one of us to the other, meaning it for us both.

"Not gonna lie," I called, crouching behind them both. "I've had better fuckin' Fridays!"

"It's Monday!" Chris called back.

"Well, fuck me; that explains a lot!" I shot back, even as Ramnik muttered and rolled her hands around and around, as if polishing an invisible crystal ball. "What are you—"

"I need five seconds when she's not targeting me!" Ramnik snapped, hands still twisting, and Chris and I looked at each other.

"I need to hold the shield," Chris said. "You got any mana left?"

"Fuck all," I admitted. My left eye still twitched with the migraine and the flaring light danced in my eyes. "I could run out there, I guess?"

"That's half a second, then she's won." Chris shook his head. "Here, grab the shield."

I did, moving up and bracing myself as Chris pulled something out of his pocket, and started to shrug out of his armor.

"What the hell are you doing?" I asked him, and he shook his head again.

"Something I didn't fucking want to, but hey, what's new!"

"Loose!" barked a voice nearby, and the snap of dozens of bowstrings could be heard above the *brrrrrp* of the dart cannons on the queen. Arrows flashed overhead—dozens, then hundreds as the highly trained archers adjusted their angles, adding to the mass overhead as they started to fall.

The last few humanoid asuras dart throwers were moving as well. Not toward us, though; instead, they were running toward the queen, grabbing scrap and carrying it toward a small section that had opened. And they all, unfortunately, totally ignored the hail of arrows.

"Take them down!" I roared, pointing, then ducking as the throwers zeroed in on me again. The shield before me juddered repeatedly. As one cannon ran dry, another took up firing, making it clear she knew where I was and was locked in tight.

Gunfire rang out, over and over. Three-round bursts tore into the cannons and the running asuras alike—even as new asuras shouldered its way free of the queen's armor, even as the arrows landed over and over on the armor, barely doing more than scratching and denting it.

It was a tank that moved out, and this fucker was clearly ready to go all out. Its cannon swiveled around, locking onto us, and I shouted a warning. "Fucking moooove!" I roared, grabbing Ramnik and disrupting her spell as I yanked her back, taking two quick steps and diving to the side, landing just as the cannon fired.

The shield was hit dead-on and torn through. The massive slab flipped over and over as it was sent flying. I dragged Ramnik up as I frantically ran. The nearest thrower adjusted, locking onto us…and coming apart under a hail of fire from Griffiths and his soldiers.

The cannon on the tank was tracking them, though, and it barked once. A slug of steel punched clean through a car fender that a soldier was hiding behind, then tore through him as well, leaving a ragged hole in his chest as he collapsed, dead.

Chris had been exposed by the shield falling, but in the maelstrom of the fight, he'd been ignored.

That was a mistake. I dragged Ramnik behind an ornamental stone planter and clapped a hand over her mouth, muting the scream, pinning her arms to her sides as she shook, trying to claw at her head. Whatever spell she'd been casting, the feedback was clearly a bitch.

I looked back, seeing Chris, the crazy bastard, as he sprinted forward, looking seriously fucking *wrong*. He'd gained at least a hundred pounds in sheer muscle, and the way he moved? His top was gone, his armor tossed aside, and the revealed body? He was striped in black lines and pale-white skin; fur erupted as he sprinted. His head shifted, bones cracking as he *shifted*.

His hands grew claws, his teeth lengthening, jaw changing shape…

He leapt over a burst of darts, landed, rolled, and then was up, dodging left and right as the tank tried to track him. It fired, once, twice.

The slugs tore through the air, slamming into the ground and arcing off, sparks flying. The terrible *boom* of each shot made the tank recoil.

Chris rolled under the last shot, and the tank clanked backward, trying to clear enough space to reacquire him, but it was too late. He was in close, diving under the front right leg, and grabbed it, heaving with all his strength. Letting loose a great roar, he lifted the ton or more of mobile murder and tilted it sideways.

As it collapsed, another scream rang out from inside the queen. The flash of light told of another asuras being born…then a line flashed out, wrapping around Chris's forearm and tightening. He roared and pulled back. But after tipping the tank, he wasn't braced, nor ready, and fell.

The line retracted fast, dragging him across the floor, even as a new scream rang out behind me—a chanting voice that made my skin crawl as a new spell was used.

This time, I knew who and what it was without looking. It could only be Yvonne, the umbramancer. Black and purple light flashed out, circling the queen and leeching the color from her shell, seeming to drag the life from her, as the steel grew ever more brittle atop the accursed ground.

Then it was the turn of the cold, and it began to grow. Kilo and his companion stalked forward, chanting and casting again and again, layering thicker and thicker layers of ice atop the armor.

I didn't know what they were doing, but I trusted Kelly, and I forced myself to my feet, closing my eyes and reaching down deep. This fucking bitch wasn't taking my friend, not while I lived.

I'd seen Markus, the old swordsman, now in his sixties if he was a fucking day, sprinting forward. His sword flashed up and around, cutting through the line that had held Chris, then two more as they shot out, trying to catch him as well.

The old bugger stood out in the open, sword spinning around up and over the shoulder, back and around, severing the lines as they flicked out, and I frantically changed the spell I was going to use.

I was out of mana—well, I had a tiny fraction, three points and counting—but I had nineteen hundred and four health. My Lightning Storm had cost me fifteen hundred mana…so I was damn well hoping for two things.

First, that Atomic Furnace also cost fifteen hundred, and secondly that the conversion of one-to-one for health to mana stayed constant.

If not…I was fucked.

"Chris, you dumb furry fuck!" I bellowed, triggering the spell and locking it down on the shell of the queen. "RUN!"

The pain as it tore through me was horrific. Where I was used to the ungentle caress of Lightning, the raging flood of Atomic Furnace was an entirely new beast.

I fell, knees hitting the asphalt. Blood ran down my cheeks; my ears, eyes, nose, and mouth released a veritable flood of blood that lifted free of me, hovering in the air, and formed a disc, then twin circles, one inside the other.

The blood flowed into the space between the rings, forming symbols that glowed with the internal light of my literal life force. Seconds passed as Ramnik screamed at me to stop, shouting for help as I continued, blinded by the pain and blood.

The disc began to spin; the center seemed to fall away like a lens, aiming. The queen was suddenly ringed in a bright light. The one-meter casting space covered a section of the armor, one that suddenly ran like a slab of butter under a flamethrower.

The steel poured inward, and the queen screeched in pain, fear, and disbelieving outrage, as she herself was burned and wounded, not just her shell.

I held on long enough that I saw the shell shatter. The overlapping layers of frozen steel were exposed to the kind of heat that was found in the depths of stars, and even though the spell's radius was contained, some of the heat bled free.

The shell shattered, warping and exploding where impurities were encountered. Shards flew in all directions.

"You crazy bastard…" I heard someone saying, and I blinked bloody tears free, looking up at Sergeant Rhodes as she dragged me back into cover.

"Damn, Matt, you look like shit!" Griffiths swore, looking at me.

"Feel it…" I croaked, looking around blearily. Jo, in the distance, ran from body to body, healing, even as the occasional high-powered round rang out.

"I bet, sir," he agreed, nodding. "Might want to hold on for this bit, though. The Dungeon Mistress had a plan, and she's got a gift for this kinda thing, even when you…oh *shit*. Well, *that's* not happy making…"

I struggled upright, Rhodes helping me, and followed her pointing finger as a new creation shouldered its way out of the queen's cover. The armor was left rent apart; the queen laid slumped inside, clearly exhausted and badly burnt. But her last creation stomped down from her side and screamed a challenge.

This one was clearly her last chance, and she'd gone all out on its design. It was humanoid, despite that it had four arms and two legs. But *damn*. The shoulders had throwers, the arms had backward sweeping blades, and the body was simply a cylinder that held the arms, with what looked to be overlapping layers of armoring.

It stalked forward, then threw its head back and let loose a shrieking buzz that tore up and down my back, making me shudder.

An answering roar rang out, clearly accepting the challenge.

CHAPTER FORTY-FIVE

It was Beta I saw stride down the steps from the dungeon, and I shook my head in disbelief.

The change that had occurred was clearly a turnkey upgrade. She was still Beta, but damn she was different again, clearly using whatever "shift" was to become an entirely new left of hard-ass, around seven foot tall and more dragon than raptor.

The colors of her scales had deepened even further. Seemingly adjusted for stealth and assassination before, all dark hues, she was golden now, or at least she had a lustrous golden hue to the scales. And her eyes glowed bright, clear even from here.

She wielded a mace and a massive shield, which was weird as I'd never seen her using either before. But fuck it.

Her wings had grown even more since I'd met her inside, and she spread them wide as she roared in response to the fucker's challenge.

It didn't pause, launching itself forward and sprinting across the ground separating them, as I felt Kelly reaching out to me.

"I'm here," I mumbled, relaxing back and closing my eyes, ignoring Rhodes's panicked questions, as she thought I was going into shock, and then the swearing as she realized what was happening and eased me down and back into cover.

"You crazy son of a bitch!" Kelly snapped at me. "I had a *plan.*"

"How's it working out?" I asked, sending her a mental hug and kiss, sharing my relief that she was okay, and that unlike me, she wasn't in the thick of the fight.

"It's…it's working fine!" she retorted, before sighing and enveloping me in her essence, the fear and sadness of losing so many, the stress of the fight; then it boiled off, and I was surrounded by a feeling of love. There was desperate annoyance and determination, pride and amazement, the image of me commanding my blood to destroy my enemies, of flying, of battling and being basically god-like when seen from the outside.

I felt it all, as well as the desperate urge for her to pin me down and slap some sense into me, to stop me taking such risks…as well as the desperate need to jump my damn bones and ride me to heaven and back, to show me just how much she adored me, and to be adored *by* me in turn.

I felt it all in a split second, and then it was gone as she got control of herself again, and suddenly she was all business.

"Jack is damaged, but he's close. Can you sense him?" she asked, and I nodded, having felt it before. He was incoming, but slowly, badly damaged. Some of the systems that relayed data were knocked out.

"I can, but no details. How did you know?" I asked, confused, floating forward. The area being inside the dungeon senses, I could see Beta and the asuras race at each other.

"I felt it as he got closer. I can't tell more, but because he's linked to you, and to the dungeon, I could just feel that something was coming and roughly how far. I guessed it must be Jack," she said. "Matt, I know Beta is important to you, she is to me as well, but…"

"But?" I asked, a sinking feeling in my chest.

"We need a few minutes, that's all. Most of the kobolds are down, half our mages are dead, and…Matt, can you feel it?"

I frowned, not knowing what she meant. Not at first. But I reached out, and sure as shit, yeah, I felt it. It was a level of exhaustion that seemed to permeate everything, and I blinked in shock, not understanding.

"It's the dungeon, Matt…" Kelly said softly. "I think we've damaged it, so much mana racing in and out so quick, so many creatures being created, and then dying so fast, the frantic researching, the core upgrades…all of it."

"Shit," I whispered. Now that I knew what I was looking for, I could feel it, all right: the pulsing core of the dungeon felt *wrong*.

"Matt!" It was Aly, suddenly there by our side, emitting a sense of desperate pride, of relief and terror all at once.

"Shitfuck!" I snapped, jerking back at seeing her and then looking back as Beta and the asuras champion slammed into each other.

She drove the shield into its chest, driving it back a few steps, but being shoved back at the same time, and swinging her mace…missing.

The champion rebounded, then leapt forward, grabbing her shield and pulling it to one side, firing a quick burst from the shoulder-mounted dart throwers.

Beta twisted, avoiding most of them, and her hardened scales helped deflect the few that hit. But she still hissed in pain, swinging the mace sideways across the front of the shield, giving it the choice of having its limbs broken, or letting go.

It leapt backward; the two lower arms folded back on themselves at the elbows. The blades jutted forward as it lunged again, grabbing the shield and driving one blade forward and around the shield.

Beta saw it coming and whipped the mace down, smashing the right arm. But the champion twisted, ignoring the wound, and stabbed the other arm forward, curving around the shield and stabbing her above her left hip.

She jumped back, hissing in pain, but the damage was done. Blood coated the blade, and she had to duck back under the shield as the shoulder throwers opened fire again, aiming for her face.

"Matt!" Aly snapped, and I glared at her, as Kelly routed more of our forces around, sending the last two assassins—Karen and Sharon—in to take out the queen.

"What?!" I snarled. My mind raced as I tried to come up with an alternative. I knew what Kelly was doing, and that she hated it as much as I did.

She was letting Beta fight alone, so that the assassins could get around her and into the queen. She was betting Beta's life that we could kill the queen. Because if we couldn't…

"I've done it!" she cried. "I've made the first rail gun! But the dungeon won't print it—it's not reacting to me!"

"Fuck!" I snarled, twisting from her to the fight, then back to stare internally at the dungeon, seeing it all in my mind at once. The cracks that had been spread across the dungeon in the massive influx and draw on its core, the too-fast upgrades, the...*life*.

It'd created so much actual life, filled with so many potentials, that without its fairy to guide it, to understand it, and to explain it to us, I'd forced it to go past its limits.

That was why it wanted the asuras!

I saw it all suddenly. The half-living, half-robotic nature of the asuras were so close to the dungeon fairies, so similar in the way they felt, that the dungeon had sensed them and their situation. It'd sensed their fear, their pain, and that they were enslaved and close to their limits, and it'd sensed a kindred spirit.

It'd sensed something that could share the burden, that could help it repair itself, and that could communicate the issues to us.

I understood at last, and it might very well be too fucking late. I took a deep breath, then shook my head as the last few sections fell into place.

What was I without the dungeon?

I was the Dungeon Lord, but without a dungeon, I was just a man. Yes, a powerful one, and yes, I might still lead the community, but it'd be a far poorer one...one that needed the dungeon far more than it needed me.

I had one last card to play, though, one last chance to pull it all out of the pot before someone flushed our chances away.

Ramnik and a handful of others let loose with their last spells, sending them hammering into the queen's shell. It shrugged them off, damaged but still going, the incredible mass of metal having a quality all of its own.

"STOP!" I ordered, loudly, overriding Kelly and Aly and everyone else in the dungeon—absorbing, feeding, summoning, researching, and more.

"Kelly, Aly...the dungeon *must* rest," I ordered, even as I revoked *all* access to the dungeon, bar the two of them. Everything from the doors to the lights, to the fucking ice cream, was locked down to everyone else. "If I don't survive this, Kelly, you lead, and Aly will advise you. But for the next day or more, only the absolute essentials, literally even opening the doors...do as little as possible."

"Matt..." Kelly said, but it was too late. I was already out.

I pushed myself to my feet, snorting and spitting blood onto the ground as I focused. Rhodes, clearly seeing something on my face, backed away, and I crouched, reaching deep inside and wrenching my life force into my mana channels.

The pain was horrific as I launched myself into the air, converting life force to mana, to storm mana, and using that to power my flight. I arced up and over to land atop the civic center, seeing what I needed to the right. But the way my health was flashing...I landed, cutting the drain on myself as I fell to my knees.

I dragged my hand across my face, splattering blood onto the rooftop as I threw it aside, forcing myself to stand and stagger to the nearest converter.

It was an Air converter, thankfully. Not as good as a Lightning one would have been, but it was better than nothing.

I drew on it. The hundred mana it contained converted as it flooded my body, banishing the mana migraine and making me take a deep breath. I straightened, seeing the other converters dotted about on the roof. I couldn't reach them all, not in time to save Beta.

I could leave her to die, to maybe win or to maybe lose against the asuras champion below. But she'd earned that evolution or spell or ability or *whatever* it was, because of her belief in me. I could give her no less than the same level of devotion.

The nearest converter along was Water, great…but I needed the mana, and at least the touch no longer brought nausea. I drained it and reached out to the next. Five I managed in short order, a hundred in each; along with the first one, that gave me six hundred mana. I moved as fast as I could—running, slipping and almost falling, grabbing onto the nearest drained converter to keep me upright.

I made it to the edge, only to see Beta fall. The champion had switched around; the lower left and upper right arms grabbed her mace and shield, yanking them out to the sides, exposing her chest as the top left arm slapped backward, bringing the blade around to the front and lunging.

Beta had already been stabbed on that side above the hip, and she threw herself back, landing lightly and yanking her crossbow from her back, cranking it in one practiced motion as the fucker threw her mace aside, flipping the shield around and using it to deflect the first crossbow bolt.

She cranked the lever, reloading it and firing again, and again, backing away as the champion caught each bolt.

Behind them, a screech of fury, buzzing with electrical feedback, rang out, and the assassins that Kelly had sent in to face the queen winked out of the dungeon sense.

"Motherfucker!" I snarled, dragging in a deep breath, even as I focused on what I had to do. I had one chance, and it needed to be done. I'd managed it once with pure mana, and I had to hope that desperate need was the catalyst I needed.

I closed my eyes, ignoring the shouts and screams from below that rang out as I forced myself to flow along my mana channels as fast as I'd ever managed.

In seconds, I was at my core, and flashing inward. The seconds it took to reach the giant superstructure that was the core seemed like hours.

I dove inward, letting my need guide me, going on instinct…*there!*

For whatever reason, fuck knows why, but I'd managed to flood myself with Lightning mana before directly from the storm, and I'd massively overfilled myself.

I'd managed that again, with the alien pure mana once, and it was like filling my veins with boiling acid; it'd nearly killed me. I had to hope, just pray, that I could do it with lightning from the spire this time.

I landed right at the base, where the lightning spire and the pure spire met, falling to my knees and laying both hands on the lightning one. I oriented myself with that, feeling the nonexistent gravity holding me to the spire as I took a deep breath, and *pulled.*

The strain built—the need, the desire for what I could literally feel pulsing under my hands, passing under me, reaching into the storage lacunas and sitting there happily. I desperately dragged on it, fighting, needing it.

Nothing!

It wouldn't come! It wouldn't react!

I knew I could do it. I knew that the pure mana would fuck me up if I tried this, while the lightning one would heal me, would energize me...

I heard a pained scream from Beta, and I swore, twisting around as gravity reoriented itself, depositing me atop the pure spire.

My hands slapped against the surface, feeling it like never before, the warmth of the stone beneath my fingers. The surface pulsed beneath me. The warm rocky surface felt like rigid glass, smooth and perfect...the warmth below warned me of the heat it truly contained.

And I drew it into myself.

I pulled the mana out of the spire, the tiniest fraction of a fraction of a percentage, and I *BURNED*.

My eyes shot open, and I staggered to my feet. My vision pulsed crazily, beating in time to my heart. My vision was golden around the edges, but that pain...my mana channels were scoured by the passage of so much mana, the purest form of it cleansing and tearing my body apart in equal measure.

The mana was seeping free of the channels, entering my body and changing it, twisting it as uncontrolled mutations brought about through the massive influx of power began, and unless I got rid of it all, and right fucking now, I was dead.

The power that flooded me wasn't meant for mortals. Nor for demi-gods.

This was the power that pushed time to roll onward. It was the wheel that turned the ages, that forced motion upon a stagnant black mass and drove it to evolve. That forced fission and fusion to occur, to bring life and death...

I felt it all, as I stared out. The pain almost robbed me of my mind. I snapped my left hand out, forcing a burst of mana into the Storm Bolt that had replaced my Lightning, and I fired it down into the asuras champion where it stood, holding Beta.

She was dangling from one hand, held in the air, her "shift" ability running out as she shrank, seeming ever more weak and frail compared to the champion holding her out for all to see, the queen directing it to make it clear that it'd won.

It'd turned to one side, clearly planning to carry Beta into the queen to be consumed...when my bolt flashed out, banishing the night with brilliant golden light.

The bolt slammed into the head and chest of the asuras, punching straight through to sink into the ground. An after-image of the destructive power burned into everyone's vision as it ended, leaving a hole in the champion a meter wide.

The head and upper right side were just gone, the beam of light having blown through them, and for a split second, the world went silent.

The battle had been so close, so fiercely contested, that it had all come down to the final few seconds. Had we been able to summon more kobolds, they'd have stormed straight through. Had the asuras been able to summon a single more champion, it'd have won.

Both sides were broken, exhausted, and fighting just to keep going. I screamed, the burning golden light of the pure ravaging me, as my health ticked inexorably down toward the end.

I had seconds left before I was dead. Unable to contain the destructive, wonderful power any longer, I channeled it all into a single blast: a scream of power and fury, determination, love and loss for those around me.

The pure mana ripped forth, twisting, taking on new life as everything I was bled into it: my need to protect my people, my love for them, for each and every goddamn one of the fuckers, from the assholes who gave me abuse day in and day out, to Kelly, who I had literally rebuilt my life around.

From the people who would never be able to pick me out in the crowd, to the ones who helped me every day—I would stand between them and this fucker. Hell, between them and anyone or thing.

They were *my* people, and anyone who wanted to fuck with them had to come through me first.

I felt it all, and I poured it out: my hatred, my pain, my love, and my fear—all filtered into the massive release of mana, and it showed.

The blast of golden light that poured forth twisted; cracking secondary colors poured up and down its length: blues and blacks, reds and purples, green and more. Colors I had no names for glowed spectral in the air, twisting around the mana that was released.

It slammed into the Red Queen and carved through her armoring like a blowtorch through rice paper. The mass of steel and more simply ceased to exist as lines were carved up and down the mass; sections tumbled inward as light leaked from their edges.

Movement was clear as the queen frantically tried to drag heavier steel across her, twisting and rolling, trying to flee…

Before screeching in agony as the light dug into her back, tearing her apart in a single final pass.

EPILOGUE

The death of the Red Queen was clear. As soon as she fell, the last of her creations, be that fighting, crawling, or whatever, simply ceased, sagging to the ground in a clatter of metal, lifeless. A sudden burst of white light broke free to dissipate into the ether.

As the last of the power left me, I fell.

The world twisted around me as I plummeted downward, crashing into the deformed remains of a tree that stood by the entrance of the dungeon.

I tumbled through the branches, smaller ones snapping, larger branches deflecting me, bouncing to the side. I fell free and crashed into the ground. My armor cushioned the last blows; blood ran from a dozen minor wounds. Seconds later, Chris crouched over me.

He had the orb that Jo had been using, and was fumbling to use it with inhuman fingers, snarling that I better damn well hang on, or he'd follow me to hell and drag me back, kicking and screaming.

I gasped, the ungentle pour of healing magic flooding me, filling me again, popping sections back into place, sealing wounds and more but…

But then it gutted out, the magic failing.

It sealed the worst of the wounds, fixed the broken bones, and resealed the body…but it could do nothing for my soul, and for my life force that I'd poured out like water upon a griddle.

I lay there, staring upward as the specter of Kelly, reaching out through the dungeon sense, called to me. Aly and others came; most were there physically, Aly and Kelly taking my orders about the dungeon to heart. But I just…couldn't.

I barely blinked at the sky overhead, seeing none of it, as time passed, and I was carried, slowly along atop a bier.

My friends were there: Chris on one side, Griffiths on another, Rhodes by my feet, and Dante across from her, each holding a section of my stretcher.

They refused to let anyone else carry me. Even Beta—now healed by the power of Jo and her team's healing magic, along with a handful of other survivors—walked alongside.

Jack fell in soon afterward, as did a battered Mike and the remains of his team. Markus and more who I'd seen fighting, then lost track of in the insanity of the battle, surrounded us, as the citizens of the Newcastle Dungeon carried me home. A small contingent of the park's forces had shown up as well, summoned at the end by Kelly, but having taken too long to travel the distance to actually join in.

I was alive, but at a terrible cost.

Inside my chest, I sensed a tiny spark of mana. The core that had blazed so powerfully before now barely glimmered.

Where I'd felt powered by my mana, strong enough to tear my way through any and all obstacles, now I felt broken, unable to summon the energy to focus my eyes. And I felt *them*.

The lives that had been lost…so many of them had been my people, or had been the souls of humans who had been torn free and wiped of their memories.

They'd been exposed as a form of energy by the asuras, and something of what I'd done exposed me to them. They were all around me, and I felt them backing away as I was carried past.

Something about the damage I'd done had opened me up, and as I passed, their energy was drawn into me. For the first time, I experienced another form of mana beyond the power of the storm, of lightning and my path as a Storm Titan.

I felt the power of the souls around me, and a new potential class reaching out to claim me.

Congratulations Matt, First Lord of the Storm!

You have unlocked a secondary evolution path…opening yourself to greater possibilities than were ever expected.

As a Storm Titan, you have the potential to become one of the most powerful entities in your system, controlling and guiding entire aspects of reality.

HOWEVER: You have scoured your soul free of all ties that bind it, and somehow you still live…

You have three choices before you.

- You may revert your soul and evolutionary path to that of a Storm Titan, gaining a single lesser boon as a reward, as well as a bonus of +2 stat points to distribute per level.

- You may shift your focus, abandoning the progress you have made toward Storm Titan, and instead begin the Path of the Ravager. Ravagers are among the rarest of all creations, able to tear and feed upon the souls of those around them, converting and controlling their life force.

  Ravagers have created some of the most terrible wonders of the known galaxy…until the weight of their creations brought them down.

  Beware, this path will result in terrible pain, but the power that will result? A single Ravager can consume entire solar systems, converting the soul essence to weapons of magnificent power, eliminating all threats to their dominion.

- You may attempt to combine both paths, choosing to work toward one or the other as your will dictates, but the soul of a Storm Titan is one born to protect. Tearing the souls of the innocent free to feed your ascension is inimical to your path. Choosing this path will permit the creation of soul-forged creations, but beware the souls you use, lest all is lost…

I stared at the options before me. Until I made this choice, I couldn't heal. But the choice?

I didn't care. I just couldn't bring myself to care about any of it. As the hours passed, I lay on our bed, staring upward. The notifications pulsed away, unread, the same text hovering before me as before, even as my life force, along with my ruptured soul, slowly leaked away.

"Matt, you have to wake up…" Kelly wept, laid by my side, candles lit all around the room, providing light in place of the mana lights of the dungeon. "You can't do this to me, to us! Don't leave us…don't go where I can't follow…please, Matt. *I love you!*"

I could feel them all around me, standing well back, but still close enough to see, to sense. The souls of those who had gone before. The souls of the recently lost, and those who'd been lost for long months and years.

Spirits that refused to pass on through the veil to their rest hovered around me, watching and waiting. I felt their hunger, as my life force bled out into the ether, and I felt their fear, that should they come too close, they'd be in range when I chose to feed on them, that the last of their life would be torn free and gobbled down.

I laid there, cold, sinking slowly away, until finally *she* came.

It started as a flare of light, as the soul at the very edge of my awareness. The one that stood alone started to move, flowing forward to stop before me, staring into my eyes.

She was tiny, weak, and furious. She'd never lived, not really. She'd been created, developed, and educated, all in preparation for her life's work, and she'd failed before she'd even started.

A single fragment of debris had punched through the metal of her containment capsule and robbed her of life, shattering the crystal that kept her in stasis.

She'd asphyxiated as her dungeon, bound into its transport container, had torn through the atmosphere, but she'd refused to leave it.

She'd reached out as best as she could, soothing the infant dungeon, guiding it without its knowledge to stretch out a tendril of power, drawing those nearby, assessing their potential.

Nothing had been found for long cycles. Creatures had come and gone, and she'd despaired, her life force leaking away as her young soul unraveled.

She'd refused to allow it, refused to fail…not now, not *ever*. She'd forced herself to leave the dungeon, despite the fear and confusion of the dim mind as she left it.

She'd scoured the area until she'd found a wounded human, bleeding out, creeping closer to death by the second, and she'd reached out, grimly sure that here was her last chance.

The final opportunity she would ever have, and none would ever know of her sacrifice, but still, she did it: she bound her soul to the human, sharing life force. She poured out her soul, healing some of his injuries, gifting him with advanced healing, as well as access to the tiny amount of mana in the area to fuel it. Forming a bridge between herself and the human, then pushing him to consciousness.

She'd spent long cycles fighting his slide toward death, finally managing to turn the corner and force him to awaken, only to have him weep and snivel over his now considerably healed injuries.

She poked and prodded him to his feet, burning more of herself to create a pull, a need, and drawing him closer and closer to the dungeon.

Hours passed as she faded, but eventually, finally, the anxiety-addled, glorified monkey reached out to the pretty light, and the dungeon was released into it, blasting it across the gully.

Days passed in a blur, then *weeks* as the dead fairy stared in mounting fury at the mismanagement of its charge, at the damage that grew from the fucking stupidity that the chosen Dungeon Lord exhibited.

The cracks that appeared grew worse and worse. The dungeon was drained and forced to gorge itself again and again with no thought to its stability.

It grew, being forced to reach for the next level before it could consolidate its gains. She howled in fury and disbelief at it all, until finally the damage was too much, and the fool who had bound itself to the dungeon finally saw the danger.

It enacted the protocols, locking the dungeon and finally, *finally* giving the dungeon time to heal and recover. Then it tore its soul wide open to protect its people.

I saw it all, and I saw it from the dungeon fairy's side. I winced, remembering forcing the dungeon to absorb her body as well.

She moved in close. Her soul hovered over me, staring at me, making sure I understood, making damn sure it was *all* clear: that the dungeon was, as I'd suspected, a living creature, and it needed to be protected, to be looked after, just as the humans and more did.

That the energy for the creation of the souls for the dungeon had to come from somewhere, and that was the core. I sensed the shape of more information, hints about the souls of others, about the possibilities for the future, and that as much as life created mana, mana *was* life.

I felt the need of the dungeon for those high-mana areas, not just to draw in the mana and to purify it, but also for the dungeon to feed.

It was all made clear, and then the fairy was there again, hanging right before me in the ether…before she struck, diving into my chest, sealing her soul to mine, and expending the last of her power all in one go.

Congratulations, Soul Titan!

As the first of your species to share a soul with another, your evolutionary path has been restructured and your choice made!

***First Lord of the Storm,* you have begun your Evolution from Thunderstorm to Soul Titan. Your specific evolutionary path stands thus:**

Thunderstorm > Reaper of the Storm > Soul Titan

New paths opened to me; the prompts flared as the notifications flashing grew wilder and wilder. But I couldn't deal with it, not right now.

The dungeon fairy…her soul had slammed into me, and I felt like one of those barrels of water the old circus divers would leap into from stupidly high up.

I felt her flashing out, pouring around me, sealing the leaking sections like a mix of glue and a searing-hot scalpel. I gasped, thrashing, and Kelly threw herself across me, holding me to the bed, pinning me down, clinging to me, fearing the worst...

Until at last the world rushed back, as did the mana I'd been without. I felt life return—caring, warmth, and need. The world around me crashed in like a tidal wave hitting the rocks of a harbor, booming and rolling, shattering and being absorbed.

I was alive, I was back, and everything had changed.

I wrapped my arms around Kelly on instinct, feeling the sob that tore from her as she felt me again, felt me really there, feeling my arms as we clung to each other. And there, in our bedroom, sheltered from the rest of the world, surrounded by the dungeon and those I loved, everything was right with the world again.

THE END
OF
BOOK 4

AGE OF FORGED STEEL

Rise of Mankind Book 5

5th May 2023

The Dungeon is wounded, the core fractured and Matts new allies are less reliable than he hoped. The Core must be made whole again, the dungeon sealed, and fixed.

The last few weeks have made it clear, Matt and the dungeon's inhabitants can no longer live as they have been, its time to focus, to grow and to rebuild.

The world outside of the dungeon walls is changing, new species have arrived, allies and enemies are rising, and the simple truths of the dungeon's minions that he always took for granted, are revealed to be terrible lies.

The Nexus Gates are opening, and the Dungeon Lord of Newcastle must learn to ride the tide, or be swept away with the rest of the debris.

The Age of Steel Continues…

https://mybook.to/AgeofForgedSteel

REVIEWS

Hey! Well, I hope you enjoyed the book? If so, please, please remember to leave a review, its massively important, as not only does it let others know about the book, it also tells Amazon that the book is worth promoting, and makes it more likely that more people will see it.

That in turn will hopefully keep me able to keep writing full time, while listening to crazy German bands screaming in my ears, and frankly, I kinda really like that!

If you want to spread the good word, that'd be amazing, and if you know of anyone that might be interested in stocking my books, I'm happy to reach out and send them samples, but honestly, if you enjoy my madness, that's massive for me.
Thank you.

FACEBOOK AND SOCIAL MEDIA

If you want to reach out, chat or shoot the shit, you can always find me on either my author page here:

www.facebook.com/JezCajiaoAuthor

<u>OR</u>

We've recently set up a new Facebook group to spread the word about cool LitRPG books. It's dedicated to two very simple rules, 1; lets spread the word about new and old brilliant LitRPG books, and 2: Don't be a Dick!
They sound like really simple rules, but you'd be amazed…
Come join us!

https://www.facebook.com/groups/litrpglegion

I'm also on Discord here: **https://discord.gg/u5JYHscCEH**

Or I'm reaching out on other forms of social media atm, I'm just spread a little thin that's all!

You're most likely to find me on Discord, but please, don't be offended when I don't approve friend requests on my personal Facebook pages. I did originally, and several people abused that, sending messages to my family and being generally unpleasant, hence, the author page:

https://www.facebook.com/JezCajiaoAuthor

I hope you understand.

PATREON!

Okay then, now for those of you that don't know about Patreon, its essentially a way to support your favorite nutcases, you can sign up for a day or a month or a year, and you get various benefits for it, ranging from my heartfelt thanks, to advance access to the books, to me sending them books, naming characters and more.

At the time of me writing this, the advanced Patreon readers are finishing up Age of Forged Steel, about to start on the next of my secret projects (They'll have access to it for about a month before I even go public with it existing) so yeah, you get plenty for the support!

There's one of my wonderful supporters out there that I have to thank personally as well; ASeaInStorm, you utter legend you. Thank you for sticking with it mate.

http://www.patreon.com/Jezcajiao

RECOMMENDATIONS

I'm often asked for personal recommendations, so if this book has whetted your appetite for more LitRPG, please have a look at the following, these are brilliant series by brilliant authors!

Ascend Online by Luke Chmilenko

The Land by Aleron Kong

Challengers Call by Nathan A Thompson

SoulShip also by Nathan

Endless Online by M H Johnson

Silver Fox and the Western Hero, also by M H Johnson

The Good Guys/Bad Guys by Eric Ugland

Condition: Evolution by Kevin Sinclair

Space Seasons by Dawn Chapman

The Wayward Bard by Lars M

MORE RECOMMENDATIONS

I know I had a page just before this of recommendations, but where those are my recommended starter list, giving you a very varied grounding in the genre, here's two more I've been enjoying:

JR Mathews: *Portal to Nova Roma*

With over 26 MILLION pages read on Kindle Unlimited, over 10,000 audiobooks sold, and more than 5,000 five star ratings on Amazon and Audible, make sure to start the Nova Roma series today!

To find peace, Alexander must first embrace war.

After tragically losing the only person he ever cared about, Alexander, a rogue artificial intelligence, opens a portal to an alternate dimension to escape his grief.

Scanning trillions of different dimensions, Alexander finally finds a world that is reminiscent of the only time he was ever happy, back when he could play virtual reality games with his only friend. He doesn't know why, or how, such a world exists, but he doesn't care. All he cares about is finding a place where he can escape the misery of Earth and start over.

Join Alexander as he risks it all by downloading his intelligence into a body made from the best stolen technology and bio-enhancements Earth has to offer and takes the plunge through a portal to another world.

Only this new world isn't full of the idyllic adventures and fantasy roleplaying he had hoped to find. Instead, Alexander finds himself trapped in the middle of an ancient city, in a divergent timeline, where monsters have ravaged the world and the only people left alive huddle behind thick walls, struggling to survive.

To save his new home, Alexander must quickly learn to adapt to his new world, melding magic with technology to give himself an edge over the unending waves of monsters assaulting the city.

To survive, Alexander must embrace war.

Read *Portal to Nova Roma* at this link!

https://www.amazon.com/Portal-Nova-Roma-J-R-Mathews-ebook/dp/B09K54TBST

Brian J Nordon's Wild Cards: *The Dread Captain*

At the District One Invitational, a rookie eSports team defied all odds and reached the finals. Their underdog story and humble beginnings elevated them to worldwide acclaim. Media corporations dubbed them, **The Paragons**.

With their main competition eliminated from the tournament during the semifinals, the rookie team sailed through the live finals and won by a landslide. Their prize was to become the first ever players in the most exclusive VR game yet, **Abidden**.

The Paragons never celebrated that semi-final victory. They lost a friend in that match, who never appeared online again. Ten years later, the gaming landscape has changed and Abidden with it. Helena is the last remaining Paragon. Her *team* now consists of celebrities, influencers and musicians. Abidden has been reduced to a shadow of its former glory, but is the most streamed and viewed game in the world, despite having only a handful of players.

None of this matters to James Sylvester. Finally out of hospital, things aren't good for James. He's found himself crippled with medical debt, his gaming licence has been revoked and he's permanently lost his place in society. He now spends his days competing in illegal slum arcades to manage the repayments. When a high-profile job comes along, James gets temporary backdoor access to his blacklisted gaming account. After reactivating it for the first time in ten years, James receives an invitation that could change his life forever.

Read *The Dread Captain* at this link!

https://www.royalroad.com/FICTION/32659/WILDCARDS-THE-DREAD-CAPTAIN

LITRPG!

To learn more about LitRPG, talk to other authors including myself, and to just have an awesome time, please join the LitRPG Group

www.facebook.com/groups/LitRPGGroup

FACEBOOK

There's also a few really active Facebook groups I'd recommend you join, as you'll get to hear about great new books, new releases and interact with all your (new) favorite authors! (I may also be there, skulking at the back and enjoying the memes…)

www.facebook.com/groups/LitRPGsociety/

www.facebook.com/groups/LitRPG.books/

www.facebook.com/groups/LitRPGforum/

www.facebook.com/groups/gamelitsociety/

www.ingramcontent.com/pod-product-compliance
Lightning Source LLC
Chambersburg PA
CBHW070346170726
48291CB00001B/207